William Diehl

SHOW
OF
EVIL

ARROW

Published in the United Kingdom in 1997 by
Arrow Books

1 3 5 7 9 10 8 6 4 2

First published in the United Kingdom in 1995 by William Heinemann
This edition first published in 1996 by Mandarin Paperbacks

Arrow Books
The Random House Group Limited
20 Vauxhall Bridge Road, London SW1V 2SA

Random House Australia (Pty) Limited
20 Alfred Street, Milsons Point, Sydney,
New South Wales 2061, Australia

Random House New Zealand Limited
18 Poland Road, Glenfield,
Auckland 10, New Zealand

Random House (Pty) Limited
Endulini, 5a Jubilee Road, Parktown 2193, South Africa

The Random House Group Limited Reg. No. 954009

www.randomhouse.co.uk

A CIP catalogue record for this book
is available from the British Library

Papers used by Random House are natural,
recyclable products made from wood grown in sustain-
able forests. The manufacturing processes conform to the
environmental regulations of the country of origin.

ISBN 0 09 942942 X

Printed and bound in Great Britain by
Bookmarque Ltd, Croydon, Surrey

In law, what plea so tainted and corrupt
But, being season'd with a gracious voice,
Obscures the show of evil?
                    – THE MERCHANT OF VENICE,
                         ACT 3, SCENE 2

SHOW
OF
EVIL

PROLOGUE

The town of Gideon, Illinois, biblical of name and temperament, squats near the juncture of Kentucky and Indiana at the edge of the Blue Ridge Mountains. A trickle of a river called the Wahoo forms the western boundary of the town, while Appalachian foothills etch its southern and eastern parameters. It was founded in the mid 1800s by a handful of farmers driven south by encroaching midwestern cities, by railroads, and by brutal winters. They were followed soon afterwards by a fire-eyed reader of the Church of Latter-Day Saints named Abraham Gideon, who had split from Brigham Young and led a small troop of followers towards the southern mountains. They had blundered onto the fledgling village, liked what they'd seen, and settled down there. It was Gideon who gave the town its name and a strict moral code that has persisted for nearly one hundred and fifty years.

Inhabited by two thousand and some citizens, most of them hardworking conservatives and many of Mormon descent, it is a town that takes care of itself and minds its own business. Its architecture is stern and simple; its streets paved only when necessity demands; its town core a collection of indispensable businesses without frills or fancies; its town meetings held at the Baptist church, the largest building in town.

The only car dealer sells Fords and farm equipment. A foreign car in Gideon is as improbable as Grandma Moses rising from the grave and running naked through the streets on Sunday morning.

The city council, a collection of dour curmudgeons, runs the town with a kind of evangelical fervour, enduring its handful of bars and taverns but drawing the line at sex, having chased away Gideon's one topless bar during the late Eighties and railing against R-rated movies so vociferously that most of the citizens watch them on cable rather than venture forth to the town's twin theatres and thereby risk the scorn of the five old men who set both the tone and moral temper of the town. The young

3

people, who silently revolt against its anachronisms, usually spend their weekends driving to nearby towns that have shopping malls and multiplex theatres, where they can buy a six-pack of beer without being recognized.

For the most part, Gideons are friendly, concerned, protective people who help their townsfolk when they are in trouble and who practise a kind of archaic combination of do-unto-others and love-thy-neighbour. And as long as its citizens sequester their more shocking vices behind closed doors and shuttered windows, nobody really gives a hoot. In short, it is a place that time, distance, and desire have cloistered from the rest of the world.

Gideons like it that way. They do not take kindly to others snooping in their business and they solve their problems without the intrusion of outsiders like state politicians or federal people or snoopy, big-time newspaper reporters.

On a Tuesday morning in October 1993, a few days before Hallowe'en, a single shocking act of violence was to change all that.

Suddenly, trust was placed by suspicion, ennui by fear, complacency by scorn. People began to lock their doors and windows during the daytime and porch lights glowed all night. And casual neighbours, who once waved friendly hellos in passing, were suddenly as cautious as strangers.

Yet like a protective family, Gideon kept this scandal behind locked doors and whispered of it only in rumours. The horrifying act itself was kept from the rest of the world – for a while, at least.

On that autumn morning, Linda Balfour prepared her husband's customary lunch: tuna fish sandwiches with mayo on white bread, a wedge of apple pie she had made the night before, potato chips, orange juice in his thermos. She had also polished his bright orange hard hat before fixing a breakfast of poached eggs, crisp bacon,

4

well-done toast, and strong black coffee, and the hat and lunch box were sitting beside his plate with the morning edition of the *St Louis Post-Dispatch* when he came down.

George Balfour was a bulky man in his early forties with a cherubic smile that hinted of a gentle and appreciative nature. A life-long resident of Gideon, he had married Linda late in his thirties after a brief courtship and regarded both his twenty-six-year-old wife and their year-old son, Adam, as gifts from God, having lived a solitary and somewhat lonely life before meeting her at a company seminar in Decatur three years earlier.

Their two-storey house was seventy years old, a spartan, white-frame place near the centre of town with a wraparound porch and a large front lawn and an old-fashioned kitchen with both a wood-burning stove and a gas range. It was George Balfour's only legacy. He had lived in the house all his life, both of his parents having died in the bedroom that Balfour now shared with his wife.

He loved coming down in the morning to those smells he remembered from his youth: coffee and burned oak slivers from the wood-burning stove, and bacon and, in the summer, the luscious odour of freshly cut cantaloupe. The TV would be set on the *Today* show. His paper would be waiting.

He was wearing what he always wore: khaki trousers, starched and pressed with a razor crease, a white T-shirt smelling of Downy, heavy, polished brogans, his cherished orange wind-breaker with SOUTHERN ILLINOIS POWER AND LIGHT COMPANY stencilled across the back and the word SUPERINTENDENT printed where the left breast pocket would normally be. Everything about his dress, his home, and his family bespoke a man who lived by order and routine. Balfour was not a man who liked surprises or change.

He kissed his son good morning, wiping a trace of

5

pabulum from the boy's chin before giving Linda a loving peck on the back of her neck. She smiled up at him, a slightly plump woman with premature wrinkles around her eyes and mouth and auburn hair pulled back and tied in a bun. The wrinkles, George often said, were because his wife laughed a lot.

Nothing about George Balfour's life was inchoate.

'Saints finally got beat yesterday,' she said as he sat down.

''Bout time,' he answered, scanning the front page of the paper. 'By the way, I gotta run up to Carbondale after lunch. They got a main transformer out. May be a little late for dinner.'

'Okay. Six-thirty? Seven?'

'Oh, I should be home by six-thirty.'

At seven-fifteen, he was standing on the porch when Lewis Holliwell pulled up in the pickup. He kissed Linda and Adam goodbye, then waved at them from the truck as Lewis drove away from the white-frame house. They turned the corner and suddenly the street was empty except for old Mrs Aiken, who waved good morning as she scampered in robe and slippers off her porch to pick up the paper, and a solitary utility man carrying a toolbox who was trudging down the alley behind the house. A bright sun was just peeking over the hills to the east, promising a day of cloudless splendour.

Thirty minutes later the Balfours' next-door neighbour, Miriam Perrone, noticed that the Balfours' back door was standing open. *Odd*, she thought, *It's a bit chilly this morning*. A little later she looked out of her dining room window and the door was still open. She went out the back door and walked across her yard to the Balfours'.

'Linda?' she called out.

No answer. She walked to the door.

'Linda?' Still no answer. She rapped on the door frame. 'Linda, it's Miriam. Did you know your back door's open?'

No answer. A feeling of uneasiness swept over her as she cautiously entered the kitchen, for she did not wish to intrude.

'Linda?'

Suddenly, she was seized with an inexplicable sense of dread. It choked her and her mouth went dry. She could hear the television, but neither Linda nor the baby was making a sound. She walked towards the door to the living room. As she approached the door, she saw the empty playpen and a second later Adam lying on his side on the carpet with his back towards her.

And then, as she stepped through the doorway, she stopped. Her lips trembled for what seemed like eternity before a low moan rose to a horrified shriek.

A few feet from the crib, Linda Balfour's butchered body was crumpled against the wall, her glazed eyes frozen in terror, her mouth gaping, a widening pond of her own blood spreading around her, while Katie Couric and Willard Scott joked about the weather in the blood-stained television set nearby.

That was how it started.

THE CITY

FOUR MONTHS LATER

One

Fog swirled around powerful spotlights in the darkest hours before dawn. Perched atop tall steel poles, they cast harsh beams out across a rancid, steaming wasteland, etching in shadow and light the buttes, knolls, and slopes of trash and refuse, of abandoned plastic bottles, Styrofoam dishes, cardboard fast-food wrappers, old newspapers, abandoned clothing, and maggot-ridden mounds of uneaten food. Like fetid foothills pointing towards the glittering skyscrapers miles away, the city's garbage formed a stunted mountain range of waste. Stinking vapours swirled up from the bacteria-generated heat of the vast landfill, while small, grey scavengers zigzagged frantically ahead of a growling bulldozer that pushed and shoved the heaps of filth into a manageably level plain.

The dozer operator, huddled deep inside layers of clothing, looked like an interplanetary alien: long johns, a flannel shirt, a thick wool sweater, a bulky jacket that might have challenged the Arctic wastelands, a wool cap pulled down over his ears, fur-lined leather and canvas gloves, a surgical mask protecting his mouth from the freezing cold and his nose from the choking odours, skier's goggles covering his eyes. Gloria Estefan's *Mi Tierra* thundered through the earphones of the Walkman in his pocket, drowning out the grinding din of the big machine.

Another hour, Jesus Suarino, who was known as Gaucho on his block, was thinking. *One more hour and I'm outa here.*

He worked the controls. Twisting the dozer in place, he lowered the blade and attacked a fresh mound of waste. The dozer tracks ground under him, spewing refuse behind the tractor as they gripped the soggy base and lurched forward. Through his misted goggles, Suarino watched the blade slice into the top of the mound, showering it into a shallow chasm just beyond. Suarino backed the machine up, dropped the blade a little lower, took off another layer of rubble. As it chopped into the pile, Suarino saw something through his smeared goggles.

He snatched the throttle back, heard the lumbering giant of a machine choke back as it slowed down and its exhaust gasp in the cold wind that swept across the range of rubble. He squinted his eyes and leaned forward, then wiped one lens with the palm of his glove.

What he saw jarred him upright. A figure rose up out of the clutter as the blade cut under it. Suarino stared at a skeletal head with eyeless sockets and strings of blonde hair streaked with grease and dirt hanging from an almost skinless skull. The head of the corpse wobbled back and forth, then toppled forward until its jaw rested on an exposed rib cage.

'Yeeeeooowww!' he shrieked, his scream of terror trapped by the mask. He tore the goggles off and leaned forward, looking out over the engine. The corpse fell sideways, exposing an arm that swung out and then fell across the torso, the fleshless fingers of the hand pointing at him.

Suarino cut off the engine and swung out of the driver's seat, dropping into the sludge and sinking almost to his knees. Ripping off the mask, he was still screaming as he struggled towards the office at the edge of the dump.

Martin Vail hated telephones. Telephones represented intrusions. Invasions of his privacy. Interruptions. But duty dictated that the city's chief prosecutor and assistant DA never be without one.

They were everywhere: three different lines in his apartment – one a hotline, the number known only to his top aide, Abel Stenner, and his executive secretary, Naomi

Chance – all with portable handsets and answering machines attached; a cellular phone in his briefcase; two more lines in his car. The only place he could escape from the dreaded devices was in the shower. He particularly hated the phone in the dead of night, and although he had all the ringers set so they rang softly and with a pleasant melodic tone, they were persistent and ultimately would drag him from the deepest sleep.

When the hotline rang, it was never good news, and the hotline had been ringing for a full minute when Vail finally rolled over onto his back and groped in the dark until he located the right instrument.

'What time is it,' he growled into the mouthpiece.

'Almost five,' Stenner's calm voice answered.

'What's that mean?'

'Four-twenty.'

'You're a sadist, Major Stenner. I'll bet you put tooth-picks under the fingernails of small children and light them. I bet you laugh at them when they scream.'

'Better wear old clothes.'

'Where are we going?'

'Twenty minutes?'

'What's going on, Abel?'

'I'll ring you from the car.'

And he hung up.

Vail verbally assaulted the phone for half a minute, then turned on the night light so he would not fall back to sleep. He stretched, kicked off the covers, and lay flat on his back in the cold room, arms outstretched, until he was fully awake.

Four-twenty in the damn morning. He got up, threw on a robe, and went to the kitchen, then ground up some Jamaican blue, poured cold water into the coffee machine, and headed for the shower. Fifteen minutes later he was dressed in corduroy slacks, a wool sweater, and hiking boots. He doctored two large mugs of coffee,

13

dumped several files from his desk into his briefcase, and when the phone rang he was ready to roll.

He snatched up the phone and said. 'This better be good,' and hung up. Throwing on a thick sheepskin car coat, he headed for the lobby ten floors below.

Major Abel Stenner sat ramrod straight behind the wheel. He was impeccably dressed in a grey pin-striped suit. When Stenner had accepted the job of Vail's chief investigator, Vail had promoted him to major, a rank rarely used except in the state police. It was a diabolical act on Vail's part – Stenner now outranked everyone in the city police but the chief. Vail handed him a mug of coffee.

'Thanks,' Stenner said.

'I thought you said to wear old clothes. You look like you're on your way to deliver a eulogy.'

'I was already dressed,' he answered as he pulled away from the kerb.

Stenner, a precise and deliberate man whose stoic expression and hard brown eyes shielded even a hint of emotion, was not only the best cop the city had ever produced, he was the most penurious with words, a man who rarely smiled and who spoke in short, direct, unflourished sentences.

'Where the hell are we going?'

'You'll see.'

Vail crunched down in the seat and sipped his coffee.

'Don't you ever sleep, Abel?'

'You ask me that once a week.'

'You never answer.'

'Why start?'

More silence. That they had become close friends was a miracle. Ten years ago, when Vail had been the top defence attorney in the state and had worked against the state instead of for it, they had been deadly adversaries. Stenner was the one cop who always had it right, who knew what it took to make a good case, who wouldn't

14

bite at the trick question and could see through the setup, and who had been broken on the stand only once – by Vail during the Aaron Stampler trial. When Vail took the job of chief prosecutor, one of his first official duties was to steal Stenner away from Police Chief Eric Eckling. He had fully expected Stenner to turn him down, their animosity had been that profound, and he had been shocked when Stenner accepted the job.

'You're on my side now,' Stenner had explained with a shrug. 'Besides, Eckling is incompetent.'

Ten years. In those years, Stenner had actually begun to loosen up. He had been known to smile on occasion and there was a myth around the DA's office, unconfirmed, that he had once cracked a joke – although it was impossible to find anyone who actually had heard it.

Vail was half asleep, his coffee mug clutched between both hands to keep it from spilling, when Stenner turned off the highway and headed down the back tar road leading to the sprawling county landfill. His head wobbled back and forth. Then he was aware of a kaleidoscope of lights dancing on his eyelids.

He opened them, sat up in his seat, and saw, against a small mountain of refuse, flashing yellow, red, and blue reflections against the dark, steamy night. A moment later Stenner rounded the mound and the entire scene was suddenly spread out before them. There were a dozen cars of various descriptions – ambulances, police cars, the forensics van – all parked hard against the edge of the landfill. Beyond them, like men on the moon, yellow-garbed cops and firemen struggled over the steamy landscape, piercing the looming piles of garbage with long poles. The acrid smell of the burning garbage, rotten food, and wet paper permeated the air. For a moment it reminded Vail of the last time he had gone home, to a place ironically called Rainbow Flats, which had been savaged by polluters who repaid the community for enduring them by poisoning the land, water, and air. First one came, then another, attracted to the place like hyenas to carrion, until it was a vast island of death surrounded by forests they had yet to destroy. He had gone home to bury his grandmother thirteen years earlier and never returned. A momentary flash of the Rainbow Flats Industrial Park supplanted the scene before him. It streaked through his mind and was gone. It had always angered him that they had had the gall to call it a park.

Three tall poles with yellow flags snapping in the harsh wind seemed to establish the parameters of the search. They were bunched in a cluster, a circle perhaps fifty yards in circumference. The sickening sour-sweet odour of death intruded on the wind and occasionally overpowered the smell of decay. Four men came over a ridge of the dump hefting a green body bag among them.

'That's three,' Stenner said.

'Bodies?'

'Where the flags are.' He nodded.

'Jesus!'

'First one was over there, in that cluster. A woman. They tumbled on the second one when I called you.'

A freezing blast of cold air swept the car as Stenner got out. Vail turned up his collar and stepped out into the predawn. He jammed his hands deep in his coat pockets and hunched his shoulders against the wind. He could feel his lips chapping as his warm breath turned to steam and blew back into his face.

Two cops, an old-timer and a rookie, were standing guard beside the yellow crime-scene ribbons as Vail and Stenner stepped over them. The wind whipped Stenner's tie out and it flapped around his face for a moment before he tucked it back under his jacket as they walked towards the landfill.

'Jesus, don't he have a coat? Gotta be ten degrees out,' said the rookie.

'He don't need a coat,' the older cop said. 'He ain't

got any blood. That's Stenner. Know what they used to call him when he was with the PD? The Icicle.'

Twenty feet away Stenner stopped and turned slowly as the cop said it and stared at him for a full ten seconds, then turned back to the crime scene.

'See what I mean,' the older cop whispered. 'Nobody ever called him that to his face.'

'Must have ears in the back of his head.'

'It's eyes.'

'Huh?'

'It's eyes. He's got eyes in the back of his head.'

'He didn't see you, he heard you,' the young cop said.

'Huh?'

'You said – '

'Jesus, Sanders, forget it. Just forget it. Coldest night of the year, I'm in the city dump, and I draw a fuckin' moron for a partner.'

'There's Shock,' Stenner said to Vail.

He nodded towards a tall, beefy uniformed cop bundled in his blue wool coat, standing at the edge of the fill. Capt. Shock Johnson was ebony black and bald, with enormous, scarred hands that were cupped in front of his mouth and shoulders like a Green Bay lineman. When he saw Vail and Stenner, he shook his head and chuckled.

'I don't believe it,' he said. 'You guys don't even have to be here.'

'What the hell's going on?' Vail asked.

'The dozer operator turned over the first one, so I decided we ought to punch around a little and, bingo, now we got three.'

'What killed them?'

'Better ask Okimoto that, he's the expert. They're a mess. Been in there awhile. Maggots have had Thanksgiving dinner on all of 'em.'

Vail groaned at the image. 'So we don't know anything yet, that it?' he asked.

17

'Know we got three stiffos been cooking down in that gunk for God knows how long.'

'May be hard to determine when these happened,' Stenner offered. 'Location will be very important.'

Johnson nodded. 'We're taking stills and video, doing measurements. If the weather's okay later I've ordered a chopper flyover. We'll get some pictures from up top.'

'Good.'

Johnson had once been Stenner's sergeant and had made lieutenant when he quit. He was now captain of the night watch, a man beholden to Stenner for years of education and for fostering in him a strong sense of intuition. He was Stenner's pipeline to a very unfriendly police department.

'Eckling here yet?' Vail asked.

'Oh yeah. He's down there in the thick of it, looking important for Channel 7. They were the first ones to get a whiff of it.'

'Nicely put,' said Vail.

'Any ideas?' Stenner asked.

'Not really. My guess is, these three here were dumped about the same time, but we can't be sure. You couldn't hardly find the same spot twice, the tractors keep moving this shit around so much.' He looked off at the ragged landscape. 'Excuse me, I gotta check that bag just came up. Besides, Eckling sees you.' He chuckled again. 'And I've had enough fun for one night.' He left.

'I'll wait in the car,' Stenner said. He had not spoken a word to his former boss since the day he quit.

The chief of police huffed up the small hill with a camera crew and a reporter trailing out behind him. He was waving his arms as he spoke and his words came out in little bursts of steam.

'I see the DA's man is here,' he sneered. 'Everybody loves a circus.'

Eckling always referred to Vail as 'the DA's man,' putting an edge to the words so that it sounded like an insult.

The three-man crew, having got everything they could out of Eckling, turned their camera on Vail. 'Any comment, Mr Vail?' asked the reporter, a small, slender man in his twenties named Billy Pearce, who peered out from the depths of a hooded parka.

'I'm just an interested spectator,' he answered.

'Care to speculate on what happened here?'

'I don't care to speculate at all, Billy. Thanks.'

Vail turned away from them and walked towards Eckling as the crew, grateful for his brevity, fled towards their van. Eckling was a tall man with the beginnings of a beer belly and eyes that glared from behind tinted spectacles.

'What's the matter, Martin, couldn't wait?' he snapped.

'You know why I'm here, Eric, we've had that discussion too many times.'

'Can't even wait until the bodies're cold,' he growled.

'That shouldn't take long in this weather.'

'Just want to get your face on the six o'clock news,' he said nastily.

'Isn't that what got you out here?' Vail said cheerily.

'Look, you can't butt in for seven days. How about leaving me and mine alone and letting us do our job?'

'I wish you could, Chief,' Vail said pleasantly.

'Go to hell,' Eckling said, and stomped away.

Vail returned to the car and shook off the cold as he got into the warm interior.

'Damn, it's bitter out there.'

'You and Eckling have your usual cordial exchange?'

'Yeah, things are improving. We didn't even bite each other.'

Two

Stenner pulled around in a tight circle and headed back towards the city.

'Go to Butterfly's,' Vail said. 'I'm starving.'

'Not open yet.'

'Go to the back door.'

Vail laid his head against the headrest and closed his eyes, thinking about Stenner, so stingy with language. Soon after Stenner had joined the bunch, he and Vail had driven to a small town to take a deposition. An hour and a half up and an hour and a half back. As he had got out, Vail had leaned back through the car window and said, 'Abel, we just drove for three hours and you said exactly twelve words, two of which were "hello" and "goodbye",' to which Stenner had replied, 'I'm sorry. Next time I'll be more succinct.' He had said it without a smile or a trace of humour. Later, Vail had realized he was serious.

They drove for fifteen minutes in silence, then: 'We're going to end up with this one,' Stenner said as they neared the city.

'Always do,' Vail said without opening his eyes.

'Very messy.'

'Most homicides are.'

Not another word was spoken until Stenner turned down the alley behind Butterfly's and stopped. While he propped the OFFICIAL CAR, DISTRICT ATTORNEY'S OFFICE placard against the inside of the windshield, Vail rapped on the door. It opened a crack and a scruffy-looking stranger, who was about six-three with machine-moulded muscles, peered out.

'We ain't open yet.'

20

'It's Martin Vail. We'll wait inside.'

'Vail?'

'New in town?' Stenner said from behind Vail.

'Yeah.'

'This man is the DA. We'll wait inside.'

'Oh. Righto. You betcha.'

'Assistant DA,' Vail corrected as they entered the steamy kitchen.

'I'm the new bartender,' the stranger said.

'What's your name?'

'Louis. But you can call me Lou.'

'Glad to meet you, Lou,' Vail said, and shook his hand. Vail and Stenner walked through the kitchen. It was a fairly large room with stainless-steel stoves and ovens and a large walk-in refrigerator with a thermal glass door. Bobby Wo, the Chinese cook, was slicing an onion so quickly, his hand was a blur. *Chock, chock, chock, chock.* Vail stopped to check the 'Special of the Day' pot.

'Shit on a shingle,' Wo said without slowing down.

'That's three times a week,' Vail complained.

'Tell the lady.' *Chock, chock, chock, chock, chock.*

'Quit bellyachin',' a growl for a voice said from across the room. Butterfly, who was anything but at five-four and two hundred and fifty pounds, entered the kitchen. 'There was a special on chipped beef, okay?'

'Know what I've been thinking about, Butterfly? Crepes.'

'*Crepes?*'

'You know, those little French pancakes, thin with—'

'A short stack,' she yelled to Bobby. 'How about you, General?'

'Major,' Stenner said. 'The usual.'

'Two soft-boiled, three and a half minutes, dry toast, burned bacon,' she yelled.

'Coffee ready?' Vail asked.

'If it wasn't, I wouldn't be this damn pleasant,' she

21

snarled, and shuffled away on flat feet encased in ancient men's leather slippers.

Vail and Stenner drew their own coffee and sat at their usual round table in the rear of the place. The morning papers were already stacked on the table.

'I'm thinking about this,' Stenner said.

Vail smiled. Of course he was. Stenner was *always* thinking.

'You mean, Why the dump?' Vail asked without looking up from the paper.

'No, I mean, Who are these people? How long have they been in there? Doesn't somebody *miss* them?'

'Disposing of them in the city dump, that's rather ironic.'

'Obvious when you think about it.'

'At least they're biodegradable,' Vail said, continuing to sip his coffee and read the paper.

Stenner stared down into his coffee cup for several seconds, then said, 'I don't think it's a pattern job. It doesn't feel right.'

'We know *anything* about these people?'

'We have two men and a woman. All ages, sizes, and shapes. A redhead, a blonde, a bald man with a glass eye.'

'Maybe it is a pattern kill. Maybe . . . they're all from the same neighbourhood, work in the same building, eat at the same restaurant . . .' Vail shrugged. He turned to the editorial pages.

'My intuition tells me this is not a pattern kill.'

'A hunch, huh?'

'A hunch is a wild guess. Intuition comes from experience.'

'Oh.'

Stenner stared at Vail for a moment, took a sip of coffee, and went on: 'They usually don't hide bodies. They leave them out where they can be found. Part of the thing.'

22

Vail ignored him.

'So what are the options?' Stenner went on. 'Three people in the landfill. Can we assume they're not there by accident?'

Vail did not look up from the paper. 'I'll give you that.'

'A burial ground?'

'For whom?'

'People who have been disposed of.'

'Murder for pay?'

'In the Thirties, Murder Incorporated buried their left-overs in a swamp in New Jersey. Dozens of them.'

Breakfast came and the conversation ended abruptly for fifteen minutes. Stenner carefully crunched up his bacon and sprinkled it into the eggs and stirred them together, then spooned the mixture onto his toast before attacking the meal with knife and fork. When he was finished, he wiped his lips with a paper napkin and finished his coffee.

'Eckling will screw it up as usual. He's looking for a quick break.'

Vail laughed. 'Sure he is. The heat's on him. This thing is going to make the national news. It's too bizarre not to.'

He finished and leaned back in his chair. 'Maybe it's a disposal service,' he ventured. 'You know? You kill your mother-in-law, make a phone call, they come pick up the baggage and dump it for you.'

'You seem to be taking this very lightly,' said Stenner. 'Maybe these are people caught up in some kind of gang war – maybe upscale gangs – the ones who go to church, wear ties.' He paused for a moment and added. 'Contribute to politicians.'

'Now there's a discomforting thought,' Vail said.

'It's a discomforting thing.'

'Abel, we have a lot on our plate. Eckling has a week before we get involved. Let's give him the week.'

'I just want to be ready.'

'I'm sure you will be,' Vail said.

Stenner thought a moment more, then said, 'Wonder what the Judge would've thought?'

For a few moments, Vail was lost in time, waiting for the Judge to stroll jauntily through the door with the *New York Times* under his arm, dressed in tweeds with a carnation in his lapel, greeting the gang sardonically before settling in for breakfast, reading, and talking law.

The Judge had had four loves: his wife, Jenny, Martin Vail, the law, and horse racing. But he had nearly been destroyed by two tragedies. His beloved Jenny, a demure Southern lady to whom he had been married for thirty-seven years, had been terminally injured in a car accident, lingering in a coma for a month before dying. The second tragedy was of his own design. To allay his grief, he had turned to a lifelong love of the ponies and had lost thirty thousand dollars to the bookies in a single month. His reputation on the bench literally lay in the palms of bookmakers. He had been saved by the devotion and respect of defence counsels, prosecutors, cops, newspaper reporters, law clerks, librarians, and politicians, all of whom respected his fairness and wisdom on the bench. They had contributed everything from dollar bills to four-figure donations and settled his debts. The Judge had quit cold turkey.

When he retired, he spent his days either as Vail's devil's advocate on cases or in the back of Wall Eye McGinty's horse parlour, which looked like the office of an uptown brokerage with a travelling neon board quoting changing odds, scratches, and those other bits of information that would be a foreign language to most humans. He always sat at the back of the room in the easy chair he himself had provided, legs crossed, his legendary black book in his lap, twirling his Montblanc pen in his fingers and studying McGinty's electronic tote board as he considered his next play.

That book! The Judge placed imaginary bets each day,

keeping elaborate records of every race, track, jockey and horse in the game, using wisdom, insight, and a staggering knowledge of statistics to run a ten-year winning streak that was recorded in the thick leather journal, a book so feared by the bookmakers that they had once banded together and offered him six figures if he would burn it. He refused but never gave tips or shared his vast knowledge of the game to anyone else. The Judge had amassed an imaginary fortune of over two million dollars, all of it on paper.

So he would spend his mornings in Butterfly's, challenging young lawyers, and his afternoons at Wall Eye McGinty's lush emporium for horse players.

His third joy was matching wits with Marty Vail. It was more than a challenge, it was a test of his forty-five years on both sides of the bar. His forays and collaborations with Vail provided an excitement unmatched by his horse playing. They would bet silver dollars arguing points of law, sliding the coins back and forth across the table as each scored a victory. After almost fifteen years, the Judge was exactly twenty-two cartwheels ahead of Vail.

A gangster client of Vail's, HeyHey Pinero, had once called the Judge swanky. 'A most swanky guy,' he had said, and it was the perfect way to describe the Judge.

A most swanky guy.

And then age and the turbulent past caught up with the old jurist. At eighty-one, a series of strokes felled him. He had survived his third stroke, but it left him arthritic and frail, unable to cook for himself or even scrounge up a snack. Ravaged by insomnia and elusive memories and trapped in his memory-drenched house, he stared out of the windows at passing traffic or dozed in front of the TV set every day until one of the regulars came by, helped him get dressed, and carried his frail bone-flesh body to the car and from there to Wall Eye McGinty's horse parlour, where the players greeted him with almost reverential solicitude. McGinty, charitable bookie that he was, always drove the Judge home when the parlour closed.

Someone came every day. Vail, his paralegal executive secretary, the incomparable Naomi, Stenner, or one of Vail's young staff lawyers. And on days when everyone seemed bogged down with other things, Vail would send a cop over to perform the duty. On those days, McGinty met the officer at the door so as not to make him uncomfortable, no questions asked. After all, McGinty's betting parlour had existed in the same place for more than twenty years. The cops would hardly have been surprised had they got to peek through the door.

Six days a week the Judge doped the horses and entered his picks in the new encyclopedia-size black book.

On the seventh day, the Judge rested. Collapsed in his wheelchair, his atrophied legs tucked under a blanket, dressed as nattily as his palsied hands and weakened eyes would permit in a tweed jacket and grey flannels, he sat in his garden, facing the sun, his eyes shielded behind black sunglasses, and tanned the grey tint of old age from paper-thin flesh.

Age had robbed him of everything but pride.

So, on a warm Sunday morning in June two years before, dressed in his nattiest outfit, the Judge sat in the garden, spoke softly to the long gone Jenny about their life together and his life without her, and told her he could no longer go on. Then he put the business end of .38 special in his mouth and pulled the trigger.

He left behind a simple note for Vail, who had watched as the detectives did their work, then rode the ambulance to the morgue with the man who was as much a father to him as anyone had ever been. When he had overseen the cruel journey, he walked out behind the hospital, sat on a bench, and wept uncontrollably for more than an hour. Stenner had stood a hundred yards away, watching over, but not wanting to impose on, his boss. Finally Vail had opened the note.

Dear Martin:

I liked you better on defence, but you're a great prosecutor. I love you as a son. You always made me proud to know you. My mind is slipping away. We all know it, right? Haven't picked a winner in weeks. Can't even eat a bagel anymore. Need I say more, my brash and brilliant friend? I won't ask for your forgiveness – nothing to forgive. Invest in Disaway, third race at Del Mar tomorrow. Buy a round for the gang on me with the proceeds.

Farewell, dear friend,
The Judge

Twenty-two silver dollars had weighted down the note. The tip had parlayed the twenty-two cartwheels into nine hundred and seventy-four dollars.

It had been one hell of a party.

'He's not coming, Martin,' Stenner said, breaking his reverie. Vail snapped around towards him, aware that he had been staring at the door revisiting the past.

'Mind reader,' Vail said.

'I sometimes have a moment . . .' Stenner started but never finished the sentence.

'I'm sure we all do from time to time,' Vail said, turning back to his paper.

To Vail, on that chilly morning, the landfill case was a curiosity, an annoyance, something else to clutter up the already crowded agenda of the district attorney's office. In fact, the landfill mystery would lead to something much bigger. Something far more terrifying than the decomposed bodies in the city dump. Something that would force Martin Vail to come to terms with his past.

A name that had haunted Vail for ten years would soon creep back into his mind.

The name was Aaron Stampler.

Three

Shana Parver rushed through the frigid morning air and climbed the steps of the county criminal courthouse. Overly sentimental and idealistic by nature, although she shielded it with a tough, aggressive facade, Parver always got a rush when she saw the front of the hulking building. 'The law is the only thing that separates us from animals,' Vail had once said. Of course, he had added his own cynical postscript: 'Although, these days, you'd never know it.' But looking up at the Doric columns soaring above the entrance, each surmounted by allegorical figures representing Law, Justice, Wisdom, Truth, Might, Love, Liberty, and Peace, reassured her faith in the sanctity of the law and reaffirmed her belief in the profession she had chosen while still in grammar school.

She was early this morning. In forty-five minutes she would be face-to-face with James Wayne Darby, and while it wasn't a courtroom, the interrogation was the next best thing, a chance to match wits with the flabby, smart-alec chauvinist. She would take a few last minutes to prepare herself mentally for the meeting.

Naomi Chance had beat her there as usual. The coffee was made in Vail's giant urn, and she was at her desk ready to do battle when Parver burst in at eight-fifteen. Naomi was always the first to arrive, walking through the sprawling office, flicking on lights before making Vail's coffee. Her look was regal and intimidating. She was a stunning ramrod-straight woman, the colour of milk chocolate, almost Egyptian-looking with high cheekbones and wide brown eyes, her black hair cut fashionably short and just beginning to show a little grey. A widow at fifty, she had the wisdom of an eighty-year-old

28

with the body of a thirty-year-old. She was a quick learner and a voracious digger. Give her a name and she'd come back with a biography. Ask for a date and she'd produce a calendar. Ask for a report and she'd generate a file. She could type 80 words a minute, take shorthand, and had earned her law degree at the age of forty-six. Her devotion to Vail superceded any notion of practising law. She had taken care of him from the beginning, knew his every whim; his taste in clothes, movies, food, women, and wine; and was, without title, his partner rather than his associate prosecutor, a title he had invented for her because it was nebulous enough to cover everything and sounded a lot more important than executive secretary.

Naomi gnawed through red tape as voraciously as a beaver gnaws through a tree bole, had no use for bureaucratic dawdling, knew where to find every public record in the city, and acted as surrogate mother and a friendly crying shoulder for the youthful staff Vail has assembled.

If Vail was the chief of staff, Naomi Chance was the commanding general of this army.

Parver was the youngest and newest member of what Vail called the Special Incident Staff – better known around town as the Wild Bunch – all of whom were in their late twenties and early thirties, all of whom had been 'discovered' by Naomi, whose vast authority included acting as a legal talent scout for the man they all called boss.

Shana Parver was the perfect compliment to Naomi Chance. She was not quite five-two but had a breathtaking figure, jet-black hair that hung well below her shoulders, and skin the colour of sand. Her brown eyes seemed misty under hooded lids that gave her an almost oriental look. She wore little makeup – she didn't need it – and she had perfect legs, having been brought up near the beaches of Rhode Island and Connecticut, where she had been a championship swimmer and basketball player in high school. She was wearing a black suit with a skirt just above the knee, a white blouse, and a string of matched pink pearls. Her hair was pulled back and tied with a white bow. Dressed as conservatively as she could get, she was still a distracting presence in any gathering, a real traffic stopper, which had almost prevented Vail from hiring her until Naomi pointed out that he was practising a kind of reverse discrimination. She had graduated *summa cum laude* from Columbia Law School and had made a name for herself as assistant prosecutor for a small Rhode Island county DA when she applied for a job on the SIS. Naomi had done the background check.

A rebellious kid who had made straight A's without cracking a book, Parver had raised almighty hell and flunked out of the upscale New England prep school her parents sent her to. Accepted in a tough, strict institution for problem kids, she had made straight A's and from then on had been an honour student all the way through college and law school.

'What happened?' Naomi had asked in their first face-to-face interview.

'I decided I wanted to be a lawyer instead of a big pain in the ass,' Parver had answered.

'Why did you apply for this job?'

'Because I wrote a graduate piece on Martin Vail. I know all his cases, from back when he was a defence advocate. He's the best prosecutor alive. Why wouldn't I want to work for him?'

She had had all the right answers. Naomi's reaction had been immediate.

'Dynamite.'

Vail had expected anything but the diminutive, smart, sophisticated, and aggressive legal wunderkind.

'I want a lawyer, I don't want to give some old man on the jury a heart attack,' he had said when he saw her picture.

'You want her to get a face drop?' Naomi had snapped.

When Parver stepped out of the lift and walked resolutely towards his office for her first interview, Vail had groaned.

'I was hoping the pictures flattered her.'

'There's no way to unflatter her,' Naomi had offered. 'Are you still going to hold her looks against her?'

'It's not just looks. This child has . . . has . . .'

'Magnetism?' Naomi had suggested.

'*Animal* magnetism. She is a definite coronary threat to anyone over forty. I speak from personal experience.'

'You going to hold her looks against her?' Naomi had asked. 'That's discrimination. Marty, this girl is the best young lawyer I've ever interviewed. She's a little too aggressive, probably self-protective, but in six months she'll be ready to take on any lawyer in the city. She has an absolute instinct for the jugular. And she wants to be a prosecutor. She doesn't give a damn about money.'

'She's rich.'

'She's well off.'

'Her old man's worth a couple million dollars – *fluid*. I call that rich.'

'Marty, this young lady reminds me so much of you when we met, it's scary.'

'She's a woman, she's rich, and she's gorgeous. The only thing we have in common is that we inhabit the same planet.'

'You better be nice to her,' Naomi had warned, leaving the office to greet her.

Six months earlier, Parver had tried two cases and blown one. Vail had told her later that she was too tough, too relentless.

'The jury likes tough, they don't like a killer,' he had said. 'You have to tone down, pull back. Study juries, juries are what it's all about. I had a friend we called The Judge who used to say that murder one is the ultimate duel. Two lawyers going at it in mortal combat – and the mortal is the defendant. Excellent analogy. Two sides completely polarized. One of them's right, the other one's

31

wrong. One of them has to perform magic, turn black into white in the minds of the jurors. In the end, the defendant's life depends on which lawyer can convince the jury that his or her perception of the facts is reality. That's what it's all about, Shana, the jury.'

Toning it down hadn't come easily.

'You ready, Miss Parver?' Naomi asked, shaking her back to the present.

Parver scowled at her. 'It's not like it's the first time I ever questioned a murder suspect, Noam.'

Parver was the primary prosecutor on the Darby case but had been in court and missed Darby's first interrogation. Now it was her turn to have a shot at him.

'This Darby is a nasty little bastard. Don't let him push you around.'

Parver smiled. 'Be nice if the creepy little slime puppy tries,' she said sweetly.

'You haven't met Rainey yet. Be careful, he's a killer. A good honest lawyer, but a killer. Don't let that smile of his fool you.'

Parver drew herself a cup of coffee, sprinkled in half a spoonful of sugar, stirred it with her finger then sucked the coffee off it.

'Somebody said he's as good as Martin was in the old days,' she said casually, and waited for the explosion.

'Ha!' Naomi snorted. 'Who the hell told you that?'

'I don't know. Somebody.'

'Don't let *somebody* kid you, nobody's that good – or is ever likely to be.'

'You never talk about those days, Naomi. How long have you been with Marty?'

'Eighteen years,' Naomi said, tracing a long black finger down Vail's calendar for the day. 'When I started with Martin, he charged fifty dollars an hour and was glad to get it. And all I knew about the law was that it was a three-letter word.' She paused for a moment, then: 'My God, wait'll I run this by him. A luncheon and a cocktail party, both on the same day. The State Lawyers Association. I'll wait to tell him, he's liable to go berserk and kill Darby if I tell him before the inquiry.'

A moment later Vail stepped out of the lift, threading his way through the crowded jungle of glass partitions, desks, file cabinets, computers, blackboards, telephones, and TV screens towards his office. It was in a rear corner of the sprawling operation, as far away from the DA Jack Yancey's office as it was possible to get and still be on the same floor.

God, Naomi thought, *he must've dressed in the dark*. Vail was wearing an old grey flannel suit, unshined loafers, and an ancient blue knit tie that looked like it had been used as a garrotte by stranglers from Bombay.

'Christ, Martin,' Naomi said, 'you look like an unmade bed.'

'I am an unmade bed,' he growled, and stomped into his office. 'How old's this coffee?'

'Fifteen minutes.'

'Good.' He went to the old-fashioned brass and chrome urn he had taken as part payment for handling a restaurant bankruptcy years ago and poured himself a mug of coffee. Parver and Naomi stood in the doorway.

His cluttered, unkempt office was a throwback to what Naomi sometimes referred to as the 'early years'. It was dominated by an enormous, hulking oak table that Vail used as a desk. Stacks of letters, case files, and books littered the tabletop, confining him to a small working area in the centre of the table. There were eight hardback chairs around the perimeter of the table. He flopped down in his high-backed leather chair, which was on wheels so he could spin around the room – to overrun bookshelves or stuffed file cabinets – without getting up. An enormous exhaust fan filled the bottom half of one window. Vail was the only smoker left on the staff and no one would come into his office unless he sat in front of the fan when he smoked.

'Stenner had me up before five taking a nature walk in the city dump,' Vail muttered, and sipped his coffee. 'Good morning, Shana.'

'You were out there?' Parver said with a look of awe. 'Is it true they found three bodies in the landfill?'

'What?' Naomi said.

'Three corpora delicti,' said Vail. 'And they were in there a looong time. Wonderful way to start the day. You don't want to hear any details.'

'Do you think it's murder?' Naomi asked.

'Okie'll let us know. Ready to take on James Wayne Darby and Paul Rainey?' Vail replied.

'Yes.' Emphatically.

'Want to talk about it? We have fifteen minutes before we go down.'

'If you do,' Parver said with confidence.

'Ah, the audacity of youth,' Naomi said, rolling her eyes. 'Oh to be thirty again.'

'I'm twenty-eight,' Parver said in a half-whisper.

'Twenty-eight,' Naomi said, shaking her head. 'I don't even want to *think* about my twenties. I'm not sure, but I think twenty-eight was one of my bad years.'

Vail casually studied the young lawyer. She was cool and steady, very self-assured for a twenty-eight-year-old. He had assembled his group of young turks carefully during the past six years, moving the assistant prosecutors from Yancey's old staff – mostly bureaucratic burnouts and unimaginative lawyers who preferred plea bargains to trials – into routine cases: drive-by gang shootings, local dope busts, assaults, robberies, burglaries, and family disputes, many of which ended in homicide. Gradually he had phased out several of them, replacing them with younger, more aggressive, yet unspectacular lawyers who preferred the long-term advantages of security to making a name for themselves before moving out into the private sector. Under Vail's careful guidance, they handled the bulk of the 2,600 murders, robberies, rapes, aggravated assaults, burglaries, car heists, child molestations, and white-collar felonies the DA's office handled every year.

The Wild Bunch was something else. Young, aggressive, litigious, and brilliant, they took on the complex, multifarious cases, acting as a team. Although they were extremely competitive, they were bonded by mutual respect, arduous hours, meagre pay, and the chance to learn from the master. Some, like Parver, had applied for the job. Others had been tracked down by the tenacious Naomi Chance. Through the four or five years they had been together, each had become a specialist in a certain area and had learned to depend on the others. They were backed up by Stenner and his investigators, seasoned cops who were experts at walking the tightrope between statutory compliance and forbidden procedures. They were all cunning, adroit, resourceful. They questioned legal theory and were not above taking tolerable risks if the payoff was high enough, and on those rare occasions when they screwed up, they did it so spectacularly that Vail, an outrageous risk-taker himself, was usually sympathetic.

The young lawyers had one thing in common: they all loved the courtroom. It was why Naomi and Vail had picked them, a prerequisite. Like it was for Vail, the law was both a religion and a contest for them; the courtroom was their church, their Roman Coliseum, the arena where all their competitive juices, their legal knowledge, their resourcefulness and cunning were adrenalized. Vail had also instilled in each an inner demand to challenge the law, to attack its canons, traditions, statutes, its very structure, while they coaxed and manoeuvred and seduced juries to accept their perception of the truth. It was his fervent belief that this legal domain had to be defied and challenged constantly if it was to endure. He insisted that they spend two or three days a month in court, studying juries and lawyers, their timing, their tricks, their opening and closing statements, and he watched with satisfaction as each developed his or her own individual styles, his or her own way of dealing with this, the most intriguing of all blood sports.

The whole team disliked James Wayne Darby intensely. He was brash, arrogant, swaggering, and flirtatious towards the women on the team and surly towards the men. His lawyer, Paul Rainey, was just the opposite, a gentleman, but a hardcase, with a strong moral streak. He believed passionately in his clients. So far, no charges had been brought against Darby.

Parver was hungry to try another case to get over her recent defeat. Darby could be it – if they could break his story. But Vail was aware that Parver's eagerness could also be her undoing.

'This is our last shot at Darby,' he told Parver. 'Just remember, Paul Rainey can kill you with a dirty look. If he gets pushy, ignore him. You know the playing field; if he gets offside, I'll jump on him. You stay focused on Darby. Just keep doing what you do best.'

'I know,' she said.

'Do you have anything new?'

'Not really. There's one thing. The phone number?'

'Phone number?'

'The slip of paper with Poppy Palmer's phone number.'

Parver went through a thick dossier of police data, coroner's reports, evidence files, and interviews, finally pulling out a copy of the slip of paper, which she laid before Vail.

'This is the note that Darby claims he found beside the phone,' she said. It was a ragged piece of notepaper with the entry: Pammer, 555–3667.

'He says Ramona Darby must have written the note because he didn't – and also Palmer's name is misspelled. Two handwriting analysts had failed to come up with a conclusive ID.'

'So . . .?'

'So suppose he wrote it and left it there for Ramona to find. Or . . . suppose he left it there *after* the fact. Supposing Ramona never called Poppy Palmer at all and there were no threats? If we can prove Ramona Darby never called Palmer and never threatened to kill Darby, we raise reasonable doubt about his whole case.'

'Only if we get him into court. There isn't any case at this point. We don't have a damn thing to take to a grand jury.'

'There's some strong evidence here,' she said defensively.

'All circumstantial,' he argued. 'You can call it whatever you want: evidence, conjecture, guesswork, insinuation, circumstance, lies, whatever, it's all for one purpose. Define the crime and lure the jury into separating your fact from the opposition's fiction – and right now we don't have one, single hard fact to nail this guy with.'

'True. But suppose we could panic Palmer? She backed up his story. If she's looking at perjury and accessory before the fact . . .'

'So you're looking to shake *her* up, not him.'

'Eventually. Start with him, then take another shot at her.'

'It's some long shot,' Vail said.

'We're busted anyway. What've we got to lose?'

'Okay, let's see how good you are.'

Four

The office where prosecutors conducted interrogations and depositions was on the third floor of the courthouse, a floor below the DA's headquarters. It was sparsely furnished: a table, six wooden chairs, an old leather sofa and a chair in one corner with a coffee table separating them. There was a small refrigerator near a window. A Mr Coffee, packets of sugar and dry cream, and a half-dozen mugs were neatly arranged on its top. The view was nothing special. No telephone. It was a pleasant room without being too comfortable. The room was also bugged and had a video camera in one corner that was focused on the table.

Vail and Parver were waiting when Paul Rainey and James Wayne Darby arrived. Rainey was a deceptively pleasant man. Tall, slender, his dark hair streaked with grey, he wore gold-rimmed glasses and an expensive dark blue suit and could have passed for a rich, Texas businessman. Darby was his antithesis, an ex-high school baseball player gone to seed: six feet tall, thirty pounds overweight, and sloppily dressed in jeans, heavy hiking boots, a flannel shirt, and a camouflage hunting jacket. Cheap aviator sunglasses hid his dull brown eyes. His dishwater-blonde hair was cropped too close and he had a beer drinker's complexion, a beer drinker's stomach, and a beer drinker's attitude. He was thirty-eight but could easily have passed for a man in his late forties. A farmer from Sandytown, a small farming community of four thousand people on the north end of the county, he had shot his wife to death with a shotgun after claiming she first tried to kill him.

Everyone on the team believed he had murdered his

wife, but they could not prove his story was phony. There were some damaging circumstances, but that was all they were: circumstances. He was having a fling with a stripper named Poppy Palmer. He had insured both himself and his wife for $250,000 six months before the shooting. And the previous two years had been a disaster. Darby, on the verge of bankruptcy, was about to lose his farm.

But there were no witnesses, so there was no way to challenge him. His story, supported by the bovine Miss Palmer, was that a hysterical Ramona Darby had called Palmer an hour or so before the shooting and threatened to kill both Darby and Palmer. A slip of paper with Palmer's number had been found near the Darbys' phone.

Vail did the introductions, which were cordial enough. Vail and Parver sat with their backs to the camcorder and Darby sat across from them, slouching down in his chair and crossing his arms over his chest. He kept the hunting jacket on. Rainey laid a slender briefcase on the table and stood behind his client, leaning on the back of his chair.

'Okay,' he said. 'Let's get this over with.'

Vail smiled. 'What's the rush, Paul? Plenty of coffee. You can smoke. Nice view.'

'Martin, I've advised my client to cooperate with you people this one, last time. He's been interrogated twice by the police – once for six hours – and previously by your department for three. He's not accused of a thing. This is beginning to feel a little like harassment. I want an agreement that this is a voluntary interrogation and that all formal requirements in connection with such are waived. Also this statement, or series of statements, by my client does not constitute a formal deposition or a sworn statement.'

'Are you implying that he can lie to us with complete immunity?' Parver asked.

'I am saying that Mr Darby has agreed to cooperate

with you in this matter. You can take his statement at face value.'

'Do you have any objections if we videotape the inquiry?'

Rainey thought for a moment. 'Only if we get a complete copy of the tape and you agree that it will not be used as evidence in a court case and will not be released to the public.'

Parver nodded. 'Acceptable.'

'Then it's acceptable to my client. We haven't got a thing to hide.'

Vail pressed a button under the table and started the camcorder.

John Wayne Darby said nothing. He stared across the table at Vail and Parver, his lips curled in a smirk.

Parver opened a file folder and took out a pencil. 'Are we ready?' she asked, trying to smile.

'Any time, little lady.'

She glared at him but did not respond. 'Please state your full name and address.'

'Sheee . . . you know my name and address.'

'Just do it, Jim,' Rainey said.

'James Wayne Darby. RFD Three, Sandytown.'

'How long have you lived at that address?'

'Uh, eight years. My daddy left it to me.'

'Age?'

'Twenty-nine.' He laughed and then said, 'Just kiddin'. I'm thirty-eight and holding.'

'Are you married?'

'I was. My wife is dead.'

'Was your wife Ramona Smith Darby?'

'That's right.'

'How long were you married?'

'Ten years.'

'Did you graduate from high school, Mr Darby?'

'Yep.'

'Did you attend college?'

40

'Yes, I did, on a baseball scholarship.'

'And did you graduate from college?'

'No. Got my leg broke in a car wreck when I was starting my third year. Couldn't play ball anymore and lost my scholarship, so I had to drop out.'

'Then what did you do?'

'Went to work on my daddy's farm.'

'Were you married at the time?'

'Yes. Ramona and I married just after I dropped out.'

'That's when you went to live at RFD Three, Sandytown?'

'Right. My daddy's farm. He built a garage apartment for us.'

'Do you have any children?'

'No.'

'Is your father still living?'

'He got a stroke four years ago.'

'And died?'

'Yeah, he died.'

'How about your mother?'

'She died when I was in college. Cancer.'

'I will ask you if you will now agree to a polygraph test.'

'Objection,' Rainey said. 'We've been over this. I've advised my client against the polygraph. It's not admissible in court and there's no advantage whatsoever to Mr Darby taking a polygraph since it cannot benefit him in any way. And let's not make an issue of this with the press, okay, Martin?'

'I assume that's a "no",' Parver said.

'That's right, little lady, it's a no,' said Darby.

Vail leaned across the table, but Parver moved a foot over his and stopped him. She stared straight at Darby and said, 'Mr Darby, I'm nobody's little lady, especially yours. Now you agreed to this interrogation. We can do this quickly or we can spend the day here. It's up to you.'

Darby's face turned a deep shade of vermilion. He

started to get up, but Rainey put a hand on his arm and nodded towards his chair. Darby sneered, then shrugged, sat back down, and fell quiet.

Parver took a diagram out of the folder and laid it before him. It showed the first floor of the Darby farmhouse. The front door lead from a wide porch into a small entrance hall. An archway opened on the left into the living room. Facing the archway was the sketch of a chair and a distance line between the arch and the chair that measured twelve feet, four inches. There were two Xs marked on the chair, two on the hallway wall opposite the chair, one on the wall next to the arch, and one that measured eight feet, seven inches marked floor to ceiling.

'I show you this sketch, Mr Darby,' Parver said. 'Is this an accurate sketch of the scene of the crime?'

'Strike the word *crime*,' said Rainey wearily. 'There isn't any crime. Nobody's been accused of a crime.'

'Would *homicide* suit you?' Parver asked.

'*Event*. I think scene of the event would be an accurate description.'

'Mr Darby, is this an accurate sketch of the scene of the event?'

Darby studied it for a minute and nodded. 'Yeah. There's some other furniture in the room.'

'It's inconsequential, is it not?'

'You mean did it enter into the shootout? No.'

'Now, Mr Darby, will you please describe for us what happened on January 7, 1993?'

'You mean getting out of bed, taking a shower . . .'

'You were going hunting . . .'

'Charlie Waters, Barney Thompson, and me went duck hunting. We go once or twice a week in the season.'

'Where did you go hunting?'

'Big Marsh.'

'What time did you get there?'

'We were in the blind by, I don't know, four-thirty, five.'

'Did you speak to your wife before you left?'

'She was asleep. I never wake her up. She made the sandwiches and stuff the night before.'

'Did you two have a fight or a disagreement the previous night?'

'Not really.'

'What do you mean, "not really"?'

'We weren't getting along. I told you that before. Things were not exactly peaches and cream around the place, but we weren't yelling at each other, nothing like that. It was just kind of cool between us. Hell, she made my lunch.'

'How long were you hunting?'

'We left Big Marsh about three P.M. We always stop on the way home and have a couple of beers, brag about who bagged the most birds, like that.'

'And it was on the way home from one of these hunting trips that you first met Poppy Palmer at the Skin Game Club, isn't that right?'

'Sure, I told you all that before.' He looked at Rainey and held his hands out and shrugged.

'Do you have anything new to ask?' Rainey said with irritation.

'There are several points we need to clear up,' Parver said quietly. Vail was impressed by her control. 'How soon after you met Poppy Palmer did you first have sexual relations with her?'

'In minutes or hours?' Darby smirked.

'Hours will be fine,' Parver answered coolly.

'Like I told you, we went into the Skin Game and she was workin' that day and we had a couple of beers and then Charlie asked her to have a beer with us only she wanted a champagne cocktail. That's the way it works, they put Coca-Cola in a glass or something and you pay five bucks for it and that's what they call champagne. So we fooled around talking until seven and she was getting off work, so I said, How about it? You want to stop

43

somewhere, have a real drink? One thing led to another and we finally went to the Bavarian Inn and got a room.' He leaned across the table towards Parver and said, 'You want all the details?'

'That won't be necessary.' She looked down at her notes. 'Not now, anyway.

Nice shot, thought Vail. *Let him think this isn't going to be the end of it. Throw him off.*

'Did you have sexual intercourse with Miss Palmer on that occasion?' Parver continued.

Darby looked at Rainey, who waved off his concern. 'Sure.'

'How many times after that did you and Miss Palmer meet?'

'I dunno, four or five. I don't remember exactly.'

She checked her notes. 'Miss Palmer says she met you at the Bavarian Inn six times. You have said five. Then six. And this time four or five. Which is it?'

'Look, what's the dif? I had a fling with her. I never tried to say I didn't. I told the cops that the first night they talked to me.'

'So was it four, five, or six?' she asked calmly.

'I just told you, I don't remember. Okay, six. Hell, it was six if Poppy says so. I don't mark my calendar, maybe she does.'

'But you always had sex with her?'

'Yeah. Why, does it turn you on hearing about it?'

'That's enough of that, Darby,' Vail snapped.

'Look, what I did was in self-defence. How many goddamn times do I have to repeat it to you people? Why don't you go out and bust some drug dealers, do something for the community?'

Vail turned to Rainey. 'This can go on forever if that's what he wants,' he said.

'Just answer the questions, yes or no,' Rainey said, still staring at Vail.

'Let's go back to the day you shot your wife,' Parver said. 'Did you to to the Skin Game Club that day?'

'No. We stopped in a beer joint out on 78. I don't know if it's got a name. The sign in front says cocktails.'

'Did you see Poppy Palmer at all that day?'

'Nope.'

'Talk to her?'

'Not before the shooting.'

'At any time?'

'I called after the police came and I found the paper with her number on it by the phone.'

'Why did you call her?'

'I wanted to tell her what happened and I wanted to know about the phone number. Where Ramona got it because Poppy's number isn't in the book and she told me Ramona had called her about four-thirty, five o'clock and went crazy on the phone. Said she was gonna fix me. You know all that, you talked to Poppy.'

'What did she tell you exactly?'

'Just that. Ramona called her and was all outta shape. And, like, blamed Poppy for what happened. And Poppy couldn't get a word in edgewise, Ramona was crying and screaming so. Said she was gonna fix my wagon. That's exactly what Poppy told me, that Ramona said she was gonna fix my goddamn wagon.'

'What time did you leave the bar on 78?'

'I don't know, about five-thirty. I wasn't watching the clock.' He chuckled. 'Usually my old lady didn't take a shot at me when I came home late.'

'Roughly what time was it?'

'It takes about a half hour to drive home and the news was coming on when I got there. I could hear Dan Rather talking on the TV when I walked in. It was just starting.'

'Show us on the diagram exactly what happened when you entered the house.'

'Damn!' He grabbed a pencil and traced his steps into the house on the diagram. As he told the story, he began talking faster. 'I come in the house here and I walk to the doorway to the living room that's, I don't know, five feet maybe, and as I look into the living room, she's . . . Ramona's . . . sitting in the easy chair here and she's aiming my .38 target pistol at me and she cuts loose! Just starts shooting! So I dive straight ahead to the other side of the arch and I'm against the wall here and she puts a shot here where this X is, and another one here, and I panic and I shove two shells in my shotgun and just then she shoots again and the bullet goes through the wall here and misses my head by a gnat's ass and I just thought, She's gonna kill me! So I charge around the corner and fire once and it kind of knocks her back in the chair and her arm flung up and she put another shot into the ceiling and I was charging right at her and I shot again. It all happened in, like, less than a minute.'

'What did you think after all the shooting was over?'

'What did I *think*? I was out of breath. I was scared. She almost killed me.'

'But what did you think while this was happening? Did you call to her, try to reason with her?'

'Hell, no, it all happened just like that. Bang, bang, bang, bang. Bullets flying through the wall. I wasn't thinking. I was trying to stay alive.'

'Did you warn her?'

'A bullet just flew that damn close to my head. Warn her about what? "Hey, Ramona here I come, ready or not"? I just panicked and I figured it's her or me and ran into the room shooting.'

'So now it's over. Your wife is lying there with two wounds, one in her head. What went through your mind?'

'At first I got choked up. I almost puked, I never shot a human being before. And she was bleeding. And I dropped the gun down and felt for a pulse in her wrist, but I, y'know, I was confused and upset, so I went in and called 911. That's when I saw where she broke into my gun cabinet and that's when I found the phone number beside the phone.'

'Was the phone number in your wife's handwriting?'

'Hell, I dunno, you think I was analysing handwriting? The cops talked to me for three, four hours that night. They took the note and I haven't seen it since.'

'But you didn't write it?'

Vail sat back in his chair and concentrated on Parver. She was doing a superb job. The handwriting of the note had not occurred to Vail – or to anyone that he was aware of. She was cool, quiet but not soft, very direct, and she was beginning to rattle Darby. She was totally focused. For a moment, she reminded Vail of Jane Venable, the prosecutor who had preceded him as chief prosecutor.

'Hell, no,' Darby snapped. 'I told you, she wasn't listed, you think I wanted my wife to call her up?'

'Do you have any idea where she might have found that number?'

'No.'

'Who else knew the number?'

'How the hell do I know?'

'Is it possible that you wrote the number down and forgot it and she found it? In a drawer or something like that?'

'I ... didn't ... write ... the goddamn number. Is that clear?'

He turned to Rainey and said plaintively, 'It's the same damn questions as last time. They know the answers, what the hell is this?' He turned back to Parver. 'I killed my wife, okay? She shot at me, I shot at her. That's it. I got nothing more to say.'

'He's right,' said Rainey. 'It's the same ground you ploughed last time.'

'I just want to make it clear to you, Mr Darby, that we have two strong motives for murder here,' Shana Parver said. She counted items off on her fingers. 'Money – a

$250,000 insurance policy, and you're about to go into bankruptcy – and infidelity. They're the biggies, Mr Darby. It's also a hard story to come to terms with, this shootout scenario. Your wife wasn't a violent woman from everything we've been told. And she also hated guns. Isn't it true that you wanted her to take shooting lessons and she refused to touch a gun?'

'Yeah. Maybe that's why she missed me,' he said with a sneer.

'The point is, Mr Darby, if we need to talk to you again, we will. We'll keep talking to you until we decide for sure whether or not this homicide was justifiable.'

He stood up angrily and leaned towards her with both hands on the table. 'It happened just the way I said it happened. Ramona and me are the only two people that were there and she's dead. Try to prove otherwise or leave me alone, *little* lady.'

He spun around and slammed out of the room.

Rainey stood and put his papers in his briefcase. He looked at Vail and shook his head.

'I object to this whole meeting, Miss Parver. The note is moot. It was there. It substantiates Miss Palmer's statement and both you and the cops have had rounds with her. Stop trying to make chicken salad out of chickenshit. You know this could just as easily have gone the other way. Jimmy could be underground and you could be going after Ramona Darby for blowing him away.' He shook his head. 'You two are whistling "Dixie" on this one.'

He followed Darby out of the room.

'Damn!' Parver said, slamming down her pencil.

'Darby's hanging tough,' Vail said. 'He doesn't have any choice.'

'You think Rainey really believes him?'

'I have no doubt he believes Darby's innocent. We haven't given him anything to change that. He knows we don't have a case.'

'Darby killed her in cold blood,' Shana Parver said. 'I know it, we *all* know it.'

'Let me tell you a little story,' Vail said, as they started back to the fourth floor. 'A few years ago an elderly man named Shuman was found in a northside apartment dead of a gunshot wound to the head. The windows and doors were all locked, but there was no weapon anywhere on the premises. The last man to see him alive was a friend of his named Turk Loudon, a junkie who had served time for robbery and assault. He had the victim's ring and fifty-seven dollars and a key to the apartment. And no alibi. He claimed the old man had told him he was sick of living and had given him the money and the ring earlier in the day. He had the key because he was homeless and Shuman let him sleep on the floor at night. He was arrested and charged with murder one.

'His *pro bono* lawyer wanted to go for a deal. Problem was, the gunshot wound to the head was a contact shot, which suggested extreme malice. A bigger problem was Loudon. He absolutely refused to plea. He claimed he was innocent, period. Nobody believed him, particularly his own lawyer.

'Then about two weeks after Loudon was arrested, some painters went to redo the apartment. They found an army .45 calibre pistol lodged behind the radiator. Shuman's prints were all over it and the bullets. Ballistics matched the gun and the bullet in Shuman's head. Shuman had shot himself, and when he did, his arm jerked out, the gun flew out of his hand and dropped behind the radiator. The cops missed it when they searched the place because they didn't think a gun would fit behind it and it was hot. So they looked under the radiator, but not behind it.'

'Were you the prosecutor?'

'No, I was the lawyer. I didn't believe my client – and I was wrong. I damn near plea-bargained him into Joliet for the rest of his life.'

'So you're saying give Darby the benefit of the doubt?'

'I'm saying if you're going to defend someone, particularly for first-degree murder, you can't afford to doubt their innocence. Paul Rainey believes Darby's innocent because he doesn't have any choice. If we can crack Darby's story, if Paul begins to doubt him? It'll gnaw on him until he finds out what the truth is. The trouble is, we can't make a dent in Darby's version of what happened.'

'So Darby sticks to his guns. . . .'

'And we're out of luck,' Vail answered. 'He got lucky. Usually amateurs like that, some little thing trips them up. Something they overlooked, a witness pops out of the cake, a fingerprint shows up where they least expect it. We've been working on this guy for a month and right now we don't have a case.'

'Let me go back to Sandytown,' she said. 'Take one more crack at it, just to make sure we haven't missed something.'

Vail sighed. He knew the frustration Shana Parver was feeling – they all were feeling – but he also had seen more than one felon walk for lack of evidence and he had to balance the time of his prosecutors and investigators against the odds of breaking Darby. The odds were in Darby's favour.

'You know, maybe it happened the way he says it did, Shana. Maybe we all dislike this guy so much we *want* him to be guilty.'

'No!' she snapped back. 'He planned it and he did her.'

'Are you ready to go up against Rainey in the courtroom?' Vail asked her.

'I can hardly wait,' she answered confidently.

'With this case?'

She thought about his question for several moments. Then her shoulders sagged. 'No,' she said finally, but her momentary depression was gone a second later. 'That's why I want to go over all the ground once more, and question Poppy Palmer again, before we shut it down,' she pleaded.

'Okay.' Vail sighed. 'One more day. Take Abel with you. But unless you come up with something significant by tomorrow night, this case is dead.'

Five

Harvey St Claire was on to something.

Vail could tell the minute he and Parver got off the lift. The heavyset man was sitting on the edge of a chair beside the main computer, leaning forward with his forearms on his thighs. And his left leg was jiggling. That was the tipoff, that nervous leg.

Sitting beside St Claire was Ben Meyer, who was as tall and lean as St Claire was short and stubby. Meyer had a long, intense face and a shock of black hair, and he was dressed, as was his custom, in a pinstriped suit, white shirt, and sombre tie. St Claire, as was *his* custom, wore a blue and yellow flannel shirt, red suspenders, sloppy blue jeans, heavy shoes, and a White Sox windbreaker.

Meyer, at thirty-two, was the resident computer expert and had designed the elabourate system that hooked the DA's office with HITS, the Homicide Investigation and Tracking System that linked police departments all over the country. St Claire, who was fifty-two, had, during his twenty-eight years in law enforcement, tracked moonshiners in Georgia and Tennessee, wetbacks along the Texican border, illegal gun smugglers out of Canada, illegal aliens in the barrios of Los Angeles and San Diego, and some of the meanest wanted crooks in the country when he was with the US Marshal's Service.

Meyer was a specialist in fraud. It was Meyer who had first detected discrepancies that had brought down two city councilmen for misappropriating funds and accepting kickbacks. Later, in his dramatic closing argument, Meyer had won the case with an impassioned plea for the rights of the taxpayers. St Claire was a hunch player, a man who had a natural instinct for link analysis –

putting together seemingly disparate facts and projecting them into a single conclusion. Most criminal investigators plotted the links on paper and in computers, connecting bits and pieces of information until they began to form patterns or relationships. St Claire did it in his head, as if he could close his eyes and see the entire graph plotted out on the backs of his eyelids. He also had a phenomenal memory for crime facts. Once he heard, read, or saw a crime item he never forgot it.

When Meyer and St Claire got together, it meant trouble. Vail ignored Naomi, who was motioning for him to come to his office, and stood behind Meyer and St Claire.

'Here's what I got in mind,' St Claire said. 'I wanna cross-match missing people and unsolved homicides, then see if we have any overlap in dates. Can we do that?'

'State level?'

'Yeah, to start with. Exclude this county for the time being.'

'Nothing to it,' Meyer said, his fingers clicking on the computer keyboard.

'What the hell're you two up to?' Vail asked.

'Hunch,' St Claire said, still watching the screen. His blue eyes glittered behind wire-rimmed glasses that kept sliding down to the end of his nose.

'Everybody's got a hunch. I had to listen to Abel's hunches all the way through breakfast. A hunch about what?'

'About this new thing,' St Claire said.

'What new thing?'

St Claire's upper lip bulged with a wad of snuff. Without taking his eyes off the big screen of the computer, he spat delicately into a silver baby cup he carried at all times for just that purpose.

'The landfill murders,' he said. 'We're trying to get a leg up on it.'

'Well, Eckling's got seven days before we officially enter the case.'

'Cold trail by then.'

'Let's wait until Okimoto tells us something,' Vail said.

'That could be a couple days,' St Claire said. 'I just wanna run some ideas through the computer network. No big thing.'

'Who says they were murdered, anyway?' Meyer said.

'Hell,' said St Claire, dropping another dollop of snuff into his baby cup and smiling, 'it's too good not to be murder.'

'What's your caseload, Ben?' asked Vail.

'Four.'

'And you're playing with this thing?'

'I don't know how to run this gadget,' St Claire complained.

Vail decided to humour him. 'You can have the whiz kid here until after lunch,' he said. 'Then Meyer's back on his cases.'

'Can't do much in three hours,' St Claire groaned.

'Then you better hurry.'

Naomi finally walked across the office and grabbed Vail by the arm. She pointed across the room to Yancey's office.

'He called ten minutes ago. I told him . . .'

'No. N-o,' Vail said, entering his office. He stopped short inside the door. Hanging on the coat tree behind the door were his dark blue suit and his tuxedo.

'What's this?'

'I had your stuff picked up for you. Didn't think you'd have time to get home and change.'

'Change for what?' he growled.

'You have to accompany Yancey to the opening luncheon of the State Lawyers Convention. He's the keynote speaker. High noon – '

'Oh, for Christ sake!'

'And the opening-night cocktail party is at the Marina Convention Center at six.'

'God*damn* it! Why didn't you tell me earlier?'

'I may as well give you all the bad news. Yancey wants to see you in his office. He wanted me to go down and get you.'

'Out of interrogation?'

'I explained that to him – again.'

'Tell him I'm tied up until lunchtime.'

'I don't think he'll buy it. Raymond Firestone's in there with him. Came in unannounced.'

Vail looked at her with a sickened expression. 'Saved the worst until last, huh? Just stood there and sandbagged me.'

'No, no, I'm not taking the rap for this one. You agreed to both the lunch and the cocktail party last summer.'

'And you're just reminding me now?'

'What did you want me to do, Marty, give you daily time ticks? Three days to go until the lawyers convention, two days, eighteen hours. Call you at home and wake you up. Nine hours to go!'

'Wake me up? I haven't been to *bed*!'

'I did not drag you out to the city dump. Parver set up the interrogation with Darby, not me. And I had nothing to do with Councilman Firestone's visit.'

Vail stared angrily across the broad expanse of the office at DA Jack Yancey's door. He knew what to expect before he walked into Yancey's office. Raymond Firestone had arrived in the city twenty years earlier with a battered suitcase, eighty dollars in his pocket, and a slick tongue. Walking door to door selling funeral insurance to the poor, he had parlayed the nickel-dime policy game into the beginnings of an insurance empire that now had offices all over the state. A bellicose and unsophisticated bully, he had, during seven years as a city councilman, perfected perfidity and patronage to a dubious art. As

Abel Stenner had once observed, 'Firestone's unscrupulous enough to be twins.'

Firestone, who was supported openly by Eckling and the police union, had let it be known soon after his first election that he was going to 'put Vail in his place'. It was a shallow threat but a constant annoyance.

Firestone was seated opposite Yancey with his back to the office door and he looked back over his shoulder as Vail entered, staring at him through narrowed dubious eyes that seemed frozen in a perpetual squint. Firestone was a man of average stature with lacklustre brown hair, which he combed forward to hide a receding hairline, a small, thin-lipped mouth that was slow to smile, and the ruby, mottled complexion of a heavy drinker.

'Hello, Raymond,' Vail said, and, ignoring the chair beside Firestone, sat down in an easy chair against the wall several feet from the desk.

Firestone merely nodded.

Yancey sat behind his desk. He was a chubby, unctuous, smooth-talking con man with wavy white hair and a perpetual smile. A dark-horse candidate for DA years before, Yancey had turned out to be the ultimate bureaucrat, capitalizing on his oily charm and a natural talent for mediation and compromise, surrounding himself with bright young lawyers to do the dirty work since he had no stomach for the vigour of courtroom battles.

'We seem to have a little problem here,' Yancey started off. 'But I see no reason why we can't work it out amicably.'

Vail didn't say a word.

Like Jane Venable before him, Vail had little respect for Yancey as a litigator but liked him personally. Abandoned ten years earlier by Venable, Yancey had eagerly accepted Vail – his deadliest opponent in court – as his chief prosecutor. Their deal was simple. Yancey handled politics. Vail handled business.

'It's about this thing between you and Chief Eckling,' Yancey continued.

Vail stared at him pleasantly. The 'thing' between Vail and Eckling had been going on since long before Vail had become a prosecutor.

'It's time to bury the goddamn hatchet,' Firestone interjected.

'Oh? In whose back?' Vail asked quietly, breaking his silence.

Firestone glared at Yancey, who sighed and smiled and leaned back in his chair, making a little steeple of his fingertips and staring at the ceiling.

'That's what we want to avoid, Martin,' he said.

'Uh-huh.'

'What we're suggesting is that you back off a little bit,' Firestone said.

'That's a compromise?'

'I thought it had been agreed that the DA's office would keep out of the chief's hair for seven days after a crime. That's the deal, he gets the week. Am I right? Did we agree to that?' Firestone looked at Yancey when he said it.

'Uh-huh,' Vail answered.

Firestone turned on him and snapped, 'Then why don't you do it?'

'We do,' Vail said flatly.

'Bullshit! You and your people show up every time a felon farts in this town,' Firestone growled.

'Now, now, Raymond,' Yancey said, 'it's not uncommon for the DA to go to the scene of a crime. Usually the police appreciate the help.'

'He ain't the goddamn DA.'

'No, but he is my chief prosecutor. It's well within his jurisdiction.'

'We're talking about cooperation here,' snapped Firestone, his face turning crimson.

'Why don't I go back to my office?' Vail suggested with

57

a smile. 'You guys are talking like I'm not even in the room. I feel like I'm eavesdropping.'

Firestone whirled on him. 'You go out of your way to make Eckling look bad,' he said, his voice beginning to rise.

'I don't have to,' Vail said. 'He does that all by himself.'

'See what I mean!' Firestone said to Yancey. 'How can Eric do his job with this smartass needling him all the time?'

'You'll excuse me,' Vail said calmly, and stood up.

'Take it easy, Marty, take it easy,' Yancey said, waving him back to his seat.

'You got a beef with me, tell me, not him,' Vail said to Firestone, his voice still calm and controlled.

'He's your boss, that's why.'

'Not in this area,' Vail said. He knew the best way to get to Firestone was to stay calm. The hint of a smile toyed with his lips. 'You know, frankly, I don't give a damn whether it pleases you or not, Raymond. You're a city boy. The county runs this office. You don't have any more clout over here than the janitor, so why don't you mind your own business and stay out of ours?'

'Jesus, Marty . . .' Yancey stammered.

'C'mon, Jack, I'm not going to listen to this windbag yell insults at me.'

'Goddamn it, I told you this was a waste of time, Jack,' Firestone said angrily. 'Vail isn't capable of cooperating with anybody.'

'Did you say that, Jack? Did you say I'd *cooperate* with them?'

'What I said was, maybe everybody could kind of stand back and cool off. What I mean is, try a little cooperation between your two departments.'

'I'm quite cool,' Vail said. 'And as far as cooperating goes, I wouldn't share my dirty socks with Eckling. He's incompetent, he's on the take, and he wouldn't know a clue if it was sitting on the end of his nose.'

'Listen here – '

'No, you listen, Councilman. I'm an officer of the court. I'm charged with the responsibility of prosecuting the cases that come before me to the best of my ability. I can't do that if I rely on Eric Eckling. Two years ago he was ready to drop the case against your two buddies on the council. We took it away from him and they're both doing hard time in Rock Island for malfeasance.' Vail stopped for a moment, then added, 'Maybe that's the problem. Maybe you're just getting jumpy, Raymond.'

Firestone began to shake with anger. His face now turned bright vermilion. He started to speak, but the words stuck in his throat.

'Tell you what,' Vail went on. 'You throw Eckling out on his ass where he belongs and put a police chief instead of a pimp in the job and you won't have a problem.'

'God*damn* you!' Firestone screamed, and stomped out of the office.

Yancey watched him leave. He blew a breath out. A line of sweat formed on his forehead. 'Jesus, Marty, you gotta be such a hard-ass?' he said.

'You and I have a deal, Jack. I run the prosecutor's office and you do the politicking. I don't ask for your help, don't ask for mine, okay?'

'He throws a lot of weight in the party.'

Yancey had, within his grasp, the thing he had yearned for all his life, an appointment to the bench. But he needed the support of every Democrat in the county, so at this moment his chief concern was keeping peace in the family. Vail knew the scenario.

'So throw just as much weight round as Firestone does. Stop acting like the Pillsbury Doughboy and kick his ass back.'

'I didn't mean for you to—'

'Sure you did. We've been through this song and dance before. You don't need Firestone anyway, his whole district's union and blue collar. Solid Democrats. They wouldn't go Republican if Jimmy Hoffa rose up from the dead and ran on the GOP ticket.'

'I just hate to look for trouble.'

'You know, the trouble with you, Jack, is you want everybody to love you. Life ain't like that, as Huckleberry Finn would say. Hell, when you're a judge you can piss everybody off and they'll smile and thank you.'

Vail started out the door.

'Marty?'

'Yeah?'

'Uh . . . are you gonna wear that suit to the luncheon?'

'Sweet Jesus,' Vail said, and left the office.

St Claire and Meyer were scatter-shooting, feeding information into the computer and looking for links, bits of information that St Claire eventually would try to connect together into patterns. Meyer was caught up in the game. It was like Dungeons and Dragons, where the players are lured through a maze of puzzles to the eventual solution.

Some of the unsolved homicides that HITS turned up were interesting, but nothing seemed to relate to the city landfill case and Meyer was getting tired. He and St Claire had been at this cross-matching game for three hours and his stomach was telling him it was lunchtime. The office was empty except for the two of them. They had developed a list of seventy-six missing persons and nineteen unsolved homicides throughout the state, but neither of the figures appeared to correlate.

'What're you after, Harvey?' Meyer asked. 'None of these cases could possibly relate to the landfill.'

'The three bodies have to be connected in some way. They were almost side by side, so they had to have been dumped at the same time, don't you agree?'

'That makes sense.'

'Well, think about it. Three people show up in the same area of the city landfill. If they were dropped at the

60

same time, in all probability they knew each other. They had something in common.'

'Yeah, they're all dead,' Meyer said.

'Also they've been in there awhile. What I'm gettin' at, son, is that if the three of them knew each other and were involved with each other in some way, and they all disappeared at the same time, don't you think *somebody* would have reported that? First thing I did this morning, I called Missing Persons and asked them one question. "You looking for three people who knew each other and were reported missing at the same time?" The answer was no.'

'Maybe – '

'Folks who are missing friends or relatives will come forward to see if they can identify these bodies. Hell, if your kid was missing, and you picked up the paper and read that three unidentified bodies were found in the city landfill, wouldn't you be curious to see if he might be one of those three? There's a lotta missing persons out there, cowboy. And at least one person looking for every one that's missing.'

'What the hell's your point, Harve?'

'Let's say we don't get an ID on these people – at least for a while. Doesn't that raise the possibility that maybe they're from someplace else?'

Meyer looked away from the screen for a moment. 'You think they're out-of-towners?'

'Maybe tourists. Conventioneers. Or assume for a minute that they were killed out of town and brought here.'

'You're reaching on this one, Harve.'

'Humour me, son. I know it's a long shot. What if they ain't local? Think about it. What if they were involved in something outside the city? A bank heist, a dope deal, some cult thing. And suppose it went sour and these John and Jane Does were killed because of this deal and they got dropped in the dump. Hell, *somebody* dumped those people out there, they didn't fall out of the sky.'

'It's a wild-goose chase.'

'Maybe,' the old-timer said, throwing his empty coffee cup into a wastebasket. He leaned back in his chair, tucked a fresh pinch of snuff in his cheek, and interlocked his pudgy fingers over his stomach. 'I'm remembering a time five, six years ago. The Seattle police turned up two white males in a common grave just outside the city. They couldn't ID the victims. Six months go by, they've about written the case off, and one day they get a call from a police chief in Arizona. A thousand miles away! Turns out the Arizona cops nabbed a guy for passing a hot fifty-dollar bill that was lifted six months before in a bank heist. The guy breaks down and not only confesses to the bank job, he says there were three of them involved and they drove up to Seattle to hide out and started squabbling and he takes them both down and buries them out in the woods and drifts back down to Phoenix. The story checks out. The Seattle police solves its case. The Arizona PD solves its bank robbery.'

'And everybody's smilin' but the guy that did the trick,' said Meyer.

'Right. The *last* place the Seattle PD would've expected to get a line on their John Does was in Arizona. So you never know. We're looking to see if anything strikes our fancy, okay?'

Meyer was back staring at the big computer screen, watching it scroll through case descriptions. Suddenly he stopped it.

'How about Satanism, Harve? Does that strike your fancy?'

'Satanism?'

'Here's a little town called Gideon down in the southern corner of the state, probably hasn't had a major homicide in twenty years. The local PD thinks Satanists killed a housewife down there.'.

62

'Gideon? There's a nice biblical name,' St Claire said. 'Seems an unlikely place for Satanists to rear their ugly heads.'

'The chief of police refused to supply any crime reports. Didn't even call in the state forensics lab – which is required by law in a case like this. According to the cover sheet, it's a small, religious community. They think it involves Satanism and they don't want any publicity about it.'

He ripped a computer printout of the cover report from the printer and read it aloud:

'UNREPORTED HOMICIDE, 7/12/93: Murder of Gideon, Ill., Housewife. Gideon is a religious community of Mormons. The population is approximately 2,000. Al Braselton, an agent with the state Bureau of Investigation, learned of the event while on an an unrelated investigation in Shelby, 12 miles north of Gideon. The Gideon police chief, Hiram Young, reluctantly turned over to Agent Braselton some photographs and the sketchy homicide report. This is all the information the Bureau has on this crime at this time. According to Chief Young, the town didn't want a lot of outsiders coming there . . .'

Meyer exclaimed, 'And this in quotes, Harve, ' "Because of the Satanism angle"! The homicide is still unresolved.'

'There's an angle I never thought about,' said St Claire. 'Satanism.' He laughed at the thought.

'My God, look at these photos,' Meyer said.

Six photographs had popped up on the computer monitor. Like all graphic police studies of violence, they depicted the stark climate of the crime without art or composition. Pornographic in detail, they appeared on the fifty-inch TV screen in two rows, three photos in each row. The three on the top were full, medium, and close-up shots of a once pleasant-looking, slightly overweight woman in her mid to late twenties. She had been stabbed and cut dozens of times. The long, establishing shot captured the nauseating milieu of the crime scene. The victim lay in a corner of the room, her head cocked crazily against the wall. Her mouth bulged open. Her eyes were frozen in a horrified stare. Blood had splattered the walls, the TV set, the floors, everything.

The medium shot was even more graphic. The woman's nipples had been cut off and her throat was slit to the bone.

But the close-up of her head was the most chilling of all.

The woman's nipples were stuffed in her mouth.

'Good lord,' St Claire said with revulsion.

'I'm glad we haven't had lunch yet,' Meyer said, swallowing hard.

The lower row of photographs were from the same perspective but were shots of her back, where the butchery had been just as vicious.

'I can see why the police chief thinks Satanists were involved,' Meyer said. 'This is obscene.'

St Claire leaned over Meyer's shoulder and together they read the homicide report filed by Chief Hiram Young:

On October 27, 1993, at approximately 8 A.M, I answered a call to the home of George Balfour, local, which was called in by a neighbour, Mrs Miriam Peronne, who resides next door. I found a white female, which I personally identified as Linda Balfour, 26, wife of George, on the floor of the living room. Mrs Balfour was DOA. The coroner, Bert Fields, attributes death to multiple stab wounds. Her son, age 1, was five feet away and unharmed. Her husband was several miles from town when the crime occurred. There are no suspects.

Meyer turned to St Claire. 'Not much there,' he said.

But St Claire did not answer. He stood up and walked close to the screen. He was looking at the close-up of the back of the woman's head.

'What's that?' he asked.

'What?'

'There, on the back of her head.' St Claire pointed to what appeared to be markings under the woman's hair.

'I'll zoom in,' Meyer said.

He isolated the photograph, then blew it up four times before it began to fall apart. Beneath the blood-mottled hair on the back of her head were what appeared to be a row of marks, but the blown-up photo was too fuzzy to define them.

'Maybe just scratches,' Meyer suggested.

'Can you clear it up any?' St Claire asked.

Meyer digitally enhanced the picture several times, the photo blinking and becoming a little more distinct each time he hit the key combinations.

'That's as far as I can take it,' Meyer said.

'Looks like numbers,' St Claire said, adjusting his glasses and squinting at the image. 'Numbers and a letter . . .'

'Looks like it was written with her blood,' Meyer said with disgust.

A familiar worm nibbled at St Claire's gut. Nothing he could put his finger on, but it was nibbling nevertheless.

'Ben, let's give this Chief Young a call. He's got to know more about this case than the network's got.'

'Harvey, I've got four cases on my desk . . .'

'I got a nudge on this, Ben. Don't argue with me.'

'A nudge? What's a nudge?'

'It's when your gut nudges your brain,' the old-timer answered.

Six

In the lobby of the Ritz Hotel, the city's three hundred most-powerful men preened like gamecocks as they headed for the dining room. They strutted into the room, pompous, jaws set, warily eyeing their peers and enforcing their standing in the power structure by flaunting condescending demeanours The State Lawyers Association Board of Directors luncheon was the city's most prestigious assembly of the year and it was – for the most powerful – a contest of attitudes. Three hundred invitations went out; invitations harder to acquire than tickets to the final game of a World Series because they could not be bought, traded, or used by anyone else. The most exclusive – and snobbish – ex officio 'club' in town established who the most powerful men in the city were. To be on the invitation list connoted acceptance by the city's self-appointed leaders. To be dropped was construed as a devastating insult.

Yancey's invitation to be the keynote speaker was a sign that he was recognized as one of the city's most valued movers and shakers. For years, he had secretly yearned to be accepted into the supercillious boys' club and he was revelling in the attention he was getting. Vail followed him into the dining room, smiling tepidly in the wake of the pandering DA as he glad-handed his way to the head table. This was Yancey's day and Vail was happy for him, even though he regarded the proceedings with disdain.

His seat was directly in front of the lectern at a table with three members of the state supreme court and the four most influential members of the legislature, an elderly, dour, and boring lot, impressed with their own importance and more interested in food and drink than intelligent conversation. Vail suffered through the lunch.

Yancey got a big hand when he was introduced. And why not? Speaking was his forte and he was renowned for spicing his speeches with off-colour jokes and supplicating plaudits for the biggest of the big shots. As he was being introduced, Yancey felt an annoying pain in the back of his head. He rubbed it away. But as he stood up to speak, it became a searing pain at the base of his skull. He shook his head sharply and then it hit again like a needle jabbing into his head. The room seemed to go out of focus; the applause became hollow. He reached for the lectern to steady himself.

Vail saw Yancey falter and shakily steady himself by gripping the lectern with one hand. With the other, he rubbed the base of his neck, twisting his head as if an imaginary bee was attacking him. He smiled, now grabbing the edge of the speaker's platform with both hands. From below him, Vail could see his hands shaking.

Yancey took all the applause, taking deep breaths to calm himself down.

'Before I begin, I'd like to take this opportunity to introduce, uh . . . my . . . m-m-my right *and* left, uh, left . . .' His speech was slurred and he was stuttering.

Vail leaned forward in his chair. *What the hell was wrong with Yancey?* he wondered.

'. . . one of this . . . this, uh . . . t-t-this country's great p-p-prosecutors, and the m-m-man who . . . uh . . .'

Yancey stopped, staring around the room helplessly, blinking his eyes. Vail got up and rushed towards the end of the head table, but even as he did, Yancey cried out, 'Oh!', pitched forward over the lectern, arms flailing, and dropped straight to the floor.

Vail rode in the ambulance with the stricken DA, after first calling St Claire and sending him to find Yancey's wife, Beryl. Yancey was grey and barely breathing. The paramedics worked over him feverishly, barking orders to each other while the driver called ahead to alert the trauma unit and summon Yancey's personal physician to the emergency room. When they arrived, they pushed Yancey's stretcher on the run into the operating room and Vail was left alone in the wash-up room.

Almost an hour passed before Yancey's doctor came out of the OR. Dr Gary Ziegler, was a tall, lean man with a craggy, portentous face studded with sorrowful eyes. He looked perpetually worried and was not a man who exuded hope to those waiting to get news of a stricken loved one. He wearily pulled off his latex gloves and swept off his cap and face mask, then pinched the bridge of his nose with a thumb and a forefinger and sighed.

'That bad, Gary?' Vail asked.

Ziegler looked over at him and shook his head.

'I hope you have a lot of energy, Martin.'

'What the hell does that mean?'

'It means you're going to be a busy man. It's going to be a long time before Jack goes back to work – if he ever does.'

'Heart attack?'

'Massive cerebral thrombosis.'

'Which is what, exactly?'

'Blockage of a main artery to the brain by a thrombus – a blood clot. Specifically, it means the cerebellum of the brain has been deprived of blood and oxygen.'

'In other words, a stroke.'

'In other words, a *massive* stroke. He's suffering severe *Hemiplegia* – we can already determine that, his reflexes are nil. And I suspect he's suffering *aphasia*, although I can't tell how bad it is yet.'

'Translate that into simple English for me,' Vail said.

Ziegler walked to the sink and began scrubbing his hands. 'Paralysis down his entire left side caused by damage to the right cerebral hemisphere. A speech deficiency caused by damage to the left hemisphere. It could have been brought on by a brain tumour, athero-sclerosis, hypertension, I can't be sure at this point. Right now we've got him stabilized, but his condition is poor and he's unconscious.'

'My God.'

'The fact that he survived the first two hours is encouraging,' Ziegler said. 'If he holds on for another week or ten days, the outlook will be greatly improved. But at this point there's no way of predicting the long-term effects.'

'What I hear you saying is, Jack could be a vegetable.'

'That's pretty rash,' Ziegler said, annoyed by Vail's description.

'It sounds pretty rash!'

'Well, nothing good can be said about a stroke of this magnitude, but until we can do an ECG, blood tests, CAT scans, an angiography, hell, I couldn't even guess at the prognosis.'

'Can I see him?'

Ziegler pointed to the door of the Intensive Care Unit.

'I'm going to clean up. If Beryl gets here before I come out, talk to her, will you? I won't be long.'

Vail looked through the window of the ICU. Yancey lay perfectly still with tubes and IV bottles attached to arms and legs, his face covered with an oxygen mask, machines beeping behind his bed. He was as still as a rock and his skin was the colour of oatmeal.

What irony, Vail thought. *One of the biggest days of his life and his brain blows out on him.*

A few moments later the lift doors opened and Beryl Yancey and her 30-year-old daughter, Joanna, accompanied by a uniformed policeman, stepped out. They looked dazed and confused and stood at the door, their hands interlocked, looking fearfully up and down the hallway. When Beryl saw Vail, she rushed to him, clutching him desperately, and chattering almost incoherently. He put his arms around her and Joanna. Beryl

Yancey knew there were frequent skirmishes between her husband and Vail, but she and Jack Yancey both liked the tough prosecutor and were well aware that his stunning record had helped keep Yancey the district attorney for the past ten years.

'I was at the beauty parlour,' Beryl babbled. 'Can you imagine, the beauty parlour? Is he alive, Martin? Oh, God, don't tell me if he's gone. I can't imagine. I won't – '

'He's hanging on, Beryl.'

'Oh, thank God, thank you, Marty . . .'

'I didn't – '

'Is he awake? Can we see him? Oh, my God, my hair must be a mess. I was right in the middle of . . .' The sentence died in her mouth as she primped her incomplete hairdo.

'Gary Ziegler's just inside the emergency room. He'll be right out. He can give you all the details.'

'They came and got me in a police car. The whole beauty parlour got hysterical when that nice man . . . Who was that man, Martin?'

'His name's Harvey. Harvey St Claire.'

'He said he would wait for you in the car.'

'Fine.'

'You're not going to leave us, are you? Nobody would say anything, you know. Mr St Claire wouldn't tell me anything! I thought . . . Oh, God, I thought everything.'

'He doesn't know anything, Beryl. Harvey doesn't know any more than you do.'

'How bad does my hair look?'

'Your hair looks fine, Mom,' her daughter said, patting her on the arm.

'You know if you need anything, anything at all, just call me. At the office, at home . . .'

'I know that, Martin. But Jack's going to be all right. I know he'll be all right. He never gets sick. Do you know, he never even gets the flu?'

A minute or two later Ziegler came out wearing a fresh

gown and the two Yancey women fled immediately to him. Vail took the lift to the first floor, but as he stepped out he saw a half-dozen reporters and a television crew clustered around the front door. He jumped back inside the lift and rode it to the basement. He took out his portable phone and punched out the car's number. It rang once and St Claire answered.

'Where are you?' he asked.

'The basement. There's press all around the front door.'

'I know. I'm looking at them as we speak.'

'I'm not ready to talk to the press.'

'Follow the arrows to the loading dock on the back side. I'll pick you up there.'

'Right,' Vail answered, following an arrow down a long, dreary tunnel. Empty dollies with bloody sheets wadded up on them lined the walls. Several of the overhead lights were burned out. The narrow, depressing shaft smelled of alcohol and dried blood. He reached the service entrance and bolted through it, raced to the loading platform, and jumped to the ground as St Claire pulled up beside him. He got in the car and St Claire pulled out into the hospital driveway, then sped off towards the courthouse.

'What was it, heart attack?' St Claire asked.

'Stroke. He can't walk, he can't talk, he's living on canned air, his brain has been deprived of oxygen and blood, and he's unconscious. When I suggested he might end up a mashed potato, Ziegler got edgy.'

'Wasn't a very professional diagnosis,' St Claire said. He spat out of the window.

'I'm not a doctor.'

'No.' St Claire chuckled. 'You're the new DA.'

'I don't have time to be DA,' Vail answered sharply. 'This is going to sound weird, but ever since this happened I keep thinking about the day Kennedy was killed, that picture of Johnson in the airplane taking the oath of office.'

'Passing of the mantle, Marty.'

'I'm not a hand squeezer and I'm too blunt in social gatherings. I don't want the mantle.'

'No, cowboy, but you sure got it.'

Chief Hiram Young sat behind his grey metal desk and drummed his fingers, staring at the phone message lying in front of him. Rose, his impressionable secretary, always responded to long-distance phone calls, especially those from big-city police departments, as if each was an omen of pending national disaster. Young even found her careful, impeccable, Palmer-method handwriting annoying, but she was the mayor's sister, so he couldn't complain. Even worse, she underlined words she felt required emphasis.

> You had an *urgent* phone call from the *District Attorney* in *Chicago* (!!) at 1:30 PM I tried to reach you in *several* places. You *must* call Mr Ben Meyer *as soon as you get in*. I took Charlotte to the dentist. Back at 3. Call *ASAP*. I *promised*!!!

The phone number was written double-size across the bottom of the memo pad.

Warily, he dialled the number and asked for Meyer.

'This is Ben Meyer,' the deep voice answered.

'Chief Hiram Young returning your call, sir,' Young replied.

'Yes, sir!' Meyer responded enthusiastically. 'Thanks for getting back to me so promptly.'

'My pleasure,' Young answered. He cradled the phone between his jaw and shoulder and leafed through the mail as they spoke.

'I hate to bother you,' Meyer said, 'but we're working a case up here you may be able to assist us with.'

'Glad to help,' Young said, opening the phone bill.

'It's in regard to the Balfour murder case.'

There was a long pause. A *long* pause.

72

Finally, 'Yes . . .?'

'We think it may relate to a case here.'

'Uh-huh.'

'Uh, would it be possible to get some additional information from your department, Chief? We have the IBI report, but it's pretty skimpy.'

'Our information is pretty skimpy.'

'Have you had any further developments? Suspects, new information . . .'

'Not a thing.'

'As I understand it, you suspect Satanists may have – '

'That was speculation,' Young said tersely.

'I see. Was there anything specific . . .'

'You seen the pictures we sent over to the IBI?'

'Yes, sir.'

'Self-explanatory, wouldn't you say?'

'So it was the nature of the crime that led you to that conclusion?'

'I said it was speculation. Some of the city fathers and local ministers came up with that idea.'

'You don't agree then?'

'Didn't say that. What's your case about?'

'Some unidentified bodies. There are some similarities. Did Mrs Balfour have any enemies? Any – '

'Nothing like that. I knew Linda since she married George up in Carbondale and came here. Three, four years ago. Nice lady. No problems. George is the salt of the earth. Bringing up that little boy all by himself. He's had enough trouble.'

'Do you have any background on Linda Balfour – you know, from before she moved to – '

'I didn't feel it was necessary to snoop into her business. Like I said, she was a nice lady. No problems.'

Meyer was floundering, trying to strike a nerve, something that would open the chief up.

Meyer said, 'And there were no suspects to speak of?'

73

'There was a utility man near the house that morning, but we never could locate him.'

'A utility man? What company – '

'Lady across the street saw him walking down the road. Fact is, we never ascertained who he worked for.'

'And that was your *only* suspect?'

'Told you, Mr Meyer, she didn't have any enemies. Nothing was stolen. Some nut comin' through town, most likely. We worked on that case for about a month.'

'Fingerprints?'

'Nothin' didn't match up with the family and their friends.'

'We're interested in the condition of the body, Chief. Can you – '

'I'm not at liberty to talk about that sir. You might talk to Dr Fields at the clinic – if he'll talk to you. He's also the coroner.'

'Thanks, Chief. Do you have that number?'

Young gave him the number and hung up. He sat and stared at the phone for several moments, started to call Fields, and then changed his mind. Doc Fields was a grown man. He could tell this Meyer fellow whatever he wanted to tell him. Young turned his attention back to the mail.

Doc Fields was staring across a tongue depressor at the most inflamed and swollen throat he had seen in recent years. He threw the wooden stick in the wastebasket and looked sternly down at the six-year-old.

'You been smoking, Mose?' he asked.

The boy's eyes bulged and his mother gasped, and then Fields laughed.

'Just jokin', young fella. Got us some bad tonsils here. Lessee, you're Baptist, aren't you, Beth?'

The mother nodded.

'Those tonsils have to come out. Sooner the better.'

The boy's eyes teared up and his lips began to tremble.

'Oh, nothin' to it, son. Besides, for a couple of days you can have all the ice cream you want to eat. How 'bout that?'

The promise of mountains of ice cream seemed to allay young Moses's fears.

'Check with Sally and see when's the best time for both of us,' Fields said. But before the woman and her son could get up to leave, Fields's secretary peeked in the door.

'You got a long-distance call, Doctor,' she said. 'It's Chicago.'

'You don't say,' said Fields. 'Probably the university school of medicine seeking my consultation.' He snatched up the phone.

'This is Dr Bert Fields. What can I do for you?' he said gruffly.

'Doctor, this is Ben Meyer. I'm a prosecutor with the DA's office. You may be able to help me.'

'You ailing?' Fields said sardonically.

Meyer laughed. 'No, sir. We have a case in progress that may relate to a homicide you had down there.'

'The Balfour murder?'

'How'd you guess?'

'Only homicide we've had hereabouts in a dozen years. In fact, the worst I ever saw and I been the town doctor since '61.'

'I understand you're the coroner.'

'Coroner, family doctor, surgeon, you name it.'

'And you performed an autopsy?'

'Of course.'

'Do you remember any of the particulars?'

'Sir, I remember every inch of that child's corpse. Not likely to forget it.'

'Would it be possible to get a copy of your report?'

Fields hesitated.

'I can assure you, we'll treat it confidentially,' Meyer hurriedly added. 'We may have a similar case up here. If this is a serial killer, it would help us greatly to stop the perp before he goes any further.'

'Perp?'

'Perpetrator.'

'Ah. Perp.' He laughed. 'It'll have to use that. It'll throw Hiram for a loop.'

'Yes, sir. I was wondering, do you have a fax machine?'

Fields got another hearty laugh out of that. 'Just got me an answer machine last year,' he said. 'Can't think of any reason why I'd need a fax machine.'

Meyer sounded depressed by the news. 'It sure would help me right now,' he said.

'Why don't I just get the report out and read it to you? Isn't that long.'

'That would be great!' Meyer answered. He reached over to the telerecorder attached to his phone and pressed the record button. 'Mind if I tape it?'

'Just like that?'

'Yes, sir, just like that. We're big-timers up here,' and they both laughed.

Fields left the phone for a minute and Meyer could hear a metal file drawer open and shut.

'This is exactly what I reported, Mr Meyer. Ready?'

'Yes.'

'The victim, Linda Balfour, is a white female, age 26. The body is 53.5 inches in length and weighs 134 pounds and has blue eyes and light brown hair. She was dead on my arrival at her home on Poplar Street, this city. The victim was stabbed, cut, and incised 56 times. There was evidence of cadaver spasm, trauma, and aero-embolism. There was significant exsanguination from stab wounds. The throat wound, which nearly decapitated Balfour, caused aero-embolism, which usually results in instantaneous death. Wounds in her hands and arms indicate a struggle before she was killed. There was also evidence of mutilation. Both of the victim's nipples and the clitoris were amputated and placed in the victim's mouth. It appears that the wounds were accomplished by a person or persons with some surgical knowledge. Also the inscription C13.489 was printed with the victim's blood on the rear of the skull, 4.6 centimetres above the base of the skull and under the hairline. The weapon was determined to be a common carving knife with an eight-inch blade found on the premises and belonging to the victim. A routine autopsy revealed no alcohol, controlled substances, or poisons in the bloodstream. The victim was nine weeks pregnant. Signed, Edward Fields, M.D. Date, 6/10/93.'

'That help any?' Fields asked.

'Yes, sir,' Meyer said, his pulse racing. 'Can you repeat the inscription on the back of the head so I'm sure I have it right?'

'C13.489. Any idea what that means?'

'Not the slightest,' Meyer said. 'But if we figure it out, I'll let you know.'

'Hope I've been some help, Mr Meyer.'

'Thank you, sir. Thank you very much. If you're ever in town give me a call. I'll buy lunch.'

'My kind of fella.'

Meyer cradled the phone and sat for a long time staring down at the scrap of paper in front of him.

C13.489. What the *hell* could that mean?

Maybe the old-timer would know.

Seven

Vail braced himself and pushed open the doors to the main salon, knowing exactly what to expect. A tidal surge of noise and heat assaulted him. He faced a thousand lawyers and their wives, all babbling at once with a calypso band somewhere on the other side of the room trying to compete with them, all enveloped in an enormous ballroom with eight food tables, each with its own towering ice sculpture, a dozen or more bars, nobody to talk to but lawyers, lobbyists, and politicians – and no place to sit. The world's biggest cocktail party. Vail, a man who despised cocktail parties, was about to take a stroll through Hades.

Vail was the most feared man in the room, for he represented a potential danger to every lawyer at the party: a loose-cannon prosecutor, unpredictable, unbuyable, unbeatable, who had spent nine years on their side of the fence before switching sides and becoming their worst nightmare, a prosecutor who knew all the tricks and was better at the game than they were. In ten years he had successfully prosecuted two city councilmen, a vice mayor and a senator for everything from bribery to malfeasance in office and had wasted a local bank for money washing. They would treat him cordially but at a distance as he worked his way through the room, subtly letting him know that he was not one of them. It was the only part of the ordeal Vail enjoyed, for he revelled in the role of the untouchable outsider.

Otherwise, he despised the annual ritual dance of the state's legal power players and their fawning associates. The corporate partners used these occasions to study the young sycophants and their wives and to reaffirm their choices. How did they handle themselves in this social bullring? Did they have the proper social graces? Did the women dress properly? Did the young lawyers drink too much? Express unacceptable political views? Hold their own in social debate with their peers? And perhaps most important of all, did they discuss the business of the company? Like pledges at a fraternity party, the young bootlickers performed for their bosses, fully aware that their performances would be discussed later and in harsh detail in the halls of the kings. Divorce had even been suggested after these forays.

They drank too much and they bragged too much and it was business. Big business. They talked about lobbying for this bill or that; which PACS they contributed to because they 'got the job done'; which congressmen and state legislators were 'spinners', those whose opinions could be influenced with a free dinner at a four-star restaurant or a hunting trip to some exclusive lodge in Wisconsin or Minnesota; which were 'bottom feeders', cheap sellouts who could be bought for a bottle of good, hearty Scotch and a box of cigars; and which were 'chicken hawk' neophytes who could be lured into the fold with flattery and attention. They scorned the 'UCs', uncooperatives whose votes were not available at any price and subtly shunned them until they were 'seasoned' and learned the first rule of the game: compromise. These conversations were not about the law, they were about business and politics, enterprises that had little use for the law or ethics or integrity.

As Vail entered the room, he passed a group of five lawyers, all performing for a tall, white-haired potentate with smooth pink skin who was obviously enjoying the playlet.

'It'll be tacked on House Bill 2641,' said one. 'Furley will take care of it, he's already spun. It'll glide right through.'

'How about Perdue and that new joker, what's his name, Eagle?' suggested another.

'Harold Eggle,' another intoned. 'A chicken hawk, nobody pays any attention to him.'

'And Perdue's a bottom feeder,' said still another. 'Send him a bottle of Chivas and forget him.'

'It's a done deal. Nobody will buck Tim Furley except the usual UCs and they'll be laughed out of the chamber,' the imperious senior partner sneered, ending the conversation.

Vail sighed as he passed them, knowing he would drift aimlessly from one group to the next, nodding hello, smiling, and moving around the room until he was close enough to a side exit to slip out and flee the event.

But tonight was different. As he walked into the room, he was deluged with handshakes, smiles, pats on the back. He was overwhelmed with goodwill. It took a few moments for it to sink in, for him to realize what was happening.

Across the room, he was being observed as he made his way through the swarms of people. Jane Venable watched with a smile. Tall, distant, untouchable, classy, arrogant, self-confident, Venable had it all. From the tip of her long, equine nose to her long, slender neck, she created a mystique that was part of her haughty allure. She was almost six feet tall and, on normal business days, disguised a stunning figure in bulky sweaters and loose-fitting jackets. But in court, the perfect showcase for her brains, beauty, and élan, she was truly in her element. There she put it all to work at once, performing in out-rageously expensive tailormade suits designed to show off the perfection of her body. From her broad shoulders to her tight buttocks, her hair pulled back into a tight bun, her tinted contact lenses accentuating her flashing green eyes, she was a tiger shark. Immaculately prepared, she was a predator waiting to slam in for the kill: the ultimate jugular artist. There was no margin for error when doing battle with her.

Like Vail, she had one rule: Take no prisoners.

On this night Venable had thrown out the rule book. She flaunted it all. Devastatingly packaged, she was encased in a dark green strapless sheath accented with spangles that embellished both her perfect figure and the flaming-red hair that cascaded down around her shoulders. She was wearing green high heels that pushed her to over six feet. In the otherwise stifling milieu of the room, she was a beacon of sex, standing half a head taller than most of the men in the room. There was no denying her; no way to ignore this brilliant amazon. Jane Venable knew exactly what buttons to push to claim the night and she was pushing them all.

The day before Venable had wrapped up one of the biggest corporate buyouts in years. It was no longer a secret that Venable had spent six months studying Japanese culture and learning the language before going to Tokyo and masterminding Mitsushi's buyout of Midland Dynamics. Her strategy had pulled the rug from under four other law firms, one of them a Washington group that everyone had assumed had the inside track. It had earned her a $250,000 bonus and moved her name to number three on the corporate letterhead.

She had been watching Vail since he entered the big room, watching the minglers part like water before him, congratulate him, pat him on the back, then swirl back to continue their conversations in his wake. And at the moment she was thinking, not about her latest legal coup, she was remembering a day ten years earlier when she had suffered one of the worst defeats in her career.

Although they occasionally traded glances from across a theatre lobby or a restaurant, it had been ten years since Venable and Vail had exchanged even a hello. It had been her last case as a prosecutor before moving to a full partnership in one of the city's platinum law firms

81

– and it was one of the most sensational cases in the city's history. A young Appalachian kid named Aaron Stampler had been accused of viciously stabbing to death one of Chicago's most revered citizens, Archbishop Richard Rushman. An open-and-shut case – except that Vail had been the defence attorney.

In a bruising trial presided over by the city's most conservative and bigoted judge, Harry Shoat – Hangin' Harry, as he was known in the profession – Vail and Venable had provided plenty of fireworks for the media. Then Vail had ambushed her. Stampler suffered from a split personality, a fact Vail had not introduced into evidence and had kept from the public. He had tricked Venable into bringing out Stampler's alter ego on the stand, and instead of the chair, Venable had had to settle for far less. Stampler was sent to the state mental institution 'until deemed cured' and she had left office a loser, at least in her own eyes.

But the case had preyed heavily on Vail's mind. After winning his points in court, Vail had had second thoughts. The outcome had troubled him, and in an ironic twist, Vail, the state's deadliest defence lawyer, had replaced Venable as chief prosecutor. Even as a prosecutor he did not get along any better with Judge Shoat. They had continued to clash in the courtroom until Hangin' Harry had been appointed to the state supreme court.

Forgiveness came hard for Venable, but she had held a grudge long enough. Vail had always attracted her, although it was years before she had admitted it to herself. Like her, he was a predator with an instinct for the jugular. In court, he was mercurial, changing moods and tactics on the whim of the moment, dazzling juries and confounding his opponents. And she was also drawn to his dark Irish good looks and those grey eyes that seemed to look right through her. Now he was not only the most dangerous prosecutor in the state, he was also *the* district attorney, and proper respect was being paid. Impetuously, she decided to end the feud.

She moved resolutely through the crowd, charting a collision course with him but staying slightly behind him so that he would not see her. Then an arm protruded through the mass of people. Massive fingers locked on Vail's elbow, steering him towards the perimeter of the ballroom and a small anteroom.

Shaughnessey, the old-timer who had carved a career from city councilman to DA to attorney general to state senator, losing only one political race in thirty years, was claiming Vail for the moment. Two years ago he had made his bid for the governor's seat only to be turned away in the primary. But it had not damaged his power. Shaughnessey was the state's high priest who with a nod could bring disaster down on the shoulders of anyone who challenged the political powers of the state house. Compared to him, most of the other state politicos were gandy dancers. The burly man, his bulk wrapped in a fifteen-hundred-dollar silk tuxedo with a trademark splash of coloured silk in its breast pocket, his fleshy face deeply tanned under a thick white mane, his thick lips curled almost contemptuously in what the unsuspecting might have mistaken for a smile, was obviously wooing the new DA.

Her curiosity piqued, she decided to wait.

Inside a small, barren room, Shaughnessey fixed his keen and deadly hooded eyes on Vail and smacked him on the arm.

'How do you like being DA?' he asked.

'I told you ten years ago, Roy, I don't want to be DA. I wanted to be chief prosecutor then and that's what I am now.'

'Not any more, my friend. You are the acting DA, you need to start acting like one.'

Vail had a sudden surge of *déjà vu*. Ten years ago. A snowy afternoon in the backseat of Shaughnessey's limo, sipping thirty-year-old brandy. The moment it had all started.

'You're the best lawyer in the state. Nobody wants to go up against you.'

'Is this some kind of an offer?'

'Let's just say it's part of your continuing education. You've got to slick up a little.'

Vail laughed. 'You mean go legit?'

'Exactly, go legit. Get a haircut, get your pants pressed, stop kickin' everybody's ass.'

'Why bother? I'm having a good time.'

'Because you want to move to the other side of town. You want what everybody wants, bow and scrape, tip their hat, call you mister and mean it. You don't want to cop pleas for gunsels the rest of your life. Yancey needs you, son. Venable's left him. He's lost all his gunslingers. His balls're hanging out. Hell, he never did have the stones for that job. He's a politician in a job that calls for an iceman. What he wants is to make judge – eight, nine years down the line – and live off the sleeve for the rest of his time. To do that, he needs to rebuild his reputation because you've been makin' him look like Little Orphan Annie. Twice in one year on headline cases – and you burned up his two best prosecutors to boot. Silverman's still in a coma from the Pinero case and Venable's on her way to Platinum City. He needs you, son.'

'Is that why you dumped this Rushman case on me?'

'Ah, you need a little humility, Martin. Besides, they want a monkey show out of that trial and you'll give it to them.'

'So that's what it's all about, getting a good show and teaching me a little humility?'

Shaughnessey just smiled.

Now, ten years later, nothing seemed to have changed.

'Now what the hell's that mean, I got to start acting like one?' Vail responded.

'This thing between you and Eric – '

'He's an incompetent ass-kisser.'

'He's chief of police. You two got to work together – '

'Listen, Roy, in my first nine months in office, I lost more cases than in the entire nine years I'd practised law. Know why? Eric Eckling.'

'Just work with him instead of going out of your way to make him look like a schmuck.'

'Eckling's cops reflect his own incompetence. They lose evidence, lie, fall apart on the witness stand, put together paper cases, violate civil rights . . .'

'Maybe that's because you stole his best cop.'

'I caught him on the way out the door. He couldn't stand Eckling, either. The only thing these guys are competent at is screwing up. We do our own investigating now. And we don't lose cases anymore.'

'Why not practise a little discretion, would that hurt anything?'

'What are you, Mr Fixit, the jolly negotiator?'

'It doesn't help anybody – this friction.'

'Hell, you're getting mellow in your old age. You used to tell, not ask.'

'Everybody else I tell. You I ask. Hell, I'm just trying to keep a little peace in the family, yuh mind?'

'Family! I'm not in any goddamn family. What is it, you been talking to Firestone?'

'He bellyaches to a mutual friend, it works its way back to me, I get a call or two. You really pissed him off, you know. What'd you do, tell him to kiss your ass?'

'No, I told him I wasn't there to kiss his.'

'He's vice chairman of the city council, for Christ sake. Do you have to *not* get along with him? It's like you and Yancey used to be.'

'Yancey and I get along fine. We have an understanding. The only time we have problems is when he forgets it.'

'Firestone is very friendly with the police and firemen. And he's not a big booster of that kindergarten of yours.'

'It's the senior high.'

'Okay, okay . . . yeah, I'm just saying – '

'You're just feeding me the same old line, Roy. Con Firestone into thinking I like him. Get along with Eckling. It's an open sore, the thing with Eckling. It's not gonna go away. Tell Firestone to butt out. It's none of his damn business. I don't work for the city, I represent the whole county.'

'Christ,' Shaughnessey said, shaking his head. 'You still hustling around trying to put all the town's big shots in jail?'

'Where'd you hear that?'

'Come ooon,' Shaughnessey answered, peeling the wrapper off a cigar the size of the Goodyear blimp.

'Maybe one of these days you'll be one of them. I warned you about that when you conned me into this job ten years ago.'

'Not a chance,' Shaughnessey said, and laughed. 'I'm out of your league now. It would take the attorney general' – he leaned forward and said softly – 'and I put him in office, too. And he's a helluva lot more grateful than you are.'

Venable was standing with her back to the anteroom door when Vail and Shaugnessey reappeared. She watched them shake hands, then Vail started back through the crowd, heading for the side entrance. She fell in behind him. When he stopped suddenly and turned to shake hands with someone, he saw her. Their eyes locked, green on grey, and this time neither of them broke the stare. Finally she thought, *What the hell*, and raised her champagne glass in a toast to him. He smiled and threaded his way through the crowd to her.

'How are you doing, Janie?' he asked.

'I think we're both doing just great,' she said, and offered him a sip of her champagne. He took it, signalled to one of the floating waiters, and got them two fresh glasses. They headed for a corner of the room, away from the crowd and the band.

'I just read about your international coup.' Vail said. 'Congratulations.'

'Thank you, Mr District Attorney.'

'Don't jump the gun,' Vail said.

'Oh, you've got the power now, Martin. Can't you tell?' She swept her arm around the crowd.

'Tomorrow'll be just another day.'

'No, it'll never be the same. You're the man they have to deal with now. And everybody knows you don't give two hoots in hell about playing politics.'

'You're a very smart lady, Janie.' He took a step backward and stared at her for several moments. 'And more handsome now than you were ten years ago, if that's possible.'

She caught her breath for just an instant but covered herself well.

'Why, Martin,' she said, 'I didn't think you noticed.'

'I'm not dead. I just overlooked it in the courtroom.'

'You certainly did.'

'Does this mean we're declaring a truce? Putting all that business behind us? Are we going to be civil to each other again?'

'We were never civil to each other.' She laughed.

'Well' – he shrugged – 'we could try.'

Her green eyes narrowed slightly. *Is he up to something?* she wondered, not yet willing to trust this apparent truce.

She's wondering what the hell I'm up to, he thought. And quickly moved to put her mind at ease. 'We'll probably never face each other in the courtroom again,' he said.

'What a shame.'

He knew exactly what she meant. Going at it before a jury one more time would be exciting. They played the staring game for a few moments longer, then she abruptly changed the subject.

'What's the real prognosis?'

Vail shrugged. 'You know doctors. He's got half a dozen specialists hovering over him and none of them'll give us a straight answer. One thing's for sure, he's got a tough road ahead of him.'

'I always liked Jack,' she said, thinking back over a decade to the obsequious, smooth-talking grifter with wavy white hair and a perpetual smile. What wasn't there to like. Yancey was not a litigator and never had been. He was a talker not a fighter, the ultimate bureaucrat who surrounded himself with smart young lawyers to do the dirty work.

'Yancey's the ultimate ass-kisser, but he's never made any bones about it,' said Vail.

'Yes,' she agreed. 'He'd kiss *anything* to stay in grace.' Venable took a long sip of champagne. 'I only let him down twice, you know. You were the reason both times.'

'Hell, that was a long time ago. Water under the dam as a friend of mine used to say.'

'Shit, you were a monster, Martin. Hell, I guess you still are. You've been prosecutor what, ten years now?'

He nodded. 'Ten years next month.'

'Long time to wait. That was the promise, wasn't it? Jack would move up to judge and you'd step in.'

'I was never promised anything except a free hand to run the prosecutor's office my way. Besides, promises aren't worth a damn in politics. You know how to tell when a politician's lying? His lips are moving.'

She laughed a throaty laugh. 'Okay,' she said, 'you know what they'd call it if all the lawyers in this room were on the bottom of a lake?'

'No, tell me.'

'A good beginning,' she said, and laughed again. 'Well,

if it did happen that way, it was brilliant of them. Taking you out of the game, putting you on their side. I'll bet Jack engineered that whole deal himself.'

'Nope. He was just along for the ride.'

'Who then? Not Shaughnessey!'

'Shaughnessey made the pitch.'

'You're kidding! Now there's a well-kept state secret.'

'It wasn't any secret. Shaughnessey made the pitch and Jack slobbered all over him agreeing. Hell, you were leaving and he didn't have a good prosecutor left.'

'Why'd you do it? You were making what? A million a year or more? You gave that up for a hundred and fifty thou?'

Her remark reminded him again about the Stampler case and the others through the years – dope pushers and mobsters, thieves and rogues he'd saved from the gallows.

'Money was never the consideration,' he said simply.

'Then why? Just tired of dealing with the scum of society? You put a lot of bad boys back on the street in your day, Mr Vail. Bargain-basement justice.'

'Justice? One thing I've learned after twenty years in the business: If you want justice, go to a whorehouse; if you want to get fucked go to court. I'm paraphrasing Thomas Jefferson.'

'A very cynical attitude for an officer of the court.'

'We're all cynics. It's the only way to survive.'

'So what's next? Finish out Jack's term as DA, run for a term to see how good you look at the polls? Then governor?'

'You sound like a campaign manager.'

She looked at him and warmth crept into her green eyes. 'It's worth a thought,' she said quietly.

He decided to take a stab at it. 'Why don't we have dinner tonight? Exchange secrets.'

'You already know all my secrets, Marty,' she said rather dolefully, but quickly recovering. 'But not tonight. Give me a call. It's an interesting thought.'

'If you change your mind, I'll be up the street at Avanti! eating dinner.'

He started to leave, then walked back and stood close to her and said in her ear, 'All by myself.' He kissed her on the cheek and was gone.

She turned back to the crowded room and the heat and noise and lawyers and calypso rhythm and her shoulders sagged.

Ah, what the hell, she thought. *Screw pride.*

Eight

Handsome, debonair, the perfect host, and master of Avanti!, the best Italian kitchen in the state, Guido Signatelli had but one flaw: outrageously tacky taste. Plastic grapes and dusty Chianti bottles dangled from phony grape arbours that crisscrossed the ceiling, and the booths that lined the walls were shaped like giant wine barrels. But Guido and Avanti! had survived on the strength of personality, discretion, and dazzling cuisine. Located three blocks from City Hall, Guido's – the regulars never referred to the place by its name – had become the lunchtime county seat and the legal profession dominated the fake landscape. Guido's personal pecking order was as precise as a genealogical chart. Starting at the bottom were the lobbyists, their mouths dry and their palms damp as they sucked up to everybody. They were followed by young lawyers eager to be seen as they cruised the room, hoping for a handshake; then the assistant prosecutors, huddled over out-of-the-way tables and whispering strategy; and finally the kingmakers, the politicos who greased the wheels of the city from behind closed doors in what was jokingly called 'executive session' – to avoid the state's sunshine laws. Many a shady executive decision had been made in the quiet of one of Guido's booths. On the top were the judges, the emperors of justice, each with his or her own preordained table, each patronized by his or her own mewling sycophants and each pandered to by the rest of the room.

Guido, a chunky, little man with a great mop of silver hair and a permanent smile, led Vail to the corner table. While still the state's most feared defence advocate, Vail had established the booth as his own. There he could eat,

91

read, or talk business in relative seclusion. A few barflies hugged the long oak and marble bar and a half-dozen tables were occupied. Conversation was a low rumble.

Vail ordered a glass of red wine and settled down to read what the *Trib* had to say about Yancey and the bodies in the city dump, both of which were prominently displayed on page one. He didn't see Jane Venable until she appeared beside him at the table. He was genuinely surprised when he looked up and saw her and it was a moment before he reacted. He stood up, throwing the paper aside.

'I don't know what I'm doing here. I must be crazy! I guess I'm as tired of that bunch of hucksters as you are and . . .'

She was babbling to cover her embarrassment, obviously having second thoughts about following the man she had ignored – and who had ignored her – for a decade. Vail held a chair for her.

'You don't have to apologize to me for anything,' he said quietly. 'Ever.'

'I'm not apologizing, I'm . . .'

'Glad to be here?' he suggested.

She glared at him for a moment and then her consternation dissolved into a sheepish grin as she sat down opposite him.

'It has been ten years,' she said sheepishly.

'Well, we've been busy,' he said casually. 'What are you drinking?'

'I'll have a glass of champagne. If I switch to something else, I'll end up on my nose.'

'Eddie,' Vail called to a nearby waiter. 'Champagne for the lady and I'll have the same. Why don't you just bring us a bottle? Taittinger '73 would be nice.'

They sat without speaking for half a minute, then both started speaking at the same time and then stopped and laughed.

'Hell, Janie, it's time we started acting like grown-ups.

92

Why not? You've been divorced for what, two years? I'm free as a bird.'

She seemed surprised that he knew anything about her personal life. 'Been keeping track of me, have you, Lawyer Vail?' she asked.

He did not answer. He was looking across the table, his eyes directly on hers. Their gazes locked for several seconds and she finally broke the stare.

'The one that got away, huh,' she said, reaching for a cigarette.

'If I thought about all the ones that got away I wouldn't have time to do anything else.'

She laughed. 'I suppose we have been acting juvenile, haven't we?'

'Maybe it's just the right time and the right place, Janie.'

'I've told you before, Martin, nobody calls me Janie.'

'Except me,' he said, taunting her. 'What're you gonna do, get me arrested? I'm the friggin' DA.'

'Somewhat reluctantly, I assume,' she answered.

'Want a job?'

'Why, are you quitting?'

He whistled softly through his teeth. 'You haven't lost your edge, I see. So why do you suppose we're sitting here, Janie?'

She shrugged. 'We're both forty . . .? she suggested.

'Plus,' he added ruefully.

'We both hate cocktail parties?'

'We both hate lawyers?'

'Good one,' she said. 'Or maybe we're both just lonelier than hell.'

'I can only speak for myself,' he said. 'I've missed you. Me and every other male who ever saw you in a courtroom. You really turned it all on. You were a real dazzler – the Hope diamond of the Cook County Courthouse. Don't you miss it? The roar of the courtroom, the smell of the crowd?'

'I still have my days in court.'

'Not like the old days. Defending polluters in civil cases really ain't the same.'

'Come on, Vail, I did one.'

'And won, unfortunately.'

'Hey . . .' she started, anger creeping into her tone.

'Sorry,' he said hurriedly. 'I'll get off the soapbox.'

She shrugged. 'Maybe I'm a little too touchy on the subject. I've always been curious about something I heard. Did they really clean your tank back when you were starting out? Is that true?'

'Oh, yeah,' he said, 'they whipped my ass good. The Chamber of Commerce sold everyone down the river, the newspaper lied to them, the bigshots bought off the judges, they brought in the heaviest, ball-busting lawyers they could find from the big town, and they turned a paradise into a killing ground. All I got out of it was a good lesson.'

'What was that?'

'It's dangerous to be blinded by idealism. The minute the hyenas find out you have integrity, they bring on their assassins in silk suits.'

'You haven't done badly. Blowing off one of the most respected banks in the city for money laundering, shutting down two chemical companies, busting half the city council for being on the sleeve. I call that getting even.'

'It's a start,' he said, and changed the subject, focusing the conversation back on them. 'What I miss are our old skirmishes, even after ten years.'

'There's something to be said for good, old-fashioned cutthroat competition.'

'You ought to know.'

'Look who's talking.'

She raised her glass and offered a toast to cutthroat competition. Their eyes locked again and this time she didn't break the stare.

'Janie,' he said, 'just how hungry are you?'

She slouched back in the booth and looked at the ceiling and closed her eyes and shook her head ever so slightly, sighed, and peered down her long nose at him.

'Cocktail parties always did ruin my appetite,' she said.

She was seeing a side of Vail he had never revealed to her before, a vulnerability, a romantic flair. He had brought home the bottle of chilled Taittinger after informing Guido that they had changed their mind about dinner. She had always been attracted to Vail, even in the old days, but had never admitted it to herself, dispelling her feelings as a combination of admiration and fear of his talent. Now, standing in his living room, watching him light the fire, she realized how much she wanted him and began to wonder if she had made a mistake. Was she rushing into something? A one-night stand? Would it turn into one of those awkward mistakes where she would awaken in the morning with a sexual hangover? But when he stood up and faced her, her fears vanished, washed away in another rush of desire. He took off her coat and tossed it over the sofa and went into the kitchen to get wineglasses.

She looked around the apartment. It was a large two-bedroom, high enough to have a nice view of the city but not ostentatious. One of the bedrooms had been converted into an office, a cluttered room of books filled with paper place markers, files stacked in the corners, magazines piled up, most of them with their wrappers still on them, scraps of notes, and newspaper clippings. A blue light glowed from the bathroom and she peered in.

It had been converted into a minigreenhouse. A six-foot-long zinc-lined sink ran along one wall, with taps and tubes running from the bathroom sink. Pots of flowers crowded the bathtub. A row of grow lights plugged into an automatic timer created the illusion of daylight twelve hours a day. Beneath the lights were bunches of small, delicate blue flowers surrounded by fernlike leaves. On the other side of the narrow room was a small plastic-covered cubicle, its sides misty with manmade dew. Through its opaque sides, she could see splashes of colour from other flowers.

She looked around the small room. 'What do you know, a closet horticulturist,' she said, half aloud.

'They're called bluebells,' he said from behind her.

She whirled around, startled, and caught her breath. 'I'm sorry. I was snooping.'

He handed her a tulip glass bubbling with champagne.

'Belles as in beautiful young ladies. They're winter flowers. Grew wild along the banks of the river where I grew up. I used to pick them and take them home to my mom and she'd put them on the piano and sometimes I'd hear her talking to them. "This is Chopin," she'd say and then play for them.'

'She sounds lovely.'

'She was. She died when I was in the eighth grade.'

'I'm sorry.'

'Long time ago.'

Her anxiety was slowly transforming back to desire. Her mouth got a little drier and she took another sip of champagne. Oddly, there was only one photograph in the bedroom, a grim, dark, foreboding picture of a murky colony of industrial plants, partially obscured by a manmade fog of steam and dirty smoke. They appeared as one long, grey mass with stacks spewing black smoke that rose to an ominous tumour of low-lying, polluted clouds hovering over the disgusting spectacle. In the foreground a scummy river with steam lurking around its edges vaguely reflected the despondent scene.

'Welcome to Rainbow Flats. Believe it or not, I used to swim in that river when I was kid.'

'So that's where they got you,' she said.

'Yeah. Ironic, isn't it? The Chamber of Commerce calls that an industrial park. I used to think a park was a cheerful place where kids play. The spin doctors destroyed that illusion.'

'Why keep a picture of it?'

'So I never get complacent.'

'I can't imagine you being complacent about anything.' She slipped off her shoes as they walked back into the living room. 'Hope you don't mind, my feet are killing me.'

'Sit down. I also give great foot.'

'Foot?'

'Best foot massage this side of Sweden.'

She sat down on the sofa and leaned back against soft, down pillows. He took one foot in both hands, first rubbing it gently, then squeezing harder, kneading his fingers into her instep. The massage was like electricity being transmitted up between her legs along the silken strands of her panty hose. She closed her eyes. Her breath was growing shorter, her pulse quickening. The champagne kicked in.

'Very good foot,' she whispered.

He slid his hand along her silken leg slowly, moving up to her calf, then to the edge of her thigh. She sat up suddenly, realizing she was completely out of breath.

'Need to stand up for a minute,' she said. She got up and walked to the fireplace. He followed her.

'Marty . . .' she started to say, but he turned her to him, took her face in both hands, and kissed her. She surrendered, responding hungrily, her mouth linked to his, their lips and tongues frantically exploring, their bodies crushed together. The allure of each to the other was hypnotic. His hands moved down her sides, around to her back, caressed her tight buttocks, then slid tentatively down the outside of her legs, urging her against him. One hand moved to the inside of her thigh, his forearm pressed between her legs, then he moved his hand higher, caressed the smooth lip of her panty hose, his fingers barely touching her. She whimpered softly, moved against his exploring fingertips and pressed against his hand, and he began to stroke her. He kissed her ears, the small place in her throat, and she responded by putting her hand behind his head and moving it slowly down to her breasts. Pent-up denial exploded. They began frantically undressing each other without ever losing the cadence of the mutual seduction, his hand moving in slight, wet circles, exploring every pore of her. He gasped for breath as she laid her hand over his exploring fingertips, guiding them. He reached behind her with his other hand and unzipped her dress. She pressed against him, taunting him, keeping the dress from falling, then pressed the flat of her hand to his stomach, slid it across the hard muscles, her thumb encircling his navel. She slid her fingers under his belt, slid her hand down until she felt him rising to meet it.

She leaned back. The dress slipped slowly down, hung for a moment on her hard nipples, then slipped over her breasts and down to her hips. They kept kissing, their eyes closed, as their hands explored each other. Their lips still locked together, she pressed his hand with hers, moved it slowly to her stomach and then down until it was between her legs, and then she pressed it hard against her and began moving it up and down, then she turned her hand, pressing the back of it against the back of his until they were stroking each other in perfect rhythm. She could feel him growing and she let her free hand glide down his back, caressing his buttocks. The tips of their nipples touched and she moved closer, felt him growing hard against her, moving her body under his fingers, tracing his hard muscle with a featherlike touch.

She ground her head into his shoulder, her muscles trembling as he continued to massage her faster and faster, and she arched her back slightly and for several minutes they stood together, moving slowly to the rhythm of her sighs.

'My God,' he whispered into her mouth, 'slow down.'

'I can't,' she whispered. '*C-can't!*' She began to grind against his hand, began stroking him faster, and he began to move with her hand. She was trembling now; she sucked in her breath and rose on her toes and he could feel her trigger getting harder and wetter under his fingers until she cried out, thrusting herself against his hand, her legs trembling with spasms.

He lowered her to the floor and lay down beside her. Her arms fell away. He was on top of her, leaning over her, his eyes closed, his biceps twitching, and she guided him into her. He took in a breath and held it, then began thrusting into her. She reached up with both arms, wrapped them around his neck, and rolled him over so that she was on top of him, sliding her hard nipples up and down his chest, straddling him, then rising slightly, she guided him back into her and leaning forward trapped his cries with her mouth. Hypnotized, they made love, stopped, held back, trembling, until they could not resist the demand any longer, until the tension was no longer bearable. He felt her wet muscles close around him. He slid his hand down between their stomachs, felt her grow even harder as he stroked her. She stiffened, stopped breathing for several seconds, then she thrust herself down on him and cried out and began to shudder, and her response was so overwhelming that all his senses spun crazily out of control. He felt a spasm, then another, and another, and still another, before he exploded.

She felt electrified, lost in time and space, and the waves began to build again.

'Oh God,' she cried, falling down across him and stretching out her long legs, tightening them and keeping them trapped while they kissed until, finally, she came again.

'Ooooh,' she slowly mumbled several times.

He lay under her, arms enfolding her, lightly scratching her back as they regained their breath, and then in a frenzied reprise, she felt him slide deeper inside her and then out, slipping against her, and she began to tighten again. Her hair fell across his face as she twisted her head from side to side, both moaning in unison as their dance built and built, until she cried out, sitting up on him, moving up and down, then she fell back against his chest.

They lay quietly for a moment while her muscles tightened and loosened with her own contractions. Her mouth was against his ear and he listened as she slowly regained her breath and finally she slid first one leg, then the other, down until she was stretched out full above him.

She lifted her head until they were almost nose to nose and she swept the tip of her tongue across his upper lip.

'God,' he whispered, still breathless, 'why did we wait so long?'

She slid off him, lying beside him with one leg over his. He put his arm around her and they lay there for several minutes watching the fire.

'Whatever happened to that gorgeous woman who worked for you,' she said, breaking the silence.

'Naomi Chance?'

'Was that her name? That's a lovely name.'

'She still works for me. You've got out of touch.'

'People used to talk about you two.'

She rolled over on her back, raised one leg up, and moved slightly so that he had a taunting view of her naked body.

'Did you two ever have a thing?' she asked.

He held up a single finger.

'Once. You did it *once*?'

He nodded. 'One night a very long time ago. She said she didn't want to keep it up, that it would ruin our professional relationship.'

Jane leaned over and bit his big toe, very lightly. 'She was nuts,' she said.

'Are you getting hungry?' he asked.

She stroked her saliva off his toe with her palm and fingers. 'I could eat a little something.'

'Will champagne and cheese do?'

'For starters. Any candles?'

'If they haven't turned to dust by now.'

'Candles, wine, and cheese. How elegant.'

'Got your appetite back, huh?'

'Oh yes,' she said softly.

She watched him as he walked to the kitchen. He had a tight, hard, rather lean body. She liked that. Not an ounce of fat, but no steroid muscles either, and a very attentive lover who knew all the buttons to push and all the doors to open. But she had suspected as much. Vail did everything with passion.

He came back in a minute or two with fresh wine-glasses dangling between his fingers, a box of stone-wheat thins, and a wedge of Brie cheese in one hand and two candles in the other. He dumped the burned-out cigarette butts out of a large ashtray, lit a candle, and dripped wax into a hot pool in the ashtray's centre. She watched intently as he twisted the candle into the pool, holding it while the wax hardened around its smooth base. He opened the package of Brie and, with his little finger, scooped out a mound from under the hard crust and held it out to her. She put his whole finger in her mouth and sucked off the cheese.

The phone rang.

'Oh sweet Jesus,' he moaned.

He tried to ignore it, but after five rings he knew Stenner was not to be denied. The man knew he was home and why.

'Shit, shit, shit,' he growled, and finally snatched up the receiver. 'Major, I'm not home at this time. If you'll leave a – '

'John Farrell Delaney.'

A pause. 'What about him?'

'He's lying in the middle of a penthouse on Lake View Drive wearing two .38-calibre slugs and nothing else. Either shot would have killed him.'

'You son of a bitch.'

'Ten minutes? Or do you need to take a shower?'

Vail thought he heard a snicker in Stenner's voice. He ignored the remark.

'Been over there yet?'

'Shock called me. What I just told you is all I know.'

'Ten minutes,' Vail said in surrender.

'I'm down front waiting.'

'I should've known.'

He hung up. She stared at him, still admiring his naked body as he started to dress. 'You don't have to go home,' she purred. 'Why don't you spend the night?'

'Very funny,' he muttered. 'It's a homicide.'

'Not very flattering.'

'What?'

'Screwing my brains out and then leaving me for a corpse.'

He pulled up his pants and angrily jerked up the zipper. 'Midnight forays in the human jungle.'

'As I recall, there were about two thousand homicides last year. Did you get out of bed for *all* of them?'

'They didn't all happen at night,' he said, looking for one of his shoes.

She sat up and groped for a cigarette.

'Shall I wait up for you?' she asked, flapping her eyelids at him like a silent-screen vamp.

'Didn't this ever happen when you were a prosecutor?' he asked.

She shook her head very slowly. 'I only had one phone and I unplugged it.'

'Suppose it was something big?' he said, putting on his socks and loafers.

She blew out a slow stream of smoke. Curiosity crept into her voice. 'How big?'

'Veeery, veeeery big.'

'Where are you going?' she asked suspiciously.

He waved her off. 'It was a rhetorical question, Janie.'

'No, no, you're not getting away with that, Vail. What happened? Where are you going at . . .' she looked at the clock – 'eleven-thirty at night?'

'John Farrell Delaney pique your interest?'

She straightened up when he said the name, surprise rounding her eyes. 'What about him?'

He looked at her, smiled, and held a finger over his lips.

'He did something! Did he do . . . No! Something was done to him.'

A brief vision from the past flashed through Vail's mind. *The Judge and Vail, facing each other across his big desk, fingers on silver dollars, as they played mind games.*

'It's classified at this point, Jane. You know I can't – '

'Don't give me that shit, Martin Vail. Ever hear of date rape? Speak up or I'll start screaming.'

'You wouldn't dare.'

'He's dead, isn't he?' She leaned over until she as an inch from his face. 'Is he dead, Marty?'

Vail nodded. 'Somebody popped two shots in his ugly, old heart.'

'Wooow!' she said slowly. 'Somebody hit *Delaney*? Oh, you do have a problem, Mr DA. We may be the only two people in the city that don't have a good reason to kill the bastard. You don't, do you?'

'No, I always get his pimp, Firestone,' Vail said. He stood up, dressed in his tuxedo but without the tie, and put on his coat. 'I never had much to do with Mr Delaney.'

'You're lucky. Well, I'll forgive you for abandoning me, but only if you promise to give me all the gory details when you get back. This is going to be the hottest gossip in town tomorrow.'

He leaned over and kissed her on the lips.

'If I'm not here when you leave, lock the door behind you.'

'Don't turn this into something cheap,' she whispered with a smile, and kissed him back.

Nine

'Was Delaney alone when they found him?' Vail asked as he got in the car. 'I mean, do they have a suspect?'

'Told you all I know,' Stenner said. He drove the few blocks from Vail's Dearborn Park townhouse to the Loft Apartments, pulling up in front of a tall, glass shaft of a building. Behind it, a hundred yards away and beyond the Hilton, the lake shimmered in the light of a half-moon. There were four police cars, an ambulance, and Okimoto's omnipresent van parked all over the street in front of the place. A small crowd weathered the cold and pressed against the crime-scene ribbons waiting for something dramatic to happen. Vail and Stenner took the lift to the thirtieth floor.

The lift opened onto a small hallway with only two doors. One was propped open with a chair and a uniformed cop stood beside it, looking back over his shoulder at the action inside.

As they entered the apartment they saw Shock Johnson, standing at the end of a long hallway, which was carpeted in white and softly illuminated with indirect lights. The big cop smiled, sauntered over to them, and stuck out a hand the size of a catcher's mitt.

'Hi, boys,' he said, leading them down the hallway towards the living room. 'We seem to be seeing a lot of each other these days.'

'Yeah, people'll think we're going steady,' said Vail.

'You're not my type,' Shock said. 'I like blondes.'

'I'll wear a wig.'

'It ain't the same.'

They reached the end of the hall and looked into a large living room with picture windows overlooking the lake. A lab man, who was on his hands and knees vacuuming the rug with a small hand machine, stood up and left as they entered. Another was dusting lamps, tables, chairs, and anything else in the room that might have gathered fingerprints. A pebbled old-fashioned glass was sitting on one of the tables, powder still clinging to it.

Except for the panoramic view of the lake, the room was cold and sterile. Black, ultramodern furniture contrasted harshly with white carpeting and walls. The three large paintings on one wall were abstracts in various configurations of black and white. The place appeared to be spotless. Spotless except for City Council Chairman Delaney, who lay flat on his back, stark naked, staring blandly at the ceiling. A lot of blood had collected under the body and dried in a large, brown stain on the carpet.

'Where's Okie?' Vail asked.

'Other room. He's guessing he got it between seven and eight-thirty.'

'Who found him?' Stenner asked.

'Delaney was the key speaker at a banquet tonight. When he didn't show up or answer his phone by the end of dinner, somebody called the office. The doorman answered, told them he hadn't seen Delaney leave the place. He checked the parking deck to make sure Delaney's car was there – you can get to it without going through the lobby. It was. There was a lot of hemming and hawing until the meeting was over. A couple of the dignitaries came over, the night manager used a passkey, and they came in. Delaney'd taken the express to Goodbye City.'

'What time was that?' Stenner asked.

'Eleven-oh-five.'

Stenner walked a little closer, leaned over, and looked down at the corpse. The right side of Delaney's face was scorched and his right eyebrow was singed off. Still leaning over, he looked back over his shoulder at Vail and Shock.

'Almost a contact shot, I'd say,' he remarked.

Shock nodded. 'Burned his eyebrow off and fried half his face. Couple of inches at best. Probably wasn't necessary. They're both insurance shots.'

'Anything happening in the bedroom?' Stenner asked.

Shock shrugged. 'Take a look.'

'Delaney doesn't look very surprised,' Vail said as Stenner walked into the other room.

'Maybe he was blinking when he got it,' Shock said.

'Probably knew who did him, wouldn't you say?'

'I'd say that's a pretty safe assumption. I mean, what the hell was he doing, anyway, traipsing around the living room with his unit hanging out?'

'Maybe his wife did him.'

'Or girlfriend?'

'Or boyfriend.'

'That, too.'

'I have a friend who says she's the only person in town that didn't have a reason to kill him.'

'You ever have a run-in with him, Marty?'

'Nah. He always sent Firestone to do his dirty work.'

'He's another one.'

'Maybe we can pin it on him.'

Shock laughed. 'I like the idea.'

'Eckling have a lot of boys working on this?'

'Half the force.'

'I'll bet he does,' Vail said. 'He can feel the heat already. This is going to give every politico in the city an enema.'

'Like maybe one of them'll be next?' Shock said, and snickered.

'Guilty conscience,' said Vail, and they both started to laugh.

'You two don't have much respect for the dead. After all, he *was* chairman of the city council, head of the finance committee, head of the city's Democratic Party . . .'

A short, dignified Japanese American with black,

107

closely cut hair and tortoiseshell glasses entered from the bedroom. Oichi Okimoto, wearing a surgeon's paper robe and plastic boots and gloves, strode back into the living room. 'How're you, Martin?' he asked as he walked past.

'I'm not getting enough sleep lately,' Vail said.

'At least it's more comfortable than the landfill.'

Okimoto, at thirty-six was one of the best forensic scientists in the business, walked across the room, carefully moved a straight-back chair to a corner, and sat down on it backward, folding his arms over its back and leaning his chin on them. He perused the room without saying a word. Vail took out his cigarette pack and Okimoto said, without turning his head, 'Don't light that, please.'

'You taking samples of the air, Okie?' Vail asked.

'It annoys me.'

Vail put the cigarettes away and everybody stood around waiting for Okimoto to finish thinking. Three minutes crept by. Finally Okimoto got up and returned the chair.

'We're through, so you may as well go home,' he said to Vail. 'Except for that mess over there, the place is immaculate. Here's what I can tell you. There's no sign of forcible entry. Wet towels on the bathroom floor. Tuxedo's laid out on the bed. He's wearing a gold, waterproofed Rolex – not a knockoff – worth about ten K, and his wallet, credit cards, et cetera, plus three hundred and eighteen dollars in cash, are on the dresser.'

He looked back at the body.

'I think – *think, okay* – somebody he knew, somebody with a key, entered the apartment while he was in the shower. Delaney finishes, gets out, towels off, comes in here to get a drink from the wet bar over there in the corner. He thinks he's alone, so he doesn't bother to put anything on – if he had answered the door or heard somebody come in, he would have put on a robe or something. He gets his drink, turns around, and our mystery guest is standing about here, in the entrance to the living room. He gets in a conversation with this somebody – or maybe he realizes he's in trouble and he's pleading for his life – anyway, he puts the drink on the table, and as he turns around, the mystery guest plugs him twice. I'm fairly certain the first shot was the torso shot; we found a spent shell casing right here. Then our somebody walked over, probably straddled him, leaned down, and popped him in the forehead. There was another shell beside the head. Robbery obviously was not the motive. And I think the culprit was a woman.'

'Why?' Vail asked.

'Imprints in the carpet. High heel, not a spike. I would say a medium heel from the configuration. We've got plenty of photos and a wax cast of the heel prints. I don't think there'll be any surprises from the autopsy. Maybe some drugs in his blood, but I doubt it, no indication of illegal substances anywhere in the place. And his stomach's probably fairly empty; he was on his way to dinner.'

'Whoever shot him came here for that purpose,' Stenner said.

'How do you figure that?' Okimoto asked.

'Because he was naked, right?' Shock offered. 'If there had been any kind of conversation, he would have gone in the bedroom and put something on.'

'That's very good,' Okimoto said.

'If it went down the way you see it, Okie,' said Vail, 'the lady really must've hated his guts. Abel's right, she came here to do him.'

'It'll all be in the autopsy,' Okimoto said. 'By the way, I won't have anything on the landfill case until tomorrow, maybe the day after. The bodies are a real mess.'

He went down the hall towards the kitchen.

'Hell, Shock,' Vail said, 'all you have to do is find

someone who hates him. According to my friend, that could be anybody in the county.'

'I have a thought,' Shock said, looking back at the body. 'He's running for re-election in the fall. Maybe he was getting some campaign photos made.'

'There you go, that's it,' Vail said. 'Hell, he's hung like a bull moose. Probably wanted to wrap up the women's vote.'

They both started to laugh.

'How about taxidermists, he could probably get them, too.'

'Yeah.' Vail stopped laughing long enough to agree. 'They could stuff it and name it after him.

'Right. The Big prick,' Shock said.

They were laughing hard when Eckling came into the apartment. He stalked down the hall and entered the death room.

'What's so goddamn funny?' he snapped. 'One of the city's leaders is lying dead on the floor and you two think it's funny? I'm surprised at you, Captain.'

'Aw, c'mon, Eric, lay off him,' Vail said. 'You know how it is around a murder scene, it's nervous laughter.'

'I already know what you think of our councilmen,' Eckling said haughtily. 'I'll remind you they represent the people. They deserve respect.'

'Why don't we bag the small talk, Eckling,' Vail said with disgust. 'It's a murder investigation. Investigate.'

'Throwing yer new weight around, Vail?' Eckling snarled.

'If I do, you'll know it. You won't have to ask.'

Eckling was distracted by Stenner as he entered from the bedroom. Stenner stopped when he saw Eckling and stood in the doorway with his arms crossed. They did not speak.

Eckling said, 'About through in here, Captain?'

'Soon as the lab boys are wrapped up,' Shock answered.

'I have people working the entire neighbourhood,' Eckling said to him. 'We'll be doing the people at City Hall and at his business first thing in the morning. I'm going to run this investigation myself, Captain Johnson. You're first in command.'

'Yes, sir.'

'His wife is on the way down now,' Eckling went on. 'Would you believe it, she didn't know he had this place. A fucking penthouse, his old lady doesn't even know it exists. She thought he was visiting somebody when I told her where he was.'

'She knows he's dead, doesn't she?' Shock asked.

'Uh, we told her there was an accident. I think Councilman Firestone was going over to tell her. They were very close.'

The lift doors shushed open behind them and Shock looked back to see Raymond Firestone enter the hallway, step back, and usher Ada Delaney into the apartment. She was a tall, stern-looking woman in her fifties, with arched eyebrows and confused eyes. Her face, stretched smooth by cosmetic surgery, still showed the sorrowful lines of a sad woman trapped in an unsatisfying life. She was dressed in a knee-length black cocktail dress and wore no make-up. She stood inside the door, looking around, then walked down the hall towards the living room.

'Jesus,' Shock said, 'somebody get a sheet. Cover that up.'

'No!' Ada Delaney demanded, standing in the entrance to the living room and looking across the room at the remains of John Farrell Delaney. 'Leave it just the way it is.'

Shock looked at Eckling and he nodded. She walked slowly into the room, stopping five or six feet from the corpse.

'He was like that?' Ada Delaney asked.

'Yes, ma'am,' Shock said.

111

She almost sneered down at the corpse. 'Typical,' she said.

There was a quick exchange of glances. Nobody said a word.

'I didn't even know about this apartment,' she said, staring out the window. She seemed transfixed by the scene of death. Her voice began to climb, not louder, but higher-pitched, and she spoke in a rush, as if she had memorized a monologue and was afraid she would forget something. Vail thought she was perhaps in some stage of shock, traumatized by the sight of her husband's corpse.

'It's quite lovely. A little severe, but quite lovely. Pretty good for a man who made a fortune running slaughter-houses.' She peered at one of the paintings. 'I never did like his taste in art. Abstracts leave me cold.' She turned to face Firestone. 'Doesn't seem quite fair, does it, Raymond? To have a beautiful place like this and not share it with the woman you supposedly love, who bore your children, shared your bed?' She paused for a moment and then added nonchalantly, 'Put up with all those lies.'

She stepped closer to the corpse until she was almost looking straight down at it.

'I married him right out of college, you know. Thirty-one years. I never knew another man – intimately, I mean. It was always just Farrell. Farrell, Farrell, Farrell. He was such an attentive suitor . . . and I did love him so . . . thirty-one years ago. He bought me an orchid for our senior prom. I don't know where he got the money. I'd never seen a real orchid before. He used to give me five orchids every anniversary. Until a few years ago.' She put her hand to her mouth. 'Oh, my, I would love to cry. But I can't even do that, I just can't seem to find my tears. You know how I feel, Raymond? I feel relieved. I'm relieved that it's over.' She looked back down at her dead husband. 'I was really growing to hate you, Farrell. And to think I didn't have to do anything. I didn't have to divorce you or go on being humiliated by you. It was done for me. What a nice . . . unexpected . . . surprise.'

She turned away from her dead husband and strolled out of the room.

'You can take me home now, Raymond,' she said.

As Vail watched her leave, he thought about Beryl Yancey, panicky with fear that her husband was dead or dying, in contrast with Ada Delaney, who couldn't even shed a tear over hers.

'Phew!' he said, as they watched the lift doors close behind her.

'Definitely a suspect,' Stenner answered.

'Oh yeah,' said Shock Johnson. 'This may turn out to be an easy one, Marty.'

'They're never easy.'

When Vail got home, there was a paper towel on the floor inside the door. On it was a lipstick print and below it Jane Venable's unlisted phone number.

No other message.

Ten

The Delaney house was in Rogers Park on Greenleaf just off Ridge Avenue, an old, columned, Italianate mansion with tall windows and bracketed eaves, which from the outside had a gloomy nineteenth-century look. Eckling left his aide in the car. The maid led him through a house that had been gutted and remodelled with large, high ceilinged rooms decorated in bright pastel colours, to a radiant atrium at the rear of the house with french doors opening onto a large garden protected by high hedge-rows. Outside, a bluejay fluttered and splashed in a concrete birdbath.

Ada Delaney, dressed appropriately in black, was seated on a bright green flowered sofa with a tall, slender man with shiny grey-black hair, olive skin, and severe, hawklike features. He was dressed in dark blue. Her confused look of the night before had been replaced with a mien of cold, controlled calm and she greeted Eckling with the attitude to go with it. Antagonism permeated the room.

'Eric.' She nodded curtly. 'Do you know Gary Angelo?'

'We've met,' Eckling said, shaking his hand.

'Mr Angelo is the family attorney,' she said. 'He's going to handle things for me. I'm sure you don't mind if he joins us.'

'Not at all,' the chief of police answered, as if he had a choice.

'Would you like coffee?' she asked, motioning towards an ornate silver service. 'Or perhaps a drink?'

'Nothing, thank you. I hope I'm not comin' at a bad time.'

'Not at all,' she said with a grim smile. 'We were just

114

discussing how well off Farrell left me and the children. At least he did something thoughtful.'

'I'm sorry, Ada – '

'Forget the compulsory grief,' she said brusquely, cutting him off. 'The fact is, you were one of his friends, Eric. You knew what was going on.'

'Uh, it wasn't my business to – '

'To what? Raymond Firestone told me all about it. Parties, poker games, weekend *retreats*, as Farrell called them, for his in crowd. You were one of them. Now you come here implying – '

'I'm not implyin' anything,' Eckling said with chagrin. 'I'm just doin' my job. These things have to be addressed.'

'Well, at least you came yourself, you didn't send one of your flunkies.'

'Please,' Eckling said, obviously ill at ease. 'I want to make this as pleasant as possible.'

'I'm sure. What is it you want to know?'

'Do you know of anyone who might have had a motive to do this to John?'

She sneered at the question. 'Don't ask stupid questions, Eric. It was very easy to hate Farrell Delaney.'

'How about, uh . . .' Eckling started, letting the sentence dangle.

'Women? Are you usually this diplomatic when you grill suspects?'

'Please, Ada.'

'Don't *please* me. That's why you're here and we both know it. I'm sure my comments last night put me at the top of the suspect list.'

'There's no list as yet.'

'Well, why don't you just get out the phone book and start with A,' she said with a sardonic smile.

Eckling looked helplessly at Angelo, who ignored him. He sat with his legs crossed, appraising freshly manicured fingernails.

'So you can't provide any leads?'

'You might start with his business partners. He was famous for screwing his friends. Or perhaps *infamous* would be a better word. Frankly, I don't really care who shot him. I hope whoever did the world that favour doesn't suffer too much for it.'

'Christ, Ada!'

'Oh, stop it. Don't be such a hypocrite, ask me what you really came here to ask.'

'Yes,' Angelo said, appraising Eckling with a cool stare. 'Why don't we cut through the felicities and get on with it. I'm sure we've all got better things to do.'

'All right, where were you between seven-thirty and nine P.M. last night?' Eckling asked bluntly.

'I was having dinner at Les Chambres with my daughter and son-in-law,' she answered with a smug smile. 'They picked me up here about seven-thirty. I had been home about thirty minutes when Raymond Firestone called me.'

Eckling mentally calculated how long it would take to get from the Delaney house in Rogers Park to the restaurant located in the Gold Coast. Thirty minutes at least. Les Chambres was ten, fifteen minutes from Delaney's penthouse. Five or ten minutes to do the trick . . .

'We arrived at the restaurant at eight,' she said. 'We were there until nearly ten-thirty. We saw several people we know.'

'You can relax, Chief,' Angelo said. 'She's airtight.'

'I see.'

'Was there anything else?' Ada Delaney said coldly.

'I guess . . . No, unless you can think of – '

'I can't, Eric. And I doubt that I will. Please don't come back here again.' She got up and left the room.

'Christ,' Eckling said to the lawyer, 'we gotta *ask* her. She oughtta realize we gotta ask her, y'know, clear her up right off the bat.'

'She has an alibi,' the lawyer said curtly. 'Check it out.

116

I'll advise her to be as cooperative as you need her to be – *after* you're satisfied she's not involved.'

'Thanks,' Eckling said.

Across town, the Wild Bunch was gathering for a staff meeting called by Shana Parver. Parver and Stenner were in her cubbyhole office talking on the phone while the rest of the bunch gathered in Vail's office, where doughnuts and coffee were waiting: Meyer; Stenner; Naomi; Hazel Fleishman, the daughter of an abusive, hard-drinking army sergeant, who, at thirty-four, was a specialist in sexual and physical abuse cases and rape and was a ferocious litigator; and Dermott Flaherty, a black Irish, streetwise, former petty thief with a gallows sense of humour. Flaherty had escaped dismal beginnings in the east and was graduated cum laude from the University of Chicago, where he had won a four-year scholarship to law school.

Missing were Bobby Hartford, the son of a black ACLU lawyer, who had spent his first ten years as a lawyer fighting civil rights cases in Mississippi and, at thirty-seven, was the oldest of the Wild Bunch; Bucky Winslow, a brilliant negotiator, whose father had lost both legs in Vietnam and died in a veterans' hospital; and St Claire.

'Where are Hartford and Winslow?' Vail asked Naomi.

'Both in court this morning.'

'St Claire?' Vail looked at Ben Meyer.

'He's checking on something over at the records building,' Meyer said.

'About that hunch of his?' Vail asked. 'Anything to it?'

'Well, uh, nothing yet,' Meyer said, not wishing to comment until St Claire was in the room.

The conversation quickly centred on Yancey's stroke and the murder of John Delaney, the landfill trio taking a backseat to these two new developments. Vail filled them in on the Delaney homicide and assured them that he had no intention of wasting a lot of time playing DA.

'This is where the action is, and this is where I intend to stay,' he insisted as Stenner and Parver finished their phone call and entered his office, she wearing a Cheshire cat grin.

'Okay, Shana,' said Vail. 'What're you so proud of?'

'I think we've got Darby,' Parver said, rather proudly. 'We can blow his story off the planet.'

'Oh?' Vail said. He walked around the desk and sat down. He leaned back in his chair and rolled a cigarette between two fingers. 'Let's hear it from the top,' he said to her. They all knew the facts of the crime, but this was the usual drill: taking it from the top so the rest of the bunch could get the whole run in perspective.

Parver gave a quick summary of the facts: that Darby was having trouble at home with his wife, Ramona, had three bad years on his farm, had lost a subsidy contract with the government, had gone through all his family's money and a fifty-thousand-dollar inheritance Ramona got a year before, and was shacking up with a nude dancer named Poppy Palmer who performed at a strip club called the Skin Game. There was also the insurance policy.

'Darby said last summer he had an accident with a harvesting machine,' she said. 'It rolled back and almost killed him, so he took out a $250,000 insurance policy on himself – and one on Ramona while he was at it.

'Now it's January third, six o'clock in the afternoon. Darby has been hunting with two of his buddies since before dawn. They stop for a couple of beers on the way home.'

Parver stood up, acting out the event as she spoke, substituting a steel ruler for the shotgun. Parver was an actress. She loved visual impact. She leaned with her back against an imaginary wall, the steel ruler pressed against her chest.

Parver: 'He gets home and walks into the house. The CBS news is just coming on. His wife, Ramona, is sitting in the living room. Before he can even say hello, she comes up with his .38 target gun and starts shooting at him. He jumps out of the doorway behind the wall of a hallway leading to the kitchen. She sends another shot through the wall. It misses him by inches. He freaks out. He slams two shells in the shotgun and rushes around the corner.'

She spun around and aimed the ruler at Fleishman.

Parver: 'And shoots her. The shot hits her in the side. Her gun hand goes up, she puts another shot into the ceiling as he charges her.'

She rushed up to Fleishman and held the steel ruler an inch away from her forehead.

Parver: '*Boom!* he shoots her right here, just above her right eye. He drops the shotgun and crosses the room to the phone and calls 911. There's a slip of paper beside the phone with Poppy Palmer's unlisted phone number on it. Later he claims he didn't write it, doesn't know where it came from. Then he goes outside and sits on the porch steps until the police arrive. That's his story. No witnesses, nobody to argue with him.'

Fleishman: 'Gunfight at the O.K. corral, right?'

Parver: 'Right. Later Darby claims he called Poppy Palmer to tell her what happened and to find out where Ramona got the unlisted number. Palmer tells him that Ramona Darby called her about five and went crazy on the phone, threatening them both.'

Vail: 'Them being . . .?'

Parver: 'Palmer and Darby.'

Vail: 'Go on.'

Parver: 'Given the motives and the nature of the individual, I don't think any of us believed it happened this way, but we don't have anything to take to the grand jury. The insurance company is about to pay off the policy. Martin and I conducted an interrogation with

119

Darby yesterday and he froze us out. So Abel and I went back out to Sandytown. We decided to take one more crack at everybody out there who might know something, *anything*.

'There's this elderly lady – she's seventy-six – lives on the opposite side of the road from Darby, about eighty yards – actually it's eighty-three – from Darby's house. It's a field that separates these two houses, a corn field in the summer – some trees line the dirt driveway leading to the Darby place, but basically it's wide open between Darby's house and hers. Her name's Shunderson, Mabel Shunderson, a widow. She's lived there more than thirty years, has known the Darbys for the entire time they lived across the road, which is . . . uh,' – she consulted her notes – 'twelve years. Mrs Shunderson saw Darby come home in his pickup truck. She was in the kitchen looking out her window, which faces the Darby place, and she had the window open because she burned something on the stove and she was shooing out the smoke. She saw Darby come home, saw him get out of the pickup carrying the shotgun, and go into the house. A minute later she heard the shots. She had told us all this before, that she heard the shots, I mean, but we never talked about the *order* of the shots.'

Vail: 'In her seventies, you say?'

Parver: 'Yes, sir. Anyway, she says she heard the shots very clearly. It was a clear night, very cold.'

Fleishman: 'She sure it was him?'

Parver: 'No question about it.'

Meyer: 'And she's sure about the time?'

Parver: 'Says the news was just coming on the television, which ties in with Darby's story and the phone call to 911, which was at six-oh-six.'

Vail: 'Okay, go on.'

Parver: 'Well, we were doing what you might call a courtesy call just to make sure we covered everything and I said to her, Did you hear all six shots, and she said yes.

She knows about guns because Gus – that's her husband, her late husband, he's been dead about six years now – did a lot of hunting and she could tell there were two guns going off. And then she said . . . '

She stopped a moment and read very carefully from her notes.

'. . . said, "I know the difference between a shotgun and a pistol, my Gus spent half his life either hunting or practising to hunt, and when I heard that shotgun, then all those pistol shots, I knew there was something goin' on down there and I thought it was maybe a burglar in the house." '

Parver looked at Vail and then around at the group. She repeated her remark.

Parver: ' "I heard that shotgun, then all those pistol shots," that's exactly what she said.'

Vail stared at her as she went on.

Parver: 'So I said to her, "You mean you heard the pistol, then the shotgun," and she said, "Young lady, I know the difference between a shotgun and a pistol. I heard the shotgun, then four pistol shots, then the shotgun again." '

Vail: 'She's saying Darby fired the first shot?'

Parver: 'Exactly.'

Flaherty: 'She's seventy-five?'

Parver: 'Six. Seventy-six.'

Flaherty: 'And the house is eighty yards from Darby's place?'

Parver: 'Eighty-three, but she knows what she heard. I don't think there's any doubt about that. But just to make sure, Abel and I did a test.'

Vail: 'A test?'

He looked at Stenner.

Stenner: 'We set up a tape recorder in her kitchen beside the open window. I went down to Darby's place and went in the barn and fired two sets of shots into some sacks of grain.'

Vails: 'Where was Darby?'

Stenner: 'He wasn't there.'

Vail: 'Uh-huh. Trespassing.'

He scribbled some notes on a legal pad.

Stenner: 'We can go back and do it legal. I just wanted to make sure we had a live one here.'

Vail: 'I know.'

Stenner: 'First I did it the way Darby says it happened. I fired three shots from the pistol, one from the shotgun, another pistol shot, and the final shotgun blast. Then I did it the way Mrs Shunderson says she heard it: the shotgun first, four pistol shots, and the final shotgun. Shana stood beside Mrs Shunderson exactly where she was standing when the event took place and taped both sets of shots.'

Parver: 'She was adamant. She says it was BOOM, bang, bang bang, bang . . . BOOM. *Not* bang, bang, bang. BOOM, bang, BOOM. Here's the tape.'

She put a small tape recorder on the desk and pressed the play button. There was silence except for the room tone. Then there were the shots, echoing very clearly in the night air.

Bang, bang, bang . . . BOOM . . . bang . . . BOOM.

'No, no. Not the way it was t'all,' came an elderly woman's firm, very positive voice. 'As I told you . . .'

Shana's voice interrupted her. 'Just a minute,' she said. 'Listen.'

BOOM . . . bang, bang, bang, bang . . . BOOM.

'Yes! That's the way it was. 'Cept there was a little more time between the last pistol shot and the shotgun.'

'You're absolutely positive?' Parver asked.

'I told you, child, I know the difference between a shotgun and a pistol.'

'And you're sure of the sequence?'

'The shotgun was first. And there was that little pause between the last pistol shot and then the shotgun again.'

Parver turned off the tape recorder.

Hazel Fleishman said, 'Wow!' The rest of the group started to talk all at once. Vail knocked on the table with his knuckles and calmed them down.

'Is she a good witness, Abel?' Vail asked.

'A crusty old lady.' Stenner nodded with a smile. 'I think she'll hold up.'

'A woman that age – ' Meyer started.

'She's positive about what she heard. And there's not a thing wrong with her hearing,' Stenner assured him.

'You think we can bring a first-degree murder case against Darby on this boom-bang testimony?' Flaherty said.

'This woman knows what she heard,' Stenner insisted.

'This is what I think happened,' Parver said. She acted out her theory again, walking to the middle of the room with her hand down at her side holding the ruler-shotgun.

'He comes home, has the shotgun loaded, walks into the house. His wife is sitting in the living room. . . .'

Parver approached Flaherty. When she was two feet away from him, she swung her arm up, aiming the imaginary gun at his forehead.

'BOOM! He walks right up to her and shoots her in the head point-blank, just like that. Then he takes the .38 – he's still got his gloves on – and he puts it in her hand and *bang, bang, bang, bang* – he puts the two shots in the hall, one in the wall, and one in the ceiling – then he backs off a few feet and hits her with the second shotgun blast. I mean, he thought of everything. Powder burns on her hand, the long shot that he claims he shot *first* after she cut loose at him. He covered everything *but* the sound.'

'It's not just the order of the shots,' Stenner said in his underplayed, quiet manner. 'It's the pauses in between them. Or lack of same. Mrs Shunderson says there was no pause between the four pistol shots. She says it was BOOM . . . bang bang bang bang . . . BOOM.

Ramona Darby was dead when he put the gun in her hand and fired the pistol.'

Vail leaned back in his chair and stared at the ceiling for a moment, then chuckled. 'Nice job, you two,' he said.

'The problem is proving premeditation,' Flaherty offered. 'We'll have to give up Shunderson in discovery so they'll know what we have. Darby'll change his story.'

'That won't hold up,' Stenner said. 'No jury will believe that he charged into her while she was shooting at him and got close enough to pop her point-blank in the head without getting hit himself. It's that point-blank head shot he has to live with.'

'He could plead sudden impulse,' Dermott Flaherty offered. 'He came in. She had the gun. She threatened him, he shot her. Then he panicked and jimmied up the rest of the story because he was afraid he couldn't prove self-defence.'

'So how do we trap him?' Vail asked.

Silence fell over the room.

Vail went on. 'Unless we have some corroborative evidence, Darby will be dancing all over the room. And Paul Rainey will jump on the strongest scenario they can come up with and stick with it.'

'Which will probably be Dermott's take on it,' Hazel Fleishman said.

Vail nodded. 'Namely that he came in, she had the gun, he freaked out and shot her but didn't kill her, blah, blah, blah.'

'Doesn't work,' Parver said. 'He can't get around the fact that for his story to work, his first shot had to hit her in the side. That shot in the face was from twelve inches, maybe less. It was cold-blooded. That shot put her away instantly.'

'Heat of the moment?' Fleishman suggested. 'The woman throws down on him, he fires in a panic – '

'And runs twelve feet across the room before he shoots

again?' Stenner asked. 'No jury'll buy that. If the farm lady's testimony holds up – if Rainey doesn't dissect her on the stand – Darby's stuck with the sequence, he'll have to change his story.'

'He's in a panic. He's exhausted. He's been out in a blind for five hours.' Flaherty lowered his head, miming Darby: 'I was cold and tired. I came in and suddenly this crazy woman's blazing away at me. I duck behind the hall wall. She keeps shooting. Finally I just charged into the room and fired. It all happened so fast. I don't remember firing that last shot. All I remember is the noise and the smoke, one of those shots coming so close to my cheek that I could feel the heat. It was over just like that.' He snapped his fingers.

Vail said, 'Very good, Dermott. You ought to be defending him.' The group laughed except for Shana Parver, who glared at Flaherty. He smiled at her and shrugged. 'Just doin' my job, Counsellor,' he said. 'I think nailing that witness was a stroke of genius.'

'No question about it,' Vail said. 'The questions we have to decide are: One, do we arrest him yet? And two, do we go for murder in the first or second?'

Shana Parver said, 'It's cold-blooded murder. We can prove premeditation. He did it the minute he walked in the door.'

'So do we arrest him?' Stenner asked. A hint of a smile played at the corners of his mouth. He watched Vail go to the urn and draw another cup of coffee. The old master, playing all the angles in his head.

Vail walked over to Shana and toyed with the ruler and said, 'How about Betty Boop? Did you talk to her about the phone call?'

Parver smiled. 'She flew the coop.'

'She did *what*?'

'We went by the club and her boss told us she left town yesterday afternoon,' Stenner said. 'Told him her sister in Texarkana is dying of cancer. We checked it out this morning, that's what we were doing on the phone. Her sister lives in San Diego. In perfect health. Last time she heard from Poppy Palmer was five years ago.'

'What do you know,' Vail said to Parver. 'Your ploy may have worked. The question you asked Darby about the phone number could have spooked her.'

'Something did,' Stenner said.

'You want to go for an indictment now?' Vail asked Parver.

She nodded.

'Fleishman?' Vail said.

'Yeah, we bust him. It'll hold up the insurance payoff and that could shake him up. And maybe Rainey, too.'

'Good point. Meyer? Indict him?'

'Pretty risky. Our whole case hangs on Shunderson's testimony. Maybe we need something more.'

'There's plenty of strong circumstantial evidence to go with it,' Parver countered.

'Abel?'

'If it gets that far.'

Vail smiled. The young lawyers looked at one another. 'What's that mean?' Parver said.

Vail stood up and circled the desk slowly. He finally lit a cigarette, then returned to the corner near the exhaust fan and blew the smoke into it. 'What we're after here is justice, right? Here's a man who killed his wife in cold blood for greed and another woman. He planned it, even down to putting the gun in her dead hand and using gloves to fire it so she'd have powder burns on her fingers. That's planning. No way around it, he didn't even have time to think about it if we believe Mrs Shunderson's testimony. He knew exactly what he was going to do when he walked into the house. That's what we have to prove to get a first-degree conviction. Flaherty's right, the whole case will hinge on whether the jury believes Shunderson *and* the time element involved. If they don't, he could walk off into the sunset with his jiggly girlfriend and two hundred and fifty thousand bucks. So, do we go to the wall with this guy? Or maybe try an end run?'

'You mean a *deal*?' Parver said with disbelief.

'Not a deal,' Vail said. '*The* deal.'

'And what's that?' she demanded. She was getting angry.

'Twenty years, no parole.'

'Part of our case is that he premeditated this,' Parver said, defending her plea for a murder-one indictment. 'Twenty years, that's a second-degree sentence.'

'No, it's a first-degree sentence with mercy. Think about it, Shana. If we go to trial and get a conviction, but the jury brings in second-degree instead of first, he could get twenty years to life and be back on the street in eight.'

'You think you can manoeuvre Rainey into twenty, no parole?' asked Flaherty.

'If we can shake his faith in Darby. Right now, he's sold on his client. Look, most defence advocates don't give a damn whether their client is guilty or innocent. It's can the state make its case and will the jury buy it. Rainey's a little different. If he finds out he's been lied to, then it comes down to whether he thinks we can prove our case. It's really not about guilt or innocence, it's about winning. If he thinks we've got him, he'll make the best deal he can for his client.'

'You think the tape will do that?'

'I don't know,' Vail said. 'But I don't know whether we can win a trial with this evidence, either. If we put the SOB away for a flat twenty, he'll be fifty-six and dead broke by the time he's back on the street.'

The room fell silent for a few moments. Vail put his feet on the edge of his table and leaned back in his chair. Stenner could almost hear his brain clicking.

'Shana,' Vail said finally, 'get an arrest warrant on James Wayne Darby. Murder one. Tell the sheriff's department we'll serve it. Naomi, set up lunch with

Rainey as soon as possible. Flaherty, check with your pals in the audio business, see if you can get the sound on that tape enhanced a little.'

'Ah, the art of the deal . . .' Stenner said softly, and smiled.

Eleven

The section known as Back of the Yards sprawled for a dozen square blocks, shouldering the stockyards for space. Its buildings, most of which were a century old, were square, muscular structures of concrete, brick, and timber behind facades of terracotta. The warehouses and old manufacturing plants were once headquarters for some of the country's great industrial powers: Goodyear and Montgomery Ward, Swift and Libby. Developers had resurrected the structures, renovating them and turning the once onerous area of canals, railroad tracks, and braying animal pens into a nostalgic and historic office park.

The Delaney building was six storeys tall and occupied a quarter of a block near Ashland. The brass plaque beside the entrance road simply: DELANEY ENTERPRISES, INC., FOUNDED 1961.

The executive offices were on the sixth floor and were reminiscent of the offices that had been there a hundred years before. As Shock Johnson stepped off the lift, he looked out on a vast open space sectioned off into mahogany and glass squares. With the exception of Delaney's office suite and the three vice presidents' offices that adjoined it, which occupied one full side of the large rectangle, all the other offices lacked both privacy and personality. Johnson thought for a moment of Dickens: he could almost see the ghost of Uriah Heep sitting atop a high stool in the corner, appraising the room to make sure everyone kept busy. The executive secretary, Edith Stoddard, was dressed to mourn in a stern, shin-length black dress. She wore very little make-up; her hair was cut in a bob reminiscent of the Thirties and was streaked

129

with grey. She was a pleasant though harsh-looking woman; her face was drawn and she looked tired.

'I've arranged for you to use three VP suites,' she said, motioning to them with her hand. 'You got the list of employees?'

'Yes, ma'am, thank you,' Johnson answered.

'We have very hurriedly called a board of directors meeting,' she said. 'I'll be tied up for an hour or two.'

'Are you on the board?' Johnson asked.

'I'm the secretary,' she said.

Three teams of detectives were assigned to the VP offices. The forty-two secretaries, sales managers, and superintendents had been divided into three lists. Each of the interrogation teams had its list of fourteen subjects. Johnson and his partner for the day, an acerbic and misanthropic homicide detective named Si Irving, took the middle office. Irving was a box of a man, half a foot shorter than his boss, with wisps of black hair streaking an otherwise bald head. He was an excellent detective but was from the old school. As he had once told Johnson, 'Catch 'em, gut 'em, and fry 'em, that's my motto.'

They suffered through a half-dozen dull men and women, none of whom would say an unkind word about 'Mr D.' and none of whom knew anything. Shock Johnson was leaning back in a swivel chair, his feet propped up on an open desk drawer, when Miranda Stewart entered the room. She was a striking woman, zaftig and blonde, wearing a smartly tailored red business suit and a black silk shirt. Her hair was tied back with a white ribbon. Johnson perked up. Irving appraised her through doleful eyes.

'Miss Miranda Stewart?' Johnson said, putting his feet back on the floor and sitting up at the desk.

'Yes,' she said.

'Please have a seat. I'm Captain Johnson of the Chicago PD and this is Simon Irving, a member of the homicide division.'

She smiled at sat down, a composed, friendly woman in her mid-thirties who seemed self-assured and perfectly at ease. She crossed her legs demurely and pulled her skirt down. It almost covered her knees.

'I want to point out that this is an informal interview,' Johnson said. 'By that I mean you will not be sworn and this session will not be transcribed, although we will be taking notes. However, if at some point in this interview we feel the necessity of reading you your rights, we will give you the opportunity to contact an attorney. This is standard operating procedure in a situation like this and we tell everyone the same thing before we start, so I don't want you to feel that bringing that up, about reading you your rights, is in any way a threat. Okay?'

'Okay,' she said in a sultry voice. She seemed to be looking forward to the experience or perhaps the attention.

'What is your full name?'

'Miranda Duff Stewart.'

'Where do you live?'

'At 3212 Wabash. Apartment 3A.'

'Are you married, Ms Stewart?'

'No. Divorced, 1990.'

'How long have you lived at that address?'

'Since 1990. Three years.'

'And how long have you worked at Delaney Enterprises?'

'Eighteen months.'

'What did you do before you came here?'

'I was the secretary to Don Weber, the vice president of Trumbell and Sloan.'

'The advertising agency?'

'Yes, in Riverfront.'

'And what is your job here at Delaney Enterprises?'

'I was recently appointed Mr Delaney's new executive secretary. Edith Stoddard – she has the job now – is getting ready to retire.'

'So you haven't started in that job yet?'

'Well, I've had some meetings with Mr Delaney. You know, about what he expects of me, my responsibilities. Things like that. I know what I'll be doing.'

'Have you been working with Mrs . . . Is it Mrs Stoddard?'

'Yes, she's married and has a daughter going to UC.'

'What's her husband do?'

'He's crippled, I understand.'

'And have you been working with Mrs Stoddard during this period?'

'No. Mr Delaney said he wanted me to start off fresh.' She smiled. 'Said he didn't want me carrying over any of her bad habits, but I think he was kidding about Edith. I mean, everybody knows how efficient she is. I think he was just, you know, looking for a change?'

'Do you know how long she's had the job?' Johnson asked.

'Not really. She's been here forever. Maybe fifteen years?'

'What we're lookin' for here, Ms Stewart, is if any bad blood might've existed between Delaney and people on his staff or maybe his business associates. Know what I mean?' Irving's voice was a raspy growl. 'Arguments, disagreements, threats . . . bad blood.'

'Well, I don't know about his business associates, you'll have to ask Edith about that. He seemed to get along fine with the people in the office . . . of course . . .' She stopped and let the sentence hang in the air.

'Of course, what?' Irving asked.

'Well, I don't think Edith was real happy about the change.'

'Was she bein' demoted, that what you mean?' said Irving.

'She was, uh, she was leaving the company.'

'Did she quit?'

'He said, Mr Delaney said, that she was taking early

132

retirement, but I got the impression that it was an either-or kind of thing.'

'Either-or?' Johnson asked.

'Either retire or, you know, you're out on your . . .' She jerked a thumb over her shoulder.

'So Mrs Stoddard wasn't happy about it?'

'I got that impression.'

Johnson said, 'Did Delaney discuss this with you?'

'No, it was just . . . just office gossip, you know how people talk. See, it wasn't really announced yet, about me taking that job.'

'So you're the only one that knew officially?'

'That I know of.'

'Did his wife know?'

'I never met his wife. She never came up here. I've seen her picture in the society pages, at charity things and stuff, but I never saw her face-to-face.'

'That wasn't the question,' Irving said bluntly. His tone was brusque and formal compared with that of Johnson, who was warmer and tended to put people at ease.

'Oh. Uh, I'm sorry, what was the question again?'

'Did his wife know you were taking Mrs Stoddard's place? That was the specific question,' Johnson said.

'Oh. I don't know.' She shrugged.

'When did he first approach you about takin' over Stoddard's position?' Irving asked.

'This was about two months ago.'

'Was it mentioned when you first came to work here? I mean, was it kinda, you know, in the works?' Irving asked.

'It was mentioned that if I lived up to my résumé, I could move up rapidly.'

'Specifically to be Delaney's exec?'

'That was mentioned. He didn't dwell on it.'

'So it was kinda like a carrot on a string for you, right? You do good, you could nail the top job? That's what it is, ain't it, the top woman's job here?'

133

'There are some women in sales, but you know how it is, working that closely to the boss and all, it's a very personal thing. A very good job. For a person with my qualifications, it was one of the best jobs in town.'

'So then, two months ago, Delaney offered you the position, that it?' said Irving.

'Yes.'

'Let me ask you something, Ms Stewart,' said Johnson. 'Are you under the impression that Mrs Stoddard was upset by all this?'

'I never talked to her about it. I worked on the first floor, she's up here on six.'

'But you said earlier, when you were talking about Mrs Stoddard leaving ... uh, you implied it was "an either-or kind of thing" ' Johnson said, checking his notes.

'That was what Mr Delaney said,' she said.

'Well, lemme put it this way,' Irving said. 'Did you ever see anything in Mrs Stoddard's attitude towards you that would indicate she was upset with *you* about the change?'

'I told you, I was at pains to keep out of her way,' she said. Annoyance was creeping into her tone.

'Whose idea was that?'

'What?'

'Whose idea to keep outta her way, yours or Delaney's?'

'His. Joh – Mr Delaney's.'

'Call him by his first name, didja?' Irving said.

'So does ... did ... Edith. That was his idea, to call him John.' She sighed. 'Look ... can I smoke? Thanks. When this first came up, about Edith retiring? He took me to lunch because he didn't want people around the office to know what he had in mind. So I never really saw much of him around the office. Sometimes just walking through the first floor, that was about it.'

'So he picks you. I mean, there was obviously a lot of other women who'd been working here longer ...' Irving let the sentence die before it became a question.

'Am I under suspicion or something?' she asked, her forehead wrinkling with apprehension.

'Not at all, Ms Stewart,' Johnson interjected. 'There's been a homicide and we're just trying to get a fix on this man, you know, the people who work around him.'

'I'm a computer expert, among other things, Captain,' she said. 'I took courses two years ago. I knew sooner or later I'd have to be an electronics whiz to get along in the world. That's one of the things that attracted him to me. On the résumé, I mean. Also that I was familiar with advertising. That appealed to him, too.'

'Okay, just to catch up,' Irving said. 'You was workin' as a VP's secretary at Trumbell and Sloan and you took courses to become computer . . . computerized . . .'

'Computer literate,' Johnson suggested.

'Computer literate, yeah. And Delaney saw that and offered you a job and mentioned the top slot might come open. Then you and Delaney slipped out to lunch and he offered you the job and implied that Edith Stoddard was given an "either-or" option, which I assume means either retire or get canned. Is that generally the way things went?'

'Yes.'

'How did he get your résumé?' Johnson asked.

'What is this?' she snapped suddenly. Blood rose to her face and her cheeks reddened. 'Why are you asking me all these personal questions? I didn't have anything to do with this. I lost a damn good job when . . . oh, when Mr Delaney was, uh, was . . .'

'Nobody's accusing you of anything,' Johnson said reassuringly. 'We're just trying to get a feel for office politics and how Delaney operated. For instance, have you ever been to Delaney's penthouse apartment over on the Gold Coast?'

'Not really . . .'

' "Not really"?' said Irving. 'I mean, either you was or you wasn't. It ain't a "not really" kinda question.'

'I don't want anybody to get the wrong impression.'

'We're not doin' impressions today, we're listenin',' Irving shot back.

'Just level with us,' Johnson said softly, with a broad, friendly, 'trust me' smile. 'Did you have a key to the penthouse apartment?'

'No!' she said, as if insulted. 'Edith was the only one I know who had a key.'

'Edith Stoddard had a key? How do you know that?'

'The time I went over there, I took a cab over at lunch. He had a desk in his bedroom and he had spreadsheets all over it. He said he worked there a lot because he never could get anything done at the office. He had some sandwiches brought in and we talked about the job. That's when he told me that Edith had a key because he was thinking of having the lock changed when she left. I mean, that's not uncommon, you know? When somebody leaves – to change the lock.'

'Did he say why she had a key?' Johnson asked.

'He told me there were times when I might have to go over there to pick something up or to sit in on meetings outside the office. He also said I was never to mention the apartment. That it was a very private place for him and he wanted to keep it that way.'

'Do you own a gun, Miss Stewart?' Irving asked suddenly.

'No!' she said, surprised. 'I hate the things.'

'You know does the Stoddard woman own a weapon?'

'I have no idea.'

'Did Delaney have any problems with Edith Stoddard recently? Over this thing, I mean?' said Johnson.

'I don't know.'

'When's the last time you saw him?' Johnson asked.

'Uh, This is Thursday? Monday. Monday or Tuesday. I was coming back from lunch as he was leaving the office. We just said hello. I told you, I didn't see him that often.'

'And when was Stoddard due to leave?'

'Today was her last day.'

When they had dismissed Miranda Stewart, Irving snatched up a phone, punched one of a dozen buttons, and tapped out a number. Johnson was going back over his notes.

'Who's this?' Irving asked. 'Hey, Cabrilla, this is Irving. No, Si Irving, not Irving whoever. Yeah, down in Homicide. I need a check on a gun purchase. Well, how often do they turn 'em in? Okay, if it was the last week I'm shit outta luck. The name is Edith Stoddard. S-t-o-d-d-a-r-d. I don't know her address, how many Edith Stoddards could there be? Yeah.' He cupped the mouthpiece with his hand. 'They turn in the gun purchases every week. He says with the new law, they're behind entering them in the comp – Yeah? Oh, hold on a minute.' He snapped on the point of his ballpoint pen and started scratching down notes. 'That it? Thanks, Cabrilla, I owe ya one.' He hung up the phone, punched out another number, spoke for a minute or two, then hung up.

'Mrs Stoddard purchased a S&W .38 police special, four-inch barrel, on January twenty-two, at Sergeant York's on Wabash. I called Sergeant York's, talked to the manager. He remembers her, says she asked who could give her shootin' lessons, and he recommended the Shootin' Club. That's that indoor range over in Canaryville, mile or so down Pershing. Wanna take a break? Tool over there?'

The Shooting Club occupied the corner building of a shopping strip a mile or so from Delaney's office. Inside, glass-enclosed islands displayed the latest in friendly firepower: pistols, automatics, shotguns, assault weapons, Russian night-vision goggles, laser scopes, zoom eyes, robo lights. Patches from US and foreign armed forces lined the top of the wall. At the rear, a steel door led to the shooting range. Viewed through tinted glass, thirty slots offered target shooters the opportunity to shoot human silhouette targets to bits. The range was soundproofed. There were three or four customers in the showroom and a half-dozen people were firing away behind the glass.

The owner was a ramrod-straight man in his forties with bad skin, wearing a tactical black camouflage parka and trousers and heavy Special Forces boots with thick lug soles. His black cap was pulled down to just above his eyes. Johnson showed his badge. The man in black introduced himself as Roy Bennett.

'No problem, is there?' he asked in a hard voice he tried to make friendly.

'We're interested in talking to whoever teaches on the range.'

'We take turns,' Bennett said. 'All our personnel are ex-military and qualified expert.'

'We're checking on a woman, probably come over either at lunch or right after work,' Irving said. 'The name Edith Stoddard wake ya up?'

'Older lady? Maybe fifty, fifty-five, 'bout yea high?' He held his hand even with his shoulder.

'Yeah,' Irving said. 'She purchased a .38 Smith & Wesson from Sergeant York's. They sent her over here to learn how to use it.'

'That's the lady.' Bennett reached under the counter and brought out an appointment book, then flipped back through it a few pages.

'Yeah, here you are. She started coming on the twenty-second of last month . . .' He flipped through the pages, running his finger down the list of names each day. 'And stopped last Monday. Fifteen days in a row. I remember her pretty good now. Didn't say a whole lot. You could tell she was uncomfortable with her weapon. Personally, I would've sold her a .25, certainly nothing heavier than a .32. That .38 was a lot of gun for her.'

'How'd she do?' Johnson asked.

'I can teach a Dodge pickup to shoot straight in two weeks,' Bennett said with a smile.

'So she done good, that what you're sayin'?' said Irving.

'She was really interested in becoming proficient at short ranges. Twenty-five yards. Yeah, she could blow the heart outta the target at twenty-five. Something happen to her?'

'Not her,' Irving said. 'But I'll tell you this, you taught her real good.'

Johnson and Irving got into the police car and headed back towards Back of the Yards.

'You wanna good-guy, bad-guy her, Shock?'

'Christ, we're not talking about Roger Touhy here, Irving, it's a fifty-year-old-woman, for God's sake.'

Irving shrugged. 'One in the pump, one in the noggin,' he said.

'So she owns a .38 and took shooting lessons. Do you know how many women in this town fit that bill? A lot of scared ladies out there.'

'A lotta scared everybody out there. But they don't all have a key to Delaney's place and they all ain't been kicked out on their ass to make room for Little Annie Fanny. It's lookin' awful good to me, Cap'n.'

'We'll talk to her, Si.'

'One in the pump, one in—'

'Yeah, yeah, yeah.'

'Do we read her her rights?'

'Damn it, Si, we're just talking at this point!'

'Okay, okay. I just don't want that fuckin' Vail pissin' in my ear over this. If we're gonna get into the gun, I say give her her Miranda.'

'Let me worry about Vail.'

What Johnson had first thought was fatigue in Edith

Stoddard's face took on different connotations as she sat across the desk from the two officers. Her eyes were flat and expressionless. The lines in her face seemed to be lines of defeat. It was the face of a woman who had been dealt badly by life; a woman tied to a crippled husband, trying to get her daughter through college, and suddenly thrown out of a prestigious job that was absolutely essential to the welfare of her family. What Shock Johnson saw in Edith Stoddard's face was humiliation, betrayal, anxiety, frustration – everything but wrath. Her anger, if she was angry, had been satisfied, if not by her, by someone.

Irving saw guilt.

He was tapping his pen nervously on the table, waiting to get past the amenities to go in for the kill. Johnson reached over without looking at him and laid his hand gently over the pen. Mrs Stoddard sat stiffly at the desk with her hands folded in front of her. Johnson repeated the same instructions he had given to the other interview subjects earlier in the day.

'You understand,' he said, 'if, at some point in this interview – see, we could stop and read you your rights, ma'am, but I don't say that as any kind of a threat. By that I mean we aren't planning to do that at this point, we tell everyone the same thing when we start, so I don't want you to feel that bringing it up now means we're going to go that far. Okay?'

She nodded.

'Please state your name.'

'Edith Stoddard.'

'Age?'

'Fifty-three in May.'

'Are you married?'

'Yes.'

'Where does your husband work?'

'He's disabled. He has a small pension.'

'Disabled in what way?' Johnson asked.

'He's a quadriplegic. Crippled from the neck down.'

'I'm sorry,' Johnson said.

'Charley loved to work around the house. He was fixing some shingles on the roof and slipped and landed flat on his back on the concrete walk. Broke his back in two places.'

'When was that?'

'In 1982.'

'He's been bedridden ever since?'

She nodded.

'And you have a daughter?'

'Angelica. She's twenty-one, a junior at UC. Studying physics.'

'Mrs Stoddard, how long did you work for Delaney? Delaney Enterprises?'

'Seventeen years.'

'And how long were you Delaney's executive secretary?'

'Nine.'

'Were you happy in that job?'

At first she looked a little confused by the question. Then finally she said, 'Yes. It was a wonderful position. Mr Delaney was . . . very helpful, sympathetic, when we had the accident.'

'You say "was", Mrs Stoddard,' Irving said. 'Is that because Delaney is, uh, deceased?'

'I was . . . Yes.'

'You was about to say . . .?'

'Nothing.'

'Ain't it true, Mrs Stoddard, that you were about to retire? That today was to be your last day here?'

She hesitated for a moment. 'Yes.'

'So when you say "was", you really meant you don't work here no more, is that correct?'

'I don't see that . . . I mean . . .'

'I think what Detective Irving is driving at here is that you were leaving the firm,' Johnson said softly.

'Yes, that's true.'

'And were you satisfied with the arrangement? Retiring, I mean?'

She did not answer. She fiddled with her fingers and her lips trembled. Irving could see her beginning to crumble and decided to go for the throat.

'Mrs Stoddard, you had a key to Delaney's penthouse on Astor, didn't you?'

'Yes.'

'Go there often, did you?'

'It was part of my job. Mr Delaney didn't like to work here in the office. Too many disruptions.'

'So you were familiar with the surroundings there, at the penthouse, I mean?'

'Yes, of course.'

'And you could more or less come and go as you please, right?'

'I only went when I was told to go there.'

'Uh-huh. Point is, ma'am, you had free access, din'cha?'

'Well, I guess you might say that.'

'And how many other people do you know had keys and access to the apartment?'

'I don't know, I wouldn't know that.'

'So what you're sayin', what you're tellin' us is, as far as you know, nobody else had that kind of access to the premises? As far as you know?' said Irving.

'As far as I know.'

'Did Mrs Delaney have a key, as far as you know?'

'I wouldn't know . . . I mean, I assume . . . uh . . .'

'Ain't it a fact, Mrs Stoddard, that you know she don't have a key, didn't even know the place existed? Isn't that right?'

'That really wasn't any of my business.'

'Uh-huh. Well, ain't it a fact you were told not to talk about that apartment? That it was kinda a secret place for him?'

'Sir, I was privy to a lot of information that was confidential. Mr Delaney never mentioned Mrs Delaney specifically.'

'But it was a confidential kinda place, right?'

'Yes.'

'Now, did you ever go over to Mr Delaney's penthouse on Astor when you weren't specifically invited?'

'Of course not!'

'Never kinda busted in on the place, y'know, looking for records or files or somethin' like that, and Mr Delaney wasn't expectin' you?'

'No. I don't understand what your point to all this is,' she said, becoming passively defensive.

'Will you excuse us for just a minute, please,' Irving said, and motioned Johnson to step outside the office. He leaned close to the captain and whispered, 'We're gettin close the skinny, here, Cap'n. I think it's time we Miranda her.'

'Not yet,' Johnson whispered back. 'She brings in a lawyer and we're in for a long haul. We'll find out as much as we can before we start that.'

'Yeah, if she starts takin' the fifth, we got problems. I just get nervous, gettin' too far into this without lettin' her know her rights. I'm goin' for the gun here any minute now, okay? Then we're into it.'

'*I'll let you know when I think it's time to Miranda her,*' Johnson said, his voice edgy and harsh.

'I just don't wanna fuck up at this stage.'

'I'll say when, Si.'

'Yes, sir.'

They returned to the room.

Edith Stoddard was slumped in her seat, her hands now in her lap, staring at the wall. Johnson thought to himself, *This lady is verging on shock*. Johnson and Irving sat down.

'Now, Mrs Stoddard,' Johnson said, 'we were talking

about your access to the apartment. Did you ever go over at night?'

'Sometimes,' she said numbly. 'If he wanted me to.'

'So this was kind of like a second workplace for you, is that correct?'

She nodded. She was still staring past them at the wall.

'And it was natural for you to spend a lot of time there?'

'I suppose you could say that.'

'Let's move on,' Irving said. 'Mrs Stoddard, do you own a gun?'

She looked at him sharply, as if suddenly drawn out of her daze by his question.

'A gun?'

'Yeah, a gun.' He pulled back his jacket and showed her his weapon. 'A gun.'

'I . . .'

Johnson stepped in. 'Mrs Stoddard, we know you purchased a .38-calibre handgun at Sergeant York's on January twenty-second of this year. Where is that gun now?'

'Oh, yes, the gun.'

'What about it?' Irving asked.

'It was stolen.'

'*Stolen?*' Irving said, turning to Johnson and raising his eyebrows.

'From my handbag.'

'You were carryin' it in your handbag?' Irving said.

'There's been a lot of crime, you know, muggings and the like, and I—'

'Do you know how to use a handgun, Mrs Stoddard?' Johnson asked.

'I thought . . . I thought it would scare them.'

'Who?'

'People who steal from people.'

'So you didn't know anything about this weapon, you just wanted it as a scare card, that it?' said Irving.

'Yes. To scare them.'

'But you were not familiar with the weapon, is that what you're saying?'

'Yes. Or no. I mean, I don't know much about guns, that's what I mean.'

Johnson looked down at his fingers for a moment and then finally he looked her straight in the eye and said, 'Mrs Stoddard, I have to interrupt these proceedings at this point and advise you that you have the right to remain silent. If you say anything more, it can, and will, be used against you in a court of law. You are entitled to an attorney. If you do not have one or – '

She cut him off. 'I killed him,' she said without emotion and without changing her expression.

Johnson and Irving were struck dumb by the admission.

'Excuse me?' Johnson said after a few seconds.

'I killed him,' she repeated without emotion.

'Christ!' Irving muttered.

'Mrs Stoddard,' Shock Johnson said firmly but quietly, 'you understand, don't you, that you are entitled to have a lawyer present now?'

She looked back and forth at them.

'I don't understand anything anymore,' she said mournfully.

Twelve

The felony and misdemeanour history of the county was stored in canyons of documents in an enormous warehouse that covered a square block near the criminal courts building. Row after row and tier upon tier of trial transcripts, bound between uniform brown covers, filled the enormous warehouse with faded and fading files. Many more had been misplaced, lost, destroyed, or misfiled; simply transposing the numbers in the index could send a record into file oblivion. Physical evidence was harder to come by. Returned to owners, lost, or destroyed, it was hardly worth the effort to track it down.

St Claire signed in and quickly found the registration number of the trial transcript: 'Case Number 83–45976432, the State versus Aaron Stampler. Murder in the first degree. Martin Vail for defence. Jane Venable for prosecution.' He was pointed down through the narrow passageways. Dust seemed to be suspended in shafts of lights from skylights. It took fifteen minutes before he found a cardbox box with STAMPLER, A. 83–45976432 scrawled on the side with a Magic Marker. He carried the box containing the transcript, three volumes of it, to a steel-framed table in the centre of the place and sat down to study Vail's most famous case.

Something had triggered St Claire's phenomenal memory, but he had yet to finger exactly what was gnawing at him: an abstract memory just beyond his grasp. But in that box St Claire was certain he would find what he was looking for, just as he now knew it would have nothing to do with the bodies in the landfill.

He started reading through the first volume but realized quickly that he would have to categorize the material in some way. He leafed through the jury selection and the mundane business of preparing the court for the trial; scanned ahead, looking for key words, piecing together bits and pieces of testimony; and made numerous trips to the copy machine. Then he began his own peculiar version of link analysis, categorizing them and working through the trial in logical rather than chronological order.

But St Claire was also interested in how Vail had conducted a defence that almost everyone believed was hopeless. And also the adversarial cross-examination of Stenner, who was the homicide detective in charge of the investigation. The fireworks began in the opening minutes of the trial.

JUDGE SHOAT: *Mr Vail, to the charge of murder in the first degree, you have previously entered a plea of not guilty. Do you now wish to change that plea?*
VAIL: *Yes sir.*
JUDGE SHOAT: *And how does the defendant now plead?*
VAIL: *Guilty but insane.*
JUDGE SHOAT: *Mr Vail, I'm sure you're aware that three professional psychiatrists have concluded that your client is sane.*
VAIL: *. . . they screwed up.*

That started what St Claire realized was ultimately a battle of titans – Venable versus Vail – both at the top of their game, both keen strategists and intractable jugular artists. Venable's opening statement to the jury was short, to the point, and almost arrogantly confident. Obviously, she figured the case was in the bag.

VENABLE: *Ladies and gentlemen of the jury, I'll be brief. During the course of this trial, you will see pictures and they will shock you. You will see overwhelming physical evidence. You will hear expert witnesses testify that Aaron Stampler – and only Aaron Stampler – could have committed this vicious and senselessly brutal murder of a revered community leader. Aaron Stampler is guilty of coldly, premeditatedly killing Archbishop Richard Rushman. In the end, I am sure you will agree with the state that anything less than the death penalty would be as great a miscarriage of justice as the murder itself.*

Vail, in sharp contrast, set up his entire defence in a complex and obviously impassioned plea to the jury.

VAIL: *Ladies and gentlemen of the jury, my name is Martin Vail. I have been charged by the court to represent the defendant, Aaron Stampler. Now, we are here to determine whether the defendant who sits before you is guilty of the loathsome and premeditated murder of one of this city's most admired and respected citizens, Archbishop Richard Rushman. In criminal law there are two types of criminals. The worst is known as* malum in se, *which means wrong by the very nature of the crime. Murder, rape, grievous bodily harm, crippling injuries – purposeful, planned, premeditated crimes against the person's body, if you will. This is such a crime. The murder of Bishop Rushman is obviously a case of* malum in se. *The accused does not deny that. You will see photographs of this crime that will sicken you. And you will be asked to believe that a sane person committed that crime. And you will be asked to render judgement on what is known as* mens rea, *which means did the accused intend to cause bodily harm – in other words, did Aaron Stampler intentionally commit the murder of Archbishop Rushman? Aaron Stampler does deny that he is guilty of* mens rea *in this murder case.... The extenuating circumstances in the case of the State versus Aaron Stampler are of an unusual nature because they involve mental disorders. And so you will be made privy to a great deal of psychological information during the course of this trial. We ask only that you listen carefully so that you can make a fair judgement on* mens rea, *for in order to make that judgement you will be asked to judge his conduct. Did Aaron Stampler suffer a defect of reason? Did he act on an irresistible impulse? ... These and many more questions will hinge on the state of Aaron Stampler's mental health at the time the crime was committed. And as you make these judgements, I would ask also that you keep one important fact in the back of your mind at all times: If Aaron Stampler was in full command of his faculties at the time of this crime, why did he do it? What was his motivation for committing such a desperate and horrifying act? And if he did, was he mentally responsible at the time? In the finally analysis, that may be the most important question of all. And so, ladies and gentlemen, your responsibility will be to rule on the believability of the evidence the prosecutor and I present to you. Whom do you believe? What do you believe? And most important of all, do you accept the evidence as truth 'beyond a reasonable doubt'? ... In the end, when you have heard all the evidence, I sincerely believe that you will find on behalf of my client, Aaron Stampler.*

St Claire had spent hours copying parts of the testimony and inventing his own chronology of the trial. The method would eventually guide him to the elusive clues he was pursuing. The initial skirmishes came quickly, during the first cross by Vail. The witness was the state's psychiatric expert, Dr Harcourt D. Bascott.

VAIL: *Are you familiar with Aaron Stampler's hometown: Crikside, Kentucky?*
BASCOTT: *It has been described to me, sir.*
VAIL: *You haven't been there?*
BASCOTT: *No, I have not.*
VAIL: *From what you understand, Doctor, is it possible that environmental factors in Crikside might contribute to schizophrenia?*
VENABLE: *Objection, Your Honour. Hearsay. And what is the relevance of this testimony?*
VAIL: *Your Honour, we're dealing with a homicide which we contend is the result of a specific mental disorder. I'm simply laying groundwork here.*
VENABLE: *Are we going to get a course in psychiatry, too?*
VAIL: *Is that an objection?*
VENABLE: *If you like.*
JUDGE SHOAT: *Excuse me. Would you like a recess so you can carry on this private discussion, or would you two like to address the court?*

So, in the opening interrogation, the tone and pace of the game was set. Stampler, St Claire learned from several witnesses, had been a physically abused, religiously disoriented, twenty-year-old Appalachian kid with a genius IQ and illiterate parents. He had been stifled in a narrow niche of a village in the Kentucky mountains, forced into the coal mines where the future was a slow death by black lung or a quick demise by explosion or poisonous gases. The thing he had feared the most was the hole, a deep mine shaft that, in his words, 'was worse than all my nightmares. I didn't know a hole could be that deep. At the bottom, the shaft was only four feet high. We had to work on our knees. The darkness swallowed up our lights.'

Forced on his ninth birthday to begin working in the hole, he had finally escaped the confines of Crikside,

Kentucky, when he was eighteen, urged by Miss Rebecca, the town's one-room-school teacher, who had nurtured his thirst for knowledge since his first day in school. In Chicago, he had been rescued by Archbishop Richard Rushman, founder of a home for runaways called Saviour House. It had been Stampler's home until he and his girlfriend decided to live together. It had turned out to be a disastrous idea. She had left and returned to her home in Ohio. Stampler had ended up in a sordid and lightless hades for the homeless called the Hollows.

VAIL: *Aaron, did you blame Bishop Rushman for that, for having to live in that awful place?*
STAMPLER: *He never said a thing about it, one way or the other.*
VAIL: *Aaron, did you ever have a serious fight with Archbishop Rushman?*
STAMPLER: *No, sir, I never had any kind of fight with the bishop. We talked a lot, mostly about things I read in books, ideas and such. But we were always friends.*
VAIL: *So the bishop did not order you out of Saviour House and you were still friends after you left?*
STAMPLER: *Yes, sir.*

St Claire next studied the testimony relating to the murder itself. There were two versions of what happened: Aaron's, which had no details, and Medical Examiner William Danielson's, which was almost pornographic in its specifics.

VAIL: *Now I want to talk about the night Bishop Rushman was murdered. There was an altar boy meeting scheduled, wasn't there?*
STAMPLER: *Yes, suh.*
VAIL: *Did any of the altar boys show up?*
STAMPLER: *No.*
VAIL: *Nobody else?*
STAMPLER: *No, sir.*
VAIL: *Was the bishop upset?*
STAMPLER: *No. He said he were tired anyway and we could meet another time.*
VAIL: *What did you do when you left?*
STAMPLER: *. . . I decided to go to the bishop's office and borrow a book to read. When I got there, I heard some noise – like people*

150

shouting — up in the bishop's bedroom, so I went up to see if everything was all right. When I got to the top of the stairs I took my shoes off and stuck them in my jacket pockets. The bishop was in the bathroom and then I realized what I heard was him singing. Then . . . I felt like there was somebody else there, beside the bishop, and that's when I lost time.

VAIL: *You blacked out?*

STAMPLER: *Yes, sir.*

VAIL: *You didn't actually see anyone else?*

STAMPLER: *No, sir.*

VAIL: *Did you see the bishop?*

STAMPLER: *No, sir. But I could hear him. He was singing in the bathroom.*

VAIL: *You just sensed that somebody else was in the room?*

STAMPLER: *Yes, sir.*

VAIL: *Then what happened?*

STAMPLER: *Next thing I knew, I was outside, at the bottom of the wooden staircase up to the kitchen, and I saw a police car and the . . . there was a flashlight flicking around, then I looked down . . . and uh, there was blood all over . . . my hands . . . and the knife . . . And . . . and then, I just ran . . . don't know why, I just ran into the church and another police car was pulling up front and I ducked into the confessional.*

VAIL: *Aaron, did you have any reason to kill Bishop Rushman?*

STAMPLER: *No, sir.*

VAIL: *Did you plan his murder?*

STAMPLER: *No, sir.*

VAIL: *To your knowledge did you kill Bishop Rushman?*

STAMPLER: *No, sir.*

Vail had started early in the trial introducing evidence and testimony implying that Stampler was not alone in the room at the time of the murder. He maintained that his client had blacked out and did not know who the mystery guest was, a contention that was hard to prove but even harder to disprove. William Danielson, the ME, filled in the blanks in his version of the killing, guided by Venable.

VENABLE: *Dr Danielson, based on the physical evidence at the scene of the homicide, what is your assessment of this crime?*

DANIELSON: *That Stampler entered through the kitchen, took off his shoes, removed the nine-inch carving knife from the tray, leaving fibres from his gloves when he did it, went down the hallway to the bedroom, and attacked the bishop. Bishop Rushman fought for his life, as witness the wounds in his hands. He was stabbed, cut, punctured, and sliced seventy-seven times. He had less than a pint of blood in his body after the attack, which is one-twelfth of the normal blood supply in the body.*

The first major battle came when Vail tried to keep photographs of the crime scene out of the testimony as prejudicial. He was overruled. The original photographs, unfortunately, were part of the physical evidence that had been misplaced or lost years before, and the copies of the pictures, which were attached with other documents at the end of the transcript, were of poor quality and told St Claire nothing. On the witness stand, Danielson went into detail of all the gruesome aspects of the crime, using a combination of photographs, physical evidence, fibre samples, bloodstains, fingerprints, the number of stab wounds and their locations, the results of certain kinds of wounds, the difference between a stab, a puncture, and an incision, and so on. Venable was painting a mural of horror.

VENABLE: *So, Dr Danielson, did you conclude that death can be attributed to several different factors?*
DANIELSON: *Yes. Body trauma, aeroembolism, cadaveric spasm, several of the stab wounds, exsanguination – that's loss of blood. All could have caused death.*
VENABLE: *Can you identify which you think was the primary cause?*
DANIELSON: *I believe it was the throat wound.*
VENABLE: *Why?*
DANIELSON: *Because it caused aeroembolism, which is the sudden exit of air from the lungs. This kind of wound is always fatal; in fact, death is usually instantaneous. And this wound was profound. Exsanguination was also a factor.*
VENABLE: *Loss of blood?*
DANIELSON: *Yes.*

As St Claire read the description, his mind flashed back to the coroner's description of Linda Balfour's body. '. . . victim was stabbed, cut, and incised 56 times . . . evidence of cadaver spasm, trauma, and aeroembolism . . . significant exsanguination from stab wounds . . . throat wound caused aeroembolism . . . evidence of mutilation . . . accomplished by a person or persons with some surgical knowledge . . .' St Claire's nudge was really kicking in, promoted further by Vail's clarification.

VAIL: *The knife entered here, just under the right ear, slashed to just under the left ear, cut through to the spinal column, severed the jugular, all the arteries and veins in his neck, the windpipe, and all muscle and tissue.*

Then Vail attacked Danielson's assertion that this throat wound was the one that killed Rushman, once again pursuing the possibility that someone else was in the room with Stampler when the bishop was killed.

VAIL: *So . . . if two of the fatal chest wounds could have been struck by one person and the rest of the wounds by another, it is also possible that one person actually struck the death wound and someone else then stabbed and cut the bishop after he was dead, right?*
DANIELSON: *I suppose . . . yes, that's true . . . but unlikely.*

St Claire frequently stopped to scribble notes to himself. He wrote, 'Was another person in the room? Ask Vail? Stenner?' And why was Vail making this point if Stampler was pleading guilty? Was the insanity plea a ploy of some kind? St Claire kept ploughing through the encyclopedia-sized transcripts, skipping occasional exchanges.

VAIL: *Aaron, are you familiar with the term 'fugue' or 'fugue state'?*
STAMPLER: *Yes, sir.*
VAIL: *What does it mean?*
STAMPLER: *Means forgetting things for a while.*
VAIL: *Do you have a term for it?*
STAMPLER: *Yes, sir. Call it losing time.*
VAIL: *And did you ever lose time?*
STAMPLER: *Yes, sir.*
VAIL: *Often?*
STAMPLER: *Yes, sir.*
VAIL: *When?*

STAMPLER: *Well, I'm not perfectly sure. At first you don't know it's happening. Then after a while, you know when you lose time.*

VAIL: *How do you know?*

STAMPLER: *Well, one minute I'd be sitting here, a second later – just a snap of a finger – I'd be sitting over there, or walking outside. Once I was in the movies with a girl and just an instant later we were walking outside the movie. I don't know how the picture ended, I was just outside on the street.*

VAIL: *Did you tell anyone about this?*

STAMPLER: *No, sir.*

VAIL: *Why not?*

STAMPLER: *I didn't think they'd believe me. Thought they'd make fun of me or maybe put me away.*

It was the question of Stampler's blackout and the 'fugue state' that stirred the liveliest cross-examination of the trial, ironically between Vail and Stenner, who was then city detective in charge of the investigation.

VAIL: *Are you familiar with the medical term 'fugue state' or hysterical amnesia?*

STENNER: *Yes, I discussed it with Dr Bascott.*

VAIL: *As a matter of fact, you don't believe in the fugue theory, do you, Lieutenant Stenner?*

STENNER: *I have no firm opinion.*

VAIL: *It is a scientific fact, Lieutenant.*

STENNER: *As I said, I have no firm opinion.*

VAIL: *Do you believe that two plus two equals four?*

STENNER: *Of course.*

VAIL: *Do you believe the earth revolves around the sun?*

STENNER: *Yes.*

VAIL: *Are you a Christian, Lieutenant?*

STENNER: *Yes.*

VAIL: *Do you believe in the Resurrection?*

STENNER: *Yes, I do.*

VAIL: *Is the Resurrection a matter of fact or a theory?*

VENABLE: *Objection, Your Honour. Lieutenant Stenner's religious beliefs have nothing to do with this case.*

VAIL: *On the contrary, Your Honour. If I may proceed, I think I can show the relevance.*

JUDGE SHOAT: *Overruled. Read the last question, please, Ms Blanchard.*

BLANCHARD: *'Is the Resurrection a matter of fact or theory?'*

VAIL: *Lieutenant?*

STENNER: *It is a matter of faith, sir.*

VAIL: *So you believe in scientific fact and you believe in religious faith, but you question the scientific reality of a psychiatric disorder which all psychologists agree exists and which is included in DSM 3, which is the standard by which all psychiatric disturbances are identified, isn't that a fact, sir?*

STENNER: *It can be faked. You can't fake two plus two, but you could sure fake a fugue state.*

VAIL: *I see. And how many people do you know for a certainty have faked a fugue state?*

STENNER: *None.*

VAIL: *How many people do you know who have had experiences with faked fugue states?*

STENNER: *None.*

VAIL: *Read a lot of examples of faking a fugue state?*

STENNER: *No.*

VAIL: *So you're guessing, right?*

STENNER: *It's logical. If there is such a thing, it could certainly be faked.*

VAIL: *Have you asked a psychiatrist if it's possible?*

STENNER: *No.*

VAIL: *So you're guessing, Lieutenant, yes or no?*

STENNER: *Yes.*

VAIL: *Ah, so your reason for doubting Aaron Stampler's statement is that you guessed he was faking – or lying, right?*

STENNER: *That is correct.*

VAIL: *So you assumed that Aaron was lying and that he killed Bishop Rushman, correct?*

STENNER: *It was a very logical assumption.*

VAIL: *I'm not questioning the logic of your assumption, just that it existed. You assumed Stampler was guilty, right?*

STENNER: *Yes.*

VAIL: *At what point, Lieutenant, were you positive from reviewing the evidence that Aaron Stampler acted alone?*

There it is again, St Claire thought. Christ, had there been someone else in the room?

STENNER: *From the very beginning.*

VAIL: *... Aaron Stampler tells you that he blacked out when he entered the bishop's room, correct?*

STENNER: *Yes.*

VAIL: *What did you do to disprove his allegation? In other words, sir, what evidence or witnesses can you produce that will verify your contention that he was alone in the room and that he acted alone?*

STENNER: *Forensics evidence, physical evidence, just plain logic . . .*

VAIL: *. . . I have a problem with some of these logical assumptions that have been made during this trial. Do you understand why?*

STENNER: *Most of the time –*

VAIL: *Lieutenant, my client's life is at stake here. 'Most of the time' won't do. And so much for logic and a preponderance of evidence. Dr Danielson says he cannot say for sure that Aaron was alone in the room, cannot say for sure that only one person actually stabbed the bishop, and cannot prove evidentially that Aaron even came in the back door or brought the knife to the murder scene. Yet you assumed Aaron Stampler lied to you because it wasn't logical, right?*

STENNER: *(No response.)*

VAIL: *The fact is, Lieutenant, that you are willing to accept on faith that Christ was crucified and died, that he arose from the dead, and went to heaven. But you don't choose to believe the fact that a person, under extreme stress or shock, can black out and enter a scientifically described limbo called a fugue state. So you never actually tried to prove that Aaron Stampler was lying, did you?*

STENNER: *It's not my job to prove the defendant is innocent, it's yours.*

VAIL: *On the contrary, Lieutenant, it's your job to prove he's guilty.*

Next St Claire got the testimony about symbols. His nudge became a reality.

VAIL: *I'd like to go back to symbols for a moment. Doctor, will you explain very simply for the jury the significance of symbols. What they are, for instance?*

BASCOTT: *Symbolic language is the use of drawings, symbols, uh, recognizable signs, to communicate. For instance, the cross is a symbol for Christianity while the numbers 666 are a universal symbol for the devil. Or to be more current, the symbols for something that is prohibited is a red circle with a slash through it. That symbol is recognized both here and in Europe. As a sign along the road, for instance.*

VAIL: *Could a symbol come in the form of words? A message, for instance?*

BASCOTT: *Possibly. Yes.*

VAIL: *So symbols can come in many forms, not just drawings or pictures?*

BASCOTT: *Yes, that is true.*

VAIL: *Now, Doctor, you have testified that you have seen the photographs of the victim in this case, Bishop Rushman?*

BASCOTT: *Yes, I have.*

VAIL: *Studied them closely?*

BASCOTT: Yes.

VAIL: Were there any symbols on the body?

BASCOTT: Uhh . . .

VAIL: Let me put it more directly. Do you think the killer left a message in the form of a symbol on the victim's body?

BASCOTT: I can't say for sure. It appears that the killer was indicating something but we never figured that out and Stampler was no help.

VAIL: Doctor, we are talking about the letter and numbers on the back of the victim's head, correct?

BASCOTT: I assumed that is what you meant. Yes.

VAIL: Do you recall what the sequence was?

BASCOTT: I believe it said 'B32.146.'

VAIL: Actually, 'B32.156.'

BASCOTT: I'm sorry. Correction, 156.

VAIL: And do you believe that this was a symbol left by the killer?

BASCOTT: Uh. Well, yes, I think we all made that assumption.

'Yeah!' St Claire said aloud. There it was. Maybe the folks in Gideon weren't too far from the truth. It was the same combination of letter and numbers that the killer had put on Linda Balfour's head. St Claire frantically read ahead. *What does it mean?* he wondered. *Did they ever figure it out?*

VAIL: And that is as far as you took it, correct?

BASCOTT: It takes years, sometimes, to break through, to decipher all these subtleties.

VAIL: In other words, you really didn't have time to examine all the facts of Mr Stampler's problems, did you?

VENABLE: Objection, Your Honour. Defence is trying to muddle the issue here. The doctor has stated that it might take years to decipher this symbol, as the counsellor calls it. We are here to determine this case on the best evidence available. This line of questioning is completely irrelevant. The numbers could mean anything – maybe even an insignificant phone number.

VAIL: Then let the doctor say so.

JUDGE SHOAT: Rephrase, Counsellor.

VAIL: Doctor, do you think this symbol is relevant?

BASCOTT: Anything is possible.

But St Claire found the answer to his question in another skirmish between Stenner and Vail.

VAIL: . . . I have only one more question, Lieutenant Stenner. You

157

stated a few minutes ago that this crime was premeditated. You said it unequivocally, as a statement of fact. Isn't that just another one of your unsupported allegations, sir?

STENNER: *No, sir, it is not.*

VAIL: *Well, will you please tell the court upon what evidence you base that supposition?*

STENNER: *Several factors.*

VAIL: *Such as?*

STENNER: *The symbols on the back of the bishop's head.*

VAIL: *And what about the symbols, Lieutenant?*

STENNER: *They refer to a quote from a book in the bishop's library. The passage was marked in the book. We found similar markings in a book retrieved from Stampler's quarters in the Hollows. Some highlighter was used and we can identify the handwriting in both books as Stampler's.*

VAIL: *Lieutenant, why do you believe these markings on the victim's head prove premeditation?*

STENNER: *Because he planned it. He wrote in blood, on the victim's head, the symbol B32.156. B32.156 is the way this book is identified, it's a method for cataloguing the books in the bishop's library.*

VAIL: *And what does it mean?*

STENNER: *It is a quote from the novel* The Scarlet Letter *by Nathaniel Hawthorne. 'No man, for any considerable period, can wear one face to himself, and another to the multitude, without finally getting bewildered as to which may be the true.'*

VAIL: *What is the significance of that quote?*

STENNER: *It is our belief that Stampler felt betrayed by Bishop Rushman, who made him leave Saviour House. His girlfriend left him, he was living in a hellhole. He felt the bishop was two-faced. So he put this symbol in blood on the victim's head to add insult to injury.*

VAIL: *I think you're reaching, Lieutenant. . . .*

STENNER: *We proved it to my satisfaction.*

VAIL: *Well, I guess we should thank our lucky stars you're not on the jury, sir. . . .*

St Claire's pause was doing double time. He wrote on his pad: 'What happened to the bishop's books?' But he kept reading until the trial came to its startling conclusion.

VENABLE: *You have quite a memory for quotations and sayings that appeal to you, don't you, Mr Stampler?*

STAMPLER: *I have a good memory, yes, ma'am.*

VENABLE: *Are you familiar with Nathaniel Hawthorne's book* The Scarlet Letter?

STAMPLER: Yes, ma'am, I know the book.

VENABLE: *And does the phrase 'B32.156' meaning anything to you?*

STAMPLER: (No response.)

JUDGE SHOAT: *Mr Stampler, do you understand the question?*

STAMPLER: Uh, I believe those are the numbers that were on the back of the bishop's head, in the pictures.

VENABLE: *Is that the first time you ever saw them?*

STAMPLER: I reckon.

VENABLE: *And you don't know what the numbers mean?*

STAMPLER: I'm not sure.

VENABLE: *You mark passages in books that appeal to you, do you not?*

STAMPLER: Sometimes.

VENABLE: *You marked passages in the books in the bishop's library, didn't you?*

STAMPLER: Sometimes.

VENABLE: *Your Honour, I'd like this marked as state's exhibit thirty-two, please.*

State's 32, a copy of Nathaniel Hawthorne's The Scarlet Letter *from Bishop Rushman's library, was so marked.*

VAIL: No objection.

VENABLE: *Recognize this book, Mr Stampler?*

STAMPLER: I reckon that's from the bishop's library.

VENABLE: *Mr Stampler, I ask you, did you or did you not mark a passage on pate 156 of this copy of* The Scarlet Letter *– indexed by the number B32?*

STAMPLER: Uh.

VENABLE: *I'll be a little more direct, Mr Stampler. Are you familiar with this quote from Nathaniel Hawthorne's* Scarlet Letter: *'No man, for any considerable period, can wear one face to himself, and another to the multitude, without finally getting bewildered as to which may be true'? Do you recognize that, Mr Stampler?*

STAMPLER: Uh.

VENABLE: *Do you recognize it? B32.156. Doesn't that strike a bell, Mr Stampler?*

STAMPLER: I don't.

VENABLE: *Mr Stampler, did you memorize that passage and print those numbers on the back of the bishop's head when you killed him?*

VAIL: Objection.

The defendant Stampler suddenly screamed and jumped over the railing separating witness from examiner, attacking Ms Venable.

STAMPLER: You lying bitch! Try to kill me.

At this point, defendant Stampler has to be overpowered by guards and the bailiff. There was general disorder in the courtroom.
JUDGE SHOAT: *Order! Order in this courtroom!*

So it was the symbol on the back of Rushman's head that had set Stampler off on the witness stand. The case had obviously been settled in the judge's chambers. When the trial reconvened, Shoat had announced that an agreement had been reached between the state and Vail. Aaron Stampler was sent to the state mental hospital at Daisyland 'until such time as the state rules that he is capable of returning to society.'

What was settled in chambers and why? St Claire wondered as he started to gather up his notes. A methodical man, he arranged them in order, scanning each of the pages as he put them in a file folder. Then he stopped for a moment, staring down at a section from early in the testimony. Suddenly his mouth went dry.

My God, he thought, *how could I have missed that! And where the hell is Aaron Stampler now?*

Thirteen

Jane Venable stared south from her thirtieth-floor office window in the glass and steel spire towards the courthouse and thought about Martin Vail. It had been a long time since she felt such passion or been as comfortable with a man. Throughout the day she kept having flashbacks of the night before, fleeting moments that blocked out everything else for an instant or two. Now, staring into the late-afternoon mist in the direction of the courthouse, she wondered if Vail was having the same kind of day.

God, I'm acting like a high school girl, she thought, and shrugged it off.

But she had a brief to be filed and she decided to take it herself rather than have her secretary do it. Then she would drop in on Vail. Why not? Her memory jumped back to an afternoon ten years earlier when Vail had shown up unannounced, in the same office that was then hers; how she had suddenly realized while they were talking that she was breathing a little faster and paying more attention to him that to what he was saying. Ten years and she still remembered that brief encounter when she had first realized that she was attracted to the rough-and-tumble, sloppy, shaggy-haired courtroom assassin.

He had slicked up a bit since then: the hair was a little shorter and his suits weren't so bagged-out, but the cutting edge was still there, just under the surface. Even as a prosecutor he was a gambler, unlike most of the lawyers she knew, who were more concerned with how close to the corner of the building their office was and what kind of car to move up to next.

161

What the hell, we started something, I'll be damned if I'm going to let it fizzle.

Then she laughed at herself.

Fizzle! It hasn't even started yet. What's the matter with you?

Aw, screw you, she said to herself.

She stuffed the brief in her attaché case and headed out the door.

On the fourth floor of the Criminal Courts Building, Abel Stenner burst out of his office and raced towards Naomi's desk.

'My God, Abel, what set you on fire?' she asked.

'Is he busy?' Stenner asked, ignoring her question.

'He's on the phone with – '

'Won't wait,' Stenner cut her off, and entered the office with Naomi trailing close behind. Vail was sitting in his chair with his back to the door, blowing smoke into the exhaust fan. He wheeled around when Stenner entered, took one look at his chief investigator, and knew something was up.

'I'll call you back,' he said, and put down the phone.

'They made a bust in the Delaney case,' Stenner announced.

'Already? Who?' Naomi asked with surprise.

'His executive secretary. Fifty-three years old. Crippled husband, daughter in college.'

'Sweet Jesus. How did they nail her so quickly?' Naomi said.

'Shock must've been on the case,' Vail answered.

'You're right. Called me from his car. They had just Mirandized her and she came out with it. Said it twice. "I killed him." They're bringing her in now. Murder one.'

Vail whistled slowly through his teeth.

'Why'd she do it?' Naomi asked.

'That's all I know. Maybe we ought to head down to Booking.'

They breezed out of Vail's office. Shana Parver was deep in a law book as Vail and Stenner passed her cubbyhole. Vail's rap on the glass startled her.

'C'mon,' said Vail.

'Where?'

'Downstairs.'

Edith Stoddard cowered as Shock Johnson and Si Irving led her through the wave of press that swarmed towards her when she got out of the car. They brought her into the booking office just as Stenner, Vail, and Parver got off the lift, which was directly across the hall from the entrance to Booking. Three TV crews, several photographers, radio interviewers, and reporters crowded through the doorway as they brought Stoddard in. Her hands were cuffed behind her and she seemed terrorized by the media and the police and the grim surroundings. Her eyes flicked from one group to another. Detectives crowded around a railing that separated the desk from the hallway to see who the celebrity was. The press shoved microphones in her face, yelled questions at her, jostled for space, while TV cameras scorched the scene with searing lights.

Shock Johnson led the stunned and frightened woman towards the booking desk as she looked around in bewilderment, flinching every time a strobe flashed, cowering under the blistering TV lights, while the press screamed at her. At that moment, Eckling appeared from a side room and took his place beside the tiny, trembling woman, displaying her like a big-game trophy. Vail watched the feeding frenzy with disgust.

'Whatever happened to innocent until proven guilty?' Shana Parver said.

'That son of a bitch is turning this into a freak show,' said Vail, and he charged into the room followed by Parver and Stenner.

In the back of the crowded room, Jane Venable eased

163

her way into the crowd of newshounds. She watched the scene with disgust, then saw Vail charge the crowd and grab Shock Johnson by the arm.

'What the hell's he doing?' Vail demanded.

'I got nothing to do with this circus,' Johnson said. It was obvious he was disgusted. 'She's a nice little lady, Marty. We were giving her Miranda. She interrupted and says, "I killed him. I killed him." '

'You sure this confession is legit, Shock?'

'She said she went in and he was taking a shower. She was standing in the entrance hall and he walked in naked and poured a drink. He saw her. When he saw the gun he put his drink down and she whacked him. Then went over and gave him the clincher.'

'What else did she tell you?'

'That's it. What I just told you is it. Marty, she's fifty-three. Got retired out early. Today was her last day. Has a crippled husband, a daughter in college, and Delaney dumped her for a thirty-year-old blonde bombshell. She bought a .38 three weeks ago, spent two weeks on a shooting range learning how to use it. She was standing right where Okie said she was when she popped him. And she flat-out confessed right after we Miranda'd her. What the hell more do you want?'

'Do you know what any good criminal attorney'll do with this? Displaying her like this, questioning her without an attorney present? We won't have a damn case left!'

Vail pushed his way to Eckling's side. 'Stop this right now,' he snarled in Eckling's ear. 'You're jeopardizing this case with this stupid stunt.'

'Goddamn it . . .' Eckling whispered back, but before he could go any further, Vail took Edith Stoddard gently by the arm and led her back into a sealed-off holding area with the press screaming questions at her as he led her away. The door shut out the sound.

'Oh,' she said, and closed her eyes.

164

Outside, as the press began to disperse, Venable headed towards the processing area. *I know that woman*, she thought.

Four years ago. Venable had settled an injury case for Delaney Enterprises. Edith Stoddard had been Delaney's private secretary. Venable remembered that she had felt very sorry for the woman. Her husband was a quadriplegic and she had a very bright daughter about to enter college. She had seemed weighed down by her world, almost self-effacing. It was in her face then, and it was worse now.

Venable could sense Stoddard's humiliation and fear.

A lot of people in this town will think she did the world a favour, she thought as he moved towards the security room.

Inside the quiet area, Vail said, 'I'm sorry, Mrs Stoddard, that was uncalled for.'

She stared up at him and the fear in her eyes was slowly replaced by stoicism.

'You're the new district attorney,' she said.

'Yes. And this is Shana Parver, one of my associates. I want Shana to explain your rights to you.'

'They read me my rights.'

'Yes, but I think you should understand what all this means.'

' Eckling burst into the room. 'What the hell do you think you're – '

Vail grabbed his arm and shoved him into an empty interrogation room, slamming the door behind them.

'Listen to me, Eckling, this is not some dipshit drug bust, this woman's going to end up with the best pro bono attorney the judge can find and *any* defence advocate worth two cents is going to make hay of that circus you just put on.'

'She confessed, fer Chrissakes!'

'So what? Does the name Menendez mean anything to you? If those brothers can walk, this woman can ride out of here on a golden chariot – and you're gonna be pulling it.' Vail speared the air with his finger. 'This woman is innocent until a jury says she's guilty or until a judge accepts her plea. That's if she doesn't change her mind, which she probably will the minute a good lawyer grabs her ear.' He started to leave and then whirled back on the chief. 'By the way, this isn't the chief prosecutor talking anymore, Eckling, it's the DA. Get your head out of your ass.'

Vail left the room. Shana Parver walked over to him as two guards led Mrs Stoddard off to be fingerprinted and processed.

'She wouldn't listen. She insists she did it and she doesn't want a trial.'

'Does she know she'll end up doing life without parole?'

'I don't think she cares, Martin.'

Behind them, the door opened and Jane Venable entered the security room. Her eyes were ablaze. It was the old Jane Venable, spoiling for a fight.

'What the hell was that all about?' she demanded. 'Eckling pilloried that woman!'

'I know, I know,' Vail said defensively. 'I just chewed his ass about it. Do you know Shana Parver? Shana, this is Jane Venable.'

'Hi,' Parver said. 'I feel like I know you, I've read the transcript of the Stampler trial several times.'

'I've had better days than that!' she said, glaring at Vail.

'What are you doing here?' Vail asked, then quickly added, 'I mean, I'm glad you're here but I'm, you know, surprised.'

'I came down to file a brief and saw the mob scene. I thought maybe they'd arrested the mayor or something.'

'Listen, Janie, you need to do that lady a favour,' Vail said.

'What do you mean?'

166

'She's determined to confess to killing Delaney. She doesn't have a lawyer. Judge Pryor will probably appoint one in the morning. In the meantime, Eckling's going to have her on the griddle as soon as they process her. If she makes a confession in there, I won't have any choice. I'll have to max her out.'

'Marty, I can't . . .'

'You can go in there and talk to this lady. Explain her options.'

Venable scowled at Vail. 'Just because I happen to walk in here, I get stuck – '

'You're the best there is and you're a woman. Maybe she'll respond to you.'

'Damn!' She blew out a breath, then walked across the room and back.

'Do you know any of the details?'

'That's moot. She needs somebody to hold her hand until she has a full-time lawyer. Give her that at least.'

'Christ, Marty, you're talking like a defence advocate.'

'Janie, she just lost her job. Her husband's lying in bed helpless from the neck down. Her daughter's in college and she probably can't afford to keep her there. Her whole world is unwinding around her. If she screws up now, she'll end up doing life without parole. That's what we'll ask for and we'll get it.'

'You're one weird prosecutor, Marty,' Venable said.

'I want all the details before I decide what we're going to do to her. If we let Eckling loose on her, I'll never have that opportunity. Talk to her, Janie.' He smiled at her. 'Then I'll buy dinner.'

'Shit,' Venable said, and walked down the hall towards the fingerprint room.

Parver looked at Vail with a smirk.

'I thought you two hated each other.'

'We're trying to get over it,' Vail said.

Harvey St Claire had made myriad phone calls to the

Catholic cathedral, the custodian, two priests, and finally to a nun named Sister Mary Alice before he finally got an answer to his question.

'Sister,' St Claire said, frustration apparent in his tone, 'I'm trying to find out what happened to all the books in Bishop Rushman's library. Nobody seems to know.'

'Who did you say this was again?' she asked.

'M'name's Harvey St Claire. I'm with the DA's office.'

'You work for Mr Vail?'

'That's right, he's m'boss. You know him?'

'I met him once, years ago,' she said. 'I know it's none of my business, but does this have anything to do with Aaron Stampler?'

'That's very incisive of you, Sister. How did you guess?'

'Well, you work for Mr Vail and he defended Aaron. A book from the bishop's library was an important part of the evidence.'

'You remember that?'

'I just remember it had something to do with the murder. That was a long time ago.'

'So do you know where those books are now?'

'Do you know the Newberry on Walton Street?'

The Newberry Library was an imposing, burly, five-storey brick building with a triple-arched entrance that occupied an entire block of West Walton. It had just celebrated its one hundredth anniversary and there was about the formidable old sentinel of a structure a sense of antiquity and conservatism. It had been endowed by businessman William Loomis Newberry to be 'an uncommon collection of uncommon collections', and so it was.

A pleasant woman who identified herself as Miss Prichard, the assistant librarian, chatted amiably as she led St Claire down hallways through arroyos of books, maps, and documents.

'Did you know this was the first electrified building in the city?' she asked, pointing towards the ceiling of the lobby. 'That's why the bulbs in that chandelier are pointed downwards, so people would know. Gas lamps won't work upside down, of course.'

'Is it always this cool in here?'

'We have climate control for twenty-one miles of books and manuscripts, Mr St Claire,' she said proudly. 'We haven't lost a book in one hundred years.'

'Quite a feat these days. Some people will steal anything.'

'I should hope that our clientele is a bit more singular than that,' she said in a very matter-of-fact tone.

The Rushman collection was in one of the rear chambers. It was a small room without windows and, except for the door, lined on all four sides with Bishop Rushman's books. An oak table contained three equally spaced brass table lamps with green shades. It occupied the centre of the room, surrounded by heavy, unpadded chairs. The place was as quiet as a mausoleum.

It was a surprisingly diverse collection. Novels by Dostoyevsky and Dante sat beside the works of Rousseau, Hobbes, and Darwin. Leather-bound codes of canon law shared space with Faulkner, Hammett, and Chandler.

St Claire eagerly pulled out a book and checked its spine. And his shoulders slumped. Rushman's peculiar method of indexing had been replaced by the Dewey decimal system. He looked around the room at the hundreds of books and realized that there was no way to identify C13 among all the volumes. He stared at the library for several minutes, trying to figure out if there was any correlation between the Dewey numbers and Rushman's old index numbers. He turned abruptly and went back to the office.

'Ms Prichard, I notice the indexing system has been changed on the books in the Rushman collection.'

'Oh yes, we had to go to the Dewey decimal system. All the books must conform, you know. What a mess it would be if we made an exception! But it was done without damage. We have never damaged a book.'

'No, you don't understand. Did the Newberry, by any chance, keep a record of the bishop's indexing system?'

'My, my, you are a purist, aren't you, Mr St Claire? Well, now, let's just go to the records.'

She opened a narrow oak drawer and her nimble fingers danced along the index cards. She pulled one out, looked at if for a moment, and then handed it to him with a smile. It was labelled 'Huckleberry Finn'. In the corner of the Dewey card was noted: 'Rushman index: J03.'

'Bless you,' St Claire said with a wide grin. 'Now all I have to do is go through all these cards, find C13, turn to page 489, and hope to hell I know what I'm looking for.'

'I remember you,' Edith Stoddard said to Jane Venable. 'You handled the Robertson injury case. That was in 1990, as I recall.' She had recovered from the booking ordeal and seemed almost relaxed. She was seated at a tattered bridge table in a small holding cell adjacent to the processing station. The room was bare except for the table and a cot in the corner. She had been fingerprinted, strip-searched, and issued a pair of orange county-issue coveralls with the word PRISONER stencilled across the back. The sleeves were rolled back several times. Stoddard would be held there until court convened in the morning. Venable had a momentary flashback, remembering these same surroundings ten years earlier. Nothing seemed to have changed. The same blue-grey paint on the walls, the small barred window in one corner.

'That's right,' Jane Venable answered.

'You were a very nice person, but you were a ferocious negotiator,' Stoddard said bluntly but unassumingly.

'That's what I get paid for – being a ferocious negotiator, I mean – not for being a nice person. Thank you for that.'

'I don't need a lawyer, Miss Venable,' the prisoner said firmly.

'Yes, you do. You never needed one more than you do right now,' Venable answered.

'I'm guilty, Miss Venable.'

'Please call me Jane.'

'Jane. I just want to plead guilty and get it over with.'

'There's more to it than that,' Venable said.

'Not really.'

'Listen to me carefully, please. You have to – may I call you Edith? Good. You have to realize that even if you did kill him – '

'I *did* kill him!'

'Okay. But you still must give your lawyer all your help so he or she can deal a proper sentence for you. Even if you don't go to trial, let whoever the judge assigns to the case save you as much time as possible.'

'I don't want a trial, I told you that,' Stoddard said as firmly as she could.

'It won't be a trial, it will be a plea bargain. It will be worked out between your lawyer and the prosecution.'

'Mr Vail?'

'Yes, or one of his prosecutors.'

'Will it be made public, the negotiations?'

'No.'

'I don't know. I just . . . I want to get it all over with. My life is ruined anyway.'

'Edith, who's going to take care of your husband? What's to become of your daughter?'

'I'll be gone for years, anyway. What's the difference?'

'If we can get this reduced down to, say, first- or possibly second-degree manslaughter, your sentence could be as light as, oh, ten years. You could be out in four or five. That gives both of them hope. It's not like you'd be going away for ever.'

Stoddard stood up and walked to the window. She stared out at the brightly lit highway in front of the criminal building, watched a semi lumber by, listened to a dog barking somewhere far off in the night. She sighed very deeply and seemed to collapse into herself.

'Will you do it?' she asked, turning back to Venable.

'Do what?'

'Handle it for me?'

'I'll get you to court tomorrow. Then – '

'No. I mean handle it all the way.'

'I have – '

'It's just sitting with Mr Vail and working it out, isn't it? Can that take so much time?'

'It's not time, it's . . . I haven't done this for years. I'm afraid I'm rusty. There are other lawyers out there more qualified than I am.'

'Then let me go ahead and tell the police what they want to know.'

Venable sighed. She looked at the small woman for a moment. 'Will you level with me?' she asked. 'Tell me everything I need to know to make the best deal for you?'

'It depends.'

'On what?'

'On what you want to know.'

Corchran's was a run-down mahogany and brass steakhouse that smelled of beer and cigarette smoke. It was located a block from the river near the old *Sun-Times* building and had been a favoured hangout of Vail's for years. Two tired middleweights were waltzing each other on the big-screen TV in one corner and there was a noisy dart game in progress near the front of the restaurant. A dozen regulars sat at the bar watching the last round of the fight and yelling at the screen as Vail and Venable entered the tavern.

'You do know all the right places, Vail,' she said, looking around the noisy watering hole.

'Best steaks in town,' Vail said. 'Come on, it's quiet in the back.'

172

They found a booth in a tiny back room that was shielded from the din. A sign over the archway into the niche said LADIES ROOM. It was decorated with facsimiles of old cigarette and beer ads.

'I can see why there's nobody back here.' She snorted. 'No self-respecting lady would be caught dead in here. They ought to be up front with it and call the place the Chauvinist Pit.' She brushed breadcrumbs off the cushions with a napkin before she sat down.

'You didn't tell me you've turned into a snob,' Vail joked.

'I like a good Irish bar as much as the next person,' she said. 'But this place hasn't seen a broom in weeks. Has the health inspector heard about it?'

'He wouldn't dare come in here,' Vail said. 'They'd throw him in the river. What do you want to drink?'

'What're we eating?'

'Steak, French fries, salad, hard rolls.'

'Alka-Selzer.'

Vail laughed. 'What'll you wash it down with.'

'A Black Jack old-fashioned.'

The waiter had a biscuit ear, knuckles the size of pinballs, and a glass eye. His smile was missing three teeth.

'Hey, Mart, how'th the boy, how'th the boy?' he lisped, plopping a brandy bottle with a candle stuck in it on the table and lighting it with a wooden kitchen match. 'Atmothphere,' he said.

'Steamroller, this is Miss Venable. She may become a regular if you treat her right.'

'Yeah?' Steamroller beamed. 'That would bring thome clath to the joint.'

'Oh, thank you,' Venable said, flashing a smile that was almost sincere. 'Not that it needs it.'

'Steamroller was heavyweight champion of Canada once,' Vail told her.

'How wonderful,' she replied.

'Yeah, I was on my way t' the top and some dinge

173

knocked my eyeball out. Then the thon of a bitch thtepped on it, kinda ground his heel on it, kin ya believe it?'

'What an engrossing tale,' Venable said. 'Ever thought about writing your memoirs?'

Steamroller stared off at the corner for a moment, thinking, then said, 'Uh . . . I can't remember 'em.' Then he shrugged. 'Oh, well. Bushmill's thtraight up and a Corona fer the champ. How about chu, Mith . . . what wath it again, Vennie, Vinnie . . .'

'Venable,' she said sweetly. 'Why don't you just call me Jane. A Black Jack old-fashioned.'

'Aw right,' he said, flashing his shattered smile. 'I like a lady knowth how to drink.' He walked away, wiping his hands on a towel stuck in his belt.

'Next time I'm taking you to Aunt Clara's Tea Room,' Venable said. 'All the waitresses are ninety and speak in old English.'

'Cucumber sandwiches and lemonade?'

'Exactly.'

'Okay, tell me about Edith Stoddard.'

'I can't do that. You're the enemy.'

'Oh God, are we back to that?' he answered.

'I'm going to represent her, Marty.'

'What! I just wanted you to give her some advice until the judge gives her a . . .' He hesitated.

'A *real* lawyer, is that what you were going to say?'

'No, no. You know, one of the courthouse heavies. This isn't your game any more.'

'It is now, and blame yourself. You sent me in there.'

'Just to get her over the rough spots.'

'Uh-huh. Well, it didn't work.'

'What the hell happened?'

'It was either me or she was going to dump the whole story on Eckling,' Venable said.

Steamroller brought the drinks and plopped them down on the table. A little of the old-fashioned slopped over and he left licking his fingers.

Venable leaned across the table and said in a low voice, 'There's something not quite kosher about this.'

'How so?'

'She's determined *not* to stand trial. She'll max out before she does.'

'Why?'

'You tell me.'

'All I know is what Shock Johnson told me. She didn't tell you *anything*?'

'If she did, I wouldn't tell you. But she didn't want to talk tonight. I told Eckling to leave her alone until morning. And I intend to make a little hay over that performance of his, you can bet your sweet ass on that, Mr District Attorney.'

'Ahhh, one hour away from that platinum law firm of yours and you're talking like the old Jane I remember.'

'I'm going to make this as tough as I can,' she said.

'Tell it to Shana Parver. It's her case.'

'What's the matter, afraid of me?'

'The experience'll do you both good.'

'How good is she?'

'Brilliant lawyer. A little too antagonistic. You two should get along fine.'

'Well, thanks.'

Streamroller wandered back to the table.

'You gonna order or are we jutht drinkin' tonight?'

'How do you like your steak?' Vail asked.

'Medium-rare.'

'Make it pink,' Vail said to Streamroller. 'She doesn't want to have to stab it to death before she eats it.'

'Do you have baked potatoes?' she asked.

'Of courth! Whaddya think?'

'And house dressing on my salad.'

Streamroller looked at Vail and his brow furrowed. 'Houth drething?' he said.

'Italian. I'll have the same.'

'Gotcha.' And he was gone again.

'Look,' said Venable, 'I haven't even seen the homicide report. All I know is what I read in the papers. And you didn't call with the details, as promised.'

'You left early.'

'I figured you'd be exhausted when you got home.'

'I was exhausted when I left,' he said with a smile, then just as quickly turned serious. 'Look, from what Shock says, she could be headed for the fryer. She bought a .38 back in January, went to a shooting gallery over in Canaryville every night for two weeks, and learned to use it. She sure as hell can't plead self-defence, he was naked as Adam when he got it. Also she plugged him twice, once here' – he pointed to his heart – 'and once here.' He placed his finger over his right eye. 'That second shot was an afterthought. Delaney was already with the angels when she capped him with the head shot.' He held his arms out at his sides. 'Now you know all I know.'

'Why would she risk life without parole rather than go on trial?' Venable mused.

'Maybe she doesn't trust her lawyer.'

'Cute.'

'I don't know,' Vail said. 'You tell me.'

Venable shrugged. 'Death before dishonour?'

'She can't dishonour Delaney, he took care of that himself a long time ago.'

'I wasn't thinking of him.'

Vail thought for a moment, then said, 'Her husband? You think she had a thing with Delaney? Nah, no way. He goes in for bodies, not brains. She's a nice lady but hardly a raving beauty.'

'Maybe he went in for *any*body. I've known men like that.'

He thought about it a little longer and shook his head. 'I can't see it. Besides, so what? I won't buy the spurned-woman defence.'

'It's worked.'

'Not with me.'

176

'How about Parver?'

'She's too hungry to buy it. And too smart. You'll have to do better than that for Stoddard to beat murder one.'

'You're singing a little different tune than you were two hours ago.'

'I said I'd be fair, I didn't say I'd give her any breaks.'

'That confession won't hold up. She was stressed out, under duress. . . .'

'Hey, you going to make a thing out of this, Janie?'

'I took the case, didn't I?'

Fourteen

The man leaned over his worktable, concentrating on the job of soldering a cobweb-thin piece of wire to a chip smaller than his fingernail. He was a husky man; his shirtsleeves were rolled up over machine-moulded biceps. A pair of magnifying goggles was perched on his nose.

'Hey, Raymond, goin' to lunch?' Terry called to him.

'Can't stop now,' Raymond answered without taking his eyes off his task.

'Want me to bring you something?'

'Yeah. Cheese crackers and a Coke.'

'You got it.'

Raymond heard the door slam shut. He finished the soldering job and placed the hot iron in a small, fireproof tray, took off the goggles, and leaned back in his chair. He stared through the window at the office across the way, watching the secretaries as they puttered around, getting ready to go to lunch. *Creatures of habit*, he thought. He could set his watch by their moves. Noon, five days a week, and they were out of there. He watched them until they left the office, then he walked across the small repair room choked with VCRs, TVs, and PCs and picked up a VCR and brought it back to the worktable. He removed the top and took out a small minicomputer and a black box about two inches square. He attached the box to the minicomputer with a short length of phone wire, then turned on the computer. He typed MODEM on the keyboard and a moment later a menu appeared on the screen. He moved the cursor to RECEIVE and hit enter. A moment later, the words ON LINE flashed in the corner of the screen. He watched the empty office across the way while he waited. Five minutes passed and

the words INCOMING CALL flashed on the screen and a
moment after that:

> ARE YOU THERE, FOX?
> HERE, HYDRA. ARE YOU PREPARED?
> ALWAYS, FOX.
> HAVE YOU SEEN THE SUBJECT?
> YES, FOX. THREE DAYS AGO.
> AND THE REFERENCE?
> IN MY HEAD.
> EXCELLENT. LEAVE TONIGHT.
> OH, THANK YOU, FOX. IT HAS BEEN SO
>   LONG.
> THE TIME IS PERFECT.
> THANK YOU, THANK YOU. IT IS AN
>   EXCELLENT PLAN.
> BE CAREFUL.
> ALWAYS.
> IN TWO DAYS. SAME TIME.
> TWO DAYS.

Fifteen

Lex was pissed off. The last trip of the day and he had to drive thirty-five miles down to Hilltown to deliver a stinking package. Thirty-five fucking miles, and he had two ladies lined up that night. Pick-and-choose time. He laughed and slapped the wheel of the minivan. Maybe he could get them both interested. Hell, what a night that would be!

But first things first. Thirty-five miles down to Hilltown. He couldn't speed.

Two tickets down, one more and I'm out.

He couldn't afford to lose his licence, the job was too good, except when they dumped a late load on him and he had to drive thirty-five miles down and thirty-five miles back. And drop off the stupid package. Seventy miles. Ten minutes to do the package. Two hours, no more. He'd be back in town by 8 P.M. Then he'd make up his mind.

Toni? Or Jessie? What a choice. Brunette or redhead?

He was thinking so hard he almost missed the turnoff. He wheeled the minivan off the main highway and headed down the last two miles on a two-lane blacktop.

Christ, who the hell would want to live out in this godforsaken place? His headlights led him to the city limits.

What a joke. City limits? A city? Twelve hundred people? The whole damn town would hardly fill up the old Paramount Theatre in St Louis. He turned on the dome light and took out the delivery slip.

Calvin Spiers. RFD 2.

Shit, the whole place was one big RFD.

He turned it over. Someone had scribbled instructions on the back. He slowed down and squinted under the dim dome light.

'Left past public library. One and a half miles to bright red mail-box just past Elmo's SuperStore.'

Well, that oughtta be easy enough.

Ten minutes later found him out on a country road on the other side of Hilltown. Elmo's SuperStore was on the right, a garish, low-slung cinder-block building with a flashing BUD sign on the roof. He drifted past it and his headlights picked up the red mailbox.

'Piece a cake,' he said aloud.

He pulled down the dirt road, peering into the darkness for signs of life. Finally he saw the house, off to the left through the trees. It was a small bungalow set back in the woods with a well-kept yard. The porch light was out, but he could see a light behind the curtains of what he assumed was the living room. He turned into the rutted driveway and beeped the horn twice, then got out, went to the other side of the van, and slid the door back. The package was about a foot square and light, no more than one or two pounds. He checked the name, took his delivery pad, and went to the front door.

Must not of heard me, he thought as he went up the steps to the porch. Then he saw the note. It was tucked in the screen door. He put the package down and pulled out the note.

UPD man: Had to run to the store. Door open. Please put package on table in den, second door on left. Thank you.

He tried the door and it swung open to reveal a long, dark hallway that led back to an open door. Light from the living room spilled over into the hall, reflected into the darkness of the hall.

Shit, I oughtta just leave it here. What the hell do they think I am?

'Anybody here?' No answer. 'Mr Spier?'

But he picked up the package and headed down the hall. He saw a light switch and flicked it, but there was no bulb in the overhead socket.

Great. Coulda left me a flashlight at least.

'Anybody here? UPD,' he called as he approached the den door.

He peered inside the darkened room, squinting his eyes to try to make out a light or a lamp. He put the box down and, facing the wall, swept his hands over its smooth surface, feeling for the light switch. He did not hear the figure emerge from the darkness behind him, moving slowly, raising its hand high. There was a flash in the light from the living room. Lex started to turn, then felt a searing pain piercing deep into his back and into his chest.

He screamed and stumbled forward, felt the blade slide out of his back as he grabbed the doorjamb. Then he felt it again, this time plunging down through his shoulder. He fell to his knees, reached out in the dark and felt the back of a chair, and grabbed it.

'Oh God,' he cried out, 'I'm just ... delivery man. UPD ... Please!'

The knife struck again. And again. And again. It ripped into his back, his side, his arm as he floundered weakly, trying to escape the deadly blade. He felt his life seeping out of him. He began to shake violently. The room became an echo chamber and he seemed to reverberate within it. He tasted salt. Sweat showered from his face.

Then he felt hot breath beside his ear and a voice whispered, 'Billy ... Peter ...'

'My ... God ...' Lex answered feebly. The last thing he felt was the deadly blade slicing into his throat, slashing through tissue and muscle. Air burst from the gaping wound and showered blood as it hissed from his lungs. With demonic glee, the assassin kept striking over and over and over in the darkness of the room.

When the deadly work was done, the executioner dipped a finger in the widening pool of blood and, lifting the hair on the back of the victim's head, printed, 'R41.102.'

Sixteen

The red rays of dawn filtered through the wooden slats of the shutters, casting long, harsh shadows across the hardwood floors. Vail lay on his back and stared up at the pickled-blonde cathedral ceiling, softly crimson in the floor's reflection of morning light. Vail turned his head. Jane lay on her side, her forehead resting against his arm. He pulled the feather comforter up over her naked shoulders and slid out of her bed, gathering up his clothes and shoes from where they were strung out across the floor.

'Whew!' he said to himself, remembering how they had got there.

Tudor Manor was one of an ensemble of mansions built in the mid-Twenties and modelled after the Tudor mansions of England. From the outside they seemed strangely incongruous with the more midwestern architecture of Rogers Park. Each building (there were four in what was collectively known as Tudor Estates) had sweeping projecting gables decorated with gargoyles and crenellations, a slate roof, ornamental chimney pots, and towering casement windows.

Inside, Venable had turned her apartment into a bright, cheery place. Its walls were painted in soft pastels, the woodwork and cabinets were pickled-white oak. There was a large living room with casement windows facing Indian Bounty Park, fifty yards away. The rear wall of the room faced a hedged courtyard and was divided by a bullet-shaped copper-and-glass atrium, which towered up to the bedroom above. Two tall ficus trees dominated its core and climbing plants adorned its glass walls. Begonias, narcissi, and impatiens wove colourful patterns between and around the two trees. There was a guest bedroom and a formal dining room and a kitchen that looked like a chef's dream.

He found filters and a pound of coffee in the freezer and started the coffee before heading into the guest bath. Thirty minutes later, dressed in the previous night's wrinkled suit and shirt, he poured two cups of coffee and took one back up the stairs to the bedroom.

He placed her cup on the night table, leaned over the bed, and kissed her on the cheek. She stirred for a moment and reached out for him. Her arm fell across the empty sheet. She opened one eye and squinted up at him.

'You're due in court in three hours,' said Vail. 'Pryor won't be happy if you're late. If you'd like to hustle, you can join me at Butterfly's for breakfast.'

She rolled over onto her back.

'I'll be busy for the next three hours,' she said sleepily.

'You got something up your sleeve, Lawyer Venable?'

She pulled the comforter slowly down until it was two inches below her navel, held her arms towards the ceiling, and wiggled them slowly.

'No sleeves,' she said.

'You're gonna catch cold.'

'I always wake up this way,' she said. 'It's too chilly to fall back to sleep. And I wouldn't dare set foot in Butterfly's this soon. It's your turf. They'd probably lynch me.'

'I thought we were putting all that behind us.'

'After Stoddard.'

'That's Shana's problem.'

'We'll see where we stand after the bail hearing.'

He leaned over her, supporting himself on both arms, and kissed her on the mouth. 'Great,' he said.

'See you in court.'

On the way out, he picked up the downstairs phone and dialled Stenner's car phone.

Stenner answered on the first ring. 'Where are you? I'm parked in front. Been calling you for fifteen minutes.'

'Pick me up on the Estes-Rockwell corner of Indian Bounty Park,' Vail said.

'What are you doing out there?'

'Jogging. I ran out of breath.'

'Damn it, what do you mean standing on a street corner in broad—'

Vail hung up. He'd heard it all before. He headed across the park towards the far side, stopped once, and looked back. The shutters were open on one of the bedroom windows and she was watching him, wrapped only in the down comforter. She didn't wave; she just watched. Vail smiled up at her and walked through the park.

Stenner's concern for Vail went back four years, just after Flaherty had joined the Wild Bunch. Vail leaned over backwards to be impartial, but in his heart Shana Parver and Dermott Flaherty were his two favourites, probably because he saw in them his own rebellious spirit. Parver rebelling against her rich parents, Flaherty against the streets where he grew up.

Flaherty had been an angry kid, always in trouble, living on the streets, getting into fistfights, shoplifting, picking pockets, and heading for big trouble. He had one saving grace: he loved school. It was the one place he could rise above his desperate life. When he was busted for picking the pocket of a Red Sox fan and scalping the two tickets from his wallet, a kindly judge, who knew about him and was impressed with his grades, sent him to a half-way house for hardcase juveniles, where they kicked his ass and wore him out with leather belts and tried to whip the anger out of the wrathful orphan. The kid never cried.

One cold night, sitting in a bare, unheated closet that served as solitary, he had a revelation: His only asset was his brain. Intelligence was the only way out of the bleak, dead-end street he was heading down. Back on the street, he scrounged for a living, earned pocket money brawling in illegal backroom bare-knuckle fights, focused his anger

186

on books. He became a voracious, self-motivated, straight-A student. Top of his class.

Once a month he hitched rides three hundred miles to Ossining to spend thirty minutes with the man who was responsible for his dreary existence.

'I'm gonna be a lawyer,' he would tell the man. 'I'm gonna get ya out.'

'Fuck lawyers,' the man would answer. 'Lawyers is why I'm here.'

He changed his name from Flavin to Flaherty, lived on fast-food hamburgers and chocolate bars to keep up his energy, avoided friendships, fearful they would find out who he was. He lived in fear of that. When he graduated from college, he decided to put distance between himself and Rochester and hitchhiked west until he ran out of money in Chicago. He applied for a scholarship, spent hours in the public library studying for the qualification tests. His scores were astronomical. For a kid of twenty-three, he seemed to have more than a passing knowledge of the law. Nobody knew why, nobody asked, but he impressed the review board enough to earn himself a full scholarship for one year, with the future hanging on what he showed during the first four quarters. He got a job as a night janitor in one of the city skyscrapers, slept on a pallet in the utility room. When he wasn't studying, he was in the courtroom, taking notes, watching the big boys in action, always rooting for the defendants and nursing an inbred hatred of prosecutors until he saw Vail in action, read about his young Wild Bunch, and realized, reluctantly, after a year that the assistant DA had become his idol. At the end of his first year he was courting a 3.8. Two more years on scholarship and he waltzed out with his law degree and with summa cum laude on his sheepskin.

He was twenty-seven at the time. Streetwise. Tough. Antisocial. Brilliant.

He had offers but chose to work for a broken-down

old warhorse named Sid Bernstein, a once blazing star in the legal world who had turned to alcohol and coke to get through the day. For one year, Flaherty honed his skills studying the old boy's cases; reading law books; and dragging the old drunk out of bed, holding him under ice-cold showers and pumping the blackest coffee into him, dressing him and getting him into the courtroom, then prompting him through each case with notes scratched out on legal pads and law books marked with self-stick notes. One morning when Bernstein failed to show up at the office, he went to Bernstein's apartment and discovered that his boss was in the hospital. Pneumonia. The old guy lasted five days.

Sitting in Bernstein's drab office after the funeral, staring at the battered law books and worn-out cardboard file folders, he looked up and saw a handsome black woman standing in the office doorway.

'Dermott Flaherty?'

'Yes.'

'Sorry about Bernstein.'

The kid didn't know how to answer that. Bernstein was a cross he had borne for a year and a half. His sympathy for the man was superficial.

'Thanks,' he said. 'What can I do for you?'

'Are you taking over the practice?'

'Nothing to take over. Just trying to figure out what to do with his stuff. Uh, was there something . . .?'

'How'd you like a job?'

'Doing what?'

'Law, what else?'

'For who?'

'Ever hear of Martin Vail?'

When he came in for his interview with Vail, he was wearing a black turtleneck, a tweed jacket he had bought at a Division Street pawnshop for six bucks, and tennis shoes. He had no expectations.

'We've been watching you in court,' said Vail. 'You've been dragging old Sid Bernstein through life for a year and a half.'

'It was a job.'

'You've got quite a transcript, Mr Flaherty. Probably could have landed a pretty good spot with some of the better law firms around town. How come you picked Sid?'

'Figured I could learn more from him.'

'You actually tried most of his cases,' Vail said, flipping through papers in a file.

'You been checking up on me?' Belligerently.

'Bother you, does it?'

Flaherty shrugged.

'You're originally from Rochester, New York?'

Flaherty hesitated, stared down at the file. Finally: 'I guess so.'

'You guess so? You don't know where you're from?' Vail said with a laugh.

'I put that behind me.'

'Why? You did pretty well for a homeless kid with no parents. How long were you on your own? When did you lose your mother and father?'

Flaherty stood up suddenly, his fists balled up, his face red with fury. His reaction surprised Vail.

'Forget it,' Flaherty said, heading for the door.

'What's your problem, son? You've got the makings of a great lawyer, but you have a chip the size of Mount Rushmore on your shoulder.'

'It won't work,' Flaherty said.

'What won't work? Sit down, talk to me. You don't want to talk about Rochester, forget it, we won't talk about Rochester.'

Flaherty sat down. 'Can I smoke?' he asked.

Vail wheeled his chair to the exhaust fan and flicked it on. He lit up, too.

'Sooner or later you'll find out.'

'Find out what, son? What kind of load are you carrying?'

'M'mom died when I was nine.'

'Okay.'

He looked at Vail and sadness seemed to invest itself in his rugged young features.

'Actually ... actually, she didn't die. Actually what happened ... See, what happened ...' And then he said out loud something he had bottled inside himself for years. 'Actually my old man killed her. Beat her to death with his bare hands. He's on death row at Sing Sing. Been there ... twenty years. I used to think ... I used to think that I'd get to be a lawyer and then ... then I'd spring him, and then I'd take him out, and then ...'

'And then what?' Vail asked softly.

'Then I'd beat him the way he beat my mom. Beat him and beat him until ...'

The young man fell silent and sat puffing on his cigarette.

'When's the last time you saw him?' Vail asked.

'Before I came out here four years ago. I used to go see him once a month. I never even wrote after I left.'

'Dermott?'

'Yeah?'

'Your father died two years ago. Heart attack.'

'You knew about all that?'

'Naomi – Naomi Chance, the lady that came to see you when Sid died? Naomi knows everything, Dermott. You're one helluva young lawyer. The thing with your father? You put that behind you. It wasn't your fault, anyway. Thing is, we're pretty tight here. What the press calls the Wild Bunch. They're very supportive of each other. They'll expect the same of you. What I'm saying is, it's too heavy a load. Maybe if you share it, maybe if you put it behind you forever, maybe you can forget it. You want a job?'

Stenner had been sceptical about the new kid, who

190

seemed sullen and involuted and dressed in black like a funeral director and who was basically, as Stenner put it, 'a street punk'. The Shoulders case had changed all that and it put Vail in jeopardy for the first time in his life.

Jake Shoulders, whose felony record prevented him from owning liquor stores, gun shops, restaurants, and bars, kept a low profile, but he was known in the DA's office. His game was blackmail and extortion and city hall was his target. Staff members, department heads, councilmen, anybody who had anything to hide, eventually appeared on Shoulders's list. Then he spread out into the restaurant business, obtained liquor licences under phony names, even got a piece of the airport action. Obviously he was paying off *somebody* in the city, somebody high up, somebody who raked it off the top and let the health and police inspectors earn their cuts by making sure the licences were nicely covered up and easily approved.

Vail and his team knew what Shoulders was up to, but they could not make the city connection. Without it, it was just another bust. By tying it to the city hall gang, they could do real damage to a corrupt bunch that had run the city for too long. Vail needed a linchpin, a witness or evidence that would tie Shoulders directly to city hall. The break came when a three-time loser named Bobby Bollinger was arrested for assault with a deadly weapon. Facing life without parole, Bollinger, who was only thirty-three, decided to toot his whistle in exchange for immunity and a ticket out of town. He called Stenner, who had arrested him his third time down. Stenner got him off the street and holed him up in a run-down hotel on Erie Street. Then Bollinger became troublesome.

'Bollinger is waffling,' Stenner told Vail one morning.

'What's his problem?'

'Perks.'

'We gave him perks.'

'He's suffering from the "more" syndrome.'

'What else?'

'Witness protection out of state. A job making one hundred thou a year. Name change and we clear his record. A new car. He says they'll be able to trace his Corvette.'

Vail chuckled. 'No yacht?'

'He says that's less than he's making now on the docks.'

'Does he also say he's guilty of a felony? Has three priors? He goes in for good this time.'

'I think he's forgot about that.'

'Remind him.'

'How far are you willing to go?'

'I'll go with the witness programme and the name change goes with it. We can probably arrange something out of state. His record goes into limbo with his old name, so he gets that. But no hundred grand. We'll support him for three months while he's in a retraining programme. After that he's on his own. And he can ride a bicycle.'

'What if he still says no?'

'We'll max him out with the judge; he's a three-time loser.'

'He came to us, Marty.'

'He came to us because if he stays around here, he's a dead man. He's looking for a ticket out and a free ride.'

'He says he can give us the link we've been looking for.'

'That's what he says. Look, I'm not going to buy a conviction for one hundred grand a year. Tell me I'm wrong on this, Abel.'

'I don't know. His way, we bring down the city hall bums, get rid of Bollinger while we're at it. Let some other state put up with him.'

Vail stopped and lit a cigarette. He walked around in a tight little circle for a minute or so.

'He'll also stand up in court,' said Stenner. 'Part of the deal.'

'Christ, I never know how you're gonna jump on these

things, Abel.' Vail leaned against the wall and blew smoke towards the floor. 'I don't like Bollinger. I don't like doing business with him. No matter where he ends up, he's always going to be up to something. He wouldn't know how to straighten out. And I'm still sceptical about whether he can link our case up. But . . . okay, give him my proposal first. Scare him with the options. If you have to, twenty-five thou for six months. And no car, that's out. Tell him to dump the Vette and use the take for a down payment.'

'Maybe I can sell that.'

'Give it a shot then. It gets sticky, we'll good-guy, bad-guy him. He already has you pegged as the negotiator, so you play the hero. Take Flaherty for the bad guy.'

'Flaherty?'

'I think he'll surprise you, Abel. Let him play it his way. When he takes over, stand back, let him do it.'

Flaherty looked tough enough to play a mean cop. He bordered on handsome with coal-black hair and dark brown eyes, but his rugged, brooding Irish features were marred by a slightly flattened nose and a scar over one eye.

In the fleabag hotel, Stenner sat talking to Bollinger, a grungy redhead with bad teeth and a worse attitude. Flaherty sat in a corner of the room watching the proceedings, wearing a .38 under his arm.

'Shit,' Bollinger snapped, 'I'm giving up everything, man. Friends, my place, my car, every fuckin' thing, and he's pissin' about one hundred grand a year and a car to replace my Vette!'

'I'll tell you what you're not giving up,' said Stenner.

'Oh yeah, what's that?'

'The rest of your life, Bobby. No parole. And when we do nail down this case, you'll be hauled in again for aiding and abetting. You won't see daylight until my son runs for president and my son hasn't been born yet.'

193

'This is great, just fuckin' great, man. I come to you with a reasonable – '

'A hundred grand a year and a new joy waggon is not reasonable. Sell your vehicle. Get something nice with the down payment.'

'What are you, my business manager?'

Stenner said, 'You could look at it that way.'

'I do this, I'm on the dodge the rest of my life.'

'Then it's Joliet. They'll pop you there – if not before. You're running. This way, we make the reservations and pick up the tab.'

'Well, then, I guess it boils down to how bad you want my information, huh?'

'No, it boils down to how bad you want to stay alive. You want to shoot craps with your life for a damn car?'

Bollinger's lips were getting dry. He licked them nervously. *That fucking DA is calling my hand.*

'How long's this gonna take?' he asked.

'As long as it takes. Could be a year before we put the case together and get into court.'

'A year! In this fuckin' funeral parlour!'

'Christ, why don't we find him a nice place out in the goddamn country,' Flaherty snarled.

Bollinger looked over at Flaherty, who was clipping his fingernails. *Who the hell is* this *guy?* He looked back at Stenner.

'No pie for a fuckin' year?' he whined.

'Pie?'

'You know . . . the old ying-yang,' Bollinger said with a lascivious grin. 'I deserve that much.'

Flaherty suddenly exploded. He threw the fingernail clippers across the room and charged at Bollinger with such fury that he surprised even Stenner. He shoved past the detective and loomed over Bollinger.

'You don't deserve shit,' he snarled.

He slid an easy chair over with his foot and sat down

in front of Bollinger, leaning forward with his face an inch from the mobster and spoke in a low, nasty monotone.

'I know all the tricks, Bobby. Know why? Because I've been there. I know what you're thinking right now. I know what you're gonna say before you say it. I'm hip, Bobby. Understand?'

Bollinger's eyes bulged with uncertainty.

'The major, here, tries to treat you like a decent human being, what'd we get? A cheap brand of grift. You been playin' us like a fiddle for two days. Well, I just took your goddamn bow away from you. Forget the fuckin' Corvette and the fuckin' one hundred grand job. You're off the goddamn sleeve. Do you understand? Am I getting through that fat head of yours?'

'I got myself—'

'You got yourself to blame, that's what you got yourself. Now here's what's gonna happen. You're gonna give up *every*thing. Names, dates, times, places, whatever the action was, you're gonna give it up. Try to con us, you lose your ticket. Dodge the questions, you lose your ticket. You tell us one goddamn lie, you lose your fuckin' ticket.'

Bollinger turned to Stenner for help. The quiet man ignored him.

'And after we make the bust, you're gonna stand up in court and sing on these guys like the canary you are—'

'Goddamn you, I had a deal working—' Bollinger started to interrupt.

'You didn't have shit. You don't cooperate, you know what we're gonna do? We're gonna drop the charges on you and turn you out on the street, and just before we do? – just before they open up those pearly fuckin' gates? – we're gonna drop dimes all over this town that you jumped on the stoolie wagon. You'll be a dead man. They'll whack you before you get to the corner.'

Stenner sat back and watched Flaherty's performance

with awe. He knew the Irishman had been a street kid, but he had never seen him in action before, not like this.

Flaherty began jabbing home his points with a forefinger. 'So we're gonna start over because right now you don't have a goddamn thing. You made some talk and we made some talk, but *nobody* said "yea", and *nobody* said "nay". Nobody said *bullshit*. Now what's it gonna be, Bobby? Do I turn on the tape recorder, or do you take a trip to the icebox?'

Bollinger looked pleadingly at Stenner.

'Man's got a point,' Stenner said casually.

'Let's hear your story,' Flaherty said. 'Now.'

Bollinger looked back and forth between his two captors and then said, 'I was the bagman.'

'For who?'

'Shoulders.'

'And who?'

Bollinger hesitated for a moment, then said, 'Roznick.'

'Vic Roznick? The city manager?' Stenner said with surprise.

'How many Roznicks you know?'

'How did you make the delivery?'

'I get a call. I go to the Shamrock Club on West Erie. Shoulders has an office on the second floor. He gives me a briefcase fulla twenties and fifties. I take it to a parking lot on Illinois near the *Trib*. The trunk's unlocked. I put the case in, that's it.'

'How do you know what was in the case?' Stenner asked.

'Christ, Jake counted it out right in fronta me. Tells me there's a fuckin' dollar missin' it's my ass.'

'And it was Roznick's car?'

'Sometimes. I sat in my car half a dozen times and watched him come out, dip into the trunk, and split with the case. Other times it was Glen Scott, Eddie Malone, Pete Yankovitch.'

'City staff?'

'Yeah. Different places for them. Shoulders had 'em all over a barrel. Stuff they did years ago. Videotape. Audio. Photos. Get 'em on a hook, then make the deal. They cooperate, he pays off and lets 'em off the spike.'

'Once they're in, they never get out,' Stenner said.

'I even shot some photos.'

'Why?' Stenner asked.

'To cover my ass, y'know, just in case.'

'You mean to do a little blackmailing of your own, don't you?' Flaherty suggested.

Bollinger shrugged but did not answer.

'You got pictures of these pickups?' Flaherty asked.

'Yeah. They oughta be worth a little extra.'

'Part of the deal,' Flaherty snapped back.

'I, uh . . . I got sompin' else maybe worth a new Vette.'

'It better be good,' said Flaherty.

'There's paper out on your boss.'

Stenner stood up, his eyes narrowed. 'Who you talking about, Yancey?'

'No, man. The piranha.'

'Piranha?' Flaherty asked.

'Vail. They're scared shitless of him. Can't be bought. Never know where he's gonna jump next.'

'You saying there's a contract out on Martin Vail?' Flaherty said fiercely. 'Who?'

'Do we have a deal on the Vette?' Bollinger asked with a smile.

With a growl, Flaherty pulled the .38 out of his shoulder holster. He jammed it under Bollinger's nose.

'Don't fuck with us. Who put out the contract and who's doing the job? You say it now or I swear to God I'll throw you out the damn window.'

'Hey, hey . . .' Bollinger said, turning pale.

Stenner reached out and laid his hand over the gun. 'Answer those two questions right now, Bobby,' he said sternly.

'Shoulders. It's like two hundred K.'

'Shoulders ordered the hit?'

'Yeah, but I think maybe they're all in on it. You know, the whole gang chipped in.'

'Who's the shooter?' Flaherty said. His voice had gone dead.

'You better cover me on this.'

'*Who's the fuckin' shooter?*'

Bollinger sighed. He was beginning to sweat. 'It's a cop, does Shoulders's tricks.'

'A cop?' Stenner said. 'What cop?'

'Look I . . . I . . .' Bollinger stammered.

'*What cop?*' Flaherty demanded.

'His name's Heintz,' Bollinger babbled.

'Lou Heintz? A sergeant?' Stenner said.

'That's the one.'

'You know him, Major?' Flaherty asked.

'Oh yes, Lou Heintz. Doesn't surprise me a bit. When is this supposed to go down?'

Bollinger shrugged. 'Whenever. It's paid for.'

'My God,' Stenner said, and headed for the phone.

'This better be the McCoy,' said Flaherty.

'Who the hell *are* you, anyways?' Bollinger whimpered.

Flaherty smiled for the first time. 'I'm the guy who's gonna make you the greatest song-and-dance man since Fred Astaire,' he said.

And he had. It had taken eighteen months, but Flaherty had successfully prosecuted Shoulders, two of his henchmen, three department heads, the city manager, and an assistant city attorney and set in motion Meyer's successful cases against the two city councilmen. All of them were still in prison.

Bollinger was in Oregon with orders never to set foot east of the Mississippi River.

Lou Heintz, the killer motorcycle cop, had vanished. And Stenner had immediately become Vail's bodyguard, picking him up every morning, delivering him to meetings, watching his back constantly, usually delivering him home at night.

About a year later, Heintz was found dead in an abandoned car in Pittsburgh with four .22s in the back of his head. It was written off as a gang hit. Nobody would ever know whether it involved the contract on Martin Vail or not.

But Stenner never stopped his surveillance. He had been Vail's constant companion ever since, except at those times when Vail managed to shake him. Like the night before.

Vail was still deep in reminiscence when Stenner pulled up in the car. He glared up at his boss and shook his head.

'Right out in the open,' he said as Vail got into the car. 'Alone. Perfect target.'

'Please, Abel. That's over. Heintz is dead, Shoulders is doing ten years.'

'Once warned . . .'

'Okay. You know I appreciate your concern. I just need a little privacy every once in a while. Kinda like sneaking out when you were a kid.'

'I never sneaked out when I was a kid.'

'I think I knew that, Abel.'

Stenner looked at Vail's wrinkled suit and twisted tie. 'You want to go home and change?' he asked.

'Hell with it,' Vail said.

'You're in court this morning and Naomi says you have a lunch with Paul Rainey.'

'Butterfly's, Major. I want breakfast. Anyway, it's not my case, it's Parver's. I'm just going to sit in the back of the courtroom and spectate.'

'How about the lunch with Rainey?'

'I'll pick up the tab. He won't care what I'm wearing.'

Seventeen

When Vail and Stenner arrived at Butterfly's, Naomi Chance and Dermott Flaherty were already there, immersed in the morning papers. Naomi looked disapprovingly at Vail as he sat down.

'Didn't get too close to your razor this morning,' she commented.

He couldn't think of an appropriate answer, so he said nothing. Instead he turned to Butterfly, who loomed over the table staring down at him.

'Two poached, sausage, white toast,' he said.

'Poached,' she snarled. 'God!' And slouched away.

'And that suit –' Naomi began.

'I don't want to hear about my suit or shaving or anything else,' Vail said.

'You can grab a quick shave in your private bath,' Naomi said.

'Screw my private bath. It's not a bathroom, it's an afterthought. They put a sink and a shower in a broom closet and called it a bathroom.'

'It's convenient.'

'It's the size of the can in an airliner.'

'There's a clean shirt and a tie in one of your file cabinets and your grey pinstripe is in the closet, take you fifteen minutes before you go down to court,' Naomi said, scanning the front page of *USA Today*.

'What is it with everybody today?' Vail grumbled. 'I'm not posing for *GQ*, you know. Why don't you pick on Flaherty? He wears that same black suit every day.'

'I have four black suits,' Flaherty said without looking up from his paper. 'I don't wear the same one every day.'

'Don't you find it a little bizarre that he dresses like

Johnny Cash *every day*?' Vail said. 'Why don't you pick on him?'

Stenner said, 'I think some variety might be in order.'

'I'm comfortable in black,' Flaherty said, ending the conversation.

Further discussion was cut short by the arrival of Okie Okimoto, who looked smug and important as he approached the table. He was carrying his briefcase.

Butterfly frowned at him. 'We don't serve sushi in here,' she growled.

'I have no desire to eat here, Madame Butterfly. Hopefully I can survive a cup of coffee.'

'Smartass,' she muttered, and dragged her feet into the kitchen.

Okimoto sat down at the round table, opened his case, and took out a file folder.

'I have here the report on the famous landfill kill,' he said, almost with a snicker. 'Or perhaps I should say *infamous* landfill kill.'

'What's so funny?' Stenner asked.

'All the fuss,' he said. 'Where's Harvey? I want him to hear this from my own two lips.'

'Must've overslept,' Naomi said.

'Hmm. Perhaps I should wait.'

'I don't think so,' said Vail. 'You've gone this far, you better finish.'

'Okay. I'll skip the anatomical details and the long medical terms for now and just give you the essence,' Okimoto said, opening the folder. 'By the way, Eckling doesn't have this yet. I assume you will be discreet with the information for at least an hour.'

'Sure. Just get on with it,' Vail answered.

'They froze to death,' Okimoto said with a smile.

'What!' Flaherty said, finally looking up from his paper.

A deadly quiet fell over the table as Stenner, Vail, Flaherty, and Naomi stared at Okimoto, waiting for the details of his surprising announcement.

'Well, the two males froze to death and the woman suffocated,' he said to the stunned group.

'Froze to death?' Stenner repeated.

'You want my expert opinion?' said Okimoto. 'I think what happened was, they crawled into a Dempsey Dumpster somewhere, probably burrowed under the junk to keep warm – this was several weeks ago, early to mid January, we had a helluva freeze for about two weeks right after New Year's if you'll remember – and by morning two of them were dead and the woman was too weak to move. They pick up the Dumpster, haul it out to the landfill, and unloaded it. The woman suffocated in the garbage, probably after she was in the dump.'

'Good God!' Flaherty said.

'So we don't have a homicide, we have a homeless tragedy?' said Vail.

'Yeah,' Okimoto said, snickering. 'So much for Harvey's murder theory.'

Then he leaned his elbows on the table. 'Know what I think? I think maybe this happens a lot. Probably other bodies out there, but I'm not going to mention it to anybody. They'll be out there digging up the whole damn landfill.'

'They froze to death,' Stenner said half aloud and shaking his head. 'Harvey's going to be crushed.'

'I hear he was on the computer network tracking down missing persons from all over the state,' Okimoto said, and started to laugh. He finished his coffee. 'Tell you what, tell Harvey the murder weapon was a refrigerator.' Then he left, still chuckling to himself.

'Harvey finally blew one,' Flaherty said, turning back to his paper. 'Him and his intuition.'

'He's usually right,' said Naomi. 'Give the devil his due.'

'Yeah, but he kind of rubs it in, don't you think?' Flaherty said. 'Anybody else notice that, that he kind of rubs our noses in it because we don't remember some oddball bit of information like the day John Dillinger was killed, something like that. Hell, John Dillinger was killed thirty years before I was born.'

'July twenty-second, 1934,' said Naomi. 'In front of the old Biograph Theatre. Actually, it's not too far from here.' She smiled at Flaherty's surprised look and added with a wink, 'It's part of our local history, darling, don't feel bad.'

When they got to the office, Parver was already there, pacing back and forth at the rear of the big room, drinking a cup of coffee and psyching herself up.

'Ready for battle?' Vail called to her as he entered his office and peeled off his jacket and tie.

She nodded and kept pacing.

'What's your plan?'

'No bail. Go to the grand jury as soon as possible.'

'She's gonna fight you,' Vail said.

'Well, we'll just have to kick ass,' Parver answered, still pacing.

Vail smiled. 'That's my girl,' he said.

Naomi took a clean shirt out of a drawer and handed it and his suit to Vail.

'There isn't room in here for me and my clothes,' he griped, and pulled the door shut behind him.

'Twenty minutes,' Naomi called out, and went to her desk.

Fifteen minutes later Parver and Vail bumped into Harvey St Claire, who was getting off the lift as they were leaving. He seemed either tired or deep in thought.

'Missed you at breakfast, Harve,' Vail said.

'May I talk to you for a minute?' St Claire answered, his tone more serious than usual.

'I have to go down to the Stoddard bail hearing with Shana. Then lunch with Rainey. Can it wait until this afternoon?'

'Uh, yeah, sure.'

'Incidentally, Okie was at Butterfly's this morning

acting the fool. The bodies in the landfill? Three homeless people got in a Dumpster and froze to death. Well, actually one of them suffocated. Anyway, you can forget working the network and get back to business.'

He and Parver headed for the lifts.

'Ohhhh, I don't think so,' St Claire drawled half aloud as he watched them leave.

Two guards led Edith Stoddard down a long, dismal hallway towards the back stairs to courtroom 3 on the second floor. Her hands were shackled behind her, but Venable had convinced the jailers not to shackle her legs by embarrassing them.

'This is a fifty-three-year-old woman,' she said. 'You think she's going to outrun you two and make a dash for the border?'

As they approached the door to the stairwell, a TV team from Channel 7 burst through the back door with lights blazing and microphone ready. Edith Stoddard cried out and lowered her face in alarm.

'Damn them,' Venable snapped, and glowered at the two jailers. It was an old media trick, slipping the security men ten bucks apiece to tell them where and when they could get a shot at the defendant. She rushed Stoddard along, but the TV crew caught them at the door. Venable opened it and urged Stoddard through, followed by the guards. Then she stood in the doorway. Questions came at her in a jumble.

'When did you take on the case?'

'Did Edith Stoddard call you?'

'Are you going for reduced bail?'

'Is it true that she's already confessed?'

And on and on. Venable finally held up a hand, and when that didn't quiet them, she raised her voice and bellowed, 'Listen!' She waited until they shut up. 'I will answer no questions. This is a bail hearing. If you want to know what's going on, go upstairs to the court like everyone else. Other than that, no comment. And I'll have no comment after the hearing, either. Is that clear?'

She stepped inside the stairwell and slammed the door in their faces. The stairwell smelled of Lysol, an odour that sickened Venable. *Why is it all of the nastier public buildings smell of Lysol? Perhaps my reaction to it is psychosomatic.*

'Please, please . . .' Edith Stoddard said. Tears welled in her eyes.

'This will take about five minutes,' Venable said. 'Just hang in there and trust me.' She held her breath until they got to the security room at the top of the stairs.

Parver was already at the prosecutor's desk. There were a thin file folder, a large yellow legal tablet, and a handful of freshly sharpened pencils on the desk in front of her. She watched as the guards led Edith Stoddard and Jane Venable to the defence desk. They sat down and Venable leaned over and spoke to her in a whisper. She did not acknowledge Shana.

In the back of the room, Vail settled back to watch the first brief skirmish between the two lawyers. Venable's objective would be to get bail as low as possible – perhaps even have her client released on her own recognizance – without giving away any of her case. Parver's objective: No bail, period.

Vail looked at Edith Stoddard. One day had beaten her down. Her shoulders were rounder, her head down. He thought for a moment about the irony of the Darby and Delaney cases. In both murders, a shot to the head was key. In Darby's case, it came first and proved premeditation; in Delaney's case, the head shot was second and proved malice.

Judge Ione Pryor, a tall, hawk-faced woman in her forties with a no-nonsense air and a steely glare behind gold-rimmed glasses, entered the courtroom and took her chair behind the bench.

'First case,' she said to the bailiff.

'The state versus Edith Stoddard. A bail hearing. Defendant was arrested yesterday on a charge of murder in the first degree.'

'Who's representing the state?' Judge Pryor asked.

Parver stood up. 'I am, Your Honour. Shana Parver, assistant prosecutor, DA's office.'

Judge Pryor looked over the top of her glasses towards the defendant's desk, settled her gaze on Venable.

'Are you representing the defendant?' she asked with surprise.

'Yes, Your Honour. Jane Venable for the defence.'

'Been a while since we've seen you in criminal courts,' the judge said.

'Yes, Your Honour.'

'Ms Parver?'

'Your Honour,' she said, standing behind her desk. 'The state has sufficient evidence to obtain a first-degree murder indictment from the grand jury against Mrs Stoddard for the slaying of John Farrell Delaney. We move that Mrs Stoddard be held without bail until the trial. This is premeditated murder, Your Honour.'

Venable stood up.

'Objection, Judge,' she said. 'The state's case consists of a statement made by my client to two police officers who were interrogating her concerning the death of her boss, John Delaney. She never mentioned Delaney by name. She said "I killed him." That's all she said.'

'If the court please,' Parver countered, 'the entire interrogation concerned Mrs Stoddard's relationship with the deceased, John Delaney. It is obvious the "him" in her confession was John Delaney. I seriously doubt she was talking about John Kennedy or Abe Lincoln.'

Pryor squinted over her glasses at Parver, considered admonishing her for a fleeting moment, then changed her mind. The young prosecutor had a strong point. She looked back at Venable.

'I would have to agree with that, Ms Venable.'

'It's moot anyway, Your Honour. The statement made by my client is inadmissible. She was under great stress at the time. She was scared to death. She had no legal representation – '

'She was given an opportunity to call a lawyer in her Miranda,' the judge said.

'I really don't think she was rational at that point. There are a great many extenuating circumstances in this matter, Judge. As far as bail goes, Mrs Stoddard has a husband who is a quadriplegic. My client is fifty-three years old and takes care of him. I don't believe she poses a danger or threat to society and, I can assure you, she's not going anywhere.'

'Excuse me, Judge Pryor,' Parver said. 'If counsel is suggesting that Mrs Stoddard be released on recognizance, the state strongly objects. I say again, this is a murder-one case. As far as Mrs Stoddard's husband is concerned, she has a twenty-one-year-old daughter who will have to take on that responsibility. And Mrs Stoddard's age is immaterial.'

The judge looked at Stoddard for a minute or two, then took off her spectacles and tapped them lightly against her jaw.

'Where is her daughter?' the judge asked. 'Is she in court today?'

'No,' Venable said.

Parver moved quickly to quell any further discussion of the specific issues of the case. 'We have a motion before the court, Judge. I suggest the counsellor wait until the trial to plead her case.'

Pow, right in the kisser, thought Venable. *Vail's taught his young lawyers well.*

The judge smothered a smile. 'Please read the motion,' she said to the court reporter, who checked the stereotape, found the motion made by Parver, and said: ' "We move that Mrs Stoddard be held without bail until the trial." '

The judge leaned back in her chair. 'When do you plan to go to the grand jury, Ms Parver?'

'As soon as possible. Hopefully, this week sometime.'

'Okay. I'm going to deny bail at this time. I agree with Ms Parver, Ms Venable. This is first-degree murder. As for the confession, the trial judge can deal with it, if and when it comes to that.'

'One more point, if it please the court,' said Venable. 'Defence would like to request that Mrs Stoddard be kept in the holding cell here in district two until the grand jury rules rather than moving her into the general prison population at this time.'

Pryor looked at Parver. Shana thought for a moment and said, 'The state has no objection.'

'Good, then that's all settled.'

Pryor rapped her gavel and called for the next case.

Venable walked across to the prosecutor's table. 'Nicely done,' she said to Parver. 'Looks like you took round one.'

'Thanks,' Parver answered.

'See you next time.'

Venable returned to Edith Stoddard as the guards prepared to handcuff her and lead her out.

'Do you boys mind cuffing her in front?' she asked. 'She isn't going to turn rabbit on you.'

The two guards exchanged glances and one of them shrugged.

'Sure, Miss Venable,' he said.

'Why did you do that?' Stoddard asked as they were leading her out of the courtroom. There was emotion in her voice for the first time, a sense of betrayal and anger. 'I told you, I want to plead guilty. I can't stand these photographers and reporters screaming at me. The pictures—'

'Edith, please trust me. Let me do this my way,' Jane Venable said. 'They will most certainly indict you for murder one. Then I'll move to throw out the confession.

They don't have the gun, so they can't prove yours was even the murder weapon. That gives me good ammunition when I go to Vail to strike a deal.'

'I just want it over with,' Stoddard said mournfully.

'And it will be soon,' Venable said with sympathy as they led Edith Stoddard out of the room.

Parver worked her way back through the reporters, who had now descended on her. Vail slipped out of the door and walked across the hall to wait for her.

Parver stopped just outside the courtroom doors.

'We will seek a murder-one indictment of Mrs Stoddard as soon as possible, hopefully before the end of the week. That's all I can tell you now.'

'Will you ask for the death penalty?' a female TV reporter asked.

Parver stared at her for several seconds. The impact of the question threw her. 'I'm not going to try this case in the media,' she said. 'I've told you all I can tell you at this time. Thank you.'

She walked away. The press swarmed off down the hall, looking for Jane Venable. Vail fell in beside Parver and they threaded their way through the crowded hall.

'I don't understand why Edith Stoddard is so determined to plead guilty,' Parver said.

'A lot of reasons,' Vail said. 'She's scared, she's depressed, she knows she's guilty. Doesn't want her family hurt any more than necessary. My guess is, she's being protective of her husband and daughter. And it's a humiliating experience, very traumatic.'

'I don't believe it's sunk in yet that she blew this man away in cold blood and she's going to pay heavily for it,' Parver said. 'She's facing life.'

'I'm sure Jane's drumming that into her, but I really don't believe that's a reality to her at this point.'

'I feel a little sorry for her,' Parver admitted, half aloud.

'You don't have that luxury,' Vail said, then added: 'There is one thing – '

'Find the gun,' Parver said.

'You're one step ahead of me.'

'Abel's working on it,' she said. 'When do I get a crack at Mrs Stoddard?'

'Let's wait until after the grand jury,' Vail said. 'Once she's indicted, when the reality of what she's up against sets in, she may begin to break down a little.'

'I don't think so,' Parver answered. 'I think she's determined to enter a plea.'

'And Venable's determined to fight it. Let's wait and see how that one plays out. Ready to take on Paul Rainey?'

'Yes, sir.'

'Have the paper?'

'Right here.' She took out the arrest warrant and gave it to Vail, who put it in the inside pocket of his jacket.

'Let's go rattle his cage,' Vail said.

Eighteen

They were at Sundance, a two-storey-high atrium covered with skylights to give the illusion of being outside when the weather was inclement or just too damn cold, as it was on this blustrey February day. The glass partitions covering the large plaza could be opened with the press of a button in the manager's office, weather permitting. It was a popular lunchtime place for downtown workers, serving the best hot dogs east of the Mississippi and mountainous salads for vegetarians. It was located behind one of the city's largest bookstores, and its old-fashioned wrought-iron tables were usually filled by noon with bookworms who bought novels or periodicals and read through lunch in the sunlit piazza.

'You really know how to entertain, Marty,' Paul Rainey said as he doctored two hot dogs with sauerkraut, relish, mustard, ketchup, and onions. He looked down at Parver. 'Does he always entertain this lavishly, Shana?'

'It's all I can afford on the assistant DA's salary,' Vail answered.

'Who're you kidding?' Rainey said. 'You made enough before you took that job to live on the tenderlion forever. I'll bet you've got the first dime you ever made. Hell, you don't own a car and you dress like a damn ragamuffin. Did you know the Lawyers Club was thinking of taking up a collection to buy you a new suit?'

'This *is* a new suit,' Vail answered a bit firmly.

'Cotton and wool. Off the rack. Two hundred tops. You know how much this outfit cost me? Two thou. Barneys.'

Vail bit into his frankfurter and chewed in silence for

a minute, then said casually, 'That's more than you're going to make off James Darby.'

Rainey looked up and rolled his eyes. 'Oh, hell, not even gonna wait until we finish this elabourate spread, are ya?' He sighed. 'Okay, Counsellors, what're we doing here?'

'You and I go back almost twenty years, right, Paul?'

'I've never counted.'

'I've seen it from both sides of the street.'

'Forget the endorsements and make your point,' Rainey said.

'Your boy Darby is guilty as sin.'

'Uh-huh. You gonna take that to the grand jury? That Darby is guilty as sin? I don't think so. And that's all you've got. Look, I don't like him any more than you do, but that doesn't make him a wife killer. So he's a putz. Half the world is a putz.'

'Paul, I'm telling you this guy carefully planned and killed his wife in cold blood. And he did it for the two worst reasons: money and a stripper with a fancy ass and 40–D cup.'

'C'mon, Marty, you fried everybody who screws around on his wife they'd only be ten men left on the planet.'

'The jury'll be back in an hour on this one.'

'What's the matter, you can't wait for the trial?' Rainey said with a laugh. 'You want to try him here over lunch? Maybe we should call over a waiter to act as judge.'

'I'm here in the interest of justice and saving the tax-payers' money,' Vail said calmly.

'Of course you are.'

'Listen a minute. Where we stand in this investigation, we have Darby saying he came in the house, his wife popped three shots at him, he shot her with a shotgun, she knocked one in the ceiling, and he finished the job with the head shot. Isn't that Darby's story?'

'It's what happened.'

212

'Well, think about that for a minute. Three shots from a .38, a shotgun blast, another .38, another shotgun blast.'

Vail opened his briefcase and took out a small tape recorder. It contained an enhanced reproduction just of Stenner's replay of the shots as Mrs Shunderson said they occurred, with the shotgun blast first. He plugged a set of headphones into the machine and handed it to Rainey.

'Listen to this,' Vail said. He waited until Rainey had the headphones adjusted and then pressed the play button. They watched as Rainey listened. He took off the 'phones and handed it back to Vail.

'So? Somebody shooting a gun.'

'It's clear that the first shot came from the shotgun,' Vail said.

'Is that what we're here about? This dummied-up tape. What kinda scam are you trying to pull, Martin?'

'I'll tell you right now, Paul, I have an unimpeachable witness who'll testify that the tape is accurate,' said Vail.

'So what,' Rainey said, obviously getting annoyed.

'So your guy's been lying to you, which is understandable, considering he killed his wife in cold blood. Point is, he hasn't been level with you. You're flying blind at this point and he's navigating you right into a mountain.'

'Where are you going with this, Marty?'

'I'm offering you a deal, Paul. We'll let him plead to second-degree murder. He gets twenty years without parole. I'm offering you twenty years and he's out. He'll be fifty-something and broke, but he'll be out. I think society will be happy with that arrangement.'

'You're crazier than a Christmas mouse, you know that?'

'I know you, Paul. I know you believe that Darby's innocent and it happened the way he said it happened. But I hate to see you get conned by your own client. Listen to the tape again.'

'I don't have to listen to the tape again. I heard the tape. It doesn't mean a damn thing.'

'It means Darby came into his house, walked over to his wife, who was watching TV, and shot her in the head. Then he put the .38 in her hand, fired four shots – one into the ceiling – and then backed off and shot her in the side with the shotgun. And it also means it was premeditated. Malice aforethought. The whole magilla.'

'If you're so damn sure you got him, you wouldn't be offering me a deal. I know you. You'd take me to the limit.'

'Look, I don't have the staff or the time for depositions and tracking down witnesses and pretrial and trial and then your appeal and on and on. I've got a desk full of cases and now I have to handle Jack's business, too. We settle this, I save the taxpayers a couple hundred thousand bucks, I save myself a lot of aggravation, you save face, and your client stays alive.'

Vail took out the warrant, laid it on the table and slid it in front of Paul Rainey.

'I'll serve this on you if you'll accept it. You can bring him in by, say, eight tonight?' he said.

Rainey opened the warrant for first-degree murder on Darby. He looked up at Vail with surprise, then looked back down at the warrant. His jaw began to spasm as his anger rose.

'I can't believe you're pulling this stunt,' he said finally.

'There's another thing,' Vail said. 'He's dead broke, I talked to Tom Smoot at New York Life last night. They're freezing the insurance funds pending the resolution of this case.'

'Never miss a trick, do you?' Rainey said, and there was ire in every word. 'Know what I think? I think you're giving up an awful lot of information, that's what I think.'

'There's a lot more,' Parver said softly.

'Oh?'

'Well, there's the slip with the phone number on it. We

214

think the phone number beside the phone was written by Darby to make it appear as though his wife called Palmer. I don't think Poppy Palmer ever talked to Ramona Darby.'

'You've had more than one shot at the Palmer woman,' said Rainey. 'You can't prove any of this. It's all conjecture. You want to talk to her again? Go ahead, be my guest.'

'We'd like to, Paul, if we could find her,' Shana Parver said in a matter-of-fact tone.

'What the hell're you talking about?'

'Poppy Palmer flew the coop,' Vail said.

Rainey's gaze jumped back and forth between Vail and Parver.

'She called her boss yesterday, about two hours after Shana questioned Darby about the slip with her phone number on it. She told him her sister was dying down in Texarkana and she had to go immediately. Her sister lives in California and is in perfect health. She hasn't heard from Poppy Palmer in five years.'

Rainey, a very shrewd lawyer, leaned back in his chair and studied Vail's face, then he looked at Parver. His eyes narrowed, but he kept quiet. At this point, he knew he would learn more by keeping his mouth shut.

'We are going to issue a subpoena on Palmer and I'm seriously considering taking out a warrant against her for perjury,' Vail said. 'She made the statement about her phone call from Ramona Darby under oath. We contend she's lying – there never was a phone call. Then I intend to go to the FBI and swear out a warrant against her for unlawful flight to avoid prosecution.'

Rainey fell deep into thought. He drummed his fingertips on the table but still maintained his silence.

'You're already in, Paul. You want to go *pro bono* from here on, representing a killer in a case you can't win? You owe it to yourself, your peace of mind, to get the truth out of him. Explain the options. Either he takes

215

twenty years, no parole, or he goes to death row and gets fried – or spends the rest of his life staring down the hall at the chair, waiting to.'

'You want me to sell out my client because he can't pay,' Rainey said with an edge.

'Not at all. What I'm saying, Paul, is you need to satisfy yourself about this. Then consider all the angles and do the best thing for you *and* your client. Either he pleads to second-degree and takes his medicine or he goes down for murder one. It's up to you. In your hands. Just one thing – if he turns rabbit, he'll never make the county line.'

Rainey slumped back in the chair. He stared at Vail, at the warrant, then back at Vail.

'He'll say he was confused,' Rainey said. 'He walked in, she was aiming the gun at him, he cut loose with the shotgun – '

Parver cut him off. 'It's the head shot,' he said. 'That's what's going to get him in the end. Do you really think any jury's going to believe she kept blazing away at him with a hole the size of Rhode Island in her side? The head shot *had* to be the first shot. Listen to the tape.'

'The hell with the goddamn tape. The tape doesn't mean shit and you know it!'

'You're an old hand at getting to the truth, Paul,' said Vail. 'If he sticks to his story' – he tapped the tape recorder – 'he's lying to you.'

Rainey took a sip of water, tapped his lips with his napkin, and dropped it on the table. He toyed with the warrant, sliding it around on the tabletop with his fingertips.

'We're playing straight up with you, Paul,' said Vail. 'I could've had the sheriff pick him up last night and he'd be sitting in the cooler right now.'

Rainey pocketed the warrant and got up.

'I'll be in touch,' he said. Then he leaned over the table and, with a smile, said very softly in Vail's ear, 'I've been in this game ten years longer than you and this is the first time a DA ever offered me a deal before he even arrested my client.'

'It's the times,' Vail said, smiling back. 'Everybody's in a hurry these days.'

'There's something not right about this,' Rainey said with a scowl.

'Yeah, your client, that's what's not right about it,' Parver said.

'I was having a pretty good day until now. You two're a real item. Buy a guy lunch, then do your best to make him lose it.'

Rainey left the table. Parver didn't say anything. She looked down at the tablecloth, moved her water glass around on it.

'Okay, what's bothering you?' Vail asked.

'Nothing.'

'Uh-huh. C'mon, spit it out.'

'Why let Darby off the hook? I mean, why even offer a plea bargain? We can take this guy, Martin. We can take him all the way, I know we can.'

'All you have is an elderly woman who heard the shots. Paul Rainey'll chew her up and spit her out. We have no backup on Mrs Shunderson and Poppy Palmer powdered on us and we haven't a clue where she is. Suppose you get a soft jury? Darby could walk. Or maybe get voluntary manslaughter, in which case he'd be back on the street in three, four years. This way, if Rainey bites, we take Darby out for twenty years.'

'I still think I can win this case.'

'You did win, Shana. Putting Darby away for twenty years without parole, that's as sweet a deal as we can ask for. Look, you just came off a case, you've got the Stoddard thing to deal with, and by tomorrow you'll probably have two more on your desk. Forget Darby, we've got him. Let's hope Rainey sees through him.'

'We just gave Rainey our whole case!' she said. 'And why didn't we let the sheriff arrest that punk?'

'We didn't give him a damn thing he wouldn't get the first day of discovery. And giving him the option to bring his man in shows good faith on our part.'

'Think the money'll have an effect on him?'

'It's a wild card. He took Darby at his word, which is natural, any lawyer will give his client the benefit of the doubt. Now he's faced with the possibility his client conned him from the front end. Paul Rainey doesn't want to feel he's been suckered by a client he doesn't even like. If he's convinced Darby lied to him, then he's faced with either defending a man he knows is guilty and not getting paid for it or getting him the best deal he can.'

'I don't think he'll buy it,' she said.

'Maybe. What really got to him, what got his attention, was Poppy Palmer running. That and the warrant. My guess is, he'll come back with a counter-offer.'

'And . . .?'

'We made him the best offer we're going to. If Rainey doesn't take it, Darby's all yours.'

'Good!' Parver said staunchly. 'I hope Rainey thumbs his nose at us. It will serve him right.'

'If he does, we better find Poppy Palmer,' Vail said. 'She'll put the nail in his coffin.'

Nineteen

Trial transcripts, autopsy reports, photographs, old police reports, and copies of book pages were all spread out on Martin Vail's large table. Naomi, Flaherty, and Harvey St Claire stood in front of the big desk, studying what St Claire called his 'exhibits.' Naomi and Dermott Flaherty stared mutely at the display, occasionally picking up a report or a photo and studying it, then slowly replacing it, obviously stunned by what St Claire had laid out on the table.

'You make a good case, Harve. You ought to be a lawyer,' Flaherty said.

'I don't make a very good impression in a courtroom. 'Cept in the witness stand. Hold m'own pretty good under oath.'

'What's Abel say?' Naomi asked.

'He's concerned,' said St Claire.

'For Abel, that's verging on panic,' Flaherty said with a chuckle.

'Am I wrong about this?' St Claire asked. 'Am I just being paranoid?'

'Paranoid! I hardly think so,' said Naomi. 'Why the hell didn't we know about this sooner?'

''Cause Gideon don't want the world t'know about it,' said St Claire. 'From what I gather, the town is run by old Fundamentalist farts. I imagine they all look like Abraham or Moses or John Brown. They don't want the world t'think Satanists are loose in their holy little village.'

'Don't they care who did it?'

'Doesn't seem so. Been about six months, ain't happened again. Guess maybe they decided to shut it outta their minds. Pray it away on Sunday mornings.'

'And they just wrote off Linda Balfour?'

'One way a puttin' it,' said St Claire.

'The first question that pops into my mind is, Who? And the second is, Why?' said Flaherty.

'Well, I can tell you who it ain't. Ain't Aaron Stampler.' St Claire dropped a wad of chewing tobacco in his silver cup. 'He's still locked up in max security at Daisyville.'

'That's Daisyland,' Naomi corrected him.

'Just as stupid,' St Claire said.

Naomi looked up as Vail, Parver, and Stenner got off the lift. 'Here comes the one person who can answer these questions if anybody can,' Naomi said, nodding towards Vail.

'What've we got here?' Vail asked as he entered the office.

They all looked at one another and then focused their attention on Harvey St Claire. He smoothed out his moustache and got rid of the wad of tobacco in his cheek.

'Tell ya how it started out,' he said. 'I was runnin' the HITS network, thinkin' maybe we could turn up something outta town on them bodies in the city dump. Missin' persons, maybe a bank heist, drug gang. Playin' a hunch, okay? And Ben Meyer runs across this brutal murder down near the Kentucky border. Town called Gideon. Ever hear of it?'

'Not that I recall,' Vail said.

'Anyway, uh, this town's run by some old religious jokers and they hushed it up. Wrote it off as Satanists. We got interested outta curiosity much as anything. The victim was a housewife. Happily married, nice solid husband. Year-old son. I thought what I'd do, I'd read the autopsy report. The police chief brushed me off, but the town doctor, he's also the coroner, was a nice old guy, most cooperative.'

St Claire searched around the table and found Doc

Fields's autopsy, which Ben had entered into the computer and printed out, and read it out loud.

'The victim, Linda Balfour, is a white female, age 26. The body is 53.5 inches in length and weighs 134 pounds and has blue eyes and light brown hair. She was dead upon my arrival at her home on Poplar Street, this city. The victim was stabbed, cut, and incised 56 times. There was evidence of cadaver spasm, trauma, and aero-embolism. There was significant exsanguination from stab wounds. The throat wound, which nearly decapitated Balfour, caused aero-embolism, which usually results in instantaneous death. Wounds in her hands and arms indicate a struggle before she was killed.'

St Claire looked up for a moment. 'Beginning to sound a little familiar, Marty?'

'Where are you taking this, Harve?'

'Okay, now listen to this. It's from the ME's testimony in Stampler's trial.'

He read excerpts from William Danielson's description of the wounds that had killed Archbishop Richard Rushman ten years before:

'*DANIELSON: Body trauma, aeroembolism, cadaveric spasm, exsanguination, that's loss of blood. All could have caused death ... The primary cause, I believe was the throat wound ... It caused aeroembolism, which is the sudden exit of air from the lungs. This kind of wound is always fatal, in fact, death is usually instantaneous. ... And the wounds indicated a knowledge of surgical techniques.*'

Vail was beginning to react. He leaned forward in his chair, his cigarette smouldering, forgotten, between his fingers.

'Now listen t' the rest of Dr Fields's report,' St Claire said, and finished reading the autopsy:

'There was also evidence of mutilation. Both the victim's nipples and the clitoris were amputated and

221

placed in the victim's mouth. It appears that the wounds were accomplished by a person or persons with some surgical knowledge. Also the inscription C13.489 was printed with the victim's blood on the rear of the skull, 4.6 centimetres above the base of the skull and under the hairline. The weapon was determined to be a common carving knife with an eight-inch blade found on the premises and belonging to the victim . . .'

'She was also nine weeks pregnant,' St Claire added, almost as an afterthought.

Vail was staring into space. He did not say anything for almost a minute.

'Where's Stampler?' he finally asked.

'Up in Daisyland, still in maximum security,' said Stenner. 'Never had a visitor, never had a letter, never made a phone call.'

'In ten years?'

'In ten years,' Stenner said. 'I talked to the head of security, Bascott and the other executives were in conferences. He wouldn't tell me much, but he volunteered that.'

'There's somethin' else,' said St Claire. 'When I was finishing up the transcripts my eye caught somethin' I missed the first time 'round. Damn near jolted me outta m'chair when I saw it. It was when you was questionin' Stampler on the witness stand. Stampler says, "My girlfriend, Linda, and I decided to live together . . ." I thought, Maybe it's just a coincidence – two women named Linda, so . . .' St Claire selected one of the photos of Linda Balfour, a close-up of her head and shoulders, and handed it to Vail. 'She look familiar?'

Vail studied the photograph for several seconds. 'That's a horrible picture. I can't really—'

'I checked the records in Carbondale, where she and

her husband got married. Maiden name's Linda Gellerman, from Akron, Ohio.'

Vail looked up at St Claire and his memory suddenly was jolted back ten years.

A tiny waiflike creature, huddled in a yellow rain slicker, her fearful eyes peering up at him as she stood in the rain.

'Mr Vail?' her tiny voice asked.

He took her inside, gave her a Coke, and asked her about her boyfriend, Aaron Stampler.

'You think Aaron killed the bishop?'

'Doesn't everybody?'

'Were you there, Linda?'

'Where?'

'At the bishop's the night he was killed?'

'Of course not!'

'Then how do you know Aaron did it?'

'Well, because he was hiding in the church with the knife and all . . .'

'How do you know it wasn't Peter or Billy Jordan?'

'You know about that?'

'About what?'

'Nothing.'

'Linda, why did you come here?'

''Cause I can't help Aaron and I want you to stop looking for me.'

'Maybe you can help him.'

'How?'

'I need you to testify.'

'About what?'

'The Altar Boys.'

She panicked, backing away from him like a cornered animal, then running for the door. Vail caught her arm as she reached for the doorknob.

'I won't do that! I'll never admit that! I'll lie. I'll tell them it isn't true.'

223

'Linda, it may help for the jury to know what really went on. What the bishop made you do.'

'Don't you understand? He didn't make us do anything! After a while it was fun. We liked it!'

She had turned and run out the door and vanished into the dark, rainswept night. He never saw her again until a moment before when he looked at the picture of the dowdy housewife, sprawled in her living room, covered with blood.

'Linda Gellerman,' said Vail. 'Aaron Stampler's girl-friend.'

'I'm thinkin' maybe we got us a copycat on our hands here,' St Claire said.

'Except for one thing,' Stenner added.

Vail finished the thought for him. 'The Altar Boys.'

Stenner nodded.

'Who the hell're the Altar Boys?' St Claire asked. 'They were never mentioned in the trial.'

'That's right, they weren't,' said Vail.

'But whoever killed Linda Gellerman knew about them. Had to,' said Stenner.

'Who were they? What did they have to do with this?' St Claire asked.

Vail snuffed out his cigarette and went to the urn for a cup of coffee.

'You have to understand, ten years ago, Archbishop Richard Rushman was known as the Saint of the Lake-view Drive,' he began. 'He wasn't liked, he was revered. He was also one of the most powerful men in the state. There was as much Richelieu in him as there was John the Baptist; as much Machiavelli as Billy Budd. But to the average person on the street, to your average juror? He was a man who awed.

'Aaron Stampler came here from a squalid little town in Kentucky. He was a true anachronism, a kid with a genius IQ and an illiterate mother and father, living in abject poverty in the coalmining hills of western Kentucky. He had to sneak to his teacher's house to read books – his father wouldn't permit books in the house except for the Bible. His father also insisted that he work in the place he feared more than anything else in the world. The hole. Shaft number five – I can still remember him talking about it – the deep-pit mines. When he finally escaped that prison, he came here. Rushman met him, took him in at Saviour House, which was a home for runaways and homeless kids. Stampler and the bishop grew very close.

'Then Aaron got himself a girlfriend. They decided to live together. And that's where the story started getting fuzzy. Jane Venable contended that the bishop was upset because these two were living in sin, so he threw them out. They were living down on the wharves in a terrible warehouse called the Hollows – it was demolished years ago. The girlfriend left Sampler, and in anger and despair he went to the church and carved up the bishop like a Christmas goose.

'Our story? Stampler left voluntarily. There was never any dispute between him and the bishop. He was in the library, thought he heard arguing up in the bishop's apartment, went up to check. When he looked into the bedroom he sensed that there was somebody else there. Then he blacked out, went into what's called a fugue state – he did it quite often, particularly under stress – and the next thing he knew, he was hiding in a confessional with the murder weapon, soaked with the bishop's blood. The girlfriend was Linda Gellerman.'

'But that wasn't the real motive,' said Stenner.

'No, there was another motive, much darker – both Venable and I knew about it – but neither of us used it in the trial.'

'Which was?' Flaherty asked.

'The bishop was a paedophile. His victims were a group called the Altar Boys. The bishop would direct movies of the Altar Boys seducing a young lady. Then he'd turn off the camera and step in and do the girl, the boys, whatever suited him. Aaron Stampler was one of the Altar Boys. Linda was the girl.'

'Why didn't that come out in the trial?' Parver asked.

'Too risky. And Venable and I agreed to destroy the tapes when the trial was over,' said Vail.

'Why?'

'To protect the bishop's good name,' Stenner said.

'Christ, a paedophile?' St Claire said. 'Why protect him?'

'You weren't there,' Stenner offered. 'He was loved by everybody. Raised millions for charity every year. Incredibly powerful man.'

'And he was dead,' said Vail. 'The tape we both had was very risky. The bishop did not appear on it, it was just his voice. Too risky for either Venable or me to introduce it. It could've been construed by the jury as a desperation move and the backlash might've lost the case. Besides, I didn't need it. Our case was that Stampler suffered multiple personality disorder—'

'Split personality?' said Flaherty.

'A misnomer, but yes. Like Sybil. His *alter ego* was a madman who called himself Roy. Stampler was this sweet, almost naïve backwoods kid. Roy was a psychotic killer. When Stampler became agitated or was abused in some way, Roy was triggered. He came out and did the dirty work. Stampler was in a fugue state and didn't know what was going on.'

'So Roy was the other person in the room when the bishop was killed,' St Claire.

Vail nodded. 'Venable was cross-examining Aaron and she triggered Roy. He came out of the witness box like a skyrocket, tried to choke her right in the courtroom.'

'You set her up, Martin,' Stenner said.

'Did she say that?'

'I say it.'

'How do you figure?'

'You knew from taping Aaron all those weeks.'

'Knew what?' asked Parver.

'That hammering on those quotes in the books would cause the switch. You started in, then backed off the quotes. She took the bait, thought you were afraid to get into it, so she did.'

'But you never bought it?'

Stenner shook his head.

'You gave Abel a real hard time on the witness stand over that there point. The fugue state 'n' everything,' Harvey St Claire said with a smile.

'I don't remember it all that well,' Stenner said brusquely. 'Ten years does tricks to your memory.'

'How about these here Altar Boys?' St Claire asked.

'There were five of them. Linda and one of them ran. Two others were killed. There were no witnesses to corroborate Rushman's voice, that's why neither of us would touch it in the courtroom.'

'Killed?' Flaherty asked.

'By Stampler–Roy,' Stenner said. 'We all knew that, too. Venable figured she had Stampler, anyway, why risk trying him for three crimes when one would do.'

'After he was put away, it became moot,' Vail added. 'Part of the plea bargain was that I turned him up for all three homicides. It was an inclusive sentence.'

'There's one more thing,' Harvey St Claire said, interrupting Vail's reminiscence. 'Found it in the bishop's library. His books're in a special collection over to th' Newberry. I didn't have any trouble when I got to page 489. The passage was marked for me.'

'Was it recent?' Stenner asked. 'What I mean was, was it marked recently?'

'I imagine Okimoto could tell us. Looked t' me like it'd been there a while.'

'What was the message?' Vail asked.

'It's from *The Merchant of Venice*,' said St Claire:

> *'In law, what plea so tainted and corrupt*
> *But, being season'd with a gracious voice,*
> *Obscures the show of evil?'*

There was a minute or two of stone silence as Vail thought about the message. *'What plea so tainted and corrupt/But, being seasoned with a gracious voice,/ Obscures the show of evil.'*

It seemed obvious to Vail that the quote was directed at him. Was his defence of Stampler tainted? Corrupt? Did his defence obscure the show of evil? Was he just being paranoid? After the Stampler trial, Vail himself had considered the possibility that his clever tactics might have obscured the truth – what the Bard called 'the show of evil'. It had taunted him for months, forced him to appraise his career as a defence attorney, to ponder about the mobsters, drug dealers, cat burglars, and other miscreants who had been his stock-in-trade. In the past he had sometimes balanced the scales in his own mind – good versus evil, truth versus deceit – always tempered with the concept of reasonable doubt. But until now Vail had never given a moment's consideration to the question Shakespeare so eloquently posed to him: Had his voice been tainted and corrupt but seasoned with gracious and masterful conviction?

Thinking back, Vail realized that Stampler himself had raised the question in Vail's mind ten years before, as he was being led away to Daisyland; a devious comment, perhaps made in jest, that had goaded Vail for months. Eventually Vail had assumed the inevitable conclusion: It was his responsibility, as an officer of the court, to provide his client with the best defence possible, and that he always had done brilliantly. And so, eventually, Vail had discarded all these ideas as abstractions.

But not, as Vail now admitted to himself, until after they had influenced his decision to take the job as chief prosecutor.

Now, in a frightening *déjà vu*, Vail could make sense out of what was happening, for there was that one piece of the puzzle only he knew, a moment in time he had never shared with anyone, and never *could* share with anyone.

His thoughts were interrupted by the phone. Naomi stepped out of the office and answered it at her desk. She came back a moment later.

'It's for you, Harve. Buddy Harris at the IBI.'

'What the hell's Buddy want?' St Claire said, half aloud, as he left the office to take the call.

'Kind of an obscure message, that Shakespeare quote,' Stenner said while St Claire was gone.

'Yeah,' Vail answered. 'In the Rushman case, the messages always referred to the archbishop. Now who's he talking about?'

St Claire returned to Vail's office, his face clouded by a frown.

'We got another one.'

'What!' said Vail.

'Where?' asked Stenner.

'Hilltown, Missouri. About thirty miles outside of St Louis. A white, male, age twenty-six. UPD man, delivering a package to a private home, was cut six ways to Sunday. Harris says St Louis Homicide is handlin' the case and they're playin' it real tight. Don't wanna give up too much to the press yet. Buddy says he was talkin' to a cop in East St Louis this mornin' about a drug case, the cop mentions they got a butcher job across the river. So Buddy calls the St Louis PD and they didn't wanna talk about it. They finally told him this UPD delivery man got sliced and diced. Buddy says it sounds like a repeat of the Gideon case.'

'Did he tell them about Balfour?'

'Nope. Didn't tell 'em anythin'. Just listened.'

'Any name attached to this victim?'

'Ain't been released yet. Can't find a next a kin. Buddy says they're obviously riled up over it.'

'Well, surprise, surprise!' said Naomi.

Vail was leaning back in his chair without moving. He stared at Stenner without blinking, deep in thought. Finally he said, 'If Stampler's behind these killings, how does he *find* these people? Gideon, Illinois? Hilltown, Missouri? You can barely find these places on the map.'

'And if he is involved, how the hell's he doin' it from maximum security at the State Hospital?' said St Claire.

'Maybe Stampler isn't behind it,' Stenner suggested. 'Perhaps it is a copycat who found about the Altar Boys.'

'And waited ten years to move on it?' Vail said.

'Maybe he's lazy,' Flaherty said with a smile.

Vail leaned forward, put his elbows on the desk, clenched his hands, and leaned his chin on his fists. He stared at St Claire for several seconds.

'Harvey, I want you to grab the red-eye to St Louis first thing in the morning and get everything you can from St Louis Homicide.'

'I can't, boss, I'm in court in the morning. The Quarrles case.'

'Abel?'

'I got two depositions tomorrow.'

'I'm between engagements,' offered Flaherty.

'Okay, you're on. Naomi, book Dermott on the early-bird, arrange for a car at the airport. Dermott, call Buddy and get some names of people you can talk to.'

'Right.'

'Naomi, get me Bascott at Daisyland. I want him personally. I don't care if he's in a conference with God, I want him on the phone *now*.'

It took Naomi ten minutes to get the director of the state mental institution on the line. Vail had forgotten how disarmingly gentle his voice was.

'Mr Vail,' he said after the usual salutations, 'Dr Samuel Woodward has been handling the Stampler case

for the past, oh, eight years now, I guess. Uh . . .
Stampler . . . is his patient and I would prefer that you
speak to him directly if you have any questions
regarding – '

'What's Stampler's condition now?' Vail asked, interrupting Bascott.

'Once again, I prefer to – '

'Dr Bascott, I have a problem down here and I need
some questions answered. If Dr Woodward is the man to
talk to, then put him on the phone.'

'He's on vacation, fishing up in Wisconsin. He'll be
back tomorrow night. I'll have him call – '

'I'll be up there day after tomorrow, first thing,' Vail
said, and there was annoyance in his tone. 'Please arrange
for me to interview both Woodward and Stampler.'

'Mr Vail, you were, uh . . . Aaron's . . . lawyer. You
haven't even been to visit him in ten years. I don't see
that – '

'Day after tomorrow,' Vail repeated. 'I'll see him then.'
And he hung up. 'Damn it,' he said. 'I'm getting the
runaround from Bascott. Naomi, arrange for the county
plane to fly me up to Daisyland at eight o'clock day after
tomorrow.'

'Done.'

At six o'clock that night, Stenner appeared, as he always
did, at Vail's office door.

'Ready to wrap it up?'

'Yeah,' Vail said wearily. But before he could get up, the
phone rang. It was Paul Rainey.

'I can't put my finger on Jim Darby,' he said.

'What do you mean, you can't put your finger on him?'

'I was tied up in court all afternoon on a sentencing.
Didn't have time to call until an hour or so ago. He's
probably out with his pals. Give me until tomorrow
morning, I'll have him there.'

Vail hesitated for a few moments.

'I'm sure I can locate him, Marty, I've just been snowed under.'

'Okay, Paul. Nine A.M. If he's not here by then, I'll have the sheriff issue a fugitive warrant on him.'

'That's not necessary.'

'Paul, I'm trying to be fair. He could be on his way to Rio for all I know.'

'Hell, he doesn't know there's a warrant out on him. He's out raising hell somewhere. I'll have him there in the morning.'

'You accepted service, he's your responsibility. Have you thought any more about our conversation at lunch?'

'I haven't even talked to him yet,' Rainey said, but there was a note of urgency in his voice.

'See you in the morning,' Vail said before he cradled the phone. He looked up at Stenner. 'We have a murder-one warrant out against James Darby and Rainey sounds a little panicky. If he doesn't deliver Darby by nine A.M., I want you to take two of your best men and a man from the sheriff's department, find Darby, and bring him in.'

Stenner nodded, but he looked pensive.

'What's bothering you?' Vail asked.

'Poppy Palmer,' Stenner said.

'What about her?'

'I was just thinking, maybe she panicked. Maybe . . .' He let the sentence hang ominously in the air.

'You have a morbid imagination, Abel.'

'I've been a cop for almost twenty-five years,' Stenner said. 'It comes with the territory.'

'What do you want to do?'

'Go out there and put some heat on, see if we can get a line on her. Darby's facing murder one and she's a key witness.'

'How about your depositions tomorrow?'

'I'll work around them.'

Vail thought for a moment and nodded. 'Okay,' he said. 'She's all yours. Go find them both.'

Twenty

The St Louis Homicide Division was almost devoid of people when Flaherty arrived at the downtown office, a stuffy room jammed with desks, telephones, file cabinets, and computers. Only two detectives were in the room: Oscar Gilanti, captain of the division, who was heading the investigation, and Sgt. Ed Nicholson, an old-timer who had the dignified demeanour and conservative look of an FBI agent.

The two detectives were more pleasant than Flaherty had expected. The captain was a short box of a man, bald except for a fringe of jet-black hair that curled around his ears. He had deep circles under his eyes, his cheeks were dark with the shadows of a two-day beard, and his suit looked like he had slept in it, which he probably had. His deep voice was raspy from lack of sleep.

'I gotta get back out to the scene,' he growled to Flaherty. 'I'm giving you Sergeant Nicholson here fer the day. Knows as much as anybody else about this mess. What was yer name again?'

'Dermott Flaherty.'

'Okay, Dermott, you wanna go anywhere, see anything, Nick'll drive yuh. I pulled a package for yuh – pictures, preliminary reports, all that shit. Autopsy won't be up probably till tomorra. We can fax it to yuh, yuh need it.'

'I can't thank you enough, Captain.'

'Hell, you know anything, we'd appreciate it. We can use all the help we can get on this one. Fuckin' nightmare.'

'I can imagine.'

'I'll be out at the scene, Nick. If Dermott here wants to come out, bring him along.'

'Right.'

The sergeant, obviously a man of habit, asked pleasantly if he had a weapon.

Flaherty smiled. 'I'm an assistant DA, Sergeant,' he said. 'Things haven't got *that* bad yet.'

The cop chuckled. He was an old pro, tall, very straight-standing, with a tanned and leathery face, gentle, alert eyes, and blondish hair turning grey. Nicholson unlocked his desk drawer and took out his 9mm H&K and slipped it into a holster on his belt. He also wore his badge pinned to his belt like an old western sheriff. He slid a thick file folder across the desk to Flaherty.

'You might take a look at this picture first, give you a point of reference. Hilltown's about thirty miles down the pike, off to the northeast of US 44. The Spier place is a couple miles out of town, little frame house, one storey, two bedrooms, kitchen, den, and big bathroom, that's about it. Sets back in the trees.'

He had picked out an aerial photo showing the house at the end of a quarter mile of dirt road that wound through scrub pines and saw grass. Behind it, the road connected with another country road that ended at a lake.

'Calvin Spier and his wife – they own the place – are out in Las Vegas. Weren't due back until the middle of next week, but they're coming back now.'

'Do the Spiers know him?' Flaherty asked.

'Spier says no. Want to go out to the scene? It's a thirty-minute drive' – he winked – 'if I put on the flasher.'

Flaherty nodded and said, 'You're the boss.'

The drive was pleasant despite a misting rain. Nicholson, a social creature, spoke in a quiet, authoritative voice, filling Flaherty in on the prologue to the killing while the young prosecutor made a cursory examination of the package. The pictures confirmed his suspicion that this killing was a repeat of the Balfour/Gellerman murder.

'Fellow owns a quick shop down the road from the road into the Spiers' place, lives behind it. He found him,' Nicholson said. 'Noticed the UPD truck through the trees when he got up yesterday morning. When it was still there at lunchtime, he strolled over to take a look. Front door was standing open. Then he heard the flies. Damn near had a heart attack when he saw that young guy in there all carved up like that. Plus he'd been dead about sixteen hours.'

'What's the victim's name?' asked Flaherty.

'Alexander Lincoln,' Nicholson answered. 'They called him Lex.'

Alex Lincoln, Flaherty thought. *The last of the Altar Boys.*

Except one. Aaron Stampler.

Rain dripped off the yellow crime ribbons that had been wrapped around a wide perimeter of the house when they got there. A sheriff's car was parked beside the driveway. A cop waved them through. Several police cars were parked single file as they approached the house.

'We're going to have to run for it,' Nicholson said, turning up the collar of his suit coat. The two men got out of the car and ran through the rain to the small porch that spanned the front of the house. Several detectives in yellow rain slickers stood under the roof. They nodded as Nicholson and Flaherty ducked under the eaves.

'It's a bitch, Nick,' one of the cops said. 'This rain has washed out footprints, tyre tracks, everything. The old man's a bear.'

Nicholson and Flaherty stood just inside the front door for a few moments. A plainclothes detective was standing beside the door jotting a note to himself in a small notebook.

'Hi, Nick,' he said. 'What a mess, huh.'

'That it is. Ray Jensen, this is Dermott Flaherty. He's a prosecutor with the Chicago DA's office.'

Jensen offered his hand. 'What brings you out here?' he asked.

'We have a thing working up in Chicago. It's a long shot, but there could be a tie-in.'

'Be a nice break for us if we could get some kind of a lead,' said Jensen. 'Right now we're sucking air.'

A hallway led to the rear of the house. Flaherty could see white chalk lines marking where the victim's legs had protruded into the hall. He held a shot of the interior of the house taken from the front door out in front of him. Lincoln's legs could be seen protruding from the door halfway down the hall.

'The Spiers left a light on in the living room,' said Jensen. 'The rest of the place was dark. My guess is the killer called Lincoln back there to do his dirty work.'

They walked past a living room that was cluttered with kewpie dolls, embroidered pillows, and dozens of photographs. The furniture was covered with plastic sheets. Flaherty smelled the acid-sweet odour of blood and death.

The death room was a small den with a fireplace. Sliding glass doors led from the room to an enclosed porch on the side of the house. Another door led into the kitchen, which dominated the rear of the place. There was blood everywhere: on the walls, the ceiling, the carpet. Flaherty found a full-length shot of the corpse. Lincoln lay on his side, his head askew. A terrible wound had almost severed his head. His mouth gaped open like that of a dead fish. The wounds were numerous and awesome. Lincoln's pants were pulled down around his knees and he had been emasculated. The results of the brutal amputation had been stuffed in his mouth.

Flaherty flipped through the pictures, found a close-up of the rear of Lincoln's head.

There it was: 'R41.102.' Flaherty showed no emotion. He kept flipping the photographs.

'How'd he get in? The killer, I mean?' he asked.

'Broke a window in back,' Jensen said. 'The way we figure it, he cased the place very carefully. Knew the back road to the lake would be abandoned this time of year, particularly after dark. He came in the back way, pulled on down to the house, and broke in through the sliding glass door leading from the little deck in the back. Here's what's interesting. It rained the night before, but there were no footprints in the house and the porch was hosed down so there were no footprints out there either. What I think, the perp took off his shoes when he came in. Then when he left he hosed off the deck so there weren't any out there, either. Probably used the hose to wash off the victim's blood, too. I mean, you look at the pictures of Lincoln, the perp had to be covered with blood.'

'Yeah, somebody did some homework on this,' Flaherty said, still flipping through the photographs. 'Whoever set up the victim knew Spier and his wife were away. Little town like this — '

'Was in the *Post-Dispatch*,' said Nicholson.

'What was?'

'About Spier and his wife going out to Vegas. A story in the people section. He drives a semi, won a trip for ten years' service without a citation or mishap.'

'How about the package?'

'Mailed from over in East St Louis, one of those wrap-and-send places,' Jensen offered. 'During lunch hour. Place was jammed, nobody remembers a damn thing about who posted it. Return name and address is a phony.'

Flaherty looked at the receipt slip. On the line that read 'sender' was the name M. Lafferty.

'Know an M. Lafferty?' the detective asked.

'Nope,' Flaherty said. 'The victim picked it up himself, huh?'

'Yeah. Was bellyaching about having to run over there after working hours and then drive down here and back after dark.'

'What about this . . . Lex Lincoln? Anything on him?'

'Young guy, twenty-six, been workin' at UPD since he moved here from Minneapolis two years ago.'

'Minneapolis? Anything there?'

'Nothing on him. No sheet. His boss – fellow named Josh Pringle – says he's a good worker, always on time, kind of a joker. No enemies we've uncovered so far. Big with the ladies – had two dates the night he was killed.'

'Maybe they ganged up on him,' Flaherty said with a smile.

The old pro laughed. 'Way I heard it, they were both really torn up over it.'

'Was anything taken?' Flaherty asked.

'Nothing from the house that we can determine,' Jensen answered. 'The Spiers will be able to tell us, but I think we can rule out robbery. This was an ambush. The only thing we know was taken was Lincoln's belt buckle.'

'His belt buckle?'

'Yes. One of a kind – an American flag, embossed on brass,' said Nicholson. 'It was cut off his belt. There's one other thing. Look here at this photo, on the back of Lincoln's head, it's written in blood. R41.102. That mean anything to you?'

Before he could answer, Gilanti came back in the house, shaking rain off his coat. He stomped down the hall, his face bunched up in a scowl, talking aloud to himself as he approached Flaherty, Jensen, and Nicholson.

'We don't have a description of the perp, we don't have a description of the vehicle, we don't have shit. And whoever done this job's been on the run for eighteen to twenty goddamn hours.' He stopped at the three men, looked down at the floor with disgust. 'Hell, the son of a bitch could be halfway to New York by now.'

Jensen said, 'We're talking to everybody in town and

in the area. We're checking all pass-through vehicles between seven and ten P.M. We're checking filling stations up and down 44. Looking for anybody suspicious.'

'Christ, that's half the world. We'll be getting calls for the next year with that description.'

'Maybe the ME'll come up with something,' said Nicholson. 'Blood, fibres, DNA sample, something.'

'Yeah, sure. And Little Bo Beep'll give us all a blow job if we're good boys. What we got is *nothing*! We don't know what or who the hell we're looking for or where he or she is going. Christ, the killer could be standing out there in the rain, looking across the ribbons, we wouldn't have a clue.'

Then he looked at Flaherty and shrugged.

'Got any ideas, Dermott?'

Flaherty gave him a lazy smile. 'I convict 'em, Captain, I'm not much at catching 'em.'

'Well, sorry I disturbed you boys. Go back to whatever you were doin'.' Gilanti moved away, then looked back at Flaherty. 'You know anything, any *fuckin'* thing at all that'll help us, Dermott, I'll name my next kid after you, even if it's a girl.'

'Thanks for your assistance, Captain.'

'Yeah, sure,' Gilanti said, and went out into the rain.

'What was in the box Lincoln delivered?' Flaherty asked Jensen.

'That's the sickest thing of all,' said Jensen. 'Just this, wrapped in a lot of tissue paper.'

Flaherty looked at the object and a sudden chill rippled up his backbone.

Chief Hiram Young was just sitting down to his evening meal when the phone rang. 'Damn,' he grumbled under his breath as he snatched up the phone. 'Abe Green's dog's probably raising cain in somebody's yard. Hello!'

'Chief Hiram Young?'

'Yes, sir,' Young answered sternly.

'Sir, my name's Dermott Flaherty. I'm an assistant DA up in Chicago.'

'I've already talked to your people. How many times I have to tell you—'

'Excuse me, sir. I just have one question.'

'I'm just settin' down t' dinner.'

'This will only take a minute. Was anything taken from the Balfour home when Linda Balfour was murdered?'

'I already told you people, robbery was not the motive.'

'I'm not talking about robbery, Chief. I'm talking about some little insignificant thing. Nothing that would be important to anyone else.'

There was a long pause. Young cradled the phone between his shoulder and jaw as he spread jam on a hot biscuit.

'Really wasn't anything,' Young said.

'What was it?'

'A stuffed fish.'

'You mean, like a fish mounted on the wall?'

'No, a little stuffed dolphin. It had ST SIMONS ISLAND, GA. printed on the side. George bought it for Linda when they were on their honeymoon.'

'Where was it? What I mean is, was it in the room where she was murdered?'

'Yes. On the mantelpiece.'

'Same room as the murder?'

'That's what I just said.'

'Thank you, sir. I appreciate your help. Goodbye.'

Young slammed down the phone.

'Something wrong, honey?' his wife asked.

'Just some big-shot DA up in Chicago tryin' to mess in our business,' he said, and returned to his dinner.

'Abel? I'm at the airport in St Louis,' Flaherty told Stenner. 'Got to hurry, my plane's loading. I'll be there at seven-oh-five.'

'I'll pick you up. Get anything?'

'A lot. I think we need to talk to Martin and Jane Venable tonight. It's the same perp, no question about it. Victim even has the symbol on the back of his head. Let me give it to you, maybe Harve can run over to the library and check it out. Got a pencil?'

'Yes.'

'It's R41.102.'

'R41.102,' Stenner repeated. 'We'll get on it right away.'

'Good. See you at seven.'

Twenty-one

Jane Venable leaned over the spaghetti pot and, pursing her lips, sucked a tiny sample of the olio off a wooden spoon. *Pretty good*, she thought, and sprinkled a little more salt in it. She looked over at the table. Earlier in the day the florist had brought an enormous arrangement of flowers with a simple note: 'These cannot compare to your beauty. Marty.'

For the first time in years, Jane felt she was beginning to have a new life outside of her office. She had made a fortune, but it had cost her any semblance of a personal life. Now, in just a few days, that had changed. She stared at the flowers and wondered silently, *My God, am I falling in love with this man?* And just as quickly she dispelled the idea. *It's just a flirtation, don't make more of it than it is.*

'I didn't think you really cooked in this chef's fantasy,' said Vail. 'Where'd you learn to cook Italian spaghetti? You're not Italian.'

'My mother was. Born in Florence. She was a translator at the Nuremberg trials when she was eighteen.'

'Ahhh, so that's where that tough streak came from.'

'My father was no slouch, either. He was a government attorney at the trials – that's where they met. And after that a federal prosecutor for fifteen years.'

'What did he think when you quit prosecuting and went private?'

'He was all for it. He said ten years was enough unless I wanted to move up to attorney general or governor. I didn't need that kind of heat.'

'Who does? There's damn little truth in politics.'

'I don't know,' she said. 'When I was a prosecutor I

honestly believed it was all about truth and justice and all that crap.'

'I repeat, there's damn little truth in politics, Janie.'

'You know what they say, truth is perception.'

'No, truth is the *jury's* perception,' Vail corrected.

'Does it ever bother you?' she asked. 'About winning?'

'What do you mean?'

'Some people say we're both obsessed with winning.'

'It's all point of view. Listen, when I was a young lawyer I defended a kid for ripping off a grocery store. The key piece of evidence was a felt hat. The prosecutor claimed my boy dropped it running out of the store. I tore up the prosecution, proved it couldn't be his hat, ate up the eyewitnesses, turned an open-and-shut case into a rout. After he was acquitted, the kid turns to me and says, "Can I have my hat back now?" It bothered me so much that one night I was having dinner with a judge – who later became one of my best friends – and I told him what had happened. Know what he said? "It wasn't your problem, it was the prosecutor's. Pass the butter, please." '

She laughed softly. 'So what's the lesson, Vail?'

Vail took a sip of wine and chuckled. 'Nobody ever said life is fair – I guess that's the lesson, if there is one.'

'That's a cynical response, Counsellor.'

'There are no guarantees. We give it the best we got no matter how good or bad the competition is. It isn't about winning anymore, it's about doing the best you can.'

'I suppose we could practise euthanasia on all the bad lawyers in the world and try to even the playing field. That's the only way we'll ever approach true justice in the courtroom. Does it ever bother you, Martin? When you *know* the opposition is incompetent?'

'Nope, it makes the job that much easier. You're not going through one of those guilt trips because you're successful, are you?'

'No,' she said, but there was a hint of doubt in her tone.

'Janie, in the years you were a prosecutor, did you ever try someone you thought was innocent?'

She was shocked by the question. 'Of course not!' she answered.

'Have you ever defended someone you thought was guilty?'

She hesitated for a long time. 'I never ask,' she said finally.

He held out his hands. 'See, point of view. I rest my case.' He lit a cigarette and leaned back in his chair. He watched her silently for a while.

'I think it's the Stoddard case,' he said.

'What do you mean?'

'That's what all this yak-yak is about, the Stoddard case. You're having a problem.'

'There's something wrong with the picture. Something doesn't make sense. This woman is forbidding me to defend her and I don't know why.'

'We probably shouldn't even be discussing this. I'm sorry I brought it up.'

'We both want to know what really happened that night in Delaney's penthouse, don't we?' she said.

'We know what happened.'

A silence fell over the table, broken finally when Venable sighed. 'You're right, we shouldn't be talking about it.'

'I'll make a deal with you. When we're together, let's keep the law books on the shelf.'

She smiled and raised her glass. 'Sounds good to me,' she said. She reached out with her other hand and stroked his cheek. He got up and moved to her side of the table and cupped her face in his hands, kissing her softly on the lips.

'How about dessert,' she whispered between kisses.

'Later.'

The phone rang.

'Let it ring,' Jane said, her eyes closed, her tongue tapping his.

The machine came on. Vail recognized the familiar voice.

'Ms Venable, this is Abel Stenner. Please forgive me for bothering you at home, but it's imperative we locate Martin Vail. . . .'

'Oh, Jesus,' he moaned.

'When you get this message, if you know his whereabouts – '

'Talk about bringing the office home with you,' she said.

Vail crossed to the corner of the kitchen counter and answered the portable phone. 'Yes, Abel.' He did not try to hide his exasperation.

'Hate to bother you, Martin, but Flaherty's back. We need to talk.'

'What, *now*?'

'Yes, sir. And I think it's time to bring Jane Venable into it.'

'Why?'

'You'll understand when we get there. I'd like to bring Harve and Dermott with me. I know it's an imposition, but it's very important.'

'Just a minute.' He held his hand over the mouthpiece. 'I'm sorry to bring my business into your home, Janie, but Abel says he needs to talk to us both immediately.'

'Both of us? What's the problem?'

He hesitated for a moment, then said, 'It concerns Aaron Stampler.'

'Oh my God,' she said, her face registering a combination of curiosity and shock. Then: 'Of course.'

'Come on,' Vail said, and hung up.

'What's this about, Martin?'

Martin told Jane about the Balfour and Missouri murders and their significance. She listened without a word,

245

her eyes growing larger as he slowly described the details of the Balfour murder.

'It's the exact MO down to the bloody references on the backs of their heads. Harvey's getting the quotes from Rushman's books, which are now in the Newberry.'

'How about Stampler?' was her first question.

'Still in max security Daisyland. As far as we know, he hasn't had any contact with the outside world for ten years.'

'Is it a copycat killer?'

Vail shrugged. 'Could be. A copycat killer could've discovered some of the quotes marked in those books. But *not* the part that Linda Gellerman played in the murders, that was never revealed in court. Did you ever show the tape to anyone?'

'Of course not. I erased it the day after the trial. How about you?'

'No. But the details *were* on the tapes Molly Arrington made during her interviews with Stampler.'

'And where are they?'

'Probably in evidence storage at the warehouse.'

'After all these years . . .' Jane said.

'Yeah.' Vail nodded. 'After all these years.'

His face got very serious. 'Listen, there's something I need to get off my chest. I've never told anybody this before. It's in the nature of client-lawyer confidentiality.'

'What is it?' she asked, obviously concerned.

'Look, I spent a couple of months setting up the perfect defence for Stampler. Multiple personality disorder. Aaron was the innocent genius-boy, Roy was the evil twin doing the bad stuff. It worked. But that day, on the way out of the courtroom, Aaron – *Aaron*, not Roy, and I could tell the difference – Aaron turned to me with this funny, almost taunting, smile and said, 'Suppose there never was an Aaron.' And he laughed as they took him away to Daisyland.'

'Oh, come on, it was probably his sick way of joking,' she said with a shrug.

'Maybe. But what if he wasn't kidding? What if it was all a con job?'

'Come on, Martin, you were just lecturing me about having an attack of conscience. Did you think he was faking?'

'No. Nor did the psychiatrist, Molly Arrington.'

'Then why worry about it? Besides, you can't tell anyone that. It *is* a confidential remark made by your client. You could be disbarred if you went public with it.'

'What if he is directing these killings in some way?'

'That's pure hunch, Counsellor. Based on incredibly circumstantial evidence. You need a lot more to go on than a chance remark, some circumstance, and an attack of conscience. Besides, you just told me he's in maximum security at Daisyland. Hasn't had any contact with the outside world in all these years. How could he do it?'

Vail shook his head. 'I have no idea,' he said.

'I just remembered something sweet, old Jack Yancey told me once. He said when he was a young lawyer he found out during the course of a murder trial that his client was guilty. He went to the judge and wanted to quit and the judge said no way, it would cause a mistrial and make a retrial impossible. Besides, it was confidential between Jack and his client. He was told to do the best he could and he did. He won the case, for a change, and his client took a hike.'

'What did Yancey think about that?'

'All he said was "Justice can't win every time." So forget it, Counsellor.' She smiled and stroked his cheek.

Flaherty, St Claire, and Stenner arrived a minute or so later, ending the conversation. They were properly apologetic.

'Good to see you again, Abel.' Jane smiled and offered her hand. 'It's been a long time.'

'Read about you a lot,' he said.

'This is Harve St Claire and Dermott Flaherty,' Vail said, completing the introductions. They moved the dishes off the dining room table and shoved the flowers back to make room for Flaherty's package.

'Nice flowers,' Flaherty said, taking the reports and photographs from his shoulder bag. 'Your birthday?'

Jane smiled. 'Nope' was all she said.

'Have you filled Ms Venable in, Marty?' Stenner asked.

'Up to Dermott leaving for St Louis. What've you got?'

'Okay,' Flaherty began. 'First, there's no question in my mind that it's the same killer. Same MO as the Balfour kill.' He spread some of the photos of Lincoln on the table. 'Same variety of stab wounds, same mutilation we had with the male victims ten years ago. The messages on the backs of the heads . . .'

He hesitated for a moment and Vail looked at him and said, 'Yeah? Go on.'

'The victim was Alexander Lincoln.'

Vail was surprised, although later he felt foolish that he hadn't guessed it sooner. 'The last of the Altar Boys,' he said.

''Cept fer Aaron Stampler,' St Claire said.

'Could there be more than one person involved?' asked Jane.

'I think this answers that question,' Flaherty answered. 'This was in the box Alex Lincoln was delivering when he was murdered.'

He handed a Polaroid photograph to Vail, who looked at it and whispered, 'Jesus!' Jane took it from him and stared at it with disgust. It was a photograph of the bloody remains of Linda Balfour, her terrified eyes staring sightlessly at the ceiling.

'My God, who *is* this?' she asked.

'Linda Gellerman Balfour,' said Flaherty. 'Obviously taken immediately after the killer finished his work. You can actually see the blood spurting from the neck wound.'

'So he or she *wants* us to know.'

'That's right, ma'am. What we got here's a bona fidey serial killer at work.'

'I want a twenty-four-hour guard on Jane starting right now,' Vail said.

'Y'think he'll be after her?' St Claire asked.

'Who the hell knows? He's cleaned out the Altar Boys, it seems logical he'll go after the principals in the trial next. I'll spend the night here for the time being. I can sleep in the guest room. That okay with you, Jane?' Vail's question was casual enough. Stenner didn't say a word. He leaned over and smelled the flowers, a move that did not go unnoticed by the rest of them.

'Whatever you feel is appropriate,' Jane said innocently.

'It will certainly solve the logistical problem,' said Stenner. 'I can pick you both up in the morning and take you to work. We'll need two men assigned outside from nightfall until I come by in the morning, one in front, one in back.'

'I'd suggest a man inside the house during the day, too, just in case the killer resorts to an invasion,' said Flaherty.

'Good idea,' Vail said.

'Might not hurt to have a man in your digs, too, Marty,' added St Claire. 'Just in case this here killer decides to lay in wait there. Point is, it'd be nice to catch the son-bitch – excuse my French, ma'am – before he tries anything. Ambush him, so t'speak.'

'Anybody else?' Vail asked.

'Shoat?' suggested Stenner.

'He's on the state supreme court now. Seems like a long shot,' said Vail. 'Warn him and let him take appropriate action if he chooses to.'

'We may as well prepare ourselves,' said Stenner. 'Some people are going to think we're crazy.'

'Let them,' said Vail.

'How about the press?' asked Flaherty.

Vail scratched his jaw for a moment. 'Just a matter of time before they put it all together. But let's not give them any help.'

'Let's look at everything we know so far,' Stenner said.

St Claire looked at Jane and said, 'The first message was the quote from *The Merchant of Venice*: And here's the latest message from the killer.' He took out his notebook and flipped through the pages. 'It's from *Hamlet*, first act, scene five:

'I could a tale unfold whose lightest word
Would harrow up thy soul, freeze thy young blood,
Make thy two eyes, like stars, start from their spheres,
Thy knotted and combined locks to part,
And each particular hair stand on end,
Like quills upon the fearful porpentine.'

Nobody responded for a few moments, letting it sink in.

'Well, he's got classical taste, I'll say that for him,' said Jane. 'As I recall, ten years ago he quoted Hawthorne and Jefferson; now it's Thoreau and Shakespeare.'

'He's already told some hair-raising tales,' Vail said.

He suddenly remembered the tapes of Molly Arrington's interviews with Aaron/Roy. He was a storyteller, all right, in either persona. He remembered the angelic Aaron, describing an early experience in his peculiar Kentucky accent.

'When I was – like maybe seven r'eight? – we had this preacher, Josiah Shackles. Big, tall man, skinny as a pole with this long black beard down t'his chest and angry eyes – like the picture y'see in history books, y'know, of John Brown when they had him cornered at Harper's Ferry? Have you seen that picture, his eyes just piercin' through you? Reverend Shackles were like that. Fire in his eyes. He didn't believe in redemption. You did one thing wrong, one thing! You told one simple lie, and you

were hellbound. He'ud stare down at me. "Look at me, boy," he'd say, and his voice were like thunder, and I'd look up at him, was like lookin' up at a mountain, and he'ud slam his finger down hard towards th'ground and say, "Yer goin' t'hell, boy!" And I believed't at th'time, I sure did. Reverend Shackles put that fear in me. Thair was no redemptionr'forgiveness in Reverend Shackles' Bible.'

Then Vail remembered something else, the images slowly seeping from his memory. It was the first time Roy had appeared during a taped interview with Molly Arrington. Aaron was off-camera and Molly was checking her notes. Suddenly she looked up. He remembered her telling him later that it had been as if all the air had been sucked out of the room. She gasped for breath. And then a shadow appeared on the wall behind her and a hand reached out and covered hers and a strange voice, a sibilant whisper, a hiss with an edge to it, an inch or two from her ear, said, 'He'll lie to you.' He was leaning forward, only a few inches from her face. But this was not Aaron. He had changed. He looked five years older. His features had become obdurate, arrogant, rigid; his eyes intense, almost feral, lighter in colour, and glistening with desire; his lips seemed thicker and were curled back in a licentious smile. 'Surprise,' he whispered, and suddenly his hand swept down and grabbed her by the throat and squeezed, his fingers digging deeply into her flesh. 'You can't scream, so don't even try.' He smiled. 'See this hand? I could twist this hand and break your neck. *Pop!* Just like that.'

More chilling moments came back in a rush to Vail: Roy, finishing the Shackles story, no longer speaking in Aaron's curious west Kentucky patois, but in the flat, Chicago street accent of Roy, Aaron's psychopathic *alter ego*, although both were compelling storytellers.

'We were up at a place called East Gorge See. Highest place around there. It's this rock that sticks out over the

ridge and it's straight down, maybe four hundred, five hundred feet, into East Gorge. You can see forever up there. Shackles used to go up there and he'd stand on the edge of the See, and he'd deliver sermons. Top of his fucking lungs, screaming about hellfire and damnation, and it would echo out and back, out and back. Over and over. He'd take Aaron up there all the time. That was the first time I ever came out. Up there. I had enough. He drags Aaron along, points down over the edge, tells him that's what it's gonna be like when he goes to hell, like falling off that cliff, and Aaron's petrified and then he grabs Aaron and shoves him down on his knees and starts going at him, like he was warming up before he started sermonizing. And when he started it was all that hate and hellfire and damnation, and all of it was aimed right at Aaron. So we ran off and hid in the woods watching him strutting around, talking to himself. Then he turns and walks back out to the cliff and he starts in again, yelling about how Aaron is hell-bound, and how rotten he is. I sneaked down on him. Hell, it was easy. He was yelling so loud he didn't even hear me. I picked up this piece of busted tree limb and I walked up behind him, jammed it in the middle of his back, and shoved. He went right over. Wheee. I couldn't tell when he stopped sermonizing and started screaming, but I watched him hit on the incline at the bottom. I didn't want to miss that. He rolled down to the bottom and all this shale poured down on top of him – what was left of him. It was wild. All that shale buried him on the spot.'

Vail should have known then, listening to that story. He should have known. . . .

And certainly later, when Roy had described the night Archbishop Richard Rushman was slaughtered.

'Aaron was by the door to the bedroom and then whoosh, it's like the hand of God reaches down inside him and

gives a giant tug and he turns inside out, and bingo, there I am. I had to take over at that point, he would have really screwed it up. I was thinking to myself, maybe this time he'll go through with it, but forget that. Not a chance. I hustled down the hall to the kitchen and checked the kitchen door. It was unlocked. I went outside on the landing and checked around and the place was deserted. I went back inside, took off my sneakers, and then got a Yoo-Hoo out of the refrigerator and drank it. My heart was beatin' so hard I thought it was going to break one of my ribs and the drink calmed me down. I opened the knife drawer and checked them out. The thick carving knife was perfect. Be like carving a turkey on Thanksgiving. I checked it and it was like a razor. I nicked my finger and sucked on it until the bleeding stopped. Then I went down the hall to the bedroom. He had the music way up. Ode to Joy. I could picture him standing in the bedroom directing that air orchestra of his. Shoulda been a goddamn orchestra conductor, maybe we never would've met him. That's just what he was doing. He had candles burning -- cleaning the air, he called it – some kind of incense. His ring was lying on the table beside the bed. He always took his ring off before he took a shower. He left his watch on, I guess it was waterproof, but he took his ring off. Make sense out of that. So there he stood, the fucking saint of the city. His naked Holiness, conducting that imaginary band of angels. The music was building. I thought, Now it's your turn. So I went over and got the ring and put it on. His Excellency was out of it. Arms flailing around, eyes closed, unaware. I just walked up behind him and tapped him on the shoulder with the knife and he turns around and I thought his eyes were going to pop out of his head when he saw the knife. He got the message real fast. I held out the hand with the ring on it and pointed the knife at it and he begins to smile. So I jabbed the knife towards the carpet and that wiped the smile off his face.

He got down on his knees and I wiggled that ring finger under his nose. The bishop slowly leaned forward to kiss the ring and I pulled away my hand and I swung that knife back with both hands and when he looked up, whack, I swung at his throat. I yelled "Forgive me, Father!" but I was laughing in his face when I said it. He moved and I didn't catch him in the throat, the knife caught his shoulder and damn near chopped the whole thing off. He screamed and held out his hands. I don't know how he even raised up that one, but he did. I started chopping on him, but I kept hitting his hands and arms. Then I cut his throat, switched and swung the knife up underhand right into his chest. It was a perfect hit. Didn't hit any ribs, just went right in to the hilt and he went, "Oh," like that, and he fell straight back and the knife pulled out of my hand. I had to put my foot on his chest to get it out. Then I took that big swipe at his neck. I couldn't stop. It was like free games on a pinball machine. Blood was flying everywhere. I know every cut I made, they were all perfect. Thirty-six stab wounds, twelve incised, seventeen cuts, and one beautiful amputation. I counted every one.'

'Oh yeah,' Vail sighed, half aloud, 'Stampler certainly can tell some stores that will make – how did Shakespeare put it? – "each particular hair stand on end like the quills of a porcupine"?'

'Close enough,' said St Claire. 'Question is, who's he talkin' to? Martin? Jane? I mean, who's this here serial killer leavin' messages fer, anyways?'

'Stampler was never a serial killer,' said Stenner. He ticked off his points on his fingers. 'He didn't pick his victims at random, he hid the crimes, he didn't collect what are known as totems – trophies from the scene of the murder.'

Vail nodded in agreement. 'When you look back at Stampler's killing spree, which lasted almost ten years, all the victims were individuals whom he thought had done him harm – and, arguably, they did. Shackles, the born-again madman, tossed over a cliff – the body was never found; his brother and ex-girlfriend, made to look like an accident; the hospital attendant in Louisville, cremated and the ashes thrown away.'

'Then you have Rushman, Peter Holloway, and Billy Jordan,' said Stenner. 'That's when he started leaving symbols. Following a specific MO'

'But he didn't hide the bodies and he didn't take totems,' said Flaherty. 'This new killer, he follows the MO to the letter, *but* he does remove items from the victim. Linda Balfour had a stuffed dolphin. It's missing. Same with Alex Lincoln's belt buckle. And the victims were meant to be found. So there are variables here.'

'So what yer sayin', this here new fella *is* a serial killer,' said St Claire.

'Enjoys it,' Stenner offered. 'Gets off on the killing. Aaron, Roy, whichever, killed for personal reasons. Anger, revenge, getting even for past hurts. This new one, he's killing for motive *and* the joy of it.'

'And Stampler's providing the motive,' said Flaherty.

'You don't think Roy enjoyed it? He certainly enjoyed describing the murders,' said Vail.

'But he had a specific motive fer everyone he killed,' said St Claire.

'These last two were specific victims,' said Flaherty.

'Not *his* victims, Stampler's victims,' said Jane.

'If Stampler's figgered out a way to trigger this here killer, what we got, we got a killer enjoys the killin' and Stampler providin' the victims,' said St Claire.

'Maybe it isn't that. Maybe it is a copycat killer. There was a composite tape of all Molly's interviews. It was the tape that was only shown in Shoat's chambers – to Jane and the judge.'

'A moment I'm not likely to *ever* forget,' she interjected.

'That tape is in evidence storage. I never got it out. Maybe somebody stumbled across it, maybe the tape is the trigger. The whole story's on that one tape.'

St Claire sighed. 'Well, here I go back to the warehouse. Talk about the needle in the ol' hay stack.'

'I'm guessing, sooner or later, Mr X is going to start picking his own prey,' Vail said.

'I don't know,' said Jane. 'Stampler could still have a few more victims on his list – you, me, Shoat. . . . Maybe that's our edge.'

'What do you mean?' Flaherty asked.

'She means he's going to go after the other principals in the trial,' Stenner answered softly. 'Jane, Martin, Shoat . . .'

'Include yourself,' Vail said to Stenner. 'You were a powerful witness.'

'Well, it isn't our case,' said Stenner. 'Gideon police are ignoring it. St Louis has juris over the Lincoln murder.'

'So the question is, who's he gonna hit next?' St Claire said.

'And where?' said Flaherty.

'And how in God's name did he *find* these people?' Jane asked. 'Gideon, Illinois? Wherever, Missouri? How did he track them down?'

'And if Stampler is involved, how the hell is he doing it?' Flaherty said.

'Hell, maybe we'll get lucky,' said St Claire hopefully. 'Maybe St Louis'll nail this nutcase 'fore he works his way back here. That's what we're all thinkin', ain't it? That he's coming' here?'

'Don't count on it,' said Vail. 'We have to assume this killer is heading here. Maybe he's here already.'

He felt Jane's hand brush against his. It was trembling and he took it gently in his and squeezed it reassuringly.

'I still remember that day in court when he came over the railing of the witness stand and grabbed me,' she said.

'It was those eyes. A moment before he grabbed me I looked into those eyes and . . .'

'And what?' Vail asked. 'What did you see?'

'They turned red for just an instant. It was like . . . like they filled with blood. I've never seen such hate, such malevolence. I still dream about those eyes.'

Suddenly Vail was no longer interested in the conversation. He stared into his coffee cup, thinking about Linda and Alex, about the Altar Boys and Bishop Rushman. All had been Stampler's friends and he had turned on them. Vail had been his friend during the trial and he was sure that this madness was being directed at him. He remembered Stampler's words again.

'Suppose there never was an Aaron.'

Stampler hadn't been joking that day, Vail was more certain of that now than ever before. And if Stampler had been cool enough and smart enough to trick all of them before, he was smart enough to figure out how to orchestrate these murders from inside Daisyland. Vail was no longer concerned about *why* Stampler was doing it or whether he, Vail, was responsible in some way for the madness. Stampler had to be stopped. And as long as he was safely tucked away in the mental institution, they had to focus on his accomplice.

Catch the accomplice, turn him against Stampler, and end it once and for all. And the accomplice was near, Vail was certain of that.

He had run out of victims everywhere else.

Twenty-two

Vail snatched up the car phone and punched out a number. Paul Rainey's smooth voice answered. 'Paul Rainey speaking.'

'It's Vail. Where is he, Paul?' Vail demanded.

'I, uh . . . I can't, uh . . .' Rainey stammered.

'You can't put your *finger* on him, right? Like you couldn't put your *finger* on him last night.'

'It's no big deal, Marty, he doesn't know there's paper out on him. Probably fishing or hunting. He's been through a lot.'

'So has his wife.' Vail snapped back. 'You're acting pretty damn cavalier for a guy with a murder-one warrant in his pocket and a client on the run.'

'He's not on the *run*, damn it!'

'You accepted service, Paul. I'm putting out an APB on him.'

'Another four hours, Marty. I'll have him there by noon.'

'Four hours for what, a tutor session? What's it going to be? He was sexually abused by his mother and took it out on his wife, or he was afraid she was going to cut off his dick because he was running around with Poppy Palmer? The Menendez or the Bobbitt defence?'

'Damn you!'

'Get off it, Paul, don't pull that indignant shit on me, I've known you too long. We're going to find him. *And* Poppy Palmer while we're at it. And the deal's off. He's going to get the needle. Goodbye.'

Vail hung up. He looked at St Claire and Stenner. 'Darby turned rabbit, I can tell. I could hear Rainey sweating over the phone.'

St Claire rubbed his hands together very slowly, stared out the window for a few seconds.

'I want a search warrant for the entire farm,' Stenner said, keeping his eyes on the road. 'We've checked airlines, buses, car rentals, trains. Nothing so far on the stripper.'

'You think he off'd her, don'cha?' asked St Claire. When Stenner nodded grimly, he said, 'Well, it ain't like he's not up to the task.'

'And he thinks he's off the hook,' Stenner said.

'Unless Rainey's got 'im in tow, maybe working' up a new yarn to get by the shot sequence.'

Vail shook his head. 'No, I don't think Rainey's up to anything. He accepted service of the warrant. If he hides Darby, he could be disbarred. The case isn't worth it to him. He's got to be thinking we have more than just the tape and he knows Darby hasn't a sou to his name. You two better get started as soon as you drop me at the airport.'

'Yeah.' St Claire snickered. 'It's almost eight-thirty. Day's half over.'

He was totally bald with a tattoo of a lizard down the middle of his skull, its tongue arched down his forehead. The sleeves of a Hawaiian shirt were rolled up tightly against his machine-tooled biceps, from which other tattoos formed a tapestry of daggers, names, and pierced hearts down to his wrists. His trousers were belted by a braided leather thong tied in a sailor's knot just below his belly button. In place of a toothpick, he had a ten-penny nail tucked in one corner of his mouth while a silver tooth gleamed from the other side. He was checking the stock behind the bar.

At ten in the morning, the bar smelled of stale cigarette smoke, old sweat, and spilled beer. A sliver of sunlight slanted through the front door, revealing an unswept floor littered with cigarette butts, wadded-up paper napkins, and dirt. Stenner held up his ID.

'I'm Major Stenner, Chicago DA's office. This is Lieutenant St Claire.'

'Major. Lieutenant. A lotta weight fer two guys,' the bartender answered with a lopsided grin.

'Is the manager around?'

'Lookin' at him. Mike Targis.'

He held out a melon-sized fist and shook hands as if he was trying to inflict pain on the two cops.

'Yer lookin' fer Poppy, I told you people all I know. She split day before yesterday, didn't even come by, called it in.'

'What time was this?'

'I dunno, lessee . . . One, maybe, one-fifteen.'

'She have any money coming?'

'Yeah. Three days, three bills.'

'She sneezed off three C's, she was in that big a hurry?' Targis shrugged. 'Easy come . . .'

'Does she have a car?' Stenner asked.

'Whaddya think? She pulls down three, four K a month in tips, plus a hundred a day salary. She's my big attraction, gents. A red mustang ragtop, last year's model.'

'Know the tag number?'

Targis gave St Claire a sucker look. 'No, and I don't know the engine number either.'

'Know where she lives?'

'Sure. Fairway Apartments, over near the golf course. Straight down 84 two miles. Can't miss it. This is about the Darby thing, right?'

'Do you know anything about it?' Stenner asked.

'Only what I read in the papers, if you can believe that.'

'You don't?'

'What, that Calamity Jane–Wild Bill Hickok shootout? Shit.'

'That's just a guess, right?'

'Oh, yeah, man.'

'Did Poppy talk about it at all?'

'You kiddin'?' He leaned across the bar and lowered his voice even though they were the only people in the room. 'She was scared shitless.'

'Of what?'

'Everything. The cops. You guys. Big Jim.'

'That's what you called Darby, Big Jim?'

'That's what Poppy called him. Everybody else picked up on it. A guy leaves a dollar tip after drinkin' for four hours? Big Jim, my ass. But who can figger women, y'know? Poppy's smart, got a figger'd give a statue a stiff, looks like Michelle ... What's her name?'

'Pfeiffer?' said Stenner.

'No, the other one. Used to be a canary.'

'Phillips,' St Claire said.

Targis jabbed a forefinger at him. 'That's the one.'

'Did she ever mention this sister of hers before?' Stenner asked.

'Uh, maybe once'r twice.'

'So you didn't get the idea they were real close?'

'I didn't get any idea at all. I don't give a shit about her sister. I got enough trouble with my own family.'

'Thanks, Mr Targis,' Stenner said, handing him a card. 'If you think of something, give us a call.'

'Is she on the lam or sompin'?'

'We just want to talk to her.'

'I thought you already did.'

'We forgot a coupla things. She happens to call in, give her that name and number, okay?'

'She ain't gonna call in. I been in this business almost twenty years, I know a goodbye call when I hear one and that call from her was definitely a goodbye call.'

'Maybe she'll call about the three hundred you owe her.'

He shook his head as he took out a towel, held it under

the spigot, then twisted it damp and started cleaning the bar.

'It mattered, she'd a come by and got it. Had to drive right past the front door on her way to the interstate.'

'That's what she told you, she was *driving* out to Texarkana?'

'Didn't say. I just figgered she drove down to O'Hare.'

'Thanks.'

'Sure. Come back later and have a drink. On the house.'

'Thanks, Mike, you're a real gent.'

On the way out the door, St Claire said, 'Targis is an ex-con.'

'How do you know?'

'He's about ten years behind in his vernacular. Besides, I know everything. I even know who Michelle Phillips is.'

'Mamas and the Papas,' Stenner said, opening the car door. St Claire stared at him with disbelief. 'I wasn't always fifty, Harve.'

They got in the car and headed back to Darby's farm to see how the search was going.

The chopper swerved off the main highway and swept down over the town of Daisyland. From the air, it was a modest village surrounded by old Victorian houses hidden among oak and elm trees. As the chopper headed north of town, the residential area became sparse and then quite suddenly the trees ended and the Stevenson Mental Health Institute appeared below them, a group of incompatible though pleasant-looking buildings separated from the town by tall, thick hedges and the brick wall that surrounded the place. Two new wings adjoined the older, rambling main structure of the hospital. Together they formed a quadrangle. Vail could see people moving about, like aphids on a large green leaf. Vail remembered one of the structures from his visits a decade earlier – a three-storey building with a peaked atrium, its slanted sides constructed of large glass squares. Maximum security – Stampler's home for the past ten years.

Down below, in one of the buildings facing the quadrangle, a man watched the chopper *chunk-chunk-chunk* overhead. He was pleasant-looking, verging on handsome, and husky, his body tooled and hardened in the workout room, and he was dressed in the khaki pants and dark blue shirt of a guard. He had intense blue eyes with blondish hair trimmed just above the ears, was clean shaven, and smelled of bay rum aftershave lotion. There was just the trace of a smile on his full lips. He stood with his arms bent at the elbows, his fists under his chin, his fingers intertwined except for the two forefingers that formed a triangle that pressed against his mouth. His attention was pure, focused intently on the chopper. He watched it veer off and disappear beyond the trees. Finally he said, in a voice just above a whisper:

'Welcome, Mr Vail.'

And his smile broadened.

'You say something, Ray?' a voice said from the hall.

'No, Ralph, just hummin' to myself,' he answered. His voice was like silk. He sat down at the worktable and went back to work.

As the chopper fluttered down on a large practice football field near the institution, a black, four-door Cadillac pulled down the service road and parked. The chopper settled lightly on the ground, its blade churning up dust devils that swirled around it.

'You could land on eggs, Sidney,' Vail said, flipping off his safety belt and opening the door.

'You say that every time,' the pilot answered.

The driver of the sedan was a trim man in his late thirties with an easy smile. He wore khaki pants and a dark blue shirt and did not look like a guard, which it turned out he was.

'I'm Tony,' he said, opening the rear door. 'I'm here to run you over to the Daisy.'

'The Daisy? They call it the Daisy?'

'Yeah,' Tony answered, holding the door for him. 'Daisyland wasn't stupid enough.'

Vail slid in and Tony slammed the door. The drive took five minutes. As they approached the sprawling complex, the large iron gates rolled back and Tony drove through and headed up a gravel road bordered on either side by knee-high winter shrubs. Vail felt vaguely uncomfortable. Perhaps subconsciously, he thought, he was afraid they would keep him there. Or, more likely, he did not look forward to seeing the unfortunate patients locked away from the world in the place cruelly known as the Daisy.

For Shana Parver, the objective of the deposition was to get as much information on the record as possible, enabling her to stand tough on a plea bargain. She was certain that Stoddard would never go to court and Venable would be manoeuvring to get in the best position for a deal. She was partly right.

Jane Venable had to defend a client who did not want to be defended and manoeuvre into position for the best plea bargain she could get. Venable had to, at the very least, convince Edith Stoddard to let her continue to whittle away at and weaken Parver's case. Getting Stoddard to recant the confession was a big step. Now, hopefully, she could prevent Stoddard from incriminating herself during the Q and A with Parver.

They had a few minutes together before Shana Parver arrived. Edith Stoddard was brought to the interrogation room in the annex by a female guard who stood outside the door. Stoddard looked wan, almost grey, her mouth turned down at the corners, her eyes deeply circled. She was wearing a formless blue dress without a belt and white, low-cut tennis shoes. Her hair was haphazardly combed. Wisps of grey and black dangled from the sides and back.

'How are you this morning?' Venable asked.

'I'm not sure,' was Stoddard's faint, enigmatic answer.

'This won't take long,' said Venable. 'Just a formality.'

'When is it going to be over? When are you going to make whatever deal you're going to make?'

'This is part of it, Edith. I'd like to make a good, solid showing here today. It will help when we discuss your plea.'

Stoddard shook her head in a helpless gesture.

'She's going to go big on the gun, Edith. I'm not going to ask you where you lost it or even *if* you lost it. When she asks about it – about losing the gun, I mean – be vague. Also she's going to bear down on where you were the night Delaney was killed. Just remember, the less Shana Parver knows, the better.'

'Why can't you just tell her . . . why can't you do whatever it is you want to do? What do you call it?'

'Plea bargain.'

'Just do it today. Get it *over* with, please.'

'Please trust me. Let me set things up right.'

'I just want it to end.'

'I understand that, Edith, but let me do my job, too. Okay?'

Stoddard's shoulders sagged. She took several deep breaths.

'Good,' Venable said. 'You'll do just fine.'

Shana Parver, dressed in a teal silk pant suit, her black hair cascading down her shoulders, arrived a few minutes later with a stenographer, a tall, slender, pleasant-looking woman from the courthouse named Chorine Hempstead. There were pleasant 'Good mornings' and offers of coffee from Hempstead, which everyone but Edith Stoddard gratefully accepted. She sat beside Jane Venable and across the table from Parver, her hands folded in front of her. She reminded Parver of a frightened bird.

Parver dropped a bulging shoulder bag on the floor, opened her briefcase, and took out a legal pad, a sheaf of notes, several pencils, and a small Sony tape recorder, all of which she placed on the table. Hempstead brought back the cups of coffee and sat at the end of the table with a shorthand tablet and waited.

'Are we ready?' Shana asked pleasantly, arranging in front of her her notes and those taken by Shock Johnson the day Stoddard had suddenly blurted out that she killed John Delaney.

'Let's get on with it,' Venable said tersely.

'For the record,' Parver began, 'I would like to state that this is a formal interrogation of Mrs Edith Stoddard, who is charged with first-degree murder in the death of Mr John Farrell-Delaney on February 10, 1994, in the city of Chicago. I am Shana Parver, representing the district attorney of Cook County. Also attending are Ms Jane Venable, representing Mrs Stoddard, and Chorine Hempstead, a clerk of the Cook County Court, who will transcribe this meeting. This interrogation is being conducted in the courthouse annex, 9 A.M., February 16, 1994. Mrs Stoddard, do you have any objection to our tape-recording this meeting?'

Stoddard looked at Jane Venable.

'No objection,' Venable said.

'Good. Please state your full name for the record.'

'Edith Hobbs Stoddard.'

'Are you married?'

'Yes.'

'What is your husband's name?'

'Charles. Charles Stoddard.'

'How long have you been married?'

'Twenty-six years.'

'And where do you live?'

'At 1856 Magnolia.'

'Do you have any children?'

'I have a daughter, Angelica.'

'How old is she?'

'Twenty-one.'

'Does she live at home?'

'She goes to the university. She lives in a dorm there, but she has a room at the house.'

'Is that the University of Chicago or the University of Illinois?'

'Chicago. She's a junior.'

'And you support her?'

'She has a small scholarship. It covers part of her tuition and her books and lab fees, but I – we – pay for her room and board and other necessities.'

'How much does that run a month?'

'Five hundred dollars. We give her five hundred a month.'

'And you have a full-time nurse for your husband?'

'Not a nurse. We have a housekeeper who attends to Charley, cooks meals, keeps the place clean.'

'Do you have separate bedrooms, Mrs Stoddard?'

'What's that got to do with anything?' Venable asked.

'A formality,' Parver answered casually.

'We have adjoining bedrooms,' Stoddard answered wearily. 'I keep the door cracked at night in case he needs something.'

'You work at Delaney Enterprises on Ashland, is that correct?'

'I did,' Stoddard said with a touch of ire.

'And how long does – did – it take to get to work every day?'

'Thirty minutes or so. Depends on the traffic.'

'You drive then?'

'Yes.'

'How long did you work for Mr Delaney?'

'Seventeen years.'

'And you were his personal secretary?'

'Executive secretary was my title,' she said proudly.

'And how long did you hold that position?'

'Nine years.'

'In that position, did you have occasion or occasions to go to Mr Delaney's apartment in the Lofts Apartments on Astor Street?'

'Yes.'

'Frequently?'

'Yes. He liked to work there, away from the bustle of the office. I frequently took files, letters to sign, or took dictation over there.'

'And did you have a key to that apartment?'

Venable started to object to the question, then thought better of it and kept quiet.

'Yes.'

'Where is that key now?'

'I, uh, it's on my keyring with my other keys.'

'And where are they?'

'The police took them when they arrested me.'

'So the police have the key now?'

'Yes.'

'Now, Mrs Stoddard, I want to ask you about the gun. You do own a gun, do you not?'

'Yes.'

'What calibre?'

'It's a .38.'

'Make?'

'Smith and Weston.'

'You mean Smith and Wesson?'

'I guess. Yes.'

'Where did you acquire this gun?'

'The Sergeant York gun store on Wabash.'

'Do you recall when you purchased it?'

'It was about a month ago. I don't remember the exact day.'

'How much did you pay for the gun in question?'

'One hundred and thirty-five dollars.'

'Why did you buy a gun?'

'For protection.'

'Did you carry this gun with you all the time?'

Pause. 'Yes.'

'You seem uncertain, Mrs Stoddard.'

'I was. I was trying to remember if I ever left it home. I don't think I did.'

'Where did you carry it?'

'I just told you, everywhere.'

'No, I mean, where did you keep the gun when you were carrying it?'

'In my handbag.'

'And when you were at the office?'

'In my middle desk drawer on the left side. I locked it.'

'And at night?'

'Under my mattress.'

'In your bedroom?'

'Yes.'

'Where is this weapon now?'

'I, uh, lost it.'

'How? I mean, if you kept it in your handbag and you locked it in the desk drawer and you kept it under the mattress at home, how did you manage to lose it? Is there a possibility that somebody stole the gun from your drawer at work?'

'I don't think . . . Maybe.'

'So what happened to the gun?'

'I guess maybe . . . it must have fallen out of my bag.'

'Was this after you shot Delaney?'

'Objection. Come on, Counsellor, there's been no admission –'

'We have Mrs Stoddard's confession –'

'Which she has recanted, as you well know. It was given under duress, she was emotionally disturbed at the time . . .'

'Did you lose the gun after Delaney was killed, Mrs Stoddard?' Parver said, cutting off Venable's objection.

269

'I still don't like the question. I would prefer that you ask her when she lost it.'

'All right, Mrs Stoddard, when did you lose the gun in question?'

'I'm not sure. I first noticed it when I got home from work Thursday night.'

'That was the night Delaney was killed, was it not?' Parver looked at the Venable and raised an eyebrow.

'Yes,' Mrs Stoddard said.

'Now, Mrs Stoddard, did you know anything about guns when you purchased this Smith and Wesson .38?'

'No.'

'Did you take lessons?'

'Yes, that's right, I took lessons.'

'To become proficient in its use, right?'

'Yes.'

'And where did you take these lessons?'

'On Pershing Street, the Shooting Club.'

'How proficient did you become, Mrs Stoddard?'

'That's a relative question, Counsellor. Would you rephrase, please?'

'Relative to what?' Parver demanded.

'Mrs Stoddard has already stated that she knew nothing about guns. She has no point of reference for a comparison.'

'Mrs Stoddard, did you stop taking lessons?'

'Yes.'

'Why?'

'The instructor told me I was good enough.'

'Everything, right? Loading, cleaning it, shooting?'

'Yes.'

'And you became good enough to discontinue the lessons, is that a fair statement?'

'I guess so.'

'Did the instructor agree that you didn't need any further lessons?'

'Yes.'

270

'And you purchased bullets for this weapon?'

'Yes.'

'Do you know how many bullets you bought?'

'Two boxes.'

'How many bullets in a box?'

'Fifty.'

'And did you keep your gun loaded?'

'Yes.'

'How many shells did it hold?'

'Six.'

'And where do you keep the remaining shells?'

'On a shelf in my bedroom closet.'

'Is that closet locked?'

'No. Why would I—'

Venable gently laid her hand over Stoddard's and shook her head, but Parver chose to ignore the comment. She opened her briefcase and took out a grey piece of paper that was folded over twice. She opened it up and laid it on the table in front of Stoddard.

'Mrs Stoddard, this is a target we obtained from the Shooting Club. You left it behind the last day you were there and they saved it. They assumed you would be back in from time to time to practice and they thought you might like to keep it.'

Venable looked down at the target, which was the customary black human silhouette on white background normally used in target ranges. There were six bullet holes, all tightly grouped in the area of the heart.

'Do you recognize the target, Mrs Stoddard?'

'That could be anyone's target, Counsellor,' Venable snapped. 'All targets look alike.'

'They don't all have your client's name and the date written on the bottom,' said Parver. She pointed to the two lines scribbled in one corner. 'They did this to identify it for her.'

'Then I guess it's mine,' Stoddard said.

'That's from twenty-five yards, Mrs Stoddard. You're pretty good.'

Edith Stoddard didn't answer immediately. Finally she shrugged. 'Most of the people at the range are that good.'

'What kind of bag do you carry, Mrs Stoddard?'

'It's a Louis Vuitton. Just a standard handbag.'

'That's the one about eight inches long and four or five inches deep, right?' Parver said, measuring out the general dimensions in the air with her hands.

'I guess.'

'And what do you normally carry in it?'

'What's the relevance of this?' Venable asked.

'Bear with me, please,' Parver said without changing her tone. She reached down to the floor and put her bulky leather bag on the desk. It was jammed with stuff. 'This is my bag, Mrs Stoddard,' Parver said, and laughed. 'As you can see, I've got everything in here but a set of the *Encyclopaedia Britannica*.'

Edith Stoddard's face softened slightly and a smile flirted briefly with her lips.

'Was your bag jam-packed like mine?'

Stoddard chuckled. 'I can't imagine having that much to carry in a handbag.'

'So your bag was fairly neat and uncluttered, would that be a fair assessment?'

'Yes. My wallet, chequebook, keys, Kleenex. Sometimes a paperback, if I was reading one. I sometimes read while eating lunch.'

'Mrs Stoddard, do you have any idea how much your gun weighed?' Parver said, checking through her notes.

'No.'

Parver hesitated a moment, then turned a page. 'One pound six ounces loaded,' she said. 'Enough to be noticeable when you were carrying it in that small, uncluttered handbag, wouldn't you agree?'

'I . . . suppose so,' Stoddard said cautiously.

'What I mean is, this gun was for your protection, isn't that what you said?'

'Yes.'

'So wouldn't it be natural to be aware of the weight, know it was there in case of trouble?'

'Objection. She carried the gun for three weeks. More than enough time to become accustomed to the weight.'

'Uh-huh. Now, Mrs Stoddard, you say you put the gun in your desk drawer and locked it. Can you recall for me the last time you specifically remember putting the gun in that drawer?'

'Come on, Counsellor, she was upset, distressed over – '

'Mrs Stoddard, when were you informed you were being retired?' Parver said, cutting off Venable.

'On Thursday.'

'You had no idea before that?'

'There was nothing official.'

'I didn't ask you that. Did you have any indication, prior to Thursday morning when Delaney replaced you, that you would be leaving?'

'There were rumours. There are always rumours.'

'And when did you first hear these rumours?'

'You know how rumours are, you don't remember when you hear a thing. I don't even remember who said it.'

'Had this been going on for a while? The rumours, I mean?'

'She just told you, Counsellor, she doesn't know when they started,' Venable said. 'I'm going to intercede here. You're dealing in hearsay. Also it's immaterial – '

'On the contrary, Ms Venable, it's quite material. Some of the other employees say it's been fairly common knowledge – that Delaney was planning to replace Edith, I mean – since just after Christmas. That's two months.'

'I am advising my client not to answer any more questions related to what she may or may not have heard or

273

when she may or may not have heard it or who she may or may not have heard it from. She's already told you, she heard it from Delaney last Thursday morning. That's when it became a fact of life for her.'

'Mrs Stoddard, on Thursday morning when Delaney told you he was replacing you, what was your immediate reaction?'

'I was, uh, I was shocked and, uh, I guess angry ... upset, confused ...'

'Confused?'

'I wanted to know why. All he said, all he *ever* said was, "Edith, it's time for a change." My whole life was ... Everything was turned topsy-turvy in just a few minutes because it was ... it was *time for a change*. Yes, I was upset and confused and angry. I was all those things!'

'When was the last time you saw Delaney?'

'He told me I would be paid for two weeks and I could have until Friday to clean out my things. I think the last time was when he left for lunch Thursday.'

'The day he was killed?'

'Yes.'

'And Friday was to be your last day?'

'Yes. I guess he thought my replacement could learn the job over the weekend and be ready to start Monday morning.' She stopped for a moment and looked down at her hands, folded on the table in front of her. 'Sorry, that was sarcastic of me. I'm sure she had been working with Mr Delaney for weeks, maybe months.'

'So now tell me, when was the last time you specifically remember locking the gun in your desk drawer?'

'I guess it was Wednesday.'

'So Thursday you kept the gun in your bag, is that it?'

'Objection. She has already stated that she doesn't remember. She's guessing it was Wednesday.'

'So you don't remember whether you had the gun Thursday or not?'

'That's what she said, Counsellor.'

'I just want to clarify, as closely as possible, when she lost the weapon.'

'It was Thursday,' Stoddard said suddenly. 'I remember putting it in my bag Thursday when I left the house. I'm just hazy about what I did with it after that. It was a very upsetting day. People coming up, telling me they were sorry. That kind of thing.'

'So let's recap for a minute. You bought the gun, took lessons, became proficient in its use' – Parver tapped the target lying on the table – 'and carried it in your bag for protection. At the office you locked it in your desk drawer and at night you kept it under your mattress. The last time you remember seeing the gun was when you put it in your bag Thursday when you left for work. Then you got to the office and Delaney called you in and retired you. And you don't remember anything about the gun or its whereabouts after that. Is that correct?'

'Yes.'

'Good. Now let's get to Thursday. Tell me in your own words what you did that day and evening – up until you went to bed that night.'

'After Mr Delaney told me, gave me the news, I went outside. There's a little picnic area behind the building. People eat lunch there, go outside to smoke, you know, a nice little place to take a break. And I sat outside for a while. I don't know how long. I think . . . I may have . . . I guess I cried. It was such a shock, finally realizing it was true, and I was trying to get my wits together – '

'Excuse me, Mrs Stoddard, I'm sorry to interrupt, but you just said, 'It was such a shock, *finally realizing it was true*.' So you were aware of the rumours, weren't you?'

'Objection,' Venable said sternly, 'that's a conclusion on your part.'

Parver's voice remained calm. 'Not *my* conclusion, Counsellor. She has admitted she heard the rumours – '

'She hasn't admitted a damn thing!'

Parver turned back to Edith Stoddard. 'You had been hearing these rumours, had you not?'

'Don't answer that,' Venable snapped.

'I . . . I . . .' Stoddard stammered.

'All right,' Parver said softly, 'we'll move on. You were saying you were trying to get your wits together?'

Stoddard, rattled, began dry-washing her hands. She licked her lips and said weakly: 'Yes, uh, trying to, you know, I have a full-time housekeeper for Charley during the day and my daughter is going to the university and she lives at the school and, uh, I was . . . I don't know how long I sat out there. Some of the people came out and talked to me, told me they were sorry. Finally I just couldn't take it any longer, so I went back upstairs and got a box and started getting my things together. One of the women, Mr Delaney asked one of the women to sit there, you know, when I gathered up my things, I guess so I wouldn't . . . wouldn't *steal* anything. I really didn't keep many personal things in the desk, anyway.'

'Did you have anything in that middle desk drawer on the left? The one you kept locked?'

'No, there were mainly backup disks from the computer and some confidential files of Mr Delaney's.'

'But you did check it?'

'Yes.'

'Was the gun in the drawer when you checked it?'

'I, uh . . .'

'We've been over this,' Venable said. 'She said she doesn't remember where the gun was.'

'I realize that. But she was getting her personal things together and she checked that drawer, and certainly if the gun was in there she would have removed it since it was a personal item. Isn't that true, Mrs Stoddard?'

'She says she doesn't remember!'

'Can she answer the question, please? Mrs Stoddard, did you take *anything* out of the drawer of a personal nature?'

276

'She . . . doesn't . . . remember,' Venable snapped.

'Well, what *did* you remove from the desk?'

'Some make-up. A Montblanc pen that was a Christmas gift. Uh, uh, some photographs of my family. A dictionary. I can't . . .'

Stoddard looked helplessly at Venable and started to shake her head. Her hands were trembling. Venable could see she was losing it, beginning to fall apart.

'Can we move on, Shana?' said Venable. 'What she took from the desk is really immaterial. She was obviously distraught . . .'

Parver leaned back and turned off the tape recorder. 'Would you like to take a break?' she asked.

'I want to get this over with,' Edith Stoddard said in almost a whisper.

Parver pressed the record button again.

'I left the office early. At lunchtime. And I drove around a while. I drove into the city, to Grant Park, and sat by the fountain for the longest time.'

'Was that the Great Lakes Fountain?'

'Buckingham.'

'So you sat by Buckingham Fountain and just cleared your mind?'

'Tried to. I just stared out at the lake.'

'Where did you park?'

'The indoor parking deck by the art institute.'

'Is it possible someone could've broken into your car while you were over by the fountain?'

'Nobody broke into my car. It was locked and nobody broke into it.'

'How long were you in the park?'

'I don't know. I got cold and left after a while. An hour, maybe.'

'Then what?'

'I went over to the gift shop at the art institute and bought Angel a shoulder bag.'

'Angel, that's what you call your daughter?'

She nodded. 'It was one of those canvas bags to carry her books in. I remembered that hers was . . . it was pretty worn and she had mentioned she needed a new one and I went into the institute to get warm and I remembered that, so I went to the gift shop and bought it. Twelve dollars.'

'It cost twelve dollars?'

'Uh-huh. And at four o'clock I went to the lab on Ellis Street – Angel has lab on Thursdays – and waited for her and we went across the street to the bookstore and had coffee and I gave her the canvas bag, and, uh . . . and then I, uh . . . I told her what happened and she was . . . she was so very . . . upset.'

Stoddard's voice broke and she stared down at her lap.

Parver snapped off the recorder again, reached into her over-stuffed bag, and slid a box of Kleenex across the table to her.

'Thank you.'

She dabbed her eyes and blew her nose and then straightened her back and nodded. Parver started the recording machine.

'You see, she has this scholarship, but it's not enough to . . . She studies very hard, A average, and maybe she'd have to get a job and she got furious over that, so we left and I took her back to the house. She cried all the way home. It was very traumatic. So sad. She didn't want to see any of her friends. So I suggested that she spend the night at home.'

'She has her own room?'

'Yes. I didn't tell my husband that night. He had a rather bad day and . . . Oh, what was the use? Why make the day worse for him? Our day lady had already fed him. We weren't hungry. He had already dozed off. So I took Alice up to the bus stop about five-thirty . . .'

'Alice is the housekeeper?'

'Yes. Alice Hightower. Been with us since the accident. And I went home. Angel had cried herself to sleep on her bed and I decided not to disturb her, so I went down to the living room and fixed myself a drink and turned on the TV, but I left the sound off. I was exhausted, too. And I guess I dozed off.'

'What time was this?'

She shrugged. 'Six or so. It was dark.'

'And what time did you wake up?'

'I guess it was, I don't know, I didn't really notice, maybe ten, ten-thirty. Diane Sawyer was on the TV when I turned it off. I went upstairs and woke Angelica up and told her to get undressed and then I went to bed.'

'So between, say, six and ten or ten-thirty, Charley was asleep in his room and Angelica was asleep in her room and you were asleep in the living room. Is that correct?'

Edith Stoddard nodded.

'And nobody saw you?'

'No.'

'Nobody called? You know, to tell you they were sorry about your leaving?'

'No.'

'Nobody called Angelica?'

'No.'

Parver looked at Jane Venable, but she was busy taking notes on a yellow legal pad and did not look up.

'So your husband and your daughter can't account for your whereabouts during that period of time – between six and ten-thirty, I mean?'

Stoddard looked at her and her face clouded up. 'Leave them out of this,' she said, her voice suddenly becoming strident and stern. 'They don't know anything, don't drag them through the mud!' She glared at Venable, her eyes watery, her lips trembling. 'I told you – ' she began, but Venable quickly cut her off.

'All right,' Venable said. 'That's enough for today. I'm advising my client to end this right now.'

'I have a few more – '

Venable slapped her hand on the table and the sharp

smack startled both Parver and Stoddard. 'I said enough!' Venable said. 'She told you about the gun and she told you where she was that night. That's all we've got to say for now.'

'I just have one more question,' Parver insisted, looking back at her notes.

'Make it quick and to the point,' Venable said edgily.

'When did you first hear that Delaney was dead?' Parver asked softly.

Stoddard looked at her for several seconds, then said, 'I heard it on the radio on my way to the office.'

Bang! Parver's strategy had paid off. She turned to Shock Johnson's notes.

'I'd like to read something from Lieutenant Johnson's report of his first meeting with you at Delaney Enterprises last Friday, Mrs Stoddard, and I'm quoting, "Mrs Stoddard, Delaney's executive secretary, was obviously very upset over the death of Delaney and was dressed in black and had a mourning ribbon on her sleeve." Unquote.

'If you had just heard about Delaney's death on the way to your office, Mrs Stoddard, why were you already dressed in mourning clothes?'

Twenty-Three

As Tony guided the Cadillac up to the main building of the Daisy, Vail saw a tall man sitting on a wooden bench beside the stairs to the administration office. He was filling a pipe, tapping the tobacco down with a small silver tool with a flat, circular tamper at the end of its stem. He seemed totally engrossed in the task, twisting the pipe between his fingers, stopping to study the tobacco, then packing it even tighter.

'That's the chief of staff, Dr Samuel Woodward,' Tony said. 'Big muckety-muck. He's waiting to greet you officially.'

'No band?' Vail said.

Tony laughed. 'They only let them out on Fridays,' he said.

As Vail got out of the car, Woodward stood. He was taller than Vail had guessed, six-three or four, and was dressed casually in dark brown corduroy slacks, a pale blue button-down shirt, open at the collar, and a black alpaca cardigan, one of its side pockets bulging with a packing of tobacco. He was a lean man with the gaunt, almost haunted face of a long-distance runner. His close-cropped, dark red hair receded on both sides to form a sharp widow's peak and he wore a beard that was also trimmed close to his face. He dropped the pipe tool in the other pocket of his cardigan and held out a hand with long, tapered, aesthetic-looking fingers.

'Mr Vail,' he said, 'Dr Sam Woodward. It's a pleasure. Sorry I wasn't here to take your call the other night.'

'My pleasure,' Vail said.

'It's such a pleasant day I thought we might stroll around the grounds and chat,' he said in a soft, faraway voice that sounded like it was being piped in from some-place else. 'No smoking inside the buildings. I quit ciga-rettes about six months ago and thought I'd taper off with a pipe. Instead of getting lung cancer, my tongue will probably rot out. You smoke?'

'I'm thinking about quitting.'

'Ummm. Well, good luck. Ferocious habit.'

He took out a small gold lighter and made a production of lighting his pipe. The sweet odour of aromatic tobacco drifted from its bowl. Vail lit a cigarette and tagged along with Woodward as he walked down the pavement that bounded the broad, manicured quadrangle formed by several buildings.

'I must say I'm curious as to why, after ten years, you should suddenly come back into Aaron Stampler's life,' Woodward said. 'You never have been to visit him.'

'I don't make a practice of seeing any of my old clients when a case is over. It's a business relationship. It ends with the verdict.'

'That's rather cold.'

'How friendly are you with your patients, Doctor? Do you go to visit them after they're released?'

'Hmmph,' he said, laughing gently. 'You do go to the point, sir, and I like a man who goes to the point, says what he thinks, so to speak. That's rare in my business. Usually it takes years carving through all the angst to get to the baseline.'

'I suppose so.'

'So why are you here?'

'Curiosity.'

'Really? Having second thoughts after all these years?'

'About what?'

'Come, come, sir. Now that you're a prosecutor, the shoe is on the other foot, so to speak. I have always found that all prosecutors think MPs are faking it.'

'Hell, Doctor, he convinced me. I saved his life.'

'And do you regret that now?'

282

The question took Vail by surprise and he thought about it for a moment before answering. 'I don't . . . No.'

'It is hard, isn't it? Accepting the absurdities of the mind.'

'That's what you call it? Absurd?'

'Well, to the average person, yes. Absurd. Ludicrous. Preposterous. Crazy. It's very easy to label anything we don't understand or like or accept as fake or insane. Insanity is what I call a phrase of convenience, nothing more than a medical description. Multiple Personality Disorder, on the other hand, ah! Now there we have a recognized mental disease, defined in DSM3, accepted by the profession, one of the true mysteries of the human condition.'

'DSM 3, that's your bible, as I recall.'

'True, sir, absolutely true. Catalogues and defines over three-hundred mental disorders. The *Gray's Anatomy* of the mind.'

'Now that you've brought it up, what does DSM 111 say about faking it?'

Woodward stopped. He did not look at Vail; he stared straight ahead and took several puffs of his pipe.

'I assume, sir, this is in the realm of an academic question. By that I mean nonspecific.'

'Of course. Generic.'

They walked down the pavement and then Woodward led Vail out across a broad expanse of lawn bordered by the buildings. From one of the buildings, Vail heard a muffled scream, a howling that quickly changed to laughter and then died away. If Woodward heard it, he made no acknowledgement of the fact. There were several inmates in the quadrangle, one pacing frantically back and forth, waving his hands and screaming silently to himself; another standing against a tree, his face a few inches from the bole, talking intently in tongues; another strapped in a wheelchair, his mouth hanging askew, his eyes half open and unfocused, staring at infinity. It was hard for Vail to ignore these human aberrations. Woodward was right. As sympathetic as Vail felt towards these unfortunate souls, they did seem strange, absurd, and ludicrous and he felt embarrassed for thinking about it.

'It's acceptable to stare, Mr Vail. Natural, in fact. They'll just stare back. You probably seem as bizarre to them as they seem to you.'

He nodded to a patient, who was picking imaginary flowers, and she smiled and nodded back.

'As to your question – about faking multiples – I presume it could be done for a short period of time. I seriously doubt that it could be sustained for very long. Too much involved, you know. My God, changing one's entire posture, body language, voice, general appearance, personality, attitude, persona. Virtually impossible to pull off over a protracted time period.'

'You said *virtually* impossible.'

Woodward smiled condescendingly. 'Hah! Forgot I was talking to a lawyer. Virtually impossible, yes, I did say that, didn't I? Well, sir, I suppose nothing is absolutely impossible anymore, technology being what it is. But I would say the chances of winning the lottery are far, far, *far* more likely than faking MPD.'

'Is Aaron Stampler capable of doing it?'

Woodward stopped again, this time staring at Vail hard before he answered. 'If he is, I wouldn't know it. Good lord, man, he was diagnosed as a dissociated multiple personality by your own psychiatrist. You were the one who uncovered this problem, Mr Vail. Now ten years later you drop out of the sky and start raising questions. Questions that, in effect, could destroy eight years of hard work and incredible research? No, this man is not acting. This man is not faking it.'

'I'm just asking, Doctor. We're just talking.'

They strolled further, Woodward puffing on his pipe, obviously deep in thought.

'Do you dream, Mr Vail?' he said finally.

'Rarely.'

'But you do dream?'

'Occasionally, yes.'

'You're in another place, another dimension, and you wake up and suddenly you're in a totally different place' – he snapped his fingers – 'just like that. Right?'

'Well, sometimes . . .'

'Instant displacement.'

'You're saying dreams are a form of losing time, Doctor? That's what Aaron called it when he went into a fugue state and changed to Roy, losing time.'

'It's a common expression used by anyone who suffers fugue events. Let me put it another way. Say you drift into a nap in the middle of a concert, next thing you know the concert's over, everybody's leaving the amphitheatre. Would you call that losing time?'

'I'd call it boredom.'

Dr Samuel Woodward laughed. 'That's because you're normal,' he said. 'Normal, of course, being a relative term. The point is, a fugue is losing time. Usually not for long, a few minutes. Five, I would say is average. It can occur over a period of years – its victims, understandably, are usually afraid to talk about it. Of course, everyone who experiences a fugue event isn't necessarily a multiple, you understand.'

'How did you end up with Aaron?' Vail asked.

'That calls for a bit of biography, not that I want to bore you. I graduated from Harvard, interned at Bellevue, did my residency at Boston General, and then I was five years in psychiatric emergency at Philadelphia Memorial. I loved it. You saw everything, something new every day. That's when I first became fascinated by multiple personalities – MPs. From Philly, I went to the Menanger. And at Menanger I began to specialize in MPD. In fact, I've written several papers on the subject. When they offered me the position here, I jumped at it, and Aaron Stampler was one of the lures.'

285

'What made him so different?'

'Everything, sir, *everything*. His background, his intelligence, the nature of his crimes, cause and effect. Absolutely fascinating case. I had read the reports prepared by Bascott, Ciaffo, and Solomon, as well as Dr Arrington's summary. There were only two personalities involved. He hadn't splintered off into five, six, or a dozen, so it was a chance to deal with the disease on a relatively elementary level. A challenge. And – most important of all – he had not been treated. A lot of interrogation, therapy sessions, that sort of thing, but no attempt to treat the disease. Put it all together? Irresistible!'

He paused for a moment to relight his pipe, then: 'I also read the trial transcript. Quite a legal feat, sir. The trial, I mean.'

'I'm not sure whether that's meant to be a compliment or not.'

'Oh yes, a compliment by all means. Back in those days, using the MPD defence was quite daring.'

'It was a sticky problem – whether the jury would buy it or not. In court, the truth sometimes can be detrimental to the health of your client.'

'Is that why you settled it in chambers?'

Vail suddenly felt cautious. The question triggered his paranoia for a second or two. *Did Woodward know Stampler had been faking it all along?* Vail wondered. Was he in on the game or had Stampler conned him, too? Vail quickly decided that Woodward had bought in to Stampler's malevolent trick.

'No,' Vail answered. 'The prosecutor triggered him. That's what put it into Judge Shoat's chambers.'

They walked a little way in silence, then Woodward said, 'Frequently, the initial reaction to multiple personality disorder is disbelief and rejection.' He paused for a moment, then added, 'And you're correct, sometimes the less the public knows about some things, the better.'

'I've often wondered who really killed the bishop,

Aaron or Roy,' Vail said. 'What I mean is, Aaron provided the motive, but Roy did the killing. Legally, a case could be made against Aaron for conspiracy to commit murder, possibly aiding and abetting.'

'I disagree, sir, most heartily. They were two different separate and distinct personalities. Aaron didn't *consciously* conspire to kill the victims. In point of fact, he was as much a victim as the victims themselves.'

Vail thought about that for a moment and nodded. 'Good legal point,' he said.

'From the beginning of his treatment, I had to deal with Aaron and Roy as two different people,' Woodward said. 'The same heart, different souls, if you believe in the soul.'

'I believe in the conscience. I suppose they could be considered the same.'

Woodward didn't respond to Vail's comment; he kept talking as if he was afraid he would lose his train of thought.

'What do you remember about the mind, Mr Vail? About the superego and the id?'

'Not much. The superego is like the monitor of our morals. The id is where all those repressed desires go.'

'Very succinct and relatively accurate, sir. When the wall between the id and the superego breaks down, the repressed desires become normal. Suddenly the idea of murder becomes normal. The mind is disordered – that's the disease – murder is just a symptom. In a manner of speaking, Roy was Aaron's id. Aaron repressed everything, Roy repressed nothing. If Aaron hated someone, Roy killed them.'

'A very convenient arrangement when you think about it,' said Vail.

'It's meant to be. That's one of the reasons human beings create other personalities, the pain becomes unbearable so they invent something to alleviate it. Look, Mr Vail – '

'Call me Martin, please.'

'Martin, I've been Aaron Stampler's shrink, confessor, friend, doctor – his only companion – for the last eight years. He was a classic mess when I came on board. Phobia, disassociation, my God, sir, Aaron had them all! He feared the dark, hated authority, distrusted his elders, dismissed his peers, was sexually confused.' Woodward stopped and shook his head. 'Did you ever hear him talk about what he called the hole, the coal mine his father forced him into?'

Vail nodded. 'The first time I ever interviewed him. Shaft number five, I'll never forget it. Creepy, crawling critters and demons.'

'What was that?'

'Creepy, crawling critters and demons. That's what he told me was waiting for him at the bottom of the shaft. That I do remember quite vividly.'

'That hole might very well be the symbol for everything in life that he dreaded. The dwelling place of his disobedient dreams. You see, when you look at Aaron, you see a madman. When I look at him, I see a person with a disease. And from the very first day I arrived, I regarded him as curable.'

Vail looked at him incredulously.

'Why do you find that hard to believe? You saved his life.'

'Couldn't let them kill the good guy just to get to the bad guy, Doctor.'

'*Touché*,' Woodward said with a laugh. Then his mood immediately became serious again. 'In point of fact, my entire professional attitude changed because of Aaron Stampler. The belief that mental illness is a disease of the mind that can be treated with talk therapy was losing credibility when I started working with him. The new thing, the new kid on the block, was biological psychiatry.'

'That's a mouthful,' Vail said, just to keep his hand in.

'Well, you know what they say, we in the medical profession can't say hello in less than five syllables.'

'And lawyers can't pronounce anything with more than one.'

'Ha! Very good, sir, very good, indeed.'

'You were talking about biological psychiatry.'

'Yes. It theorizes that mental illness is caused by a chemical imbalance in the brain, that it can be medicated. So you had – still have – polarized viewpoints. Cure by talk or cure by pills. I was of the old school, a talker – old habits die hard, as they say – but I decided to go into the Stampler case with an open mind, to try everything and anything.'

Woodward waved his arms around, clicked off numbers on his fingers, closed his eyes, lifted his eyebrows as he rambled on.

'The list seemed endless at times. Thorazine, Prozac, Xanax, Valium, Zoloft, Halcion. We have bezodiazepines, which are addictive, and Haldol to treat hallucinations and delusions. There are antipsychotic drugs and antidepressants and antianxiety drugs, and I tried them all, every damn one that I felt was applicable. I tried behavioural therapy, recreational therapy, occupational therapy. I tried shock treatments . . .'

He stopped and lit his pipe again, each draw making a gurgling noise, and blew the smoke towards the blue sky.

'And I spent two hours a day, five days a week, for eight years with Aaron. Nobody, sir, *no*body knows him as I do.'

Woodward began talking intimately about Aaron Stampler, a rambling discourse that brought back, in a rush, details that Vail had forgot. Woodward described Stampler as a misplaced child who had grown into a gifted but frustrated young intellectual, his accomplishments scorned by a stern and relentless father determined that the boy follow him into the hell of the coal mines.

His mother considered Aaron's education akin to devil's play; a boy to whom the strap and the insults of his parents had done little to discourage him from a bold and persistent quest for knowledge. That quest was abetted by a sympathetic schoolteacher, Rebecca, who saw in the lad a glimmering hope that occasionally there might be resurrection from a bitter life sentence in the emotionally barren and aesthetically vitiated Kentucky hamlet, and who ultimately seduced him. Aaron was a loner, attracted to both the professions and the arts, who had wanted – as do most young people at one time or another – to be lawyer, doctor, actor, and poet – but whose dreams were constantly thwarted by everyone except his mentor, Rebecca.

And Woodward talked about the schoolteacher who appeared to be Crikside's only beacon, a lighthouse of lore and wisdom in an otherwise bleak and tortured place; a woman who threatened the bigotry of their narrow and obdurate heritage, a notion possibly vindicated by Rebecca's 'education' of Aaron Stampler. And finally he talked about the sexual liberation of Aaron Stampler, first by Rebecca, then later in a perverse and tormenting way by the paedophile, Bishop Rushman.

'It's easy to understand how this could have happened, considering what we know about Aaron's childhood and teen years. The simplified assumption was that Aaron created Roy to assume the guilt and responsibility for acts that Aaron couldn't perform himself. He transferred his guilt to Roy. As I said, this is an oversimplification of a very complex problem. We're dealing with the human mind, remember. The science isn't as obvious as DNA or fingerprints, which are unequivocal.'

'Look, Dr Woodward, I wasn't in any way demeaning your – '

'I understand that. I just want *you* to understand that work with him isn't a twice-a-week gabfest. This young man has dominated my professional life. I'm not complaining, it has also been most rewarding. But just achieving transference with him took three years.'

'Transference?' Vail said.

'A form of trust. When it works, the patient comes to regard the analyst as a figure from the past, a parent or a mentor, somebody they relate to. Trust is transferred from the mentor to the therapist.'

'You just said Aaron transferred his guilt to Roy. Is this the same kind of thing?'

'Yes. He simply created his own avenger. There is a downside, there always is. It creates a subconscious fear that old injuries and insults will be repeated – what we call re-experiencing. Fear of reliving pain from children, friends, husband, wives, just about anybody.'

'So all the pain is transferred from past to present?'

'Everything. Pain, anger frustration, unreasonable expectations. But it is important because it permits us to make connections between the past and the present. Drugs can ease the fear. And, of course, at times the pain.'

'What's the ultimate objective, Doctor? What did you call it, the baseline?'

'Free association. Encouraging the subject to concentrate on inner experiences ... thoughts, fantasies, feelings, pain. Hopefully creating an atmosphere in which the subject will say absolutely everything that comes to mind without fear of being censored or judged.'

'How does that help you?' Vail said.

'Well, what you're getting is their mental topography, like a roadmap to their secrets. They remember things from the deep past – traumatic events, painful encounters – very clearly, re-experience the fears and feelings that go with them. And, we hope, learn to accept them. Doesn't always happen, of course. Ours is not a perfect science like mathematics, where two and two always equals four. No, no, sometimes when dealing with the human mind two and two equals eight or twelve ...'

'Or one?'

'Or one – or a half. In Aaron's case, remembering some of the horrible acts committed by Roy and learning to deal with the knowledge was the product of re-experiencing and free association.'

'So you *have* made progress?'

Woodward stopped, knocked the dead embers from his pipe into a trash barrel, and stuffed the pipe in his cardigan pocket. 'I would say so,' he said. 'I want you to meet someone. His name is Raymond Vulpes.'

'Who's Raymond Vulpes?'

'The only other person alive who knows – as I do – every intimate detail of the lives of Aaron and Roy.'

They walked across the yard to what was known as MaxSec. The first thing Vail noticed was that the windows had no bars, they were made of thick, bulletproof glass. It was an attractive-looking structure and obviously built to provide the most pleasant circumstances possible. Maximum security was at the end of a long, wide hallway that connected it to one of the wards in the newer wing. There was an office off to one side of the hall with a wire-mesh door and Woodward led Vail to it, took out a bunch of keys, unlocked the door, and entered. As Vail stepped through the doorway, he was instantly seized with an overwhelming sense of evil.

The air seemed suddenly to be sucked out of the room.

A wet, icy chill swept through it.

The hair bristled on the back of Vail's neck.

Gooseflesh rippled up his arms.

Sweat burst from the pores in his forehead – a frigid sweat, like water dribbling down the torso of a melting snowman.

He shivered spasmodically.

He unconsciously gasped for air.

And then it was over.

Vail was rooted in place for a moment, as if his legs had suddenly atrophied.

What was it? A rampant chimera let loose by his imagination?

A subconscious fear of the uncharted and unpredictable minds in this community of the deranged?

An omen of some kind?

He quickly regaining his bearings, wondering if Woodward had had the same reaction. But it was obvious that Vail had been the only one who had experienced... whatever it was. They were in a fairly confined space, an electronic repair shop littered with TVs, VCRs, oscilloscopes, and computers lined up on workbenches and tables and further cramping the limited space.

A man in his mid to late twenties leaned over a worktable in a corner near the room's single window. A gooseneck lamp curved down beside his face, its light revealing the insides of a dismantled computer. He had the smooth, muscular build of a swimmer, dark blond hair, and pale eyes, and he was wearing the khaki pants and dark blue cotton shirt of a guard, the shirt's sleeves hitched halfway to his elbows. He looked up as Woodward and Vail entered the room and grinned, a wide, boyish grin, full of straight white teeth.

'Mr Vail, I'm Raymond Vulpes,' he said, sticking out his hand. 'Can't tell you what a great thrill it is to meet you.'

Vail took the hand and looked into Vulpes's face and in that moment realized that he was shaking hands with Aaron Stampler.

Twenty-Four

Caught off guard and shocked, Vail stepped back from Vulpes and turned to Woodward, who was leaning against a bench, smiling. For an instant he thought perhaps this was a perverse joke; that they were all mad and Woodward was the maddest one of all; that when Vail tried to leave, they would slam the doors and trap him inside with the other lunatics.

'I wanted you two to meet,' Woodward said casually. 'We're going to the vistor's suite, Raymond. I'll send Terry up for you in a few minutes.'

'Fine, I have to finish changing a couple of chips in Landberg's machine.'

'Excellent.'

'See you then, Mr Vail,' Vulpes said, flashing another million-dollar grin as they left the repair room.

'What the hell's going on?' Vail asked as Woodward locked the door.

'Recognized him, eh?'

'Ten years hasn't changed him that much. He's a lot heavier and he seems to be in great shape.'

'Works out an hour a day. Part of the regimen.'

'What regimen? Is this some kind of bizarre joke?'

'Joke? Hardly. Relax, Martin, all in good time.'

MaxSec was sealed from the hallway and the rest of the ward by a wall with a single, solid, sliding steel door. The security officer, a skinny young man named Harley, smiled as Woodward and Vail approached. He pushed a button under his desk. The heavy door slid open. Harley waved them in without bothering with the sign-in sheet.

The wide hallway continued inside the steel-guarded entrance. Light streamed in through the glass-panelled roof. The walls on both sides were lined with locked rooms. There was moaning behind one of the doors, but the hall itself was empty. Woodward led them into the first room on the right.

The room contained a small desk with two chairs, a padded wooden chair, a table and a TV, and a cot. The window was five feet above floor level. The entire space and everything in it – walls, furniture, and floor – was painted pure white.

Vail remembered the room. Except possibly for a slight rearrangement of the furniture, it had not changed in ten years.

'Is this, uh, what's his name again?'

'Raymond Vulpes.'

'Is this his room?'

'No, no, this is the visitor's suite, as we jokingly call it.'

'So they have visitors here.'

'Yes. Patients in max are not permitted any visitors in their quarters, so we provide this homey little visitor's room. They're not permitted to associate with other patients, either.'

'Can't they talk to each other?'

'No, sir. Sounds a bit medieval, I know. The reason, of course, is that they are in various stages of recovery. Social intercourse could be disastrous.'

'I should think total isolation would be just as disastrous.'

'There are people around,' Woodward said with a shrug. 'Therapists, security people, some staff. It's not solitary confinement. And they can spend an hour or two a day outside.'

'They just can't communicate with each other?'

'Quite right.'

'So Aaron hasn't had any communication with the outside world in ten years?'

'You mean Raymond.'

'Raymond, Aaron,' Vail said with annoyance.

'It's an important, even crucial distinction. Sit down, Martin. I hope that what I'm about to tell you will give you a sense of pride.'

'Pride?'

'You had a part in it. Had it not been for you, Raymond would never have existed. The host would certainly have been dead by now, either by electrocution or terminal injection.'

'Who *is* Vulpes?'

'Raymond is what is known as a resulting personality.'

'A what?'

'Resulting personality. Roy was a resulting personality. Now Raymond is one.'

'So Aaron's split into a third person?'

'Yes and no. He's certainly a third person. However, the others no longer exist. It's not a unique case, although it well might become one.'

'How?'

'If we've stabilized Raymond. By that I mean he won't split again. They usually do.'

'Where did Raymond come from and when?'

'He was created to mediate the problems between Roy and Aaron. He first appeared almost three years ago.'

'Who created him?'

'Aaron was always the host.'

'Another escape mechanism?'

'Not an escape. An alternative. Another form of transference. As I explained to you, transference is the conscious or subconscious mirroring of behaviour patterns from one individual to another. This also applies to personae in a split personality. It's a form of denial. The schizoid places guilt on another individual, in this case, a new person – *voilà*, Raymond.'

'*Voilà*.' Vail said it with obvious distaste. 'What if Roy had transferred to Raymond instead of Aaron?'

'It wouldn't have happened. Raymond didn't want

296

that. Abhorrent behaviour patterns can be mirrored only to individuals who would normally accept the transference.'

'In other words, the receiver must be capable of such behaviour to begin with?'

'Correct. Raymond doesn't need Roy, never did.'

'And Aaron transferred to you, right?'

'Yes. That was a major breakthrough, I might add. It was not an easy transition. My strategy was to appeal to his need to be appreciated by his supervisors. That was what attracted him to Rushman. Aaron had transferred his need – as a child – for approval from his parents to the bishop. My problem, of course, was Rushman, who had betrayed that trust. Aaron didn't trust me for several years. The advantage, of course, is that Roy would come out, so I got to deal with them both. Then when Raymond emerged, the transference was complete. Aaron and Roy eventually disappeared.'

'And now you have Raymond, the perfect specimen.'

Woodward was surprised by the remark. He nervously stroked his beard with both hands, then said, 'There's no need for sarcasm, Martin. He'll be down in a minute. Talk to him before you judge him.'

'I just mean it sounds like Raymond encompasses all the best of Aaron – his intelligence, his dreams, desires . . .'

'Exactly. Aaron always saw himself as an innocent victim. He had no control over Roy. He couldn't even communicate with him. I was the pipeline between them.'

'There were two tapes. Do you know about them?'

'You mean the Altar Boys tapes?'

'You *do* know about that.'

'Of course.'

'Both the original and one copy were erased by mutual agreement with the prosecutor.'

'Why?'

'To protect the Catholic church. Rushman was dead,

the case was resolved. It wasn't necessary to drag all that up.'

'That was very civilized of you two. I'm not sure it was in my patient's best interest.'

'Why not? You could always get the information from the horse's mouth. I assume Roy went into detail about those events.'

'That's true,' Woodward agreed.

'Let's get back to Raymond. Where did the name come from?'

'That's what he called himself the first time he appeared. I said, "Who are you?" and he said, "I'm Raymond Vulpes."'

'So Roy dominated Aaron and Raymond dominated Roy.'

Woodward nodded. 'Aaron never did confront either Roy or Raymond directly. As I said, I was the pipeline. But when Raymond appeared, I was able to bring both Raymond and Roy out. It was absolutely fascinating, watching them switch back and forth. They would interrupt each other, argue, an incredible clash of the two egos. And Raymond was as normal as you or I. His ego and id were all in the right places – he was totally in control. He completely frustrated Roy. Put him in his place. Roy was impotent in Raymond's presence.'

'How about Aaron?'

'He stepped out of it and left Raymond to deal with Roy.'

'How convenient.'

'Understandable. Raymond isn't pained. Raymond didn't go through the agonies of re-experiencing; Aaron did. And what Aaron ultimately came to terms with – from all that pain – Raymond learned from him. Raymond could step back, study the clash between Aaron and Roy objectively, rationally. He accepted Aaron and Roy as one, not as a split personality. The horror that Aaron had to deal with did not infect Raymond. Raymond was capable of happiness. Raymond was, and is, everything Aaron wanted to be. So Raymond took over and ultimately destroyed Roy – and, incidentally, was perfectly happy to be rid of both of them.'

'I'll bet,' Vail snapped. 'So you can't bring either one of them out anymore?'

'Precisely. For the past eighteen months, Raymond's been psychologically stable. No fugue events, no more appearances by either Aaron or Roy. In fact, for the last several months, Raymond has rarely mentioned them. He's become far more interested in the present and the future than the past.'

'What you're telling me is that Raymond Vulpes is sane?'

'As sane as we are. In this case a very troubled teenager has been replaced by a charming, educated, intelligent man. A charming fellow with a genius level IQ and a remarkable memory. He's rational, well-adjusted, has a stunning spectrum of interests. We're good friends, Raymond and I. We play chess together, discuss movies and books – he reads incessantly, everything from text-books, magazines, fiction, nonfiction, how-to-books. His thirst for information is unquenchable.' Woodward stopped and smiled.

Looking at Woodward's smug, self-satisfied grin, Vail's uneasiness towards him changed to contempt. When he talked about Raymond, Woodward sounded like a modern Frankenstein who had taken Aaron's skin and bones and fashioned them into a human being on his own design.

'My question was, has he had visitors, communication, letters, phone calls, *anything* from the outside world?' Vail asked.

'Basically, no. We have had, in the past few months, visiting doctors who have come to observe what we've done with him. Always, of course, in concert with members of the staff. It's purely academic. Q and A, no social involvement whatsoever.'

'No phone calls?'

'Who would call him? He hasn't received a letter, not even a postcard, in a decade.'

'And he doesn't correspond with *anyone*?'

'To tell you the truth, Martin, I don't think there's anyone Raymond *wants* to correspond with. Look at it this way: He knows a great deal about his past, but not everything. He knows enough to understand what happened to Aaron and why Roy appeared. Some things don't interest him. I suppose in a way you could compare Raymond to an amnesiac. He's learned enough about his past to be comfortable with himself. He doesn't need or want to know any more.'

Woodward stood up and walked to the door. 'I'll send Max to get him,' he said. 'Excuse me for a minute.'

Vail took out a cigarette and toyed with it. Everything Woodward said seemed perfectly logical. It was medically plausible, not even that uncommon. It all made perfect sense.

Sure it did, Vail thought. Here was a psychotic madman living comfortably in an insane asylum, where he has convinced all the doctors that he has been miraculously transformed into a real sweetheart named Raymond Vulpes, who was perfectly sane.

Talk about the inmates running the asylum.

Vail didn't believe a word of it. And he was prevented from discussing Aaron's remark after the trial by the rules of confidentiality.

A few minutes later, Max entered with Vulpes. He was still smiling, but his joviality had been replaced with a subtle caution.

'Anybody care for something to drink?' Max asked pleasantly.

'I'll have a Coke,' Vulpes said. He was standing on the opposite side of the table facing Vail.

300

'Evian for me,' Woodward said.

'Coke sounds good,' Vail said. They sat down, Vail and Vulpes facing each other and Woodward at one end of the table, like the moderator on a talk show.

Vail did not know what to say. Congratulations on your new persona? Welcome to the world, Raymond? Whatever he said would be hypocritical at best.

'Well, you wanted to meet Raymond. Here he is,' Woodward said proudly.

'You'll have to forgive me, Raymond,' Vail said, 'I'm a bit overwhelmed by miracles of science.'

The smile faded from Woodward's face. Vulpes did not react at all. There was still a hint of the smile on his lips. His eyes bored into Vail.

'Most are,' Vulpes said. 'The doc is doing a book on me. Could win him a Pulitzer Prize, right, Sam?'

'Well, we'll see about that,' Woodward said, feigning modesty.

'It seems strange to me,' Vail said. 'For instance, you just appeared. Don't you ever wonder who your mother was?'

Without hesitation Vulpes said, 'My mother was Mnemosyne, goddess of memory and mother of the nine muses.' Then he chuckled.

Woodward laughed. 'Raymond has a wonderful sense of humour,' he said, as if Vulpes was not in the room.

Vail said, 'And you simply got rid of Roy?'

'Let's just say he had enough,' Vulpes said. 'He retired.'

'So what did you learn from Roy and Aaron?'

'Well, Roy wasn't as intelligent as Aaron, but he was a hell of a lot smarter.'

'You mean street-smart?'

'I mean he wasn't naïve.'

'And Aaron was?'

'You know that.'

'Do I?'

301

'The way you ambushed that prosecutor, what was her name?'

'Is that what Roy said? That I ambushed her?' Vail said without answering the question. Vulpes knew damn well what her name was.

'That's what *I* say.'

'Really.'

'I've read the trial transcripts. And Roy told me you played it just right. Started to ask about the symbols, then backed off. No wonder they called you a brilliant strategist.'

'Did Aaron and Roy ever talk about killing the old preacher . . . uh, I can't think of his name, its been ten years.'

'Shackles.'

'Shackles, right.'

'Roy bragged about that one, all right. They really hated that old man.'

'That's an understatement,' Vail said.

Vulpes almost smiled and nodded. 'Guess you're right about that. He was their first, you know.'

'So I heard.'

'Why, hell, Mr Vail, you probably know more about the two of them than I do.'

'Oh, I think not.'

Their eyes met for just a second. Nothing. Not a blink, not a flinch. *It's the eyes*, Vail thought. *His eyes don't laugh when the rest of his face does. They never change. Ice-cold blue.*

'How about the others? Did he talk about them?'

'You mean his brother and Aaron's old girlfriend, Mary Lafferty?'

'I'd forgotten her name, too,' Vail said.

Vulpes looked him directly in the eye. 'Lafferty,' he repeated. 'Mary Lafferty.'

'Oh yes,' Vail said.

'Actually, Roy also talked about Peter Holloway and Billy Jordan,' Vulpes said. 'The Altar Boys.'

Vail stared into Vulpes's barren eyes, devoid of everything but hate. Bile soured his throat as his mind darted back ten years to the night he had found the devastated remains of the two young men. The flashback was a collage of horrors: the dark, ominous, two-storey lodge framed by the moon's reflection rippling on the lake; fingers of light probing an enormous den in the basement, a sweeping fireplace separating it into two rooms; a large raccoon racing past Vail followed by the rats, flushed by the light, squealing from behind a sofa; a hand rising up from behind the sofa, its fingers bent as if clawing the air, the flesh dark blue, almost black; the rest of the arm, a petrified limb stretched straight up, and then the naked, bloated torso; the face, or what was left of it, swollen beyond recognition, the eyes mere sockets, the cheeks, lips, and jaw gnawed and torn by furry night predators, the gaping mouth, a dark tunnel in an obscene facsimile of something once human; the throat sliced from side to side, further mutilated by the creatures that had feasted upon it, and the stabs, cuts, and incisions and the vast sea of petrified blood, black as tar, and the butchered groin. And the fossilized corpse next to it – a smaller version of the same.

I am responsible for this human ghoul, he thought. It took a moment for him to regain his composure and go on with the confrontation.

'So you discussed the Altar Boys,' he said finally.

'Of course, that's what it was all about, right?'

'It was all about a lot of things. How about Alex, did they discuss Alex with you?'

'Alex?'

'Lincoln. Alex Lincoln?'

'Lincoln.' Not a glimmer when he spoke Lincoln's name. 'You mean the other Altar Boy? I don't recall Roy ever said much about Lincoln.'

If the eyes are a window to the soul, Vail thought, *Raymond has no soul*. Aaron may have passed on his IQ and his fantastic memory to Raymond Vulpes, and all that sweetness and light, but he hadn't passed on his soul because Aaron had had no soul to pass on.

'How about Linda? Did anyone talk about her?'

Vulpes stared out the window for a moment, then said, 'Gellerman. Her name was Linda Gellerman. Aaron had a warm spot for her, even though she ran out on him.'

'He said that, that she ran out on him.'

'Perhaps I'm paraphrasing,' Vulpes said.

'Did Roy ever tell you the last thing he said to me?'

Vulpes stared at him blankly, then slowly shook his head. 'I don't think he ever mentioned it. What was it about?'

'Nothing, really. An aimless remark. Kind of a joke.'

'I'm always up for a good laugh.'

'Some other time, maybe.'

Vulpes's jaw tightened and he sat a little straighter. 'Must've been pretty good for you to remember it after ten years.'

'You know how it is, some things stick in your mind.'

Woodward sensed the animosity growing between the two. 'Raymond, tell Martin about your first trip downtown,' he said.

This time it was Vail's jaw that tightened. He stared across the table at Vulpes and their eyes locked.

'You've been outside?' Vail asked, trying to sound indifferent.

'Just three times,' Woodward interjected. 'Under close supervision.'

'When was this?'

'During the last two weeks,' Vulpes said. His eyes were as expressionless as a snake's. 'You don't know what it's like, to walk into an ice cream store and have your choice of twenty-eight different flavours and hot fudge covered with . . . with those little chocolate things.'

What was wrong with that statement? Vail thought. Then he realized there had been no joy in his tone. No excitement, no animation. Vulpes was emotionless, making words, doing his best to create the perfect conundrum, a man so calm his equanimity invoked thoughts of the nightmare sleepwalker in *The Cabinet of Dr Caligari*. Control. Raymond Vulpes had perfected control.

'Sprinkles,' Vail said.

'Sprinkles,' Vulpes repeated.

'That's what excited you about your first day of freedom in ten years, an ice cream with sprinkles?' Vail asked.

'Metaphorically. It's having the choice,' Vulpes answered. 'Here, it's chocolate or vanilla.'

'Another metaphor,' Vail said. 'Black and white, like most choices in life when you carve away all the bullshit.'

Their eyes never strayed. They sat three feet apart, their gazes locked in a hardball game of flinch. Black and white choices, Vail thought, and his mind leapt back to the last day of the trial. There was a clear black and white choice. Vail and his team had spent weeks struggling to prove that Aaron Stampler was really two personalities in one body: Aaron, the sweet kid from Crikside, Kentucky, who had suffered every imaginable kind of abuse; and Roy, the evil *alter ego* with an insatiable lust for murder and revenge. Vail had won for Stampler, rescued him from almost certain death in the electric chair or from a needle filled with terminal sleep. Venable, realizing she was beat, had agreed to the plea bargain: Aaron Stampler would be sent to Daisyland until such time as he was deemed cured and his evil psychological twin, Roy, was purged.

Vail had been elated with his victory. Then, on the way out of the courthouse, Stampler had turned to him, leering, and whispered: 'Suppose there never was an Aaron.' And laughed as they had led him away.

He wants me to know. He wants me to know but not be able to do anything about it. Just like that day after the trial. It was not enough that he had created the nightmare, he wanted to haunt me with it, knowing there was nothing I could do about it, nobody I could tell.

It had been their dark secret for ten years, a cruel umbilical that, even at this moment, bound them together.

Stampler had an insatiable ego. Vail understood that now. That was the game. The dare.

Stop me if you can. Catch me if you can.

Vail did not break the stare. 'And what else did you do beside get a hot fudge sundae?' he asked.

'Went to a record store and bought a couple of CDs. Then we went to Data City, checked out the latest CD-ROMs We went to Belk's and I bought a pair of jeans. My own choice, the colour I wanted, the style I wanted. Two hours of freedom that first day, except, of course, Max was in my shadow all the time. And the next time and the next. Day before yesterday we went to the movies. It was astounding. That enormous screen. Digital sound. Instead of that tiny postage stamp of an image on my eleven-inch screen. Quite an experience.'

'I'll bet,' Vail said. Vail didn't ask what picture he saw although he knew Vulpes was dying to tell him. He was making conversation. He already knew what he had come to find out. The sooner he got out of there, the better.

'Where'd you get the money?' Vail asked, hoping to nick Vulpes's pride, to humiliate him just a little.

'I earned it,' Vulpes answered calmly.

'Earned it?'

'Raymond has become a remarkably proficient electronics repairman. VCRs, TVs, computers . . .'

'Telephones?' Vail said, raising his eyebrows.

What passed for a smile toyed with Vulpes's lips. 'The telephone company takes care of their own communications,' he answered.

'Raymond earns seventy-five cents an hour repairing all our electronics equipment. So we let him branch out,

306

repair equipment for people on the outside. They bring the stuff to the front desk – '

'I've got nine thousand and change in the bank,' Vulpes interrupted in his silky tone. 'The doc deposits it for me. They keep me busy.'

'He's the best in the area. It's almost like a full-time job,' Woodward said proudly.

And then Vulpes said, 'Soon will be.'

The comment froze Vail. Nothing in Vulpes's face changed, but the eyes twinkled for a moment.

'I don't understand,' Vail said.

'Well, that's the real news,' said Woodward. 'In three more days, Raymond's on furlough.'

'Furlough?' said Vail.

'Six weeks. He's got a job in an electronics repair place on Western – '

'He's coming to Chicago?' Vail interrupted.

'We have a halfway house there,' said Woodward. 'Full-time supervision, ten o'clock curfew, some group therapy – we think Raymond's ready for that now, right?'

'I'm sure I can handle it.'

Vail felt as if an enormous hand were squeezing his chest. He modulated his breathing so as not to indicate it had suddenly become stifled. His hands became cold and he was sure the colour had drained from his face. He took a sip of Coke.

'I'll bet you can,' he finally managed to say.

'If it works out, I mean, if he makes it through those first weeks without incident, the board has elected to release him for good.'

'Well, I guess congratulations are in order,' Vail said.

'Maybe we can have lunch one day,' said Vulpes. 'After all, you *are* responsible for my . . . well, for my very existence, aren't you?'

'Sounds like a splendid idea,' Woodward chimed in.

'Maybe so.'

'Well, what do you think, Mr . . . Martin?' Woodward

asked. 'Does the news give you renewed belief in redemption and resurrection?'

'Resurrection?'

'Raymond, here, resurrected from the ashes, so to speak.' Woodward said it with such anomalous pride that Vail was chilled again, not by Vulpes, this time by the egocentric doctor, a man so obviously dazzled by his own brilliance that he was blind to Vulpes's true nature. But then, ten years before, Vail had been just as pleased with himself for having saved Aaron Stampler from certain death.

Vail hardly heard the rest of the conversation. It was unimportant. He was just biding time until he could diplomatically get out of there.

'Well, I think that should be it for the day,' Vail heard Woodward say. 'I'm sure we all need to get back to work.'

'Yes,' Vail said, managing a meagre smile.

Woodward went to the door and called out to Max. Vail got up and walked around the table until he was behind Vulpes. He leaned over and said, ever so softly, 'Raymond?'

Vulpes didn't turn around. He stared straight ahead. 'Yes?'

'Supposing there never was an Aaron?'

Raymond continued to look at the wall on the opposite side of the room. He smiled, but Vail could not see it.

He knows. He knows and there's not a thing he can do about it. I'm a free man and he can't stop that because nobody would believe him.

Half a minute passed before Vulpes turned around. He stood up, his face inches from Vail's. He was smiling, but suddenly, for just an instant, his eyes turned to stone. Hatred glittered in them and the irises turned bloodred.

Like the chill he had felt when he entered the repair room, it came and went in the blink of an eye, but it was enough to send an icicle straight into Vail's heart.

Venable was right. Now he had seen it. It was like

looking into the mind of – whomever? Aaron, Roy, Raymond – and realizing that he was no different, no less malevolent and invidious, no less capable of *anything* than the youth Vail had saved from death ten years before. The only difference was, now he was older, more dangerous, and about to go free.

'There'll always be an Aaron in my heart,' Vulpes said softly, tapping his chest. 'Just as there will always be a Martin in there. I owe everything I am to the two of you.' He said in his silken voice, smiling his sincerest smile, 'Thank you.'

Vulpes stood at the window and watched them walk back across the wide courtyard, Vail striding resolutely towards the entrance. He could guess what Vail was saying. He could almost hear his protest.

But he was wrong. Vail knew there was no percentage in arguing with Woodward. It was, as they say, a done deal and he was powerless to stop it.

'The press will have a field day with this,' he told Woodward.

'The press won't know anything about it. The release order has been signed by a local judge who is very sympathetic to our work. Raymond Vulpes will be released. The press knows Aaron Stampler. They don't even know Raymond Vulpes exists.'

For one fleeting moment, Vail toyed with the notion of bringing up the murders of Linda Balfour and Alex Lincoln, but he decided against it. It was only a matter of time before that news would come out. But Raymond had the perfect alibi. They would be chalked up as copycat killings.

Perfect. Vulpes had thought of everything. He hadn't missed a note.

'I assume you'll honour the confidentiality of this meeting,' Woodward said.

'Confidentiality?'

'Well, legally speaking, you're still his attorney.'

Vail shook his head. 'Conflict of interest,' he answered sardonically. 'As a prosecutor, I'd have to resign the job.'

'Give the boy a chance,' Woodward asked.

'He's not a boy anymore, Woodward,' Vail said.

They shook hands and Vail walked to car, where Tony waited beside the open door.

Tony drove him back to the football field and the pilot cranked up the chopper as he got out of the Cadillac and ran towards it. Vail ducked down under the blades, slid into the seat beside him, and snapped on his seat belt.

'Christ,' the pilot said, 'you look like you saw a ghost.'

'I did,' Vail said. 'Let's get the hell out of here.'

Twenty-Five

ARE YOU THERE, HYDRA?
YES, FOX.
YOU HAVE DONE EXCEPTIONALLY WELL.
  BEYOND EXPECTATIONS.
THANK YOU, FOX.
YOU HAVE STUDIED THE PLAN?
YES, FOX, THE BEAUTIFUL PLAN.
AND ARE YOU PREPARED?
YES, YES.
AND DO YOU HAVE THE MESSAGE?
YES, FOX.
EXCELLENT. ARE YOU EXCITED?
ALWAYS.
IT IS TIME, AGAIN.
THANK YOU. I DON'T LIKE WAITING.
HOW DO YOU FEEL TODAY?
I FEEL EXCEPTIONALLY ANXIOUS.
GOOD. YOU MUST BE MORE CAUTIOUS
  THAN EVER.
DOES HE KNOW?
YES. DO NOT CONCERN YOURSELF. IT IS AS
  WE EXPECTED.
I WILL BE CAUTIOUS.
GOOD. SOON, HYDRA.
YES, YES, YES!
UNTIL THEN . . .

Twenty-Six

Parver came into the office as dusk was ending. The last thin shafts of daylight pierced the windows, casting crimson streaks through the gloom of the office. It was empty except for Vail, who was sitting alone in his office. He was slumped in his chair, his legs stretched out stiffly in front of him, his elbows on the arms of his chair, the fingers of both hands entwined and resting on his chest. His desk lamp was the only illumination on the entire floor and he had pulled the expensive black, cantilevered light down so its beam was swallowed up by the dark wood of his table. He was staring into space.

She approached his office cautiously and rattled on the jamb with her fingers. He looked up, his eyes gleaming in the shadows.

'Ms Parver,' he said with a nod.

'You busy?' she asked.

He thought about that for a couple of seconds and said, 'Yeah. I'm working real hard at being relaxed. I'm into sudden-death overtime at doing absolutely nothing.'

'It can wait,' she said, and started to leave.

'Too late,' he said. 'Come on in here and sit down. What's on your mind?'

'It's about the Stoddard case,' she said, looking across the chaotic mess of his desk. She noticed, lying in front of him, a small tape recorder about the size of a credit card and perhaps half an inch thick attached to a fountain pen by a thread of wire.

'What about Stoddard?' Vail said.

'I'm not sure, I think the case is still loose in places. Some of it, I don't . . . it doesn't quite . . .' She stopped, looking for the proper word.

'Make sense?' he offered.

'Yes. I know you want a perfect case.'

'I don't expect perfection from us mortals,' Vail said with a wry smile. 'Perfection is a perfect sunrise on a clear day. A baby born whole and healthy. Mortals have nothing to do with it.'

'Some people . . .' she said, and then aborted the sentence.

'Some people what?'

'It was a bad thought. I shouldn't have started—'

'Some people *what*, Parver?'

She took a deep breath and her cheeks puffed as she blew it out.

'Some people say you only go to court when you have a sure thing.'

Vail thought about that for a few moments. 'I suppose you might look at it that way,' he said.

'How do you look at it?'

He took out a cigarette and twirled it between two fingers for a while. Finally he said, 'What I expect is a case without any holes. I don't want to get halfway through a trial and discover we're prosecuting an innocent person. I want to *know* they're guilty – or forget it. If that's playing it safe, so be it. On the other hand, if we know, if we're absolutely, no-shit positive that the party is guilty, like Darby, I'll send them to hell or burn out my brain trying.'

'Can we ever be that sure, Marty?' she asked.

'What do you mean?'

'I mean, if it's not absolutely open-and-shut, can we ever be sure?'

'We're sure about Darby.'

'You're going to make a deal.'

'Because we don't have a case yet. Even with old Mrs What'shername's fantastic auricle sense. Rainey will have the son of a bitch back on the street before the time changes. I told you at the time, better to get him off the street for twenty years than have him back at Poppy Palmer's bar with two hundred fifty K in the bank.'

'Maybe that's what they're talking about.'

'Who are "they"? Who've you been talking to?'

She shrugged. 'I swear I don't even remember. Some smartass young lawyer at the bar in Guido's.'

'Did it bother you?'

'Made me mad,' she said, her forehead gathering into seams.

'That's being bothered.' He laughed and after a minute or so she joined him. 'Who cares what those loudmouth suits think, anyway?' he said.

When their laughter had run its course, he fell quiet again. She looked across the desk at him and it occurred to her that she had never, since she had started working for him, seen him really blow up. When he was truly angry, he became the ultimate poker player. His face became a mask. He quieted up. Only his eyes showed anything. His eyes did the thinking. They became alert and feral. Otherwise, his attitude had always been typically Irish: either 'Don't sweat the little ones' or 'Don't get mad, get even.'

His eyes were alert and feral right now.

'What's bugging you?' she asked, surprised that she had asked the question and concerned that perhaps she had crossed the line between business and personal things. He stared almost blankly across the desk, not at her, at some object on the other side of the room. He put the cigarette between his lips but did not light it.

'Stampler,' he said after a while.

'Stampler?'

'I saw him today.'

'Why is he bugging you?'

'Because he's a liar. Because he's amoral and he knows it and he's comfortable with it. Because he's a psychopathic schemer and a killer and he's about to be set free *on our turf* and he already knows who he's going to kill

314

and how and when. And he knows I know he's going to do it and there's not a goddamn thing I can do to stop him.'

Her eyebrows arched higher and higher as he spoke, and when he finished, she said, 'Ooo-kaaay.'

'Nobody else knows this yet,' he said. 'Keep it to yourself until I go public with it.'

'Is that what the tape recorder was for? I mean, is that legal?'

He stared down at it and then back to her. 'It's for reference,' he said, and ended that part of the conversation.

'What are you going to do about him?' she asked.

'If I knew the answer to that, I wouldn't be sitting here in the dark, I'd be over at Janie's scarfing down homemade spaghetti and thinking about what a lovely evening it's going to get to be later on.'

'Can I help?'

'Shana, you may have a short fuse and you may be hell on wheels in court, but this is not something you want to get involved in. This is not like looking at pictures of murder victims or going eyeball to eyeball with some drive-by shooter. This is devil's play and whatever innocence you still harbour will surely be destroyed if you come too close.'

She did not answer and a silence fell on the room. After a while she squirmed in her chair and cleared her throat and started to get up, and he suddenly sat straight up in the chair and snapped his fingers so loudly it startled her.

'Okay,' he said. 'Thanks for listening to that. I'm going over to Jane Venable's now and try to forget all of this for a few hours. As for Edith Stoddard, you're right. As Jane says, there's something wrong with the picture. Figure out what it is. I'd like to know, too.'

'Thanks,' she said, rather flatly.

'It's your case, Parver. Was there anything substantial you wanted to discuss?'

'No, just needed to talk, I guess, and here you were.'

'You want to talk some more?'

She smiled and shook her head. 'Nope, and I'm sure you don't, either.'

Vail stood up and stretched his arms. 'Absolutely right,' he said. 'Come on, we'll share a cab. I'll buy.'

'I'll pay my share,' she said, somewhat defensively.

'Hey,' Vail said, 'you want to be that way about it, you can pay the whole damn tab.'

Harvey St Claire watched the day dying through the farmhouse window. Near the edge of a pine thicket half a mile away he saw the beams of flashlights begin to dance in the dusk. They had been at the search for Poppy Palmer six hours.

'They're not gonna find her, Abel.'

'I know.'

'So why're we wasting time out here?'

'I could be wrong.'

Stenner had been seated at Darby's desk for two hours, painstakingly going through bills, mail, notebooks, everything he could find.

St Claire swung a wooden chair around and sat backward on it. 'No airline reservation. No cab ride. Her car's parked at the apartment – '

Stenner said, 'He could've driven her down to O'Hare.'

'No airline reservation,' St Claire repeated. 'And no sister in Texarkana.'

'To wherever she went.'

'No airline reservation – '

'Paid cash, gave a phoney name.'

'Her photo's been flashed at every ticket counter at the airport. Nobody recognized her.'

'Maybe she wore a wig.'

'You're a very strange guy, Abel.'

'I've worked for Martin Vail for ten years. You get to think that way after a while. It's the way he thinks. He hates surprises.'

'So if she ain't here and she didn't leave, where the hell is she?'

Stenner did not answer. He continued his boring chore in silence.

'Sometimes I wish to hell I never heard of Miranda,' St Claire said. 'Sometimes I yearn fer a little Texas justice.'

'What is Texas justice?' Stenner said, and was almost immediately sorry he asked. He was carefully sorting through the stacks of opened mail on the desk. He had piled the day's delivery, unopened, on the opposite corner of the desk.

'Back when I was in the US Marshall's, this was, hell, eighteen, twenty years ago,' St Claire started, 'I got sent down to the Mexican border to sniff out a runner named Chulo Garciez, who got himself busted for running illegals across the border and selling 'em to migrant farms. Two of my best friends were carryin' him up to San Antonio and what they didn't know, Chulo's girl-friend had smuggled him a watch spring in a candy bar. Was a Mars bar, I think, or maybe a Baby Ruth.'

Stenner looked up at him dolefully for an instant and then went back to the mail.

St Claire went on, 'Chulo secrets this here spring in the back of his belt, knowing he would be cuffed behind his back in the back-seat of the car, and he picks the cuffs with the spring, reaches over the front seat, hauls out Freddy Corello's .45, puts two in his head, and empties the other four into Charley Hinkle, who was driving, jumps over the seat, kicks Charley out, pulls onto the verge, kicks Freddy out, and heads back to the border in the government car. They find it about ten miles from Eagle Pass right on the border. So I go down to the Border Patrol station in Eagle Pass and that's where I met Harley Bohanan, who was about six-seven and weighed two-fifty and made John Wayne look like a midget. Carried an old-fashioned .44 low on his hip, like Wayne.'

'Uh-huh.'

'I tell my story to ol' Harley and he says he knows Garciez and he is one bad-ass Mex and maybe he can help me and he puts me up in this awful goddamn adobe motel outside a town with roaches as big as wharf rats and no air conditionin'. Has a damn ceiling fan so big it'd suck yer eyeballs out. You had to keep your eyes closed when you laid under it.'

'Uh-huh.'

'Two nights later Harley is bangin' on my door at four in the mornin' and we drive out towards Quemado and right there on the river in a little boxed canyon there's a dozen wannabe wetbacks, all shot in the back of the head, stripping clean, even had their gold teeth knocked out. Harley is snoopin' around and suddenly he says, "One of 'em got away." Sure enough, we pick up some barefoot tracks and we follow them for a couple hours and finally come on this illegal cowerin' in a little cave in the desert. Poor son-bitch dyin' a thirst.'

'Uh-huh.'

'He tells us they were set up by a federalee captain name a . . . hell what was his name? . . . uh, Martino, Martinez, something like that, *and* a guy named Chulo, who was supposed to pick 'em up at the border and take 'em to find work on this side, only instead Chulo and the federalee started shootin' them. This fella just lucked out. Harley knows who this federalee is. That night we ford the Rio Grande – it's about a inch deep there – in his Jeep and the federalee is drinkin' in a cantina. We wait till he comes out and Harley grabs him like you'd grab a puppy by the back of the neck and throws him in the back of the Jeep and we drive back down to the river and he throws the Mex out into the river and then pulls down his pants. He pulls out that .44 and it don't have any front sight on it. Filed off. He goes into the chest on the back of the Jeep, takes out an old, dirty can of ten-weight motor oil, dips the muzzle of the .44 in the can, and then shoves this federalee down on the knees and bends him over and, as I stand here, swear t'God, sticks the muzzle of the pistol about an inch and a half up the federalee's ass and says, "Where's Chulo? I count t'three and I don't know, I'm gonna blow your brains out the hard way." '

'Uh-huh,' Stenner said, still examining the mail.

'An hour later we're outside a cantina on the US side. There's Chulo's truck and he's inside drinkin' beer and playin' with some little hot-stuff *señorita* and Harley pulls out a knife the size of Mount Everest and carves a hole outta the rear tyre on the truck. I stroll into the bar and order a Corona and I say, in Mex, "That truck out there's got a flat." Chulo gets up and stomps out the door, me kinda amblin' behind him. He goes to the back a the truck and he's leaning over examinin' the damage and Harley steps around from behind it with his .44 drawn and says, "Garciez, yer under arrest fer draft dodgin'," and Chulo jumps up and makes th' mistake of reachin' under his arm and *kaBOOM*, ol' Harley blows a hole through that sorry son-bitch you could drive his truck through. And y' know what ol' Harley says? "Costs twenty bucks a day to house a US prisoner and Chulo was lookin' at twenty years. Hell, Harve, we just saved the taxpayers about a hundred grand." That's what I mean by Texas justice.'

Stenner still did not look up from the bills and letters.

'That was some long story just to explain two words,' he said when St Claire finished this epic.

'Thought you'd appreciate the details,' St Claire said. 'Ain't like we're runnin' late for a ballgame or nothin'.' He walked to a window, threw it open, and sent a long squirt of tobacco juice out on the lawn.

'You were Darby,' Stenner said, 'wanted to get lost for a week or two, where would you go, Harvey?'

'I dunno. Hawaii. One of the Caribbean islands?'

'Can't afford it. Insurance company has him on hold, bank account's almost empty. He's surely maxed out his credit cards. And he was still here yesterday, mail's open.'

Stenner handed St Claire two phone bills. 'How about a little hunting trip?' he said. 'Red Marsh Lodge, on the Pecatonica River about eighty miles from here. Called them twice last month and just a couple of days ago, last entry on the bill that came today.'

He dialled the number.

'Red Marsh,' answered a soft-spoken man with a slightly Swedish accent.

'Yes,' Stenner said. 'We're friends of Jim Darby's, Mr James Darby? We were supposed to go on this trip with him, but we thought we had to work. We got off early. Is he still there?'

'He's down riggin' out his boat. Take me a bit to get 'im back up here.'

'No, we don't want to talk to him. We thought we'd drive on up and surprise him in the morning. Do you have a double open?'

'Sure do. Cabin eight, right next to him.'

'He's in seven?'

'Nine.'

'Good. Now don't tell him about the call, we want to surprise the hell out of him at breakfast.'

'You'll have to get here mighty early then. He's takin' the boat out to the blind at four-thirty. Wants t'be there at first light. Most of the boys do.'

'You have a boat rental open?'

'Sure do.'

'Hold that for us, too. The name's Stenner. A. Stenner.'

'Abe Stenner. Gotcha.'

'Right, Abe Stenner.' He hung up, looked at St Claire, and almost smiled.

'We got him,' he said.

*

Later that night, in bed, with Jane Venable nestled under his arm, one of her long legs thrown over one of his, and her breathing soft and steady in his ear, Vail thought how quickly and naturally their first furious lovemaking had turned into an untroubled, easy partnership. The passion was always sudden and furious and overwhelming, but there was also a sense of comfort when they were together. Perhaps it was because they were both in their forties and love – if that was what this was, neither of them had tampered with the word yet – was like finding some small treasure each of them had lost and both had given up hope of ever finding again. For the first time in years, Vail was thankful when the day was over, when he could flee the office and come to her and delight in her presence. He lay on his back, half smiling, and stared up through the darkness at the vaulted ceiling. But soon his thoughts began turning in on him and they drifted away from Jane Venable and back to Aaron Stampler – or Raymond Vulpes – or whoever the hell he was, and he thought: *Not this time, you son of a bitch. You did it to me once. That time was on me. This time it's on you.*

Twenty-Seven

The fog was so cotton-thick as they neared the marshes guarding the river that Stenner was reduced to driving at twenty miles an hour. He leaned forward, eyes squinted, trying to discern the white line down the middle of the country road. He had missed the turnoff to the lodge in the soupy mist and they had to double back, driving slowly along the blacktop road, flicking the lights between high and low so they could see through the earthbound clouds. Eventually they saw the sign, a small wooden square at the intersection of the main road and an unpaved lane that disappeared into the trees. They were running late, four-thirty having come and gone.

RED MARSH LODGE, it said in black letters on a mud-spattered white sign. A thick red arrow below the letters pointed down the dirt road. Even on low beam, the headlights turned the fog into a blinding mirror and they crept through the forest on the winding, rutted road for almost two miles before the rustic main building of the lodge suddenly jumped out at them through the haze.

Quarter to five.

Walt Sunderson, a heavyset Swede with a florid complexion and a thick red moustache that dropped down almost to his jaw, stepped out on the porch of the log cabin. He was dressed in overalls and a thick flannel shirt under a padded Arctic jacket.

'Abe Stenner?' he called out, the word sounding flat and without resonance in the thick grey condensation.

'Yes, sir,' the detective said, getting out of the car.

'Just missed him,' Sunderson said in the melodramatic cadence peculiar to the Swedish. 'Darby hauled outta here ten, fifteen minutes ago. I got your boat ready, though, and a map of the marshes and blinds. Won't take you hardly any time at all to get rigged out. You can unpack when you get back. Don't even have to lock your car.'

'That's right civilized,' St Claire said, shoving a wad of tobacco under his lip with his thumb.

'Got plenty hot coffee, you betcha, ready for you in a thermos. Hope you like it black?'

They both nodded. Although Stenner preferred a pinch of two of sugar in his, they were eager to get started. Stenner and St Claire retrieved two shotguns in black leather cases from the trunk. St Claire was wearing a fur-lined ammo vest, its slots filled with 12-gauge shotgun shells. Stenner stuffed another box of rounds in one of the pockets of his army field jacket while Sunderson got the quart thermos. He led them down a long, narrow floating deck.

'Careful, fellas, can't see a thing in this soup.'

'Is it always this thick?' St Claire asked.

'Not in the daytime.'

The boat, a ten-foot, flat-bottomed skiff with a thirty hp motor riveted to the stern, lolled in the still water, barely distinguishable in the darkness and mist despite the heavy beam of a one hundred-watt floodlight nearby. Sunderson checked the floor of the skiff and, scowling and muttering to himself, went to a small shed at the end of the dock. He came back with a coil of heavy rope looped over his shoulder.

'Could have sworn I put an anchor and chain in your boat last night,' he said. 'I'll hitch up this line for you. There's lots of trees and stumps out there, you won't have any trouble finding something to tie up to.'

'That'll be fine,' Stenner said, clambering aboard behind St Claire, who had taken the stern and tiller. They set off into the windless, oppressive darkness, their faces and jackets dripping with condensation before they had travelled fifty yards.

'Kinda eerie,' St Claire said, following the beam of a small headlight mounted on the bow.

'Ah, "death, to feel the fog in my throat, the mist in my face",' Stenner said softly.

'Didn't know you were a poet, Abel,' St Claire chuckled.

'I'm not. Robert Browning was.'

They fell silent and the boat moved slowly up the narrow creek, the motor gurgling behind them. Stenner held a small map trying to figure out where they were. Twenty minutes later Stenner could see another boat vaguely through the damp, shifting, strands of mist. It was tied to a fallen tree.

'Two of them,' Stenner whispered as they approached the blind.

The two hunters were dressed in camouflage suits and had thrown their life jackets into the stern of the boat. Neither one was Darby. Rushes swished along the sides of the skiff as St Claire guided it towards the blind. One of the men, who was tall and dissipated-looking, was taking a long pull from a gallon jug, holding it high in the crook of his arm and tilting his head back, letting the amber fluid run easily into his mouth. A large black lab with friendly eyes sat on the seat beside the other man and ruffed when he saw them coming through the fog.

'Morning,' the man beside the dog said cheerfully. He was a short fellow, bordering on fat, with a jowly face that became almost cherubic when he smiled.

'Morning,' Stenner said as St Claire reversed the engine and angled in beside their boat. The drinker lowered the jug and wiped his mouth with the back of his hand.

'Care for a swig?' he asked, offering the bottle. 'Home-made cider. It'll sure take the edge of this chill.'

Stenner said, 'Thanks, anyway.' St Claire reached out and took the jug and, holding up his elbow, expertly dropped it into the angle of his arm and took a long swig. He shuddered as he lowered the container and handed it back.

'Sure right about that,' he said. 'It warms ya right through to yer bones. Thanks.'

'You seen another hunter out here this morning?' Stenner asked.

'You mean Jim Darby. He went on up to six. 'Bout half an hour ago.'

'What's six?' Stenner asked.

'The blinds are numbered. On that map you got there. Old Walt hand-drew the sorry thing. Six is down the creek half a mile or so just before it dumps into the river. This is four here and that one over on the far side of the creek is five.'

'How far away is six?' Stenner asked.

'Half-mile, maybe.'

'Couldn't take more then ten minutes to go up there, could it?'

'More like five, even in the fog.'

'Thanks.'

'You friends of his?' one of them asked.

'Yeah,' St Claire said. 'Thought we'd surprise him. Well, thanks for the help.'

'Sure. Good hunting.'

'Same to you.'

St Claire throttled up and angled the small boat back out into the creek and headed for the six blind. Five minutes later they picked out a small sign on a crooked post with a solitary 6 hand-painted on it. St Claire turned into the tall river grass and cut the engine. The blind was empty.

'Hear that?' St Claire said. Stenner listened keenly and through the fog could hear the low mutter of an engine. Then a dog started barking and a moment later they heard a muffled splash. The engine picked up a little speed and gradually got louder.

'Here he comes,' Stenner whispered.

The sputtering sound of the motor moved slowly towards them and then the skiff emerged through the fog almost directly in front of them. Darby was hunched in the back of the skiff. He seemed preoccupied and did not see them until the dog, a spotted spaniel of some kind, started barking.

'Jesus,' he said with surprise, and cut his motor. He had a 12-gauge shotgun turned down-side-up in his lap, snapping shells into the chamber. St Claire eased a 9mm Glock out of its shoulder holster and casually laid hand and gun on his thigh. As the other boat neared his Darby squinted through the gauzy wisps of fog and suddenly recognized Stenner. He sat up, scowling, as he drew abreast of them. Stenner reached out and grabbed the gunwale of Darby's boat and pulled them together.

'Good morning, Mr Darby,' he said. He reached into his jacket pocket and took out the warrant. As he did, St Claire raised up on one knee and held the pistol out at arm's length, pointing straight at Darby's face.

'Kindly put that scattergun down on the bottom of that skiff,' he said with harsh authority.

'We have a warrant for your arrest, Mr Darby,' Stenner said, and held the warrant in front of his face.

Darby was obviously startled. Even in the fog and predawn gloom, they could see the colour in his face drain from ruddy to pasty-white.

'That's no good up here,' he snarled. The dog snarled menacingly in the front of the boat. 'Shut up, Rags.' The dog whined into silence.

'Sheriff'll be waiting when we get back t'camp,' said St Claire. 'You wouldn't want to add unlawful flight to your problems, now, would ya?'

'I'm not fleeing. Do I look like I'm fleeing to you? I got nothin' to flee about.'

'This warrant charges you with first-degree murder in the death of your wife. You have a right to remain silent – '

326

'I know the drill,' he hissed, and put the shotgun aside. 'I heard it all before.'

'I'd like you to turn around and put your hands behind your back, please,' Stenner said formally. 'I have to cuff you.'

'I'm not going anywhere,' Darby said.

'Procedure.'

'Don't do that, please,' he said. His tone had changed suddenly from arrogant to almost solicitous.

'I told you, it's procedure.'

'Not behind my back, okay? Where would I go?'

'Don't give us any guff, son,' St Claire said.

'I'm asking you, please don't tie my hands behind my back,' he begged. 'I . . . I can't swim.'

St Claire looked at Stenner, who in turn looked at Darby, who was plainly terrified. The dog walked unsteadily back and started to growl again.

'I said, shut up!' Darby bellowed, and smacked the dog in the face. It yelped and curled up on the floor of the skiff. 'Please,' he pleaded.

'Cuff him in front, Harve,' Stenner said in a flat, no-nonsense monotone. St Claire holstered his pistol and moved up beside him.

'Thanks,' Darby said, holding his hands out for St Claire to shackle. Once cuffed, Darby laid on the bottom of the boat with his head barely visible over the side. The abused Rags crawled up beside him and licked his face.

'Dogs'll forgive anything,' St Claire said, shaking his head. He looked down at Darby. 'What were ya doin' out there in the marsh?' he asked.

'Took a dump,' Darby said sullenly.

'Helluva dump. Sounded like the *Titanic* goin' down.' He swung the bow light around, letting its beam cut through the rising fog. Darby's boat had left a pathway through the water grass. 'Lookee there,' St Claire said with a grin. 'He left us a little trail t'foller.'

He tied Darby's boat to the back of their skiff and

headed back through the marsh grass. To the east, the rising sun bloodied the mist and cast long, dim shadows across the marsh. A snake glided past them, unconcerned, looking for breakfast, its head sticking up, perusing the terrain. Off in the still persistent fog, a bird squawked and they could hear its big wings flapping through the grey, awakening morning. Presently the path ended. The grass was folded down in a large circle. At one end, the skeletal fingers of a tree branch reached up out of the water.

'Think this here's the place,' he told Stenner. 'Why don't I tie down here and wait for you to take him back to the lodge and bring the sheriff and a coupla drag lines out here.'

'Fair enough,' Stenner answered, and swung the two boats together. 'I'm coming over there,' he told Darby. 'Keep your dog in tow.'

'He's all noise,' Darby said. 'What's this all about, anyway?'

'Poppy Palmer,' Stenner said, and Darby's face turned the colour of wet cement as Stenner stepped into the skiff.

'What're you talking about?' Darby whined. 'She went to see her sister in Texarkana.'

'She ain't got a sister in Texarkana.'

'That ain't my fault!'

'Now there's a goddamn non sequitur for ya.' St Claire laughed.

'Back as fast as I can, Harve,' Stenner said. 'You'll be okay?'

St Claire looked at him balefully and took a swig of coffee as the other skiff rumbled off through the grass and into the crimson morning.

Sun and wind had sent the fog swirling away and the morning had dawned bright and cold when St Claire saw the thirty-foot powerboat cruising up the creek. He put two fingers in the corners of his mouth and whistled shrilly and waved. They turned into the marsh and slid quietly up to his boat. Stenner was standing beside the sheriff, a tall, bulky man in a dark blue jacket wearing a brown campaign hat with his badge pinned to the crown.

'Mornin' gentlemen,' St Claire said. 'Thanks fer comin' by.'

The sheriff's boat churned to a stop as he walked to the bow and, leaning over, took St Claire's hand.

'Jake Broadstroke,' he said in a voice that sounded like it came from his toes. 'Sorry we took so long, had to round up a couple of divers. Hope you two know what you're talking about.'

'Well, it's a hunch,' St Claire said. 'But I got thirty years a hunches under m'belt and I ain't often wrong.'

One of the divers, dressed in a black wet suit and a face mask, slipped over the side of the big boat. The water was waist-deep.

'Hell, Sheriff, I doubt we'll need the drag lines. Bottom's a little murky, but we oughtta be able to tread it out. Somebody hand me a light.'

He took the waterproof lamp, adjusted his face mask, and went under, joined a minute or two later by the other diver. Everybody settled back and waited. Nobody said anything. The only sound was the wind rattling the weeds.

Half an hour crept by. The sheriff gnawed on the remains of a cigar. St Claire spat freely into the wind-rippled water. Stenner said nothing. All eyes gazed out over the reeds. Then the muddy swamp churned a bit and a woman's head suddenly broke the surface, rising up out of the water. Wet-dark hair streaked down over a bloated, blue-grey face, partially covering a gaping mouth filled with mud. Black links of chain were gnarled around her throat. Water dribbled from her glassy eyes and for just a moment or two she appeared to be weeping. Poppy Palmer had danced her last striptease.

'Ah, Jesus,' St Claire said.

'Yes,' Stenner said, almost inaudibly. 'I was hoping we were wrong, too.'

Twenty-Eight

Vail was behind the closed door of his office, a signal to the rest of the staff that he wanted to be left alone. Naomi called it 'diving'. It was as if Vail were underwater, in a different world, one without sound or distraction, one in which all the data and facts of the case were jumbled together. He sought to categorize them, to rearrange them into a logical chronology until they formed a picture that made sense to him. Like a legal jigsaw puzzle, the picture would eventually become clear even though some of the pieces were missing. Only one thing was on his mind: Aaron Stampler – or Raymond Vulpes – one and the same, unchanged, he was certain.

Vail had not yet broached the problem of Stampler/Vulpes with the staff and would not until he had analysed his meeting with Vulpes and Woodward and formed a beginning strategy for dealing with the situation. He was wearing earphones, listening to the tape he had made of the interview with the psychiatrist and his 'creation'. He knew that somewhere in that tape Vulpes had revealed himself – purposely – to taunt Vail. Somewhere on that tape was a clue that Vail would recognize. Nothing incriminating, just Vulpes letting Vail know that he was still Aaron Stampler and that he had successfully scammed them all. If Vail knew anything he knew that Stampler's ego would ultimately be his undoing.

He had been behind his closed doors for hours when he got the call from Stenner. He and St Claire would be in the office momentarily with details, but they wanted Vail to know that Darby was in custody and that they had discovered Poppy Palmer's body. Vail had to put Stampler/Vulpes aside for now and deal with the Darby case. Twenty minutes later Stenner and St Claire blew into the office like a March wind.

My God, Vail thought, *did I just see Stenner smile?*

Vail waved Parver into his office and leaned back in his chair. 'Okay,' he said to his two chief investigators, 'let's hear it.'

'He spilled his guts,' St Claire said. 'We had him pegged right on his wife's murder, Shana, the old lady's hearing was perfect. Thing is, Rainey never got hold of Darby, so he didn't know we were after his ass. He thought he was home free except for Poppy Palmer.'

Stenner picked up the story: 'Stretched his luck. Picked her up, told her he was taking her to the airport, drove to his barn, strangled her on the spot.'

'Then the miserable son-bitch threw her in the boot and drove around for the better part of a day with her body,' St Claire continued. 'Spent the night in a motel outside Rockford, and this mornin' he wrapped her up in an anchor chain and dropped her in the marsh up along the Pecatonica.'

'Congratulations,' Vail said. 'You two did a great job.'

'We had some luck,' said Stenner. 'We were actually so close to him, we heard him drop her body in the water.' He turned to Shana Parver. 'But now you've got him.' He held up two fingers. 'Twice.'

'Rainey was waitin' at county jail when we brought him down,' said St Claire. 'Says he wants t'talk.'

Vail laughed. 'Sure he does. Well, the hell with Rainey, it's too late now.' He turned to Shana Parver. 'Okay, Shana, you got your way. Darby's all yours. I assume you'll want to max him out?'

She looked up and smiled, but there was little mirth in the grin. 'Of course . . .' she said.

'You have a different idea?'

'No, sir!'

'Everything in order?' Vail asked Stenner. 'About the arrest, I mean?'

'We served the warrant on him, Mirandized him, and used the sheriff in Stephenson County to locate the body.'

Parver sat quietly in the corner, nibbling on the corner of one lip.

'What is it, Shana?' Vail asked.

'I can't help thinking if we had taken him down right after the deposition, Poppy Palmer'd still be alive.'

'We didn't have anything to take him down *with* after the deposition,' Vail answered, a bit annoyed. 'Hell, by the time we got the warrant, she was already dead.'

Parver did not reply to Vail's comment.

'Shana?'

'Yes, sir.'

'If she hadn't lied to us, she'd still be alive.'

'I know.'

'There's no looking back on this. Tell Rainey for me the girl's blood is on his hands, not ours. If he had delivered his man to us when he said he would, Poppy Palmer would be alive today.'

'I'll tell him that.' She nodded.

'Good. No more plea bargains. You wanted to take him all the way? Do it. Take him all the way to the chair.'

'Yes, sir.'

St Claire trudged through the chilly sunset to the records warehouse two blocks away. He had seen the sun rise and now was watching it set, but he was still too adrenalized to quit for the night. He decided to take a stab at finding the missing Stampler tapes among the mountains of records and files and boxes in the chaos that was the trial records warehouse. It would be impossible, he knew, but maybe he would get lucky twice in one day.

He walked wearily through the dim, two-storey-high crisscross of corridors lined high with boxes and files and illuminated only by green-shaded bulbs high above the walkways. He heard the muffled tones of Frank Sinatra singing 'Come Fly With Me' echoing from one of the corridors and the dim reflection of a light casting long shadows into the main walkway. When he reached the corner and looked down the aisle, he saw a police sergeant seated in a rocking chair under an old-fashioned floor lamp with a fringed shade. He was listening to a small transistor radio with his feet propped against a grey metal desk, gently rocking himself.

'Hi, there,' St Claire said, his voice reverberating down the corridor.

'The old cop jumped. 'God*damn*,' he said. 'Scare a man half to death.'

'Sorry,' said St Claire, walking down the box-lined corridor. 'M'name's Harve St Claire, DA's office.'

The cop lowered his feet and turned the radio volume down. A handprinted sign on a doubled-over piece of white shirt-board read C. FELSCHER, CUSTODIAN.

'Sgt. Claude Felscher at your service.' He stuck out his hand.

He was a large, bulky man, overweight and rumpled, his uniform unpressed, his pants sagging under a beer belly, his tie askew and not pulled tight enough to hide the missing top button on his blue uniform shirt. A tangled fringe of grey hair curled over his ears. He looked dusty and forgotten, like a fossil lost in the shadowy corner of a museum. Only his badge added an incongruous touch to the gloomy scene. It was polished and it twinkled under the dim bulb of the old lamp.

St Claire wedged a healthy chew under his lip and offered the plug to the old cop, who shook his head.

'How long've you been custodian here, Claude?'

'Hell, I been here since Cain knocked off Abel.'

'Must be the loneliest job in town.'

'Oh, I dunno,' the old-timer said. 'Look around you. I got all these famous cases to keep me company. Remember Speck? Richard Speck?'

'Sure.'

'Right over there in aisle 19. Gacy is down in 6. George

Farley, killed twelve women, remember? Pickled them, kept them in jars in the basement? Over on 5. Even got a file on Dillinger, from when he was locked up after that bank robbery outside Gary. They had a touch of class about them, not like the bums these days. Drive-by shootings, easy store stickups, for Christ sake! World's really fucked up, Harve.'

'I couldn't agree more. You remember the Rushman case?'

'The archbishop? Hell, that was like yesterday. That what you're looking for?'

St Claire nodded. 'State versus Aaron Stampler. Trial ended in late March.'

'Anything specific?'

'Physical evidence.'

'Aw, shit. Let me tell you about physical evidence. By the time it gets here, it's pretty well picked over. All we get is what hasn't been claimed. And it's not in any particular order. Look around you. I couldn't tell you how many cases are stored in here – thousands, hell, hundreds of thousands – a lot of it misplaced or misfiled.'

'I was afraid of that. Thought maybe I'd luck out.'

'Well, hell, don't give up so easy.' The sergeant got a flashlight from a desk drawer and led St Claire down through the caverns of records. The odour of mildew and damp paper stung St Claire's nose. Felscher found the cardboard boxes filled with the Stampler records.

'I been down here before,' St Claire said. 'Must've been your day off. There wasn't any evidence here, it's all paper.'

'You're right,' Felscher said, sliding several of the boxes out of their nesting places, checking them, and pushing them back. 'What exactly are you after, anyway?'

'Some videotapes.'

'Sorry. But you're welcome to look around the place.' He swept his arm in a semicircle and laughed.

'Forget it. Thanks for your help, Claude.' They shook

hands and St Claire started back down the dreary corridor of files.

'Don't feel too bad, Harve. They'd probably be pretty well deteriorated by now, anyway. This isn't exactly what you'd call a humidity-controlled facility.'

'I didn't wanna look at 'em, I was hopin' to find out if they were disposed of. And to whom.'

'Oh, now wait just a minute. Why didn't you say so? That's a little different story. You might still luck out.'

Felscher walked down the corridor to a series of bookshelves lined with long rows of canvas-bound ledgers identified by dates. He ran his forefinger along the spines. 'Let's see, September first to tenth, '82 . . . December . . . February . . . Here we go, March twentieth through thirtieth, 1983.' Felscher pulled a mildewed and roach-gnawed ledger from the shelf. 'These are the index ledgers. Not a lot of help when you're looking for something, but . . .'

He opened the book and carefully turned the pages, which were yellowed with age and faded, the entries handwritten by the clerk of the court.

'Got to be careful. These old books'll fall apart on you. Stampler, Stampler, yeah, that was some big case, all right? Wonder whatever happened to him?'

'Still in Daisyland.'

'Good. The way he carved up the old bishop, they ought to keep him there forever.'

'Yeah,' St Claire agreed.

'Okay, here we go, March twenty-third . . . State versus Aaron Stampler, murder in the first. Here's the inventory. Let's see, got some bloody clothes, shoes, a kitchen knife, couple of books, and a ring, they were returned to the cathedral out on Lakeview, 2/4/83. What d'ya know, Harve, you did get lucky. Here we go, twenty-three videotapes. They were released to a Dr Molly Arrington, Winthrop, Indiana, 26/4/83.'

'Well, I'll be damned,' St Claire said, and his heart jumped a beat. 'She's got the whole damn tape library.'

The office was abandoned except for Parver, who was sitting alone in her small office. The thick Darby file lay on the desk in front of her, but she had tired of looking at it and had pulled the Stoddard file. She really did not want to deal with either of them. She was tired and had no place to go but home, and so she sat alone in her big office, fighting off what was a mounting malaise. Behind her, the lift door opened and Flaherty stepped off, carrying a battered old briefcase. He went to his office, threw the case on his desk, and only then noticed that Parver was still there. He ambled back to her cubbyhole and stood in the doorway with his hand stuffed in his pockets.

'Good news about Darby,' he said. 'I can hardly wait to hear your summation to the jury.'

She looked at him, her face bunched up as if she were in pain. 'Did you hear about Poppy Palmer?'

'It's all over the afternoon editions,' he said. 'I hear Eckling is scorched. He's saying if his department had handled it, the girl never would have been killed.'

'What do you expect? If he'd handled the case, Darby probably would have killed half the county before Eckling got his head far enough out of his ass to figure it out.'

Flaherty whistled low through his teeth. 'You okay?' he asked.

'Why?' she snapped back.

'Hey, excuse me, I should have knocked.' He started to leave.

'Where are you going?' she demanded.

'I don't know, you seem a little . . .' He paused, searching for the right word. 'Pensive?'

'Pensive?' She considered that and said, half smiling. 'I guess I am a little pensive right now.'

'Can I help?'

She stared up at him from behind her desk for a moment, then wheeled her chair back and stood up. 'How'd you like to go over to Corchran's? I'll buy you a drink.'

'No, I'll buy you a drink.'

'Ah, one of those, huh? Tell you what, Flaherty, I'll toss you for it.'

'You mean, like, throwing coins against the wall?'

'Uh-huh.' She reached into her purse and took out two quarters. She handed him one. 'Back in the computer room, there's no carpet on the floor.'

'You sound like a pro.'

'I have my days.'

They walked back to the computer room and stood ten feet from the bare back wall.

'How do you do this?' he asked innocently.

'They don't pitch quarters in Boston?'

'I rarely had a quarter when I lived in Boston.'

'You just pitch the coin. One who gets closest to the wall wins. Want a practice shot first?'

'Nah, let's just do it. Winner buys?'

'Winner buys.'

'You go first, I'll see how it's done.'

She leaned over, put one hand on her knee, held the coin between her thumb and forefinger, and scaled it side-hand. It hit the wall, bounced back three inches, and spun around several times before it dropped.

'Looks pretty good,' he said.

'Not bad.'

'Like this, huh,' he said, assuming the same stance she had except that he used his left hand.

'You're a southpaw,' she said. 'I never noticed that before.'

'You never noticed a lot about me, Parver,' he answered.

The remark surprised her.

'Just kind of flip it, huh?'

'Uh-huh.'

He leaned way over, held his hand at arm's length, and sighted down his arm, then tossed the coin overhand. It flipped through the air, twanged into the juncture of the floor and wall, and died. There wasn't a quarter of an inch between the coin and the wall.

'What d'ya know,' he said. 'Beginner's luck.'

Parver's eyes narrowed suspiciously. 'You hustled me, Flaherty,' she said through clenched teeth.

'Never!'

'I saw the way you did that. You definitely hustled me!'

He grinned, picked up the quarters, and handed them to her. 'Shall we?'

They took a cab to Corchran's and went back to the Ladies Room. Steamroller gave them a gap-toothed smile and led them to a corner booth. He swept the table off with the damp rag stuck in his belt and looked at them with his good eye.

'Drinkin'? Eatin'?' he asked.

'We'll start with drinks, and see what happens.'

'Thwell, what'll it be?'

'Martini, very dry, straight up, no condiments,' Parver said.

'Condi-what?'

'No fruit or vegetables,' said Flaherty.

'Gotcha. Mithter Flaherty, the uthual?'

'Yep.'

'On the way, sluggerth.' Steamroller swaggered off towards the bar.

'Okay, Parver, what's eating you? Hell, you got everything you could want. You got Darby wired, you got Stoddard. Two capital cases. Want to give me one of them?'

'No, thank you very much,' she said haughtily.

'So what's the problem?'

'It hit me for the first time today, when Marty asked me if I was ready to max out Darby.'

'What do you want to do, throw the switch, too?'

Steamroller brought the drinks and set them on the table. She downed hers and ordered a second.

'That's not what I mean,' she said, then squished up her face. 'Damn! Martinis taste like ether or something.'

'You never drank a martini before?'

'Nope. Usually drink Cuba Libres.'

'Jesus, you dusted that off like it was a glass of milk. Those things are deadly.'

'They come in a real small glass. Nothing to 'em. What were we talking about?'

'You had just said, uh, "That's not what I mean," after I said that thing about throwing the switch.'

'Oh, yes, now I remember. The thing is, I've never tried a capital case, Flaherty.'

'You getting stagefright?' Flaherty laughed. 'Kickass Parver's getting weak knees? Come on, it's just another case – think of it as a misdemeanour.'

'That's not what I mean. I'm not worried about winning, that's not it at all. I just . . . I never really thought about it before.'

'What? What the hell're you talking about?'

'Asking for the death penalty.'

'Ah, so that's it. Anticipating an attack of conscience, are you? Come on, this guy walked up to his wife and shot her in the face with a shotgun. And he choked the little dancer to death. Think about that, he was looking in her face while he was killing her.'

'Stop it, Dermott.'

'No. We're prosecutors, Shana. The last things standing between civilization and the jungle. We don't make the laws, we just uphold them, and the law says that if Darby's convicted of murder one, he's a wrap.'

'I know all that, for God's sake,' she said angrily. 'I didn't come here to hear a rehash of Philosophy 101.' She suddenly got up to leave.

He reached out and gently grabbed her arm. 'Hey, I'm

sorry,' he said plaintively. 'Sometimes I get too cynical for my own good. Old habits die hard. I promise no more platitudes. Please . . . don't leave.'

She looked down at him and smiled. 'No more shit?'

'No more shit.'

'Good.' She sat back down and finished her second martini.

'Let me ask you something,' he said. 'If you were on a jury panel and they asked if you if you were in favour of the death penalty, what would you say?'

'That's moot.'

'Hell it is. Think about it for a minute.' He turned back to his Coke. They were silent for a full minute before she answered.

'I'd say I'm not sure whether I am or not, but I wouldn't let that influence my judgement. It's the evidence that counts.'

'Good. And would you go into court if you had doubts about the defendant's guilt?'

'God, you sound like Martin. He asked me the same thing the other night.'

'It's what prosecutors fear more than anything else – convicting an innocent man.'

'Or woman.' She held a finger up to the waiter and dipped it towards her glass.

'Or woman. Point is, if you got 'em – and you've got Darby – then what's the dif? You do your job. How would you feel, knowing what you know about Darby, if he beat the rap? Suppose he walked?'

'Won't happen,' she said defensively.

'I mean, supposing someone else was trying him and they blew the case?'

She thought for a moment, then decided to ignore the question. She suddenly changed the subject. 'Then there's Edith Stoddard,' she said.

'What about her?'

341

'Something's wrong there, Flaherty. She doesn't even want to put up a fight.'

'That's her option. Not much to fight about. According to your preliminary report, she bought the gun, spent two weeks learning to use it, and then popped him – twice. One would've been enough. The second shot was malicious. That's murder one, hot-shot. She's good as cooked.'

'You'd send her to the chair?'

'Pretty open and shut. She obviously planned to waste him for at least two weeks. No sudden impulse, no temporary insanity, no imminent danger. She got pissed, planned it, and whacked him.'

'She's so pitiful. There's something real . . . sad . . . about her.'

'What's sad is she's looking twenty thousand volts in the eye. These things are not supposed to get personal, Shana.'

'Well it *is* personal, okay. I'm taking it very personal.'

'Maybe you should let somebody else handle it.'

'Not on your life, Irish. I'll do it and do it right.'

'Hell, I wouldn't worry about it. Venable's handling the case. She hasn't tried a criminal case in ten years.'

Parver finished her third martini and slid the glass to the edge of the table. 'Think it's going to be cakewalk, do you? Let me tell you, she's good. Ten years or not, she's good.' She stopped and leaned across the table and said cautiously, 'I think Marty's got a thing with her.'

'Get outta here,' he said with mock surprise, remembering the flowers on Venable's dining-room table.

Parver nodded emphatically and winked.

'Will wonders never cease,' he said, and laughed.

The waiter brought her a new drink and took the empty away.

'That's your fourth martini,' Flaherty said. 'And I happen to know the bartender has a very heavy hand.

It's none of my business, but I don't think you understand about martinis.'

'Well, I may just get a li'l drunk tonight, Flaherty.' She paused, took a sip, and then said, 'Y'know, that's an awful long name. Flahar-ty. That's almost three syl'bles. I'm going to call you Flay. Anyway, Flay, can you handle it, if I get a little snockered?'

He smiled at her. 'I've never been drunk,' he said, somewhat sheepishly.

'You're kidding?'

'Nope. Pot was my drug of choice.'

'Pot's illegal.'

'That's why I quit.'

She held up her glass. 'This isn't.'

'That doesn't make a lot of sense, either.'

'First time I tried grass, I sat in front of the oven in my friend's kitchen for an hour waiting for Johnny Carson to come on.'

Flaherty laughed hard and nodded. 'That must've been some good stuff.'

'I dunno, never tried it again,' she said, and realized her speech was getting a little slurred and Flaherty was suddenly transforming into twins. She closed one eye and focused across the table on his ruggedly handsome face. 'How come you never asked m'out?'

'I just did.'

'Uh-huh, six months later. I know you're not gay.'

'Nope.'

'And I, uh, I know I'm not *that* unesrable.' She stopped and giggled. 'Un-desir-able.'

'Oh no,' he said softly, and smiled.

'Well?'

'They don't have courses in the social graces on the streets of Boston – or in the state reformatory.'

'You were *that* bad?'

'I was pretty bad.'

'Wha's the worst thing y'ever did? Or maybe I shouldn't ask.'

'Boosting cars.'

'You stole cars?'

He nodded. 'Me and my buddies.'

'Can you do tha' thing they do in the movies, y'know, where they rip all th'wires out f'the dashboard and make 'em spark and start th'car? Can you do that?' She closed one eye again and focused hard on him.

'You mean hot-wiring?' he said, nodding. 'Sixty seconds, anything on wheels.'

'Y'r kiddin'!'

'Nope.'

'Wow. Why'd you quit?'

'I had a revelation. God appeared at the foot of my bed one night and told me if I kept it up I was gonna die young.'

'And . . .'

'I took him seriously.'

'She didn't really,' Parver said sceptically.

'She?'

'God.'

'Oh.' Flaherty smiled and made rings on the table with his wet glass. 'In a way she did. One of my best friends went to the chair. He was robbing a grocery store and killed a cop. I mean, we were close, Ernie and I had done jobs together.'

'That was his name, Ernie?'

'Ernie Holleran. There were five of us, hung out together, did stuff together. Ernie was one of us. But he did that thing and they maxed him out and the night they did it to him, we took the bus up to the state pen and we found this hill where you could see the prison and got two-six packs and sat there drinking and waiting until they did it. You can tell because when they throw the switch, the lights fade out, then come back on. They do it twice, just to make sure. We sat there until the Black

344

Maria left with him and we threw empty beer cans at the hearse and then we took the bus back home. That's the night God spoke to me. I decided I wasn't going out *that* way.'

She was staring at him with one eye still closed, her mouth half open, mesmerized by his story.

'Know what?' she said after a while. 'I'm not inter'sted, in-ter-ested, in social graces, Flay.' She finished half her drink and slapped the glass back down on the table. 'I'm in-ter-ested in scilnit, sincilat – '

'Scintilating?'

'Thank you . . . conversation, and, uh, and a beaut'ful man with lovely eyes and dark bl'ck hair and . . . sufer, sulper – '

'Superficial?'

'Than'you, su-per-fi-cial things like that. How come you always wear black, Flay? Why d'you have this Johnny Cash symrom . . . sidro..syn-drome.'

He sighed and sipped his Coke and stared into her liquid eyes. 'The truth?'

'What else is there?'

'I don't have any colour sense. Don't know what goes with what. Long as I wear black, I'm safe.'

'You really care about that, huh?'

He sat without comment for a minute, then nodded. 'I guess I do,' he said, and his cheeks began to colour.

'Why, Couns'lor, I do b'lieve you're blushing,' she said, and snickered. 'You're somp'in else, Flay.'

He laughed away the colour. 'And you're loaded.'

'My embarr'sing you?'

'Never.'

They stared across the table for a long moment, then she cast her eyes down. 'Think we . . . I . . . could get outta here with't fallin' on m'face?'

'I'd never let you fall on your face, Hotshot.'

'Ho'shot, s'cute, I like it.'

'Want to go for it?'

'Go f'r th'gold.' She snickered. 'Jus' one min't.'

'How about a cup of coffee?'

'Yuck!'

'Okay, we'll just sit here until you get it together.'

'Ma'be Steamroller c'n get us a cab? Think?'

'Wait right here.'

'Nooo, I'm gonna wait waaaay over there,' she said, pointing across the room, and had a sudden fit of the giggles. The waiter got the cab and Flaherty helped her to her feet and put his arm under hers and pulled her against him.

'Make believe we're snuggling up, nobody'll pay any attention to us,' he said, tilting her head against his shoulder and leading her towards the door.

'Sng'ling up, that what they call't in Boston?'

'Yeah,' he said. They made it to the front door without incident, but as they walked outside a frigid blast of air swept off the river.

'Wow!' she said. 'Wah' was'at?'

'Fresh air.'

'I th'nk m'legs're goin',' she said, sagging as he led her to the cab. He slid her into the backseat.

'Flay?'

'Yeah?'

'Th'nks.'

'For what?'

'List'nin' t'me.'

'I'll listen to you anytime,' he said, sliding in beside her.

'Really?'

'Sure.'

'Th'n lissen caref'lly 'cause . . . I'm gonna try t'remember . . . what m'address is.'

She got the address right on the third try and slid down in the seat and put her head on his shoulder and stared at him through her one eye and said, 'Tell you secret,

Mist Flar'ty. I have cov'ted you from afar ev'since th' first time I saw you. That okay?'

He put his arm around her and drew her closer.

'I think it's great,' he whispered, but did not tell her that he, too, had coveted her for just as long.

'Good,' she murmured, and a moment later was sound asleep.

She lived in a second-floor apartment on the corner of West Eugenie and North Park, a two-storey brick building with a pleasant nineteenth-century feel to it. Flaherty paid the cab driver and found her key in her purse and then got out, leaning into the backseat and gathering her up in his arms.

'Need some help?' the cabbie asked.

'Nah, she doesn't weigh more'n a nickel,' Flaherty said, and carried her into the apartment building. He found her apartment without incident and, bracing one knee against the wall, balanced her against it while he opened the door, then carried her in and kicked it shut.

It was a bright, cheery one-bedroom, furnished with expensive and flawless taste and bright colours. Waterford and Wedgwood abounded and the furniture was warm and inviting. The kitchen, which was small but efficient, was separated from the main room by a small breakfast counter. The walls were covered with numbered prints by Miró, Matisse, and Degas. A single lamp glowed near the window. He carried her to the bedroom and flicked on the light switch with his elbow. It was a mess, the bed unmade, a dirty dish with the remains of a pizza on the night-table, books piled high haphazardly in the corner. He laid her on the bed and she stirred and gazed up sleepily.

'M'home?' she asked.

'Yep.'

'You carried me up all those stairs?'

'Uh-huh.'

'Sir Gagalad . . . oh, what'shisname. Tha's you. Glori-

347

ous knight.' She tried to sit up but flopped back on the feather mattress with her arms stretched out and sighed.

'Mouth's full a feathers,' she said, and giggled softly.

'I'll get you some water.'

'I'll try t'get undress'd while you're gone.'

He went into the kitchen, found a pebbled glass in the cabinet, and drew ice cubes out of the icemaker in the refrigerator door. He poured cold water over them and swished the glass around a few times.

'How're you doing?' he called to her.

'Better'n 'spected.'

'Let me know when you're in bed.'

'Just any ol' time,' she answered.

When he returned to the room, she was lying half under the covers, her clothes strewn on the floor. One leg was draped over the side of the bed. Her pantyhose hung forlornly from the leg.

'Almos' made it,' she said. 'That left leg was a real bitch.' She wiggled the leg and laughed weakly. 'Wow,' she said. 'You're right 'about martoonies.'

He put the glass of water on the night-table beside the bed and went to the window to close the blinds and suddenly a chill rippled across the back of his neck. He spread the blinds with his hands and scanned the street below.

Empty except for a single car parked across the street. It was also empty.

Paranoia, he thought. If the copycat killer was loose in Chicago, Shana Parver was certainly far down on his list. He closed the blinds.

'Flay?'

'Yeah.' He looked at her and she turned her head towards him and peered through one half-open eye.

'Don' leave me, please. Don' wanna wake up lonesome in t'morning. 'Kay?'

'Okay.'

'Wadda guy.'

348

He walked over to the bed and helped her sit up and take a sip of water.

'Mmmm,' she said, and fell back on the mattress. 'Not gonna leave me?'

'No, I'm not going to leave you.'

She smiled and immediately fell asleep again. Flaherty sat down on the bed and very carefully rolled the remaining leg of her pantyhose over her ankle and slipped it off her foot. He took her toes in his fingers and stroked them very gently.

God, he thought, *even her toes are gorgeous*.

In the backseat of the company limo, Jane Venable was already missing Martin. She had had a business meeting with her Japanese clients and Vail had decided he should spend at least an occasional night in his own apartment.

She was spoiled already. Spoiled by his attentiveness, spoiled by their passionate and inventive lovemaking, spoiled by just having him there. She stared out the window, watching the night lights streak by. When they stopped at a light, she suddenly sat up in her seat.

'Larry,' she said, 'pull over in front of the Towers, please.'

The driver pulled over and parked in front of the glittering shaft of glass and chrome. He jumped out and opened the door for her.

'I'll be back in a couple of minutes,' she said, and hurried into the apartment building. The night manager sat behind a desk that looked like the cockpit of an SST. A closed-circuit videocamera system permitted him to scan the halls of each of the thirty floors. He was slender, his face creased with age, his brown but greying hair combed straight back. He wore a blue blazer with a red carnation in its lapel and looked more like the deskman at an exclusive hotel than the inside doorman of an apartment building.

'May I help you?' he asked in a pseudo-cultured British accent, his eyes appraising the black limo.

Venable put on her most dazzling smile. 'Hi,' she said. 'What's your name?'

'Victor,' he said with a guarded smile.

'Well, Victor, I'm Jane Venable,' she said, taking a sheet of paper from her purse and sliding it across the polished desk in front of him. 'I'm an attorney. My client has been charged with the murder of John Delaney. I have a court order here permitting me access to the scene of the crime. I know this is a terrible imposition, but would you let me in?'

'What? Now? You want to inspect the premises *now?*'

She laid the folded fifty-dollar bill on the document.

'I just happened to be in the neighbourhood. I doubt I'll be fifteen minutes.'

He looked at the court order, cast another glance at the limo, then smiled at her as he palmed the fifty.

'How can I resist such a dazzling smile, Ms Venable,' he said. He opened the desk drawer, took out a ring of keys, and led her to the lift.

'Terrible thing,' he said as the lift climbed to the thirtieth floor.

'Dreadful,' she said, remembering that Delaney's death had probably been cause for celebrating all over the city. 'Did you know him well?'

Victor raised an eyebrow and smiled. 'He said "Hello" coming in and "Good evening" going out and gave me a bottle of Scotch for Christmas. That's how well I knew Mr Delaney.'

'Was it good Scotch?'

'Chivas.'

'Nice.'

They arrived at the thirtieth floor and Victor unlocked the door. The crime ribbons had been removed.

'Take your time, I'm on until two,' Victor said. 'The door will lock when you leave.'

'You're a dream, Victor.'

'Thank you, Ms Venable.' He left, pulling the door shut behind him.

A crazy notion, she thought, *coming here in the middle of the night.* But when she had looked through the car window and realized she was in front of the place – well, what the hell, she wasn't in any rush to get back to her empty condo anyway.

It had been years since Venable had visited the scene of a homicide and her adrenaline started pumping the instant she started down the hallway to the living room. She stood a few feet away from the black outline on the floor. It seemed to box in the wide, dark brown stain in the carpet.

She wasn't really looking for anything in particular; she felt it was her responsibility to Edith Stoddard to familiarize herself with the murder scene. She walked into the bedroom, noticed there were scratches on the spindles of the headboard. She stood in the bathroom. His toothbrush, a razor, and an Abercrombie and Fitch shaving bowl and brush were on one side of the marble-top sink and a bottle of bay rum aftershave lotion was on the other side. A towel hung unused on a gold rack near the shower.

She went into the kitchen, checked the refrigerator. Someone had emptied it out and cleaned it. There were canned foods in the small pantry. Delaney, it seemed, had a passion for LeSueur asparagus and Vienna sausages. She went back to the bedroom, checked through his desk and drawers and found nothing of interest. She found an ashtray, carried it back to the bedroom, and sat down on the end of the bed facing the closet. She decided to have a cigarette before she left. Smoking was not permitted in company vehicles.

Stupid, she thought. *But at least I got this little junket out of the way.*

Did Edith Stoddard's sense of betrayal over losing her

job really precipitate Delaney's death? she wondered anew. It was a persistent question in her mind. The other facts in the case seemed blatant, but the motive seemed so bland. But then she remembered reading about other cases not dissimilar, like the postman who lost his job, went back to the post office with an assault weapon, and killed nine people before turning it on himself. Perhaps it wasn't as bland as she thought.

Thinking about Edith Stoddard, she stared into the closet. From where she was sitting, she could see the entire area, which was adjacent to, and formed a small hallway into, the bathroom; a large closet, empty except for a suit, a couple of shirts on hangers, a bathrobe, a pair of leather slippers, and a pair of black loafers.

But something else caught her attention. As she stared at it, she realized that the closet wall was off balance. One side of the closet was deep, stretching to the wall, the other side was just wide enough to hang a suit. It was at least two feet narrower.

She stared at it for a full two minutes, her old instincts working, a combination of paranoia and nosiness that had made her the best prosecutor of her time.

'Why is that closet off centre,' she said aloud to herself.

She went into the bathroom and checked to see if there were shelves behind the wall, but the commode was located behind it and that wall was tiled. She went back into the bedroom, entered the closet and turned on the light. *Only a woman would be curious about this odd bit of interior architecture*, she thought. *Only a woman would be concerned about the loss of that much closet space*. She rapped on the wall with her knuckles, thinking perhaps it was a riser, but the tapping was hollow.

A hollow space, two feet deep and five feet wide? A safe, perhaps? Secret files, something incriminating? Something she could use in court to taint the victim? She traced the seam where the two walls joined but found nothing. She stood at the juncture of the two walls and shoved against one of them.

It gave a little. She shoved harder. It bowed a little at the top.

The wall panel was not nailed; it was locked in the middle. She stepped back and once again scanned the seams, top, bottom, and sides. It was a door. Now she had to figure out how to open it.

She ran her fingertips around the doorsill and along the carpeting. Nothing.

She sighed and sat back down on the end of the bed and stared some more. She looked at the clothes rod. There were no clothes on the narrow side of the closet. She went back in, reached up, and jiggled the rod, then twisted it. The rod was threaded. She turned it four full turns before the whole end of the rod pulled away from the wall. She laid it on the floor and examined the receptacle. There was a button recessed in the threaded rod holder. She pushed it, heard a muffled *click*, and then the panel popped open an inch or two. A light blinked on inside the smaller closet. She swung it open.

Her breath came in a gasp. Her mouth gaped for a moment as she stared with shock and disbelief at its contents.

'My God,' she whispered.

Then her eyes moved down to the floor of the secret compartment.

The gun.

Twenty-nine

Jane Venable arrived at Vail's office at exactly ten o'clock. The lift doors parted and she stepped out, decked out in an emerald-green silk suit that made her red hair look like it was on fire. She had a tan Coach leather shoulder bag slung over one shoulder. She strode towards his office with the authority and assurance of a show horse prancing past the judges' stand. Everyone in the office suddenly found something to do that would put her directly in their line of sight. Every eye followed her to Naomi's desk.

'Hi,' she said with a bright smile. 'You must be Naomi. I'm Jane Venable.' She thrust her hand out.

Vail came out of his office and greeted her, ignoring the momentary smirk Jane flashed at him, a look Naomi did not miss. *Marty*, she thought, *you're dead in the water.* Vail had included Venable in the special meeting because she was an integral part of the emerging Stampler crisis. They entered his office.

'Last night was the pits,' she said, faking a big smile.

He smiled back. 'I smoked a pack of cigarettes trying to go to sleep.'

'That'll teach you to take a night off.'

'We're being watched,' he said, flicking his eyes towards the rest of the staff.

'I know. Isn't it fun?'

'Coffee?'

'Sure.'

'I checked on you last night – to make sure your guardian angels were there,' Vail said.

'I don't know what my neighbours think,' she said. 'One guy parks in front of the house all night and the other one parks on my terrace and cruises the grounds with a flashlight every hour on the hour.'

'Just makes you even more mysterious than you already are.'

'I don't know why I even brought it up, I've never met any of my neighbours.' Her mood seemed to change suddenly when he turned his back to her to draw the coffee. He could see her reflection in the windowpane. She became less ebullient, more introspective, as if she had very quickly fallen into deep thought.

The Stoddard case was heavy on Venable's mind. The discovery of the secret compartment in Delaney's apartment presented her with a peculiar dilemma. As Stoddard's defender, she was not required to tell the prosecution what she had found. On the other hand, the gun was integral to the case and she could be accused of concealing evidence. Her decision had been not to touch anything. She had closed up the secret room and left; her argument would be that she had not been sure whose gun was in the closet. And she still had to deal with Edith Stoddard about her discovery. She decided to put the problem aside for the moment; obviously Vail's meeting would rule the agenda this morning. *Loosen up*, she told herself.

Vail poured a spoonful of sugar in her coffee cup. She quickly brightened again when he returned with her coffee. As she put the cup on the table in front of her, he said, 'Something bothering you?'

'You haven't known me that long.'

'How long?'

'Long enough to tell if something's got my goat.'

'Ah! So something *has* got your goat,' he said. He walked around the table and sat down, tilting his chair back with one foot on the corner of the desk.

She leaned across the table and stared at him through half-closed eyes and said, with mock sarcasm, 'I don't have a goat, Mr District Attorney.'

He laughed, and she asked, 'Did you miss me?' looking as if she were asking the time of day.

'Nah, although it did occur to me that some corporate samurai warrior might steal your heart away at dinner last night.'

She laughed at him. 'You can't get rid of me that easily, Vail.'

'I don't want to get rid of you at all.'

They were keeping up the facade of two people casually making conversation, a pantomime for the staff, which was still working very hard to make it appear as if they were disinterested in the scene behind the glass partition.

'Good,' she said, shaking her head so her hair flowed down over her shoulders.

He whistled very low in appreciation of her studied wiles. 'You are a science unto yourself,' he said.

'I suppose a good-morning kiss would stop traffic up here.'

'It would probably stop traffic in Trafalgar Square.'

'Pity.'

'Let's let the Wild Bunch in and get started. I'm sure they're all sitting outside this fishbowl reading our lips. Besides, they're all dying to meet the legendary Jane Venable.'

'Sure.'

'Absolutely. They know all about you. They've all read the transcript of the Stampler trial.'

'Well, that's just great!' she snapped. 'The one trial where Mr Wonderful whipped my ass and *that's* what they know about me?'

'Actually twice. I whipped your ass twice. Have you forgotten . . .?'

'Just call them in, okay?' she said, cutting him off.

'I did miss you last night,' he whispered as he walked past her.

'It was your decision.'

'That's right, rub it in.'

He opened the office door and waved at those of the staff who were in the office. They finished phone calls, put away files, and dribbled into the room over the next five minutes, each pleasantly greeting Venable, though regarding her with respectful suspicion since she was considered a potential threat in the courtroom. They drew coffee from the big urn, doctored it, grabbed a doughnut from the box provided by Naomi, and settled down, some in chairs, some on the floor, waiting expectantly. Vail rarely called an emergency staff meeting like this. Only Hazel Fleishman and Bucky Winslow were absent; both were in court.

The last to enter the room was Bobby Hartford, a tall, ramrod-straight black man from Mississippi whose father, Nate Hartford, a field rep for the NAACP, had been shot to death in front of Bobby. He'd been nine years old at the time. Now, at thirty-eight, Hartford was the oldest member of the Wild Bunch and its only married man (Fleishman was also married). He had about him an almost serene air despite his traumatic early years – Vail had never heard him raise his voice. He sat on the floor beside Flaherty.

'I asked Jane Venable here today because she's deeply involved in what we're about to discuss,' Vail began. He turned to Venable. 'This is what we call a brain scan. The rules are the same for all of us. If you have something to ask, clarify, or contribute, jump in anytime. You'll probably hear some challenges, some devil's advocacy, that's the way we do it here, okay?'

He paused to take a sip of coffee and light a cigarette, blowing the smoke at the exhaust fan.

'All right, here's the situation. I assume you've all read Dermott's report on the Balfour and Lincoln murders. You've also read the trial transcripts of the Stampler trial, so by now you are aware of the more than coincidental nexus of these crimes. And although the latest two killings are way out of our jurisdiction, we're going to

357

become involved in this situation whether we like it or not. I'm convinced Stampler wanted me to know that he had conned us all – and he's still conning us. So when I went up to see him and his shrink, Dr Woodward, I wired myself. Taped the conversations I had with them.'

'Was that legal?' Hartford asked.

'We're not planning to use it in court.'

'Not what I asked, Counsellor,' Hartford challenged.

Vail regarded him balefully for a few moments, then shook his head. 'No, it wasn't.' Then he grinned. 'Want to leave the room when I play it?'

'Oh, hell, no,' Hartford said with a laugh. 'I just wanted to know where you're coming from.'

There was a ripple of laughter in the room.

'Fear is where I'm coming from,' Vail said seriously. 'I fear this man. He is very dangerous. I hope I can convince you of that before this meeting's over. Before I play the tape, here's what we know. We know that Stampler hasn't had any contact with the outside world for ten years, no phone calls, no letters, no visitors. We know the killer is printing messages in code on the back of his victim's heads in blood, just as Stampler did. And the quotes are keyed to Rushman's old library books, which are now in the Newberry, just as Stampler's were. All those coincidences can reasonably be explained. Newspaper accounts, trial records, that sort of thing – none of that information is secret.

'But we also know that whoever killed Balfour and Lincoln was privy to information that could *only* have come from Stampler. What the public never knew was that Rushman was a paederast. He had a group called the Altar Boys – four boys and a girl – whom he directed in pornographic videos, then stepped in and took his pleasure with the girl or one of the boys, or all of them, whatever suited him. Stampler was one of the Altar Boys. He murdered two of them. But Alex Lincoln got away. So did Stampler's girlfriend, Linda, who was the young lady in the group. She later became Mrs Linda Balfour. Now they're dead and the MO is exactly the same as the murders Stampler committed.'

'There is one difference,' Stenner interjected. 'This killer takes trophies – like mementoes of his tricks. He took a stuffed toy that belonged to Linda Balfour and Lincoln's belt buckle. My feeling is the copycat is a true serial killer.'

'He also left a Polaroid shot of Linda Balfour's body when he killed Lincoln,' Flaherty said, 'so there would be no doubt he committed both crimes.'

'None of the information about Rushman was ever revealed in the trial,' Vail went on. 'There were two tapes of one of the Altar Boys sessions. Jane and I each had one and we both erased them after the trial.

'Our theory is that Stampler is triggering this killer, but we don't know how he's doing it or how he originally made contact with the surrogate. I think somewhere in my conversation with Stampler he dropped a clue, something very subtle to let me know he's the real killer.'

'Why?' Meyer asked.

'Because he's playing games with me. He's a psychopath. I think you better listen to the tape before you ask any more questions. Maybe I'm too close, maybe one of you will hear something I'm missing.'

'Or maybe you're wrong,' Flaherty said, half grinning. 'Maybe he didn't plant a clue at all.'

'You mean I'm paranoid, Dermott?'

'Something like that.'

Vail shrugged and smiled. 'Very possible. The question is, is my paranoia justified? You guys decide.'

He punched the play button and the conversation with Woodward began. The group, including Venable, leaned forwards, rapt in the conversation, zeroing in on every word as Woodward described his almost decade-long experience with Aaron Stampler. The revelation that Aaron Stampler had become Raymond Vulpes created the biggest buzz among the group. Then well into the interview between Vail and Stampler/Vulpes, Dermott Flaherty abruptly sat up and said, 'Hold it! Stop it there.'

Vail punched the stop button.

'Back it up a little and replay,' Flaherty said.

Vail snapped the rewind button, let it run a few feet, and punched Play.

VAIL: *Did Aaron and Roy ever talk about killing the old preacher . . . uh, I can't think of his name, it's been ten years.*
VULPES: *Shackles.*
VAIL: *Shackles, right.*
VULPES: *Roy bragged about that one, all right. They really hated that old man.*
VAIL: *That's an understatement.*
VULPES: *Guess you're right about that. He was their first, you know?*
VAIL: *So I heard.*
VULPES: *Why, hell, Mr Vail, you probably know more about the two of them than I do.*
VAIL: *Oh, I think not. How about the others? Did he talk about them?*
VULPES: *You mean his brother and Aaron's old girlfriend, Mary Lafferty?*
VAIL: *I'd forgot her name, too.*
VULPES: *Lafferty. Mary Lafferty.*

'There's your clue,' Flaherty said. 'He repeats Mary Lafferty's name three times. I never knew about Mary Lafferty, that's why I didn't catch it at the time. And I didn't include it in my report, so you never knew about it, Marty.'

'Catch what? What are you talking about?' Venable asked.

'The name on the package that Lincoln was delivering when he was killed – the addressor was M. Lafferty. There's no way Stampler could know that, none of those details have been released to the press yet.'

The revelation caused a flurry of conversation. St Claire was the most excited.

'Ain't that enough to stall ol' Woodward in his tracks?'

he asked. 'I mean, doesn't that prove Vulpes or whoever the hell he is knew about these killings?'

'It makes no difference. I was Stampler's lawyer of record,' Vail said. 'I can't take any legal action against him, I can't even testify against him in court. Anyway, all we have at this point is circumstantial evidence and hunches, and I guarantee, it would take a lot more than that to stop Woodward. He regards Vulpes as his personal medical victory and Vulpes knows it. But you're right about the package, Dermott, Vulpes thought I knew about the return address. It was his way of letting me know that he was at least involved in the deaths of Alex Lincoln and Linda Balfour.'

'There's something else,' Jane Venable said. 'Does the name Vulpes ring anybody's bell?'

They all looked at one another and shook their heads.

'*Vulpes* is Latin – it's the genus for a fox.'

'The craftiest of all creatures,' Stenner intoned.

'Another goddamn message,' St Claire growled.

'Janie,' said Vail, 'I saw those red eyes you talked about – for just the flash of a second, I saw pure hate. I saw murder. I saw the damn four *horsemen* for an instant.'

'Well, I've got a tidbit of information that should give us all a chuckle at Mr Vulpes's expense,' said Naomi. 'It's in the report submitted to the judge who signed the order for Vulpes's furlough.'

'How did you get that?' Vail asked.

'I went to a seminar once with the court clerk up there, she faxed it to me,' Naomi said, and winked. She flipped through the pages. 'Here it is, listed under the heading "Miscellaneous".' She looked up. 'Mr Stampler, it seems is phobic.'

'Phobic? What kind of phobia?' Vail asked.

'He's afraid of the dark,' she said, and snickered.

'Afraid of the dark?' Parver said with disbelief. Flaherty broke into a hearty laugh as thoughts of the madman, cowering in the dark, flashed through his mind.

'Afraid of the dark,' Naomi repeated. 'He's had special permission to sleep with the lights on ever since he was admitted to Daisyland.'

'Is he still sleeping with the lights on?' asked Vail.

She nodded. 'According to Doctors Woodward, Ciaffo, and Bascott, who petitioned for his furlough, it's called a nonaggressive phobic reaction. They attribute it to childhood traumas.'

'According to Woodward, Raymond never went through re-experiencing; Aaron did,' said Parver. 'He says on the tape that Raymond doesn't suffer any of either Aaron's or Roy's psychological problems.'

'So how come he picked up Stampler's phobia?' St Claire asked.

'Because it's the one thing Stampler can't hide,' Vail said.

'How could Woodward have missed it?' Naomi asked.

'Because he wanted to miss it,' said Vail. 'Woodward's already got a spot on his wall for the Nobel Prize in medicine.'

'Or because he wasn't looking for it,' suggested Venable, taking a more practical approach to the question. 'Stampler had been sleeping with the lights on for years and Raymond just kept doing it. That miscellaneous note in the report was probably part of an earlier evaluation.'

'Afraid of the dark,' said Stenner. 'Makes perfect sense – the thing Stampler feared most in life was the coal mines.'

'And nothin' could be darker than the hole,' said St Claire.

'Except maybe Aaron Stampler's soul,' said Jane Venable.

'I think I can answer one big question: I know how he tracked down Lincoln and Balfour,' Bobby Hartford said quietly. 'I'm going into my office and make a phone call. You guys can listen to it on Marty's speakerphone.'

'Who are you calling?' asked Flaherty.

'Minnesota Department of Motor Vehicles.'

Hartford went to his office and dialled the number. A high-pitched, somewhat comical, voice answered.

'DMV. Sergeant Colter speaking.'

'Hey, Sergeant, this is Detective John Standish down in Chicago. How you doing?'

'Good, neighbour, what can I do you for?'

'We're looking for a witness in an old homicide case, dropped out of sight a couple of years ago. We just got a tip somebody saw him up in your neck of the woods. Can you run him through the computer for me?'

'Got a name?'

'Alexander Sanders Lincoln. White, male, twenty-six.'

'Hang on a minute.'

They could hear the keys of a computer board clicking in the background.

'You're out of luck, friend. We had him up until 1991, then his licence expired. Wait a minute, there's an entry here – the Missouri DMV requested a citation report on him in November '91. He probably applied for a commercial driver's licence. He was clean up here.'

'Good, I'll try Missouri. Thanks, Sergeant. You've been a big help.'

'Anytime.'

Hartford hung up. He dialled another number.

'Illinois Department of Motor Vehicles, Officer Anderson. How may I help you?'

'Hi, Anderson, this is Detective John Standish, Chicago PD.'

'Morning, Standish, what's the problem?'

'We've got an old warrant here, the statute's about to run out. Woman named Linda Gellerman, white, female, twenty-six. We got a tip she's back in Illinois. Run it through your computer, will you, see if she pops up.'

'Gellerman? Two *l*s?'

'Right.'

Another pause, then: 'Yeah. Linda Gellerman . . . married two years ago and had the licence reissued in her married name. That's Linda Balfour, 102 Popular Street, Gideon, Illinois.'

'Hey, that was easy. I may take the rest of the day off.' Anderson laughed. 'I should be so lucky.'

'Thanks, brother. Come see us.'

'Yes, sir. S'long.'

Hartford hung up and returned to Vail's office. He snapped his fingers as he entered and sat back down on the floor.

'It's an old trick. Used to take down the licence numbers of Ku Klux Klanners, find out who they were, and call 'em on the phone, tell him we were FBI and they better keep their noses clean,' Hartford said. 'Put the sweats on 'em for a while.'

'Stampler could have done it from Daisyland if he had access to a phone,' said Flaherty.

'He doesn't have access to a phone,' Vail said.

'How about the repair shop?'

'No phone line.'

'The killer coulda done it,' St Claire said.

'I got the chills when he talked about Linda Gellerman,' Parver said. 'Two years ago she thought she had her whole life ahead of her.'

'She did,' Naomi said. 'She just didn't know how short it was going to be.'

'You think he's been faking all along, Marty?' Flaherty asked.

'What do you believe, Abel?' Vail asked the stoic detective.

'I don't believe there was ever a Roy, never have. I believe Raymond Vulpes is a myth. Stampler was and is a clever, cold-blooded, psychopathic killer.'

'Could you be a little more explicit?' Venable said with a smile. The group broke into nervous laughter, relieving the tension that had been building in the room.

'Hellacious trick, and I'd hate to prove it in court, but

I agree with Abel,' said Vail. 'I think he's been pulling everyone's chain for the last ten years.'

St Claire said, 'Everything that son-bitch does sends a message to us.'

'Including his name – the Fox,' said Hartford scornfully.

'Well, the new message is "Catch me if you can",' Vail said solemnly. 'Because tomorrow morning Raymond Vulpes will be leaving Daisyland for six weeks. And he's coming here. Abel, I want two men on the Fox – around the clock – not too close, but close enough to videotape him. Let's see who he talks to, who he contacts, where he goes.'

'That's kinda flirtin' with harassment, ain't it?' St Claire asked casually, spitting into his baby cup.

'No,' said Vail, just as casually. 'Harassment is if we drag him into an alley and beat the living shit out of him.'

Vail's response caught everyone off guard. They had never heard their boss so vitriolic, so openly angry.

'There's still the big question,' said Flaherty. 'How did he locate the serial killer and how does he trigger him?'

'There's somethin' we're all overlookin',' said St Claire. 'There were twenty-three other tapes admitted into evidence in the Stampler trial.'

'Twenty-three other tapes?' Vail said.

'I remember that,' Venable said. 'Don't you remember, Marty? Judge Shoat wanted to review all the tapes Dr Arrington made with Stampler to justify the agreement to send Stampler to Daisyland.'

'Hell, I forgot all about it,' said Vail. 'I never got them back.'

'Molly Arrington did,' said St Claire. 'About a week after the trial ended. She's had 'em for ten years, if she kept 'em.'

'Why wouldn't she?' Parver offered. 'Seems to me they'd be great research material.'

'Which brings up a point,' suggested Venable. 'Maybe you've been going about this problem backwards.'

'What do you mean?' Stenner asked.

'Maybe Stampler didn't locate the serial killer,' Venable answered. 'Maybe the killer came to him.'

Thirty

'What say, Raymond?' Terry asked. 'Want to go down to the commissary, eat with the inmates once before you leave?'

'I've gone ten years without eating with them,' Vulpes answered, 'why break my string now? I'll wait until we get downtown, have a hot fudge sundae and a hot dog.'

Terry laughed. 'You and your hot fudge sundaes. Gotta lock the door behind me. Y'know, rules.'

'Sure. What's one more hour, more or less. Besides, I got to pack up my tools.'

'Right. I'm proud of you, Raymond.'

'Thanks, Terry. I'm going to miss you.'

'Me, too.' He laughed. 'Hell, you're the only one I can talk to around here, gives me an answer that makes any sense. I'll bring you back a Coke.'

'Thanks.'

Terry pulled the gate closed behind him and key-locked it. Vulpes listened to his footsteps fade down the hallway. He opened one of the cabinets in the repair shop, took out a VCR, and put it on his worktable. He then took a small screwdriver and removed four screws from each side of the machine's cover and slid it off. He placed the cover on its side, so as to obscure the machine from the doorway.

He looked across the quadrangle at the purchasing office opposite his window. It was a small office run by three women. Two of them were standing in the doorway. The third, Verna Mableton, was pacing back and forth in front of the windows, talking on her portable phone. She waved the other two women on and they left. She sat on the corner of her desk and kept talking.

Vulpes watched her without any expression. Occasionally he glanced at the door to the repair shop.

Inside the VCR was a small, handmade computer. It was six inches long, four inches wide, and two inches deep and looked like a small keyboard with a tiny, oblong digital-readout screen above the keys. Beside it was a black box, three inches square and two inches deep. He took the two units out, laid them on the desk, and monitored the door while he attached the black box to the minicomputer with a two-inch piece of telephone wire.

Vulpes was proud of the minicomputer. It was basically a modem with a keyboard and he had made it from scratch. He was even prouder of the transmission box. He had waited patiently for more than a year until one of the purchasing department's computers had gone down. He suggested waiting until Saturday to repair it, when nobody was in the office. The guard had waited outside, sitting in the sun. Vulpes had dismantled the portable phone and sketched the circuitry. It had taken him five months, getting a piece at a time with his regular orders so they wouldn't become suspicious, to get the materials he needed. It took another four months to duplicate the radio phone in the purchasing office. Basically it was nothing more than a dialling device for the modem.

He looked back across the quad at the office. Verna stood up, nodded, and placed the portable phone on its stand. She took her purse and left the office. Vulpes turned the microcomputer on and typed MODEM. It hummed for a second and then ENTER appeared in the small screen. He typed in a phone number and waited. The numbers blinked out and after a few seconds the word CONTACT blinked three times. He began typing.

ARE YOU THERE, HYDRA?
YES, FOX, AS ALWAYS.
IT IS TIME.

OH, THANK YOU, FOX.
ARE YOU READY?
YES, FOX, ALWAYS READY.
HAVE YOU RESEARCHED THE LIST?
ALL FOUR OF THEM.
AND?
TAKE YOUR PICK.
EXCELLENT, AS USUAL, HYDRA.
THANK YOU, FOX. WHO SHALL IT BE?
DO YOU HAVE A CHOICE?
WHATEVER MAKES YOU HAPPY, FOX.
I THINK . . .
YES?
I THINK IT WILL BE TONIGHT.
OH, FOX, TONIGHT! THANK YOU. THANK
    YOU, FOX.
HYDRA?
YES, FOX.
YOU KNOW WHAT TO DO AFTER?
OH YES, FOX, I KNOW WHAT TO . . .
    SOMEONE COMING.
DO NUMBER THREE.
NUMBER THREE! YES, YES, FOX, YES!
    SOON . . .

Vulpes typed END on the screen and the screen blinked
off. His heart was beating in his mouth. His penis was
erect. He sat down, leaning forward so his face was
hidden by the VCR cover. He was panting. And then
suddenly he was released. He gasped, blew out a long
breath, and finally sat up straight. He took several deep
breaths and hummed very slowly to himself, reducing the
tempo of his humming until it was a mere rattle in his
throat. His heart slowed to normal. He sighed.

He disconnected the small box and removed the tray
from his toolbox. He wrapped the minicomputer and

the transmission box in lead foil and placed them in the bottom of the chest, covering them with tools.

There, it's over for now.

Thirty-One

The pilot put the twin-engine plane down on a grass strip
in a little town called Milford in southern Indiana. There
was no Tony in a Cadillac to greet him, so Vail and St
Claire rented a car at the small airport and drove six
miles south across the Flatrock River to the Justine Clinic.
The hospital was a pleasant departure from the Daisy. It
was shielded from the highway by a half-mile-deep stand
of trees, at the end of a gravel road. As Vail and St Claire
burst out of the miniforest, Justine spread out before
them, looking more like a collective farm than a mental
hospital. A cluster of old brick buildings surrounded a
small lake. A tall, brick silo stood alone and solitary,
like a sentinel in the middle of the sprawling field that
separated the facility from the woods. A tall chain-link
fence behind the buildings on one side of the lake formed
what appeared to be an enormous playground. Several
children were hanging on a spinning whirligig, while a
woman in a thick red jacket sat nearby reading a book.
A boat dock with a tin-roofed boathouse at its end
stretched out into the lake and a floating raft drifted
forlornly about twenty yards from the shore. It was a
pleasant-seeming place, unlike the cold, foreboding
penal-colony atmosphere of the Daisy.

'Looks like a summer camp I went to once when I was
a kid,' St Claire said.

'Somehow I never thought of you as a kid, Harve,' Vail
said.

'I was about nine. Damn, I hated it. We had to swim
in this lake, musta been forty below. M'lips were blue
the whole two weeks I was there.' He paused to spit
out the car window. 'What's this guy's name again?'

371

'Lowenstein. Dr Fred Lowenstein. He's the director.'

'Sound like a nice guy?'

'He was very pleasant on the phone.'

'And she wouldn't talk to you, huh?'

'Her secretary said she was in a meeting, so I asked for the director.'

'He knows what's goin' on?'

'Vaguely.'

They pulled up to what appeared to be the main building, a sprawling brick barn of a place with a slate roof, and parked beside several other cars on a gravelled oval in front of the structure. Gusts of wind whined off the lake and swirled into dancing dust monkeys as they got out of the car. A young boy in his early teens was hosing down a battered old pickup truck nearby.

'We're looking for Dr Lowenstein,' Vail said to him. 'Is his office in here?' The boy nodded and watched them enter.

The lobby of the building was an enormous room with a soaring ceiling and a great open fireplace surrounded by faded, old, fluffy sofas and chairs. The receptionist, a chunky woman in her late forties with wispy blue-grey hair held up by bobby pins, sat behind a scarred maple desk angled to one side of the entrance. A Waterford drinking glass sat on one corner of her desk stuffed with a half-dozen straw flowers. Behind her, a large Audobon print of a cardinal hung slightly lopsided on the wall. The only thing modern in the entire room was the switchboard phone.

'Help you?' she asked pleasantly.

'Martin Vail to see Dr Lowenstein. I have an appointment.'

'From Chicago?'

'Right.'

'Boy, didn't take you long t'get here,' she said, lifting the phone receiver.

'The miracle of flight,' St Claire said, his eyes twinkling.

She looked at him over rimless glasses for a second, then: 'Doc, your guests are here from the Windy City, Uh-huh, I mentioned that. It's the miracle of flight. 'Kay.' She cradled the phone. 'First door on the right,' she said, motioning down a hall towards an open door and smiling impishly at St Claire.

Lowenstein was a great moose of a man with burly shoulders and shaggy brown hair that swept over his ears and curled around the collar of a plaid shirt. The sleeves were turned up halfway to his elbows and his battered corduroy pants had shiny spots on the knees. He had a pleasant, ruddy face and warm brown eyes, and there was about him a pleasant, haphazard attitude unlike the measured mien of the pipe-smoking Woodward. He was sitting at a roll-top desk, leaning over a large yellow butterfly mounted on a white square of cardboard, studying it through a magnifying glass. A cup of tea sat forgotten among stacks of papers and pamphlets that cluttered the desktop. He looked up as Vail tapped on the door frame.

'Dr Lowenstein? Martin Vail. This is Harve St Claire.'

'Well, you certainly didn't waste any time getting here,' he said in a gruff rumble of a voice.

'We have a twin-engine Cessna available when the occasion demands,' Vail said. 'An hour beats driving for three hours.'

'I would say.' He put down the magnifying glass and offered a calloused hand that engulfed Vail's.

'Pretty thing,' St Claire said, nodding to the mounted butterfly.

'Just a common monarch,' Lowenstein said. 'Found it on the windowsill this morning. Thought the kids might enjoy studying it. Can I get you anything? Tea, coffee?'

'No thanks,' Vail said.

Lowenstein sat back at the desk and swept a large paw towards two wooden chairs.

'I appreciate your help on this, Doctor,' said Vail. 'I

wouldn't have bothered you except that Molly wouldn't take my call.'

'I understand the nature of your problem, Mr Vail, but I don't know a hell of a lot about the Stampler case. It's my feeling that you and Molly need to address the problem. I'm also certain she would have refused a meeting if you had reached her by phone.'

'Why?'

'Molly had a breakdown four years ago. A combination of exhaustion, depression, and alcohol. She was a patient here for a year and a half.'

'I'm sorry, I had no idea . . .'

'She overcame the major problems. There were some side effects. She was agoraphobic for about a year. Lived on the grounds. Wouldn't leave. To her credit, she overcame that, too. Has a little house down the road. Bought herself a car. She's working mainly with children now, and quite successfully. Avoids pushing herself. She's a brilliant woman, as you know. Graduated *magna cum laude* from Indiana State. A very compassionate lady.'

'I know that, sir,' said Vail. 'She did a remarkable job on the Stampler case.'

'That's what I'm driving at. I think it left its scars.'

'In what way?'

'I've never been quite sure. She was, uh, very subdued when she first came back. Didn't want to talk about the experience for a long time. In fact, never has except in the most clinical terms. It's certainly not an experience she cares to relive.'

'Why did you invite us over if she won't speak to us?'

'Because your problem is serious. She's strong enough now to deal with it and put it behind her.'

'Are you her therapist?'

'I have been. She is also a dear friend, has been for fifteen years. Her brother's problems contributed to the breakdown. Are you familiar with that?'

Vail nodded. 'Delayed stress syndrome from Vietnam?'

374

'Yes. He's catatonic. Never has recovered. Pretty tough to deal with.'

'This is certainly a pleasant atmosphere,' Vail said. 'If she had to suffer through that experience I can't think of a better place to do it. It's certainly a far cry from Daisyland.'

'Thanks. We're not much for show here,' he said.

'So Molly agreed to the meeting?'

'I told her it was a grave situation. No details. She trusts my judgement.'

'Thanks.' Vail and St Claire stood to leave. Vail turned at the door. 'By the way, Doctor, could you describe a psychopath for me? Not in heavy psychotalk, just the basics.'

Lowenstein regarded Vail for a moment, slowly nodded. 'Totally amoral, usually paranoid, harbours great rage – which he can successfully hide. Remember the boy in the Texas tower? Nobody knew how angry he was until he turned the town into a shooting gallery. Psychopaths also tend to consider others inferior, have contempt for their peers, and they're antisocial, pathological liars. Laws don't count to them.'

'Homicidal?'

'Can be. Depends on the extent of the rage. They can also be charming, intelligent, witty, often socially desirable. Why?'

'I think Aaron Stampler fits the profile perfectly.'

'A real charmer, eh?'

Vail nodded.

'Well, that's what keeps us in business, Mr Vail,' Lowenstein said, turning back to his butterfly. 'Second door on the left. She's expecting you.'

Dr Molly Arrington's sitting room adjoined her office and was a study in simple elegance. It was a small room, cosy and inviting, dominated by a forest-green chesterfield sofa with overstuffed cushions and pillows. Two dark-oak Kennedy rocking chairs balanced the seating arrangement and a large antique coffee table held the group together. The walls were papered with a grey-and-white striped pattern. A shaggy blanket with a silly-looking, wall-eyed black and white cow knitted in its centre was thrown over one arm of the sofa and there was a tube vase holding a single, enormous yellow daisy on one corner of the table. Soft light filtered through a single window, forming deep shadows in the corners of the room.

'Hello, Martin,' she said, stepping out of the shadows, her voice just above a whisper. Vail was taken aback by Molly Arrington's appearance. She was smaller than Vail remembered, her once unblemished skin creased with the ridges of time and tragedy, her ash-brown hair streaked with grey and cropped close to her ears. Her pale blue eyes had an almost haunted look. It was obvious that a year and a half in the institution had taken a toll, and yet there was about her an aura of uncompromising stubbornness in the jut of her chin and the brace of her shoulders.

'Hi, Molly. Good to see you again.'

'Ten years,' she said. 'Such a long time. You haven't changed a bit. Come in and sit down.' She smiled at St Claire. 'I'm Molly.'

'Harve St Claire, Doctor. A real pleasure.'

Vail sat on the sofa and St Claire eased himself into one of the rockers and leaned back with a sigh.

'This place is delightful,' Vail said. 'Reminds me of a funky New England prep school. I can understand why you love it here.'

'Fred calls it the campus,' she said. 'I lived out here for a while.'

'He told us.'

'I live in town now. Go shopping, go to the movies,' she said with a rueful smile. 'I'm not agoraphobic any more.'

'I'm sorry you were ill. I didn't know.

'Thanks. It was a strange experience, being one of them instead of one of us. Gave me a different perspective on life,' she said, ending any further discussion of her hard times. She took an ashtray from a drawer and put it on the coffee table. 'You may smoke in here,' she said. She seemed so calm, Vail wondered if she was on some kind of tranquillizer.

'Whatever happened to Tommy Goodman?' she asked. 'Is he still with you?'

'Tommy met a wine princess from Napa Valley, got married, and is now the vice president of her old man's wine company. He drives a Rolls and has a three-year-old son who looks like a ferret.'

She laughed, a pleasant, loose kind of laugh, throwing her head back and closing her eyes.

'Tommy a mogul, hard to believe. And you?'

'I'm the district attorney.'

'You're kidding.'

'Afraid not. Harve, here, is one of my top investigators. He helped track down Pancho Villa.'

'I ain't quite that old, ma'am.' St Claire chuckled.

'Naomi?'

'Still running the ship.'

'I know about the Judge, he was a friend of my aunt's. How sad. He was such a gentleman. Always had that fresh carnation in his lapel.'

'I miss him a lot,' Vail said. 'It's not as much fun any more.'

'What?'

For a moment, Vail seemed stumped by the question, then he said, 'Everything, I guess.'

She got up and walked across the room to a small refrigerator in the corner. 'How about a Coke or some fruit juice?'

'Sure, I'll take a Coke.'

'Same, ma'am,' St Claire said.

'Okay in the bottle?'

'Only way to drink 'em,' St Claire said with a smile.

She opened three bottles, carefully cleaned the tops of them with a paper towel, wrapped the bottles with linen napkins, and brought them back. She sat down and lit a cigarette.

'This involves Aaron Stampler, doesn't it? Your coming here?'

'Yes.'

'Are they letting him out?'

'How'd you guess?'

'Well, it's been ten years . . .'

'What's that mean?'

'They could have effected a cure in that time.'

'There's no way to cure Stampler.'

'You thought so ten years ago.'

'I wanted to know that if he *was* cured, he would be freed, not sent to Rock Island to finish his sentence. But I never figured it would happen.'

'What's the diagnosis?'

'Ever heard of a resulting personality?'

'Of course.'

'His psychiatrist claims he has developed a new persona named Raymond Vulpes. Aaron and Roy, it seems, have gone to that great split-personality place in hell.'

'That's pretty cynical, Martin. Don't you ever feel some sense of redemption, knowing that you saved him?'

'No.'

'Why, for heaven's sake?'

'Because I don't believe him. I don't believe there ever was a Roy and I think Raymond is a figment of Aaron's imagination, not his psyche – aided by Woodward's ego.'

'Sam Woodward? He's his doctor?'

'Has been for almost ten years. You know Woodward?'

'Only by reputation.'

'Which is . . .?'

'Excellent. He's highly respected in the community. You

think Aaron Stampler tricked Sam Woodward and you and me and the state psychiatrist, the prosecutor, the judge – '

'All of us. Yes, I believe that. I believe he's a raving psychopath and one helluva actor.'

'That's impossible, Martin.'

'You remember telling me the instant before Roy first appeared to you, the room got cold and you couldn't breathe? Do you remember that?'

'Yes, I remember that quite well. I had never experienced anything quite like it.'

'It happened to me when I walked into the room and met Stampler – or Vulpes – for the first time in ten years. It was like an omen. Like I was in the presence of tremendous evil. Nothing like that ever happened to me, either.'

'Anticipation. You obviously have a vivid memory of my description. You expected it and – '

'It happened before I saw him. I didn't even know he was in the room.'

There was a pause, then she asked, 'Did you have any sense of anxiety when you went up there?'

'I was uncomfortable.'

'About seeing Aaron again?'

'That may have been a small part of it. Mainly, I don't like Daisyland.'

'You're not supposed to like it, Martin. It's not like going to the theatre.'

'That's not what I mean. There's a . . . I don't know . . . a sense of hopelessness about the place.'

He was leading her up to the reason they were there, trying to get the dialogue flowing easily, renewing her trust in him, and not doing too well.

He turned to St Claire. 'Harve, do you mind stepping outside for a minute?' The old-timer excused himself and left the room.

'What I'm about to tell you would normally violate

the confidentiality between client and lawyer,' Vail said, 'but since you were his psychiatrist, I can tell you with immunity. You're also bound by confidentiality.'

He told her about Aaron's last words to him after the trial.

'He wasn't kidding,' Vail said as he finished. 'I think his ego had to let me know.'

'Why didn't you tell me at the time?'

'Why? Hell, it wouldn't have done a bit of good. Stampler could have stood on the courthouse steps five minutes after the trial and told the world he was sane and he killed those three people in cold blood and there's not a damn thing anyone could have done about it. He pleaded guilty to three murders and his sentence was passed and final. Nothing could have changed that, Molly, it's called double jeopardy.'

'You also told me it was your job to find the holes and use them against the law so it would be changed.'

'In a court of law. Don't you understand, we can't *get* Raymond Vulpes in court. You and I are both bound by the tenets of confidentiality. If I had gone to Judge Shoat and told him that I had made a mistake based on Stampler's comment, I could have been disbarred – and considering how Shoat despised me, probably would've been. So what possible good would have come from telling *you* what Stampler said? There wasn't a damn thing you could do about it, either.'

'So now the time's come to free him and you want to keep him inside because of some remark he made ten years ago.'

'It's a much more complex problem than that.'

'Not *my* problem, Martin.'

'That's right, but I need all the help I can get right now. Vulpes is going to walk. There's nothing I can do to stop him and Vulpes knows it. Woodward is convinced that Stampler and Roy no longer exist. He believes in Raymond Vulpes. And he's convinced the state board.'

'It's uncomfortable to think about. I love medicine as much as you love the law. If this is true, I feel, I don't know, as if we both perverted our professions.'

'Not you. You did your job.'

'Not very well, I'm afraid.'

'He faked us both out, Molly. But I wanted to be faked, I wanted to believe him because it was the one way to beat the case. Ironic, isn't it? The thing I fear most is prosecuting an innocent person, but I have to live with the fact that I am responsible for saving a guilty one.'

'Then be practical about it. If there's nothing that can be done, put it behind you. It's not your business any more.'

'It's my business because *he* wants it that way.'

'What do you mean, *he* wants it that way?'

Vail asked St Claire to rejoin them. 'What do you remember most about the murder of the bishop?' Vail asked.

'Most vividly? The pictures,' she said. 'They were ghastly.'

'What else? How about the Altar Boys? Do you remember their names?'

'Afraid not. I remember he killed them.'

'Not all. One got away. His name was Alex Lincoln. Do you remember Stampler's girlfriend?'

'Yes. I met her once. At that shelter . . .'

'Saviour House. Her name was Linda Gellerman.'

'She was very frightened. And she was pregnant. She was going to have an abortion, as I recall.'

'That's right. She straightened her life out, married a nice guy two years ago, and had a little boy.'

She smiled. 'It's nice to hear a story with a happy ending.'

'Unfortunately, the story doesn't end there. A few months ago somebody walked into her house one morning and chopped her to bits in front of her child.'

'Oh . . .'

'Now somebody has done the same thing to Alex Lincoln. Exactly the same MO as the Stampler murders, including the genital mutilation and the symbols on the back of the head. We know the same person committed both murders – one in southern Illinois, the other one outside St Louis. But Stampler's still in the maximum security wing and he hasn't had a letter or a visitor in almost ten years.'

'But you think he's involved in some way?'

'Something like that.'

'How could he be?'

'We don't know how and we don't know why. But I'm positive he's directing a copycat killer. We – Harve and I – think it may have something to do with transference.'

'Transference? I don't understand.'

'Isn't it true that transference sometimes causes the patient to have irrational expectations from the people they work and live with? That re-experiencing can cause problems?'

'It can. There are other reasons. People naturally seek approval from their parents or supervisors. Frustration of these expectations may evoke rage or other immature behaviour patterns.'

'Or worse?'

'Yes.'

'And these tendencies wouldn't be immediately obvious to the psychiatrist, would they?'

'Usually the symptoms of abnormal behaviour are what put the patient into treatment in the first place.'

'I didn't ask you that.'

'What are you suggesting?'

'That perhaps someone you were treating may have had mental problems far more severe than – '

Her cheeks began to colour and her tone took on an edge. 'You really don't think much of my ability, do you, Martin?'

'Of course I do!'

'You didn't even use me as a witness in the trial.'

'You served your purpose, Molly. Hell, if it weren't for you . . .' He stopped, realizing where his thought was heading.

'If it weren't for me, you wouldn't be in this fix, is that what you were going to say?'

'No, no, no.' He shook his head. 'I'm responsible for the problem, nobody else.'

'Then stop implying – '

'I'm not implying anything!'

'You're implying one of *my* patients is this killer of yours.'

'No, we think it's *possible*, that's all. Do you still have the tapes you made with Stampler?'

'Yes, I do.'

'Where are they?'

'Under lock and key.'

'Where?'

'In my office.'

'May we see them?'

'What are you trying to prove?'

'May we see them, please?'

She got up and opened the door to her private office. The walls were lined with oak book cabinets with glass doors. They were filled with reports, files, and near the end of one shelf the Stampler tapes, twenty-three of them, each in his own black box with the date on the spine. There were also several locked file cabinets.

'I also keep audiotapes of most of my interviews,' she said with a touch of sarcasm. 'They're in the locked files.'

'Do you ever leave them open? You know, during the day when you're getting stuff out of them?'

'The tapes have never been out of this office.'

'Have you ever discussed them with anyone?'

'I've discussed the case, in strictly medical terms.'

'No details on, for instance, the Altar Boys?'

'Absolutely not. Never. They're confidential. And

they're invaluable as a research tool.' She stopped, her brow bunched up in a scowl. 'You're questioning me as if I were on the witness stand and I resent it!'

'I'm trying to figure out how the copycat killer knew about Linda and Alex. The tapes are a very logical possibility. Did you ever mention anything about the motive for Rushman's murder to – '

'You know I couldn't do that even if I wanted to. I have a responsibility to my patient. You're asking me to violate confidentiality.'

'Don't play games with me, Molly,' Vail said, and anger was creeping into his tone. 'This isn't about shrink-patient relationships, it's about slaughter. Not just murder – *slaughter!* Stampler is a mass murderer. Want a list? Shackles. His brother. Mary Lafferty, his old girlfriend. Some guy in Richmond, we don't even know his name, for God's sake. Rushman, Peter Holloway, Bill Jordan. Alex Lincoln, and poor little Linda Gellerman trying to make sense out of a screwed-up life in some little nowhere town. Count 'em up, lady, that's nine – that we *know* about! Don't tell me about confidentiality when there are two butchers on the loose.'

'How dare you talk to me like that! How dare . . .'

'Molly, someone you treated or worked with may be a serial killer taking orders from Stampler. Think about it – both of them could be *your* clients. You want to protect them by invoking doctor-patient confidentiality?'

'You would, if they were your clients,' she snapped back.

Vail hesitated for a moment. Suddenly he became calm, speaking just above a whisper. 'Stampler *was* my client,' he said. 'I made a mistake. Now I'm trying to rectify it. We don't want details. We want names. We can check them out discreetly. We're not going to hurt or embarrass anyone, but we have to stop the killing.'

She did not answer. Instead she got up and slunk back into the shadows of the room, becoming a fragile silhouette in the corner. St Claire shifted uneasily in his chair, astounded by Vail's attack on Molly Arrington. He needed a chew. The silence in the room was unsettling. Then as suddenly as his temper had erupted, Vail became quiet. His shoulders sagged and he shook his head. The silent stalemate lasted a full five minutes. It was Molly who finally spoke.

'It's all supposition, anyway,' she said feebly.

'I would have to disagree, ma'am,' St Claire said softly, finally breaking his silence. 'I believe in my heart that the copycat killer came from here, just like I believe Stampler's makin' a fool of you like he's makin' a fool of us. I don't pretend t'understand why, I reckon you're the only one in this room could even make a stab at figgerin' that out. But there ain't any doubt in m'mind that he's a genuine, full-blown monster. He don't deserve an ounce of pity or sympathy or compassion. And whoever it is – doin' his biddin'? – is just as bad.'

'How would you know?' she asked from the safety of her dark penumbra. 'I mean, even if I gave you names, how would you know if one of them . . .' She let the sentence trail off.

'You'd just have t'trust us on that. Have to be some-body had access to your tapes. Somebody who may have even come here lookin' for 'em, who looked on Stampler as a hero.'

'Somebody who was in a position to kill Linda Balfour and Alex Lincoln on the days they were murdered,' Vail said.

'And you think Aaron Stampler turned this person into a serial killer?'

'Not at all. I think the potential was there, all Stampler did was capitalize on it. I think maybe, somehow, trans-ference played a key role in this.'

Molly stepped back out of the shadows and sat down on the rocker facing St Claire and Vail. She said, 'You keep bringing up transference.'

'It's something Woodward said.' Vail, who had taken notes of the audiotape, took out his notebook and flipped through the pages. 'Here it is. He was talking about the downside of transference, how it creates a subconscious fear that old injuries and insults will be repeated. He said it's a double-edged sword, that the fear of re-experiencing all past injuries can turn the patient against the therapist. And then he said, and this is a quote, "Abhorrent behaviour patterns can be mirrored only to individuals who would normally accept the transference." '

'That's true,' she said. 'Nobody can transmit abnormal moral standards to another unless the receiver is capable of such behaviour to begin with.'

'See, ma'am, what we think happened, and understand this here's a rank amateur talking, what we think is that this copycat killer was in therapy and reacted adversely to re-experiencing. So that person sought out Stampler for assurance, and Stampler was brilliant enough to become the killer's mentor.'

'The killer transferred to Stampler?'

'Yes. And Stampler capitalized on the killer's insta-bility,' said Vail.

'We ain't sure just how the killer contacted Stampler, Doctor, we don't know at this point how that was accomplished, but that seems the likely scenario since Stampler wasn't in any position to contact anyone on the outside. What I mean, somebody came to him, he didn't go t'them.'

'Why do you think that person was here?'

' 'Cause of the tapes. The tapes are the one place the copycat coulda learned about Rushman and the Altar Boys. And about Linda.' St Claire paused for a minute, then said, 'I just had a thought. S'posin' this person wasn't a full-time patient – '

'An outpatient?' Molly interrupted.

'Or maybe an employee. Somebody who was workin' here and who was also bein' treated for some kinda mental problem. Got into the files, studied Stampler . . . and then maybe left here – maybe got a job at Daisyland for a while . . .'

'And was proselytized by Stampler.' Vail finished the sentence.

'It coulda happened. Ain't much else makes any sense.'

'Is that possible, Molly?' Vail asked.

'Well, there's certainly no rule that says a patient always transfers to a doctor.'

'So what we're lookin' for here is someone who is your basic psychopath and left here . . .'

'Or was on vacation or leave on the days when Balfour and Lincoln were killed,' Vail added.

'You mean this person might still be here?'

'No, ma'am. We think – and once again we're guessin' – that the killer's in Chicago waitin' for Stampler–Vulpes – to get out.'

'And he gets out today, Molly.'

'We're also guessin' he's got a list of future victims.'

'A list drawn up by Vulpes.'

Vail put his briefcase on the couch beside him, opened it, and removed a large manila envelope. He took out three photographs. He handed her the photo of Linda Balfour's corpse, taken by the police. She looked at it in horror and turned her head as she handed it back to him.

'Alex Lincoln was a delivery man for UPD. He was lured to a house near St Louis and killed. This photograph was in a box that Alex Lincoln was delivering. The real residents of the house were out of town at the time.'

He handed her the Polaroid shot of Balfour. Her eyes widened as she realized it had been taken by the killer.

'My God.'

'You're a psychiatrist, Molly,' said Vail. 'How do you figure this? The same MO as Stampler's murders. Messages in blood on the backs of both heads. References to Rushman's books, which are now in a private library. And the last surviving members of the Altar Boys. That information was never brought out in the trial. How did the killer even know about them?'

'Thing is, Dr Arrington, we ain't askin' to look in no files or ask about specifics. What we need to find out is if there's a chance that a patient or an employee here coulda got a squint at those tapes, and if so, where we can locate that person now. Hell, could be a half-dozen or a dozen fits the bill. Our job'd be to narrow it down, find out if any of 'em coulda been in Gideon, Illinois, and St Louis, Missouri, on the dates those two folks was killed. We sure ain't lookin' to drag a whole buncha folks in and have 'em psychologically evaluated, if that's what you're worried about.'

'And you think this killer went from here to Daisyland?'

'Possibly,' said Vail. 'Maybe not directly from here, but ultimately managed to make contact with Stampler there.'

'When would this killer have been here?'

'Not sure, ma'am. Could go way back, but the first killin' occurred last October, so my best guess is two, three years ago.'

'How many people are on the grounds – staff and inmates?' Vail asked.

'Patients, not inmates, please.'

'Sorry.'

'Our patient list is held to three hundred fifty. There's a medical staff of twenty-two and another twenty in the kitchen, security, main office. About four hundred altogether.'

'Big turnover?'

'On staff? Not really. It's a pleasant place to work, the wages are excellent.'

'Patients?'

'I'm guessing – I would say the average stay would be two to three years. We have some long-termers and we have some who are gone in six months. Also about a third of them are children, three to twenty-one.'

'Tell you what'd help, ma'am. If we could get us a list of the staff and patients for the past three years.'

'We can't release the names of our patients. This is a private hospital, patients are guaranteed anonymity.'

'How about a list of staff and anyone on staff who might have been undergoing treatment while they were employed here?' Vail suggested.

She thought about that for a bit, then excused herself and went towards her office. She stopped at the door and said, 'I'm not playing prima donna. These people have very fragile egos. They need all the breaks they can get. It doesn't always have a happy ending, sometimes they end up back here – or someplace worse. We're not infallible, you know, it's not like treating mumps.'

She went into the office and closed the door.

St Claire leaned over and whispered, 'You realized we could be chasin' the biggest wild-goose in history.'

'Got a better idea?' Vail whispered back.

'Hell, no, it was my idea to begin with.'

They could hear her muffled voice as she spoke on the phone. Vail lit a cigarette. Ten minutes crept by before she came back. She sat down in the rocking chair.

'I'm not comfortable with this,' she said. 'I talked to Lowie – Fred – and our personnel director, Jean Frampton, and they agreed to give up the staff records. They left it up to me, whether to discuss staffers who were also outpatients. That's what I'm uncomfortable about. These people, when they reveal themselves to us, that's the ultimate in trust. To violate that . . .'

'I understand that, ma'am, and we certainly appreciate your feelings. Could I make one suggestion, please? If there are staffers who were patients, maybe we could discuss 'em in general terms, not necessarily by name, unless they become real strong candidates.'

'We'll see.'

'Fair 'nuff.'

Thirty minutes later they had a computer printout of the staff members going back for the past five years. They spread the sheet on the coffee table and she began going down the list. It was divided into sections: Name, address, age, sex, education, qualifications, previous employment. There was also a check box marked References and another marked Photograph. There were fifty-five names on the list. Thirty-eight had been employed the entire three years. Six others had been there at least two years, four were relative newcomers, and seven had been dismissed or had resigned.

'Let's start with them,' St Claire suggested.

Molly had a remarkable memory for all the staffers, knew their backgrounds and temperaments, how proficient they were. 'When you see the same forty people every day for years, you get to know them very well,' she explained. They went down the list, checking backgrounds, discussing each of the people as if he or she was a candidate for office. As the afternoon wore on, she became increasingly interested in the project, gradually cutting down the list, occasionally making a discreet phone call to clarify questions that arose. St Claire was beginning to question his hunch, although not out loud. They finally eliminated all but three prospects, two women and a man.

'Jan Rider,' said Molly. 'She was an inpatient for several years, then lived in a halfway house as an outpatient for about six months. She was a housekeeper. Borderline psychotic. Delusionary, disassociated. Her neighbours had her committed when she went into the backyard stark naked and prayed to a tree. She believed it was the Virgin Mary.'

'Do you know where she is now?'

'The state hospital in Ohio. She was one of our failures.'

'Are you sure she's still there?'

'Yes.'

'Next.'

'Sidney Tribble. I'll tell you right off the top, he is from St Louis and he went back there after he got his ticket. Tribble has a sister there, they're quite close. He's got a good job making an acceptable salary. No psychological recurrences so far.'

'Why was he here?'

'Schizoid, paranoid, dissociative.'

'Why was he committed?'

'Court order. His wife left him and he began to delude. Thought she and her new boyfriend were taunting him. He stabbed a man in a shopping mall, someone he didn't even know, he just picked up a pair of shears in a hardware department and attacked him.'

'Did he kill him?'

She shook her head. 'The wounds were relatively superficial. The judge ordered confinement and treatment and his sister paid to have him committed here instead of the state hospital.'

'How long was he here?'

'A year in treatment, a little over two years as an employer and an outpatient. He worked here as our electrician. Went back to St Louis about a year ago.'

St Claire cast a glance at Vail, then made a note beside Tribble's name: 'Possible.'

'Okay, who's next?' Vail asked.

'Rene Hutchinson. She was also on the housekeeping staff. Very bright; in fact, she taught a class of ten-year-olds and was quite good at it, but she didn't want the responsibility. She worked as a housekeeper, then later she assisted in the infirmary. Pretty woman, kind of raw-boned. Pioneer stock.'

'How old was she?'

'Late thirties.'

'What was her problem?'

391

'She wasn't my patient,' Molly said. 'I would prefer you ask Dr Salzman. He treated her.'

'Think he'll talk to us?'

'We'll find out,' she said, and went to the phone.

Orin Salzman was a small man with a greying Vandyke beard and neatly cropped black hair. His shoulders were stooped and rounded as if weighted by the burden of his patients. He wore a black turtleneck sweater, khaki slacks, and a tweed jacket with leather patches on the elbows and seemed a bit put out at being interrupted. He appeared at Molly's door, hands stuffed in his pockets, staring at them through thick tortoiseshell glasses. Molly offered him a drink, which he declined.

'What's this about?' he asked in a stern tone, leaning against the doorjamb.

Molly introduced Vail and St Claire and explained the situation briefly, without going into too many details. Salzman was superficially familiar with the Stampler case, which helped.

'They're interested in Rene Hutchinson's case,' Molly said.

'You know I can't divulge my work with Rene,' he said.

'Look, Doctor,' St Claire said, 'we ain't lookin' to cause this Hutchinson woman any grief. But we gotta check all these people out. If we ask anythin' that you feel is privileged, jest say so, we'll back off.'

'Hmm,' he said. He slowly eased himself into the room and sat on the opposite end of the couch from Vail. 'So I gather you're looking for people with psychopathic tendencies, that it?'

'Kinda.'

He drummed his fingers on the coffee table for a few moments, then said, 'Well, if Molly says okay, I'm willing to listen.'

'What can you tell us – off the top – about her?' Vail asked.

'Her father was an army man, sergeant as I recall. She was born out west somewhere, lived all over the world. Left home when she was fairly young. Went to college for two years. University of Colorado. Very bright woman with an extremely fragile psyche.'

'Did you ever figure out why?'

'Not really. She had suffered a nervous breakdown before she came here, which she concealed from us when she applied for the job. It came out after she'd been here about two years. She was working the night clean-up staff here and going to school in the daytime, got exhausted and almost had a relapse. Then she was arrested for shoplifting.'

'What'd she steal?'

'Something inconsequential, a cheap purse as I remember. Kleptomania is often a cry for attention.'

'And how long was she here?'

'She worked here about three years. She was in therapy for the last six months of her employment, mainly to mend a damaged ego and shaky self-image and build back her strength.'

'What's her background?'

'Well, she wasn't particularly anxious to discuss her past.'

'Isn't that why she came to you?'

'She came to me because she had to. The judge ordered her to get psychiatric help.'

'For how long?'

'Six months.'

'Did she resent these sessions with you?'

'No. She was in pain, and believe me, mental disorders are as painful as your pain would be if you broke a leg. It's not the kind of pain you can take an aspirin for or rub away, and you can't take antibiotics to cure it, but the hurt is very real to those who are suffering.'

'How did she deal with her past?'

'She didn't. I never did really connect with her. The re-experiencing process is the most painful of all. It requires the individual to deal with their darkest side, examine motives and actions they'd rather forget.'

'And Rene resisted it?'

'Wasn't really interested. I strongly suspect she was sexually abused by her father although she never admitted that. She did tell me once that her father was physically and mentally abusive, but that was as far as she took it.'

'So she was uncooperative?'

'No, she was friendly and talkative, she just didn't want to deal with the past, and six months wasn't enough time to earn her trust.'

'You liked her, then?'

'I didn't dislike her. She was a patient I saw for three hours a week. We never got beyond her shielding, which is not uncommon at all.'

'Did you ever consider her dangerous?'

'No – well, to herself, perhaps, when she first came to me. She was verging on manic-depression, there's always a danger of suicide in depression cases. But I never considered her capable of purposely hurting someone else.'

'So you feel she was cured?'

'Let's just say we stopped the problem before it got too bad. She was never an inpatient, she just met with me for three hours a week and I had her on some antidepressant medication.'

'Worked at night, you say?' asked Vail.

He nodded. 'Five nights a week for four hours and eight hours on the weekends. She was the night house-keeping staff, cleaned the offices and meeting rooms.'

'So she would have had access to keys to the offices, for clean-up purposes?' said Vail.

'Uh-huh . . .'

394

'You say she was goin' t'school. Remember what she was studyin'?'

'Data processing. The wave of the future, she called it.'

'Where was that, here in Winthrop?' Vail asked.

Salzman chuckled. 'Obviously you've never seen Winthrop. It's about the size of your hand. She commuted to Shelbyville, about fifteen miles up the Indy highway. Drove an old Pontiac Firebird.'

'Do you know where she went when she left here?'

'Sorry. We lost track of her after she left. You might check with Jean in Personnel on the off-chance somebody asked for a reference.' Molly excused herself and went into her office. They could hear her talking to someone on the phone.

'One more thing,' said St Claire to Salzman. 'Did ya ever get any indication that Rene Hutchinson might have been psychotic, or have psychotic tendencies?'

'No, but that doesn't mean she wasn't. Psychopaths are consummate liars, among other things. She was aloof and could be very guarded at times. And she had mood swings, but then, who doesn't.'

'Anything else you can think of?'

'Well, no, not really. She was excellent with young people, particularly in the eight-to-fifteen age range. They seemed to relate to her, if that means anything.'

'Did she ever mention Aaron Stampler or a fella named Vulpes? Raymond Vulpes?' St Claire asked.

'Not that I recall.'

Vail gave Salzman his card. 'If you think of anything else, would you give me a call?' he asked.

Salzman lifted his glasses, propping them on his forehead as he studied the card. 'DA, huh? What's your interest in Stampler?'

'I defended him,' said Vail. 'Before I became a prosecutor.'

'Huh,' said the psychiatrist, lowering his glasses. 'That's kind of a sticky wicket, isn't it?'

'I think you could say that,' said Vail with a smile.

'Well, tell Molly I'll see her later. Will you two be around for a while?'

'No, we'll be leaving shortly. Thanks for your help.'

'Not much help, I'm afraid, but it was nice to see you,' Salzman said, and left the office.

When Molly came back, she said, 'I have a little information for you. Jean says she got a request for a recommendation for Rene about two months after she left. It was from City General Hospital in Terre Haute. I just talked to the personnel director there. He says she worked there for four months, left around the first of the year. They've had no further contact with her.'

'So she was there at the time of the Balfour kill,' said St Claire.

'And it was just a nervous breakdown, she didn't show signs of any other mental problems?' Vail said.

'Maybe,' said St Claire, 'she was an adroit liar, as Dr Lowenstein would say.'

'You really think she was psychotic?' Molly asked.

'I'm askin' you, ma'am,' St Claire said, and smiled.

Molly lit another cigarette, considered his question carefully before she answered. 'If she was, Orin didn't detect it,' she said finally.

'Where did she come from before she worked here?' Vail asked.

'Accordin' to her record on this sheet, she came here from Regional General Hospital in Dayton, Ohio. General housekeeping,' St Claire answered, checking the computer printout. 'You also got a picture of her, if that's what this here checkmark means.'

'I'll have Jean pull it,' Molly said.

'May I show you something?' St Claire said. He led them into her office. 'Got a couple of hair pins?' he asked Molly.

She laughed. 'Afraid I don't use them.'

'How about paperclips. I need two.'

He took the two paperclips she gave him and straightened them out, then inserted them into the bookcase lock. Working with both hands, he moved the two wires around until he felt the tumblers in the lock. He twisted both clips and the door clicked open. It took about thirty seconds. He reached in, took out one of the tape boxes, and removed the tape, then put the empty box back. He turned to Molly and handed her the tape. 'When's the last time ya looked at one of these, Doctor?'

'I have no idea,' Molly answered. 'I haven't looked at them since I got my ticket. Four years, maybe longer.'

'She was workin' at night, had a key to the office, came in, popped the lock, took a tape, maybe two or three, returned them the next night. Nothin' to it. You never woulda known the dif, 'less a'course you happened to check the particular box she borrowed. That's if it was Hutchinson, a'course.'

'You think she knew how to pick a lock?'

'No big secret, ma'am. I mean, it ain't some inside cop thing. I read it in one of those books, y'know the kind? *101 Things You Always Wanted to Know How to Do But Nobody'd Tell You* kinda books? Point is, she coulda got into the tapes, she was missin' for two months before she applied for work in Terre Haute, and she had mental problems. Nobody else here fits the bill except Tribble.'

They returned to the sitting room. The personnel director had sent 3 × 5 colour mug shots of Rene Hutchinson and Tribble to the office. Molly handed them to Vail and then turned over the photograph of Linda Balfour's body, which was lying facedown on the table. She stared down at it.

'You think a woman is capable of this?' she asked.

'Ma'am,' said St Claire, 'I think a woman can do anything a man can do but sire a child – and I ain't even too sure 'bout that any more.'

Thirty-Two

Angelica Stoddard was short and resembled her mother. She had a trim, tight body, good posture, and blue eyes so pale she almost looked blind – a striking young woman in an extra-large sweater that hung down halfway to the knees of her bleached-out jeans. She wore jogging shoes with white sweat socks that sagged over the tops and a black felt hat over ash-blonde hair. The hat was pulled down almost to her ears. She looked sombre and walked quickly with her head down. Venable fell in beside her. Angelica paid no attention at first but finally turned and looked up at Venable.

'Hi,' said Venable, 'I'm Jane Venable. I'm your mother's lawyer. Can we go somewhere and talk for a few minutes?'

'Not here,' the young woman answered in a whisper, looking around furtively.

'Anywhere you say.'

'Anywhere but here,' Angelica said.

Venable had her car drive them to a coffee shop off campus. They found a table in the back of the small café. Angelica ordered cappuccino and Venable had black coffee.

'Why did you come to the school?' Angelica Stoddard said. 'Why didn't you call first?'

'I tried, but I couldn't get through.'

Angelica's shoulders sagged. 'Oh, yeah, it's a hall phone,' she said, shaking her head. 'It's always busy. I'm sorry I said that, but I . . . I'm so embarrassed by all this. I know it's wrong, but I can't help it.'

'It's okay, Angelica. It's absolutely understandable, you don't have to apologize to me.'

'What do you want?'

'I need your help.'

'To do what?'

'I want you to come with me to see your mother.'

The young woman looked shocked. 'I can't do that,' she said urgently, but still speaking almost in a whisper. 'She absolutely forbids me to—'

'Angelica, she must put up a fight.'

'You don't know my mother. Once she makes up her mind . . .'

'Look, for God's sake, she's not deciding what kind of car to buy, her life is on the line here.'

'What can I do?'

'Tell her to defend herself.'

'She won't listen to me, and she won't change her mind. I know her, Ms Venable. I talked to her. They let her call me. She kept saying, "This is the only way." '

'You've got to go with me to see her and back me up.'

'She'd kill me!' Angelica said, then quickly added, 'Figuratively speaking, I mean.'

'Angelica . . . do they call you Angel?' The young student nodded. 'Angel, you tell her you and your dad need her. She can't just stand by and get maxed out by the state. If she'll put up a fight we can win this case. Do you want her to spend the next twenty years in state prison?'

'No! Oh no. Oh God, what's happening to us?' Angelica shook her head and started to cry.

'Trust me,' Venable said. 'Just do exactly what I tell you to do and trust me.'

Vail had secured wiretapping permits for the pay phone in the hall outside Vulpes's door and in his room. The two electronics experts in the investigative department had set up a listening and watching post in an empty loft across the street from the halfway house. One of them, Bob Morris, had graduated from electronics school and had attended the FBI academy. His partner, Reggie Solomon, was a classic nerd, who was interested only in the mysteries of electronic surveillance. A second team comprised of Randy Dobson, a young, lean detective who wore baggy khakis and an Atlanta Braves T-shirt under a leather jacket, and Kirby Grosso, a tallish, raw-boned woman wearing a jogging outfit – the two best shadows on the DA's investigative staff – was on standby in a car a block away. Grosso had a Hi8 videocamera secreted in her athletic bag so she could videotape Vulpes without being detected.

They watched Terry bring Vulpes to the halfway house and help him carry his belongings to the second-floor room. Vulpes had a large old-fashioned leather suitcase, a stereo, TV, and VCR, his tool chest and two large cardboard boxes of books and tapes. They listened on the monitor when Vulpes entered his room, and Morris, using a 500mm telephoto lens, videotaped him through the open window of the room. They heard the supervisor running down the rules and regulations, the most important of which was a 10 P.M. curfew that was strictly enforced. The supervisor, whose name was David Schmidt, had a pleasant, reassuring voice.

'You'll do just fine, Raymond,' he said as he left the room.

'Thanks,' Vulpes answered. A few moments later he appeared at the window of his room. He leaned on the sill and looked up and down the street. He closed his eyes and took a deep breath of fresh air.

Actually, Vulpes was studying the terrain. He was certain the phone and his room were bugged, just as he was certain that he was being observed from somewhere in the old building across the street. Excellent. Vail had taken the bait.

Then he closed the window, pulled down the shade, and turned on his CD player. In the loft across the street, the sounds of a Judas Priest album roared into Solomon's earphones and he pulled them off.

'Well, shit,' Morris said. 'There goes our sound and picture.' He snatched up his portable phone and punched out the number of the chase car.

Grosso answered. 'Yeeees?' she said pleasantly.

'This is Bird Watch. Got Fox in his den, shades drawn, music drowning out our sound. Suggest you cover the back door.'

'Way ahead of you, Bird Watch. Got it in view.'

'See ya.'

'Over and out.'

Morris and Solomon settled back to watch and wait.

'You sure he can't see in here?' Solomon said.

'Not with his shades drawn.'

'How about when the shades are up?'

'Not unless he's Superman.'

'What are we on this guy about, anyway?'

'I dunno,' said Morris. 'All I know, Stenner said he's dangerous, whatever the hell that means.'

Vulpes stood in the middle of his room and surveyed his surroundings. It was large enough to include a bed, dresser, night table, and lamp. On the opposite side of the room was a small loveseat covered with a blanket and an easy chair with a battered coffee table between them. Against the wall was a table large enough to hold his TV. He lifted the blanket on the loveseat. Grey duct tape held a large rip together.

What the hell, he thought, *it's just for the night*. He kept the volume on his CD player as loud as he felt was safe. He moved the small night table to the wall beside the door. He unpacked his minicomputer, set it up on the table, and plugged it in. He went into the hall with a small tape recorder, lifted the receiver off the phone, and taped the sound as he dropped a quarter into the slot. When he got a dial tone, he dialled the Time of Day and then hung up. He went back to his room. The halfway house was almost empty, everyone was at work at that time of day. He looked at his watch.

Ten minutes. He had ten minutes. He had to take the chance.

He went back to the hall, unscrewed the cover of the phone, found the external line into the phone, and unplugged it. If the phone was tapped they wouldn't even know it was momentarily out of service. He worked quickly. He detached four coloured wires leading to the small magnet in the phone and attached one wire to the 'in' screws of the radio component he had made at Daisyland then the others to the 'out' side. The component successfully acted as a conduit between the external line and the line of the phone. He plugged the external line back in and quickly slipped the cover back and screwed it into place. He stepped back into his room and closed the door.

It had taken seven minutes.

He opened his suitcase and removed a city map from a pocket in the top of the bag and spread it out on the bed. There were four crosses marked in red on the map. He smiled and refolded the map and put it back in its pocket.

He was ready.

Stoddard looked grey, her mouth slack and her eyes swollen from lack of sleep. Her grey-black hair was straggly and had not been combed for several days. The female guard, a slender black woman with her hair pulled back and held by a barrette, led her out of the cell and towards the visitor's room.

'Listen, I heard you talking to your daughter on the phone,' the guard said. 'Sorry about that, I was standing there and couldn't help overhearing you. I heard you tell her not to come, but she's here.'

'What!'

'Ma'am, I got a daughter and a son and if I was in

your shoes, they'd come whether I liked it or not. Stop here a minute.'

They stopped at the check-in desk while the guard unlocked a drawer and removed her bag.

'I got some powder and lipstick and a comb in here and a little mirror,' she said. 'Why don't you do a little repair job on your face. Make both of you feel good.'

'I don't want her to be here.'

'Well, she is, honey, so give her a break.' The guard handed her a small compact, a mirror, and a comb. Edith took them haltingly, stared in the tiny mirror, and shuddered. She started to dab her face with powder.

'Here,' the guard said, taking the compact, 'let me do that.' She started working on Stoddard's face.

'What's your name?' Stoddard asked.

'Cheryl Williams,' the guard answered. 'Used to work in a beauty parlour before I decided to become a cop.'

She powdered the pallor away, put a thin line of lipstick on Stoddard's lips, and combed her straggly hair back, then took off her own barrette and, pulling Stoddard's hair tight, slipped it on. She stepped back and admired her work.

'There,' she said. 'You put a smile on and she'll leave here a lot happier than when she came.' She held the mirror up so Stoddard could check herself out. Stoddard smiled for the first time in days.

'Thank you,' she said.

'Sure. Tell her the food's good. They seem to worry a lot about that.'

When Edith Stoddard entered the small visitor's cell and saw Venable and Angelica, she stopped cold, her shackled arms dropping stiffly in front of her and her eyes blazing with fury.

'I told you, I didn't want her . . .' she started, but she didn't finish the sentence. Angelica, overwhelmed at the sight of her mother in the drab prison clothes and handcuffs, rushed to her and wrapped her arms around her.

403

'Oh, Mama!' she sobbed. 'I love you. Please listen to Ms Venable. We need you, Mama. I need you.' She clung to Edith Stoddard, her shoulders shaking as tears suddenly flooded her face.

Stoddard looked at Jane Venable, her face clouded with anger, but finally her eyes closed and her lips trembled and tears crept from her closed eyes.

'Oh, Angel,' she said in a shaky voice. 'I love you so much.'

'Then please, *please* listen to Ms Venable. Please do as she says. Please trust her.'

Stoddard pushed her daughter away and fixed a hard stare at her.

'Now, Angie, you listen to me. I *know* what I'm doing. You trust *me*.'

'I want you to come home,' the young woman sobbed.

'Well, that's not going to happen, dear. You must adjust to that. You're going to have to spend a little more time with Dad and keep his spirits up.'

Angelica suddenly pulled back from her. 'And who keeps *my* spirits up, Mom? You just sit here and do nothing. You let them write about you in the papers and everybody at school says you must be guilty because—'

'I *am* guilty, Angie. Get it through that thick little head of yours. Let me handle this.'

'Fine,' her daughter spat at her. 'Handle it, then. And the hell with the rest of us.' She whirled around and banged on the door. The guard opened it and she left the room.

Edith Stoddard sank into a chair. 'Why did you do that? What possible reason could you have for doing that to both of us?' she asked Venable.

'Edith, look at me.'

The older woman slowly raised her eyes, eyes filled with anger.

'I found the room, Edith.'

Stoddard said nothing. The expression in her eyes changed from anger to fear.

'I found the room in the closet, you know the room I'm talking about.'

Stoddard said nothing.

'How long did Delaney keep you in this kind of bondage?'

'It wasn't like that.'

'Oh, come on! I saw the handcuffs, the leather straps, the whips, the corsets, the garter bells. How long were you in sexual bondage to Delaney?'

Stoddard turned away from Venable.

'Do they have to know?'

'Who? Vail? Parver? The police? It's significant evidence in a murder investigation, I can be disbarred if I don't report it. And even if I didn't tell them, somebody's going to tumble across that closet just like I did, carpenters or painters redoing the room. How did this start, Edith? Did he make you do these things in order to keep your job?'

'They don't have to know,' she said, turning to Venable and pleading. 'They don't have to know you found out.'

'What about the gun?'

'The gun? Oh yes, the gun . . .'

'Would you like me to throw it in the lake? Hell, Edith, I'm your lawyer, not your accomplice.'

Stoddard slumped in her chair. 'Why didn't you mind your own business?'

'This *is* my business. What do you fear, Edith? Are you worried about what your husband and daughter will think? You were a bonded slave, for God's sake. You think I can't make hay out of that? We can beat this rap, Edith.'

'Never!' Edith Stoddard glared at her angrily. Venable stared back at her just as hard.

'If you think I'm going to let the state put you away for twenty years to life, you're out of your mind. I have a responsibility to you and the court.' She sat down facing Stoddard and reached for her cuffed hands, but Stoddard pulled them away. 'Edith, listen to me. Even if we don't go all the way to trial, I'll be able to bargain very strongly in your favour with this information. Martin Vail is a very smart lawyer. He'll see the possibilities, too. But I must tell them, do you understand that?'

'Not if I fire you.'

'Even if you fired me, I'd have to give up this knowledge.'

'So the whole world will know . . .'

'The police and the district attorney will know. And, yes, it will make the press – there will be a police report. So what do you have to lose? Let me fight the good fight, Edith. I don't want you to go to jail at all.'

Stoddard stared at her for several long moments, then said, 'You don't understand. At first it was humiliating, but then . . .'

'Yes?'

'But then I began to look forward to it. I wasn't a slave. I began to look forward to the times I'd go over there and he'd come out of that closet in that garter belt and hand me the handcuffs and I would hook his hands over his head to the headboard and do whatever I wanted to him.'

'You don't have to tell me this, Edith—'

'I *want* to tell you,' Stoddard said, cutting her off. 'Don't you understand, I haven't had sex with my husband for more than ten years. *Ten years!* There were no other men, I didn't cheat on him. I . . . I just considered . . . it . . . part of my job. One of my *duties*. And when it was over, I whipped him. *I* whipped *him*. "You bad boy," I'd say, and I'd take the whip and he would bend over and I would give him several hard lashes across his backside. It was like getting even for all the humiliation. You understand what I'm saying, Ms Venable? I *enjoyed* it. What do you think the prosecutors are going to think about that?'

'The prosecutor will never know,' Venable said emphatically. 'You don't have to tell them *anything*. We will bargain this out. You will never testify.'

Edith Stoddard stood slowly and walked to the door and tapped on it. Officer Williams opened it. As she left, Stoddard turned to Jane and said, 'You betrayed me, Ms Venable.'

Rudi Hines had manipulated the clean-up schedule so as to arrive at the billing office in City Hospital at five minutes to three. The billing office worked from six-thirty to two-thirty on weekends and usually everyone was out of there before three o'clock. Nobody ever worked overtime. But on this day the manager of the department, Herman Laverne, was still in the office on the phone. Hines immediately panicked but decided to go ahead with the usual procedure.

God, get out of here before three.

Laverne looked up as Hines shuffled in. Hines, wearing coveralls, was slightly built with short red hair under a Red Sox cap turned backwards. The bucket was on wheels and Hines directed it into the office with the mop. It rattled past Laverne, who cupped his hand over the mouthpiece of the phone.

'I'll be outta here in a minute,' he said.

Hines nodded, went to the back of the room, and began mopping the floor, all the while watching the screen of one of the three computers in the back of the room. That particular computer had a modem and was left on all night to receive bills, order confirmations, or messages. The clock on the wall crept closer to three o'clock and Laverne was still yapping on the phone.

At exactly three o'clock, Vulpes typed FONCOM into his mini-computer and immediately got the dial tone of the hall phone. He held the tape recorder up to the small mike built into the machine and pressed play. The sound of a quarter dropping into the phone slot played into the mike and from there to the phone. In an instant he had a dial tone. He dialled 555–7478. It rang once and then the word CONNECT flashed on the screen. He typed DIRCOM into his machine and the screen went blank.

Across the street Morris heard the phone operate, heard the coin drop, and then heard the dial tone.

'He's on the horn again,' Morris said. He turned on the monitor. Solomon put the paperback novel he was reading aside. They listened to Vulpes dial. The phone rang once and as soon as it was answered, there was a hum on the line.

'What the hell's that?' Solomon said.

'Sounds like he got a bad connection.'

'Can't you do something with all that stuff you got, you know, get it on another frequency or something?'

'What do you mean, another frequency? We got a bug in the damn phone. He dialled wrong or got a bad connection.'

In his room, Vulpes began talking to the computer on the other end of the line as soon his screen went blank.

At City Hospital, Laverne was about to leave the billing office when he heard the computer beep.

'What's that?' he said, half aloud, and walked back to the computer. Rudi Hines stood back against the wall, eyes staring at the screen, terrified, squeezing the mop handle with both hands.

HYDRA, FOX IS FREE. The message appeared on the screen.

'What the hell is that?' Laverne said. 'Hydra? Fox? Some hackers must be screwing around.'

HYDRA?

'This is ridiculous.' Laverne snapped.

HYDRA?

Laverne leaned over the keyboard and typed: WHO THE HELL IS HYDRA? AND WHO ARE YOU?

In his room, Vulpes immediately typed DISCON and the program returned to READY. He sat and stared at the computer for several seconds. Someone must have come in and seen the computer screen. Vulpes would not try again. Everything was ready. If Hydra was there, the message was clear. Vulpes was free. That was the only reason for the call.

Across the street in the loft, Solomon was getting nervous.

'Why isn't he hanging up?'

'Maybe he's stupid,' Morris said.

'What's he doing, sitting over there listening to a dead line?'

'I don't know what the hell he's – '

The line suddenly went dead.

'There. Stupid schmuck finally figured it out,' Solomon said. He picked up his paperback and started reading again.

In his room, Vulpes unplugged the minicomputer, put it back in the toolbox, and returned the night table to its place. He looked at his watch.

Three-ten. Time to go.

And at the hospital Laverne muttered. 'Just some crazy kid hackers,' as he headed out the door. And to Hines: 'Be sure the door locks behind you when you finish up.'

Hines nodded and watched Laverne go. Hines sighed with relief. It was all right, Laverne was annoyed but not concerned by the message from Fox. Fox was free, that was all that mattered. The clock on the wall said 3:20.

Only six more hours.

Ten minutes later Vulpes left the halfway house. Morris dialled Grósso.

'Present,' she said.

409

'Fox is out of the den. Heading towards the Loop.'

'Keep me on the line,' she said. Morris watched the corner. The grey Mustang drifted into sight, turned, and drove past the listening post. A block away Vulpes climbed the stairs to the elevated train stop.

'He's taking the el,' Grosso said a moment later on the phone. 'We're on foot. Call traffic and tell 'em not to bust our car. We'll contact Icicle as soon as he lights somewhere.'

'Rodge. Over and out,' Morris answered.

Grosso and Dobson followed Vulpes to a three-storey open-atrium mall in the downtown section. Vulpes seemed to be in no hurry. Grosso stayed half a city block behind Vulpes while Dobson tracked him from the opposite side of the atrium. Occasionally Grosso would enter a store and snoop around while Dobson kept Vulpes in view. Dobson stopped occasionally and window-shopped, watching Vulpes in the reflection of the store window. When Grosso was back on track, Dobson would enter a store. They both wore beepers and each had dialled in the other's number. If either of them lost Vulpes or got in trouble, they would simply push the send button and immediately beep the other. They were a good team: cautious, savvy, alert.

Vulpes strolled the first floor of the mall, engrossed in window-shopping, occasionally stopping and watching the shoppers. The mall was crowded. Winter sales. Vulpes went to the second floor of the mall, entered an ice cream store, and came out with a hot fudge sundae piled with whipped cream and sprinkles. He sat on a bench and ate it slowly, savouring every bite. He went to a record store and bought two CDs, then went to a men's clothing store, where he bought a black turtleneck sweater. He rented a copy of *Sleepless in Seattle* from the video rental store, then went to a one-dollar movie theatre in the mall and bought a ticket for *Schindler's List*. He got a hot dog and a Coke at one of the food counters that surrounded the entrance to the theatre and sat at a small table eating. Dobson and Grosso rendezvoused out of his line of sight.

'Shit, I saw that picture,' Dobson complained. 'It's three hours long!'

'Well, you're about to see it again,' Grosso answered. 'And don't talk about the movie while it's on. I hate people who tell me what's going to happen.'

When Vulpes finished eating, he checked his watch and went into the theatre.

'I'll get the tickets, you get the popcorn,' Grosso said.

'I'm getting the short end of the deal,' Dobson complained.

'For a change,' Grosso answered, and headed for the ticket window.

Stenner was waiting at the county airport when Vail and St Claire landed from their trip to the Justine Clinic.

'I brought Jane with me,' Stenner said, adding, almost as an apology, 'Didn't want to leave her by herself.'

'How about the house guard?' Vail asked.

Stenner looked at his watch. 'Just coming on now.'

He opened the back door of the car and Jane peered out. Vail smiled when he saw her. The tension that had ridged his face with hard lines seemed to ease a bit.

'You okay?' he asked, climbing in beside her.

'Of course. Hey, Mr DA, I wanted to come, okay?'

'I'm a little stressed out. Sorry,' he said. 'Let's swing by the office on the way home, Abel.'

She wrapped both arms around one of his arms. 'You can relax. Your bad boy is sitting in the movies as we speak.'

'The movies?'

'Our two best tails are baby-sitting through *Schindler's List*,' Stenner said, driving away from the airport. 'If he stays for the whole show, they'll be getting out about now.'

'And he has to be in by ten,' said Venable. 'That's a little over an hour from now.'

'What did he do before the movie?'

'Went shopping, rented a movie, ate some ice cream.'

'Him and his damn ice cream,' said Vail. 'How about phone calls?'

'Morris says nothing significant.'

'Get him on the phone,' Vail said.

'Y'know, if he is tied in with our copycat, the old Fox could be bidin' his time,' St Claire said, tapping out the number on the car phone. 'Makes us wait until we get a little lax, then hit.'

'That's why we're not going to get lax, Harve,' Vail said.

'Here's Morris,' St Claire answered, stretching the cord and handing the phone back to Vail.

'This is Martin Vail, Bobby. Who did Vulpes call?'

'Only made two calls, Mr Vail. He called and got the time and then he made a call and got a bad connection. That's it. Then he left.'

'Thanks,' Vail said with disgust, cradling the receiver. 'He only made two calls and one of them was a bad connection.'

'We drew a bad connection at Daisyland, too,' said Stenner. 'They have an enormous cleaning staff and a fairly regular turnover. Over eight hundred patients. Delivery people, visiting firemen, a constant flow of traffic. Trying to go back two years?' He shook his head. 'Impossible.'

'So the only leads we got left are Hutchinson and Tribble. Both of 'em as long as a shot gets,' St Claire grumbled.

'Flaherty ran both of them through the state payroll computer after you called,' said Stenner. 'There's no record either of them ever worked at Daisyland. St Louis isn't doing any better. Flaherty talked to his pal, Sergeant Nicholson, this afternoon. They haven't got the first clue. Not a fingerprint, no blood samples, nobody saw anything, nobody heard anything.'

'We're dealin' with a real pro here, Marty,' St Claire said.

'No, we're dealing with Stampler. He's calling every turn.'

'Maybe you're puttin' too much emphasis on Stampler,' St Claire said. 'Maybe it is just a copycat killer, saw the tapes in Arrington's office, knew how it was done, found out about the bishop's library . . .'

'It's Stampler,' Vail said flatly. 'I saw him, I talked to him. He's running it and he's going to keep running it.'

'So we just wait, that it?' Stenner said.

'That's it. Everybody on the staff covered?'

'Yes, sir,' said Stenner. 'They're either under surveillance or with their families. Flaherty's keeping an eye on Shana – a task he seems to be enjoying, as does she, I might add.'

'Y'know, I don't like to bring this up,' said St Claire, 'but it's gonna get right costly – all this surveillance, I mean, if we gotta keep it up for long.'

Vail glared at the back of his head.

'You got a better idea, Harve?'

'I don't even have an idea half as good.'

Grosso and Dobson sat two rows apart in the back of the theatre so they could keep Vulpes in view and get out quickly when he got up to leave. He sat through the entire picture. He stood up as the credits rolled and Grosso and Dobson slipped out.

Outside, Grosso grabbed for her cigarettes.

'Three hours without a smoke,' she said. 'I'm having a seizure. You better get lost.'

'Too late,' Dobson said. Grosso turned and was face-to-face with Vulpes. His eyes were like stones.

'Excuse me,' he said, 'can I trouble you for a light?' He put a cigarette between his lips.

'Sure.'

'Did you enjoy the film?'

'It's a great picture,' she said calmly.

He smiled. 'Thanks for the light,' he said, and walked off towards the mall exit.

'He made us,' Grosso growled to Dobson.

'How? Man, we were practically invisible.'

'I don't know how, but he made us. Not only that, but he wants us to know it. Shit, we're off the detail.'

'Well, he's probably on his way home. Let's tuck him in and let the electronics wizards take over. Stenner will decide what to do with us.'

'He's going to pull us off the case, Randy.'

'What case? Is this a case? Hell, nobody knows why we're even following this guy.'

'Stenner says he's dangerous.'

'That's it? We're following him because he's dangerous? Half the people in the city are dangerous, for Christ sakes.'

'He's spooky-looking,' Grosso said. 'Did ya see those eyes?'

'Oh, we're following him because he's spooky-looking and dangerous. I feel much better.'

On the train heading back to his room, Vulpes checked his watch. Eight-thirty. He smiled. Hydra would strike in half an hour.

The game he had been waiting ten years to play was about to begin.

Thirty-Three

In the hazy light of an almost full moon, gargoyles and harpies and strange mythical creatures lurked in the spires of the Gothic buildings forming one of the University of Chicago's many quadrangles. Staring up at them, Naomi Chance felt a sudden thrust of fear, as if they were harbingers of doom. The medieval beasts seemed to be taunting her. She quickly shook it off and turned up the collar of her coat against the brisk wind that funnelled between the buildings, assaulting her as she left the library and started across the quad towards the parking lot a block away. The monthly meeting of the Association of Legal Secretaries had been particularly dull, but she had presided with her usual élan and kept the proceedings moving as briskly as possible.

As she approached 57th Street, she saw the glow of a cigarette among the trees and shrubs near the street. A moment later the butt arced to the ground. A man was huddled in the shadows, his hands buried in his pockets. A car was parked by the kerb ten or twelve feet away.

She gripped the small can of Mace she always kept handy in her pocket and subconsciously quickened her pace. Normally, she would not have noticed him, but tonight was different. Tonight she saw omens everywhere. *Hell*, she thought, *everybody's jumpy because of Stampler's release*. As she approached the figure huddled in the bushes, she gripped the Mace even tighter and steered a course away from the bushes and trees. But before she got to the street, a voice said, 'Naomi Chance.'

'Who's that?' she demanded when he said it, increasing the pace.

'Hold up a minute, please.'

She glared into the darkness as a large, bulky man moved away from the shrubs. He was tall and muscular, a powerful black man, his features obscured by the dark.

'What the hell do you want?' Naomi demanded, and took her hand out of her pocket. 'Keep your distance, this is a can of Mace.'

'Whoa,' the big man said, and stopped in his tracks, fumbling in his coat pocket. 'Man, they warned me you were rough and ready,' he said in a deep voice, and laughed. He held out his hand and flipped open his wallet. A gold badge twinkled in the streetlights.

'Detective Zack Lyde, Chicago PD,' he said. 'My boss, Shock Johnson, loaned us out to the DA and the DA says keep an eye on you. So that's just what my partner and I are doin', Ms Chance, keepin' an eye on you.'

Naomi's breath came out in a rush. 'You scared the shit out of me, son,' she said.

'I'll tell you, that can of Mace gave my pulse a little kick, too. Look, why not let us drive you home? We need to clear your apartment when we get there and then just kinda, you know . . .'

'Keep an eye on me?' she said, finishing the sentence for him.

'Yeah.' He said, chuckling, in his deep, gruff voice. 'My pard can follow us in your car. I'd feel a lot better that way.'

'Why don't you just drive with me and let your pard follow us,' she suggested.

'Fair enough,' Lyde said. As they walked towards his unmarked police car, Naomi saw Judge Harry Shoat leaving the library after his weekly graduate-school seminar. His driver trotted up to him as Shoat started down the walk.

'How about Judge Shoat over there? Watching him, too?' Naomi asked.

'Hell, he just laughed at us,' Lyde said. 'Says Mr Vail looks for spooks under his bed before he goes to sleep.'

'You mean you don't?' she said with a grin, and followed her protector to the car to fill his partner in on the plan.

A block away Jefferson Hicks, a city patrolman assigned as Shoat's driver and bodyguard, rushed up to him and took his briefcase.

'How'd it go, Your Honour?' he asked.

'Excellent, as always,' Shoat said, exuding self-assurance. 'Although for the life of me, I don't see how some of those oafs ever hope to pass the bar.'

'Yes, sir,' said the driver.

Hicks had a black belt in karate and had attended a special course in antiterrorism. He had been assigned to Shoat for four months, ever since an irate taxpayer, who felt he had been treated unjustly in court, had shot and nearly killed one of Shoat's peers. Hicks belonged to the city; the sedan belonged to the judge.

Once inside the four-door Mercedes, Shoat reached into the pocket in back of the shotgun seat, took out a bottle of Napoleon brandy and a snifter, and poured himself a drink. He savoured the brandy, swirling the snifter around, sniffing the aroma and gauging his sips so the drink would last the thirty minutes it took to get to his condominium in the Edgewater district.

'I got another call from the DA's office while you were in lecturing,' Hicks said. 'About that Stampler guy.'

'Vail!' Shoat snapped with disdain. Before he became a state supreme court judge, back when he was known as Hanging Harry Shoat, the ultraconservative jurist was a 'max-out' judge known for meeting out harsh sentences, often tainted with racism. An impatient and humourless perfectionist, he dispensed justice with a callous disregard for the situations or circumstances of defendants and had been passed over three times for the supreme court before his impressive knowledge of the law and precedents had made it impossible to snub him further.

417

He huddled down in the back seat, a stern man with a razor-slim moustache and black hair tinted to hide its grey streaks. He and Vail had gone to the mat many times in the courtroom. Shoat still harboured resentment towards the man who defied convention and challenged the law with consistent fervour. Even as a prosecutor Vail had an arrogant attitude about authority that rankled the jurists. Now that he had changed sides, Vail was slandering his own client, implying the man should not be freed, even though the state's leading psychiatrists had approved the release.

'Wants it both ways,' Shoat muttered, taking a sip of brandy, remembering with distaste how Vail had ambushed Venable in the Stampler trial. 'The hell with Vail,' he said aloud.

'Yes, sir,' Hicks agreed.

'He's baaack,' Morris said as Vulpes entered the house. He trained the videocamera on the open window and waited until he saw Vulpes enter the room before he started shooting.

'Been shopping,' Solomon said, watching through binoculars. He saw Vulpes dump out the contents of two shopping bags on the bed. 'Got himself a couple CDs, looks like a sweater.'

'He's got a videotape, too,' Morris said, squinting into the eyepiece. 'Looks like ... *Sleeping* ...'

'*Sleepless in Seattle*,' Solomon said. 'That's a funny picture.'

'I hope it *sounds* funny because we're probably gonna have to listen to it.'

'Got some pretty good music in it, It's got Jimmy Durante singing "As Time Goes By".'

'Who's Jimmy Durante?'

'He's an old-time movie actor. Big nose. Voice like a gravel grinder. You'll hear.'

'He's putting the tape in the VCR,' Solomon said.

'I can see that, Solomon, I don't need a play-by-play.'

Vulpes started to get undressed, then almost as an afterthought he went to the window and closed the blind.

'Well, shit,' said Morris. 'We're back on ear-time.'

They could hear Vulpes whistling softly, moving around the room, heard the bed groan as he lay down on it, then they heard the TV turn on, following by a preview at the beginning of the tape.

Morris turned off the camera and leaned back in his chair.

'What a way to make a living,' Solomon said. 'Listening to movies you can't see.'

In his room, Vulpes quickly switched to the black turtleneck after pulling down the shade. He took a small tape recorder from the tool chest and put it on the night table. He had made the audiotape while still at Daisyland, playing the movie through several times, stopping it at any funny spots and taping his laughter, timing it perfectly. He even sang along with Durante.

Vulpes waited until the film started and on a precise cut he pressed the play button and the audio recorder. The movie and the tape, now perfectly in sync, were about two hours long. He set the TV so it would turn off at eleven. The audio recorder would turn itself off. With luck, nobody would know he was gone until morning.

He opened the door to his room and looked down the stairs. He could hear Schmidt moving around in the kitchen. He went down the stairs.

'Hi, Raymond,' Schmidt said.

'Hi. Thought I'd get a Coke.'

'Sure. Well, I'm packing it in,' said Schmidt. 'Lock the door after me, will you?'

'Sure. Good night.'

'You're gonna be happy here, Raymond. I'm sure of it,' said Schmidt.

Vulpes smiled and nodded. 'Already love it,' he said.

At nine-fifteen Morris saw Schmidt leave the halfway house, huddled in his plaid lumber jacket. Five minutes later the lights on the first floor of the halfway house blinked out. And five minutes after that Vulpes slid open the side window in the kitchen, slipped over the sill, and dropped silently into the shrubs beside the house.

Stenner had never seen Vail this edgy. He had double-checked everyone in the Wild Bunch to make sure they were protected. He was jumpy about Naomi going to the meeting at the University of Chicago until he was assured she was in capable hands. And he insisted that Parver, Flaherty, and Meyer, who lived alone, stay together for the night.

'Why don't I take you home,' Stenner said to Vail. 'Vulpes is tucked in watching a movie on TV.'

'I have a nudge,' said Vail. 'The kind of nudge Harvey gets. And you, too, only you call it instinct.'

'I got a nudge, too,' said St Claire. 'Had it ever since we got to the office.'

'What kind of nudge, Harve?' Flaherty asked.

St Claire said, with a touch of annoyance, 'How many times I gotta tell ya, Dermott, if I knew, it wouldn't be a nudge, it'd be a reality.'

'Last time you had one of your nudges, you turned up the Linda Balfour case,' Stenner said.

'The last time you had a nudge, we turned over Poppy Palmer,' St Claire countered.

'I agree with Abel, let's go home,' Venable said to Vail. 'But I want to talk to you for a minute before we leave.'

Surprised at how serious she seemed, Vail led her into his office and closed the door.

'Something got your goat?' he joked.

'I have to tell you something,' she said. 'And this isn't about Aaron Stampler.'

'So . . . tell.'

'I went to Delaney's apartment. Out of a sense of duty, I suppose. Wanted to experience the scene of the crime. And I discovered something. There's a hidden compartment built into the closet in the bedroom.'

'What kind of compartment?'

'It's about two feet deep and five feet long. It's a hiding place for Delaney's toys.'

'What kind of toys?'

'Whips, handcuffs, garter belts – '

'*What*?'

'And a .38-calibre Smith and Wesson. It's on the floor. Looks like it was just thrown there. I didn't touch any of it.'

'The gun is in this room?'

Venable nodded. 'I assume it's the murder weapon.'

'How did you find it?'

'Probably only a woman would have noticed it – women are very conscious of closet space. I was sitting on the bed, staring at the closet, and I realized that it's lopsided. I mean, there's a lot more room on one side than the other. So I snooped around and couldn't figure out why. And I snooped around some more and felt the door give. And I kept snooping. To open it, you unscrew the hanging rod and take it out. There's a button recessed in the fixture it screws into.'

'That's very sneaky, Venable. You want a job?'

'I have a job – defending Edith Stoddard.'

'If this is going to be a bargaining session I'd like to bring Shana in on it, it's her case.'

'We're not going to bargain, Marty. We're going to trial.'

'Janie, you probably turned up the murder weapon. That's all we need to burn this lady.'

'She was a victim for almost ten years, Martin. He degraded her and she took it so she could keep her job. Then he tossed her over for a younger model and ruined her life. I can make that add up to a walk.'

'On what grounds?'

'Name it. How about the McNaghten Rule. Namely that Stoddard was labouring under such a defect of reason, caused by the circumstances, that she didn't know the nature and quality of the act she was committing. Then we have the concept of irresistible impulse – she was so distressed she couldn't control her actions. Or how about temporary insanity? She was degraded and humiliated and finally thrown away like a piece of garbage.'

'Save your closing statement for the jury,' he said. He lit two cigarettes and handed her one. 'And you're forgetting we have premeditation. And I thought Stoddard was determined to cop a plea?'

'I never was.'

'She's the client.'

'And I'm an officer of the court charged with giving my client the best advice and defence possible. That's what I'm going to do. You want to settle for involuntary manslaughter?'

Vail laughed. 'I can't do that, I'd be disbarred for incompetence. Either she's not guilty or she's guilty of *some*thing.'

'Then I guess it's Parver and me,' she said. 'Unless you're going to step in.'

'I don't step in on my prosecutors' cases,' he said. 'I'll send St Claire and Parver over to investigate the secret room. Then maybe you and Parver can have a sit-down.'

'What do you think she'll do?'

'Go for the jugular.'

'Trained her well, huh?'

'Didn't have to, it comes naturally with her. Thanks for telling me.'

'You wouldn't have told me?'

'Sure. But it still had to give you some bad moments, considering the options, I mean.'

'There weren't any options and you know it.'

'Ain't ethics hell?' He grinned.

'Yeah, ain't they,' she said, and after a moment, 'You never cease to amaze me, Mr Vail.' She was obviously relieved.

'Why? Did you expect me to throw a temper tantrum?'

'I know some men who would.'

'Look, we'll both do what we have to do, Janie. Hell, in a way, I got you into this.'

'In a *way*?' she said, raising her eyebrows. They both laughed.

St Claire tapped on the door and Vail waved him into the office.

'I just figured out what my nudge is,' he said. 'Something you said about Vulpes's phone calls strikes me as odd.'

'What's that?'

'You said he made a phone call and got a bad connection?'

'That's what Morris told me.'

'Well, if he got a bad connection, how come he didn't try the call again?'

Vail stared across the room at him, then looked at Venable.

'He's right,' she said. 'It's not like he didn't have time to dial again. If I made a call and got a bad connection –'

'You'd either call the operator or try again, right?' St Claire finished the sentence.

Hicks entered Shoat's elegant two-bedroom condo first. He flicked on the lights and walked down the short entrance hall to the living room. He put Shoat's briefcase on his desk. Shoat had bought the condo after his wife died, preferring to get rid of the old house near Loyola University with its painful memories. The two-bedroom condo near the lake was convenient, was in a proper neighbourhood, and was on the ground floor. It suited his purpose perfectly. It had a small deck at the rear that was secluded by a high redwood fence. He enjoyed sitting on this rustic terrace, reading cases and writing out his opinions in longhand. Hicks pulled back the thin, white cotton drapes, flicked on the lights, and slid open the door, checking the deck then closing the door and pulling the drapes closed again. He checked the living room, the master and guest bedrooms and baths, all the closets, and the small sitting room the judge used as an office.

'All clear,' he told his boss.

'Very good, Hicks,' the judge said. 'Don't know what I'd do without you.'

'Look, you want I should maybe spend the night in the guest room what with all this hoopla over . . .?'

'Don't be silly.' Shoat said, waving him off. 'I'm going to get in bed and watch Court TV for an hour or so. I'll be sound asleep by ten.'

'Right, sir. Seven o'clock in the morning?'

'As usual.'

He followed Hicks to the door, pulling on the night chain and twisting the dead bolt after letting his body-guard out. He made himself a Scotch and water, turned off the lights, and went into the bedroom.

Shoat was fastidious in his nightly ritual. He set out his clothes for the next day, placed his Scotch and water on the night table, brushed his teeth and scrubbed his face, and changed into scarlet silk pyjamas. He folded his silk bathrobe carefully over a chair within arm's reach of the bed, lined up his slippers side by side exactly where he expected his feet to hit the floor when he arose, piled three goose-down pillows, and fluffed them up just right before finally turning down the covers and slipping side-ways between the flannel sheets so as not to wrinkle them. He propped himself up and pulled the feather com-forter up under his chin and turned on the television, flicking the remote control to the Court TV channel. Settling down, he sipped his drink and watched with the sound turned low. Within minutes, he was trying to keep awake. He finished the drink and clicked off the TV.

He was dozing when suddenly the room seemed to be flooded with cold air. He lay in bed, staring sleepily into the dark. It got colder.

Then he thought he heard something. The sound seemed to be coming from the living room, although he was sleepy and confused in the dark.

'Hicks, is that you?' he called out, thinking perhaps his bodyguard had come back for something and was at the front door. He waited and listened.

There it was again. Was someone talking outside the condo?

Disoriented in the dark, he groped for the lamp and instead grabbed his bathrobe. He stumbled out of bed in the dark, his feet padding the floor of the darkened room in search of his slippers. The room was frigid and he gave up on the slippers and floundered his way towards the living room.

A frosty draught sighed past him as he reached the bedroom door. He looked across the room. The door to the terrace had blown open. The white cotton curtains, flapping and twisting in the wind, looked like apparitions in the ghostly moonlight.

Damn! he thought. *Hicks forgot to lock the door to the terrace.*

He started towards the door. Then he heard a voice.

'*Order. Order in the court.*' And a gavel smacking against wood.

The voice seemed to come from the dervish curtains, swirling in the wind. He stepped closer, squinting his eyes to get a clearer look. And then he saw something, a vague shape hidden within the gossamer panels. Shoat was suddenly hypnotized with fear. The shape slowly materialized into a dark form that seemed to emerge from within the whirling folds. It moved towards him. Shoat's mouth turned to sand. His feet would not move.

'W-w-who's that?' he stammered.

The figure, silhouetted by the moonlight against the shimmering drapes, raised its hand. There was a click and the same voice, the same husky whisper he had heard a moment before said:

> 'The prince who keeps the world in awe;
> The judge whose dictates fix the law;
> The rich, the poor, the great, the small,
> Are levelled – death confounds them all.'

There was a slight pause, then: 'Greetings from Daisy-land, Judge.'

'Oh, my God!' the judge shrieked. He turned and rushed towards a table near the door, pulled open a drawer, thrust his hand in, and felt the cold steel of his .32-calibre pistol. But before he could pull it from its hiding place, he felt a hand grab his hair and his head was snapped back.

Shoat felt only a slight burning sensation when the knife sliced through his throat. But when he opened his mouth to scream, all he heard was a rush of air from beneath his chin. And then the taste of salt flooded his mouth.

When the pain struck, it was too late for Shoat to feel it.

Thirty-Four

It was easy to trace the phone number. Morris had attached a digital readout to the monitor and had the number listed in his log. Stenner made one phone call and got the rest of the information.

'City Hospital,' he said. 'The last three digits, 4–7–8, is the office extension. He was calling the billing department.'

'Why in hell was he calling the billing department at City Hospital?' Vail wondered aloud.

'And why'd he get a bad connection?' asked St Claire.

Meyer, the computer expert, had been sitting in the corner listening to the discussion. He turned to his computer and entered the modem program, then brought up the menu. He dialled the phone number, 555–7478, and listened to it ring as he watched his computer screen. The screen went black for a moment, then the word CONNECT flashed on and another menu appeared across the top of the screen.

'There's your answer,' he said. 'He was calling a modem line. Vulpes was talking to a computer.'

'With what?' Parver asked.

'Yeah. Where'd he get a computer?' St Claire asked.

'I don't know, but that's what the call was all about, that's the hum on the line,' said Meyer. 'If he stayed on for ninety seconds and he's a computer expert, he knew exactly what he was doing.'

'Maybe we ought to roust him and ask him,' said Flaherty.

'On what grounds?' Vail said. 'He's a free man. If he does have a computer, it's understandable. It's his business. But if he's using it to trigger the copycat, then we got him.'

He dialled Morris.

'Yes, sir?'

'This is Martin, Bobby. What's Vulpes up to right now?'

'He's watchin' a video. *Sleepless in Seattle*.'

'You're sure he's there?'

'We can hear him laughing. Few minutes ago he was singing "As Time Goes By" with Jimmy Durante.'

'Is the back door covered?'

'Sure.'

'You stay on top of this guy, Bobby. He makes any phone calls or does anything out of the ordinary, call the office immediately.'

'Absolutely.'

Vail hung up. 'He's in his room watching a video, they can hear him on the room tap.'

He paced his office for a few moments. 'All right, here's what we're going to do,' he said. 'Harve and Ben, come with me. We'll check out the billing department at the hospital. Shana and Dermott, stay here in the office and monitor the phones. And call Naomi right now just to make sure she's protected. Anything happens? Any calls from Morris or anybody else, call me on the portable. Abel, I want you to take Jane home and stay with her, and I mean in the house with her until I get back. I don't trust anyone else but you to protect her. And I want the house guard to patrol the entire perimeter. Any questions? Good. Let's get on with it.'

The emergency ward at City Hospital looked like a battle zone. Three ambulances were parked at the entrance, one with its red light still blinking. Once inside, Vail, Meyer, and St Claire were greeted with a rush of noise and motion. An aide raced by pushing a young woman on a gurney. Her face was covered by an oxygen mask and IVs were protruding from both arms. Her eyes were half open and her head wobbled back and forth with the movement of the stretcher. A young doctor was racing along beside it, shouting orders to a nurse who held open the door to the OR preparation station.

'I got a compound fracture of the lower leg, possible head injuries, I need a CAT scan before we go to OR.'

'We're ready for her,' the nurse yelled back.

Another doctor dashed from the receiving room, his gown streaked with blood, and headed up the hall.

'Excuse me,' Vail said, but the MD waved him off. 'Not now,' he said, and ran off towards the operating room.

Vail looked through the door of Receiving and saw a nurse pull a sheet over a body. Two feet away, a team of doctors and nurses worked frantically to prepare another victim for treatment. A nurse burst out of the room carrying a clipboard.

'Excuse me,' Vail said. 'We're trying to find the night superintendent.'

'Down the hall, lift to the first floor, third door on your left, Mrs Wilonski,' she said without looking at them or slowing down.

'Thanks,' Vail said.

They found the night superintendent's station and a nurse paged Eve Wilonski, the super on duty, then raced off, advising them to stay put.

'If you don't, she'll never find you,' she said.

'Doesn't anybody around here *walk*?' Meyer asked.

The lift door swung open and a short, square woman in a rigidly starched uniform marched towards them. Her stern face wore the ferocious expression of a bulldog.

'Gentlemen, I'm Eve Wilonski, night super. Sorry I'm in a rush right now, we've got a mess in Emergency.'

'We came up that way. I'm Martin Vail, acting DA'

'Yes, sir, I recognized you from pictures in the paper.'

'These are two of my associates, Ben Meyer and Harve St Claire.'

'Gentlemen,' she said with a nod.

'What happened?'

'Three-car pileup on LaSalle,' she said. 'Three dead, six trying to stay alive. A drive-by on the south side with a dead three-year-old and her mother hanging on by her fingernails. We got two heart attacks and they just brought one in for this psych ward who was standing on the marquee of the Chicago Theatre peeing on people walking by on the sidewalk. That's in the last forty minutes and it isn't even eleven o'clock yet. It's just warming up out there.'

'Sorry to bother you when things are so crazy,' said Vail.

'It's always crazy down there,' she said casually. 'Do we have a problem with the district attorney's office, too?'

'No, *we* do. I need to take a look at your billing office and also find out if anyone was in there at three o'clock this afternoon.'

'That office closes at two-thirty on weekends,' she said.

'I know. But we have reason to believe that someone was in there at three. It's imperative we know who that person was.'

'Maybe a cleaning person, somebody like that?' St Claire suggested.

'That's quite possible,' she said. 'If it's an emergency, I can call Mr Laverne at home. He's the billing supervisor. Someone could have been working overtime.'

'That would help a lot,' Vail said.

'May I ask what this is about?'

'A hacker,' Meyer said casually. 'We have reason to believe someone may be hacking into your billing computer. The consequences could be serious.'

'Oh, my God,' she said. She flipped through a staff telephone directory, her finger tracking down the rows of staffers and stopping at Laverne's name. She dialled the number and waited for what seemed an eternity.

'He's not home,' St Claire moaned.

'Mr Laverne?' she said suddenly. 'I'm sorry to bother you at home, this is Eve Wilonski. I have the district attorney here. He'd like to speak to you.' She handed the phone to Vail.

'Mr Laverne, this is Martin Vail.'

'Yes, Mr Vail.'

'Mr Laverne, we're checking on a computer problem and we need to know if anyone in your department worked overtime today.'

'I did.'

'You did? Were you there at three o'clock?'

'Yes, sir, I was talking to a pharmaceutical company on the West Coast.'

'Was anyone else in the room at the time?'

'Uh, yes. Hines, I think is the name. Cleans up. Is this about the hacker?'

His question surprised Vail. 'You know about that?'

'I was there when the message came across the modem line.'

'What message?'

'Well, it was crazy. Something about a fox and someone named Hydra.'

'Hydra? Do you remember exactly what the message said?'

'Let's see. First it said "Hydra, Fox is free." Then it repeated the name Hydra a couple of times. Then I jumped in and asked who Hydra was and who was on-line and the connection went dead.'

'And you say Hines was in there at the time?'

'Yes. Came in while I was on the phone.'

'Thank you, Mr Laverne. You've been a great help.'

'It was a hacker, right?'

'Yes. We're investigating it.'

'I knew it. Too nutty to be anything else. You people always work this late at night?'

'When it's something this important. Thanks, Mr Laverne. Goodbye.' He cradled the phone. 'Do you know someone in clean-up named Hines?'

'Yes. Rudi Hines.'

'Show Ms Wilonski the picture of Tribble,' Vail said to St Claire.

Harvey took a flat wallet out of his pocket and removed the photograph of Tribble supplied by the Justine Clinic.

'Is this Rudi Hines?' Vail asked.

She looked at the photograph and shook her head. 'No, this is a man. Rudi Hines is a woman.'

Her answer stopped conversation for a moment. Vail looked at St Claire. 'Show her the other one,' he said. St Claire showed her the photo of Rene Hutchinson. She studied it for a moment and then slowly nodded. 'Yes, her hair's darker and much shorter, but that's Rudi.'

'Can we take a look at the billing office?'

'Of course.' She took a ring of keys out of a drawer and led them down a maze of hallways to a fairly large room with several desks and a bank of computers at the rear. The screens faced away from the door. Meyer walked straight back to them and stopped short.

'Christ, look at this,' he said. They all crowded around the screen and read the message:

> Very Clever . . .
> The prince who keeps the world in awe;
> The judge whose dictates fix the law;
> The rich, the poor, the great, the small,
> Are levelled – death confounds them all.
>
> Hydra

'I don't know what the hell it is, but it'll be in one of Rushman's books, that's for damn sure,' St Claire said.

'What's it mean?' Eve Wilonski asked. 'Who is Hydra?'

'Greek mythology, ma'am,' St Claire answered. 'Hydra was a demon with two heads. Every time Ulysses cut one of 'em off, she grew two more in its place.'

432

'Or maybe grew a new name whenever things got hot?' suggested Vail.

'Maybe,' agreed St Claire.

'He's telling us something, Harve. Everything he does sends a message – names, quotes, *everything*. He's taunting us.' Vail read it again and then a chill rippled through him. He repeated the second line aloud: ' "*The judge whose dictates fix the law.*" '

'Shoat?'

'What other judge could it be? I'll get Shock Johnson on the portable.'

St Claire turned back to Eve Wilonski. 'Tell you what the message really means, ma'am. It means we need an address on this here Rudi Hines ASAP,' he said.

Stenner parked the car in front of Venable's house and opened the door for her. As they approached the front door, he drew his gun. Venable was surprised. Stenner always seemed so totally in control, it was hard to imagine him armed. He took her gently by the arm, stepped in front of her at the door, and held out his hand for the key. She gave it to him and he unlocked the door, then swung it open with his foot. He moved cautiously into the foyer, then moved quickly and professionally through the first floor, checking the living room, kitchen, guest bedroom, and all the closets.

'We're clear down here,' he said. The outside guard was sitting on the terrace with his back to the door. He was wearing earphones and listening to a Walkman.

'I could have walked out there and pulled the chair out from under him, he wouldn't know the difference,' Stenner said, walking to the door of the terrace. 'I want him to stay in here with you while I check the second floor.'

He opened the door and tapped the house guard on the shoulder. The man pulled off the earphones.

He stood up and turned around.

His face wore a hideous grin.

It was a moment or two before Stenner, with a shock, recognized the grinning face of Aaron Stampler.

By then it was too late.

'Welcome home,' Stampler hissed. The knife slashed the air as he swung it underhanded. It pierced Stenner just over his belt, its deadly point angled upward, slicing towards his heart. The two men stumbled back into the living room and crashed into the wall.

Gasping, Stenner grabbed Stampler's wrist to keep him from withdrawing the blade. Stampler, his face inches away from Stenner's, curled his lips in a leer. He shoved his other hand into Stenner's coat pocket, felt his car keys, and grabbed them.

As they burst into the room, Venable fell back against the wall. She gaped with horror when she saw the knife buried in Stenner's side. Then rage took over. She grabbed a heavy brass lamp from an end table and charged Stampler, swinging it like a club. It smashed the ridge of his jaw and split it open. Stenner slid from his grasp and fell at their feet, the knife still embedded in his side.

Stampler roared with pain. He grabbed the lamp and with his other hand hit Venable on the jaw. The blow knocked her backwards against the other wall. Stampler grabbed the lamp with both hands and swung it overhanded.

She felt the heavy metal hit her cheek, felt the bones crush and a searing pain in her eye. Blood flooded down into her mouth. Her legs gave out and she fell to the floor, looking up at the enraged killer through one eye.

Stampler turned to get the knife, but Stenner had rolled over. It was under him. The madman ran around the corner into the kitchen, grabbed a dish towel, and pressed it against the wound in his jaw. He pulled open a drawer, dumped its contents on the floor. He pulled out another and another and finally found the knife drawer. He snatched up a vicious-looking boning knife and raced

434

back into the living room. But as he did, Stenner rolled over and, with great effort, slid his 9mm pistol across the hardwood floor to Venable. She grabbed it as Stampler rushed into the room from the kitchen. Half conscious and in pain, she swung the gun up and fired. It tore a corner off the kitchen cabinet. Stampler dived into the living room, scrambling for cover. She fired again and again. He skittered along behind a sofa. A shot ripped into it, bursting through the other side in a cloud of cotton and foam rubber. Stampler grabbed a chair. Hunched over, he ran towards a window, shoved the chair through it, dived through the shower of glass, and ran towards Stenner's car.

Inside, Venable rolled over on her stomach. She stared through her good eye at Stenner, who had the knife in his hand. He went limp and the knife slipped out of his grasp. He fell forward.

Outside, she heard Stenner's car start and roar away.

'Abel . . .' Venable moaned, and passed out.

Thirty-Five

When Shock Johnson arrived at Judge Harry Shoat's condominium, three patrol cars were already there. The six patrolmen had searched the grounds around the perimeter of the two-storey building, but on Johnson's instructions had not attempted to enter the condo.

'We knocked on the door and tried him on the phone,' said a sergeant who had taken charge of the small force. 'No answer from inside and no answer on the phone.'

'Shit,' Johnson grumbled. He tucked his hands in his rear pockets and stared at the house.

'What's the layout, Sergeant?' he asked, without taking his eyes off the condo.

'One-floor condominium. The people upstairs are wintering in Georgia, so he's the only one in the building right now. There's a terrace with a six-foot fence around there on the side, windows in back and on that side. The place is dark and his car's in the garage.'

'Where the hell's his goddamn bodyguard? What's his name?'

'Hicks, sir. I called him. The judge dismissed him, told him to go home. Hicks drives his car here every morning and they travel in the judge's Mercedes, that's why it's in the garage.'

'Wasn't Shoat warned?'

'Hicks said he laughed at Vail.'

'Christ. Eckling's gonna have me for lunch when he gets back from Atlanta.'

'The chief's in Atlanta?'

'Yeah, at some lawmen's convention. Free drinks and food what that's about.' He looked around, pointed to a young, athletic patrolman. 'What's your name, son?' he asked.

'Jackowitz, sir.'

'Take that fence and see if you can see anything through the terrace door. I don't wanna go kickin' in anythin' until I'm sure he's in there.'

'Yes, sir.'

'Take a walkie-talkie and be cautious.'

Jackowitz took the fence like a pro, jumping up and grabbing the top slat, chinning himself, and swinging first one leg then the other over the top. He dropped down onto the terrace.

Johnson waited.

The walkie-talkie crackled to life.

'Terrace door's unlocked, sir.' Jackowitz reported.

'Oh, shit,' Johnson moaned. 'You got a flashlight?'

'Yes, sir.'

'Take a look inside, but be careful.'

'Going in.'

There was a minute or two of silence, then: 'Oh, sweet Jesus, Lieutenant, I ain't believing this. I'm opening the front door.'

Johnson walked to the entrance and a moment later the front lights flickered on and the door swung open and Jackowitz stared out at them. Even in the dim light he was pale and swallowing hard.

'I been on the force twelve years, sir, I never seen anything the likes of this.'

Johnson walked into the foyer and turned into the living room. Shoat was lying in the middle of the room, naked, his arms folded across his chest as if he had been laid out by a funeral director. The destruction of the body was profound, from the wounds on his torso, legs, and arms, to the emasculation of his private parts. There was blood everywhere. Johnson stared at the scene for a full two minutes, the muscles in his jaw twitching.

Finally he said, 'Where the hell's his head?' to nobody in particular.

'Good question,' Jackowitz answered in a hoarse whisper.

Vulpes held the towel hard against his jaw to stem the bleeding. It was already beginning to swell and pain was etched into the side of his face. He had the city map on his lap marked with the route from the halfway house to Venable's place and back to Hydra's apartment. He watched his speed. He had to ditch Stenner's car fast, forced to assume that Venable had called in the report and his situation had suddenly became desperate.

What shitty luck, he thought. First, Stenner had brought her home instead of Vail. And then the bitch had screwed everything up. That was twice she had tried to kill him. Once in court, where she tried to send him to the chair, and again tonight.

Okay, so he had got Stenner instead of Vail. And he had smashed the bitch up good, maybe scrambled her brains. Poetic justice. As his own brain raced, he momentarily forgot the pain in his jaw.

He was cautious when he got to Hydra's apartment. He drove past it. The street looked safe. He parked at the opposite end of the street. Too bad Hydra didn't have a phone; he could have called her, told her to split, to follow him until he could find a good spot to ditch the car. He would have to take a chance, go up to her place and get her out of there.

As he got out of the car, he saw the police car. It was a block away and it cruised in quietly, parking perpendicular to the street he was on. Two cops got out, strolled to the corner, and crossed to Hydra's apartment building. They looked around, went in the front door.

They're on to her, he thought. *How the hell did they get on to her?* He decided he had to abandon Hydra. But she knew the plan. He didn't think she would talk, though she was now so far over the edge he couldn't be sure. He got back in, pulled the door shut, and started the car. Then he saw the two policemen come around the side of the house and return to their car.

He sat in Stenner's darkened sedan. Maybe they were just answering a disturbance call. Maybe it was just a coincidence and they would leave. He decided to give them a few minutes.

Meyer drove the car to the row-house apartment south of Garfield Park. Vail sat in the backseat, twirling an unlit cigarette between his fingers. St Claire turned in the shotgun seat and looked back at him.

'What about Vulpes?' he asked. 'We got enough to pull him in?'

'For talking to a computer? We need the woman, then we'll decide. We're still not positive she's the copycat.'

'He's not going anywhere,' said Meyer. 'He's home singing duets with Jimmy Durante.'

'Okay,' said St Claire.

'You disagree?' Vail asked.

'Nope, just thinkin' out loud.'

'You got another nudge?' asked Meyer.

'Kinda.'

'What's a kinda nudge?' Meyer asked.

'It's just, you know, a kinda nudge. Ain't a full-fledged nudge yet.'

'Your nudges make me nervous, Harve,' Vail said.

'Why?'

'Because most of the time they turn out to be harbingers of doom.'

'Can't help it, just happens.'

'I'm not knocking it, I'm just saying they make me nervous.'

The police car was parked a block away from Rudi Hines's apartment. The driver was an old-timer named

John Bohane. His partner, Richard Luscati, was a rookie, two months on the job.

'Lieutenant Johnson said we should wait here for you, Mr Vail, so as not to rile anybody up. We did walk down there and look around.'

'And . . .?'

'Her car's parked around back in an alley. Bonnet's warm. And there's a lot of blood on the front seat.'

'Uh-oh,' St Claire said.

'You think she's in there then?' Vail asked.

'Yes, sir, I do.'

'Okay, let's do this cautiously. This lady should be considered armed and dangerous.'

'Right.'

Meyer pulled the car in front of the patrol car and parked. The five men walked up the quiet deserted street to the converted row house.

'That's her apartment,' Bohane said, pointing to the corner of the second floor.

'There a back door?' St Claire asked.

'Uh-huh.'

'Whyn't you two go in the back, we'll take the front, just in case she decides to take a drive.'

'Right.'

The two patrolmen disappeared quietly down the paved walk that separated the two houses. Vail, St Claire, and Meyer walked quietly to the front door.

Vulpes watched as the second car pulled up beside the police car. He couldn't see what was going on. Then the new arrival pulled over to the kerb in front of the patrol car and three men got out. The cops joined them. They started across the street towards the apartment building. As they passed under the street light, he recognized Vail.

His pulse throbbed in his jaw, increasing the pain, but

he ignored it. He was overwhelmed with hatred. There was Vail, a block away, and he could do nothing about it.

Damn you, damn you, Vail! You figured it out faster than I gave you credit for.

Well, perhaps the police did not know about the attack on Stenner and Venable yet. Stenner was surely dead. Venable was out cold, so probably Stenner's car wasn't hot yet.

Maybe I hurt the bitch more than I thought. He laughed thinking about it. Still, he had to ditch the car in a hurry.

It was too late to help Hydra. Hopefully she was so far over the edge, she wouldn't give away the rest of the plan. *Too bad*, he thought. It was such a perfect plan and she had carried it out flawlessly until now. But Venable had screwed him up and now Vail had beat him to her.

He had to get away from there, lift another car and ditch Stenner's. He checked the map and found a group of high-rise apartments. *Perfect*, he thought. He had to find a parking lot and heist another car.

Goodbye, Hydra. Sorry it didn't work out.

He wheeled the car into a U-turn and headed for North River.

'Lemme go first,' St Claire said, arcing a wad of chewing tobacco into the grass.

'How come you go first?' Meyer asked.

''Cause I got the gun,' St Claire said. He drew a .357 Magnum from under his coat and led the way inside. A poorly lit hallway was swallowed up by darkness and a flight of stairs on one side led to the second floor. A moment later the two patrolmen emerged from the other end of the hall.

'We're clear,' Bohane said. 'Her car's still back there.' The patrolmen led the way, followed by St Claire, Meyer, and Vail. Bohane knocked on the door.

'Ms Hines?' he called out.

Inside the apartment Rudi Hines was in the bathroom. She stood naked in front of the sink, scrubbing her hands, the water pouring off her hands tinged with red. When she heard the rap on the door, she hurriedly threw on a cotton housecoat and stepped from the bathroom into the living room.

It was sparsely furnished. A sofa with its springs sagging to the floor, a round kitchen table with two chairs, two easy chairs in the same disrepair as the sofa. The only light came from the 60 watt bulb in a floor lamp near the door.

'Is it you?' she cried eagerly.

She heard the muffled reply. 'Ms Hines, it's the police. We need to talk to you. It's about your car.'

She went back into the bathroom and emerged a moment later with a large carving knife clutched in one hand. She backed into a dark corner of the room.

'Look, ma'am,' St Claire said, standing near the door. 'We don't wanna have to bust up your door. Just open up and talk to us for a minute.'

'Go away.'

In the hall, St Claire looked at Vail and shrugged. He turned to Bohane. 'Waste it,' he ordered.

The two cops drew their revolvers. Bohane stepped back and slammed his foot into the door an inch or two from the knob. It burst open. Somewhere down the hall a door opened and a dim face peered out.

'Go back inside,' Vail said. 'And stay there.'

The face disappeared and the door closed.

The two patrolmen jumped inside the room. Bohane first, Luscati covering him, then St Claire behind them. St Claire saw her first, standing in the shadows.

'Lemme do the talking,' he said softly, and to her, 'Now why'd you make us go and do that?'

'What do you want?' she said. She saw Vail enter the room. Her eyes blazed in the dim light.

'I know who you are,' she hissed.

'Ms Hines, I'm Martin Vail, acting district attor—'

'I *know* who you are. Why aren't you out there?'

'Out where?'

'What do you *want*?'

'Ma'am, do you also go under the name Rene Hutchinson?' St Claire asked.

She backed further into the corner, her eyes peering at them from the darkness. She lurked in the shadows, but Vail could see one hand in the spilled light from the lamp. It was still covered with dried blood.

' "*Vengeance with its sacred light shines upon you.*" Sophocles,' she whispered.

'Miss Hines, do you also go by the name—'

'I am Hydra,' she said. She held the knife tight at her side, within the folds of the housecoat.

'Do you know Aaron Stampler?'

'There's no such person.'

'Do you know Raymond Vulpes?'

' "*Revenge is sweeter than flowing honey.*" Homer.'

'Do you know the Fox?' St Claire said, cutting her off.

' "*Punishment is justice for the unjust.*" '

'Listen here, ma'am . . .'

She glared from the darkness at Vail. 'What are you *doing* here?' she demanded.

'Where should I be?' Vail asked.

'With her.'

'With who?'

' "*To die is a debt we must all pay.*" '

The two patrolmen looked at each other quizzically. Meyer looked around the room. On a table near the door he saw a small tape recorder. It was caked with blood.

'Look here, ma'am, we know you're Rene Hutchinson. Wouldn't you like to tell us where Fox is?' He took a step towards her. 'We need to talk to you and Fox.'

'I taught him everything he knows,' she whispered suddenly and with pride.

'What was that?' St Claire asked.

'I taught him everything he knows.'

Meyer moved sideways to the table. He took out a pencil and punched the play button of the recorder.

'Stop that!' she shrieked.

'*Order. Order in the courtroom.*' The hollow sound of a gavel rapping. Then:

> *The prince who keeps the world in awe;*
> *The judge whose dictates fix the law;*
> *The rich, the poor, the great, the small,*
> *Are levelled; death confounds them all.*
> *Greetings from Daisyland, Judge.*'

Vail immediately recognized the voice on the tape. It was Vulpes.

'Miss Hutchin – ' St Claire started to say, but the woman suddenly charged out of the darkness. She rushed straight towards Vail. The knife glittered in her hand.

St Claire moved quickly in front of him, aiming his gun at Hydra as she charged.

'Hold it!' he ordered, but she didn't stop.

The rookie cop panicked and shot her in the chest.

She screamed. The knife twirled from her hand and she was knocked backward, landing flat on her back on the floor. She lay there, gasping for breath, staring at the ceiling.

'Thank you,' she whispered. 'Thank you . . .'

The rookie lost it. He stared down at her in horror. 'Oh God! Oh sweet God, why didn't you stop when I told you?' he screamed at her.

'Shut up, Ritch. Call the medics.'

'She charged us with a knife,' the rookie babbled. 'I didn't . . . didn't . . .'

His cheeks suddenly ballooned. He clasped his hand over his nose and mouth and raced to the bathroom.

'I got eighteen years in, never fired my gun except on the range,' Bohane said disgustedly. 'He's on the street two months and shoots a woman.' He shook his head. 'I'll call an ambulance.'

'Use this,' Vail said, handing him the portable phone. The cop dialled 911.

St Claire kneeled down beside Hydra.

'Rene Hutchinson?' he asked.

'I am Hydra,' she said faintly.

'Who named you that?'

'Fox. Fox knows everything. But I taught him everything he knows.'

St Claire's 'kinda' nudge suddenly became a reality. He was remembering some notes he had read among the files on Stampler. Notes that Tommy Goodman had written ten years before after his return from a trip to Kentucky, to do background on Stampler.

'How did you meet him?' St Claire asked Hydra.

'I have known him forever.'

'You're Rebecca, aren't you?'

'I am . . . Hydra.'

'Before that. You were Rebecca?'

Her voice faded to a whisper. 'Taught him every . . . thing he knows,' she said.

'Jesus, you're his teacher, ain't ya?'

She didn't answer.

'When did you first contact him, Rebecca?'

For just an instant her memory streaked back to the young boy with the brutal strap marks on his buttocks who sat in the corner of her living room, devouring her books and the passages *she* had marked for *him*; to a time when it had been just the two of them, alone in the sanctuary of her house, sheltered from the brutal world around them as they made love in front of the fire. Then, suddenly, the moment dissolved into a clear, hot, white light.

As St Claire stared at her, her eyes suddenly crossed slightly. Life blinked out of them and they turned to

445

stone. St Claire held his fingers against her throat, but he knew there would be no pulse.

'She was Stampler's schoolteacher, Marty,' said St Claire. 'I remembered readin' the notes Goodman wrote when he came back from Kentucky. It's the last entry in the report. She told him, "I taught Aaron everything he knows." She was as crazy as he is.'

'He isn't crazy, Harve. He's a cold-blooded killer, that's all he ever was. Call Morris. Tell him to go across the street and take the son of a bitch down.'

'My pleasure.'

The rookie staggered to the doorway of the bathroom, wiping his lips with a washcloth.

'Mr Vail, there's something in here for Major Stenner.'

Vail went into the bathroom. There was a box addressed to Stenner sitting in the bathtub. Below the name was scrawled:

> *What are fears but voices airy,*
> *whispering harm where harm is not.*
> *And deluding the unwary,*
> *until the fatal bolt is shot.*

Vail opened the box and stared into the face of Harry Shoat.

Thirty-Six

Morris and Soloman banged on the door of the halfway house until a young man with long hair tied back in a ponytail stumbled down the stairs and cracked open the door.

'Huh?' he said.

Morris showed him his ID. 'Police, open up,' he said.

'Police!' the young man said in a panic.

'We're just checking on the new man,' Morris said as he and Solomon brushed past him and went up the stairs. Through the door, they heard Vulpes's raspy voice singing a duet with Durante.

'Make someone happy . . .'

'Open up, police!' Morris demanded. He tried the door. It was unlocked. The titles of the movie were rolling as they burst into the room. Morris froze when he saw the tape recorder.

'Make just someone happy . . .'

Solomon stared bleakly into the empty room. 'Shit, he bluffed us out, Bobby,' he moaned.

Vail was just leaving Rebecca Hutchinson's apartment when the phone rang. He listened while Morris babbled on the other end. His mind raced ahead of the conversation.

'Get the Chicago PD over there right now and give them a full report,' he said. 'I'll be back at the office.'

The question now: Where was Vulpes?

Shock Johnson answered that question with more bad news.

'Where are you?' the police lieutenant asked.

'In the car heading back to the office,' Vail answered.

'Go straight to the hospital, Marty. Stampler got Jane

447

Venable and Abel. They're alive but just barely. Should be arriving in Emergency about now. He killed our house guard.'

'Goddamn! God*damn* him!' Vail cried. 'What happened?' he asked Johnson.

'He killed our man and jumped Abel and Jane when they arrived at her house. She got a couple of shots off and sent him packing in Stenner's car. That's all she told us before she passed out. Some neighbours heard the shots and called it in. We have an APB out on him now, but our pictures are all ten years old.'

'Get your artist to put twenty pounds and ten years on him and get it to the media. Also I suggest a five-state alarm. If he breaks out of Chicago, God knows how long it may take to track him down.'

'Done. I heard about what happened with the woman. We found the rest of Shoat out at his place. She must've been doing Shoat while Stampler was doing his dirty work at Venable's house.'

'Stampler faked my people out,' said Vail. 'Sneaked out of the halfway house.'

'Christ, what the *hell's* goin' on, Marty?'

'Stampler is what's going on. He's on the loose and who knows *what* he's got in mind.'

'What do we tell the press?'

'You tell them the truth, Shock. How's Eckling reacting to all this?'

'He's at a convention in Atlanta. I haven't talked to him yet.'

'Well, we've got three dead people, including a cop and a judge, two people in the hospital, and a mass murderer on the loose. You better break the news before he sees it on TV.'

'See you at the hospital.'

'Yeah.' Vail hung up.

Meyer, not a cowboy behind the wheel by any means,

took off like an antic teenager, threading through traffic with his hand on the horn.

'Doesn't this car have a siren?' Vail yelled.

'No, sir.'

'Harvey, get a damn siren put on this thing tomorrow!'

'Yes, sir. What'd he say about Abel?'

'They're both hanging on, whatever the hell that means.'

Ten minutes later Meyer screeched into the emergency parking lot and pulled up against a brick wall near the entrance. Vail was out of the car before Meyer set the brakes, taking the steps to the loading dock two at a time and pushing open the swinging doors, startling the short, chubby nurse with round eyes and heart-shaped lips who was sitting at the receiving desk.

'I'm Martin Vail. Any report on Jane Venable or Abel Stenner?'

'They're both in the OR,' the nurse said. 'That's all I can tell you at this time.'

'I'm the DA. These people are on my staff. Can't you do a little better than that? How bad are they?'

'You'll have to wait until the doctors came out,' she answered apologetically. 'I really don't know anything. I'm sorry.'

Meyer and St Claire joined him a moment later. Vail paced the hall, staring at the operating-room doors. The nurse, obviously accustomed to relatives and friends of emergency victims in the halls, leaned across the desk and in a half-whisper said to St Claire, 'There's a visitors' room down the hall. Coffee machine, soft chairs, a TV. I'll call you soon as I – '

'Thank ya, ma'am. I don't think he's gonna leave this hall till he knows something.'

'That could be a while.'

'I know th' man real good. He ain't movin' till he knows the score. What's happening?'

'They took them into prep about fifteen minutes ago. I expect they're both in surgery by now.'

'Thanks.'

Vail leaned against the wall and stared up at a clock over the operating-room doors. It was eleven-twenty. Stampler had been free less than twelve hours.

Aaron Stampler lurked in the darkness, watching the gate. He was on the first-floor landing of a six-storey deck that provided private parking for tenants in the attached apartment building. The gate was activated by a card similar to a credit card. Stampler had lucked on to the building after dumping Stenner's car. It was nearly midnight. He reasoned that anyone coming in now was probably in for the evening and would not miss his or her car until morning. It was a perfect setup for him.

He had passed up a car with two couples in it. It seemed risky to him. He decided to wait. Ten minutes passed and a two-door BMW pulled up to the gate. In it was a man and he was by himself. Perfect.

As the car drove past and started up the ramp to the second floor, Stampler ran up the stairs. He peered through the door. He was in luck. The BMW was pulling into a parking space in a dark corner. Stampler threw the bloody towel into a waste can, ran across the lighted section of the deck, and ducked behind a row of cars, then crept down the row towards the parked car. The driver got out. He lowered the driver's seat and leaned into the back of the car, taking out a leather satchel. He put it on the ground and locked the car door.

Stampler was hunched behind the car next to his. He waited until the driver passed him, then he moved like an animal, soundlessly, taking two long steps, and grabbed the man's head with both hands, one under his chin, the other on the back of his head. He snapped the driver's neck like a breadstick. The man sagged as Stampler

450

caught him under the arms and dragged him back to the car.

Down below, he heard the gate open and a car drive through. Stampler looked around frantically. The driver's satchel was sitting in the middle of the driveway. He quickly opened the trunk of the car, rolled the driver's body inside, then ran and picked up the satchel. He unlocked the door of the BMW just as the car approached the second-floor deck. Stampler jumped in and lay across the front seat just as the car circled onto the second floor. The car's lights swept past the windshield, then continued on up the ramp.

Stampler sat up and studied the instrument panel of the car. Until tonight he had not driven an automobile in ten years. The car had everything: a tape and CD player, cruise control, heat, air, and a telephone. He opened the leather satchel. The first thing he saw was the stethoscope.

He had killed a doctor.

He rooted through the satchel, found bandages and hydrogen peroxide. He had to duck down twice as other cars entered the parking facility. He finished cleaning his wound. His jaw was already swollen and beginning to discolour. He covered the gash with a thin bandage. There were several kinds of painkillers, but Stampler ignored them. He had to stay alert.

He got out of the car, opened the trunk, retrieved the dead man's wallet, and got back in the car. He searched through the wallet One hundred and eighty-seven dollars and several credit cards. Not bad. The man's name was Steven Rifkin. According to his ID, he was a staff doctor at the University Medical Center. Under 'person to notify in case of an accident': his mother.

God, am I in luck, thought Stampler. *He lives alone. Nobody's waiting up for him.* If his luck held, it could be late morning before the doctor was missed.

Stampler took two maps from his inside pocket,

stretched them out on the seat next to the city map, and found his location. With his finger, he traced a route to Interstate 80. He felt suddenly secure. Once he got on the Interstate, he could get lost in traffic. He looked at the dashboard clock: 11:25. He started the car and left the parking lot.

As Stampler was making his way towards the interstate, Shock Johnson arrived at the emergency room, looking harried and unhappy.

'We got two TV stations and a radio reporter outside,' he said. 'They're at Shoat's place and at the Hutchinson woman's apartment. They're on this story like ants on honey. What's the news here?'

'No news yet,' Vail said, and began pacing the hallway outside the operating rooms again.

'I called Eckling,' Johnson went on, falling in beside Vail. 'He's doing barrel rolls over this. He's taking the red-eye back here. Gets in at six. He says to stall the press.'

'How the hell can you stall he press? We need the media now. We have to put the heat on Stampler.'

'We found Stenner's car parked in a dead-end alley off Wabash.'

'He's going to lift another set of wheels, bank on it,' said Vail. 'He's too smart to stay around here.'

'I talked to the state police. They've alerted Wisconsin, Iowa, Indiana, Ohio, and Missouri. I got Cal Murphy updating the photo. We should have it on HITS in another two, three hours.'

A youthful doctor with his hair askew and his gown blood splattered came out of the OR. He fell against the wall, pulled down his face mask, and pinched exhaustion from his eyes. He dug under the robe and took out a cigarette. Vail walked over to him and offered a light.

'Thanks,' the doctor said, drawing in the smoke and blowing it towards the ceiling with a sigh. He stared at Vail, his eyes etched with weariness.

'You're the DA, aren't you?' he said.

'Yes, Martin Vail. This is Lieutenant Johnson, Chicago PD.'

'You here about Venable and Stenner?'

Vail nodded. 'What can you tell us?'

'Stenner's still on the table in three. It may be a while before we know anything. He has a deep stab wound, entered here – ' he pointed to his side just under his rib cage – 'angled up towards his heart. It's a rough one.'

'Is he going to make it?'

'It's a toss-up. He's on the edge.'

'How about Jane?'

'She's going to live, but she took a terrible blow to the right cheek. The bones in her face are crushed and we pulled a bone splinter from her right eye. She may lose it. She also has a concussion. She's in for the long haul, constructive surgery, cosmetic work. What happened to her?'

'The same madman that stabbed Stenner hit her with something,' said Johnson. 'We're not sure yet, probably a brass lamp.'

'Christ, what're people coming to?' he said, as much to himself as to Vail and Johnson. 'I've got to go outside, we're not supposed to smoke in here.'

'Can I see her?'

'Wait until they take her out of Recovery, okay? It's a madhouse in there right now. Probably an hour or so.'

'Thanks.'

'Sure.'

Eve Wilonski, the night supervisor, came striding down the hall, her face looking like an angry bulldog's.

'Well, Mr Vail, you're becoming a fixture around here,' she growled.

'I hardly have any choice,' Vail answered, and there was anger in his tone.

'Is all this related in some way to your earlier visit?' she asked, her voice softening.

'Unfortunately. I'm afraid we're going to be around here for a while,' Vail said. 'Sorry if we're screwing things up.'

'It's the press, sir,' she said. 'They're making a nuisance of themselves.'

Vail looked at Shock Johnson.

'I guess it's time to make an official statement,' he said, then turned to Mrs Wilonski. 'Is there someplace we can hold a quick press conference without turning the hospital inside out?'

'We have a press room on the first floor,' she said. 'It's all yours.'

Five miles away Stampler guided the stolen BMW onto Interstate 80. It was fairly crowded with people returning from dinner and the theatre. He manoeuvred into the fast-moving outside lane. It was eleven-thirty-five. With a self-satisfied smile, he headed east.

Thirty-Seven

The driving was going well, a breeze, in fact. Stampler
had figured out the cruise control and set it on 70, a safe
speed according to Rebecca. Hold it to 70, be sure to use
your turn indicator when you pass, do not drive errati-
cally, she had told him. It's like swimming, she had told
him. You never forget how. Don't worry.

Worry? He never worried. Worry was destructive. He
remembered a quote from Emerson. '*What fears you
endured, from evils that never arrived.*' Worry sapped
his strength, fear drained his energy. Together they were
destructive forces, distractions he could never afford.

He turned his thoughts to Daisyland, to Max and
Woodward, patronizing him, telling him how 'well' he
was doing. Panderers. Treating him like a child. His grip
on the steering wheel tightened until his knuckles almost
glowed in the dark. God, would he like to see their faces
now.

The news was coming on and he turned up the radio.

'Good morning, this is Jerry Quinn with the two A.M.
edition of the news. Updating the hottest story of the
hour, in a bizarre murder case that is still unfolding,
Supreme Court Judge Harry Shoat was brutally murdered
in his Lakeshore condominium earlier tonight and his
killer, a deranged woman, was shot and killed while
resisting arrest less than an hour later. During a hastily
called press conference at midnight, Lt. Shock Johnson
of the Chicago Police Homicide Division told reporters
Shoat was brutally murdered about 9 P.M.

'According to Johnson, Shoat's body was mutilated
and he was beheaded. His head was found an hour later
in the apartment of Rebecca Hutchinson at 3215 Grace

Avenue. Ms Hutchinson was killed when she attacked one of the arresting officers with the same knife she allegedly used to kill Judge Shoat.

'Acting District Attorney Martin Vail, who joined Johnson at the press conference, said that his office has issued a murder warrant against Raymond Vulpes, aka Aaron Stampler, of a central city address. The warrant will charge Vulpes/Stampler with the murder of police officer John Rischel and the attempted murders of attorney Jane Venable and special officer Maj. Abel Stenner.

'Vail said these attacks took place at approximately the same time Shoat was killed by Hutchinson. Vail identified Vulpes as Aaron Stampler, confessed killer of Bishop Richard Rushman. Vail said Stampler was released from the state mental institution at Daisyland earlier in the day. Stampler has been a patient at Daisyland since the Rushman murder ten years ago. Ironically, Vail defended Stampler in the Rushman murder trial before becoming chief prosecutor of the district attorney's office.

'Vail said Stampler will also be charged with one count of murder and two counts of attempted murder and mayhem in the attacks on well-known attorney Jane Venable and Maj. Abel Stenner, head of the DA's Special Investigation Squad, both of whom also figured prominently in the Rushman case. Here is a portion of acting DA Vail's statement.

' "We have reason to believe that Aaron Stampler, during the past several years, communicated by computer with Ms Hutchinson, who was his teacher in grammar school. We also believe Stampler abetted Ms Hutchinson in two other murders. The murder of Mrs Linda Balfour at her home in Gideon, Illinois, last October, and Alex Lincoln, a UPD delivery person, in Hilltown, Missouri, a few weeks ago. In both cases, the MO was exactly the same as was used in the Rushman murder. Stampler also attacked attorney Jane Venable and detective Abel Stenner at Ms Venable's home. Both are in critical condition in the Intensive Care Unit of City Hospital but are expected to survive."

'Police have issued a five-state alarm for Stampler and will have an updated photograph of him in about an hour. Stampler is thirty-five years old, five-nine, weighs one hundred and fifty pounds, and has blue eyes and blond hair. According to Ms Venable, she struck Vulpes during the attack and he has a severe laceration on the left side of his jaw. Police said Stampler should be considered armed and extremely dangerous – '

Stampler snapped the radio off.

'Son of a bitch,' he said aloud. 'Son of a bitch!' *They killed Rebecca! How did Vail track her down? What had gone wrong?* He slammed a fist into the steering wheel. His eyes glittered with hatred. Venable and Stenner, who sat on the witness stand and told the court that Stampler was faking it, had survived.

Well, he'd show them. Get-even time. *Get-fucking-even time!*

He passed the sign on the edge of the interstate: SHELBYVILLE, NEXT EXIT.

This time there wouldn't be any mistakes.

He pulled into a sprawling truck-stop complex and parked in a dark area off to the side of the restaurant. He checked his map and stuffed it in his pocket, then went through the doctor's satchel again. He opened a flat leather case and his eyes gleamed. It was a set of scalpels. He took out the largest one, tapped his thumb on the blade, and drew a drop of blood. He sucked it off and slipped the razor-sharp tool in his breast pocket. He also took a hypodermic needle, a vial of morphine, and a large roll of adhesive tape from the bag. He got out of the car and locked it. He looked around. Nobody was near him. He hastily opened the trunk and threw the doctor's satchel on top of Rifkin's body. He slammed the trunk shut and walked off into the darkness.

Vail sat next to Jane Venable in the ICU. The entire right side of her face was swathed in bandages. IVs protruded from both arms, the narrow tubes, like snakes, curling up to bottles attached to the back of her head. Behind her, machines beeped and hummed as they measured her life signs. An oxygen mask covered her mouth and nose. Her limp hand, which he clutched between both of his, seemed cold and lifeless.

He watched the clock on the wall. It was nearly 2:30 A.M. Stenner had been in surgery for more than four hours. An hour earlier, one of the doctors had stepped briefly into the hall.

'We're doing everything we can,' the weary surgeon had told Vail. 'He's a lucky man. The point of that knife missed his heart by a quarter of an inch. If it had nicked the aorta he would have bled to death before the medics got to him.'

'But he's going to make it, right?' Vail said, almost pleadingly.

'It's touch and go. He's still opened up, we're having to do a lot of microsurgery. But he's strong, in excellent physical condition, that's going to help.'

Since then the tortured minutes had crawled by.

Outside the ICU the entire staff had gathered at the hospital, monitoring phone calls in a small office Mrs Wilonski had hastily cleared out for them. But in the outside world there was nothing but silence. Stampler had simply vanished into the night. Was he holed up somewhere in the city? Had he stolen another car? Vail was overwhelmed with anxiety, guilt, and hatred towards the man who had so successfully conned them all and was now on a madhouse killing spree.

He felt a slight pressure from Jane's hand and looked over at her. Her lips moved under the oxygen mask.

'Take it off,' her lips said.

'Can't do that, Janie.'

'Just a minute,' the lips said.

'Okay, just for a minute.' Vail reached over and slid the face mask down to her chin. She squeezed his hand again.

'Hi,' Vail said.

'Abel?' she asked, her speech blurred by drugs.

'He's carved up pretty badly, but they think he's going to make it.'

'Sav'd m'life, Marty.'

'And you saved his.'

'D'you catch Stampler?'

'Not yet. Just a matter of time. I can't stay long. I'm not even supposed to be in here.'

'Pull rank, you're th' DA...'m I all smashed up, Marty?'

'Nah. I know a good body shop, they'll knock the dents out in no time.'

She smiled up at him.

' 'Fraid m' goin' t'sleep again.'

'Sleep well, my dear. I'll be here when you wake up.'

'Marty?'

'Yeah?'

'Kiss me?'

He leaned over and gently touched her lips with his.

'I love you.'

'And I love you, Janie.'

And she drifted off again.

She was in a deep, deep sleep, dreaming the dream she always dreamed: She was walking through dense fog, hearing the voices but never quite seeing the faces that went with them, those harpy songs that taunted her, luring her deeper and deeper into the mist. *Help me, help me, help me*, the voices cried until the sense of futility overwhelmed even her dreams, until suddenly she stepped into the hole and fell through the clouds, tumbling towards oblivion until she awakened with a start.

This time as she moved through the cottony mist, her

feet froze in place and the haze blazed into light just before she fell. She awoke with a start. The bed-table light was on and her feet were tied to the foot of the bed. She tried to scream, but her mouth was bound with tape. Fear turned sour in her mouth.

She looked around and saw, a few inches from her face, a scalpel.

Its blade twinkled as it was twisted in the light's beam. Her eyes gradually refocused on the face behind the scalpel's edge.

'Hi, Miss Molly,' he said in the innocent Appalachian accent he had discarded years before. ' 'Member me?'

She recognized Stampler immediately. Time had not changed him that much. Molly Arrington's heart was pounding in her throat, her temples, her wrists. She was having trouble breathing through her nose. Behind him, she saw the open window, the curtains wafting lazily in the draft. She peered at him in terror, but then just as quickly – as she adjusted to waking up – she grew calm. Questions assaulted her mind. *How did he get here? What was he doing?*

'Listen to me,' he said, and his voice was cold, calculating, without accent or tone. 'I'm going to take that tape off your mouth, but if you scream, if you talk above a whisper, I'll make an incision right here' – he put the point of the blade against her throat – 'and cut out your vocal cords. It won't kill you, unless maybe you drown in your own blood, but it will be almighty painful. Do we have an understanding?'

She slowly nodded.

He picked a corner of the tape up with the tip of his little finger and then ripped it off. It tore her lips. Tears flushed her eyes, but she did not scream.

'That's good, that's very, very good,' he said. 'I always did admire your spunk. I suppose you have some questions?'

She did not answer but instead stared down in shock

at him. He was stark naked and erect, sitting in a chair beside the bed.

'Cat got your tongue?' He chuckled. He moved the scalpel to the neckline of her silk nightshirt and drew the sharp blade slowly down the length of the shirt. It spread open in the wake of the incision until he had split it all the way to her knees. He took the knife and flipped first one side of the shirt, then the other, aside.

'There,' he said, staring lasciviously at her naked body. 'Now we're even.'

Still not a sound from her.

'Can't you even say hello?'

She did not look at him. She stared at the ceiling.

'*Talk to me!*' he roared.

She turned her head slowly towards him.

'Martin was right,' she said.

'Oh, *Martin was right. Martin was right*,' he mimicked her. 'Martin was *finally* right, you should say. And only because I let him know. I gave him the clues and he *finally* figured it all out.'

'That's what he said.'

'Bright boy. Well, Doc, I don't have much time. Got a lot to do before I'm on my way. Got to be waiting when he comes.'

'Comes where?'

He just smiled.

She did not ask again.

He held the scalpel up again and regarded it with sensual pleasure. 'Know what I like about knives, Doctor? I like the way they feel. I like their power. People have a visceral fear of knives. And they're so efficient. All you have to do . . .' – he slashed the scalpel through the air – '. . . is that. *Swish*, and it's all over. Exsanguination. Instant rigor mortis. *Instant*! All the air rushes out of the lungs. It's such a . . . a pure sound. *Whoosh*. Ten, fifteen seconds and it's all over. And this? This is a masterpiece. A scalpel. The ultimate blade. So beautiful.'

'It's nice to know you killed them first, before you—'

'Oh, she can talk. Before I what? Before I cleansed them? Before I blooded them?'

'So that's what you did. Cleansed them,' she said with sarcasm.

'Oh, we're going to push it, are we?'

'Push what?' she answered wearily. 'I don't doubt for a minute you're going to kill me.'

'I might surprise you.'

'You can't surprise me any more,' she said.

He stood up and began to stroke himself. His lips were twitching around a sickening leer.

'You always wanted it, didn't you? Huh? Wanted me to throw you down on the floor of that cell and fuck your brains out.'

'You're delusionary.'

The smile vanished. The eyes went dead.

'Rebecca was right. Rebecca was always right. She was right about my brother and Mary. *Get rid of them*, she told me. *Get rid of the hate*. She was there when I stuffed the towels in the car window. And when they were cold and stiff, we did it in the front seat, right in front of them. *Now you're even*, she said. *Now you can forget them*. Just like I forgot Shackles and Rushman and Peter and Billy. Just like I finally could forget Linda and that creepy little coward, Alex Lincoln. She told me you were in the pit, too, that you were just as nuts as the rest of us. You know what it's like, don't you? To be smarter than all of them, listen to them pampering, pandering, so *righteous*. So fucking proud of themselves playing God. And they were all wrong. All of you were *wrong*. That's the best part of it all. Now everybody will know, the whole *world* will know.'

'I was wrong,' Molly said. 'You're not delusionary, you're demonic.'

'Demonic,' he sneered, raising his eyebrows.

'Demonic,' he repeated, savouring the word. 'I like that. Is that a medical term?'

'You want to kill the people that kept you alive.'

'Alive. You call ten years in bedlam *alive*?'

'Would you have preferred the electric chair?'

'I would have preferred freedom. He played games with me.'

'He did the best he – '

'He *fucked* me to protect that miserable faggot Rushman. He had the tape. Not a woman on that jury would have found me guilty if they had seen the tape. Christ, after that he had plenty of room for reasonable doubt. A second person in the room, temporary insanity, irresistible impulse. But nooo, he had to play the clever boy, protecting Rushman's good name, sucking that prosecutor into his game. And you went along with it.'

'You tricked yourself. *You* provided the multiple personality defence . . .'

'I didn't know you two would use it to sell me out. I knew when he came up to see me in Daisyland the other day he was going to try and ruin me. Hell, he would have looked like a fool if he tried to stop me from leaving, but he was too smart for that. We had the perfect plan, Hydra and me. Hydra got Shoat and I was supposed to get Venable. I could have been back in the room with a perfect alibi. I could've laughed at Vail. I could've got them all – Venable, Shoat, Stenner, you – all but Vail. I would've let him live in his own hell. Then that *bitch*, Venable, screwed me up. Look at my face. She did that!'

Molly said nothing. She stared at him in disgust as he straddled her, resting on his knees.

'He should've pleaded temporary insanity. I could have walked out of there free and clear.'

'That's ridiculous, he couldn't – '

'*Don't speak to me like that!*'

'I'm sorry.'

'You're not sorry. You're patronizing me. You should know better.

She shut up and stared at the ceiling again.

'Vail was so fucking clever, playing all those little legal games of his in court, dicking around with that insufferable Shoat. Jesus, *I* could have done better.'

No answer.

'Ten years of drugs and shock treatments, egomaniac doctors, panderers, panderers, they were all fucking *panderers*.'

He turned to the night table and put the scalpel down. He picked up a hypodermic needle, stared at its point. He picked up the vial of morphine, inserted the needle into it, working the plunger until it was full of the deadly painkiller.

'Well, now, Mr Vail understands what it's like to hate enough to kill. And it's going to get worse.' He settled down on her and held the needle in front of her face. 'One hundred ccs, Doc. Permanent sleep, like the shot they give you when they put you away like a dog. I'll give it to you a little bit at a time, so the pain won't be so bad. *A cc here, a cc there, here a cc, there a cc . . .*' he sang.

He had lost it, she realized. Disassociated. Calm replaced by rage. Whatever he was going to do, he would do, she knew that now. She closed her eyes and waited with an eerie calm for the inevitable. She hardly felt the needle when it pierced her arm.

Thirty-Eight

An exhausted young surgeon walked out of operating room three. He was surprisingly young, a tall, lean man with his long black hair tucked up under his green surgical cap. His surgical gown and shoe mittens were blood-spattered. His eyes were bloodshot. He pulled off his mask and breathed a sigh of relief. Vail approached him.

'Doctor? I'm Martin Vail. Any news?'

The young doctor smiled and held out a large hand with long, delicate fingers. 'It's a pleasure, Mr Vail. I'm Alex Rosenbloom. Your man Stenner is one tough cookie.'

'He's going to make it, then?'

Rosenbloom nodded. 'But an hour ago I wouldn't have bet on it. We almost lost him twice.'

'Thank you, sir. Thank you very much.'

The young doctor slapped Vail on the shoulder. 'I'm thankful I didn't have to bring bad news out,' he said. 'Look, I know you've been very patient. They're taking him into Recovery now. You can stick your head in for just a minute.'

'Thanks. There are a lot of us here that thank you.'

'I heard the whole DA's staff is here,' Rosenbloom said. 'He must be a very special person.'

'Yes, he is.'

Vail entered the small recovery room. Stenner seemed frighteningly tiny and frail. He looked grey and vulnerable with his arms attached to a half-dozen IV tubes and various machines beeping and humming beside his bed. Vail took his hand.

'Welcome back,' he said softly.

Stenner groaned.

'Can you hear me, Abel?'

Stenner's eyes opened a hair and he stared, unfocused, at his friend. He blinked his eyes once.

'You're going to be okay, my friend. And so is Janie. Thank you. Thank you.'

Stenner slowly blinked his eyes again.

'We've got Stampler in our sights,' Vail lied. 'Just a matter of time.'

Under the oxygen mask, he saw Stenner's lips form the word 'Good.' Then his hand slipped out of Vail's and he fell asleep.

Vail stood by the window, staring out at the first red signs of dawn. It was nearing 5 A.M. and everyone was exhausted. But the crisis seemed to be over. Both Stenner and Venable were holding their own and for that Vail was grateful. He gathered the troops together.

'I think it's safe to call it a night – or a morning,' he said with an attempt at a smile. 'I'd like to work in shifts, keep somebody here around the clock. Naomi, work up a schedule, okay? I'm going to hang in here for a while longer.'

'I ain't goin' nowheres,' St Claire said emphatically.

'Me neither,' Meyer joined in.

'Look, we all need to get some rest,' Naomi said, taking command. 'Let's not forget we still have an office to run.'

'I'm going outside and have a cigarette,' Vail said. He went down the long hallway and out on the emergency dock. There was very little activity. The chaos of the night before had been replaced by an eerie calm. He lit up and watched the sky begin to brighten. Parver and Flaherty joined him.

'I hate to bring this up,' Parver said, 'but Stoddard is up for arraignment tomorrow. What're we going to do?'

'Postpone it until we see how Jane is doing. Hell, I don't want to deal with that right now.'

'I'm sorry,' she answered. 'I'll take care of it.'

'You're still having mixed feelings about Stoddard, aren't you?'

She thought for a minute and nodded. 'After finding that stuff in that closet room, I . . .' She hesitated for a moment, then finished the sentence. 'Don't worry, I'll handle it properly.'

'I know you will.' He smiled at Flaherty, who stood quietly by, holding her hand. 'You two take care of each other. Time has a bad habit of running out when you least expect it.'

'Yes, sir.'

'Better go home and get some shut-eye.'

The emergency doors swung open and St Claire peered out.

'I think we got us a break,' he said.

Buddy Harris was on the phone. The state police officer had been up all night, fielding false alarms and the usual nut calls that result from an APB. It seemed everybody in the city of Chicago had seen Stampler during the long night.

'But I think we got a live one,' he told Vail. 'I just got a call from the Indiana HP. They think they've tumbled on a stolen car with Illinois plates and an MD's tag. Probably wouldn't have noticed it for hours except the dumb bastard parked in a handicapped space next to a diner. It was spotted by a waitress a little after two A.M., so it's been parked there for a couple of hours. They ran the registration. It's owned by a Dr Steven Rifkin. There's no answer at his house, so I called the University Medical Center. They say he checked out of there about ten-thirty last night. Apparently he had a really hard day and was going straight home to bed.'

'You say Indiana has the car?'

'Yeah. In a place outside Indianapolis called Shelbyville.'

Vail thought for a moment. The name struck a chord.

Then he remembered the shrink at the Justine Clinic telling him Rene Hutchinson had taken computer lessons in Shelbyville.

'Jesus, Buddy, that's only a few miles from the Justine Clinic. My God! He's going after Molly Arrington. Call the Indiana patrol, tell them to get an address on a Dr Molly Arrington in Winthrop and get over there on the double. I'm going out to the airport and fly down there.'

'Hell, that isn't necessary, Marty, they got—'

'I'll call you from the airport. Just get on it, Buddy.'

Vail turned to Naomi. 'Call Hawk Permar and tell him we need the chopper. There's going to be three of us and we're going about thirty miles southeast of Indianapolis, a town called Winthrop. If he starts bitching, tell him I'll personally throw in a two-hundred-dollar bonus.'

'Three passengers?' St Clare said.

'You, me, and Flaherty. We're going down there to find that son of a bitch and bring him back.'

They were airborne, swinging south from the airport and following Interstate 65 towards Indianapolis. The pilot, Matt Permar, who had earned the nickname Hawk flying choppers in Vietnam, was grumbling about not getting enough sleep as he followed the interstate straight towards Indianapolis. A chunky, good-humoured man, he was an excellent pilot who loved to gripe – a hangover from his army days.

'What'ya mumblin' about?' St Claire asked.

'Cockamamie DA, never does anything at *normal* hours. It's always the middle of the night or dawn. Always spur of the moment – '

'Blah, blah, blah,' said Vail. 'You can always say no.'

'You pay too well,' Hawk answered.

'Then stop bellyaching,' Vail said.

'Bellyaching is good. Bellyaching is normal. I love to bellyache. If I didn't bellyache, I'd be a fruitcake by now.'

'Ain't nobody ever told ya, Hawk. You *are* a fruitcake,'

St Claire said, and stuffed a wad of tobacco under his lip.

The gripe session was cut short by the squawk of the radio. It was Harris, who was still on duty.

'I got some bad news from Winthrop, Marty,' he said, his voice getting hoarse from lack of sleep.

'I'm prepared for that. Lay it on me.'

'Molly Arrington's dead, Martin. Spread-eagled on her bed, body mutilated, probably was raped. The weirdest thing about it is, he pumped her full of enough morphine to kill her even if he hadn't cut her up. He also printed in blood on her torso the words "I'm waiting". Does any of that make sense to you?'

Vail was thinking about Molly. Gentle Molly, who had never hurt a soul in her life. 'Nothing that bastard does makes any sense,' he said angrily.

'He stole her car, probably been on the road at least two, maybe three hours. There's nothing you can do there, Marty. The creep could be anywhere.'

Vail did not answer immediately. He thought about the message.

'*I'm waiting.*' And then suddenly it did make sense. There was only one place Stampler *could* go. He couldn't go back to Chicago and by now the whole country knew the story. He would go back to where it had started. Vail grabbed the sectional map and traced a path with his finger south from Shelbyville. His finger finally found what he was looking for.

'I know where to find him,' he said. 'We'll pass on Winthrop. Head for Crikside, Kentucky.'

'Huh?' Hawk said.

'Where?' Harris said.

'Crikside, spelling C-r-i-k-s-i-d-e. Call the Kentucky HP and fill them in. Hold on a minute.' He made an arch with his thumb and forefinger and measured the distance south of Indianapolis.

'About one hundred and seventy-five miles and we're

469

still one hundred miles from Indianapolis. How about it, Matt, how long?'

'What, two hundred and seventy-five miles? Hour and a half, maybe two. What's the weather like down there?'

'Who cares?' said Vail.

'I care!' Hawk hunched down in his seat and shoved the throttles forward. 'I know the weather's for shit,' he said.

'Just keep flying south towards Louisville.'

'You really think that's where the son-bitch's headin'?' St Claire said.

'There's no place else left for him to go,' Vail said. 'He had this thing planned out perfectly. He sneaked out of the halfway house. His plan was to kill Jane and me while Rebecca killed Shoat. She sneaks back to her place, he sneaks back into the halfway house, and we would be his alibi.'

'How about Rebecca takin' off Shoat's head?'

'She collected trophies, remember?' said Flaherty. 'It's what serial killers do, just like hunters collect antlers or animal heads. That was her trophy, Harve. She was going to send it to Abel, the way she left the photo of Linda Balfour when she killed Alex Lincoln.'

'Stampler only made one mistake,' said Vail.

'The call to the hospital,' said Flaherty.

'Right,' agreed Vail. 'And he underestimated Jane Venable. When he couldn't kill her, he was on the run, his plan was blown. His face is on every TV station in the country by now. My guess is, he's playing head games with me now.'

'And he killed Molly Arrington –' Flaherty started to say.

'To goad me. He's finished and he knows it.' Vail finished the sentence. 'He's going to make catching him as tough as he can. Let's say he snatched the doctor's car at eleven, eleven-thirty. That put him in Shelbyville at around two A.M., about the time a waitress spotted the car parked in a handicapped zone. Winthrop's just outside the outskirts of Shelbyville. He could've walked to Arrington's house from there in, say, half an hour. That puts him at Arrington's at between two-thirty and three. An hour to do his dirty work and get out with her car. From there to Louisville is about a hundred miles, say another two hours.'

'So he was in Louisville maybe half an hour ago,' Hawk calculated.

'It's another one hundred and twenty miles to Crikside. If he gets through the weather he could be in Crikside, say, two and a half, three hours from now. With luck we may just catch him while he's still on the road.'

'We gotta stop and refuel,' Hawk said.

'Do it in Louisville,' said Vail.

'Mind if I ask a question?' Flaherty said.

'What's that?' Vail answered.

'We don't even have a warrant for Stampler. Is this legal?'

'I'm making a citizen's arrest,' said Vail.

'Citizen's arrest?'

'That's right. I'm arresting him for stealing Molly Arrington's car. We'll charge him with the rest of his sins when we get him back to Chicago.'

'Citizen's arrest.' St Claire laughed. 'You sound like Barney Fife.'

'Sounds like kidnapping to me,' grumbled Hawk.

'Well, keep that notion to yourself,' Vail said.

The radio squawked to life again. Harris's calm voice reported the latest developments. 'We've alerted the Kentucky state cops and the sheriff of the county, but they got traffic problems down there. They got themselves a spring snowstorm and a lot of traffic problems.'

'A snowstorm! I knew it. I *knew* it!' Hawk howled.

'Just keep flying,' said Vail.

'They aren't all steamed up over the possibility that he *might* have killed a woman and he *might* be on his way

471

to Crikside,' Harris continued. 'They said they'll get somebody over to check it out by noon or one o'clock.'

'Shit,' Vail snapped.

'I got some more bad news,' Harris went on. 'Indiana HP popped the trunk on that car. The doctor's body was inside. Broken neck.'

'That makes three so far he's personally killed,' Vail said bitterly.

'One other thing, Arrington's car is a '93 black Camaro two-door, licence: J32 576. Got that?'

'Got it.'

'And be careful, you're flying into the Cumberland Mountains down there. Good luck.'

'Thanks for the help, Buddy. Over and out.'

'Snow and mountains,' Hawk groaned. 'Two of my favourite things. All we need now's a little ground fire to make this a dream vacation.'

Thirty-Nine

The chopper swung over the low ridge and dropped down closer to the road. Snow flurries splattered against the windshield. Below them the two-lane blacktop was still discernible although the snow was beginning to cover it. They had seen only three cars in the last twenty minutes. Hawk's gaze jumped from window to windshield as he roared two hundred feet over the rugged terrain. Beside him, Vail was navigating from a roadmap. They were following the state road that led to Crikside. Behind them, St Claire and Flaherty also scanned the road, Flaherty with a pair of binoculars. Hawk glanced at the clock.

Nine-twenty-two.

'How am I doing?' he yelled.

'We're about ten miles from the place. It's just over the next ridge.'

'I can't even see the next ridge,' Hawk said.

'It's eight or nine miles ahead of us. He can't be far ahead of us, not with the road conditions the way they are.'

'I thought we'd pick him up before this,' Hawk answered. 'He must be driving like a madman – *if* he's coming here.'

'He's coming here,' Vail answered with finality. 'He just stopped off in Winthrop long enough to satisfy his blood lust, claim another victim.'

'I think we missed him,' Hawk said.

'We ain't missed him,' said St Claire. 'Marty's right, been right all along.'

'You having one of your nudges?' Flaherty asked without taking his eyes off the road.

'This ain't a nudge, it's a reality,' Vail said, imitating St Claire's gruff voice. Their laughter eased the tension.

Flaherty leaned forward, the binoculars tapping the side window. 'I got some tracks,' he said.

'Where?' the others asked, almost in unison.

'Right under us. They're blowing off the road, but there's a car somewhere in front of us. Can we get lower?'

'This thing don't do well underground,' Hawk answered. But he dropped down another fifty feet.

'See anything?' Flaherty asked Vail.

'I can't see that far up the road. I'm not sure how close we are to that ridge. Maybe we ought to gain a little altitude. I can't tell exactly where we are on this map.'

'There it is,' said Flaherty.

They peered down in front of the chopper. Through the rushing snowflakes a car was visible racing through the storm.

Flaherty said, 'It's black . . . I can't tell the make, but it's a two-door.'

'Gotta be the son-bitch,' St Claire said. He stuffed a fresh wad of tobacco into his cheek.

'We're coming up on that ridge,' Hawk said. 'We could be a couple hundred feet short.' He pulled back on the throttle, easing the chopper's speed.

'You're right on top of him,' said Vail. 'Slow her down a little more.'

Hawk cut the power a little more. He was heading for the ridge at about fifty miles an hour.

Below them, Stampler heard the unmistakable sound of a helicopter. He looked out the car window. It was no more than a hundred feet above him. To his right was another ridge, thick with pine trees. Ahead of him he saw a turnoff. A faded sign said:

KC&M
HILLSIDE DIVISION

Stampler hit the brakes and almost lost it. The car skittered across the road, showered up snow as it ripped through a low drift, and then swung back on the road. He got the car under control and turned into the road. A wooden horse was stretched across the entrance. Stampler tore through it, showering bits of wood into the trees. The macadam road was pitted by disuse and bad weather. He was having trouble keeping the sedan on the road. But he was climbing up the side of the ridge, forcing the chopper to gain altitude.

But it didn't. He could hear it, *chung, chung, chung, chung* over his head. The car skewed beneath him, its wheels spinning helplessly on the snow-packed road. He lost control, slammed on the brakes, and sent the car into a wild spin. It teetered on the edge of a ditch, then spun out the other way and plunged off the road. Stampler saw the trees hurtling towards him, crossed his arms over the steering wheel, and put his head against them as the car swiped one tree and crashed into the one beyond it. The bonnet flew up and shattered the windshield. Stampler's arms took the brunt of the blow. Numbly, he felt for the door handle, pulled it back, and tumbled out of the car. Small whirlwinds of snow spun around him and he looked up. The chopper was fifty feet over his head. He dived into the trees and started running.

Hawk looked around at the forest that encroached on him. Tree limbs reached treacherously out over the road.

'I'm not sure I've got enough room to put down here,' he yelled. 'But it's a helluva lot safer than trying to follow him up this damn mountain.'

He lowered the helicopter slowly to the ground. The rotors thrashed at the tree limbs, snapping them off, scattered the debris into the air. Hawk eased it down, felt the skids hit the ground and settle in.

'Okay, we're down,' he said, and Vail, Flaherty, and St Claire scrambled out. Vail vaulted the ditch and took off after Stampler, with Flaherty close behind. St Claire wasn't as lucky. He slipped on the muddy bank and fell, twisting his ankle.

'KeeRIST!' he yelled. Vail turned, raced back to him.

'Just get goin',' St Claire said. 'It ain't broke. Here, take this.'

He pulled the .357 from under his arm and handed it to Vail. When Vail hesitated, St Claire said, 'Hell, you might not use the damn thing, but it's one helluva good scare card.'

Vail took the gun and ran off into the forest.

Stampler stumbled out into a clearing, gasping for breath, clutching at the pain in his side. He was in front of the shambles of a wooden office building, boarded up and rotting. He stared around at the snowy landscape. His gaze settled on the muscular steel framework of a lift. It was vaguely familiar, the relic, now idle and rusted. A large sign said:

CLOSED

TRESPASSERS WILL BE PROSECUTED
KENTUCKY COAL AND MINING COMPANY

Even obscured by snow, the place began to take on an air of familiarity. Memories began nibbling at his mind and with them a gnawing sense of apprehension. In his mind, he heard the sound of the lift clinking and groaning as it lowered men into the guts of the earth. Blackened faces and haunted eyes filtered through his flashback like demons in a nightmare.

He remembered awakening on his ninth birthday, seeing the hard hat with the ominous lamp on the front perched on the chair beside his bed, and the fear that went with his 'present'. He remembered shrinking down on the bed, trying to keep from crying, knowing that on this day he was going down into the hole, that fearful pit, for the first time; being so terrified, he threw up on

476

the way there; and the boss man standing right where he was standing now in front of the office, looking down at him, grinning, telling him today he was going to become a man.

'Stampler!'

Stampler turned and, there, across the snowy clearing, stood Vail. Perhaps fifty yards away, on the opposite side of the clearing. From the corner of his eye he saw another man emerge from the forest, a younger man, who joined Vail. They stood and waited for him.

Stampler started across the clearing, past the ghostly silhouette of the lift shaft, heading for the opposite side of the clearing, the snow squeaking underfoot as he made his way across a low mound that separated him from his nemesis.

'Stampler!'

Vail raised his hand. He was aiming a gun at him. The other one, the younger one, also had a pistol, but he stood with his gun hand lowered at his side.

The ground seemed to groan underfoot.

Vail aimed the gun over Stampler's head and fired a shot. Its thunder echoed through the trees and snow showered down from the limbs. Stampler stopped, glared across the white expanse at Vail.

'You wouldn't shoot an unarmed man, would you, Counsellor?'

'Don't kid yourself.'

Stampler leered at him. 'Know what it's like, now, don't you, Marty? Blood for blood. We're not that different, you and me.'

Vail did not answer. He pondered the question, thinking about the carnage of the last twelve hours; about Abel and Jane fighting for their lives; about Shoat and Dr Rifkin and a good cop and poor Molly Arrington, innocents all, sacrificed on Stampler's altar of vengeance. And about Rebecca, who had planted the seeds of Stampler's hate and also had the blood of Alex and Linda on

477

her hands. Five people dead, three in just half a day, and two gravely injured. And of all his targets only Vail had escaped the madman's wrath.

Stampler slipped back into his Crikside accent for a moment. 'Now, yuh know what I main, Marty. Feel it, don't yuh? A hurtin' in the chest. Yer stomach's on fire. Head feels like it's in a vice and somebody's squaizin' it tighter and tighter. Got a hard-on waitin' fer it t' happen. You feel it, don't yuh, Marty? The urge to kill.'

Vail's finger tightened on the trigger.

'Or maybe I shouldn't call you Marty? Too familiar. How about *Mr* Vail? Or *Mr* Counsellor? *Mr* Prosecutor? *Martin*? Oh, help me, Martin,' he jibed, slipping easily from one accent to the other. 'Ah'm so scairt and confused. I lost time, Martin, and Ah jest *know* sompin' terrible has happened. Plaise help me, suh.'

Hate ate up Vail's insides, assaulted his head, gnawed at his heart. Stampler was right, he wanted to squeeze the trigger, watch the bullet rip into his chest. He wanted to watch Stampler die.

'Marty?' Flaherty said behind him.

'Stay out of it, Dermott.'

'Let me go bring him in. You're making me nervous.'

'How 'bout it, *Martin*? Can yuh help me, suh?' Stampler began to laugh. 'I'm goan turn 'round now, I'm jes' gonna walk away from you. Go ahead, shoot an unarmed man in the back. That's what you want to do, isn't it?'

'He's pushing you, Marty.'

Vail felt the cold trigger against his finger. His fist tightened a little more.

'I know what he's doing,' Vail said.

'I'm going out there and get him.'

'Stay right there, Dermott, can't you read the sign?'

The sign, weather-scarred and leaning sideways in the drifting snow, said:

DANGER   UNSAFE   DANGER

This mine shaft has been sealed
No admittance to this area

DANGER   UNSAFE   DANGER

And behind it the mound in the snow was the cover that had been placed over the shaft years before. Vail called out to Stampler. 'Put your hands behind your head and walk towards me.'

Stampler walked away from them. 'Ah'm leavin now, Martin.' He laughed harder. 'Catch me if you can.'

'You're standing right over mine shaft five, Stampler,' Vail called to him. 'The hole. Remember the hole?' He pointed to an old sign lying near the shed: KC&M MINE NUMBER FIVE.

Stampler hesitated. He looked back at Vail and Flaherty, then at the rusting lift mount. The groaning, clinking, awful sound it used to make rang again in his ears. He looked down at his feet and his gaze pierced the snow and boards and plummeted into the darkness. He saw twelve men – eleven men and a boy – suspended under the steel mount, being lowered from the land of the living into that pit of pure darkness; men, old long before their years, bent over and stooped from chopping away at walls of coal; saw the light at the top of the shaft as it shrank, growing smaller and smaller until he couldn't see it any more; dropped into air that smelled of bad eggs, with his mouth so dry his tongue stuck to his teeth. Dropping down into hell. A pitch-black hell.

'What's with him?' said Flaherty. 'He's just staring at the ground.'

The boards under Stampler's feet whimpered and sagged ever so slightly. Stampler stared at his feet. Snow cascaded between the boards. His jaw began throbbing as his pulse increased. He took a step forward. The ancient boards, ruined by years of bad weather and neglect, groaned as Stampler's weight tortured them. The platform sagged even more. He stopped – afraid to move ahead and afraid to stay in place. He took a giant step, put his foot down gently, leaned forward, and swung the other leg beside it. There was a crack under his feet. It sounded like a rifle shot as the board underfoot broke.

'Oh, Jesus,' Stampler said to himself. He started to run and with each step the rotted platform collapsed underfoot, disintegrating behind him as he dashed madly towards the trees. Then his leg crashed through the platform and he fell forward, felt the platform behind him start to fall away. He started to crawl and it cracked again. This time the platform began disappearing from under him. He leaned forward, reaching out, trying to find something to grab. His fingers burst through the snow, dug into the rotten wood. He pulled himself forward and another section broke away. He looked over his shoulder. Behind him, like an enormous, obscene black mouth, the hole kept spreading.

'Aw, Jesus!' he screamed. He started to fall and he dug his fingernails deeper into the wood. His weight pulled at the nails, but they began to slide, and splinters, like needles, pierced his fingertips, jutted under his fingernails, and punctured the quick. He was too terrified to cry out in pain. He was scrambling for his life as the decayed platform disintegrated completely around him.

The last boards gave way.

Stampler looked back for an instant. His eyes locked on to Vail's. His fingers scratched across the disintegrating platform and he vanished into the black maw.

He did not scream. He did not utter a sound. He plunged soundlessly down, down, down.

It was a very long time before they heard the dull, faraway thump; the faint clatter of wood slats as they plunged down behind him. Then it was deathly still except for the wind rattling the dead limbs of the trees.

'God almighty,' Flaherty whispered.

'Save your prayers for somebody who deserves them,'

Vail said. He turned and walked away from the gaping hole in the snow.

They followed the road back to the chopper, which was waiting with its rotors idling. Vail and Flaherty helped St Claire into the helicopter and climbed aboard behind him.

'Where's Stampler?' he asked.

'Where he belongs,' Vail answered. 'In hell.'

The chopper lifted off and climbed towards the top of the ridge. Vail watched mine shaft five pass below them. He stared down at the black circle surrounded by fresh snow. It looked like the bull's-eye of a target. He watched it until the chopper swept over the top of the ridge and he could no longer see Aaron Stampler's grave.

EPILOGUE

The mixed aromas of ether, antiseptics, and disinfectant permeated the silent hallways of the hospital. Doctors and nurses consulted in hushed conversation at doorways. Visitors wandered from rooms, some smiling and encouraged, other teary-eyed and wan as they struggled to comprehend bad news. Elation and melancholy walked hand-in-hand, and the atmosphere was charged with emotion. Nothing seemed commonplace in these corridors where strangers were drawn together by the common bonds of disease, misfortune, and mishap.

Vail avoided everyone, speaking briefly when he could not avoid it, usually merely nodding to those he recognized as regulars or staff. He rushed to the hospital at the end of each day, first checking on Jane and Abel, then eating tasteless food in the cafeteria or standing outside the emergency door to grab a smoke.

Martin Vail had always detested hospitals because they reminded him of the blackest and most agonizing days of his past. They evoked images, in sharp and painful focus, of his mother as they put her in an ambulance and carried her out of his life forever, the intensive care unit where his father lay dead from a coronary, the pale blue room in which he said farewell to Ma Cat, the grandmother who had raised him, as she lay dying of cancer. Ironically, those images now had been replaced by relief and thanksgiving and by the sheer joy of knowing that Jane Venable and Able Stenner had been saved by the surgeons, nurses, and attendants in the emergency room at Chicago General.

A few days after the demise of Stampler, Jack Yancey died as the result of his stroke, and Vail officially became the district attorney. Dr Samuel Woodward, under fire for his role in the release of Stampler, held a press conference and, bolstered by half a dozen colleagues, weaseled out of the situation with long-winded psychobabble.

During the weeks that followed, Vail kept a nightly vigil between the hospital rooms of Jane Venable and

Abel Stenner, sleeping in the chair in Venable's room and going home only to shower and change clothes on his way to work. Sometimes he sat beside Jane's bed, holding her hand for an hour at a time, convinced that he was to blame for her pain and suffering, as well as Stenner's. After all, he would reason to himself, he had been the instrument of Stampler's bloody revenge, having provided in his plea bargain during Stampler's trial the method that was used ten years later to free the monster.

Stenner was making a remarkable recovery. By the end of the third week he would be taking short walks down the halls with the help of a walker. Jane, who faced several weeks of torturous facial reconstruction, seemed in constant good spirits despite the painful injuries and the loss of her eye. Weak but ebullient, her face swathed in bandages from her forehead to her jaw and bruises tainting her nose and throat, she was indomitable. Aaron Stampler dominated their talks. Ironically, it was Jane who bolstered Vail's spirits during the long nights in the hospital as he fought with his conscience.

'Boy,' she said one night, 'I'll bet Aaron Stampler's sitting down in hell, laughing his buns off about now.'

'What do you mean?'

'Because he's still getting to you, darling. He's reaching out of his grave and pulling your chain. He conned everyone, Marty. Everybody bought his lie, why should you be any different?'

'Because I helped manufacture the lie.'

'He *conned* you, Marty. Admit it and forget it. Stampler isn't worth five minutes of bad time. You're a great lawyer. You did exactly what the law prescribes, you gave Stampler the best possible defence. You beat me fair and square, and believe me, I've thought a lot about the way you sandbagged me in the years since the trial. It was perfect. It was textbook stuff. The fact that the son of a bitch was guilty is beside the point.'

'Beside the point?'

486

'Marty, how many lawyers do you know who ask their clients whether they're guilty or not?'

'What's that got to do with anything? It's immaterial.'

'No, it's practical. If the client did it, he'll lie to you, so why bother to ask? You presume innocence and gather evidence to support that assumption, which you did brilliantly.'

'You're talking like a college professor.'

'And you're acting like a student. I remember a quote from an article about you – years ago,' Venable said. 'I don't remember the exact words, but in essence you said the only way for the law to remain strong is if we constantly attack its weaknesses.'

'You have a good memory.'

'Don't you still feel that way?'

'It doesn't have a damn thing to do with the courtroom. It has to do with acting. The courtroom has become the theatre of the absurd. Which lawyer gives the best performance? How good is the judge? How gullible is the jury? The truth gets lost in the shuffle.'

'Reality is what the jury perceives as truth. You also said that.'

'Well, I was young and brash in those ... do you remember everything you read?'

'Just the stuff I agree with.' She tried to laugh but it was painful. 'Sure, it's theatre. Sure, it's the best man – or woman – wins. And yes, it's all about swaying the jury. So what? Those are the rules. And you're hellaciously good at pushing the rules to the limit no matter what side you're on.' She paused a moment and winked her good eye. 'It's one of the reasons I love you,' she said.

'I can't even begin to list all the reasons I love you, Janey,' he said. He leaned over and kissed her gently on the mouth.

'Don't go away,' she whispered. 'Kiss me some more. Unless you'd like to lock the door and slide in beside me.'

'You're under sedation,' he whispered back.

'It wore off.'

Characteristically, when he brought up the subject with Stenner, the detective's response was short and direct.

'You made a mistake ten years ago. You think you're infallible, Marty?'

But the subject of Stampler could not be ignored.

St Claire and Naomi had stayed on the phone for the first week or so, sorting through police records in Colorado, San Francisco, and Kentucky and putting together a background profile on Rebecca, a sorrowful and sordid story in itself. Gradually the saga of Rebecca and Aaron Stampler began to make sense.

Harvey St Claire, with his baby cup in hand and a wad of tobacco in his cheek, settled back in a chair on his nightly visit to Abel and gave him all the details.

'We've managed to trace her back as far as high school. That was Denver, 1965,' he began. 'Her mother died when she was twelve, her father was regular Air Force. An NCO, rose up through the ranks, ultimately made captain. He was killed in a burglary in their apartment in early 1965. She vanished right after that. Accordin' to a retired homicide detective named Ashcraft, she was a suspect – there were reports of sexual and physical abuse by the old man – but they couldn't make anythin' stick. The murder was never solved.'

'How was he killed?' Stenner mumbled.

'Stabbed to death.

'Not usually . . . burglar's choice of weapons.'

St Claire nodded. 'It was a messy job. I got the feelin' talkin' to Ashcraft that they deep-sixed the investigation because everyone assumed Rebecca did him but they couldn't put a case together. Anyway, she popped up on the computer in San Francisco two years later – a dope bust in the Haight-Ashbury. Paid a menial fine, seventy-five bucks. Nothin' else until she accepted a teachin' job in Crikside in 1970. Stampler was in the first grade then – that's when she became his teacher and later mentor and finally lover.'

'When was Stampler born?' asked Stenner.

'Sixty-five, coincidentally the same year Rebecca's father was killed and she took a hike. We went back over Tommy Goodman's notes from his meetin' with her – he went down there and talked to her when Vail was preparin' Stampler's defence. She mentioned some drug problems to him and there was somethin' about living in a commune in New Mexico for awhile and teaching kids there, but we couldn't put that together, most of those communes appeared and disappeared like sand gnats back in the late Eighties. And there's no further arrest records on her – that we could uncover – so she's litreally a cipher until she showed up in Crikside. What attracted her to the job was they didn't ask for references. I assume Crikside was beggin' and not too choosy. The state has no employment or health records on her, and social security didn't turn up anythin' on her until she went to work teachin' school. Apparently they needed a teacher so bad they overlooked certain fundamentals, like a teaching certificate and a background check. The locals say she was a good teacher.'

'Depends on what she was teaching,' Stenner said.

'Well, she sure taught Stampler a few tricks you don't normally learn in school, like Murder 101. Anyway, she taught there until 1991, then she just left. Boarded up this little house she owns one weekend and vanished into the night, just like in Denver. But interestingly enough, she paid her taxes every year by money order, so the house is still in her name.'

'I missed the last act,' said Stenner. 'You think that's where Stampler was heading when you caught up with him?'

'He was ten miles from her house when we nailed him. You tell me.'

As the weeks drifted by, the subject of Aaron Stampler took a backseat to the Edith Stoddard case. When Vail was not there, Venable stared at the blank TV screen or out of the window, thinking about the night she discovered the hidden closet in Delaney's apartment, about the paraphernalia. About the gun. And she wondered whether Edith Stoddard was a victim or a willing participant in the bizarre sexual games Delaney obviously liked to play. If Stoddard contended that she was victimized by the dead man, Venable could build a strong case in her favour.

She sent notes to Stoddard, advising her not to discuss the case with *anyone* until Venable was back on her feet and able to discuss the case with her. Stoddard never answered the notes and refused to recant the confession she made to Shock Johnson.

Shana Parver, with the assistance of Dermott Flaherty, continued to construct the murder one case against Edith Stoddard, whose arraignment had been postponed for a month because Jane Venable was in the hospital. Parver was the strategist, Flaherty the pragmatist.

'Venable will use the insanity defence,' Flaherty guessed.

'It's still premeditated murder,' Shana snapped back.

'But extenuated. Venable will argue that she was a sexual victim of Delaney. That he kept her in sexual bondage. That her job was at stake. And then he cut her loose and she was mentally unstable because of her daughter and husband.'

'We still have her confession,' Parver countered.

'Which Venable will get thrown out. She was distraught, scared, anguished . . .'

'Oh blah, blah, blah,' Parver said.

Flaherty laughed. 'C'mon,' he said. 'I'll buy you dinner.'

'No, I'll buy you dinner. I'm the primary on this case. And don't let me order a martini.'

'Oh, I don't know,' he laughed. 'You get very lovable when you're loaded.'

She cast a dubious glance at him. 'I don't have to be loaded to be lovable, Flay,' she said.

Trees trembled before a warm spring breeze as Vail drove along Lakeshore Drive. He stopped and bought several bunches of spring flowers from a street vendor before entering the hospital. Jane was sitting up in bed and Stenner, who could now get around with the help of a cane, was sitting across the room.

'I got my walking papers today,' Stenner said. 'They're going to parole me an hour early so I can come to court in the morning.'

'Nothing to see,' Vail said. 'We're going to ask for a continuation of the arraignment until Jane's well enough to go to court.'

'That was thoughtful of you,' Venable said. 'Do I see signs of a crack in your armour?'

'It was Shana's idea,' Vail said with a smile. 'And I don't see so much as a blemish in her armour.'

'She's a tough little cookie, Marty,' Jane said. 'You taught her well.'

'I didn't teach her anything,' Vail laughed. 'She was born tough. Wait'll she gets John Wayne Darcy in court.'

'How about Edith Stoddard?' Jane asked.

'That's between the two of you. I'm not involved in that one, thank God.'

'You're involved in everything that goes on in the DA's office, Marty. Who are you trying to kid?'

'I didn't come here to talk business,' Vail said. He handed her the bouquet of spring flowers. 'I came to tamper with your affections.'

'You can tamper with my affections anytime,' she said and took the dead flowers from a vase on the table beside

491

the bed and dropped them in the wastebasket. Vail took the vase to the sink in the corner and filled it with water.

'I think I'll go back to my room and spend a little time,' Stenner said. 'Been there four weeks. Be like leaving home. Goodnight.'

'I'll drop by and tuck you in,' Vail said.

'My nurse takes care of that,' Stenner responded brusquely, walking as jauntily as he could from the room.

'I'm jealous of Abel,' Venable said. 'He's going home and I have two more operations to go.'

Vail sat down beside her and ran a finger gently down the bandage on her face. 'A few more weeks and it will all be behind us,' he said gently.

He stood up and walked to the window.

'Still have Stampler on your mind, don't you?' she said softly.

'You know,' he said, 'there was a moment there . . . there was a moment when . . . when it was a catharsis. For a minute or two I had the power of life and death over him. I had him in my sights. God knows, I wanted to kill him. I wanted to shoot him over and over again. A bullet for every one he butchered. The trigger had an eight-of-an-inch to go and I knew what he wanted, Janey, I knew he *wanted* me to put him down, to pull me down to his level. Then I saw the sign and eased off and let the devil have him.'

'Well, it's over, my dear,' she said and patted the bed beside her.

Maybe, he thought. *And maybe it will never be over.*

The next morning, Shana Parver and Dermott Flaherty sat at the prosecutor's table, prepared to ask for another continuance of the arraignment of Edith Stoddard. Vail, Naomi, and St Claire, accompanied by Abel Stenner, sat beside them in the first row. Edith Stoddard's daughter, Angelica, sat on the opposite side of the courtroom, nervously awaiting the hearing to start. She kept staring back at the entrance to the courtroom.

At exactly 9 A.M., Judge Thelma McElroy, a handsome black woman whose glittering, intelligent eyes hid behind round, wire-rimmed glasses, entered the room. A fair judge, she was known for her stern, no-nonsense approach to the law.

Edith Stoddard was led into the courtroom and took a seat at the defence table. She was drawn and thin. It was obvious her weeks in jail had worn her down. She folded her hands on the table and stared down at them.

A moment later there was a rumble from the rear of the courtroom, and Vail turned to see what the commotion was about.

Jane Venable entered the courtroom in a wheelchair. She was resplendent in an emerald green silk business suit, her red hair pulled back in a tight bun, a black patch over her eye, the side of her face covered with a fresh bandage.

She wheeled down the centre aisle, cast her good eye at Vail, smiled, and winked as she headed for the defendant's table. Vail could not conceal his surprise. Shana Parver was even more surprised. She looked back at Vail, who just raised his eyebrows and shrugged.

'What the hell . . .' he mumbled under his breath.

'I think we're in trouble,' Stenner said.

'We were in trouble when she took the case,' Vail answered.

Judge McElroy lowered her head and peered over her glasses at Venable.

'Well, Ms Venable, this is a surprise. Welcome back.'

'Thank you, Your Honour,' Venable answered.

'Are we ready to proceed?' the judge asked.

'Quite,' Venable answered.

'We were prepared to seek a postponement because of Ms Venable's injuries, Your Honour . . .'

'That won't be necessary,' Venable answered. 'The defendant is prepared to answer the charges.'

'The State is ready, Your Honour,' Shana Parver stammered as Flaherty dug into his briefcase and began pulling out files.

The judge looked down at her agenda sheet.

'This is an arraignment, correct?'

'Yes,' Parver answered.

'Any motions before we proceed?'

'Your Honour,' Venable began, 'if it please the court, the defence asks that we be permitted to introduce one witness for the defence.'

'Before we even start?' the Judge said.

'We will seek bond for the defendant, Edith Stoddard, Your Honour. She has been incarcerated for almost two months without relief. We would seek permission for a character witness to appear in her behalf.'

'Your Honour . . .' Parver began, but the judge raised her hand and cut her off.

'Just one minute, Counsellor,' she said, and to Venable, 'who is this witness, Ms Venable?'

'Her daughter, Angelica, Your Honour.'

'Your Honour, this is highly irregular,' Parver snapped back. 'This is an arraignment. We are prepared to present grand jury findings supporting the state's contention that Mrs Stoddard committed the offence of first-degree murder. There can be no bond.'

'Your Honour, there are extenuating circumstances in this case,' Venable countered. 'My client has no previous criminal record. She was a valued executive secretary for years and has supported a daughter in college and a husband who is a paraplegic. Certainly the court and the prosecution can not object to hearing her daughter's plea. Fifteen minutes, Your Honour, that's all we ask?'

Judge McElroy leaned back in her chair and took off her glasses.

'I assume the defence is prepared to enter a plea,' she said, staring down at Venable.

'Yes, Your Honour.'

'And you want to introduce this witness *before* the prosecution makes its presentments?'

'I think it would be appropriate to do it now,' Venable answered.

'Huh,' McElroy said. She picked up a pencil and tapped the point on a pad for several seconds. 'Well, I agree with the prosecution. It certainly is an unusual departure from normal procedure. On the other hand, I do not wish this court to appear without compassion. Ms Parver, I'm going to overrule your objection. Keep in mind there is no jury here. The question of bail rests with my discretion.'

Although she was angry, Parver realized it would be foolish to stir the judge's wrath this early in the game.

'Yes, Your Honour,' Parver said.

'Thank you. All right, the defence may call its witness,' she said.

'Defence calls Angelica Stoddard.'

Angelica Stoddard was pale and nervous. Her hands were shaking as she took the oath and sat down in the witness box. Her eyes were fixed on Venable as she wheeled her chair to the front of the courtroom. Edith Stoddard stared suspiciously at Venable.

'Just relax,' Venable said softly. 'I know you're nervous but this will only take a few minutes. Give your name, please.'

'Angelica Stoddard.'

'How old are you, Angelica?'

'Twenty-one.'

'And where do you reside?'

'In Chalmers Dormitory. I attend Chicago University.'

'And how long have you been attending college?'

'Three years.'

'What kind of grades do you make, Angelica?'

495

'I have a 3.2 going into my senior year.'

'An A-student?'

'Well, yes. I've made a couple of B's, but mostly A's.'

'You have a scholarship, do you not?'

'Yes. It pays tuition and books.'

'And who pays your room and board?'

'My mother.'

'Mrs Edith Stoddard?'

'Yes.'

'What is your father's name?'

'Charles. Charles Stoddard.'

'Is your father employed?'

'No. My father is paralysed from the neck down.'

'And he lives with your mother?'

'Yes.'

'*So*, your mother is the sole support of both you and your father, is that correct?'

'Yes.'

'And until recently, she worked at Delaney Enterprises?'

'Yes. Mister Delaney fired her.'

'Who takes care of your father during the day?'

'We had a nurse who was also our housekeeper. She came at eight in the morning and left at five.'

'So your mother takes care of him from eight on?'

'Yes. Except when she has to . . . had to, work at night. Once or twice a week I went to the house when she had to work after five.'

'So you both take care of him.'

'Yes, but mainly my mom watches . . . watched over him.'

'And have things changed since your mother's arrest?'

'Yes. Our nurse quit. The insurance wasn't enough to cover her wages anyway.'

'And do you take care of your father now?'

'Yes. I dropped out of school and moved back to the house.'

496

'So when your mother lost her job, it changed your lifestyle radically, is that true?'

'Yes.'

'And this happened when your mother was arrested?'

Angelica nodded and stared down at her lap. 'Doctor Saperstein – he's my father's doctor – says we should put him in a nursing home.' She began to cry and dabbed at her eyes with a tissue.

'Can you afford that? I mean, if your insurance doesn't cover the nurse, how could you afford a nursing home?'

'I will . . . would get a job. Sell the house . . .'

She stopped for a moment, stared down again, and seemed to gather her composure. Then she looked up and her expression had changed from sorrow to anger.

'It's so unfair . . .' she said, then hesitated for a moment and looking straight at Edith Stoddard, her voice stronger and her eyes flashing, she said. 'It's unfair because my mother didn't kill Delaney, I did! She confessed to protect me!'

The judge was jolted back in her chair. Venable seemed shocked. Edith Stoddard leapt to her feet.

'That's a lie,' she yelled. 'She's trying to protect me! I killed Delaney, I confessed to killing Delaney. The police have my confession on record. Stop this now!'

'No, you stop it, Mama,' Angelica yelled back. 'I was the one he kept in bondage. Since I was eighteen. He held your job over my head. He threatened me . . .'

The courtroom was in bedlam. Parver was on her feet.

'Objection, Your Honour, *objection*!'

Venable stammered: 'Your Honour, I had no idea . . .'

Naomi turned to Vail. 'Holy shit!' she whispered. But Vail did not answer. He stared at Venable with absolute awe.

'It's true,' Angelica Stoddard screamed. 'I went there that night to plead with him to give her job back and he forced me to . . .'

'*Objection*, Your Honour,' Parver yelled.

McElroy slammed her gavel several times. 'Quiet in this courtroom,' she demanded, her eyes flashing with rage. 'Quiet, NOW! Counsellors – in my chambers, now. This court is in recess.'

'Excuse me, Your Honour, may we have ten minutes before you meet with the attorneys?' Parver asked.

Judge McElroy still flushed with ire, glanced at Venable. 'All right, allll-*right*,' she snapped. 'Fifteen minutes, ladies. Then I'll see you both in chambers.'

She fled the bench.

Vail looked across the room at Venable, who held her hands out at her side as if to say, 'I'm just as confused as you are.' Vail smiled at her and shook his head.

Vail led Parver, Naomi, St Claire, Stenner, and Flaherty into a small holding office beside the courtroom.

'Okay,' Shana,' Vail said after pulling the door shut, 'now what're you going to do? Punt or play?'

She looked him straight in the eyes and said, 'I'll be damned if I know. I can't even figure out what the options are.'

'Do you think Venable planned this, or is she just as surprised as we are?' Naomi asked.

'I don't think she planned it,' Vail said. 'But I think there's a chance she knew it was going to happen.'

'Shock defence,' Flaherty said.

'Theatre of the law,' Vail answered.

'You should know,' Stenner said. 'You pulled the same kind of stunt on Jane ten years ago.'

'Maybe so, Abel,' Shana agreed, 'but who do we deal with? What's your gut feeling? Which one of them did it?'

Stenner made a practical decision. 'The mother did it. The other way is too convoluted.'

'I say the mother,' Flaherty said. 'But I think the daughter was involved with Delaney, just as she said she was on the stand, and the mother killed him to set her free.

All this can come out in discovery. I say we postpone the arraignment and go back to the drawing board.'

'The daughter did it and the mother's covering for her,' St Claire said. 'I don't care how convoluted it is.'

'I think Angelica did it,' Parver agreed.

'I think Edith did it for a lot of reasons,' Naomi said.

'They're both giving the same story, both say the other one knew nothing about it, they have the same motive, the same opportunity, and neither one of them has an alibi,' Stenner said.

'That's ridiculous,' said St Claire. 'We got Stoddard's fingerprints all over the weapon.'

Vail stared at the ceiling. 'Why wouldn't Stoddard's fingerprints be all over the weapon, it's her gun?' he asked of nobody in particular.

'How about the bullets?' Flaherty asked.

'Same story,' Vail said. 'It's her gun. Naturally, she loaded it.'

'And the daughter?' asked Flaherty. 'How about her prints?'

'She'll say she wore gloves,' Shana said. 'If she wants to stick with her story.'

'Indict 'em both, see if we can break one of 'em down before we get to court,' suggested St Claire.

Vail laughed. 'Oh sure, I can see that. What do you think the grand jury will say if we go back in there and tell 'em we want to indict two people because we're not sure which one committed the crime?'

'I think it's a setup,' said Stenner. 'Either they were in it together or they're confusing the issue now.'

'Can we crack one story?' said Flaherty. 'Find a chink in Edith Stoddard's story and see if the daughter stays with the wrong yarn?'

Shana Parver shifted uneasily in her chair. She stared down at the floor but said nothing.

'Okay, Parver,' Vail said. 'What's bugging you? Out with it.'

'I think,' she started, hesitated for a moment, then went on, 'I think he deserved what he got no matter who shot him.'

That quieted the room down. They all looked at each other, then back at Shana.

'Let me ask you all something,' said Vail. 'Do any of you think Edith Stoddard would willingly have become involved in Delaney's sex games?'

'Why?' Shana asked.

'Because that may be the key to this whole mess,' Vail said. 'Delaney shined to the daughter and dazzled her. Look, she's a kid, all of a sudden she's getting attention from her mother's boss who is a big shot in town. He lures her in, the next thing you know he's playing kinky sex games with her. She doesn't tell anybody, certainly not her mother. Delaney was naked when he was hit. Supposing he was with the daughter and Edith Stoddard came in and caught them. She goes off the wall, pulls the gun, and drops Delaney. Then she hustles Angelica out of there, dumps the gun and splits. The next day during Johnson's interrogation, she realizes she can't buffalo the pros so she cops to the crime, says she lost it because Delaney got rid of her, and hopes it will end there. That way she protects her husband and her daughter.'

'Pretty good scenario,' Stenner said.

'Except we know the truth,' said Flaherty.

'Do we?' St Claire offered. 'All we know is that Delaney was one sick son of a bitch and whoever whacked him knew about his closet full of goodies. Either way, he comes off in court as a greaseball and the ladies get the sympathy.'

'Gonna be hard to get a unanimous decision on this,' Naomi said. 'If half the jurors are women, they'll hang that jury up for ever.'

'I think Naomi's right,' Vail said. 'The question here is, what do *we* want. Do we want to put Edith or Angelica Stoddard away for the rest of their lives?'

'Compassion?' Stenner said, eyeing Vail.

'Expedience,' Flaherty offered. 'I say make the best deal we can, otherwise she may walk.'

'Shana?' Vail said. 'It's your call.'

'First-degree manslaughter. Ten to twenty.'

'Venable won't buy it,' said Vail. 'She'll take her chances with the jury.'

'You're overlooking Edith Stoddard,' said Shana. 'She doesn't want to go to trial. She sure as hell doesn't want what happened in the courtroom this morning to be repeated. Her whole thing now is to protect her daughter and her husband.'

'You think she'll go for manslaughter one?' Naomi asked.

'I think Janey wants her client to walk out of this courtroom a free woman,' said Vail.

'So?' Shana said.

'So, I think it's time to make a deal,' Vail said.

'And I think no matter what happens, justice is going to get another swift kick in the ass,' Stenner said.

And it was the first time anyone in the room ever saw him smile.

'What the hell are you pulling, Ms Venable?' Judge McElroy asked, scowling across her desk at Venable.

'I swear, I had no idea she was going to say that,' Venable answered. 'She asked if she could be a character witness, to help her mother get bail.'

'I certainly hope so. I don't take kindly to lawyers who try to turn my courtroom into a carnival.' Judge McElroy glared at her for a few seconds more.

'You have my word,' Venable replied firmly.

'All right,' McElroy said. 'What are we going to do about this mess?'

'I think that's up to Ms Venable,' Shana answered immediately.

'Me?' Venable said.

'Yes,' Parver said. 'You can't defend them both. That

means Angelica will have to get her own lawyer. Are you prepared in your defence to lay this off on Angelica Stoddard?'

'What do you mean?' Venable answered, her voice getting edgy.

'That's the only way you can walk Edith out of here,' said Parver. 'Either we assume Edith Stoddard is guilty and try to work something out, or you're going to have to convince your client that you should go after her own daughter. Only one of them's guilty.'

'Then we'll go to the jury,' Venable snapped.

'And wash all that dirty laundry in front of the press?' Shana answered. 'I don't think so. We still have a confession, Counsellor. Your client hasn't recanted that yet.'

'No jury in the world will convict Edith Stoddard,' Venable said.

'That isn't the point, is it?' Shana said.

'What is the point?'

'We have a clear case of premeditated murder. We have a powerful civic leader who has a lot of friends in high places. The only way to break that down is to drag Edith through the mud, too. Think about it.'

McElroy leaned back in her chair, making a pyramid of her fingertips and leaning her chin on them. She smothered a smile. This Parver child was slick and tough, she thought. Inwardly, she admired both women. She stood finally.

'If you two will excuse me,' she said, 'I'm going to step outside for a few minutes. I would like to think that when I get back we can resolve this problem.'

She left the room.

'Okay, what are you offering?' Venable said.

'Manslaughter one. Ten to twenty. She could be out in six or seven years.'

'Not a chance. I'd be betraying my client. We'll take second degree. Five to ten.'

'I can't do that.'

'What does Martin want?'

'This is my case, not his.'

'He didn't make a recommendation?'

'Nope.'

Venable smiled. 'What a guy,' she said.

'We agree on that,' Shana said, and finally smiled too.

'So – what's the answer, Shana? We can wrap it up here and now.'

'Your way?'

'Hell, girl, you got me into this in the first place,' Venable said with a smile. 'I was perfectly happy sitting up in platinum city making a fortune. I think the question is, do you really want to go to trial on this?'

Shana Parver did not answer immediately. She stared at the ceiling, as Vail often did, thinking. Finally she said, 'How about a compromise? Plead her guilty to first-degree manslaughter if the judge will agree to five to twenty. She could be out in three years.'

'Minimum security prison?'

'I have no problem with that.'

Venable smiled and stuck out her hand.

'Deal,' she said. 'You're a helluva lawyer, Shana.'

'Look who's talking.'

A few days after the arraignment, the governor of Kentucky ordered the state patrol to recover Stampler's body from mine shaft number five. Spring rains had washed away the snow, leaving behind a muddy oasis in the forest with the gaping hole, like a bull's-eye, in the centre of the timbers that covered the old lift shaft. A small crowd of Crikside residents stood in the periphery, watching with anticipation the way crowds will, although there was nothing much to see but a small crane with lights and a video camera that was lowered into the bowels of the Kentucky mountainside, and a half dozen state troopers staring at the video monitor.

The mine shaft was empty.

1

Last night I dreamt I went to Manderley again. It seemed to me I stood by the iron gate leading to the drive, and for a while I could not enter, for the way was barred to me. There was a padlock and a chain upon the gate. I called in my dream to the lodge-keeper, and had no answer, and peering closer through the rusted spokes of the gate I saw that the lodge was uninhabited.

No smoke came from the chimney, and the little lattice windows gaped forlorn. Then, like all dreamers, I was possessed of a sudden with supernatural powers and passed like a spirit through the barrier before me. The drive wound away in front of me, twisting and turning as it had always done, but as I advanced I was aware that a change had come upon it; it was narrow and unkept, not the drive that we had known. At first I was puzzled and did not understand, and it was only when I bent my head to avoid the low swinging branch of a tree that I realized what had happened. Nature had come into her own again and, little by little, in her stealthy, insidious way had encroached upon the drive with long, tenacious fingers. The woods, always a menace even in the past, had triumphed in the end. They crowded, dark and uncontrolled, to the borders of the drive. The beeches with white, naked limbs leant close to one another, their branches intermingled in a strange embrace, making a vault above my head like the archway of a church. And there were other trees as well, trees that I did not recognize, squat oaks and tortured elms that straggled cheek by jowl with the beeches, and had thrust themselves out of the quiet earth, along with monster shrubs and plants, none of which I remembered.

The drive was a ribbon now, a thread of its former self, with gravel surface gone, and choked with grass and moss. The trees had thrown out low branches, making an impediment to progress; the gnarled roots looked like skeleton claws. Scattered here and again amongst this jungle growth I would recognize shrubs that had been landmarks in our time, things of culture and grace, hydrangeas whose blue heads had been famous. No hand had checked their progress, and they had gone native now, rearing to monster height without a bloom, black and ugly as the nameless parasites that grew beside them.

On and on, now east now west, wound the poor thread that once had been our drive. Sometimes I thought it lost, but it appeared again, beneath a fallen tree perhaps, or struggling on the other side of a muddied ditch created by the winter rains. I had not thought the way so long. Surely the miles had multiplied, even as the trees had done, and this path led but to a labyrinth, some choked wilderness, and not to the house at all. I came upon it suddenly; the approach masked by the unnatural growth of a vast shrub that spread in all directions, and I stood, my heart thumping in my breast, the strange prick of tears behind my eyes.

There was Manderley, our Manderley, secretive and silent as it had always been, the grey stone shining in the moonlight of my dream, the mullioned windows reflecting the green lawns and the terrace. Time could not wreck the perfect symmetry of those walls, nor the site itself, a jewel in the hollow of a hand.

The terrace sloped to the lawns, and the lawns stretched to the sea, and turning I could see the sheet of silver placid under the moon, like a lake undisturbed by wind or storm. No waves would come to ruffle this dream water, and no bulk of cloud, wind-driven from the west, obscure the clarity of this pale sky. I turned again to the house, and though it stood inviolate, untouched, as though we ourselves had left but yesterday, I saw that the garden had obeyed the jungle law, even as the woods had done. The rhododendrons stood fifty feet high, twisted and entwined with bracken, and they had entered into alien marriage with a host of nameless shrubs, poor, bastard things that clung about their roots as though conscious of their spurious origin. A lilac had mated with a copper beech, and to bind them yet more closely to one another the malevolent ivy, always an enemy to grace, had thrown her tendrils about the pair and made them prisoners. Ivy held prior place in this lost garden, the long strands crept across the lawns, and soon would encroach upon the house itself. There was another plant too, some half-breed from the woods, whose seed had been scattered long ago beneath the trees and then forgotten, and now, marching in unison with the ivy, thrust its ugly form like a giant rhubarb towards the soft grass where the daffodils had blown.

Nettles were everywhere, the vanguard of the army. They choked the terrace, they sprawled about the paths, they leant, vulgar and lanky, against the very windows of the house. They made indifferent sentinels, for in many places their ranks had been broken by the rhubarb plant, and they lay with crumpled heads and listless stems, making a pathway for the rabbits. I left the drive and went on to the terrace, for the nettles were no barrier to me, a dreamer. I walked enchanted, and nothing held me back.

Moonlight can play odd tricks upon the fancy, even upon a dreamer's fancy. As I stood there, hushed and still, I could swear that the house was not an empty shell but lived and breathed as it had lived before.

Light came from the windows, the curtains blew softly in the night air, and there, in the library, the door would stand half open as we had left it, with my handkerchief on the table beside the bowl of autumn roses.

The room would bear witness to our presence. The little heap of library books marked ready to return, and the discarded copy of *The Times*. Ash-trays, with the stub of a cigarette; cushions, with the imprint of our heads upon them, lolling in the chairs; the charred embers of our log fire still smouldering against the morning. And Jasper, dear Jasper, with his soulful eyes and great, sagging jowl, would be stretched upon the floor, his tail a-thump when he heard his master's footsteps.

A cloud, hitherto unseen, came upon the moon, and hovered an instant like a dark hand before a face. The illusion went with it, and the lights in the windows were extinguished. I looked upon a desolate shell, soulless at last, unhaunted, with no whisper of the past about its staring walls.

The house was a sepulchre, our fear and suffering lay buried in the ruins. There would be no resurrection. When I thought of Manderley in my waking hours I would not be bitter. I should think of it as it might have been, could I have lived there without fear. I should remember the rose-garden in summer, and the birds that sang at dawn. Tea under the chestnut tree, and the murmur of the sea coming up to us from the lawns below.

I would think of the blown lilac, and the Happy Valley. These things were permanent, they could not be dissolved. They were memories that cannot hurt. All this I resolved in my dream, while the clouds lay across the face of the moon, for like most sleepers I knew that I dreamed. In reality I lay many hundred miles away in an alien land, and would wake, before many seconds had passed, in the bare little hotel bedroom, comforting in its very lack of atmosphere. I would sigh a moment, stretch myself and turn, and opening my eyes, be bewildered at that glittering sun, that hard, clean sky, so different from the soft moonlight of my dream. The day would lie before us both, long no doubt, and uneventful, but fraught with a certain stillness, a dear tranquillity we had not known before. We would not talk of Manderley, I would not tell my dream. For Manderley was ours no longer. Manderley was no more.

2

We can never go back again, that much is certain. The past is still too close to us. The things we have tried to forget and put behind us would stir again, and that sense of fear, of furtive unrest, struggling at length to blind unreasoning panic – now mercifully stilled, thank God – might in some manner unforeseen become a living companion, as it had been before.

He is wonderfully patient and never complains, not even when he remembers . . . which happens, I think, rather more often than he would have me know.

I can tell by the way he will look lost and puzzled suddenly, all expression dying away from his dear face as though swept clean by an unseen hand, and in its place a mask will form, a sculptured thing, formal and cold, beautiful still but lifeless. He will fall to smoking cigarette after cigarette, not bothering to extinguish them, and the glowing stubs will lie around on the ground like petals. He will talk quickly and eagerly about nothing at all, snatching at any subject as a panacea to pain. I believe there is a theory that men and women emerge finer and stronger after suffering, and that to advance in this or any world we must endure ordeal by fire. This we have done in full measure, ironic though it seems. We have both known fear, and loneliness, and very great distress. I suppose sooner or later in the life of everyone comes a moment of trial. We all of us have our particular devil who rides us and torments us, and we must give battle in the end. We have conquered ours, or so we believe.

The devil does not ride us any more. We have come through our crisis, not unscathed of course. His premonition of disaster was correct from the beginning; and like a ranting actress in an indifferent play, I might say that we have paid for freedom. But I have had enough melodrama in this life, and would willingly give my five senses if they could ensure us our present peace and security. Happiness is not a possession to be prized, it is a quality of thought, a state of mind. Of course we have our moments of depression; but there are other moments too, when time, unmeasured by the clock, runs on into eternity and, catching his smile, I know we are together, we march in unison, no clash of thought or of opinion makes a barrier between us.

We have no secrets now from one another. All things are shared. Granted that our little hotel is dull, and the food indifferent, and that day after day dawns very much the same, yet we would not have it otherwise. We should meet too many of the people he knows in any of the big hotels. We both appreciate simplicity, and we are sometimes bored – well, boredom is a pleasing antidote to fear. We live very much by routine, and I – I have developed a genius for reading aloud. The only time I have known him show impatience is when the postman lags, for it means we must wait another day before the arrival of our English mail. We have tried wireless, but the noise is such an irritant, and we prefer to store up our excitement; the result of a cricket match played many days ago means much to us.

Oh, the Test matches that have saved us from ennui, the boxing bouts, even the billiard scores. Finals of schoolboy sports, dog racing, strange little competitions in the remoter counties, all these are grist to our hungry mill. Sometimes old copies of the *Field* come my way, and I am transported from this indifferent island to the realities of an English spring. I read of chalk streams, of the mayfly, of sorrel growing in green meadows, of rooks circling above the woods as they used to do at Manderley. The smell of wet earth comes to me from those thumbed and tattered pages, the sour tang of moorland peat, the feel of soggy moss spattered white in places by a heron's droppings.

Once there was an article on wood pigeons, and as I read it aloud it seemed to me that once again I was in the deep woods at Manderley, with pigeons fluttering above my head. I heard their soft, complacent call, so comfortable and cool on a hot summer's afternoon, and there would be no disturbing of their peace until Jasper came loping through the undergrowth to find me, his damp muzzle questing the ground. Like old ladies caught at their ablutions, the pigeons would flutter from their hiding-place, shocked into silly agitation, and, making a monstrous to-do with their wings, streak away from us above the tree-tops, and so out of sight and sound. When they were gone a new silence would come upon the place, and I – uneasy for no known reason – would realize that the sun no longer wove a pattern on the rustling leaves, that the branches had grown darker, the shadows longer; and back at the house there would be fresh raspberries for tea. I would rise from my bed of bracken then, shaking the feathery dust of last year's leaves from my skirt and whistling to Jasper, set off towards the house, despising myself even as I walked for my hurrying feet, my one swift glance behind.

How strange that an article on wood pigeons could so recall the past and make me falter as I read aloud. It was the grey look on his face that made me stop abruptly, and turn the pages until I found a paragraph on cricket, very practical and dull – Middlesex batting on a dry wicket at the Oval and piling up interminable dreary runs. How I blessed those solid, flannelled figures, for in a few minutes his face had settled back into repose, the colour had returned, and he was deriding the Surrey bowling in healthy irritation.

We were saved a retreat into the past, and I had learnt my lesson. Read English news, yes, and English sport, politics, and pomposity, but in future keep the things that hurt to myself alone. They can be my secret indulgence. Colour and scent and sound, rain and the lapping of water, even the mists of autumn and the smell of the flood tide, these are memories of Manderley that will not be denied. Some people have a vice of reading Bradshaws. They plan innumerable journeys across country for the fun of linking up impossible connexions. My hobby is less tedious, if as strange. I am a mine of information on the English countryside. I know the name of every owner of every British moor, yes – and their tenants too. I know how many grouse are killed, how many partridge, how many head of deer. I know where trout are rising, and where the salmon leap. I attend all meets, I follow every run. Even the names of those who walk hound puppies are familiar to me. The state of the crops, the price of fat cattle, the mysterious ailments of swine, I relish them all. A poor pastime, perhaps, and not a very intellectual one, but I breathe the air of England as I read, and can face this glittering sky with greater courage.

The scrubby vineyards and the crumbling stones become things of no account, for if I wish I can give rein to my imagination, and pick foxgloves and pale campions from a wet, streaking hedge.

Poor whims of fancy, tender and un-harsh. They are the enemy to bitterness and regret, and sweeten this exile we have brought upon ourselves.

Because of them I can enjoy my afternoon, and return, smiling and refreshed, to face the little ritual of our tea. The order never varies. Two slices of bread and butter each, and China tea. What a hide-bound couple we must seem, clinging to custom because we did so in England. Here, on this clean balcony, white and impersonal with centuries of sun, I think of half past four at Manderley, and the table drawn before the library fire. The door flung open, punctual to the minute, and the performance, never-varying, of the laying of the tea, the silver tray, the kettle, the snowy cloth. While Jasper, his spaniel ears a-droop, feigns indifference to the arrival of the cakes. That feast was laid before us always, and yet we ate so little.

Those dripping crumpets, I can see them now. Tiny crisp wedges of toast, and piping-hot, floury scones. Sandwiches of unknown nature, mysteriously flavoured and quite delectable, and that very special gingerbread. Angel cake, that melted in the mouth, and his rather stodgier companion, bursting with peel and raisins. There was enough food there to keep a starving family for a week. I never knew what happened to it all, and the waste used to worry me sometimes.

But I never dared ask Mrs Danvers what she did about it. She would have looked at me in scorn, smiling that freezing, superior smile of hers, and I can imagine her saying: 'There were never any complaints when Mrs de Winter was alive.' Mrs Danvers. I wonder what she is doing now. She and Favell. I think it was the expression on her face that gave me my first feeling of unrest. Instinctively I thought, 'She is comparing me to Rebecca'; and sharp as a sword the shadow came between us . . .

Well, it is over now, finished and done with. I ride no more tormented, and both of us are free. Even my faithful Jasper has gone to the happy hunting grounds, and Manderley is no more. It lies like an empty shell amidst the tangle of the deep woods, even as I saw it in my dream. A multitude of weeds, a colony of birds. Sometimes perhaps a tramp will wander there, seeking shelter from a sudden shower of rain and, if he is stout-hearted, he may walk there with impunity. But your timid fellow, your nervous poacher – the woods of Manderley are not for him. He might stumble upon the little cottage in the cove and he would not be happy beneath its tumbled roof, the thin rain beating a tattoo. There might linger there still a certain atmosphere of stress . . . That corner in the drive, too, where the trees encroach upon the gravel, is not a place in which to pause, not after the sun has set. When the leaves rustle, they sound very much like the stealthy movement of a woman in evening dress, and when they shiver suddenly, and fall, and scatter away along the ground, they might be the patter, patter, of a woman's hurrying footstep, and the mark in the gravel the imprint of a high-heeled satin shoe.

It is when I remember these things that I return with relief to the prospect from our balcony. No shadows steal upon this hard glare, the stony vineyards shimmer in the sun and the bougainvillaea is white with dust. I may one day look upon it with affection. At the moment it inspires me, if not with love, at least with confidence. And confidence is a quality I prize, although it has come to me a little late in the day. I suppose it is his dependence upon me that has made me bold at last. At any rate I have lost my diffidence, my timidity, my shyness with strangers. I am very different from that self who drove to Manderley for the first time, hopeful and eager, handicapped by a rather desperate gaucherie and filled with an intense desire to please. It was my lack of poise of course that made such a bad impression on people like Mrs Danvers. What must I have seemed like after Rebecca? I can see myself now, memory spanning the years like a bridge, with straight, bobbed hair and youthful, unpowdered face, dressed in an ill-fitting coat and skirt and a jumper of my own creation, trailing in the wake of Mrs Van Hopper like a shy, uneasy colt. She would precede me in to lunch, her short body ill-balanced upon tottering, high heels, her fussy, frilly blouse a compliment to her large bosom and swinging hips, her new hat pierced with a monster quill aslant upon her head, exposing a wide expanse of forehead bare as a schoolboy's knee. One hand carried a gigantic bag, the kind that holds passports, engagement diaries, and bridge scores, while the other hand toyed with that inevitable lorgnette, the enemy to other people's privacy.

She would make for her usual table in the corner of the restaurant, close to the window, and lifting her lorgnette to her small pig's eyes survey the scene to right and left of her, then she would let the lorgnette fall at length upon its black ribbon and utter a little exclamation of disgust: 'Not a single well-known personality, I shall tell the management they must make a reduction on my bill. What do they think I come here for? To look at the page boys?' And she would summon the waiter to her side, her voice sharp and staccato, cutting the air like a saw.

How different the little restaurant where we are today to that vast dining-room, ornate and ostentatious, the Hôtel Côte d'Azur at Monte Carlo; and how different my present companion, his steady, well-shaped hands peeling a mandarin in quiet, methodical fashion, looking up now and again from his task to smile at me, compared to Mrs Van Hopper, her fat, bejewelled fingers questing a plate heaped high with ravioli, her eyes darting suspiciously from her plate to mine for fear I should have made the better choice. She need not have disturbed herself, for the waiter, with the uncanny swiftness of his kind, had long sensed my position as inferior and subservient to hers, and had placed before me a plate of ham and tongue that somebody had sent back to the cold buffet half an hour before as badly carved. Odd, that resentment of servants, and their obvious impatience. I remember staying once with Mrs Van Hopper in a country house, and the maid never answered my timid bell, or brought up my shoes, and early morning tea, stone cold, was dumped outside my bedroom door. It was the same at the Côte d'Azur, though to a lesser degree, and sometimes the studied indifference turned to familiarity, smirking and offensive, which made buying stamps from the reception clerk an ordeal I would avoid. How young and inexperienced I must have seemed, and how I felt it, too. One was too sensitive, too raw, there were thorns and pin-pricks in so many words that in reality fell lightly on the air.

I remember well that plate of ham and tongue. It was dry, unappetizing, cut in a wedge from the outside, but I had not the courage to refuse it. We ate in silence, for Mrs Van Hopper liked to concentrate on food, and I could tell by the way the sauce ran down her chin that her dish of ravioli pleased her.

It was not a sight that engendered into me great appetite for my own cold choice, and looking away from her I saw that the table next to ours, left vacant for three days, was to be occupied once more. The *maître d'hôtel*, with the particular bow reserved for his more special patrons, was ushering the new arrival to his place.

Mrs Van Hopper put down her fork, and reached for her lorgnette. I blushed for her while she stared, and the newcomer, unconscious of her interest, cast a wandering eye over the menu. Then Mrs Van Hopper folded her lorgnette with a snap, and leant across the table to me, her small eyes bright with excitement, her voice a shade too loud.

'It's Max de Winter,' she said, 'the man who owns Manderley. You've heard of it, of course. He looks ill, doesn't he? They say he can't get over his wife's death . . .'

3

I wonder what my life would be today, if Mrs Van Hopper had not been a snob.

Funny to think that the course of my existence hung like a thread upon that quality of hers. Her curiosity was a disease, almost a mania. At first I had been shocked, wretchedly embarrassed; I would feel like a whipping boy who must bear his master's pains when I watched people laugh behind her back, leave a room hurriedly upon her entrance, or even vanish behind a Service door on the corridor upstairs. For many years now she had come to the Hôtel Côte d'Azur, and, apart from bridge, her one pastime which was notorious by now in Monte Carlo, was to claim visitors of distinction as her friends had she but seen them once at the other end of the post-office. Somehow she would manage to introduce herself, and before her victim had scented danger she had proffered an invitation to her suite. Her method of attack was so downright and sudden that there was seldom opportunity to escape. At the Côte d'Azur she staked a claim upon a certain sofa in the lounge, midway between the reception hall and the passage to the restaurant, and she would have her coffee there after luncheon and dinner, and all who came and went must pass her by. Sometimes she would employ me as a bait to draw her prey, and, hating my errand, I would be sent across the lounge with a verbal message, the loan of a book or paper, the address of some shop or other, the sudden discovery of a mutual friend. It seemed as though notables must be fed to her, much as invalids are spooned their jelly; and though titles were preferred by her, any face once seen in a social paper served as well. Names scattered in a gossip column, authors, artists, actors, and their kind, even the mediocre ones, as long as she had learnt of them in print.

I can see her as though it were but yesterday, on that unfor-gettable afternoon – never mind how many years ago – when she sat at her favourite sofa in the lounge, debating her method of attack. I could tell by her abrupt manner, and the way she tapped her lorgnette against her teeth, that she was questing possibilities. I knew, too, when she had missed the sweet and rushed through dessert, that she had wished to finish luncheon before the new arrival and so install herself where he must pass. Suddenly she turned to me, her small eyes alight.

'Go upstairs quickly and find that letter from my nephew. You remember, the one written on his honeymoon, with the snapshot. Bring it down to me right away.'

I saw then that her plans were formed, and the nephew was to be the means of introduction. Not for the first time I resented the part that I must play in her schemes. Like a juggler's assis-tant I produced the props, then silent and attentive I waited on my cue. This newcomer would not welcome intrusion, I felt certain of that. In the little I had learnt of him at luncheon, a smattering of hearsay garnered by her ten months ago from the daily papers and stored in her memory for future use, I could imagine, in spite of my youth and inexperience of the world, that he would resent this sudden bursting in upon his solitude. Why he should have chosen to come to the Côte d'Azur at Monte Carlo was not our concern, his problems were his own, and anyone but Mrs Van Hopper would have understood. Tact was a quality unknown to her, discretion too, and because gossip was the breath of life to her this stranger must be served for her dissection. I found the letter in a pigeon-hole in her desk, and hesitated a moment before going down again to the lounge. It seemed to me, rather senselessly, that I was allowing him a few more moments of seclusion.

I wished I had the courage to go by the Service staircase and so by roundabout way to the restaurant, and there warn him of the ambush. Convention was too strong for me though, nor did I know how I should frame my sentence. There was nothing for it but to sit in my usual place beside Mrs Van Hopper while she, like a large, complacent spider, spun her wide net of tedium about the stranger's person.

I had been longer than I thought, for when I returned to the lounge I saw he had already left the dining-room, and she, fearful of losing him, had not waited for the letter, but had risked a bare-faced introduction on her own. He was even now sitting beside her on the sofa. I walked across to them, and gave her the letter without a word. He rose to his feet at once, while Mrs Van Hopper, flushed with her success, waved a vague hand in my direction and mumbled my name.

'Mr de Winter is having coffee with us, go and ask the waiter for another cup,' she said, her tone just casual enough to warn him of my footing. It meant I was a youthful thing and unimportant, and that there was no need to include me in the conversation. She always spoke in that tone when she wished to be impressive, and her method of introduction was a form of self-protection, for once I had been taken for her daughter, an acute embarrassment for us both. This abruptness showed that I could safely be ignored, and women would give me a brief nod which served as a greeting and a dismissal in one, while men, with large relief, would realize they could sink back into a comfortable chair without offending courtesy.

It was a surprise, therefore, to find that this newcomer remained standing on his feet, and it was he who made a signal to the waiter.

'I'm afraid I must contradict you,' he said to her, 'you are both having coffee with me'; and before I knew what had happened he was sitting in my usual hard chair, and I was on the sofa beside Mrs Van Hopper.

For a moment she looked annoyed — this was not what she had intended — but she soon composed her face, and thrusting her large self between me and the table she leant forward to his chair, talking eagerly and loudly, fluttering the letter in her hand.

'You know I recognized you just as soon as you walked into the restaurant,' she said, 'and I thought, "Why, there's Mr de Winter, Billy's friend, I simply must show him those snaps of

14

Billy and his bride taken on their honeymoon", and here they are. There's Dora. Isn't she just adorable? That little, slim waist, those great big eyes. Here they are sun-bathing at Palm Beach. Billy is crazy about her, you can imagine. He had not met her of course when he gave that party at Claridge's, and where I saw you first. But I dare say you don't remember an old woman like me?'

This with a provocative glance and a gleam of teeth.

'On the contrary I remember you very well,' he said, and before she could trap him into a resurrection of their first meeting he had handed her his cigarette case, and the business of lighting-up stalled her for the moment. 'I don't think I should care for Palm Beach,' he said, blowing the match, and glancing at him I thought how unreal he would look against a Florida background. He belonged to a walled city of the fifteenth century, a city of narrow, cobbled streets, and thin spires, where the inhabitants wore pointed shoes and worsted hose. His face was arresting, sensitive, medieval in some strange inexplicable way, and I was reminded of a portrait seen in a gallery, I had forgotten where, of a certain Gentleman Unknown. Could one but rob him of his English tweeds, and put him in black, with lace at his throat and wrists, he would stare down at us in our new world from a long-distant past – a past where men walked cloaked at night, and stood in the shadow of old doorways, a past of narrow stairways and dim dungeons, a past of whispers in the dark, of shimmering rapier blades, of silent, exquisite courtesy.

I wished I could remember the Old Master who had painted that portrait. It stood in a corner of the gallery, and the eyes followed one from the dusky frame . . .

They were talking though, and I had lost the thread of conversation. 'No, not even twenty years ago,' he was saying. 'That sort of thing has never amused me.'

I heard Mrs Van Hopper give her fat, complacent laugh. 'If Billy had a home like Manderley he would not want to play around in Palm Beach,' she said. 'I'm told it's like fairyland, there's no other word for it.'

15

She paused, expecting him to smile, but he went on smoking his cigarette, and I noticed, faint as gossamer, the line between his brows.

'I've seen pictures of it, of course,' she persisted, 'and it looks perfectly enchanting. I remember Billy telling me it had all those big places beat for beauty. I wonder you can ever bear to leave it.'

His silence now was painful, and would have been patent to anyone else, but she ran on like a clumsy goat, trampling and trespassing on land that was preserved, and I felt the colour flood my face, dragged with her as I was into humiliation.

'Of course you Englishmen are all the same about your homes,' she said, her voice becoming louder and louder, 'you depreciate them so as not to seem proud. Isn't there a minstrels' gallery at Manderley, and some very valuable portraits?' She turned to me by way of explanation. 'Mr de Winter is so modest he won't admit to it, but I believe that lovely home of his has been in his family's possession since the Conquest. They say that minstrels' gallery is a gem. I suppose your ancestors often entertained royalty at Manderley, Mr de Winter?'

This was more than I had hitherto endured, even from her, but the swift lash of his reply was unexpected. 'Not since Ethelred,' he said, 'the one who was called Unready. In fact, it was while staying with my family that the name was given him. He was invariably late for dinner.'

She deserved it, of course, and I waited for her change of face, but incredible as it may seem his words were lost on her, and I was left to writhe in her stead, feeling like a child that had been smacked.

'Is that really so?' she blundered. 'I'd no idea. My history is very shaky and the kings of England always muddled me. How interesting, though. I must write and tell my daughter; she's a great scholar.'

There was a pause, and I felt the colour flood into my face. I was too young, that was the trouble. Had I been older I would have caught his eye and smiled, her unbelievable behaviour

16

making a bond between us; but as it was I was stricken into shame, and endured one of the frequent agonies of youth.

I think he realized my distress, for he leant forward in his chair and spoke to me, his voice gentle, asking if I would have more coffee, and when I refused and shook my head I felt his eyes were still on me, puzzled, reflective. He was pondering my exact relationship to her, and wondering whether he must bracket us together in futility.

'What do you think of Monte Carlo, or don't you think of it at all?' he said. This including of me in the conversation found me at my worst, the raw ex-schoolgirl, red-elbowed and lanky-haired, and I said something obvious and idiotic about the place being artificial, but before I could finish my halting sentence Mrs Van Hopper interrupted.

'She's spoilt, Mr de Winter, that's her trouble. Most girls would give their eyes for the chance of seeing Monte.'

'Wouldn't that rather defeat the purpose?' he said, smiling.

She shrugged her shoulders, blowing a great cloud of ciga-rette smoke into the air. I don't think she understood him for a moment. 'I'm faithful to Monte,' she told him; 'the English winter gets me down, and my constitution just won't stand it. What brings you here? You're not one of the regulars. Are you going to play "Chemy", or have you brought your golfclubs?'

'I have not made up my mind,' he said; 'I came away in rather a hurry.'

His own words must have jolted a memory, for his face clouded again and he frowned very slightly. She babbled on, impervious. 'Of course you miss the fogs at Manderley; it's quite another matter; the west country must be delightful in the spring.' He reached for the ash-tray, squashing his cigarette, and I noticed the subtle change in his eyes, the indefinable something that lingered there, momentarily, and I felt I had looked upon some-thing personal to himself with which I had no concern.

'Yes,' he said shortly, 'Manderley was looking its best.'

A silence fell upon us during a moment or two, a silence that brought something of discomfort in its train, and stealing a glance

17

at him I was reminded more than ever of my Gentleman Unknown who, cloaked and secret, walked a corridor by night. Mrs Van Hopper's voice pierced my dream like an electric bell.

'I suppose you know a crowd of people here, though I must say Monte is very dull this winter. One sees so few well-known faces. The Duke of Middlesex is here in his yacht, but I haven't been aboard yet.' She never had, to my knowledge. 'You know Nell Middlesex of course,' she went on. 'What a charmer she is. They always say that second child isn't his, but I don't believe it. People will say anything, won't they, when a woman is attractive? And she is so very lovely. Tell me, is it true the Caxton-Hyslop marriage is not a success?' She ran on, through a tangled fringe of gossip, never seeing that these names were alien to him, they meant nothing, and that as she prattled unaware he grew colder and more silent. Never for a moment did he interrupt or glance at his watch; it was as though he had set himself a standard of behaviour, since the original lapse when he had made a fool of her in front of me, and clung to it grimly rather than offend again. It was a page-boy in the end who released him, with the news that a dress-maker awaited Mrs Van Hopper in the suite.

He got up at once, pushing back his chair. 'Don't let me keep you,' he said. 'Fashions change so quickly nowadays they may even have altered by the time you get upstairs.'

The sting did not touch her, she accepted it as a pleasantry. 'It's so delightful to have run into you like this, Mr de Winter,' she said, as we went towards the lift; 'now I've been brave enough to break the ice I hope I shall see something of you. You must come and have a drink some time in the suite. I may have one or two people coming in tomorrow evening. Why not join us?' I turned away so that I should not watch him search for an excuse.

'I'm so sorry,' he said, 'tomorrow I am probably driving to Sospel, I'm not sure when I shall get back.'

Reluctantly she left it, but we still hovered at the entrance to the lift.

'I hope they've given you a good room; the place is half empty, so if you are uncomfortable mind you make a fuss. Your valet has unpacked for you, I suppose?' This familiarity was excessive, even for her, and I caught a glimpse of his expression.

'I don't possess one,' he said quietly; 'perhaps you would like to do it for me?'

This time his shaft had found its mark, for she reddened, and laughed a little awkwardly.

'Why, I hardly think . . .' she began, and then suddenly, and unbelievably, she turned upon me, 'Perhaps you could make yourself useful to Mr de Winter, if he wants anything done. You're a capable child in many ways.'

There was a momentary pause, while I stood stricken, waiting for his answer. He looked down at us, mocking, faintly sardonic, a ghost of a smile on his lips.

'A charming suggestion,' he said, 'but I cling to the family motto. He travels the fastest who travels alone. Perhaps you have not heard of it.'

And without waiting for her answer he turned and left us.

'What a funny thing,' said Mrs Van Hopper, as we went upstairs in the lift. 'Do you suppose that sudden departure was a form of humour? Men do such extraordinary things. I remember a well-known writer once who used to dart down the Service staircase whenever he saw me coming. I suppose he had a penchant for me and wasn't sure of himself. However, I was younger then.'

The lift stopped with a jerk. We arrived at our floor. The page-boy flung open the gates. 'By the way, dear,' she said, as we walked along the corridor, 'don't think I mean to be unkind, but you put yourself just a teeny bit forward this afternoon. Your efforts to monopolize the conversation quite embarrassed me, and I'm sure it did him. Men loathe that sort of thing.'

I said nothing. There seemed no possible reply. 'Oh, come, don't sulk,' she laughed, and shrugged her shoulders; 'after all, I am responsible for your behaviour here, and surely you can accept advice from a woman old enough to be your mother. *Eh bien,*

Blaize, je viens . . .' and humming a tune she went into the bedroom where the dressmaker was waiting for her.

I knelt on the window-seat and looked out upon the afternoon. The sun shone very brightly still, and there was a gay high wind. In half an hour we should be sitting to our bridge, the windows tightly closed, the central heating turned to the full. I thought of the ash-trays I would have to clear, and how the squashed stubs, stained with lip-stick, would sprawl in company with discarded chocolate creams. Bridge does not come easily to a mind brought up on Snap and Happy Families; besides, it bored her friends to play with me.

I felt my youthful presence put a curb upon their conversation, much as a parlour-maid does until the arrival of dessert, and they could not fling themselves so easily into the melting pot of scandal and insinuation. Her men-friends would assume a sort of forced heartiness and ask me jocular questions about history or painting, guessing I had not long left school and that this would be my only form of conversation.

I sighed, and turned away from the window. The sun was so full of promise, and the sea was whipped white with a merry wind. I thought of that corner of Monaco which I had passed a day or two ago, and where a crooked house leant to a cobbled square. High up in the tumbled roof there was a window, narrow as a slit. It might have held a presence medieval; and, reaching to the desk for pencil and paper, I sketched in fancy with an absent mind a profile, pale and aquiline. A sombre eye, a high-bridged nose, a scornful upper lip. And I added a pointed beard and lace at the throat, as the painter had done, long ago in a different time.

Someone knocked at the door, and the lift-boy came in with a note in his hand. 'Madame is in the bedroom,' I told him but he shook his head and said it was for me. I opened it, and found a single sheet of note-paper inside, with a few words written in an unfamiliar hand.

'Forgive me. I was very rude this afternoon.' That was all. No signature, and no beginning. But my name was on the envelope, and spelt correctly, an unusual thing.

20

'Is there an answer?' asked the boy.

I looked up from the scrawled words. 'No,' I said. 'No, there isn't any answer.'

When he had gone I put the note away in my pocket, and turned once more to my pencil drawing, but for no known reason it did not please me any more; the face was stiff and life-less, and the lace collar and the beard were like props in a charade.

4

The morning after the bridge party Mrs Van Hopper woke with a sore throat and a temperature of a hundred and two. I rang up her doctor, who came round at once and diagnosed the usual influenza. 'You are to stay in bed until I allow you to get up,' he told her; 'I don't like the sound of that heart of yours, and it won't get better unless you keep perfectly quiet and still. I should prefer', he went on, turning to me, 'that Mrs Van Hopper had a trained nurse. You can't possibly lift her. It will only be for a fortnight or so.'

I thought this rather absurd, and protested, but to my surprise she agreed with him. I think she enjoyed the fuss it would create, the sympathy of people, the visits and messages from friends, and the arrival of flowers. Monte Carlo had begun to bore her, and this little illness would make a distraction.

The nurse would give her injections, and a light massage, and she would have a diet. I left her quite happy after the arrival of the nurse, propped up on pillows with a falling temperature, her best bed-jacket round her shoulders and be-ribboned boudoir cap upon her head. Rather ashamed of my light heart, I telephoned her friends, putting off the small party she had arranged for the evening, and went down to the restaurant for lunch, a good half hour before our usual time. I expected the room to be empty – nobody lunched generally before one o'clock. It was empty, except for the table next to ours. This was a contingency for which I was unprepared. I thought he had gone to Sospel. No doubt he was lunching early because he hoped to avoid us at one o'clock. I was already half-way across the room and could not go back. I had not seen him since we disappeared in the lift the day before, for wisely he had avoided dinner in the restaurant, possibly for the same reason that he lunched early now.

It was a situation for which I was ill-trained. I wished I was older, different. I went to our table, looking straight before me, and immediately paid the penalty of gaucherie by knocking over the vase of stiff anemones as I unfolded my napkin. The water soaked the cloth, and ran down on to my lap. The waiter was at the other end of the room, nor had he seen. In a second though my neighbour was by my side, dry napkin in hand.

'You can't sit at a wet tablecloth,' he said brusquely; 'it will put you off your food. Get out of the way.'

He began to mop the cloth, while the waiter, seeing the disturbance, came swiftly to the rescue.

'I don't mind,' I said, 'it doesn't matter a bit. I'm all alone.'

He said nothing, and then the waiter arrived and whipped away the vase and the sprawling flowers.

'Leave that,' he said suddenly, 'and lay another place at my table. Mademoiselle will have luncheon with me.'

I looked up in confusion. 'Oh, no,' I said, 'I couldn't possibly.'

'Why not?' he said.

I tried to think of an excuse. I knew he did not want to lunch with me. It was his form of courtesy. I should ruin his meal. I determined to be bold and speak the truth.

'Please,' I begged, 'don't be polite. It's very kind of you but I shall be quite all right if the waiter just wipes the cloth.'

'But I'm not being polite,' he insisted. 'I would like you to have luncheon with me. Even if you had not knocked over that vase so clumsily I should have asked you.' I suppose my face told him my doubt, for he smiled. 'You don't believe me,' he said; 'never mind, come and sit down. We needn't talk to each other unless we feel like it.'

We sat down, and he gave me the menu, leaving me to choose, and went on with his *hors d'œuvre* as though nothing had happened.

His quality of detachment was peculiar to himself, and I knew that we might continue thus, without speaking, throughout the meal and it would not matter. There would be no sense of strain. He would not ask me questions on history.

'What's happened to your friend?' he said. I told him about the influenza. 'I'm so sorry,' he said, and then, after pausing a moment, 'you got my note, I suppose. I felt very much ashamed of myself. My manners were atrocious. The only excuse I can make is that I've become boorish through living alone. That's why it's so kind of you to lunch with me today.'

'You weren't rude,' I said, 'at least, not the sort of rudeness she would understand. That curiosity of hers – she does not mean to be offensive, but she does it to everyone. That is, everyone of importance.'

'I ought to be flattered then,' he said; 'why should she consider me of any importance?'

I hesitated a moment before replying.

'I think because of Manderley,' I said.

He did not answer, and I was aware again of that feeling of discomfort, as though I had trespassed on forbidden ground. I wondered why it was that this home of his, known to so many people by hearsay, even to me, should so inevitably silence him, making as it were a barrier between him and others.

We ate for a while without talking, and I thought of a picture postcard I had bought once at a village shop, when on holiday as a child in the west country. It was the painting of a house, crudely done of course and highly coloured, but even those faults could not destroy the symmetry of the building, the wide stone steps before the terrace, the green lawns stretching to the sea. I paid twopence for the painting – half my weekly pocket money – and then asked the wrinkled shop woman what it was meant to be. She looked astonished at my ignorance.

'That's Manderley,' she said, and I remember coming out of the shop feeling rebuffed, yet hardly wiser than before.

Perhaps it was the memory of this postcard, lost long ago in some forgotten book, that made me sympathize with his defensive attitude. He resented Mrs Van Hopper and her like with their intruding questions. Maybe there was something inviolate about Manderley that made it a place apart; it would not bear discussion. I could imagine her tramping through the rooms, perhaps paying sixpence for admission, ripping the quietude with her sharp, staccato laugh. Our minds must have run in the same channel, for he began to talk about her.

'Your friend,' he began, 'she is very much older than you. Is she a relation? Have you known her long?' I saw he was still puzzled by us.

'She's not really a friend,' I told him, 'she's an employer. She's training me to be a thing called a companion, and she pays me ninety pounds a year.'

'I did not know one could buy companionship,' he said; 'it sounds a primitive idea. Rather like the Eastern slave market.'

'I looked up the word "companion" once in the dictionary,' I admitted, 'and it said "a companion is a friend of the bosom."'

'You haven't much in common with her,' he said.

He laughed, looking quite different, younger somehow and less detached. 'What do you do it for?' he asked me.

'Ninety pounds is a lot of money to me,' I said.

'Haven't you any family?'

'No – they're dead.'

'You have a very lovely and unusual name.'

'My father was a lovely and unusual person.'

'Tell me about him,' he said.

I looked at him over my glass of citronade. It was not easy to explain my father and usually I never talked about him. He was my secret property. Preserved for me alone, much as Manderley was preserved for my neighbour. I had no wish to introduce him casually over a table in a Monte Carlo restaurant.

There was a strange air of unreality about that luncheon, and looking back upon it now it is invested for me with a curious glamour. There was I, so much of a schoolgirl still, who only the day before had sat with Mrs Van Hopper, prim, silent, and subdued, and twenty-four hours afterwards my family history was mine no longer, I shared it with a man I did not know. For some reason I felt impelled to speak, because his eyes followed me in sympathy like the Gentleman Unknown.

My shyness fell away from me, loosening as it did so my reluctant tongue, and out they all came, the little secrets of childhood, the pleasures and the pains. It seemed to me as though he understood, from my poor description, something of the vibrant personality that had been my father's, and something too of the love my mother had for him, making it a vital, living force, with a spark of divinity about it, so much that when he died that desperate winter, struck down by pneumonia, she lingered behind him for five short weeks and stayed no more. I remember pausing, a little breathless, a little dazed. The restaurant was filled now with people who chatted and laughed to an orchestral background and a clatter of plates, and glancing at the clock above the door I saw that it was two o'clock. We had been sitting there an hour and a half, and the conversation had been mine alone.

I tumbled down into reality, hot-handed and self-conscious, with my face aflame, and began to stammer my apologies. He would not listen to me.

'I told you at the beginning of lunch you had a lovely and unusual name,' he said. 'I shall go further, if you will forgive me, and say that it becomes you as well as it became your father. I've enjoyed this hour with you more than I have enjoyed anything for a very long time. You've taken me out of myself, out of despondency and introspection, both of which have been my devils for a year.'

I looked at him, and believed he spoke the truth; he seemed less fettered than he had been before, more modern, more human; he was not hemmed in by shadows.

'You know,' he said, 'we've got a bond in common, you and I. We are both alone in the world. Oh, I've got a sister, though we don't see much of each other, and an ancient grandmother whom I pay duty visits to three times a year, but neither of them make for companionship. I shall have to congratulate Mrs Van Hopper. You're cheap at ninety pounds a year.'

'You forget', I said, 'you have a home and I have none.'

26

The moment I spoke I regretted my words, for the secret, inscrutable look came back in his eyes again, and once again I suffered the intolerable discomfort that floods one after lack of tact. He bent his head to light a cigarette, and did not reply immediately.

'An empty house can be as lonely as a full hotel,' he said at length. 'The trouble is that it is less impersonal.' He hesitated, and for a moment I thought he was going to talk of Manderley at last, but something held him back, some phobia that struggled to the surface of his mind and won supremacy, for he blew out his match and his flash of confidence at the same time.

'So the friend of the bosom has a holiday?' he said, on a level plane again, an easy camaraderie between us. 'What does she propose to do with it?'

I thought of the cobbled square in Monaco and the house with the narrow window. I could be off there by three o'clock with my sketchbook and pencil, and I told him as much, a little shyly perhaps, like all untalented persons with a pet hobby.

'I'll drive you there in the car,' he said, and would not listen to protests.

I remembered Mrs Van Hopper's warning of the night before about putting myself forward and was embarrassed that he might think my talk of Monaco was a subterfuge to win a lift. It was so blatantly the type of thing that she would do herself, and I did not want him to bracket us together. I had already risen in importance from my lunch with him, for as we got up from the table the little *maître d'hôtel* rushed forward to pull away my chair. He bowed and smiled – a total change from his usual attitude of indifference – picked up my handkerchief that had fallen on the floor, and hoped 'mademoiselle had enjoyed her lunch'. Even the page-boy by the swing doors glanced at me with respect. My companion accepted it as natural, of course; he knew nothing of the ill-carved ham of yesterday. I found the change depressing, it made me despise myself. I remembered my father and his scorn of superficial snobbery.

'What are you thinking about?' We were walking along the

corridor to the lounge, and looking up I saw his eyes fixed on me in curiosity.

'Has something annoyed you?' he said.

The attentions of the *maître d'hôtel* had opened up a train of thought, and as we drank coffee I told him about Blaize, the dressmaker. She had been so pleased when Mrs Van Hopper had bought three frocks, and I, taking her to the lift afterwards, had pictured her working upon them in her own small salon, behind the stuffy little shop, with a consumptive son wasting upon her sofa. I could see her, with tired eyes, threading needles, and the floor covered with snippets of material.

'Well?' he said smiling, 'wasn't your picture true?'

'I don't know,' I said, 'I never found out.' And I told him how I had rung the bell for the lift, and as I had done so she had fumbled in her bag and gave me a note for a hundred francs. 'Here,' she had whispered, her tone intimate and unpleasant, 'I want you to accept this small commission in return for bringing your patron to my shop.' When I had refused, scarlet with embarrassment, she had shrugged her shoulders disagreeably. 'Just as you like,' she had said, 'but I assure you it's quite usual. Perhaps you would rather have a frock. Come along to the shop some time without Madame and I will fix you up without charging you a sou.' Somehow, I don't know why, I had been aware of that sick, unhealthy feeling I had experienced as a child when turning the pages of a forbidden book. The vision of the consumptive son faded, and in its stead arose the picture of myself had I been different, pocketing that greasy note with an understanding smile, and perhaps slipping round to Blaize's shop on this my free afternoon and coming away with a frock I had not paid for.

I expected him to laugh, it was a stupid story, I don't know why I told him, but he looked at me thoughtfully as he stirred his coffee.

'I think you've made a big mistake,' he said, after a moment.

'In refusing that hundred francs?' I asked, revolted.

'No – good heavens, what do you take me for? I think you've

made a mistake in coming here, in joining forces with Mrs Van Hopper. You are not made for that sort of job. You're too young, for one thing, and too soft. Blaize and her commission, that's nothing. The first of many similar incidents from other Blaizes. You will either have to give in, and become a sort of Blaize yourself, or stay as you are and be broken. Who suggested you took on this thing in the first place?' It seemed natural for him to question me, nor did I mind. It was as though we had known one another for a long time, and had met again after a lapse of years.

'Have you ever thought about the future?' he asked me, 'and what this sort of thing will lead to? Supposing Mrs Van Hopper gets tired of her "friend of the bosom", what then?'

I smiled, and told him that I did not mind very much. There would be other Mrs Van Hoppers, and I was young, and confident, and strong. But even as he spoke I remembered those advertisements seen often in good class magazines where a friendly society demands succour for young women in reduced circumstances; I thought of the type of boarding-house that answers the advertisement and gives temporary shelter, and then I saw myself, useless sketch-book in hand, without qualifications of any kind, stammering replies to stern employment agents. Perhaps I should have accepted Blaize's ten per cent.

'How old are you?' he said, and when I told him he laughed, and got up from his chair. 'I know that age, it's a particularly obstinate one, and a thousand bogies won't make you fear the future. A pity we can't change over. Go upstairs and put your hat on, and I'll have the car brought round.'

As he watched me into the lift I thought of yesterday, Mrs Van Hopper's chattering tongue, and his cold courtesy. I had ill-judged him, he was neither hard nor sardonic, he was already my friend of many years, the brother I had never possessed. Mine was a happy mood that afternoon, and I remember it well. I can see the rippled sky, fluffy with cloud, and the white whipped sea. I can feel again the wind on my face, and hear my laugh, and his that echoed it. It was not the Monte Carlo I had known,

or perhaps the truth was that it pleased me better. There was a glamour about it that had not been before. I must have looked upon it before with dull eyes. The harbour was a dancing thing, with fluttering paper boats, and the sailors on the quay were jovial, smiling fellows, merry as the wind. We passed the yacht, beloved of Mrs Van Hopper because of its ducal owner, and snapped our fingers at the glistening brass, and looked at one another and laughed again. I can remember as though I wore it still my comfortable, ill-fitting flannel suit, and how the skirt was lighter than the coat through harder wear. My shabby hat, too broad about the brim, and my low-heeled shoes, fastened with a single strap. A pair of gauntlet gloves clutched in a grubby hand. I had never looked more youthful, I had never felt so old. Mrs Van Hopper and her influenza did not exist for me. The bridge and the cocktail parties were forgotten, and with them my own humble status.

I was a person of importance, I was grown up at last. That girl who, tortured by shyness, would stand outside the sitting-room door twisting a handkerchief in her hands, while from within came that babble of confused chatter so unnerving to the intruder – she had gone with the wind that afternoon. She was a poor creature, and I thought of her with scorn if I considered her at all.

The wind was too high for sketching, it tore in cheerful gusts around the corner of my cobbled square, and back to the car we went and drove I know not where. The long road climbed the hills, and the car climbed with it, and we circled in the heights like a bird in the air. How different his car to Mrs Van Hopper's hireling for the season, a square old-fashioned Daimler that took us to Mentone on placid afternoons, when I, sitting on the little seat with my back to the driver, must crane my neck to see the view. This car had the wings of Mercury, I thought, for higher yet we climbed, and dangerously fast, and the danger pleased me because it was new to me, because I was young.

I remember laughing aloud, and the laugh being carried by

the wind away from me; and looking at him, I realized he laughed no longer, he was once more silent and detached, the man of yesterday wrapped in his secret self.

I realized, too, that the car could climb no more, we had reached the summit, and below us stretched the way that we had come, precipitous and hollow. He stopped the car, and I could see that the edge of the road bordered a vertical slope that crumbled into vacancy, a fall of perhaps two thousand feet. We got out of the car and looked beneath us. This sobered me at last. I knew that but half the car's length had lain between us and the fall. The sea, like a crinkled chart, spread to the horizon, and lapped the sharp outline of the coast, while the houses were white shells in a rounded grotto, pricked here and there by a great orange sun. We knew another sunlight on our hill, and the silence made it harder, more austere. A change had come upon our afternoon; it was not the thing of gossamer it had been. The wind dropped, and it suddenly grew cold.

When I spoke my voice was far too casual, the silly, nervous voice of someone ill at ease. 'Do you know this place?' I said. 'Have you been here before?' He looked down at me without recognition, and I realized with a little stab of anxiety that he must have forgotten all about me, perhaps for some considerable time, and that he himself was so lost in the labyrinth of his own unquiet thoughts that I did not exist. He had the face of one who walks in his sleep, and for a wild moment the idea came to me that perhaps he was not normal, not altogether sane. There were people who had trances, I had surely heard of them, and they followed strange laws of which we could know nothing, they obeyed the tangled orders of their own subconscious minds. Perhaps he was one of them, and here we were within six feet of death.

'It's getting late, shall we go home?' I said, and my careless tone, my little ineffectual smile would scarcely have deceived a child.

I had misjudged him, of course, there was nothing wrong after all, for as soon as I spoke this second time he came clear

31

of his dream and began to apologize. I had gone white, I suppose, and he had noticed it.

'That was an unforgivable thing for me to do,' he said, and taking my arm he pushed me back towards the car, and we climbed in again, and he slammed the door. 'Don't be frightened, the turn is far easier than it looks,' he said, and while I, sick and giddy, clung to the seat with both hands, he manoeuvred the car gently, very gently, until it faced the sloping road once more.

'Then you have been here before?' I said to him, my sense of strain departing, as the car crept away down the twisting narrow road.

'Yes,' he said, and then, after pausing a moment, 'but not for many years. I wanted to see if it had changed.'

'And has it?' I asked him.

'No,' he said. 'No, it has not changed.'

I wondered what had driven him to this retreat into the past, with me an unconscious witness of his mood. What gulf of years stretched between him and that other time, what deed of thought and action, what difference in temperament? I did not want to know. I wished I had not come.

Down the twisting road we went without a check, without a word, a great ridge of cloud stretched above the setting sun, and the air was cold and clean. Suddenly he began to talk about Manderley. He said nothing of his life there, no word about himself, but he told me how the sun set there, on a spring afternoon, leaving a glow upon the headland. The sea would look like slate, cold still from the long winter, and from the terrace you could hear the ripple of the coming tide washing in the little bay. The daffodils were in bloom, stirring in the evening breeze, golden heads cupped upon lean stalks, and however many you might pick there would be no thinning of the ranks, they were massed like an army, shoulder to shoulder. On a bank below the lawns, crocuses were planted, golden, pink, and mauve, but by this time they would be past their best, dropping and fading, like pallid snowdrops. The primrose was more vulgar, a homely pleasant creature who appeared in every cranny like a weed. Too early yet for bluebells, their heads were still hidden beneath last year's leaves, but when they came, dwarfing the more humble violet, they choked the very bracken in the woods, and with their colour made a challenge to the sky.

He never would have them in the house, he said. Thrust into vases they became dank and listless, and to see them at their best you must walk in the woods in the morning, about twelve o'clock, when the sun was overhead. They had a smoky, rather bitter smell, as though a wild sap ran in their stalks, pungent and juicy. People who plucked bluebells from the woods were vandals; he had forbidden it at Manderley. Sometimes, driving in the country, he had seen bicyclists with huge bunches strapped before them on the handles, the bloom already fading from the dying heads, the ravaged stalks straggling naked and unclean.

The primrose did not mind it quite so much; although a creature of the wilds it had a leaning towards civilization, and preened and smiled in a jam-jar in some cottage window without resentment, living quite a week if given water. No wild flowers came in the house at Manderley. He had special cultivated flowers, grown for the house alone, in the walled garden. A rose was one of the few flowers, he said, that looked better picked than growing. A bowl of roses in a drawing-room had a depth of colour and scent they had not possessed in the open. There was something rather blowzy about roses in full bloom, something shallow and raucous, like women with untidy hair. In the house they became mysterious and subtle. He had roses in the house at Manderley for eight months in the year. Did I like syringa, he asked me? There was a tree on the edge of the lawn he could smell from his bedroom window. His sister, who was a hard, rather practical person, used to complain that there were too many scents at Manderley, they made her drunk. Perhaps she was right. He did not care. It was the only form of intoxication that appealed to him. His earliest recollection was of great branches of lilac, standing in white jars, and they filled the house with a wistful, poignant smell.

The little pathway down the valley to the bay had clumps of azalea and rhododendron planted to the left of it, and if you wandered down it on a May evening after dinner it was just as though the shrubs had sweated in the air. You could stoop down and pick a fallen petal, crush it between your fingers, and you had there, in the hollow of your hand, the essence of a thousand scents, unbearable and sweet. All from a curled and crumpled petal. And you came out of the valley, heady and rather dazed, to the hard white shingle of the beach and the still water. A curious, perhaps too sudden contrast . . .

As he spoke the car became one of many once again, dusk had fallen without my noticing it, and we were in the midst of light and sound in the streets of Monte Carlo. The clatter jagged on my nerves, and the lights were far too brilliant, far too yellow. It was a swift, unwelcome anticlimax.

Soon we would come to the hotel, and I felt for my gloves in the pocket of the car. I found them, and my fingers closed upon a book as well, whose slim covers told of poetry. I peered to read the title as the car slowed down before the door of the hotel. 'You can take it and read it if you like,' he said, his voice casual and indifferent now that the drive was over, and we were back again, and Manderley was many hundreds of miles distant.

I was glad, and held it tightly with my gloves. I felt I wanted some possession of his, now that the day was finished.

'Hop out,' he said. 'I must go and put the car away. I shan't see you in the restaurant this evening as I'm dining out. But thank you for today.'

I went up the hotel steps alone, with all the despondency of a child whose treat is over. My afternoon had spoilt me for the hours that still remained, and I thought how long they would seem until my bed-time, how empty too my supper all alone. Somehow I could not face the bright inquiries of the nurse upstairs, or the possibilities of Mrs Van Hopper's husky interrogation, so I sat down in the corner of the lounge behind a pillar and ordered tea.

The waiter appeared bored; seeing me alone there was no

need for him to press, and anyway it was that dragging time of day, a few minutes after half past five, when the normal tea is finished and the hour for drinks remote.

Rather forlorn, more than a little dissatisfied, I leant back in my chair and took up the book of poems. The volume was well worn, well thumbed, falling open automatically at what must be a much-frequented page.

> I fled Him, down the nights and down the days;
> I fled Him, down the arches of the years;
> I fled Him, down the labyrinthine ways
> Of my own mind; and in the midst of tears
> I hid from Him, and under running laughter.
> Up vistaed slopes I sped
> And shot, precipited
> Adown Titanic glooms of chasmed fears,
> From those strong feet that followed, followed after.

I felt rather like someone peering through the keyhole of a locked door, and a little furtively I laid the book aside. What hound of heaven had driven him to the high hills this afternoon? I thought of his car, with half a length between it and that drop of two thousand feet, and the blank expression on his face. What footsteps echoed in his mind, what whispers, and what memories, and why, of all poems, must he keep this one in the pocket of his car? I wished he were less remote; and I anything but the creature that I was in my shabby coat and skirt, my broad-brimmed school-girl hat.

The sulky waiter brought my tea, and while I ate bread-and-butter dull as sawdust I thought of the pathway through the valley he had described to me this afternoon, the smell of the azaleas, and the white shingle of the bay. If he loved it all so much why did he seek the superficial froth of Monte Carlo? He had told Mrs Van Hopper he had made no plans, he came away in rather a hurry. And I pictured him running down that pathway in the valley with his own hound of heaven at his heels.

I picked up the book again, and this time it opened at the title-page, and I read the dedication. 'Max – from Rebecca. 17 May', written in a curious slanting hand. A little blob of ink marred the white page opposite, as though the writer, in impatience, had shaken her pen to make the ink flow freely. And then as it bubbled through the nib, it came a little thick, so that the name Rebecca stood out black and strong, the tall and sloping R dwarfing the other letters.

I shut the book with a snap, and put it away under my gloves; and stretching to a nearby chair, I took up an old copy of *L'Illustration* and turned the pages. There were some fine photographs of the chateaux of the Loire, and an article as well. I read it carefully, referring to the photographs, but when I finished I knew I had not understood a word. It was not Blois with its thin turrets and its spires that stared up at me from the printed page. It was the face of Mrs Van Hopper in the restaurant the day before, her small pig's eyes darting to the neighbouring table, her fork, heaped high with ravioli, pausing in mid-air.

'An appalling tragedy,' she was saying, 'the papers were full of it of course. They say he never talks about it, never mentions her name. She was drowned you know, in the bay near Manderley . . .'

5

I am glad it cannot happen twice, the fever of first love. For it is a fever, and a burden, too, whatever the poets may say. They are not brave, the days when we are twenty-one. They are full of little cowardices, little fears without foundation, and one is so easily bruised, so swiftly wounded, one falls to the first barbed word. Today, wrapped in the complacent armour of approaching middle age, the infinitesimal pricks of day by day brush one lightly and are soon forgotten, but then – how a careless word would linger, becoming a fiery stigma, and how a look, a glance over a shoulder, branded themselves as things eternal. A denial heralded the thrice crowing of a cock, and an insincerity was like the kiss of Judas. The adult mind can lie with untroubled conscience and a gay composure, but in those days even a small deception scoured the tongue, lashing one against the stake itself.

'What have you been doing this morning?' I can hear her now, propped against her pillows, with all the small irritability of the patient who is not really ill, who has lain in bed too long, and I, reaching to the bedside drawer for the pack of cards, would feel the guilty flush form patches on my neck.

'I've been playing tennis with the professional,' I told her, the false words bringing me to panic, even as I spoke, for what if the professional himself should come up to the suite, then, that very afternoon, and bursting in upon her complain that I had missed my lesson now for many days?

'The trouble is with me laid up like this you haven't got enough to do,' she said, mashing her cigarette in a jar of cleansing cream, and taking the cards in her hand she mixed them in the deft, irritating shuffle of the inveterate player, shaking them in threes, snapping the backs.

'I don't know what you find to do with yourself all day,' she went on; 'you never have any sketches to show me, and when I do ask you to do some shopping for me you forget to buy my Taxol. All I can say is that I hope your tennis will improve; it will be useful to you later on. A poor player is a great bore. Do you still serve underhand?' She flipped the Queen of Spades into the pool, and the dark face stared up at me like Jezebel.

'Yes,' I said, stung by her question, thinking how just and appropriate her word. It described me well. I was underhand. I had not played tennis with the professional at all. I had not once played since she had lain in bed, and that was a little over a fort-night now. I wondered why it was I clung to this reserve, and why it was I did not tell her that every morning I drove with de Winter in his car, and lunched with him, too, at his table in the restaurant.

'You must come up to the net more; you will never play a good game until you do,' she continued, and I agreed, flinching at my own hypocrisy, covering the Queen with the weak-chinned Knave of Hearts.

I have forgotten much of Monte Carlo, of those morning drives, of where we went, even our conversation; but I have not forgotten how my fingers trembled, cramming on my hat, and how I ran along the corridor and down the stairs, too impatient to wait for the slow whining of the lift, and so outside, brushing the swing doors before the commissionaire could help me.

He would be there, in the driver's seat, reading a paper while he waited, and when he saw me he would smile, and toss it behind him in the back seat, and open the door, saying, 'Well, how is the friend-of-the-bosom this morning, and where does she want to go?' If he had driven round in circles it would not have mattered to me, for I was in that first flushed stage when to climb into the seat beside him, and lean forward to the wind-screen hugging my knees, was almost too much to bear. I was like a little scrubby schoolboy with a passion for a sixth-form prefect, and he kinder, and far more inaccessible.

'There's a cold wind this morning, you had better put on my coat.'

I remember that, for I was young enough to win happiness in the wearing of his clothes, playing the schoolboy again who carries his hero's sweater and ties it about his throat choking with pride, and this borrowing of his coat, wearing it around my shoulders for even a few minutes at a time, was a triumph in itself, and made a glow about my morning.

Not for me the languor and the subtlety I had read about in books. The challenge and the chase. The sword-play, the swift glance, the stimulating smile. The art of provocation was unknown to me, and I would sit with his map upon my lap, the wind blowing my dull, lanky hair, happy in his silence yet eager for his words. Whether he talked or not made little difference to my mood. My only enemy was the clock on the dashboard, whose hands would move relentlessly to one o'clock. We drove east, we drove west, amidst the myriad villages that cling like limpets to the Mediterranean shore, and today I remember none of them.

All I remember is the feel of the leather seats, the texture of the map upon my knee, its frayed edges, its worn seams, and how one day, looking at the clock, I thought to myself, 'This moment now, at twenty past eleven, this must never be lost,' and I shut my eyes to make the experience more lasting. When I opened my eyes we were by a bend in the road, and a peasant girl in a black shawl waved to us; I can see her now, her dusty skirt, her gleaming, friendly smile, and in a second we had passed the bend and could see her no more. Already she belonged to the past, she was only a memory.

I wanted to go back again, to recapture the moment that had gone, and then it came to me that if we did it would not be the same, even the sun would be changed in the sky, casting another shadow, and the peasant girl would trudge past us along the road in a different way, not waving this time, perhaps not even seeing us. There was something chilling in the thought, something a little melancholy, and looking at the clock I saw that five more minutes had gone by. Soon we would have reached our time limit, and must return to the hotel.

'If only there could be an invention', I said impulsively, 'that bottled up a memory, like scent. And it never faded, and it never got stale. And then, when one wanted it, the bottle could be uncorked, and it would be like living the moment all over again.' I looked up at him, to see what he would say. He did not turn to me, he went on watching the road ahead.

'What particular moments in your young life do you wish uncorked?' he said. I could not tell from his voice whether he was teasing me or not. 'I'm not sure,' I began, and then blundered on, rather foolishly, not thinking of my words, 'I'd like to keep this moment and never forget it.'

'Is that meant to be a compliment to the day, or to my driving?' he said, and as he laughed, like a mocking brother, I became silent, overwhelmed suddenly by the great gulf between us, and how his very kindness to me widened it.

I knew then that I would never tell Mrs Van Hopper about these morning expeditions, for her smile would hurt me as his laugh had done. She would not be angry, nor would she be shocked; she would raise her eyebrows very faintly as though she did not altogether believe my story, and then with a tolerant shrug of the shoulder she would say, 'My dear child, it's extremely sweet and kind of him to take you driving; the only thing is – are you sure it does not bore him dreadfully?' And then she would send me out to buy Taxol, patting me on the shoulder. What degradation lay in being young, I thought, and fell to tearing my nails.

'I wish,' I said savagely, still mindful of his laugh and throwing discretion to the wind, 'I wish I was a woman of about thirty-six dressed in black satin with a string of pearls.'

'You would not be in this car with me if you were,' he said; 'and stop biting those nails, they are ugly enough already.'

'You'll think me impertinent and rude I dare say,' I went on, 'but I would like to know why you ask me to come out in the car, day after day. You are being kind, that's obvious, but why do you choose me for your charity?'

I sat up stiff and straight in my seat and with all the poor pomposity of youth.

'I ask you,' he said gravely, 'because you are not dressed in black satin, with a string of pearls, nor are you thirty-six.' His face was without expression, I could not tell whether he laughed inwardly or not.

'It's all very well,' I said; 'you know everything there is to know about me. There's not much, I admit, because I have not been alive for very long, and nothing much has happened to me, except people dying, but you – I know nothing more about you than I did the first day we met.'

'And what did you know then?' he asked.

'Why, that you lived at Manderley and – and that you had lost your wife.' There, I had said it at last, the word that had hovered on my tongue for days. Your wife. It came out with ease, without reluctance, as though the mere mention of her must be the most casual thing in all the world. Your wife. The word lingered in the air once I had uttered it, dancing before me, and because he received it silently, making no comment, the word magnified itself into something heinous and appalling, a forbidden word, unnatural to the tongue. And I could not call it back, it could never be unsaid. Once again I saw the inscription on the fly-leaf of that book of poems, and the curious slanting R. I felt sick at heart and cold. He would never forgive me, and this would be the end of our friendship.

I remember staring straight in front of me at the windscreen, seeing nothing of the flying road, my ears still tingling with that spoken word. The silence became minutes, and the minutes became miles, and everything is over now, I thought, I shall never drive with him again. Tomorrow he will go away. And Mrs Van Hopper will be up again. She and I will walk along the terrace as we did before. The porter will bring down his trunks, I shall catch a glimpse of them in the luggage lift, with new-plastered labels. The bustle and finality of departure. The sound of the car changing gear as it turned the corner, and then even that sound merging into the common traffic, and being lost, and so absorbed for ever.

I was so deep in my picture, I even saw the porter pocketing his tip and going back through the swing-door of the hotel, saying something over his shoulder to the commissionaire, that I did not notice the slowing-down of the car, and it was only when we stopped, drawing up by the side of the road, that I brought myself back to the present once again. He sat motionless, looking without his hat and with his white scarf round his neck, more than ever like someone medieval who lived within a frame. He did not belong to the bright landscape, he should be standing on the steps of a gaunt cathedral, his cloak flung back, while a beggar at his feet scrambled for gold coins.

The friend had gone, with his kindliness and his easy *camaraderie*, and the brother too, who had mocked me for nibbling at my nails. This man was a stranger. I wondered why I was sitting beside him in the car.

Then he turned to me and spoke. 'A little while ago you talked about an invention,' he said, 'some scheme for capturing a memory. You would like, you told me, at a chosen moment to live the past again. I'm afraid I think rather differently from you. All memories are bitter, and I prefer to ignore them. Something happened a year ago that altered my whole life, and I want to forget every phase in my existence up to that time. Those days are finished. They are blotted out. I must begin living all over again. The first day we met, your Mrs Van Hopper asked me why I came to Monte Carlo. It put a stopper on those memories you would like to resurrect. It does not always work, of course; sometimes the scent is too strong for the bottle, and too strong for me. And then the devil in one, like a furtive peeping Tom, tries to draw the cork. I did that in the first drive we took together. When we climbed the hills and looked down over the precipice. I was there some years ago, with my wife. You asked

42

me if it was still the same, if it had changed at all. It was just the same, but – I was thankful to realize – oddly impersonal. There was no suggestion of the other time. She and I had left no record. It may have been because you were with me. You have blotted out the past for me, you know, far more effectively than all the bright lights of Monte Carlo. But for you I should have left long ago, gone on to Italy, and Greece, and further still perhaps. You have spared me all those wanderings. Damn your puritanical little tight-lipped speech to me. Damn your idea of my kindness and my charity. I ask you to come with me because I want you and your company, and if you don't believe me you can leave the car now and find your own way home. Go on, open the door, and get out.'

I sat still, my hands in my lap, not knowing whether he meant it or not.

'Well,' he said, 'what are you going to do about it?'

Had I been a year or two younger I think I should have cried. Children's tears are very near the surface, and come at the first crisis. As it was I felt them prick behind my eyes, felt the ready colour flood my face, and catching a sudden glimpse of myself in the glass above the windscreen saw in full the sorry spectacle that I made, with troubled eyes and scarlet cheeks, lank hair flopping under broad felt hat.

'I want to go home,' I said, my voice perilously near to trembling, and without a word he started up the engine, let in the clutch, and turned the car round the way that we had come.

Swiftly we covered the ground, far too swiftly, I thought, far too easily, and the callous countryside watched us with indifference. We came to the bend in the road that I had wished to imprison as a memory, and the peasant girl was gone, and the colour was flat, and it was no more after all than any bend in any road passed by a hundred motorists. The glamour of it had gone with my happy mood, and at the thought of it my frozen face quivered into feeling, my adult pride was lost, and those despicable tears rejoicing at their conquest welled into my eyes and strayed upon my cheeks.

I could not check them, for they came unbidden, and had I reached in my pocket for a handkerchief he would have seen I must let them fall untouched, and suffer the bitter salt upon my lips, plumbing the depths of humiliation. Whether he had turned his head to look at me I do not know, for I watched the road ahead with blurred and steady stare, but suddenly he put out his hand and took hold of mine, and kissed it, still saying nothing, and then he threw his handkerchief on my lap, which I was too ashamed to touch.

I thought of all those heroines of fiction who looked pretty when they cried, and what a contrast I must make with blotched and swollen face, and red rims to my eyes. It was a dismal finish to my morning, and the day that stretched ahead of me was long. I had to lunch with Mrs Van Hopper in her room because the nurse was going out, and afterwards she would make me play bezique with all the tireless energy of the convalescent. I knew I should stifle in that room. There was something sordid about the tumbled sheets, the sprawling blankets, and the thumped pillows, and that bedside table dusty with powder, spilt scent, and melting liquid rouge. Her bed would be littered with the separated sheets of the daily papers folded anyhow, while French novels with curling edges and the covers torn kept company with American magazines. The mashed stubs of cigarettes lay everywhere – in cleansing cream, in a dish of grapes, and on the floor beneath the bed. Visitors were lavish with their flowers, and the vases stood cheek-by-jowl in any fashion, hot-house exotics crammed beside mimosa, while a great beribboned casket crowned them all, with tier upon tier of crystallized fruit. Later her friends would come in for a drink, which I must mix for them, hating my task, shy and ill-at-ease in my corner hemmed in by their parrot chatter, and I would be a whipping-boy again, blushing for her when, excited by her little crowd, she must sit up in bed and talk too loudly, laugh too long, reach to the portable gramophone and start a record, shrugging her large shoulders to the tune. I preferred her irritable and snappy, her hair done up in pins,

44

scolding me for forgetting her Taxol. All this awaited me in the suite, while he, once he had left me at the hotel, would go away somewhere alone, towards the sea perhaps, feel the wind on his cheek, follow the sun; and it might happen that he would lose himself in those memories that I knew nothing of, that I could not share, he would wander down the years that were gone.

The gulf that lay between us was wider now than it had ever been, and he stood away from me, with his back turned, on the further shore. I felt young and small and very much alone, and now, in spite of my pride, I found his handkerchief and blew my nose, throwing my drab appearance to the winds. It could never matter.

'To hell with this,' he said suddenly, as though angry, as though bored, and he pulled me beside him, and put his arm round my shoulder, still looking straight ahead of him, his right hand on the wheel. He drove, I remember, even faster than before. 'I suppose you are young enough to be my daughter, and I don't know how to deal with you,' he said. The road narrowed then to a corner, and he had to swerve to avoid a dog. I thought he would release me, but he went on holding me beside him, and when the corner was passed, and the road came straight again he did not let me go. 'You can forget all I said to you this morning,' he said; 'that's all finished and done with. Don't let's ever think of it again. My family always call me Maxim, I'd like you to do the same. You've been formal with me long enough.' He felt for the brim of my hat, and took hold of it, throwing it over his shoulder to the back seat, and then bent down and kissed the top of my head. 'Promise me you will never wear black satin,' he said. I smiled then, and he laughed back at me, and the morning was gay again, the morning was a shining thing. Mrs Van Hopper and the afternoon did not matter a flip of the finger. It would pass so quickly, and there would be tonight, and another day tomorrow. I was cocksure, jubilant; at that moment I almost had the courage to claim equality. I saw myself strolling into Mrs Van Hopper's bedroom rather late for my bezique, and when questioned by her, yawning carelessly, saying, 'I forgot the time. I've been lunching with Maxim.'

I was still child enough to consider a Christian name like a plume in the hat, though from the very first he had called me by mine. The morning, for all its shadowed moments, had promoted me to a new level of friendship, I did not lag so far behind as I had thought. He had kissed me too, a natural business, comforting and quiet. Not dramatic as in books. Not embarrassing. It seemed to bring about an ease in our relationship, it made everything more simple. The gulf between us had been bridged after all. I was to call him Maxim. And that afternoon playing bezique with Mrs Van Hopper was not so tedious as it might have been, though my courage failed me and I said nothing of my morning. For when, gathering her cards together at the end, and reaching for the box, she said casually, 'Tell me, is Max de Winter still in the hotel?' I hesitated a moment, like a diver on the brink, then lost my nerve and my tutored self-possession, saying, 'Yes, I believe so – he comes into the restaurant for his meals.'

Someone has told her, I thought, someone has seen us together, the tennis professional has complained, the manager has sent a note, and I waited for her attack. But she went on putting the cards back into the box, yawning a little, while I straightened the tumbled bed. I gave her the bowl of powder, the rouge compact, and the lip-stick, and she put away the cards and took up the hands glass from the table by her side. 'Attractive creature,' she said, 'but queer-tempered I should think, difficult to know. I thought he might have made some gesture of asking one to Manderley that day in the lounge, but he was very close.'

I said nothing. I watched her pick up the lip-stick and outline a bow upon her hard mouth. 'I never saw her,' she said, holding the glass away to see the effect, 'but I believe she was very lovely. Exquisitely turned out, and brilliant in every way. They used to give tremendous parties at Manderley. It was all very sudden and tragic, and I believe he adored her. I need the darker shade of powder with this brilliant red, my dear: fetch it, will you, and put this box back in the drawer?'

And we were busy then with powder, scent, and rouge, until the bell rang and her visitors came in. I handed them their drinks, dully, saying little; I changed the records on the gramophone, I threw away the stubs of cigarettes.

'Been doing any sketching lately, little lady?' The forced heartiness of an old banker, his monocle dangling on a string, and my bright smile of insincerity: 'No, not very lately; will you have another cigarette?'

It was not I that answered, I was not there at all. I was following a phantom in my mind, whose shadowy form had taken shape at last. Her features were blurred, her colouring indistinct, the setting of her eyes and the texture of her hair was still uncertain, still to be revealed.

She had beauty that endured, and a smile that was not forgotten. Somewhere her voice still lingered, and the memory of her words. There were places she had visited, and things that she had touched. Perhaps in cupboards there were clothes that she had worn, with the scent about them still. In my bedroom, under my pillow, I had a book that she had taken in her hands, and I could see her turning to that first white page, smiling as she wrote, and shaking the bent nib. Max from Rebecca. It must have been his birthday, and she had put it amongst her other presents on the breakfast table. And they had laughed together as he tore off the paper and string. She leant, perhaps, over his shoulder, while he read. Max. She called him Max. It was familiar, gay, and easy on the tongue. The family could call him Maxim if they liked. Grandmothers and aunts. And people like myself, quiet and dull and youthful, who did not matter. Max was her choice, the word was her possession; she had written it with so great a confidence on the fly-leaf of that book. That bold, slanting hand, stabbing the white paper, the symbol of herself, so certain, so assured.

How many times she must have written to him thus, in how many varied moods.

Little notes, scrawled on half-sheets of paper, and letters, when he was away, page after page, intimate, *their* news. Her voice, echoing through the house, and down the garden, careless and familiar like the writing in the book.

And I had to call him Maxim.

6

Packing up. The nagging worry of departure. Lost keys, unwritten labels, tissue paper lying on the floor. I hate it all. Even now, when I have done so much of it, when I live, as the saying goes, in my boxes. Even today, when shutting drawers and flinging wide an hotel wardrobe, or the impersonal shelves of a furnished villa, is a methodical matter of routine, I am aware of sadness, of a sense of loss. Here, I say, we have lived, we have been happy. This has been ours, however brief the time. Though two nights only have been spent beneath a roof, yet we leave something of ourselves behind. Nothing material, not a hair-pin on a dressing-table, not an empty bottle of Aspirin tablets, not a handkerchief beneath a pillow, but something indefinable, a moment of our lives, a thought, a mood.

This house sheltered us, we spoke, we loved within those walls. That was yesterday. Today we pass on, we see it no more, and we are different, changed in some infinitesimal way. We can never be quite the same again. Even stopping for luncheon at a wayside inn, and going to a dark, unfamiliar room to wash my hands, the handle of the door unknown to me, the wallpaper peeling in strips, a funny little cracked mirror above the basin; for this moment, it is mine, it belongs to me. We know one another. This is the present. There is no past and no future. Here I am washing my hands, and the cracked mirror shows me to myself, suspended as it were, in time; this is me, this moment will not pass.

And then I open the door and go to the dining-room, where he is sitting waiting for me at a table, and I think how in that moment I have aged, passed on, how I have advanced one step towards an unknown destiny.

We smile, we choose our lunch, we speak of this and that, but – I say to myself – I am not she who left him five minutes ago. She stayed behind. I am another woman, older, more mature . . .

I saw in a paper the other day that the Hôtel Côte d'Azur at Monte Carlo had gone to new management, and had a different name. The rooms have been redecorated, and the whole interior changed. Perhaps Mrs Van Hopper's suite on the first floor exists no more. Perhaps there is no trace of the small bedroom that was mine. I knew I should never go back, that day I knelt on the floor and fumbled with the awkward catch of her trunk.

The episode was finished, with the snapping of the lock. I glanced out of the window, and it was like turning the page of a photograph album. Those roof-tops and that sea were mine no more. They belonged to yesterday, to the past. The rooms already wore an empty air, stripped of our possessions, and there was something hungry about the suite, as though it wished us gone, and the new arrivals, who would come tomorrow, in our place. The heavy luggage stood ready strapped and locked in the corridor outside. The smaller stuff would be finished later. Waste-paper baskets groaned under litter. All her half empty medicine bottles and discarded face-cream jars, with torn-up bills and letters. Drawers in tables gaped, the bureau was stripped bare.

She had flung a letter at me the morning before, as I poured out her coffee at breakfast. 'Helen is sailing for New York on Saturday. Little Nancy has a threatened appendix, and they've cabled her to go home. That's decided me. We're going too. I'm tired to death of Europe, and we can come back in the early fall. How d'you like the idea of seeing New York?'

The thought was worse than prison. Something of my misery must have shown in my face, for at first she looked astonished, then annoyed.

'What an odd, unsatisfactory child you are. I can't make you out. Don't you realize that at home girls in your position without any money can have the grandest fun? Plenty of boys and excitement. All in your own class. You can have your own little set of friends, and needn't be at my beck and call as much as you are here. I thought you didn't care for Monte?'

'I've got used to it,' I said lamely, wretchedly, my mind a conflict.

'Well, you'll just have to get used to New York, that's all. We're going to catch that boat of Helen's, and it means seeing about our passage at once. Go down to the reception office right away, and make that young clerk show some sign of efficiency. Your day will be so full that you won't have time to have any pangs about leaving Monte!' She laughed disagreeably, squashing her cigarette in the butter, and went to the telephone to ring up all her friends.

I could not face the office right away. I went into the bathroom and locked the door, and sat down on the cork mat, my head in my hands. It had happened at last, the business of going away. It was all over. Tomorrow evening I should be in the train, holding her jewel case and her rug, like a maid, and she in that monstrous new hat with the single quill, dwarfed in her fur-coat, sitting opposite me in the wagon-lit. We would wash and clean our teeth in that stuffy little compartment with the rattling doors, the splashed basin, the damp towel, the soap with a single hair on it, the carafe half-filled with water, the inevitable notice on the wall '*Sous le lavabo se trouve une vase*', while every rattle, every throb and jerk of the screaming train would tell me that the miles carried me away from him, sitting alone in the restaurant of the hotel, at the table I had known, reading a book, not minding, not thinking.

I should say good-bye to him in the lounge, perhaps, before we left. A furtive, scrambled farewell, because of her, and there would be a pause, and a smile, and words like 'Yes, of course, do write', and 'I've never thanked you properly for being so kind', and 'You must forward those snapshots', 'What about your address?' 'Well, I'll have to let you know.' And he would light a cigarette casually, asking a passing waiter for a light, while I thought, 'Four and a half more minutes to go. I shall never see him again.'

Because I was going, because it was over, there would suddenly be nothing more to say, we would be strangers, meeting for the last and only time, while my mind clamoured painfully, crying 'I love you so much. I'm terribly unhappy. This has never come to me before, and never will again.' My face would be set in a prim, conventional smile, my voice would be saying, 'Look at that funny old man over there; I wonder who he is; he must be new here.' And we would waste the last moments laughing at a stranger, because we were already strangers to one another. 'I hope the snapshots come out well,' repeating oneself in desperation, and he 'Yes, that one of the square ought to be good; the light was just right.' Having both of us gone into all that at the time, having agreed upon it, and anyway I would not care if the result was fogged and black, because this was the last moment, the final good-bye had been attained.

'Well,' my dreadful smile stretching across my face, 'thanks most awfully once again, it's been so ripping . . .' using words I had never used before. Ripping: what did it mean? – God knows, I did not care; it was the sort of word that schoolgirls had for hockey, wildly inappropriate to those past weeks of misery and exultation. Then the doors of the lift would open upon Mrs Van Hopper and I would cross the lounge to meet her, and he would stroll back again to his corner and pick up a paper.

Sitting there, ridiculously, on the cork mat of the bathroom floor, I lived it all, and our journey too, and our arrival in New York. The shrill voice of Helen, a narrower edition of her mother, and Nancy, her horrid little child. The college boys that Mrs Van Hopper would have me know, and the young bank clerks, suitable to my station. 'Let's make Wednesday night a date.' 'D'you like Hot music?' Snub-nosed boys, with shiny faces. Having to be polite. And wanting to be alone with my own thoughts as I was now, locked behind the bathroom door . . .

She came and rattled on the door. 'What are you doing?'

'All right – I'm sorry, I'm coming now,' and I made a pretence of turning on the tap, of bustling about and folding a towel on a rail.

She glanced at me curiously as I opened the door. 'What a time you've been. You can't afford to dream this morning, you know, there's too much to be done.'

He would go back to Manderley, of course, in a few weeks; I felt certain of that. There would be a great pile of letters waiting for him in the hall, and mine amongst them, scribbled on the boat. A forced letter, trying to amuse, describing my fellow passengers. It would lie about inside his blotter, and he would answer it weeks later, one Sunday morning in a hurry, before lunch, having come across it when he paid some bills. And then no more. Nothing until the final degradation of the Christmas card. Manderley itself perhaps, against a frosted background. The message printed, saying 'A happy Christmas and a prosperous New Year from Maximilian de Winter.' Gold lettering. But to be kind he would have run his pen through the printed name and written in ink underneath 'from Maxim', as a sort of sop, and if there was space, a message, 'I hope you are enjoying New York.' A lick of the envelope, a stamp, and tossed in a pile of a hundred others.

'It's too bad you are leaving tomorrow,' said the reception clerk, telephone in hand; 'the Ballet starts next week, you know. Does Mrs Van Hopper know?' I dragged myself back from Christmas at Manderley to the realities of the wagon-lit.

Mrs Van Hopper lunched in the restaurant for the first time since her influenza, and I had a pain in the pit of my stomach as I followed her into the room. He had gone to Cannes for the day, that much I knew, for he had warned me the day before, but I kept thinking the waiter might commit an indiscretion and say: 'Will Mademoiselle be dining with Monsieur tonight as usual?' I felt a little sick whenever he came near the table, but he said nothing.

The day was spent in packing, and in the evening people came to say good-bye. We dined in the sitting-room, and she went to bed directly afterwards. Still I had not seen him. I went down to the lounge about half past nine on the pretext of getting luggage labels and he was not there. The odious reception clerk smiled when he saw me. 'If you are looking for Mr de Winter we had a message from Cannes to say he would not be back before midnight.'

'I want a packet of luggage labels,' I said, but I saw by his eye that he was not deceived. So there would be no last evening after all. The hour I had looked forward to all day must be spent by myself alone, in my own bedroom, gazing at my Revelation suit-case and the stout hold-all. Perhaps it was just as well, for I should have made a poor companion, and he must have read my face.

I know I cried that night, bitter youthful tears that could not come from me today. That kind of crying, deep into a pillow, does not happen after we are twenty-one. The throbbing head, the swollen eyes, the tight, contracted throat. And the wild anxiety in the morning to hide all traces from the world, sponging with cold water, dabbing eau-de-Cologne, the furtive dash of powder that is significant in itself. The panic, too, that one might cry again, the tears swelling without control, and a fatal trembling of the mouth lead one to disaster. I remember opening wide my window and leaning out, hoping the fresh morning air would blow away the tell-tale pink under the powder, and the sun had never seemed so bright, nor the day so full of promise. Monte Carlo was suddenly full of kindliness and charm, the one place in the world that held sincerity. I loved it. Affection overwhelmed me. I wanted to live there all my life. And I was leaving it today. This is the last time I brush my hair before the looking-glass, the last time I shall clean my teeth into the basin. Never again sleep in that bed. Never more turn off the switch of that electric light. There I was, padding about in a dressing-gown, making a slough of sentiment out of a commonplace hotel bedroom.

'You haven't started a cold, have you?' she said at breakfast.

'No,' I told her, 'I don't think so,' clutching at a straw, for this might serve as an excuse later, if I was over-pink about the eyes.

'I hate hanging about once everything is packed,' she grumbled; 'we ought to have decided on the earlier train. We could get it if we made the effort, and then have longer in Paris. Wire

Helen not to meet us, but arrange another *rendezvous*. I wonder' – she glanced at her watch – 'I suppose they could change the reservations. Anyway it's worth trying. Go down to the office and see.'

'Yes,' I said, a dummy to her moods going into my bedroom and flinging off my dressing-gown, fastening my inevitable flannel skirt and stretching my home-made jumper over my head. My indifference to her turned to hatred. This was the end then, even my morning must be taken from me. No last half-hour on the terrace, not even ten minutes perhaps to say good-bye. Because she had finished breakfast earlier than she expected, because she was bored. Well then, I would fling away restraint and modesty, I would not be proud any more. I slammed the door of the sitting-room and ran along the passage. I did not wait for the lift, I climbed the stairs, three at a time, up to the third floor. I knew the number of his room, 148, and I hammered at the door, very flushed in the face and breathless.

'Come in,' he shouted, and I opened the door, repenting already, my nerve failing me; for perhaps he had only just woken up, having been late last night, and would be still in bed, tousled in the head and irritable.

He was shaving by the open window, a camel-hair jacket over his pyjamas, and I in my flannel suit and heavy shoes felt clumsy and over dressed. I was merely foolish, when I had felt myself dramatic.

'What do you want?' he said. 'Is something the matter?'

'I've come to say good-bye,' I said, 'we're going this morning.'

He stared at me, then put his razor down on the washstand. 'Shut the door,' he said.

I closed it behind me, and stood there, rather self-conscious, my hands hanging by my side. 'What on earth are you talking about?' he asked.

'It's true, we're leaving today. We were going by the later train, and now she wants to catch the earlier one, and I was afraid I shouldn't see you again. I felt I must see you before I left, to thank you.'

They tumbled out, the idiotic words, just as I had imagined them. I was stiff and awkward; in a moment I should say he had been ripping.

'Why didn't you tell me about this before?' he said.

'She only decided yesterday. It was all done in a hurry. Her daughter sails for New York on Saturday, and we are going with her. We're joining her in Paris, and going through to Cherbourg.'

'She's taking you with her to New York?'

'Yes, and I don't want to go. I shall hate it; I shall be miserable.'

'Why in heaven's name go with her then?'

'I have to, you know that. I work for a salary. I can't afford to leave her.' He picked up his razor again, and took the soap off his face. 'Sit down,' he said. 'I shan't be long. I'll dress in the bathroom, and be ready in five minutes.'

He took his clothes off the chair and threw them on the bathroom floor, and went inside, slamming the door. I sat down on the bed and began biting my nails. The situation was unreal, and I felt like a lay-figure. I wondered what he was thinking, what he was going to do. I glanced round the room, it was the room of any man, untidy and impersonal. Lots of shoes, more than ever were needed, and strings of ties. The dressing-table was bare, except for a large bottle of hair-wash and a pair of ivory hair-brushes. No photographs. No snapshots. Nothing like that. Instinctively I had looked for them, thinking there would be one photograph at least beside his bed, or in the middle of the mantelpiece. One large one, in a leather frame. There were only books though, and a box of cigarettes.

He was ready, as he had promised, in five minutes. 'Come down to the terrace while I eat my breakfast,' he said.

I looked at my watch. 'I haven't time,' I told him. 'I ought to be in the office now, changing the reservations.'

'Never mind about that, I've got to talk to you,' he said.

We walked down the corridor and he rang for the lift. He can't realize, I thought, that the early train leaves in about an hour and a half. Mrs Van Hopper will ring up the office, in a moment, and ask if I am there. We went down in the lift, not talking, and so out to the terrace, where the tables were laid for breakfast.

'What are you going to have?' he said.

'I've had mine already,' I told him, 'and I can only stay four minutes anyway.'

'Bring me coffee, a boiled egg, toast, marmalade, and a tangerine,' he said to the waiter. And he took an emery board out of his pocket and began filing his nails.

'So Mrs Van Hopper has had enough of Monte Carlo,' he said, 'and now she wants to go home. So do I. She to New York and I to Manderley. Which would you prefer? You can take your choice.'

'Don't make a joke about it; it's unfair,' I said; 'and I think I had better see about those tickets, and say good-bye now.'

'If you think I'm one of the people who try to be funny at breakfast you're wrong,' he said. 'I'm invariably ill-tempered in the early morning. I repeat to you, the choice is open to you. Either you go to America with Mrs Van Hopper or you come home to Manderley with me.'

'Do you mean you want a secretary or something?'

'No, I'm asking you to marry me, you little fool.'

The waiter came with the breakfast, and I sat with my hands in my lap, watching while he put down the pot of coffee and the jug of milk.

'You don't understand,' I said, when the waiter had gone; 'I'm not the sort of person men marry.'

'What the devil do you mean?' he said, staring at me, laying down his spoon.

I watched a fly settle on the marmalade, and he brushed it away impatiently.

'I'm not sure,' I said slowly. 'I don't think I know how to explain. I don't belong to your sort of world for one thing.'

'What is my world?'

'Well – Manderley. You know what I mean.'

He picked up his spoon again and helped himself to marmalade.

'You are almost as ignorant as Mrs Van Hopper, and just as unintelligent. What do you know of Manderley? I'm the person to judge that, whether you would belong there or not. You think I ask you this on the spur of the moment, don't you? Because you say you don't want to go to New York. You think I ask you to marry me for the same reason you believed I drove you about in the car, yes, and gave you dinner that first evening. To be kind. Don't you?'

'Yes,' I said.

'One day,' he went on, spreading his toast thick, 'you may realize that philanthropy is not my strongest quality. At the moment I don't think you realize anything at all. You haven't answered my question. Are you going to marry me?'

I don't believe, even in my fiercest moments, I had considered this possibility. I had once, when driving with him and we had been silent for many miles, started a rambling story in my head about him being very ill, delirious I think, and sending for me and I having to nurse him. I had reached the point in my story where I was putting eau-de-Cologne on his head when we arrived at the hotel, and so it finished there. And another time I had imagined living in a lodge in the grounds of Manderley, and how he would visit me sometimes, and sit in front of the fire. This sudden talk of marriage bewildered me, even shocked me I think. It was as though the King asked one. It did not ring true. And he went on eating his marmalade as though everything were natural. In books men knelt to women, and it would be moonlight. Not at breakfast, not like this.

'My suggestion doesn't seem to have gone too well,' he said. 'I'm sorry. I rather thought you loved me. A fine blow to my conceit.'

'I do love you,' I said. 'I love you dreadfully. You've made me very unhappy and I've been crying all night because I thought I should never see you again.'

When I said this I remember he laughed, and stretched his hand to me across the breakfast table. 'Bless you for that,' he said; 'one day, when you reach that exalted age of thirty-six which you told me was your ambition, I'll remind you of this moment. And you won't believe me. It's a pity you have to grow up.'

I was ashamed already, and angry with him for laughing. So women did not make those confessions to men. I had a lot to learn.

'So that's settled, isn't it?' he said, going on with his toast and marmalade; 'instead of being companion to Mrs Van Hopper you become mine, and your duties will be almost exactly the same. I also like new library books, and flowers in the drawing-room, and bezique after dinner. And someone to pour out my tea. The only difference is that I don't take Taxol, I prefer Eno's, and you must never let me run out of my particular brand of tooth-paste.'

I drummed with my fingers on the table, uncertain of myself and of him. Was he still laughing at me, was it all a joke? He looked up, and saw the anxiety on my face. 'I'm being rather a brute to you, aren't I?' he said; 'this isn't your idea of a proposal. We ought to be in a conservatory, you in a white frock with a rose in your hand, and a violin playing a waltz in the distance. And I should make violent love to you behind a palm tree. You would feel then you were getting your money's worth. Poor darling, what a shame. Never mind, I'll take you to Venice for our honeymoon and we'll hold hands in the gondola. But we won't stay too long, because I want to show you Manderley.'

He wanted to show me Manderley . . . And suddenly I realized that it would all happen; I would be his wife, we would walk in the garden together, we would stroll down that path in the valley to the shingle beach. I knew how I would stand on the steps after breakfast, looking at the day, throwing crumbs to the birds, and later wander out in a shady hat with long scissors in my hand, and cut flowers for the house. I knew now why I had bought that picture post-card as a child; it was a premonition, a blank step into the future.

He wanted to show me Manderley . . . My mind ran riot then, figures came before me and picture after picture – and all the while he ate his tangerine, giving me a piece now and then, and watching me. We would be in a crowd of people, and he would say, 'I don't think you have met my wife.' Mrs de Winter. I would be Mrs de Winter. I considered my name, and the signature on cheques, to tradesmen, and in letters asking people to dinner. I heard myself talking on the telephone: 'Why not come down to Manderley next week-end?' People, always a throng of people. 'Oh, but she's simply charming, you must meet her—' This about me, a whisper on the fringe of a crowd, and I would turn away, pretending I had not heard.

Going down to the lodge with a basket on my arm, grapes and peaches for the old lady who was sick. Her hands stretched out to me, 'The Lord bless you, Madam, for being so good,' and my saying, 'Just send up to the house for anything you want.' Mrs de Winter. I would be Mrs de Winter. I saw the polished table in the dining-room, and the long candles. Maxim sitting at the end. A party of twenty-four. I had a flower in my hair. Everyone looked towards me, holding up his glass. 'We must drink the health of the bride,' and Maxim saying afterwards, 'I have never seen you look so lovely.' Great cool rooms, filled with flowers. My bedroom, with a fire in the winter, someone knocking at the door. And a woman comes in, smiling; she is Maxim's sister, and she is saying, 'It's really wonderful how happy you have made him; everyone is so pleased, you are such a success.' Mrs de Winter. I would be Mrs de Winter.

'The rest of the tangerine is sour, I shouldn't eat it,' he said, and I stared at him, the words going slowly to my head, then looked down at the fruit on my plate. The quarter was hard and pale. He was right. The tangerine was very sour. I had a sharp, bitter taste in my mouth, and I had only just noticed it.

'Am I going to break the news to Mrs Van Hopper or are you?' he said.

He was folding up his napkin, pushing back his plate, and I wondered how it was he spoke so casually, as though the matter was of little consequence, a mere adjustment of plans. Whereas to me it was a bomb-shell, exploding in a thousand fragments.

'You tell her,' I said; 'she'll be so angry.'

We got up from the table, I excited and flushed, trembling already in anticipation. I wondered if he would tell the waiter, take my arm smilingly and say, 'You must congratulate us, Mademoiselle and I are going to be married.' And all the other waiters would hear, would bow to us, would smile, and we would pass into the lounge, a wave of excitement following us, a flutter of expectation. But he said nothing. He left the terrace without a word, and I followed him to the lift. We passed the reception desk and no one even looked at us. The clerk was busy with a sheaf of papers, he was talking over his shoulder to his junior. He does not know, I thought, that I am going to be Mrs de Winter. I am going to live at Manderley. Manderley will belong to me. We went up in the lift to the first floor, and so along the passage. He took my hand and swung it as we went along. 'Does forty-two seem very old to you?' he said.

'Oh, no,' I told him, quickly, too eagerly perhaps. 'I don't like young men.'

'You've never known any,' he said.

We came to the door of the suite. 'I think I had better deal with this alone,' he said; 'tell me something – do you mind how soon you marry me? You don't want a trousseau, do you, or any of that nonsense? Because the whole thing can be so easily arranged in a few days. Over a desk, with a licence, and then off in the car to Venice or anywhere you fancy.'

'Not in a church?' I asked. 'Not in white, with bridesmaids, and bells, and choir boys? What about your relations, and all your friends?'

'You forget,' he said, 'I had that sort of wedding before.'

We went on standing in front of the door of the suite, and I noticed that the daily paper was still thrust through the letter-box. We had been too busy to read it at breakfast.

'Well?' he said, 'what about it?'

'Of course,' I answered, 'I was thinking for the moment we would be married at home. Naturally I don't expect a church, or people, or anything like that.'

61

And I smiled at him. I made a cheerful face. 'Won't it be fun?' I said.

He had turned to the door though, and opened it, and we were inside the suite in the little entrance passage.

'Is that you?' called Mrs Van Hopper from the sitting-room. 'What in the name of Mike have you been doing? I've rung the office three times and they said they hadn't seen you.'

I was seized with a sudden desire to laugh, to cry, to do both, and I had a pain, too, at the pit of my stomach. I wished, for one wild moment, that none of this had happened, that I was alone somewhere, going for a walk, and whistling.

'I'm afraid it's all my fault,' he said, going into the sitting-room, shutting the door behind him, and I heard her exclamation of surprise.

Then I went into my bedroom and sat down by the open window. It was like waiting in the ante-room at a doctor's. I ought to turn over the pages of a magazine, look at photographs that did not matter and read articles I should never remember, until the nurse came, bright and efficient, all humanity washed away by years of disinfectant: 'It's all right, the operation was quite successful. There is no need to worry at all. I should go home and have some sleep.'

The walls of the suite were thick, I could hear no hum of voices. I wondered what he was saying to her, how he phrased his words. Perhaps he said, I fell in love with her, you know, the very first time we met. We've been seeing one another every day.' And she in answer, 'Why, Mr de Winter, it's quite the most romantic thing I've ever heard.' Romantic, that was the word I had tried to remember coming up in the lift. Yes, of course. Romantic. That was what people would say. It was all very sudden and romantic. They suddenly decided to get married and there it was. Such an adventure. I smiled to myself as I hugged my knees on the window seat, thinking how wonderful it was, how happy I was going to be. I was to marry the man I loved. I was to be Mrs de Winter. It was foolish to go on having that pain in the pit of my stomach when I was so happy. Nerves of course.

62

Waiting like this; the doctor's ante-room. It would have been better, after all, more natural surely to have gone into the sitting-room hand in hand, laughing, smiling at one another and for him to say 'We're going to be married, we're very much in love.'

In love. He had not said anything yet about being in love. No time perhaps. It was all so hurried at the breakfast table. Marmalade, and coffee, and that tangerine. No time. The tangerine was very bitter. No, he had not said anything about being in love. Just that we would be married. Short and definite, very original. Original proposals were much better. More genuine. Not like other people. Not like younger men who talked nonsense probably, not meaning half they said. Not like younger men being very incoherent, very passionate, swearing impossibilities. Not like him the first time, asking Rebecca . . . I must not think of that. Put it away. A thought forbidden, prompted by demons. Get thee behind me, Satan. I must never think about that, never, never, never. He loves me, he wants to show me Manderley. Would they ever have done with their talking, would they ever call me into the room?

There was the book of poems lying beside my bed. He had forgotten he had ever lent them to me. They could not mean much to him then. 'Go on,' whispered the demon, 'open the title-page; that's what you want to do, isn't it? Open the title-page.' Nonsense, I said, I'm only going to put the book with the rest of the things. I yawned. I wandered to the table beside the bed. I picked up the book. I caught my foot in the flex of the bedside lamp, and stumbled, the book falling from my hands on to the floor. It fell open, at the title-page. 'Max from Rebecca.' She was dead, and one must not have thoughts about the dead. They slept in peace, the grass blew over their graves. How alive was her writing though, how full of force. Those curious, sloping letters. The blob of ink. Done yesterday. It was just as if it had been written yesterday. I took my nail scissors from the dressing-case and cut the page, looking over my shoulder like a criminal.

I cut the page right out of the book. I left no jagged edges, and the book looked white and clean when the page was gone.

A new book, that had not been touched. I tore the page up in many little fragments and threw them into the waste-paper basket. Then I went and sat on the window seat again. But I kept thinking of the torn scraps in the basket, and after a moment I had to get up and look in the basket once more. Even now the ink stood up on the fragments thick and black, the writing was not destroyed. I took a box of matches and set fire to the fragments. The flame had a lovely light, staining the paper, curling the edges, making the slanting writing impossible to distinguish. The fragments fluttered to grey ashes. The letter R was the last to go, it twisted in the flame, it curled outwards for a moment, becoming larger than ever. Then it crumpled too; the flame destroyed it. It was not ashes even, it was feathery dust . . . I went and washed my hands in the basin. I felt better, much better. I had the clean new feeling that one has when the calendar is hung on the wall at the beginning of the year. January the 1st. I was aware of the same freshness, the same gay confidence. The door opened and he came into the room.

'All's well,' he said; 'shock made her speechless at first, but she's beginning to recover, so I'm going downstairs to the office, to make certain she will catch the first train. For a moment she wavered; I think she had hopes of acting witness at the wedding, but I was very firm. Go and talk to her.'

He said nothing about being glad, about being happy. He did not take my arm and go into the sitting-room with me. He smiled, and waved his hand, and went off down the corridor alone. I went to Mrs Van Hopper, uncertain, rather self-conscious, like a maid who has handed in her notice through a friend.

She was standing by the window, smoking a cigarette, an odd, dumpy little figure I should not see again, her coat stretched tight over her large breasts, her ridiculous hat perched sideways on her head.

'Well,' she said, her voice dry and hard, not the voice she would have used to him. 'I suppose I've got to hand it to you for a double-time worker. Still waters certainly run deep in your case. How did you manage it?'

I did not know what to answer. I did not like her smile. 'It was a lucky thing for you I had the influenza,' she said. 'I realize now how you spent your days, and why you were so forgetful. Tennis lessons my eye. You might have told me, you know.'

'I'm sorry,' I said.

She looked at me curiously, she ran her eyes over my figure. 'And he tells me he wants to marry you in a few days. Lucky again for you that you haven't a family to ask questions. Well, it's nothing to do with me any more, I wash my hands of the whole affair. I rather wonder what his friends will think, but I suppose that's up to him. You realize he's years older than you?'

'He's only forty-two,' I said, 'and I'm old for my age.'

She laughed, she dropped cigarette ash on the floor. 'You certainly are,' she said. She went on looking at me in a way she had never done before. Appraising me, running her eyes over my points like a judge at a cattle show. There was something inquisitive about her eyes, something unpleasant.

'Tell me,' she said, intimate, a friend to a friend, 'have you been doing anything you shouldn't?'

She was like Blaize, the dressmaker, who had offered me that ten per cent.

'I don't know what you mean,' I said.

She laughed, she shrugged her shoulders. 'Oh, well . . . never mind. But I always said English girls were dark horses, for all their hockey-playing attitude. So I'm supposed to travel to Paris alone, and leave you here while your beau gets a marriage licence? I notice he doesn't ask me to the wedding.'

'I don't think he wants anyone, and anyway you would have sailed,' I said.

'H'm, h'm,' she said. She took out her vanity case and began powdering her nose. 'I suppose you really do know your own mind,' she went on; 'after all, the whole thing has been very hurried, hasn't it? A matter of a few weeks. I don't suppose he's too easy, and you'll have to adapt yourself to his ways. You've led an extremely sheltered life up to now, you know, and you can't say that I've run you off your feet. You will have your work cut out as mistress of Manderley. To be perfectly frank, my dear, I simply can't see you doing it.'

Her words sounded like the echo of my own an hour before.

'You haven't the experience,' she continued, 'you don't know that milieu. You can scarcely string two sentences together at my bridge teas, what are you going to say to all his friends? The Manderley parties were famous when she was alive. Of course he's told you all about them?'

I hesitated, but she went on, thank heaven, not waiting for my answer.

'Naturally one wants you to be happy, and I grant you he's a very attractive creature but – well, I'm sorry; and personally I think you are making a big mistake – one you will bitterly regret.'

She put down the box of powder, and looked at me over her shoulder. Perhaps she was being sincere at last, but I did not want that sort of honesty. I did not say anything. I looked sullen, perhaps, for she shrugged her shoulders and wandered to the looking-glass, straightening her little mushroom hat. I was glad she was going, glad I should not see her again. I grudged the months I had spent with her, employed by her, taking her money, trotting in her wake like a shadow, drab and dumb. Of course I was inexperienced, of course I was idiotic, shy, and young. I knew all that. She did not have to tell me. I suppose her atti-tude was deliberate, and for some odd feminine reason she resented this marriage; her scale of values had received a shock.

Well, I would not care, I would forget her and her barbed words. A new confidence had been born in me when I burnt that page and scattered the fragments. The past would not exist for either of us; we were starting afresh, he and I. The past had blown away like the ashes in the waste-paper basket. I was going to be Mrs de Winter. I was going to live at Manderley.

Soon she would be gone, rattling alone in the wagon-lit without me, and he and I would be together in the dining-room of the hotel, lunching at the same table, planning the future. The brink of a big adventure. Perhaps, once she had gone, he would talk to me at last, about loving me, about being happy. Up to now there had been no time, and anyway those things are not easily said, they must wait their moment. I looked up, and caught her reflection in the looking-glass. She was watching me, a little tolerant smile on her lips. I thought she was going to be generous after all, hold out her hand and wish me luck, give me encouragement and tell me that everything was going to be all right. But she went on smiling, twisting a stray hair into place beneath her hat.

'Of course,' she said, 'you know why he is marrying you, don't you? You haven't flattered yourself he's in love with you? The fact is that empty house got on his nerves to such an extent he nearly went off his head. He admitted as much before you came into the room. He just can't go on living there alone . . .'

7

We came to Manderley in early May, arriving, so Maxim said, with the first swallows and the bluebells. It would be the best moment, before the full flush of summer, and in the valley the azaleas would be prodigal of scent, and the blood-red rhododendrons in bloom. We motored, I remember, leaving London in the morning in a heavy shower of rain, coming to Manderley about five o'clock, in time for tea. I can see myself now, unsuitably dressed as usual, although a bride of seven weeks, in a tan-coloured stockinette frock, a small fur known as a stone marten round my neck, and over all a shapeless mackintosh, far too big for me and dragging to my ankles. It was, I thought, a gesture to the weather, and the length added inches to my height. I clutched a pair of gauntlet gloves in my hands, and carried a large leather handbag.

'This is London rain,' said Maxim when we left, 'you wait, the sun will be shining for you when we come to Manderley'; and he was right, for the clouds left us at Exeter, they rolled away behind us, leaving a great blue sky above our heads and a white road in front of us.

I was glad to see the sun, for in superstitious fashion I looked upon rain as an omen of ill-will, and the leaden skies of London had made me silent.

'Feeling better?' said Maxim, and I smiled at him, taking his hand, thinking how easy it was for him, going to his own home, wandering into the hall, picking up letters, ringing a bell for tea, and I wondered how much he guessed of my nervousness, and whether his question 'Feeling better?' meant that he understood. 'Never mind, we'll soon be there. I expect you want your tea,' he said, and he let go my hand because we had reached a bend in the road, and must slow down.

I knew then that he had mistaken my silence for fatigue, and it had not occurred to him I dreaded this arrival at Manderley as much as I had longed for it in theory. Now the moment was upon me I wished it delayed. I wanted to draw up at some wayside inn and stay there, in a coffee-room, by an impersonal fire. I wanted to be a traveller on the road, a bride in love with her husband. Not myself coming to Manderley for the first time, the wife of Maxim de Winter. We passed many friendly villages where the cottage windows had a kindly air. A woman, holding a baby in her arms, smiled at me from a doorway, while a man clanked across a road to a well, carrying a pail.

I wished we could have been one with them, perhaps their neighbours, and that Maxim could lean over a cottage gate in the evenings, smoking a pipe, proud of a very tall hollyhock he had grown himself, while I bustled in my kitchen, clean as a pin, laying the table for supper. There would be an alarm clock on the dresser ticking loudly, and a row of shining plates, while after supper Maxim would read his paper, boots on the fender, and I reach for a great pile of mending in the dresser drawer. Surely it would be peaceful and steady, that way of living, and easier, too, demanding no set standard?

'Only two miles further,' said Maxim; 'you see that great belt of trees on the brow of the hill there, sloping to the valley, with a scrap of sea beyond? That's Manderley, in there. Those are the woods.'

I forced a smile, and did not answer him, aware now of a stab of panic, an uneasy sickness that could not be controlled. Gone was my glad excitement, vanished my happy pride. I was like a child brought to her first school, or a little untrained maid who has never left home before, seeking a situation. Any measure of self-possession I had gained hitherto during the brief seven weeks of marriage, was like a rag now, fluttering before the wind; it seemed to me that even the most elementary knowledge of behaviour was unknown to me now, I should not know my right hand from my left, whether to stand or sit, what spoons and forks to use at dinner.

'I should shed that mackintosh,' he said, glancing down at me, 'it has not rained down here at all, and put your funny little fur straight. Poor lamb, I've bustled you down here like this, and you probably ought to have bought a lot of clothes in London.'

'It doesn't matter to me, as long as you don't mind,' I said.

'Most women think of nothing but clothes,' he said absently, and turning a corner we came to a cross-road, and the beginning of a high wall.

'Here we are,' he said, a new note of excitement in his voice, and I gripped the leather seat of the car with my two hands.

The road curved, and before us, on the left, were two high iron gates beside a lodge, open wide to the long drive beyond. As we drove through I saw faces peering through the dark window of the lodge, and a child ran round from the back, staring curiously. I shrank back against the seat, my heart beating quickly, knowing why the faces were at the window, and why the child stared.

They wanted to see what I was like. I could imagine them now, talking excitedly, laughing in the little kitchen. 'Only caught sight of the top of her hat,' they would say, 'she wouldn't show her face. Oh, well, we'll know by tomorrow. Word will come from the house.' Perhaps he guessed something of my shyness at last, for he took my hand, and kissed it, and laughed a little, even as he spoke.

'You mustn't mind if there's a certain amount of curiosity,' he said; 'everyone will want to know what you are like. They have probably talked of nothing else for weeks. You've only got to be yourself and they will all adore you. And you don't have to worry about the house, Mrs Danvers does everything. Just leave it all to her. She'll be stiff with you at first, I dare say, she's an extraordinary character, but you mustn't let it worry you. It's just her manner. See those shrubs? It's like a blue wall along here when the hydrangeas are in bloom.'

I did not answer him, for I was thinking of that self who long ago bought a picture post-card in a village shop, and came out into the bright sunlight twisting it in her hands, pleased with her purchase, thinking 'This will do for my album. "Manderley", what a lovely name.' And now I belonged here, this was my home. I would write letters to people saying, 'We shall be down at Manderley all the summer, you must come and see us,' and I would walk along this drive, strange and unfamiliar to me now, with perfect knowledge, conscious of every twist and turn, marking and approving where the gardeners had worked, here a cutting back of the shrubs, there a lopping of a branch, calling at the lodge by the iron gates on some friendly errand, saying, 'Well, how's the leg today?' while the old woman, curious no longer, bade me welcome to her kitchen. I envied Maxim, careless and at ease, and the little smile on his lips which meant he was happy to be coming home.

It seemed remote to me, and far too distant, the time when I too should smile and be at ease, and I wished it could come quickly; that I could be old even, with grey hair and slow of step, having lived here many years – anything but the timid, foolish creature I felt myself to be.

The gates had shut to with a crash behind us, the dusty high-road was out of sight, and I became aware that this was not the drive I had imagined would be Manderley's, this was not a broad and spacious thing of gravel, flanked with neat turf at either side, kept smooth with rake and brush.

This drive twisted and turned as a serpent, scarce wider in places than a path, and above our heads was a great colonnade of trees, whose branches nodded and intermingled with one another, making an archway for us, like the roof of a church. Even the midday sun would not penetrate the interlacing of those green leaves, they were too thickly entwined, one with another, and only little flickering patches of warm light would come in intermittent waves to dapple the drive with gold. It was very silent, very still. On the high-road there had been a gay west wind blowing in my face, making the grass on the hedges dance in unison, but here there was no wind. Even the engine of the car had taken a new note, throbbing low, quieter than before. As the drive descended to the valley so the trees came in upon us, great beeches with lovely smooth white stems, lifting their myriad branches to one another, and other trees, trees I could not name, coming close, so close that I could touch them with my hands. On we went, over a little bridge that spanned a narrow stream, and still this drive that was no drive twisted and turned like an enchanted ribbon through the dark and silent woods, penetrating even deeper to the very heart surely of the forest itself, and still there was no clearing, no space to hold a house.

The length of it began to nag at my nerves; it must be this turn, I thought, or round that further bend; but as I leant forward in my seat I was for ever disappointed, there was no house, no field, no broad and friendly garden, nothing but the silence and deep woods. The lodge gates were a memory, and the high-road something belonging to another time, another world.

Suddenly I saw a clearing in the dark drive ahead, and a patch of sky, and in a moment the dark trees had thinned, the name-less shrubs had disappeared, and on either side of us was a wall of colour, blood-red, reaching far above our heads. We were amongst the rhododendrons. There was something bewildering, even shocking, about the suddenness of their discovery. The woods had not prepared me for them. They startled me with their crimson faces, massed one upon the other in incredible profusion, showing no leaf, no twig, nothing but the slaughter-ous red, luscious and fantastic, unlike any rhododendron plant I had seen before.

I glanced at Maxim. He was smiling. 'Like them?' he said.

I told him 'Yes,' a little breathlessly, uncertain whether I was speaking the truth or not, for to me a rhododendron was a homely, domestic thing, strictly conventional, mauve or pink in colour, standing one beside the other in a neat round bed. And these were monsters, rearing to the sky, massed like a battalion, too beautiful I thought, too powerful; they were not plants at all.

We were not far from the house now, I saw the drive broaden to the sweep I had expected, and with the blood-red wall still flanking us on either side, we turned the last corner, and so came to Manderley. Yes, there it was, the Manderley I had expected, the Manderley of my picture post-card long ago. A thing of grace and beauty, exquisite and faultless, lovelier even than I had ever dreamed, built in its hollow of smooth grassland and mossy lawns, the terraces sloping to the gardens, and the gardens to the sea. As we drove up to the wide stone steps and stopped before the open door, I saw through one of the mullioned windows that the hall was full of people, and I heard Maxim swear under his breath. 'Damn that woman,' he said; 'she knows perfectly well I did not want this sort of thing,' and he put on the brakes with a jerk.

'What's the matter?' I said. 'Who are all those people?'

'I'm afraid you will have to face it now,' he said, in irritation. 'Mrs Danvers has collected the whole damned staff in the house and on the estate to welcome us. It's all right, you won't have to say anything, I'll do it all.'

I fumbled for the handle of the door, feeling slightly sick, and cold now too from the long drive, and as I fumbled with the catch the butler came down the steps, followed by a footman, and he opened the door for me.

He was old, he had a kind face, and I smiled up at him, holding out my hand, but I don't think he could have seen, for he took the rug instead, and my small dressing-case, and turned to Maxim, helping me from the car at the same time.

'Well, here we are, Frith,' said Maxim, taking off his gloves. 'It was raining when we left London. You don't seem to have had it here. Everyone well?'

'Yes, sir, thank you, sir. No, we have had a dry month on the whole. Glad to see you home, and hope you have been keeping well. And Madam too.'

'Yes, we are both well, thank you, Frith. Rather tired from the drive, and wanting our tea. I didn't expect this business.' He jerked his head to the hall.

73

'Mrs Danvers' orders, sir,' said the man, his face expressionless.

'I might have guessed it,' said Maxim abruptly. 'Come on' — he turned to me — 'it won't take long, and then you shall have your tea.'

We went together up the flight of steps, Frith and the footman following with the rug and my mackintosh, and I was aware of a little pain at the pit of my stomach, and a nervous contraction in my throat.

I can close my eyes now, and look back on it, and see myself as I must have been, standing on the threshold of the house, a slim, awkward figure in my stockinette dress, clutching in my sticky hands a pair of gauntlet gloves. I can see the great stone hall, the wide doors open to the library, the Peter Lelys and the Vandykes on the walls, the exquisite staircase leading to the minstrels' gallery, and there, ranged one behind the other in the hall, overflowing to the stone passages beyond, and to the dining-room, a sea of faces, open-mouthed and curious, gazing at me as though they were the watching crowd about the block, and I the victim with my hands behind my back. Someone advanced from the sea of faces, someone tall and gaunt, dressed in deep black, whose prominent cheek-bones and great, hollow eyes gave her a skull's face, parchment-white, set on a skeleton's frame.

She came towards me, and I held out my hand, envying her for her dignity and her composure; but when she took my hand hers was limp and heavy, deathly cold, and it lay in mine like a lifeless thing.

'This is Mrs Danvers,' said Maxim, and she began to speak, still leaving that dead hand in mine, her hollow eyes never leaving my eyes, so that my own wavered and would not meet hers, and as they did so her hand moved in mine, the life returned to it, and I was aware of a sensation of discomfort and of shame.

I cannot remember her words now, but I know that she bade me welcome to Manderley, in the name of herself and the staff, a stiff, conventional speech rehearsed for the occasion, spoken in a voice as cold and lifeless as her hands had been. When she had finished she waited, as though for a reply, and I remember blushing scarlet, stammering some sort of thanks in return, and dropping both my gloves in my confusion. She stooped to pick them up, and as she handed them to me I saw a little smile of scorn upon her lips, and I guessed at once she considered me ill-bred. Something, in the expression of her face, gave me a feeling of unrest, and even when she had stepped back, and taken her place amongst the rest, I could see that black figure standing out alone, individual and apart, and for all her silence I knew her eye to be upon me. Maxim took my arm and made a little speech of thanks, perfectly easy and free from embarrassment, as though the making of it was no effort to him at all, and then he bore me off to the library to tea, closing the doors behind us, and we were alone again.

Two cocker spaniels came from the fireside to greet us. They pawed at Maxim, their long, silken ears strained back with affection, their noses questing his hands, and then they left him and came to me, sniffing at my heels, rather uncertain, rather suspicious. One was the mother, blind in one eye, and soon she had enough of me, and took herself with a grunt to the fire again, but Jasper, the younger, put his nose into my hand, and laid a chin upon my knee, his eyes deep with meaning, his tail a-thump when I stroked his silken ears.

I felt better when I had taken my hat off, and my wretched little fur, and thrown them both beside my gloves and my bag on to the window seat. It was a deep, comfortable room, with books lining the walls to the ceiling, the sort of room a man would move from never, did he live alone, solid chairs beside a great open fireplace, baskets for the two dogs in which I felt they never sat, for the hollows in the chairs had tell-tale marks. The long windows looked out upon the lawns, and beyond the lawns to the distant shimmer of the sea.

There was an old quiet smell about the room, as though the air in it was little changed, for all the sweet lilac scent and the roses brought to it throughout the early summer. Whatever air came to this room, whether from the garden or from the sea, would lose its first freshness, becoming part of the unchanging room itself, one with the books, musty and never read, one with the scrolled ceiling, the dark panelling, the heavy curtains.

It was an ancient mossy smell, the smell of a silent church where services are seldom held, where rusty lichen grows upon the stones and ivy tendrils creep to the very windows. A room for peace, a room for meditation.

Soon tea was brought to us, a stately little performance enacted by Frith and the young footman, in which I played no part until they had gone, and while Maxim glanced through his great pile of letters I played with two dripping crumpets, crumbled cake with my hands, and swallowed my scalding tea.

Now and again he looked up at me and smiled, and then returned to his letters, the accumulation of the last months I supposed, and I thought how little I knew of his life here at Manderley, of how it went day by day, of the people he knew, of his friends, men and women, of what bills he paid, what orders he gave about his household. The last weeks had gone so swiftly, and I – driving by his side through France and Italy – thought only of how I loved him, seeing Venice with his eyes, echoing his words, asking no questions of the past and future, content with the little glory of the living present.

For he was gayer than I had thought, more tender than I had dreamed, youthful and ardent in a hundred happy ways, not the Maxim I had first met, not the stranger who sat alone at the table in the restaurant, staring before him, wrapped in his secret self. My Maxim laughed and sang, threw stones into the water, took my hand, wore no frown between his eyes, carried no burden on his shoulder. I knew him as a lover, as a friend, and during those weeks I had forgotten that he had a life, orderly, methodical, a life which must be taken up again, continued as before, making vanished weeks a brief discarded holiday.

I watched him read his letters, saw him frown at one, smile at another, dismiss the next with no expression, and but for the grace of God I thought, my letter would be lying there, written from New York, and he would read it in the same indifferent fashion, puzzled at first perhaps by the signature, and then tossing it with a yawn to the pile of others in the basket, reaching for his cup of tea. The knowledge of this chilled me; how narrow a chance had stood between me and what might-have-been, for he would have sat here to his tea, as he sat now, continuing his home life as he would in any case, and perhaps he would not have thought of me much, not with regret anyway, while I, in New York, playing bridge with Mrs Van Hopper, would wait day after day for a letter that never came.

I leant back in my chair, glancing about the room, trying to instil into myself some measure of confidence, some genuine realization that I was here, at Manderley, the house of the picture post-card, the Manderley that was famous. I had to teach myself that all this was mine now, mine as much as his, the deep chair I was sitting in, that mass of books stretching to the ceiling, the pictures on the walls, the gardens, the woods, the Manderley I had read about, all of this was mine now because I was married to Maxim.

We should grow old here together, we should sit like this to our tea as old people, Maxim and I, with other dogs, the successors of these, and the library would wear the same ancient musty smell that it did now. It would know a period of glorious shabbiness and wear when the boys were young – our boys – for I saw them sprawling on the sofa with muddy boots, bringing with them always a litter of rods, and cricket bats, great clasp-knives, bows-and-arrows.

On the table there, polished now and plain, an ugly case would stand containing butterflies and moths, and another one with birds' eggs, wrapped in cotton wool. 'Not all this junk in here,' I would say, 'take them to the schoolroom, darlings,' and they would run off, shouting, calling to one another, but the little one staying behind, pottering on his own, quieter than the others.

My vision was disturbed by the opening of the door, and Frith came in with the footman to clear the tea. 'Mrs Danvers wondered, Madam, whether you would like to see your room,' he said to me, when the tea had been taken away.

Maxim glanced up from his letters. 'What sort of job have they made of the east wing?' he said.

'Very nice indeed, sir, it seems to me; the men made a mess when they were working, of course, and for a time Mrs Danvers was rather afraid it would not be finished by your return. But they cleared out last Monday. I should imagine you would be very comfortable there, sir; it's a lot lighter of course on that side of the house.'

'Have you been making alterations?' I asked.

'Oh, nothing much,' said Maxim briefly, 'only redecorating and painting the suite in the east wing, which I thought we would use for ours. As Frith says, it's much more cheerful on that side of the house, and it has a lovely view of the rose-garden. It was the visitors' wing when my mother was alive. I'll just finish these letters and then I'll come up and join you. Run along and make friends with Mrs Danvers; it's a good opportunity.'

I got up slowly, my old nervousness returning, and went out into the hall. I wished I could have waited for him, and then, taking his arm, seen the rooms together. I did not want to go alone, with Mrs Danvers. How vast the great hall looked now that it was empty. My feet rang on the flagged stones, echoing to the ceiling, and I felt guilty at the sound, as one does in church, self-conscious, aware of the same constraint. My feet made a stupid pitter-patter as I walked, and I thought that Frith, with his felt soles, must have thought me foolish.

'It's very big, isn't it?' I said, too brightly, too forced, a school-girl still, but he answered me in all solemnity.

'Yes, Madam, Manderley is a big place. Not so big as some, of course, but big enough. This was the old banqueting hall, in old days. It is used still on great occasions, such as a big dinner, or a ball. And the public are admitted here, you know, once a week.'

'Yes,' I said, still aware of my loud footsteps, feeling, as I followed him, that he considered me as he would one of the public visitors, and I behaved like a visitor too, glancing politely to right and left, taking in the weapons on the wall, and the pictures, touching the carved staircase with my hands.

A black figure stood waiting for me at the head of the stairs, the hollow eyes watching me intently from the white skull's face. I looked round for the solid Frith, but he had passed along the hall and into the further corridor.

I was alone now with Mrs Danvers. I went up the great stairs towards her, and she waited motionless, her hands folded before her, her eyes never leaving my face. I summoned a smile, which was not returned, nor did I blame her, for there was no purpose to the smile, it was a silly thing, bright and artificial. 'I hope I haven't kept you waiting,' I said.

'It's for you to make your own time, Madam,' she answered, 'I'm here to carry out your orders,' and then she turned, through the archway of the gallery, to the corridor beyond. We went along a broad, carpeted passage, and then turned left, through an oak door, and down a narrow flight of stairs and up a corresponding flight, and so to another door. This she flung open, standing aside to let me pass, and I came to a little ante-room, or boudoir, furnished with a sofa, chairs, and writing-desk, which opened out to a large double bedroom with wide windows and a bathroom beyond. I went at once to the window, and looked out. The rose-garden lay below, and the eastern part of the terrace, while beyond the rose-garden rose a smooth grass bank, stretching to the near woods.

'You can't see the sea from here, then,' I said, turning to Mrs Danvers.

'No, not from this wing,' she answered; 'you can't even hear it, either. You would not know the sea was anywhere near, from this wing.'

She spoke in a peculiar way, as though something lay behind her words, and she laid an emphasis on the words 'this wing', as if suggesting that the suite where we stood now held some inferiority.

'I'm sorry about that; I like the sea,' I said.

She did not answer; she just went on staring at me, her hands folded before her.

'However, it's a very charming room,' I said, 'and I'm sure I shall be comfortable. I understand that it's been done up for our return.'

'Yes,' she said.

'What was it like before?' I asked.

'It had a mauve paper, and different hangings; Mr de Winter did not think it very cheerful. It was never much used, except for occasional visitors. But Mr de Winter gave special orders in his letters that you would have this room.'

'Then this was not his bedroom originally?' I said.

'No, Madam, he's never used the room in this wing before.'

'Oh,' I said, 'he didn't tell me that,' and I wandered to the dressing-table and began combing my hair. My things were already unpacked, my brushes and comb upon the tray. I was glad Maxim had given me a set of brushes, and that they were laid out there, upon the dressing-table, for Mrs Danvers to see. They were new, they had cost money, I need not be ashamed of them.

'Alice has unpacked for you and will look after you until your maid arrives,' said Mrs Danvers. I smiled at her again. I put down the brush upon the dressing-table.

'I don't have a maid,' I said awkwardly; 'I'm sure Alice, if she is the housemaid, will look after me all right.'

She wore the same expression that she had done on our first meeting, when I dropped my gloves so gauchely on the floor.

'I'm afraid that would not do for very long,' she said; 'it's usual, you know, for ladies in your position to have a personal maid.'

I flushed, and reached for my brush again. There was a sting in her words I understood too well. 'If you think it necessary perhaps you would see about it for me,' I said, avoiding her eyes; 'some young girl perhaps, wanting to train.'

'If you wish,' she said. 'It's for you to say.'

There was silence between us. I wished she would go away. I wondered why she must go on standing there, watching me, her hands folded on her black dress.

'I suppose you have been at Manderley for many years,' I said, making a fresh effort, 'longer than anyone else?'

'Not so long as Frith,' she said, and I thought how lifeless her voice was, and cold, like her hand when it had lain in mine; 'Frith was here when the old gentleman was living, when Mr de Winter was a boy.'

'I see,' I said; 'so you did not come till after that?'

'No,' she said, 'not till after that.'

Once more, I glanced up at her and once more I met her eyes, dark and sombre, in that white face of hers, instilling into me, I knew not why, a strange feeling of disquiet, of foreboding. I tried to smile, and could not; I found myself held by those eyes, that had no light, no flicker of sympathy towards me.

'I came here when the first Mrs de Winter was a bride,' she said, and her voice, which had hitherto, as I said, been dull and toneless, was harsh now with unexpected animation, with life and meaning, and there was a spot of colour on the gaunt cheek-bones.

The change was so sudden that I was shocked, and a little scared. I did not know what to do, or what to say. It was as though she had spoken words that were forbidden, words that she had hidden within herself for a long time and now would be repressed no longer. Still her eyes never left my face; they looked upon me with a curious mixture of pity and of scorn, until I felt myself to be even younger and more untutored to the ways of life than I had believed.

I could see she despised me, marking with all the snobbery of her class that I was no great lady, that I was humble, shy, and diffident. Yet there was something beside scorn in those eyes of hers, something surely of positive dislike, or actual malice?

I had to say something, I could not go on sitting there, playing with my hair-brush, letting her see how much I feared and mistrusted her.

'Mrs Danvers,' I heard myself saying, 'I hope we shall be friends and come to understand one another. You must have patience with me, you know, because this sort of life is new to me, I've lived rather differently. And I do want to make a success of it, and above all to make Mr de Winter happy. I know I can leave all household arrangements to you, Mr de Winter said so, and you must just run things as they have always been run; I shan't want to make any changes.'

I stopped, a little breathless, still uncertain of myself and whether I was saying the right thing, and when I looked up again I saw that she had moved, and was standing with her hand on the handle of the door.

'Very good,' she said; 'I hope I shall do everything to your satisfaction. The house has been in my charge now for more than a year, and Mr de Winter has never complained. It was very different of course when the late Mrs de Winter was alive; there was a lot of entertaining then, a lot of parties, and though I managed for her, she liked to supervise things herself.'

Once again I had the impression that she chose her words with care, that she was feeling her way, as it were, into my mind, and watching for the effect upon my face.

'I would rather leave it to you,' I repeated, 'much rather,' and into her face came the same expression I had noticed before, when first I had shaken hands with her in the hall, a look surely of derision, of definite contempt. She knew that I would never withstand her, and that I feared her too.

'Can I do anything more for you?' she said, and pretended to glance round the room. 'No,' I said. 'No, I think I have everything. I shall be very comfortable here. You have made the room so charming' – this last a final crawling sop to win her approval. She shrugged her shoulders, and still she did not smile. 'I only followed out Mr de Winter's instructions,' she said.

She hesitated by the doorway, her hand on the handle of the open door. It was as though she still had something to say to me, and could not decide upon the words, yet waited there, for me to give her opportunity.

I wished she would go; she was like a shadow standing there, watching me, appraising me with her hollow eyes, set in that dead skull's face.

'If you find anything not to your liking you will tell me at once?' she asked.

'Yes,' I said. 'Yes, of course, Mrs Danvers,' but I knew this was not what she had meant to say, and silence fell between us once again.

'If Mr de Winter asks for his big wardrobe,' she said suddenly, 'you must tell him it was impossible to move. We tried, but we could not get it through these narrow doorways. These are smaller rooms than those in the west wing. If he doesn't like the arrangement of this suite he must tell me. It was difficult to know how to furnish these rooms.'

'Please don't worry, Mrs Danvers,' I said. 'I'm sure he will be pleased with everything. But I'm sorry it's given you so much trouble. I had no idea he was having rooms redecorated and furnished. He shouldn't have bothered. I'm sure I should have been just as happy and comfortable in the west wing.'

She looked at me curiously, and began twisting the handle of the door. 'Mr de Winter said you would prefer to be on this side,' she said, 'the rooms in the west wing are very old. The bedroom in the big suite is twice as large as this; a very beautiful room too, with a scrolled ceiling. The tapestry chairs are very valuable, and so is the carved mantelpiece. It's the most beautiful room in the house. And the windows look down across the lawns to the sea.'

I felt uncomfortable, a little shy. I did not know why she must speak with such an undercurrent of resentment, implying as she did at the same time that this room, where I found myself to be installed, was something inferior, not up to Manderley standard, a second-rate room, as it were, for a second-rate person.

'I suppose Mr de Winter keeps the most beautiful room to show to the public,' I said. She went on twisting the handle of the door, and then looked up at me again, watching my eyes, hesitating before replying, and when she spoke her voice was quieter even, and more toneless, than it had been before.

'The bedrooms are never shown to the public,' she said, 'only the hall and the gallery, and the room below.' She paused an instant, feeling me with her eyes. 'They used to live in the west wing and use those rooms when Mrs de Winter was alive. That big room, I was telling you about, that looked down to the sea, was Mrs de Winter's bedroom.'

Then I saw a shadow flit across her face, and she drew back against the wall, effacing herself, as a step sounded outside and Maxim came into the room.

'How is it?' he said to me. 'All right? Do you think you'll like it?'

He looked round with enthusiasm, pleased as a schoolboy. 'I always thought this a most attractive room,' he said. 'It was wasted all those years as a guest-room, but I always thought it had possibilities. You've made a great success of it, Mrs Danvers: I give you full marks.'

'Thank you, sir,' she said, her face expressionless, and then she turned, and went out of the room, closing the door softly behind her.

Maxim went and leant out of the window. 'I love the rose-garden,' he said; 'one of the first things I remember is walking after my mother, on very small, unsteady legs, while she picked off the dead heads of the roses. There's something peaceful and happy about this room, and it's quiet too. You could never tell you were within five minutes of the sea, from this room.'

'That's what Mrs Danvers said,' I told him.

He came away from the window, he prowled about the room, touching things, looking at the pictures, opening wardrobes, fingering my clothes, already unpacked.

'How did you get on with old Danvers?' he said abruptly.

I turned away, and began combing my hair again before the looking-glass. 'She seems just a little bit stiff,' I said, after a moment or two; 'perhaps she thought I was going to interfere with the running of the house.'

'I don't think she would mind your doing that,' he said. I looked up and saw him watching my reflection in the looking-glass, and then he turned away and went over to the window again, whistling quietly, under his breath, rocking backwards and forwards on his heels.

'Don't mind her,' he said; 'she's an extraordinary character in many ways, and possibly not very easy for another woman to get on with. You mustn't worry about it. If she really makes herself a nuisance we'll get rid of her. But she's efficient, you know, and will take all housekeeping worries off your hands. I dare say she's a bit of a bully to the staff. She doesn't dare bully me though. I'd have given her the sack long ago if she had tried.'

'I expect we shall get on very well when she knows me better,' I said quickly; 'after all, it's natural enough that she should resent me a bit at first.'

'Resent you? Why resent you? What the devil do you mean?' he said.

He turned from the window, frowning, an odd, half angry expression on his face. I wondered why he should mind, and wished I had said something else.

'I mean, it must be much easier for a housekeeper to look after a man alone,' I said. 'I dare say she had got into the way of doing it, and perhaps she was afraid I should be very over-bearing.'

'Overbearing, my God . . .' he began, 'if you think . . .' and then he stopped, and came across to me, and kissed me on the top of my head.

'Let's forget about Mrs Danvers,' he said; 'she doesn't interest me very much, I'm afraid. Come along, and let me show you something of Manderley.'

I did not see Mrs Danvers again that evening, and we did not talk about her any more. I felt happier when I had dismissed her from my thoughts, less of an interloper, and as we wandered about the rooms downstairs, and looked at the pictures, and Maxim put his arm around my shoulder, I began to feel more like the self I wanted to become, the self I had pictured in my dreams, who made Manderley her home.

My footsteps no longer sounded foolish on the stone flags of the hall, for Maxim's nailed shoes made far more noise than mine, and the pattering feet of the two dogs was a comfortable, pleasing note.

I was glad, too, because it was the first evening and we had only been back a little while and the showing of the pictures had taken time, when Maxim, looking at the clock, said it was too late to change for dinner, so that I was spared the embarrassment of Alice, the maid, asking what I should wear, and of her helping me to dress, and myself walking down that long flight of stairs to the hall, cold, with bare shoulders, in a dress that Mrs Van Hopper had given me because it did not suit her daughter. I had dreaded the formality of dinner in that austere dining-room, and now, because of the little fact that we had not changed, it was quite all right, quite easy, just the same as when we had dined together in restaurants. I was comfortable in my stockinette dress, I laughed and talked about things we had seen in Italy and France, we even had the snapshots on the table, and Frith and the footman were impersonal people, as the waiters had been; they did not stare at me as Mrs Danvers had done.

We sat in the library after dinner, and presently the curtains were drawn, and more logs thrown on the fire; it was cool for May, I was thankful for the warmth that came from the steady burning logs.

It was new for us to sit together like this, after dinner, for in Italy we had wandered about, walked or driven, gone into little cafés, leant over bridges. Maxim made instinctively now for the chair on the left of the open fireplace, and stretched out his hand for the papers. He settled one of the broad cushions behind his head, and lit a cigarette. 'This is his routine,' I thought, 'this is what he always does: this has been his custom now for years.'

He did not look at me, he went on reading his paper, contented, comfortable, having assumed his way of living, the master of his house. And as I sat there, brooding, my chin in my hands, fondling the soft ears of one of the spaniels, it came to me that I was not the first one to lounge there in possession of the chair; someone had been before me, and surely left an imprint of her person on the cushions, and on the arm where her hand had rested. Another one had poured the coffee from that same silver coffee pot, had placed the cup to her lips, had bent down to the dog, even as I was doing.

Unconsciously, I shivered as though someone had opened the door behind me and let a draught into the room. I was sitting in Rebecca's chair, I was leaning against Rebecca's cushion, and the dog had come to me and laid his head upon my knee because that had been his custom, and he remembered, in the past, she had given sugar to him there.

8

I had never realized, of course, that life at Manderley would be so orderly and planned. I remember now, looking back, how on that first morning Maxim was up and dressed and writing letters, even before breakfast, and when I got downstairs, rather after nine o'clock, a little flurried by the booming summons of the gong, I found he had nearly finished, he was already peeling his fruit.

He looked up at me and smiled. 'You mustn't mind,' he said; 'this is something you will have to get used to. I've no time to hang about at this hour of the day. Running a place like Manderley, you know, is a full-time job. The coffee and the hot dishes are on the sideboard. We always help ourselves at breakfast.' I said something about my clock being slow, about having been too long in the bath, but he did not listen, he was looking down at a letter, frowning at something.

How impressed I was, I remember well; impressed and a little overawed by the magnificence of the breakfast offered to us. There was tea, in a great silver urn, and coffee too, and on the heater, piping hot, dishes of scrambled eggs, of bacon, and another of fish. There was a little clutch of boiled eggs as well, in their own special heater, and porridge, in a silver porringer. On another sideboard was a ham, and a great piece of cold bacon. There were scones too, on the table, and toast, and various pots of jam, marmalade, and honey, while dessert dishes, piled high with fruit, stood at either end. It seemed strange to me that Maxim, who in Italy and France had eaten a *croissant* and fruit only, and drunk a cup of coffee, should sit down to this breakfast at home, enough for a dozen people, day after day probably, year after year, seeing nothing ridiculous about it, nothing wasteful.

I noticed he had eaten a small piece of fish. I took a boiled egg. And I wondered what happened to the rest, all those scrambled eggs, that crisp bacon, the porridge, the remains of the fish. Were there menials, I wondered, whom I should never know, never see, waiting behind kitchen doors for the gift of our breakfast? Or was it all thrown away, shovelled into dustbins? I would never know, of course, I would never dare to ask.

'Thank the Lord I haven't a great crowd of relations to inflict upon you,' said Maxim, 'a sister I very rarely see, and a grandmother who is nearly blind. Beatrice, by the way, asks herself over to lunch. I half expected she would. I suppose she wants to have a look at you.'

'Today?' I said, my spirits sinking to zero.

'Yes, according to the letter I got this morning. She won't stay long. You'll like her, I think. She's very direct, believes in speaking her mind. No humbug at all. If she doesn't like you she'll tell you so, to your face.'

I found this hardly comforting, and wondered if there was not some virtue in the quality of insincerity. Maxim got up from his chair, and lit a cigarette. 'I've a mass of things to see to this morning, do you think you can amuse yourself?' he said. 'I'd like to have taken you round the garden, but I must see Crawley, my agent. I've been away from things too long. He'll be in to lunch, too, by the way. You don't mind, do you? You will be all right?'

'Of course,' I said, 'I shall be quite happy.'

Then he picked up his letters, and went out of the room, and I remember thinking this was not how I imagined my first morning; I had seen us walking together, arms linked, to the sea, coming back rather late and tired and happy to a cold lunch, alone, and sitting afterwards under that chestnut tree I could see from the library window.

I lingered long over my first breakfast, spinning out the time, and it was not until I saw Frith come in and look at me, from behind the service screen, that I realized it was after ten o'clock. I sprang to my feet at once, feeling guilty, and apologized for sitting there so late, and he bowed, saying nothing, very polite, very correct, and I caught a flicker of surprise in his eyes. I wondered if I had said the wrong thing. Perhaps it did not do to apologize. Perhaps it lowered me in his estimation. I wished I knew what to say, what to do. I wondered if he suspected, as Mrs Danvers had done, that poise, and grace, and assurance were not qualities inbred in me, but were things to be acquired, painfully perhaps, and slowly, costing me many bitter moments.

As it was, leaving the room, I stumbled, not looking where I was going, catching my foot on the step by the door, and Frith came forward to help me, picking up my handkerchief, while Robert, the young footman, who was standing behind the screen, turned away to hide his smile.

I heard the murmur of their voices as I crossed the hall, and one of them laughed – Robert, I supposed. Perhaps they were laughing about me. I went upstairs again, to the privacy of my bedroom, but when I opened the door I found the housemaids in there doing the room; one was sweeping the floor, the other dusting the dressing-table. They looked at me in surprise. I quickly went out again. It could not be right, then, for me to go to my room at that hour in the morning. It was not expected of me. It broke the household routine. I crept downstairs once more, silently, thankful of my slippers that made no sound on the stone flags, and so into the library, which was chilly, the windows flung wide open, the fire laid but not lit.

I shut the windows, and looked round for a box of matches. I could not find one. I wondered what I should do. I did not like to ring. But the library, so snug and warm last night with the burning logs, was like an ice-house now, in the early morning. There were matches upstairs in the bedroom, but I did not like to go for them because it would mean disturbing the house-maids at their work. I could not bear their moon faces staring at me again. I decided that when Frith and Robert had left the dining-room I would fetch the matches from the sideboard. I tiptoed out into the hall and listened. They were still clearing, I could hear the sound of voices, and the movement of trays.

Presently all was silent, they must have gone through the service doors into the kitchen quarters, so I went across the hall and into the dining-room once more. Yes, there was a box of matches on the sideboard, as I expected. I crossed the room quickly and picked them up, and as I did so Frith came back into the room. I tried to cram the box furtively into my pocket, but I saw him glance at my hand in surprise.

'Did you require anything, Madam?' he said.

'Oh, Frith,' I said awkwardly, 'I could not find any matches.' He at once proffered me another box, handing me the cigarettes too, at the same time. This was another embarrassment, for I did not smoke.

'No, the fact is,' I said, 'I felt rather cool in the library, I suppose the weather seems chilly to me, after being abroad and I thought perhaps I would just put a match to the fire.'

'The fire in the library is not usually lit until the afternoon, Madam,' he said. 'Mrs de Winter always used the morning-room. There is a good fire in there. Of course if you should wish to have the fire in the library as well I will give orders for it to be lit.'

'Oh, no,' I said, 'I would not dream of it. I will go into the morning-room. Thank you, Frith.'

'You will find writing-paper, and pens, and ink, in there, Madam,' he said. 'Mrs de Winter always did all her correspondence and telephoning in the morning-room, after breakfast. The house telephone is also there, should you wish to speak to Mrs Danvers.'

'Thank you, Frith,' I said.

I turned away into the hall again, humming a little tune to give me an air of confidence. I could not tell him that I had never seen the morning-room, that Maxim had not shown it to me the night before. I knew he was standing in the entrance to the dining-room, watching me, as I went across the hall, and that I must make some show of knowing my way. There was a door to the left of the great staircase, and I went recklessly towards it, praying in my heart that it would take me to my goal, but when I came to it and opened it I saw that it was a garden room, a place for odds and ends: there was a table where flowers were done, there were basket chairs stacked against the wall, and a couple of mackintoshes too, hanging on a peg. I came out, a little defiantly, glancing across the hall, and saw Frith still standing there. I had not deceived him, though, not for a moment.

'You go through the drawing-room to the morning-room, Madam,' he said, 'through the door there, on your right, this side of the staircase. You go straight through the double drawing-room, and turn to your left.'

'Thank you, Frith,' I said humbly, pretending no longer.

I went through the long drawing-room, as he had directed; a lovely room this, beautifully proportioned, looking out upon the lawns down to the sea. The public would see this room, I supposed, and Frith, if he showed them round, would know the history of the pictures on the wall, and the period of the furniture. It was beautiful of course, I knew that, and those chairs and tables probably without price, but for all that I had no wish to linger there; I could not see myself sitting ever in those chairs, standing before that carved mantelpiece, throwing books down on to the tables. It had all the formality of a room in a museum, where alcoves were roped off, and a guardian, in cloak and hat like the guides in the French châteaux, sat in a chair beside the door. I went through then, and turned to the left, and so on to the little morning-room I had not seen before.

I was glad to see the dogs there, sitting before the fire, and Jasper, the younger, came over to me at once, his tail wagging, and thrust his nose into my hand. The old one lifted her muzzle at my approach, and gazed in my direction with her blind eyes, but when she had sniffed the air a moment, and found I was not the one she sought, she turned her head away with a grunt, and looked steadily into the fire again. Then Jasper left me, too, and settled himself by the side of his companion, licking his side. This was their routine. They knew, even as Frith had known, that the library fire was not lit until the afternoon. They came to the morning-room from long custom. Somehow I guessed, before going to the window, that the room looked out upon the rhododendrons. Yes, there they were, blood-red and luscious, as I had seen them the evening before, great bushes of them, massed beneath the open window, encroaching on to the sweep of the drive itself. There was a little clearing too, between the bushes, like a miniature lawn, the grass a smooth carpet of moss, and in the centre of this, the tiny statue of a naked faun, his pipes to his lips.

The crimson rhododendrons made his background, and the clearing itself was like a little stage, where he would dance, and play his part. There was no musty smell about this room, as there had been in the library. There were no old well-worn chairs, no tables littered with magazines and papers, seldom if ever read, but left there from long custom, because Maxim's father, or even his grandfather perhaps, had wished it so.

This was a woman's room, graceful, fragile, the room of someone who had chosen every particle of furniture with great care, so that each chair, each vase, each small, infinitesimal thing should be in harmony with one another, and with her own personality. It was as though she who had arranged this room had said: 'This I will have, and this, and this,' taking piece by piece from the treasures in Manderley each object that pleased her best, ignoring the second-rate, the mediocre, laying her hand with sure certain instinct only upon the best. There was no inter-mingling of style, no confusing of period, and the result was perfection in a strange and startling way, not coldly formal like the drawing-room shown to the public, but vividly alive, having something of the same glow and brilliance that the rhododendrons had, massed there, beneath the window. And I noticed then that the rhododendrons, not content with forming their theatre on the little lawn outside the window, had been permitted to the room itself. Their great warm faces looked down upon me from the mantelpiece, they floated in a bowl upon the table by the sofa, they stood, lean and graceful, on the writing-desk beside the golden candlesticks.

The room was filled with them, even the walls took colour

from them, becoming rich and glowing in the morning sun. They were the only flowers in the room, and I wondered if there was some purpose in it, whether the room had been arranged originally with this one end in view, for nowhere else in the house did the rhododendrons obtrude. There were flowers in the dining-room, flowers in the library, but orderly and trim, rather in the background, not like this, not in profusion. I went and sat down at the writing-desk, and I thought how strange it was that this room, so lovely and so rich in colour, should be, at the same time, so business-like and purposeful. Somehow I should have expected that a room furnished as this was in such exquisite taste, for all the exaggeration of the flowers, would be a place of decoration only, languorous and intimate.

But this writing-table, beautiful as it was, was no pretty toy where a woman would scribble little notes, nibbling the end of a pen, leaving it, day after day, in carelessness, the blotter a little askew. The pigeon-holes were docketed, 'letters unanswered', 'letters-to-keep', 'household', 'estate', 'menus', 'miscellaneous', 'addresses'; each ticket written in that same scrawling pointed hand that I knew already. And it shocked me, even startled me, to recognize it again, for I had not seen it since I had destroyed the page from the book of poems, and I had not thought to see it again.

I opened a drawer at hazard, and there was the writing once more, this time in an open leather book, whose heading 'Guests at Manderley' showed at once, divided into weeks and months, what visitors had come and gone, the rooms they had used, the food they had eaten. I turned over the pages and saw that the book was a complete record of a year, so that the hostess, glancing back, would know to the day, almost to the hour, what guest had passed what night under her roof, and where he had slept, and what she had given him to eat. There was notepaper also in the drawer, thick white sheets, for rough writing, and the notepaper of the house, with the crest, and the address, and visiting cards, ivory white, in little boxes.

I took one out and looked at it, unwrapped it from its thin

tissue of paper. 'Mrs M. de Winter' it said, and in the corner 'Manderley'. I put it back in the box again, and shut the drawer, feeling guilty suddenly, and deceitful, as though I were staying in somebody else's house and my hostess had said to me, 'Yes, of course, write letters at my desk,' and I had unforgivably, in a stealthy manner, peeped at her correspondence. At any moment she might come back into the room and she would see me there, sitting before her open drawer, which I had no right to touch.

And when the telephone rang, suddenly, alarmingly, on the desk in front of me, my heart leapt and I started up in terror, thinking I had been discovered. I took the receiver off with trembling hands, and 'Who is it?' I said, 'who do you want?' There was a strange buzzing at the end of the line, and then a voice came, low and rather harsh, whether that of a woman or a man I could not tell, and 'Mrs de Winter?' it said, 'Mrs de Winter?'

'I'm afraid you have made a mistake,' I said; 'Mrs de Winter has been dead for over a year.' I sat there, waiting, staring stupidly into the mouthpiece, and it was not until the name was repeated again, the voice incredulous, slightly raised, that I became aware, with a rush of colour to my face, that I had blundered irretrievably, and could not take back my words. 'It's Mrs Danvers, Madam,' said the voice. 'I'm speaking to you on the house telephone.' My *faux pas* was so palpably obvious, so idiotic and unpardonable, that to ignore it would show me to be an even greater fool, if possible, than I was already.

'I'm sorry, Mrs Danvers,' I said, stammering, my words tumbling over one another; 'the telephone startled me, I didn't know what I was saying, I didn't realize the call was for me, and I never noticed I was speaking on the house telephone.'

'I'm sorry to have disturbed you, Madam,' she said; and she knows, I thought, she guesses I have been looking through the desk. 'I only wondered whether you wished to see me, and whether you approved of the menus for today.'

'Oh,' I said. 'Oh, I'm sure I do; that is, I'm sure I approve of the menus. Just order what you like, Mrs Danvers, you needn't bother to ask me.'

'It would be better, I think, if you read the list,' continued the voice; 'you will find the menu of the day on the blotter, beside you.'

I searched feverishly about me on the desk, and found at last a sheet of paper I had not noticed before. I glanced hurriedly through it: curried prawns, roast veal, asparagus, cold chocolate mousse – was this lunch or dinner? I could not see; lunch, I suppose.

'Yes, Mrs Danvers,' I said, 'very suitable, very nice indeed.'

'If you wish anything changed please say so,' she answered, 'and I will give orders at once. You will notice I have left a blank space beside the sauce, for you to mark your preference. I was not sure what sauce you are used to having served with the roast veal. Mrs de Winter was most particular about her sauces, and I always had to refer to her.'

'Oh,' I said. 'Oh, well . . . let me see, Mrs Danvers, I hardly know; I think we had better have what you usually have, whatever you think Mrs de Winter would have ordered.'

'You have no preference, Madam?'

'No,' I said. 'No, really, Mrs Danvers.'

'I rather think Mrs de Winter would have ordered a wine sauce, Madam.'

'We will have the same then, of course,' I said.

'I'm very sorry I disturbed you while you were writing, Madam.'

'You didn't disturb me at all,' I said; 'please don't apologize.'

'The post leaves at midday, and Robert will come for your letters, and stamp them himself,' she said; 'all you have to do is ring through to him, on the telephone, if you have anything urgent to be sent, and he will give orders for them to be taken in to the post-office immediately.'

'Thank you, Mrs Danvers,' I said. I listened for a moment, but she said no more, and then I heard a little click at the end of the telephone, which meant she had replaced the receiver. I did the same. Then I looked down again at the desk, and the notepaper, ready for use, upon the blotter. In front of me stared the ticketed pigeon-holes, and the words upon them 'letters unanswered', 'estate', 'miscellaneous', were like a reproach to me for my idleness. She who sat here before me had not wasted her time, as I was doing. She had reached out for the house telephone and given her orders for the day, swiftly, efficiently, and run her pencil perhaps through an item in the menu that had not pleased her. She had not said 'Yes, Mrs Danvers,' and 'Of course, Mrs Danvers,' as I had done. And then, when she had finished, she began her letters, five, six, seven perhaps to be answered, all written in that same curious, slanting hand I knew so well. She would tear off sheet after sheet of that smooth white paper, using it extravagantly, because of the long strokes she made when she wrote, and at the end of each of her personal letters she put her signature, 'Rebecca', that tall sloping R dwarfing its fellows.

I drummed with my fingers on the desk. The pigeon-holes were empty now. There were no 'letters unanswered' waiting to be dealt with, no bills to pay that I knew anything about. If I had anything urgent, Mrs Danvers said, I must telephone through to Robert and he would give orders for it to be taken to the post. I wondered how many urgent letters Rebecca used to write, and who they were written to. Dressmakers perhaps – 'I must have the white satin on Tuesday, without fail,' or to her hairdresser – 'I shall be coming up next Friday, and want an appointment at three o'clock with Monsieur Antoine himself. Shampoo, massage, set, and manicure.' No, letters of that type would be a waste of time. She would have a call put through to London. Frith would do it. Frith would say 'I am speaking for Mrs de Winter.' I went on drumming with my fingers on the desk. I could think of nobody to write to. Only Mrs Van Hopper. And there was something foolish, rather ironical, in the realization that here I was sitting at my own desk in my own home with nothing better to do than to write a letter to Mrs Van Hopper, a woman I disliked, whom I should never see again. I pulled a sheet of notepaper towards me. I took up the narrow, slender pen, with the bright pointed nib. 'Dear Mrs Van Hopper,' I began. And as I wrote, in halting, laboured fashion, saying I hoped the voyage had been good, that she had found her daughter better, that the weather in New York was fine and warm, I noticed for the first time how cramped and unformed was my own handwriting; without individuality, without style, uneducated even, the writing of an indifferent pupil taught in a second-rate school.

9

When I heard the sound of the car in the drive I got up in sudden panic, glancing at the clock, for I knew that it meant Beatrice and her husband had arrived. It was only just gone twelve; they were much earlier than I expected. And Maxim was not yet back. I wondered if it would be possible to hide, to get out of the window, into the garden so that Frith, bringing them to the morning-room, would say, 'Madam must have gone out,' and it would seem quite natural, they would take it as a matter of course. The dogs looked up inquiringly as I ran to the window, and Jasper followed me, wagging his tail.

The window opened out on to the terrace and the little grass clearing beyond, but as I prepared to brush past the rhododendrons the sound of voices came close, and I backed again into the room. They were coming to the house by way of the garden, Frith having told them doubtless that I was in the morning-room. I went quickly into the big drawing-room, and made for a door near me on the left. It led into a long stone passage, and I ran along it, fully aware of my stupidity, despising myself for this sudden attack of nerves, but I knew I could not face these people, not for a moment anyway. The passage seemed to be taking me to the back regions, and as I turned a corner, coming upon another staircase, I met a servant I had not seen before, a scullery-maid perhaps; she carried a mop and pail in her hands. She stared at me in wonder, as though I were a vision, unexpected in this part of the house, and 'Good morning,' I said, in great confusion, making for the stairway, and 'Good morning, Madam,' she returned, her mouth open, her round eyes inquisitive as I climbed the stairs.

They would lead me, I supposed, to the bedrooms, and I could find my suite in the east wing, and sit up there a little while, until I judged it nearly time for lunch, when good manners would compel me to come down again.

I must have lost my bearings, for passing through a door at the head of the stairs I came to a long corridor that I had not seen before, similar in some ways to the one in the east wing, but broader and darker – dark owing to the panelling of the walls.

I hesitated, then turned left, coming upon a broad landing and another staircase. It was very quiet and dark. No one was about. If there had been housemaids here, during the morning, they had finished their work by now and gone downstairs. There was no trace of their presence, no lingering dust smell of carpets lately swept, and I thought, as I stood there, wondering which way to turn, that the silence was unusual, holding something of the same oppression as an empty house does, when the owners have gone away.

I opened a door at hazard, and found a room in total darkness, no chink of light coming through the closed shutters, while I could see dimly, in the centre of the room, the outline of furniture swathed in white dust-sheets. The room smelt close and stale, the smell of a room seldom if ever used, whose ornaments are herded together in the centre of a bed and left there, covered with a sheet. It might be too that the curtain had not been drawn from the window since some preceding summer, and if one crossed there now and pulled them aside, opening the creaking shutters, a dead moth who had been imprisoned behind them for many months would fall to the carpet and lie there, beside a forgotten pin, and a dried leaf blown there before the windows were closed for the last time. I shut the door softly, and went uncertainly along the corridor, flanked on either side by doors, all of them closed, until I came to a little alcove, set in an outside wall, where a broad window gave me light at last. I looked out, and I saw below me the smooth grass lawns stretching to the sea, and the sea itself, bright green with white-tipped crests, whipped by a westerly wind and scudding from the shore.

It was closer than I had thought, much closer; it ran, surely, beneath that little knot of trees below the lawns, barely five minutes away, and if I listened now, my ear to the window, I could hear the surf breaking on the shores of some little bay I could not see. I knew then I had made the circuit of the house, and was standing in the corridor of the west wing. Yes, Mrs Danvers was right. You could hear the sea from here. You might imagine, in the winter, it would creep up on to those green lawns and threaten the house itself, for even now, because of the high wind, there was a mist upon the window-glass, as though someone had breathed upon it. A mist salt-laden, borne upwards from the sea. A hurrying cloud hid the sun for a moment as I watched, and the sea changed colour instantly, becoming black, and the white crests with them very pitiless suddenly, and cruel, not the gay sparkling sea I had looked on first.

Somehow I was glad my rooms were in the east wing. I preferred the rose-garden, after all, to the sound of the sea. I went back to the landing then, at the head of the stairs, and as I prepared to go down, one hand upon the banister, I heard the door behind me open, and it was Mrs Danvers. We stared at one another for a moment without speaking, and I could not be certain whether it was anger I read in her eyes or curiosity, for her face became a mask directly she saw me. Although she said nothing I felt guilty and ashamed, as though I had been caught trespassing, and I felt the tell-tale colour come up into my face.

'I lost my way,' I said, 'I was trying to find my room.'

'You have come to the opposite side of the house,' she said; 'this is the west wing.'

'Yes, I know,' I said.

'Did you go into any of the rooms?' she asked me.

'No,' I said. 'No, I just opened a door, I did not go in. Everything was dark, covered up in dust-sheets. I'm sorry. I did not mean to disturb anything. I expect you like to keep all this shut up.'

'If you wish to open up the rooms I will have it done,' she

said; 'you have only to tell me. The rooms are all furnished, and can be used.'

'Oh, no,' I said. 'No. I did not mean you to think that.'

'Perhaps you would like me to show you all over the west wing?' she said.

I shook my head. 'No, I'd rather not,' I said. 'No, I must go downstairs.' I began to walk down the stairs, and she came with me, by my side, as though she were a warder, and I in custody.

'Any time, when you have nothing to do, you have only to ask me, and I will show you the rooms in the west wing,' she persisted, making me vaguely uncomfortable. I knew not why. Her insistence struck a chord in my memory, reminding me of a visit to a friend's house, as a child, when the daughter of the house, older than me, took my arm and whispered in my ear, 'I know where there is a book, locked in a cupboard, in my mother's bedroom. Shall we go and look at it?' I remembered her white, excited face, and her small, beady eyes, and the way she kept pinching my arm.

'I will have the dust-sheets removed, and then you can see the rooms as they looked when they were used,' said Mrs Danvers. 'I would have shown you this morning, but I believed you to be writing letters in the morning-room. You have only to telephone through to my room, you know, when you want me. It would only take a short while to have the rooms in readiness.'

We had come down the short flight of stairs, and she opened another door, standing aside for me to pass through, her dark eyes questing my face.

'It's very kind of you, Mrs Danvers,' I said. 'I will let you know some time.'

We passed out together on to the landing beyond, and I saw we were at the head of the main staircase now, behind the minstrel's gallery.

'I wonder how you came to miss your way?' she said, 'the door through the west wing is very different to this.'

'I did not come this way,' I said.

'Then you must have come up the back way, from the stone passage?' she said.

'Yes,' I said, not meeting her eyes. 'Yes, I came through a stone passage.'

She went on looking at me, as though she expected me to tell her why I left the morning-room in sudden panic, going through the back regions, and I felt suddenly that she knew, that she must have watched me, that she had seen me wandering perhaps in that west wing from the first, her eye to a crack in the door. 'Mrs Lacy, and Major Lacy, have been here some time,' she said. 'I heard their car drive up shortly after twelve.'

'Oh!' I said. 'I had not realized that.'

'Frith will have taken them to the morning-room,' she said: 'it must be getting on for half past twelve. You know your way now, don't you?'

'Yes, Mrs Danvers,' I said. And I went down the big stairway into the hall, knowing she was standing there above me, her eyes watching me.

I knew I must go back now, to the morning-room, and meet Maxim's sister and her husband. I could not hide in my bedroom now. As I went into the drawing-room I glanced back, over my shoulder, and I saw Mrs Danvers still standing there at the head of the stairs, like a black sentinel.

I stood for a moment outside the morning-room, with my hand on the door, listening to the hum of voices. Maxim had returned, then, while I had been upstairs, bringing his agent with him I supposed, for it sounded to me as if the room was full of people. I was aware of the same feeling of sick uncertainty I had experienced so often as a child, when summoned to shake hands with visitors, and turning the handle of the door I blundered in, to be met at once, it seemed, with a sea of faces and a general silence.

'Here she is at last,' said Maxim. 'Where have you been hiding? We were thinking of sending out a search party. Here is Beatrice, and this is Giles, and this is Frank Crawley. Look out, you nearly trod on the dog.'

Beatrice was tall, broad-shouldered, very handsome, very much like Maxim about the eyes and jaw, but not as smart as I had expected, much tweedier; the sort of person who would nurse dogs through distemper, know about horses, shoot well. She did not kiss me. She shook hands very firmly, looking me straight in the eyes, and then turned to Maxim. 'Quite different from what I expected. Doesn't answer to your description at all.'

Everyone laughed, and I joined in, not quite certain if the laugh was against me or not, wondering secretly what it was she had expected, and what had been Maxim's description.

And 'This is Giles,' said Maxim, prodding my arm, and Giles stretched out an enormous paw and wrung my hand, squeezing the fingers limp, genial eyes smiling from behind horn-rimmed glasses.

'Frank Crawley,' said Maxim, and I turned to the agent, a colourless, rather thin man with a prominent Adam's apple, in whose eyes I read relief as he looked upon me. I wondered why, but I had no time to think of that, because Frith had come in, and was offering me sherry, and Beatrice was talking to me again. 'Maxim tells me you only got back last night. I had not realized that, or of course we would never have thrust ourselves upon you so soon. Well, what do you think of Manderley?'

'I've scarcely seen anything of it yet,' I answered; 'it's beautiful, of course.'

She was looking me up and down, as I had expected, but in a direct, straightforward fashion, not maliciously like Mrs Danvers, not with unfriendliness. She had a right to judge me, she was Maxim's sister, and Maxim himself came to my side now, putting his arm through mine, giving me confidence.

'You're looking better, old man,' she said to him, her head on one side, considering him; 'you've lost that fine-drawn look, thank goodness. I suppose we've got you to thank for that?' nodding at me.

'I'm always very fit,' said Maxim shortly, 'never had anything wrong with me in my life. You imagine everyone ill who doesn't look as fat as Giles.'

'Bosh,' said Beatrice; 'you know perfectly well you were a perfect wreck six months ago. Gave me the fright of my life when I came and saw you. I thought you were in for a breakdown. Giles, bear me out. Didn't Maxim look perfectly ghastly last time we came over, and didn't I say he was heading for a breakdown?'

'Well, I must say, old chap, you're looking a different person,' said Giles. 'Very good thing you went away. Doesn't he look well, Crawley?'

I could tell by the tightening of Maxim's muscles under my arm that he was trying to keep his temper. For some reason this talk about his health was not welcome to him, angered him even, and I thought it tactless of Beatrice to harp upon it in this way, making so big a point of it.

'Maxim's very sunburnt,' I said shyly; 'it hides a multitude of sins. You should have seen him in Venice having breakfast on the balcony, trying to get brown on purpose. He thinks it makes him better-looking.'

Everyone laughed, and Mr Crawley said, 'It must have been wonderful in Venice, Mrs de Winter, this time of year,' and 'Yes,' I said, 'we had really wonderful weather. Only one bad day, wasn't it, Maxim?' the conversation drawing away happily from his health, and so to Italy, safest of subjects, and the blessed topic of fine weather. Conversation was easy now, no longer an effort. Maxim and Giles and Beatrice were discussing the running of Maxim's car, and Mr Crawley was asking if it were true that there were no more gondolas in the canals now, only motorboats. I don't think he would have cared at all had there been steamers at anchor in the Grand Canal, he was saying this to help me, it was his contribution to the little effort of steering the talk away from Maxim's health, and I was grateful to him, feeling him an ally, for all his dull appearance.

'Jasper wants exercise,' said Beatrice, stirring the dog with her foot; 'he's getting much too fat, and he's barely two years old. What do you feed him on, Maxim?'

'My dear Beatrice, he has exactly the same routine as your

dogs,' said Maxim. 'Don't show off and make out you know more about animals than I do.'

'Dear old boy, how can you pretend to know what Jasper has been fed on when you've been away for a couple of months? Don't tell me Frith walks to the lodge gates with him twice a day. This dog hasn't had a run for weeks. I can tell by the condition of his coat.'

'I'd rather he looked colossal than half-starved like that half-wit dog of yours,' said Maxim.

'Not a very intelligent remark when Lion won two firsts at Cruft's last February,' said Beatrice.

The atmosphere was becoming rather strained again, I could tell by the narrow lines of Maxim's mouth, and I wondered if brothers and sisters always sparred like this, making it uncomfortable for those who listened. I wished that Frith would come in and announce lunch. Or would we be summoned by a booming gong? I did not know what happened at Manderley.

'How far away from us are you?' I asked, sitting down by Beatrice; 'did you have to make a very early start?'

'We're fifty miles away, my dear, in the next county, the other side of Trowchester. The hunting is so much better with us. You must come over and stay, when Maxim can spare you. Giles will mount you.'

'I'm afraid I don't hunt,' I confessed. 'I learnt to ride, as a child, but very feebly; I don't remember much about it.'

'You must take it up again,' she said. 'You can't possibly live in the country and not ride: you wouldn't know what to do with yourself. Maxim says you paint. That's very nice, of course, but there's no exercise in it, is there? All very well on a wet day when there's nothing better to do.'

'My dear Beatrice, we are not all such fresh-air fiends as you,' said Maxim.

'I wasn't talking to you, old boy. We all know you are perfectly happy slopping about the Manderley gardens and never breaking out of a slow walk.'

'I'm very fond of walking too,' I said swiftly. 'I'm sure I shall never get tired of rambling about Manderley. And I can bathe too, when it's warmer.'

'My dear, you are an optimist,' said Beatrice. 'I can hardly ever remember bathing here. The water is far too cold, and the beach is shingle.'

'I don't mind that,' I said. 'I love bathing. As long as the currents are not too strong. Is the bathing safe in the bay?'

Nobody answered, and I realized suddenly what I had said. My heart thumped, and I felt my cheeks go flaming red. I bent down to stroke Jasper's ear, in an agony of confusion. 'Jasper could do with a swim, and get some of that fat off,' said Beatrice, breaking the pause, 'but he'd find it a bit too much for him in the bay, wouldn't you, Jasper? Good old Jasper. Nice old man.' We patted the dog together, not looking at one another.

'I say, I'm getting infernally hungry. What on earth is happening to lunch?' said Maxim.

'It's only just on one now,' said Mr Crawley, 'according to the clock on the mantelpiece.'

'That clock was always fast,' said Beatrice.

'It's kept perfect time now for months,' said Maxim.

At that moment the door opened and Frith announced that luncheon was served.

'I say, I must have a wash,' said Giles, looking at his hands.

We all got up and wandered through the drawing-room to the hall in great relief, Beatrice and I a little ahead of the men, she taking my arm.

'Dear old Frith,' she said, 'he always looks exactly the same, and makes me feel like a girl again. You know, don't mind me saying so, but you are even younger than I expected. Maxim told me your age, but you're an absolute child. Tell me, are you very much in love with him?'

I was not prepared for this question, and she must have seen the surprise in my face, for she laughed lightly, and squeezed my arm.

'Don't answer,' she said. 'I can see what you feel. I'm an interfering bore, aren't I? You mustn't mind me. I'm devoted to Maxim, you know, though we always bicker like cat and dog when we meet. I congratulate you again on his looks. We were all very worried about him this time last year, but of course you know the whole story.' We had come to the dining-room by now, and she said no more, for the servants were there and the others had joined us, but as I sat down, and unfolded my napkin, I wondered what Beatrice would say did she realize that I knew nothing of that preceding year, no details of the tragedy that had happened down there, in the bay, that Maxim kept these things to himself, that I questioned him never.

Lunch passed off better than I had dared to hope. There were few arguments, or perhaps Beatrice was exercising tact at last; at any rate she and Maxim chatted about matters concerning Manderley, her horses, the garden, mutual friends, and Frank Crawley, on my left, kept up an easy patter with me for which I was grateful, as it required no effort. Giles was more concerned with food than with the conversation, though now and again he remembered my existence and flung me a remark at hazard.

'Same cook I suppose, Maxim?' he said, when Robert had offered him the cold soufflé for the second time. 'I always tell Bee, Manderley's the only place left in England where one can get decent cooking. I remember this soufflé of old.'

'I think we change cooks periodically,' said Maxim, 'but the standard of cooking remains the same. Mrs Danvers has all the recipes, she tells them what to do.'

'Amazing woman, that Mrs Danvers,' said Giles, turning to me; 'don't you think so?'

'Oh, yes,' I said. 'Mrs Danvers seems to be a wonderful person.'

'She's no oil painting though, is she?' said Giles, and he roared with laughter. Frank Crawley said nothing, and looking up I saw Beatrice was watching me. She turned away then, and began talking to Maxim.

'Do you play golf at all, Mrs de Winter?' said Mr Crawley.

'No, I'm afraid I don't,' I answered, glad that the subject had been changed again, that Mrs Danvers was forgotten, and even though I was no player, knew nothing of the game, I was prepared to listen to him as long as he pleased; there was something solid and safe and dull about golf, it could not bring us into any difficulties. We had cheese, and coffee, and I wondered whether I was supposed to make a move. I kept looking at Maxim, but he gave no sign, and then Giles embarked upon a story, rather difficult to follow, about digging a car out of a snow-drift – what had started the train of thought I could not tell – and I listened to him politely, nodding my head now and again and smiling, aware of Maxim becoming restive at his end of the table. At last he paused, and I caught Maxim's eye. He frowned very slightly and jerked his head towards the door.

I got up at once, shaking the table clumsily as I moved my chair, and upsetting Giles's glass of port. 'Oh, dear,' I said, hovering, wondering what to do, reaching ineffectively for my napkin, but 'All right, Frith will deal with it,' said Maxim, 'don't add to the confusion. Beatrice, take her out in the garden; she's scarcely seen the place yet.'

He looked tired, rather jaded. I began to wish none of them had come. They had spoilt our day anyway. It was too much of an effort, just as we returned. I felt tired too, tired and depressed. Maxim had seemed almost irritable when he suggested we should go into the garden. What a fool I had been, upsetting that glass of port.

We went out on to the terrace and walked down on to the smooth green lawns.

'I think it's a pity you came back to Manderley so soon,' said Beatrice, 'it would have been far better to potter about in Italy for three or four months, and then come back in the middle of the summer. Done Maxim a power of good too, besides being easier from your point of view. I can't help feeling it's going to be rather a strain here for you at first.'

'Oh, I don't think so,' I said. 'I know I shall come to love Manderley.'

She did not answer, and we strolled backwards and forwards on the lawns.

'Tell me a bit about yourself,' she said at last; 'what was it you were doing in the south of France? Living with some appalling American woman, Maxim said.'

I explained about Mrs Van Hopper, and what had led to it, and she seemed sympathetic but a little vague, as though she was thinking of something else.

'Yes,' she said, when I paused, 'it all happened very suddenly, as you say. But of course we were all delighted, my dear, and I do hope you will be happy.'

'Thank you, Beatrice,' I said, 'thank you very much.'

I wondered why she said she hoped we would be happy, instead of saying she knew we would be so. She was kind, she was sincere, I liked her very much, but there was a tiny doubt in her voice that made me afraid.

'When Maxim wrote and told me,' she went on, taking my arm, 'and said he had discovered you in the south of France, and you were very young, very pretty, I must admit it gave me a bit of a shock. Of course we all expected a social butterfly, very modern and plastered with paint, the sort of girl you expected to meet in those sort of places. When you came into the morning-room before lunch you could have knocked me down with a feather.'

She laughed, and I laughed with her. But she did not say whether or not she was disappointed in my appearance or relieved.

'Poor Maxim,' she said: 'he went through a ghastly time, and let's hope you have made him forget about it. Of course he adores Manderley.'

Part of me wanted her to continue her train of thought, to tell me more of the past, naturally and easily like this, and something else, way back in my mind, did not want to know, did not want to hear.

'We are not a bit alike, you know,' she said, 'our characters are poles apart. I show everything on my face: whether I like people or not, whether I am angry or pleased. There's no reserve about me. Maxim is entirely different. Very quiet, very reserved. You never know what's going on in that funny mind of his. I lose my temper on the slightest provocation, flare up, and then it's all over. Maxim loses his temper once or twice in a year, and when he does – my God – he *does* lose it. I don't suppose he ever will with you, I should think you are a placid little thing.'

She smiled, and pinched my arm, and I thought about being placid, how quiet and comfortable it sounded, someone with knitting on her lap, with calm unruffled brow. Someone who was never anxious, never tortured by doubt and indecision, someone who never stood as I did, hopeful, eager, frightened, tearing at bitten nails, uncertain which way to go, what star to follow.

'You won't mind me saying so, will you?' she went on, 'but I think you ought to do something to your hair. Why don't you have it waved? It's so very lanky, isn't it, like that? Must look awful under a hat. Why don't you sweep it back behind your ears?'

I did so obediently, and waited for her approval. She looked at me critically, her head on one side. 'No,' she said. 'No, I think that's worse. It's too severe, and doesn't suit you. No, all you need is a wave, just to pinch it up. I never have cared for that Joan of Arc business or whatever they call it. What does Maxim say? Does he think it suits you?'

'I don't know,' I said, 'he's never mentioned it.'

'Oh well,' she said, 'perhaps he likes it. Don't go by me. Tell me, did you get any clothes in London or Paris?'

'No,' I said, 'we had no time. Maxim was anxious to get home. And I can always send for catalogues.'

'I can tell by the way you dress that you don't care a hoot what you wear,' she said. I glanced at my flannel skirt apologetically.

'I do,' I said. 'I'm very fond of nice things. I've never had much money to spend on clothes up to now.'

'I wonder Maxim did not stay a week or so in London and get you something decent to wear,' she said. 'I must say, I think it's rather selfish of him. So unlike him too. He's generally so particular.'

'Is he?' I said; 'he's never seemed particular to me. I don't

111

think he notices what I wear at all. I don't think he minds.'

'Oh,' she said. 'Oh, well, he must have changed then.'

She looked away from me, and whistled to Jasper, her hands in her pockets, and then stared up at the house above us.

'You're not using the west wing then,' she said.

'No,' I said. 'No, we have the suite in the east wing. It's all been done up.'

'Has it?' she said. 'I didn't know that. I wonder why.'

'It was Maxim's idea,' I said, 'he seems to prefer it.'

She said nothing, she went on looking at the windows, and whistling. 'How do you get on with Mrs Danvers?' she said suddenly.

I bent down, and began patting Jasper's head, and stroking his ears. 'I have not seen very much of her,' I said; 'she scares me a little. I've never seen anyone quite like her before.'

'I don't suppose you have,' said Beatrice.

Jasper looked up at me with great eyes, humble, rather self-conscious. I kissed the top of his silken head, and put my hand over his black nose.

'There's no need to be frightened of her,' said Beatrice; 'and don't let her see it, whatever you do. Of course I've never had anything to do with her, and I don't think I ever want to either. However, she's always been very civil to me.'

I went on patting Jasper's head.

'Did she seem friendly?' said Beatrice.

'No,' I said. 'No, not very.'

Beatrice began whistling again, and she rubbed Jasper's head with her foot. 'I shouldn't have more to do with her than you can help,' she said.

'No,' I said. 'She runs the house very efficiently, there's no need for me to interfere.'

'Oh, I don't suppose she'd mind that,' said Beatrice. That was what Maxim had said, the evening before, and I thought it odd that they should both have the same opinion. I should have imagined that interference was the one thing Mrs Danvers did not want.

112

'I dare say she will get over it in time,' said Beatrice, 'but it may make things rather unpleasant for you at first. Of course she's insanely jealous. I was afraid she would be.'

'Why?' I asked, looking up at her, 'why should she be jealous? Maxim does not seem to be particularly fond of her.'

'My dear child, it's not Maxim she's thinking of,' said Beatrice; 'I think she respects him and all that, but nothing more very much.

'No, you see,' – she paused, frowning a little, looking at me uncertainly – 'she resents your being here at all, that's the trouble.'

'Why?' I said, 'why should she resent me?'

'I thought you knew,' said Beatrice; 'I thought Maxim would have told you. She simply adored Rebecca.'

'Oh,' I said. 'Oh, I see.'

We both went on patting and stroking Jasper, who, unaccustomed to such attention, rolled over on his back in ecstasy.

'Here are the men,' said Beatrice, 'let's have some chairs out and sit under the chestnut. How fat Giles is getting, he looks quite repulsive beside Maxim. I suppose Frank will go back to the office. What a dull creature he is, never has anything interesting to say. Well, all of you. What have you been discussing? Pulling the world to bits, I suppose.' She laughed, and the others strolled towards us, and we stood about. Giles threw a twig for Jasper to retrieve. We all looked at Jasper. Mr Crawley looked at his watch. 'I must be off,' he said; 'thank you very much for lunch, Mrs de Winter.'

'You must come often,' I said, shaking hands.

I wondered if the others would go too. I was not sure whether they had just come over for lunch or to spend the day. I hoped they would go. I wanted to be alone with Maxim again, and that it would be like we were in Italy. We all went and sat down under the chestnut tree. Robert brought out chairs and rugs. Giles lay down on his back and tipped his hat over his eyes. After a while he began to snore, his mouth open.

'Shut up, Giles,' said Beatrice. 'I'm not asleep,' he muttered, opening his eyes, and shutting them again. I thought him unattractive. I wondered why Beatrice had married him. She could never have been in love with him. Perhaps that was what she was thinking about me. I caught her eye upon me now and again, puzzled, reflective, as though she was saying to herself 'What on earth does Maxim see in her?' but kind at the same time, not unfriendly. They were talking about their grandmother.

'We must go over and see the old lady,' Maxim was saying, and 'She's getting gaga,' said Beatrice, 'drops food all down her chin, poor darling.'

I listened to them both, leaning against Maxim's arm, rubbing my chin on his sleeve. He stroked my hand absently, not thinking, talking to Beatrice.

'That's what I do to Jasper,' I thought. 'I'm being like Jasper now, leaning against him. He pats me now and again, when he remembers, and I'm pleased, I get closer to him for a moment. He likes me in the way I like Jasper.'

The wind had dropped. The afternoon was drowsy, peaceful. The grass had been new-mown; it smelt sweet and rich, like summer. A bee droned above Giles's head, and he flicked at it with his hat. Jasper sloped in to join us, too warm in the sun, his tongue lolling from his mouth. He flopped beside me, and began licking his side, his large eyes apologetic. The sun shone on the mullioned windows of the house, and I could see the green lawns and the terrace reflected in them. Smoke curled thinly from one of the near chimneys, and I wondered if the library fire had been lit, according to routine.

A thrush flew across the lawn to the magnolia tree outside the dining-room window. I could smell the faint, soft magnolia scent as I sat here, on the lawn. Everything was quiet and still. Very distant now came the washing of the sea in the bay below. The tide must have gone out. The bee droned over us again, pausing to taste the chestnut blossom above our heads. 'This is what I always imagined,' I thought, 'this is how I hoped it would be, living at Manderley.'

I wanted to go on sitting there, not talking, not listening to the others, keeping the moment precious for all time, because we were peaceful, all of us, we were content and drowsy even as the bee who droned above our heads. In a little while it would be different, there would come tomorrow, and the next day, and another year. And we would be changed perhaps, never sitting quite like this again. Some of us would go away, or suffer, or die; the future stretched away in front of us, unknown, unseen, not perhaps what we wanted, not what we planned. This moment was safe though, this could not be touched. Here we sat together, Maxim and I, hand-in-hand, and the past and the future mattered not at all. This was secure, this funny fragment of time he would never remember, never think about again. He would not hold it sacred; he was talking about cutting away some of the under-growth in the drive, and Beatrice agreed, interrupting with some suggestion of her own, and throwing a piece of grass at Giles at the same time. For them it was just after lunch, quarter past three on a haphazard afternoon, like any hour, like any day. They did not want to hold it close, imprisoned and secure, as I did. They were not afraid.

'Well, I suppose we ought to be off,' said Beatrice, brushing the grass from her skirt; 'I don't want to be late, we've got the Cartrights dining.'

'How is old Vera?' asked Maxim.

'Oh, same as ever, always talking about her health. He's getting very old. They're sure to ask all about you both.'

'Give them my love,' said Maxim.

We got up. Giles shook the dust off his hat. Maxim yawned and stretched. The sun went in. I looked up at the sky. It had changed already, a mackerel sky. Little clouds scurrying in forma-tion, line upon line.

'Wind's backing,' said Maxim.

'I hope we don't run into rain,' said Giles.

'I'm afraid we've had the best of the day,' said Beatrice.

We wandered slowly towards the drive and the waiting car.

'You haven't seen what's been done to the east wing,' said Maxim.

'Come upstairs,' I suggested; 'it won't take a minute.'

We went into the hall, and up the big staircase, the men following behind.

It seemed strange that Beatrice had lived here for so many years. She had run down these same stairs as a little girl, with her nurse. She had been born here, bred here; she knew it all, she belonged here more than I should ever do. She must have many memories locked inside her heart. I wondered if she ever thought about the days that were gone, ever remembered the lanky pig-tailed child that she had been once, so different from the woman she had become, forty-five now, vigorous and settled in her ways, another person . . .

We came to the rooms, and Giles, stooping under the low doorway, said, 'How very jolly; this is a great improvement, isn't it, Bee?' and 'I say, old boy, you have spread yourself,' said Beatrice: 'new curtains, new beds, new everything. You remember, Giles, we had this room that time you were laid up with your leg? It was very dingy then. Of course Mother never had much idea of comfort. And then, you never put people here, did you, Maxim? Except when there was an overflow. The bachelors were always dumped here. Well, it's charming, I must say. Looks over the rose-garden too, which was always an advantage. May I powder my nose?'

The men went downstairs, and Beatrice peered in the mirror.

'Did old Danvers do all this for you?' she said.

'Yes,' I said. 'I think she's done it very well.'

'So she should, with her training,' said Beatrice. 'I wonder what on earth it cost. A pretty packet, I bet. Did you ask?'

'No, I'm afraid I did not,' I said.

'I don't suppose it worried Mrs Danvers,' said Beatrice. 'Do you mind if I use your comb? These are nice brushes. Wedding present?'

'Maxim gave them to me.'

'H'm. I like them. We must give you something of course. What do you want?'

'Oh, I don't really know. You mustn't bother,' I said.

116

'My dear, don't be absurd. I'm not one to grudge you a present, even though we weren't asked to your wedding!'

'I hope you did not mind about that. Maxim wanted it to be abroad.'

'Of course not. Very sensible of you both. After all, it wasn't as though . . .' she stopped in the middle of her sentence, and dropped her bag. 'Damn, have I broken the catch? No, all is well. What was I saying? I can't remember. Oh, yes, wedding presents. We must think of something. You probably don't care for jewellery.'

I did not answer. 'It's so different from the ordinary young couple,' she said. 'The daughter of a friend of mine got married the other day, and of course they were started off in the usual way, with linen, and coffee sets, and dining-room chairs, and all that. I gave rather a nice standard lamp. Cost me a fiver at Harrods. If you do go up to London to buy clothes mind you go to my woman, Madame Carroux. She has damn good taste, and she doesn't rook you.'

She got up from the dressing-table, and pulled at her skirt.

'Do you suppose you will have a lot of people down?' she said.

'I don't know. Maxim hasn't said.'

'Funny old boy, one never quite knows with him. At one time one could not get a bed in the house, the place would be chock-a-block. I can't somehow see you . . .' she stopped abruptly, and patted my arm. 'Oh, well,' she said, 'we'll see. It's a pity you don't ride or shoot, you miss such a lot. You don't sail by any chance, do you?'

'No,' I said.

'Thank God for that,' she said.

She went to the door, and I followed her down the corridor.

'Come and see us if you feel like it,' she said. 'I always expect people to ask themselves. Life is too short to send out invitations.'

'Thank you very much,' I said.

We came to the head of the stairs looking down upon the

117

hall. The men were standing on the steps outside. 'Come on, Bee,' shouted Giles. 'I felt a spot of rain, so we've put on the cover. Maxim says the glass is falling.'

Beatrice took my hand, and bending down gave me a swift peck on my cheek. 'Good-bye,' she said; 'forgive me if I've asked you a lot of rude questions, my dear, and said all sorts of things I shouldn't. Tact never was my strong point, as Maxim will tell you. And, as I told you before, you're not a bit what I expected.' She looked at me direct, her lips pursed in a whistle, and then took a cigarette from her bag, and flashed her lighter.

'You see,' she said, snapping the top, and walking down the stairs, 'you are so very different from Rebecca.'

And we came out on to the steps and found the sun had gone behind a bank of cloud, a little thin rain was falling, and Robert was hurrying across the lawn to bring in the chairs.

We watched the car disappear round the sweep of the drive, and then Maxim took my arm and said, 'Thank God that's that. Get a coat quickly, and come out. Damn the rain, I want a walk. I can't stand this sitting about.' He looked white and strained, and I wondered why the entertaining of Beatrice and Giles, his own sister and brother-in-law, should have tired him so.

'Wait while I run upstairs for my coat,' I said.

'There's a heap of mackintoshes in the flower room, get one of them,' he said impatiently, 'women are always half an hour when they go to their bedrooms. Robert, fetch a coat from the flower room, will you, for Mrs de Winter? There must be half a dozen raincoats hanging there left by people at one time or another.' He was already standing in the drive, and calling to Jasper, 'Come on, you lazy little beggar, and take some of that fat off.' Jasper ran round in circles, barking hysterically at the prospect of his walk. 'Shut up, you idiot,' said Maxim. 'What on earth is Robert doing?'

Robert came running out of the hall carrying a raincoat, and I struggled into it hurriedly, fumbling with the collar. It was too big, of course, and too long, but there was no time to change it, and we set off together across the lawn to the woods, Jasper running in front.

'I find a little of my family goes a very long way,' said Maxim. 'Beatrice is one of the best people in the world, but she invariably puts her foot in it.'

I was not sure where Beatrice had blundered, and thought it better not to ask. Perhaps he still resented the chat about his health before lunch.

'What did you think of her?' he went on.

'I liked her very much,' I said; 'she was very nice to me.'

'What did she talk to you about out here, after lunch?'

'Oh, I don't know. I think I did most of the talking. I was telling her about Mrs Van Hopper, and how you and I met, and all that. She said I was quite different from what she expected.'

'What the devil did she expect?'

'Someone much smarter, more sophisticated, I imagine. A social butterfly, she said.'

Maxim did not answer for a moment; he bent down, and threw a stick for Jasper. 'Beatrice can sometimes be infernally unintelligent,' he said.

We climbed the grass bank above the lawns, and plunged into the woods. The trees grew very close together, and it was dark. We trod upon broken twigs, and last year's leaves, and here and there the fresh green stubble of the young bracken, and the shoots of the bluebells soon to blossom. Jasper was silent now, his nose to the ground. I took Maxim's arm.

'Do you like my hair?' I said.

He stared down at me in astonishment. 'Your hair?' he said. 'Why on earth do you ask? Of course I like it. What's the matter with it?'

'Oh, nothing,' I said, 'I just wondered.'

'How funny you are,' he said.

We came to a clearing in the woods, and there were two paths, going in opposite directions. Jasper took the right-hand path without hesitation.

'Not that way,' called Maxim; 'come on, old chap.'

The dog looked back at us and stood there, wagging his tail, but did not return. 'Why does he want to go that way?' I asked.

'I suppose he's used to it,' said Maxim briefly; 'it leads to a small cove, where we used to keep a boat. Come on, Jasper, old man.'

We turned into the left-hand path, not saying anything, and presently I looked over my shoulder and saw that Jasper was following us.

'This brings us to the valley I told you about,' said Maxim, 'and you shall smell the azaleas. Never mind the rain, it will bring out the scent.'

He seemed all right again now, happy and cheerful, the Maxim I knew and loved, and he began talking about Frank Crawley and what a good fellow he was, so thorough and reliable, and devoted to Manderley.

'This is better,' I thought; 'this is like it was in Italy', and I smiled up at him, squeezing his arm, relieved that the odd strained look on his face had passed away, and while I said 'Yes,' and 'Really?' and 'Fancy, darling,' my thoughts wandered back to Beatrice, wondering why her presence should have disturbed him, what she had done; and I thought too of all she had said about his temper, how he lost it, she told me, about once or twice a year.

She must know him, of course; she was his sister. But it was not what I had thought; it was not my idea of Maxim. I could see him moody, difficult, irritable perhaps, but not angry as she had inferred, not passionate. Perhaps she had exaggerated; people very often were wrong about their relatives.

'There,' said Maxim suddenly, 'take a look at that.'

We stood on a slope of a wooded hill, and the path wound away before us to a valley, by the side of a running stream. There were no dark trees here, no tangled undergrowth, but on either side of the narrow path stood azaleas and rhododendrons, not blood-coloured like the giants in the drive, but salmon, white, and gold, things of beauty and of grace, drooping their lovely, delicate heads in the soft summer rain.

The air was full of their scent, sweet and heady, and it seemed to me as though their very essence had mingled with the running waters of the stream, and become one with the falling rain and the dank rich moss beneath our feet. There was no sound here but the tumbling of the little stream, and the quiet rain. When Maxim spoke, his voice was hushed too, gentle and low, as if he had no wish to break upon the silence.

'We call it the Happy Valley,' he said.

We stood quite still, not speaking, looking down upon the

clear white faces of the flowers closest to us, and Maxim stooped, and picked up a fallen petal and gave it to me. It was crushed and bruised, and turning brown at the curled edge, but as I rubbed it across my hand the scent rose to me, sweet and strong, vivid as the living tree from which it came.

Then the birds began. First a blackbird, his note clear and cool above the running stream, and after a moment he had answer from his fellow hidden in the woods behind us, and soon the still air about us was made turbulent with song, pursuing us as we wandered down into the valley, and the fragrance of the white petals followed us too. It was disturbing, like an enchanted place. I had not thought it could be as beautiful as this.

The sky, now overcast and sullen, so changed from the early afternoon, and the steady insistent rain could not disturb the soft quietude of the valley; the rain and the rivulet mingled with one another, and the liquid note of the black bird fell upon the damp air in harmony with them both. I brushed the dripping heads of azaleas as I passed, so close they grew together, bordering the path. Little drops of water fell on to my hands from the soaked petals. There were petals at my feet too, brown and sodden, bearing their scent upon them still, and a richer, older scent as well, the smell of deep moss and bitter earth, the stems of bracken, and the twisted buried roots of trees. I held Maxim's hand and I had not spoken. The spell of the Happy Valley was upon me. This at last was the core of Manderley, the Manderley I would know and learn to love. The first drive was forgotten, the black, herded woods, the glaring rhododendrons, luscious and over-proud. And the vast house too, the silence of that echoing hall, the uneasy stillness of the west wing, wrapped in dust-sheets. There I was an interloper, wandering in rooms that did not know me, sitting at a desk and in a chair that were not mine. Here it was different. The Happy Valley knew no trespassers. We came to the end of the path, and the flowers formed an archway above our heads. We bent down, passing underneath, and when I stood straight again, brushing the raindrops from my hair, I saw that the valley was behind us, and the azaleas, and the trees, and, as Maxim had described to me that afternoon many weeks ago in Monte Carlo, we were standing in a little narrow cove, the shingle hard and white under our feet, and the sea was breaking on the shore beyond us.

Maxim smiled down at me, watching the bewilderment on my face.

'It's a shock, isn't it?' he said; 'no one ever expects it. The contrast is too sudden; it almost hurts.' He picked up a stone and flung it across the beach for Jasper. 'Fetch it, good man,' and Jasper streaked away in search of the stone, his long black ears flapping in the wind.

The enchantment was no more, the spell was broken. We were mortal again, two people playing on a beach. We threw more stones, went to the water's edge, flung ducks and drakes, and fished for driftwood. The tide had turned, and came lapping in the bay. The small rocks were covered, the seaweed washed on the stones. We rescued a big floating plank and carried it up the beach above high-water mark. Maxim turned to me, laughing, wiping the hair out of his eyes, and I unrolled the sleeves of my mackintosh caught by the sea spray. And then we looked round, and saw that Jasper had disappeared. We called and whistled, and he did not come. I looked anxiously towards the mouth of the cove where the waves were breaking upon the rocks.

'No,' said Maxim, 'we should have seen him, he can't have fallen. Jasper, you idiot, where are you? Jasper, Jasper?'

'Perhaps he's gone back to the Happy Valley?' I said.

'He was by that rock a minute ago, sniffing a dead sea-gull,' said Maxim.

We walked up the beach towards the valley once again. 'Jasper, Jasper?' called Maxim.

In the distance, beyond the rocks to the right of the beach, I heard a short, sharp bark. 'Hear that?' I said. 'He's climbed over this way.' I began to scramble up the slippery rocks in the direction of the bark.

'Come back,' said Maxim sharply; 'we don't want to go that way. The fool of a dog must look after himself.'

I hesitated, looked down from my rock. 'Perhaps he's fallen,' I said, 'poor little chap. Let me fetch him.' Jasper barked again, further away this time. 'Oh, listen,' I said, 'I must get him. It's quite safe, isn't it? The tide won't have cut him off?'

'He's all right,' said Maxim irritably; 'why not leave him? He knows his own way back.'

I pretended not to hear, and began scrambling over the rocks towards Jasper. Great jagged boulders screened the view, and I slipped and stumbled on the wet rocks, making my way as best I could in Jasper's direction. It was heartless of Maxim to leave Jasper, I thought, and I could not understand it. Besides, the tide was coming in. I came up beside the big boulder that had hidden the view, and looked beyond it. And I saw, to my surprise, that I was looking down into another cove, similar to the one I had left, but wider and more rounded. A small stone breakwater had been thrown out across the cove for shelter, and behind it the bay formed a tiny natural harbour. There was a buoy anchored there, but no boat. The beach in the cove was white shingle, like the one behind me, but steeper, shelving suddenly to the sea. The woods came right down to the tangle of seaweed marking high water, encroaching almost to the rocks themselves, and at the fringe of the woods was a long low building, half cottage, half boat-house, built of the same stone as the breakwater.

There was a man on the beach, a fisherman perhaps, in long boots and a sou'wester, and Jasper was barking at him, running round him in circles, darting at his boots. The man took no notice; he was bending down, and scraping in the shingle. 'Jasper,' I shouted, 'Jasper, come here.'

The dog looked up, wagging his tail, but he did not obey me. He went on baiting the solitary figure on the beach.

I looked over my shoulder. There was still no sign of Maxim. I climbed down over the rocks to the beach below. My feet made a crunching noise across the shingle, and the man looked up at the sound. I saw then that he had the small slit eyes of an idiot, and the red, wet mouth. He smiled at me, showing toothless gums.

'G'day,' he said. 'Dirty, ain't it?'

'Good afternoon,' I said. 'No. I'm afraid it's not very nice weather.'

He watched me with interest, smiling all the while. 'Diggin' for shell,' he said. 'No shell here. Been diggin' since forenoon.'

'Oh,' I said, 'I'm sorry you can't find any.'

'That's right,' he said, 'no shell here.'

'Come on, Jasper,' I said, 'it's getting late. Come on, old boy.'

But Jasper was in an infuriating mood. Perhaps the wind and the sea had gone to his head, for he backed away from me, barking stupidly, and began racing round the beach after nothing at all. I saw he would never follow me, and I had no lead. I turned to the man, who had bent down again to his futile digging.

'Have you got any string?' I said.

'Eh?' he said.

'Have you got any string?' I repeated.

'No shell here,' he said, shaking his head. 'Been diggin' since forenoon.' He nodded his head at me, and wiped his pale blue watery eyes.

'I want something to tie the dog,' I said. 'He won't follow me.'

'Eh?' he said. And he smiled his poor idiot's smile.

'All right,' I said; 'it doesn't matter.'

He looked at me uncertainly, and then leant forward, and poked me in the chest.

'I know that dog,' he said; 'he comes fro' the house.'

'Yes,' I said. 'I want him to come back with me now.'

'He's not yourn,' he said.

'He's Mr de Winter's dog,' I said gently. 'I want to take him back to the house.'

'Eh?' he said.

I called Jasper once more, but he was chasing a feather blown by the wind. I wondered if there was any string in the boat-house, and I walked up the beach towards it. There must have been a garden once, but now the grass was long and overgrown, crowded with nettles. The windows were boarded up. No doubt the door was locked, and I lifted the latch without much hope. To my surprise it opened after the first stiffness, and I went inside, bending my head because of the low door. I expected to find the usual boat store, dirty and dusty with disuse, ropes and blocks and oars upon the floor. The dust was there, and the dirt too in places, but there were no ropes or blocks. The room was furnished, and ran the whole length of the cottage. There was a desk in the corner, a table, and chairs, and a bed-sofa pushed against the wall. There was a dresser too, with cups and plates. Bookshelves, the books inside them, and models of ships standing on the top of the shelves. For a moment I thought it must be inhabited – perhaps the poor man on the beach lived here – but I looked around me again and saw no sign of recent occupation. That rusted grate knew no fire, this dusty floor no footsteps, and the china there on the dresser was blue-spotted with the damp. There was a queer musty smell about the place. Cobwebs spun threads upon the ships' models, making their own ghostly rigging. No one lived here. No one came here. The door had creaked on its hinges when I opened it. The rain pattered on the roof with a hollow sound, and tapped upon the boarded windows. The fabric of the sofa-bed had been nibbled by mice or rats. I could see the jagged holes, and the frayed edges. It was damp in the cottage, damp and chill. Dark, and oppressive. I did not like it. I had no wish to stay there. I hated the hollow sound of the rain pattering on the roof. It seemed to echo in the room itself, and I heard the water dripping too into the rusted grate.

I looked about me for some string. There was nothing that would serve my purpose, nothing at all. There was another door at the end of the room, and I went to it, and opened it, a little fearful now, a little afraid, for I had the odd, uneasy feeling that I might come upon something unawares, that I had no wish to see. Something that might harm me, that might be horrible.

It was nonsense of course, and I opened the door. It was only a boat store after all. Here were the ropes and blocks I had expected, two or three sails, fenders, a small punt, pots of paints, all the litter and junk that goes with the using of boats. A ball of twine lay on a shelf, a rusted clasp knife beside it. This would be all I needed for Jasper. I opened the knife, and cut a length of twine, and came back into the room again. The rain still fell upon the roof, and into the grate. I came out of the cottage hurriedly, not looking behind me, trying not to see the torn sofa and the mildewed china, the spun cobwebs on the model ships, and so through the creaking gate and on to the white beach.

The man was not digging any more; he was watching me, Jasper at his side.

'Come along, Jasper,' I said; 'come on, good dog.' I bent down and this time he allowed me to touch him and pull hold of his collar. 'I found some string in the cottage,' I said to the man.

He did not answer, and I tied the string loosely round Jasper's collar.

'Good afternoon,' I said, tugging at Jasper.

The man nodded, staring at me with his narrow idiot's eyes. 'I saw 'ee go in yonder,' he said.

'Yes,' I said; 'it's all right, Mr de Winter won't mind.'

'She don't go in there now,' he said.

'No,' I said, 'not now.'

'She's gone in the sea, ain't she?' he said; 'she won't come back no more?'

'No,' I said, 'she'll not come back.'

'I never said nothing, did I?' he said.

'No, of course not; don't worry,' I said.

He bent down again to his digging, muttering to himself. I went across the shingle and I saw Maxim waiting for me by the rocks, his hands in his pockets.

'I'm sorry,' I said. 'Jasper would not come. I had to get some string.'

He turned abruptly on his heel, and made towards the woods.

'Aren't we going back over the rocks?' I said.

'What's the point? We're here now,' he said briefly.

We went up past the cottage and struck into a path through the woods. 'I'm sorry I was such a time; it was Jasper's fault,' I said, 'he kept barking at the man. Who was he?'

'Only Ben,' said Maxim; 'he's quite harmless, poor devil. His old father used to be one of the keepers; they live near the home farm. Where did you get that piece of twine?'

'I found it in the cottage on the beach,' I said.

'Was the door open?' he asked.

'Yes, I pushed it open. I found the string in the other room, where the sails were, and a small boat.'

'Oh,' he said shortly. 'Oh, I see,' and then he added, after a moment or two: 'That cottage is supposed to be locked, the door has no business to be open.'

I said nothing; it was not my affair.

'Did Ben tell you the door was open?'

'No,' I said, 'he did not seem to understand anything I asked him.'

'He makes out he's worse than he is,' said Maxim. 'He can talk quite intelligibly if he wants to. He's probably been in and out of the cottage dozens of times, and did not want you to know.'

'I don't think so,' I answered; 'the place looked deserted, quite untouched. There was dust everywhere, and no footmarks. It was terribly damp. I'm afraid those books will be quite spoilt, and the chairs, and that sofa. There are rats there, too; they have eaten away some of the covers.'

Maxim did not reply. He walked at a tremendous pace, and the climb up from the beach was steep. It was very different from the Happy Valley. The trees were dark here and close together, there were no azaleas brushing the path. The rain dripped heavily from the thick branches. It splashed on my collar and trickled down my neck. I shivered; it was unpleasant, like a cold finger. My legs ached, after the unaccustomed scramble over the rocks. And Jasper lagged behind, weary from his wild scamper, his tongue hanging from his mouth.

'Come on, Jasper, for God's sake,' said Maxim. 'Make him walk up, pull at the twine or something, can't you? Beatrice was right. The dog is much too fat.'

'It's your fault,' I said, 'you walk so fast. We can't keep up with you.'

'If you had listened to me instead of rushing wildly over those rocks we would have been home by now,' said Maxim. 'Jasper knew his way back perfectly. I can't think what you wanted to go after him for.'

'I thought he might have fallen, and I was afraid of the tide,' I said.

'Is it likely I should have left the dog had there been any question of the tide?' said Maxim. 'I told you not to go on those rocks, and now you are grumbling because you are tired.'

'I'm not grumbling,' I said. 'Anyone, even if they had legs of iron, would be tired walking at this pace. I thought you would come with me when I went after Jasper anyway, instead of staying behind.'

'Why should I exhaust myself careering after the damn dog?' he said.

'It was no more exhausting careering after Jasper on the rocks than it was careering after the driftwood on the beach,' I answered. 'You just say that because you have not any other excuse.'

'My good child, what am I supposed to excuse myself about?'

'Oh, I don't know,' I said wearily; 'let's stop this.'

'Not at all, you began it. What do you mean by saying I was trying to find an excuse? Excuse for what?'

'Excuse for not having come with me over the rocks, I suppose,' I said.

'Well, and why do you think I did not want to cross to the other beach?'

'Oh, Maxim, how should I know? I'm not a thought-reader. I know you did not want to, that's all. I could see it in your face.'

'See what in my face?'

'I've already told you. I could see you did not want to go. Oh, do let's have an end to it. I'm sick to death of the subject.'

'All women say that when they've lost an argument. All right, I did not want to go to the other beach. Will that please you? I never go near the bloody place, or that God-damned cottage.

And if you had my memories you would not want to go there either, or talk about it, or even think about it. There. You can digest that if you like, and I hope it satisfies you.'

His face was white, and his eyes strained and wretched with that dark lost look they had had when I first met him. I put out my hand to him, I took hold of his, holding it tight.

'Please, Maxim, please,' I said.

'What's the matter?' he said roughly.

'I don't want you to look like that,' I said. 'It hurts too much. Please, Maxim. Let's forget all we said. A futile silly argument. I'm sorry, darling. I'm sorry. Please let everything be all right.'

'We ought to have stayed in Italy,' he said. 'We ought never to have come back to Manderley. Oh, God, what a fool I was to come back.'

He brushed through the trees impatiently, striding even faster than before, and I had to run to keep pace with him, catching at my breath, tears very near the surface, dragging poor Jasper after me on the end of his string.

At last we came to the top of the path, and I saw its fellow branching left to the Happy Valley. We had climbed the path then that Jasper had wished to take at the beginning of the afternoon. I knew now why Jasper had turned to it. It led to the beach he knew best, and the cottage. It was his old routine.

We came out on to the lawns, and went across them to the house without a word. Maxim's face was hard, with no expression. He went straight into the hall and on to the library without looking at me. Frith was in the hall.

'We want tea at once,' said Maxim, and he shut the library door.

I fought to keep back my tears. Frith must not see them. He would think we had been quarrelling, and he would go to the servants' hall and say to them all, 'Mrs de Winter was crying in the hall just now. It looks as though things are not going very well.' I turned away, so that Frith should not see my face. He came towards me though, he began to help me off with my mackintosh.

'I'll put your raincoat away for you in the flower-room, Madam,' he said.

'Thank you, Frith,' I replied, my face still away from him.

'Not a very pleasant afternoon for a walk, I fear, Madam.'

'No,' I said. 'No, it was not very nice.'

'Your handkerchief, Madam?' he said, picking up something that had fallen on the floor. 'Thank you,' I said, putting it in my pocket.

I was wondering whether to go upstairs or whether to follow Maxim to the library. Frith took the coat to the flower-room. I stood there, hesitating, biting my nails. Frith came back again. He looked surprised to see me still there.

'There is a good fire in the library now, Madam.'

'Thank you, Frith,' I said.

I walked slowly across the hall to the library. I opened the door and went in. Maxim was sitting in his chair, Jasper at his feet, the old dog in her basket. Maxim was not reading the paper, though it lay on the arm of the chair beside him. I went and knelt down by his side and put my face close to his.

'Don't be angry with me any more,' I whispered.

He took my face in his hands, and looked down at me with his tired, strained eyes. 'I'm not angry with you,' he said.

'Yes,' I said. 'I've made you unhappy. It's the same as making you angry. You're all wounded and hurt and torn inside. I can't bear to see you like this. I love you so much.'

'Do you?' he said. 'Do you?' He held me very tight, and his eyes questioned me, dark and uncertain, the eyes of a child in pain, a child in fear.

'What is it, darling?' I said. 'Why do you look like that?'

I heard the door open before he could answer, and I sank back on my heels, pretending to reach for a log to throw on the fire, while Frith came into the room followed by Robert, and the ritual of our tea began.

The performance of the day before was repeated, the placing of the table, the laying of the snow-white cloth, the putting down of cakes and crumpets, the silver kettle of hot water placed on its little flame, while Jasper, wagging his tail, his ears stretched back in anticipation, watched my face. Five minutes must have passed before we were alone again, and when I looked at Maxim I saw the colour had come back into his face, the tired, lost look was gone, and he was reaching for a sandwich.

'Having all that crowd to lunch was the trouble,' he said. 'Poor old Beatrice always does rub me up the wrong way. We used to scrap like dogs as children. I'm so fond of her too, bless her. Such a relief though that they don't live too near. Which reminds me, we'll have to go over and see Granny some time. Pour out my tea, sweetheart, and forgive me for being a bear to you.'

It was over then. The episode was finished. We must not speak of it again. He smiled at me over his cup of tea, and then reached for the newspaper on the arm of his chair. The smile was my reward. Like a pat on the head to Jasper. Good dog then, lie down, don't worry me any more. I was Jasper again. I was back where I had been before. I took a piece of crumpet and divided it between the two dogs. I did not want it myself, I was not hungry. I felt very weary now, very tired in a dull, spent way. I looked at Maxim but he was reading his paper, he had folded it over to another page. My fingers were messy with the butter from the crumpet, and I felt in my pocket for a handkerchief. I drew it out, a tiny scrap of a thing, lace-edged. I stared at it, frowning, for it was not mine. I remembered then that Frith had picked it up from the stone floor of the hall. It must have fallen out of the pocket in the mackintosh. I turned it over in my hand. It was grubby; little bits of fluff from the pocket clung to it. It must have been in the mackintosh pocket for a long time. There was a monogram in the corner. A tall sloping R, with the letters de W interlaced. The R dwarfed the other letters, the tail of it ran down into the cambric, away from the laced edge. It was only a small handkerchief, quite a scrap of a thing. It had been rolled in a ball and put away in the pocket and forgotten.

I must have been the first person to put on that mackintosh since the handkerchief was used. She who had worn the coat then was tall, slim, broader than me about the shoulders, for I had found it big and overlong, and the sleeves had come below my wrist. Some of the buttons were missing. She had not bothered then to do it up. She had thrown it over her shoulders like a cape, or worn it loose, hanging open, her hands deep in the pockets.

There was a pink mark upon the handkerchief. The mark of lip-stick. She had rubbed her lips with the handkerchief, and then rolled it in a ball, and left it in the pocket. I wiped my fingers with the handkerchief, and as I did so I noticed that a dull scent clung about it still. A scent I recognized, a scent I knew. I shut my eyes and tried to remember. It was something elusive, something faint and fragrant that I could not name. I had breathed it before, touched it surely, that very afternoon.

And then I knew that the vanished scent upon the handkerchief was the same as the crushed white petals of the azaleas in the Happy Valley.

The weather was wet and cold for quite a week, as it often can be in the west country in the early summer, and we did not go down to the beach again. I could see the sea from the terrace, and the lawns. It looked grey and uninviting, great rollers sweeping in to the bay past the beacon on the headland. I pictured them surging into the little cove and breaking with a roar upon the rocks, then running swift and strong to the shelving beach. If I stood on the terrace and listened I could hear the murmur of the sea below me, low and sullen. A dull, persistent sound that never ceased. And the gulls flew inland too, driven by the weather. They hovered above the house in circles, wheeling and crying, flapping their spread wings. I began to understand why some people could not bear the clamour of the sea. It has a mournful harping note sometimes, and the very persistence of it, that eternal roll and thunder and hiss, plays a jagged tune upon the nerves. I was glad our rooms were in the east wing and I could lean out of my window and look down upon the rose-garden. For sometimes I could not sleep, and getting softly out of bed in the quiet night I would wander to the window, and lean there, my arms upon the sill, and the air would be very peaceful, very still.

I could not hear the restless sea, and because I could not hear it my thoughts would be peaceful too. They would not carry me down that steep path through the woods to the grey cove and the deserted cottage. I did not want to think about the cottage. I remembered it too often in the day. The memory of it nagged at me whenever I saw the sea from the terrace. For I would see once more the blue spots on the china, the spun webs on the little masts of those model ships, and the rat holes on the sofa bed. I would remember the pattering of the rain on the roof. And I thought of Ben, too, with his narrow watery blue eyes, his sly idiot's smile. These things disturbed me, I was not happy about them. I wanted to forget them but at the same time I wanted to know why they disturbed me, why they made me uneasy and unhappy. Somewhere, at the back of my mind, there was a frightened furtive seed of curiosity that grew slowly and stealthily, for all my denial of it, and I knew all the doubt and anxiety of the child who has been told, 'these things are not discussed, they are forbidden.'

I could not forget the white, lost look in Maxim's eyes when we came up the path through the woods, and I could not forget his words. 'Oh, God, what a fool I was to come back.' It was all my fault, because I had gone down into the bay. I had opened up a road into the past again. And although Maxim had recovered, and was himself again, and we lived our lives together, sleeping, eating, walking, writing letters, driving to the village, working hour by hour through our day, I knew there was a barrier between us because of it.

He walked alone, on the other side, and I must not come to him. And I became nervous and fearful that some heedless word, some turn in a careless conversation should bring that expression back to his eyes again. I began to dread any mention of the sea, for the sea might lead to boats, to accidents, to drowning . . . Even Frank Crawley, who came to lunch one day, put me in a little fever of fear when he said something about the sailing races in Kerrith harbour, three miles away. I looked steadily at my plate, a stab of sickness in my heart at once, but Maxim went on talking quite naturally, he did not seem to mind, while I sat in a sweat of uncertainty wondering what would happen and where the conversation would lead us.

It was during cheese, Frith had left the room, and I remember getting up and going to the sideboard, and taking some more cheese, not wanting it, so as not to be at the table with them, listening; humming a little tune to myself so I could not hear.

I was wrong of course, morbid, stupid; this was the hypersensitive behaviour of a neurotic, not the normal happy self I knew myself to be. But I could not help it. I did not know what to do. My shyness and gaucherie became worse, too, making me stolid and dumb when people came to the house. For we were called upon, I remember, during those first weeks, by people who lived near us in the county, and the receiving of them, and the shaking hands, and the spinning out of the formal half-hour became a worse ordeal than I first anticipated, because of this new fear of mine that they would talk about something that must not be discussed. The agony of those wheels on the drive, of that pealing bell, of my own first wild rush for flight to my own room. The scrambled dab of powder on my nose, the hasty comb through my hair, and then the inevitable knock on the door and the entrance of the cards on a silver salver.

'All right. I'll be down immediately.' The clap of my heels on the stairs and across the hall, the opening of the library door or, worse still, that long, cold, lifeless drawing-room, and the strange woman waiting there, or two of them perhaps, or a husband and a wife.

'How do you do? I'm sorry; Maxim is in the garden somewhere, Frith has gone to find him.'

'We felt we must come and pay our respects to the bride.'

A little laughter, a little flurry of chat, a pause, a glance round the room.

'Manderley is looking as charming as ever. Don't you love it?'

'Oh, yes, rather . . .' And in my shyness and anxiety to please, those schoolgirls' phrases would escape from me again, those words I never used except in moments like these, 'Oh, ripping'; and 'Oh, topping'; and 'absolutely'; and 'priceless'; even, I think, to one dowager who had carried a lorgnette 'cheerio'. My relief at Maxim's arrival would be tempered by the fear they might say something indiscreet, and I became dumb at once, a set smile on my lips, my hands in my lap. They would turn to Maxim then, talking of people and places I had not met or did not

136

know, and now and again I would find their eyes upon me, doubtful, rather bewildered.

I could picture them saying to one another as they drove away, 'My dear, what a dull girl. She scarcely opened her mouth,' and then the sentence I had first heard upon Beatrice's lips, haunting me ever since, a sentence I read in every eye, on every tongue – 'She's so different from Rebecca.'

Sometimes I would glean little snatches of information to add to my secret store. A word dropped here at random, a question, a passing phrase. And, if Maxim was not with me, the hearing of them would be a furtive, rather painful pleasure, guilty knowledge learnt in the dark.

I would return a call perhaps, for Maxim was punctilious in these matters and would not spare me, and if he did not come with me I must brave the formality alone, and there would be a pause in the conversation while I searched for something to say. 'Will you be entertaining much at Manderley, Mrs de Winter?' they would say, and my answer would come, 'I don't know, Maxim has not said much about it up to the present.' 'No, of course not, it's early yet. I believe the house was generally full of people in the old days.' Another pause. 'People from London, you know. There used to be tremendous parties.' 'Yes,' I would say. 'Yes, so I have heard.' A further pause, and then the lowered voice that is always used about the dead or in a place of worship, 'She was so tremendously popular, you know. Such a personality.' 'Yes,' I would say. 'Yes, of course.' And after a moment or so I would glance at my watch under cover of my glove, and say, 'I'm afraid I ought to be going; it must be after four.'

'Won't you stay for tea? We always have it at quarter past.'

'No – No, really, thanks most awfully. I promised Maxim . . .' my sentence would go trailing off into nothing, but the meaning would be understood. We would both rise to our feet, both of us knowing I was not deceived about her offer to tea nor she in my mention of a promise to Maxim. I had sometimes wondered what would happen if convention were denied, if, having got into the car and waved a hand to my hostess on the doorstep,

I suddenly opened it again, and said, 'I don't think I'll go back after all. Let's go to your drawing-room again and sit down. I'll stay to dinner if you like, or stop the night.'

I used to wonder if convention and good county manners would brave the surprise, and whether a smile of welcome would be summoned to the frozen face, 'But of course! How very delightful of you to suggest it.' I used to wish I had the courage to try. But instead the door would slam, the car would go bowling away down the smooth gravel drive, and my late hostess would wander back to her room with a sigh of relief and become herself again. It was the wife of the bishop in the neighbouring cathedral town who said to me, 'Will your husband revive the Manderley Fancy Dress ball, do you suppose? Such a lovely sight always; I shall never forget it.'

I had to smile as though I knew all about it and say, 'We have not decided. There have been so many things to do and to discuss.'

'Yes, I suppose so. But I do hope it won't be dropped. You must use your influence with him. There was not one last year of course. But I remember two years ago, the bishop and I went, and it was quite enchanting. Manderley so lends itself to anything like that. The hall looked wonderful. They danced there, and had the music in the gallery; it was all so in keeping. A tremendous thing to organize, but everybody appreciated it so.'

'Yes,' I said. 'Yes, I must ask Maxim about it.'

I thought of the docketed pigeon-hole in the desk in the morning room, I pictured the stack upon stack of invitation cards, the long list of names, the addresses, and I could see a woman sitting there at the desk and putting a V beside the names she wanted, and reaching for the invitation cards, dipping her pen in the ink, writing upon them swift and sure in that long, slanting hand.

'There was a garden party, too, we went to one summer,' said the bishop's wife. 'Everything always so beautifully done. The flowers at their best. A glorious day, I remember. Tea was served at little tables in the rose-garden; such an attractive original idea. Of course, she was so clever . . .'

She stopped, turning a little pink, fearing a loss of tact; but I agreed with her at once to save embarrassment, and I heard myself saying boldly, brazenly, 'Rebecca must have been a wonderful person.'

I could not believe that I had said the name at last. I waited, wondering what would happen. I had said the name. I had said the word Rebecca aloud. It was a tremendous relief. It was as though I had taken a purge and rid myself of an intolerable pain. Rebecca. I had said it aloud.

I wondered if the bishop's wife saw the flush on my face, but she went on smoothly with the conversation, and I listened to her greedily, like an eavesdropper at a shuttered window.

'You never met her then?' she asked, and when I shook my head she hesitated a moment, a little uncertain of her ground. 'We never knew her well personally, you know: the bishop was only inducted here four years ago, but of course she received us when we went to the ball and the garden party. We dined there, too, one winter. Yes, she was a very lovely creature. So full of life.'

'She seems to have been so good at everything too,' I said, my voice just careless enough to show I did not mind, while I played with the fringe of my glove. 'It's not often you get someone who is clever and beautiful and fond of sport.'

'No, I suppose you don't,' said the bishop's wife. 'She was certainly very gifted. I can see her now, standing at the foot of the stairs on the night of the ball, shaking hands with everybody, that cloud of dark hair against the very white skin, and her costume suited her so. Yes, she was very beautiful.'

'She ran the house herself, too,' I said, smiling, as if to say, 'I am quite at my ease, I often discuss her.' 'It must have taken a lot of time and thought. I'm afraid I leave it to the housekeeper.'

'Oh, well, we can't all do everything. And you are very young, aren't you? No doubt in time, when you have settled down. Besides, you have your own hobby, haven't you? Someone told me you were fond of sketching.'

'Oh, that,' I said. 'I don't know that I can count it for much.'

'It's a nice little talent to have,' said the bishop's wife; 'it's not everyone that can sketch. You must not drop it. Manderley must be full of pretty spots to sketch.'

'Yes,' I said. 'Yes, I suppose so,' depressed by her words, having a sudden vision of myself wandering across the lawns with a camp-stool and a box of pencils under one arm, and my 'little talent' as she described it, under the other. It sounded like a pet disease.

'Do you play any games? Do you ride, or shoot?' she asked.

'No,' I said, 'I don't do anything like that. I'm fond of walking,' I added, as a wretched anticlimax.

'The best exercise in the world,' she said briskly; 'the bishop and I walk a lot.' I wondered if he went round and round the cathedral, in his shovel hat and his gaiters, with her on his arm. She began to talk about a walking holiday they had taken once, years ago, in the Pennines, how they had done an average of twenty miles a day, and I nodded my head, smiling politely, wondering about the Pennines, thinking they were something like the Andes, remembering, afterwards, they were that chain of hills marked with a furry line in the middle of a pink England on my school atlas. And he all the time in his hat and gaiters.

The inevitable pause, the glance at the watch unnecessary, as her drawing-room clock chimed four in shrill tones, and my rise from the chair. 'I'm so glad I found you in. I hope you will come and see us.'

'We should love to. The bishop is always so busy, alas. Please remember me to your husband, and be sure to ask him to revive the ball.'

'Yes, indeed I will.' Lying, pretending I knew all about it; and in the car going home I sat in my corner, biting my thumb nail, seeing the great hall at Manderley thronged with people in fancy dress, the chatter, hum, and laughter of the moving crowd, the musicians in the gallery, supper in the drawing-room probably, long buffet tables against the wall, and I could see Maxim standing at the front of the stairs, laughing, shaking hands, turning to someone who stood by his side, tall and slim, with dark hair, said the bishop's wife, dark hair against a white face, someone whose quick eyes saw to the comfort of her guests, who gave an order over her shoulder to a servant, someone who was never awkward, never without grace, who when she danced left a stab of perfume in the air like a white azalea.

'Will you be entertaining much at Manderley, Mrs de Winter?' I heard the voice again, suggestive, rather inquisitive, in the voice of that woman I had called upon who lived the other side of Kerrith, and I saw her eye too, dubious, considering, taking in my clothes from top to toe, wondering, with that swift downward glance given to all brides, if I was going to have a baby.

I did not want to see her again. I did not want to see any of them again. They only came to call at Manderley because they were curious and prying. They liked to criticize my looks, my manners, my figure, they liked to watch how Maxim and I behaved to each other, whether we seemed fond of one another, so that they could go back afterwards and discuss us, saying, 'Very different from the old days.' They came because they wanted to compare me to Rebecca . . . I would not return these calls any more, I decided. I should tell Maxim so. I did not mind if they thought me rude and ungracious. It would give them more to criticize, more to discuss. They could say I was ill-bred. 'I'm not surprised,' they would say; 'after all, who was she?' And then a laugh and a shrug of the shoulder. 'My dear, don't you know? He picked her up in Monte Carlo or somewhere; she hadn't a penny. She was a companion to some old woman.' More laughter, more lifting of the eyebrows. 'Nonsense, not really? How extraordinary men are. Maxim, of all people, who was so fastidious. How could he, after Rebecca?'

I did not mind. I did not care. They could say what they liked. As the car turned in at the lodge gates I leant forward in my seat to smile at the woman who lived there. She was bending down, picking flowers in the front garden. She straightened up as she heard the car, but she did not see me smile. I waved, and she stared at me blankly. I don't think she knew who I was. I leant back in my seat again. The car went on down the drive.

When we turned at one of the narrow bends I saw a man walking along the drive a little distance ahead. It was the agent, Frank Crawley. He stopped when he heard the car, and the chauffeur slowed down. Frank Crawley took off his hat and smiled when he saw me in the car. He seemed glad to see me. I smiled back at him. It was nice of him to be glad to see me. I liked Frank Crawley. I did not find him dull or uninteresting as Beatrice had done. Perhaps it was because I was dull myself. We were both dull. We neither of us had a word to say for ourselves. Like to like.

I tapped on the glass and told the chauffeur to stop.

'I think I'll get out and walk with Mr Crawley,' I said.

He opened the door for me. 'Been paying calls, Mrs de Winter?' he said.

'Yes, Frank,' I said. I called him Frank because Maxim did, but he would always call me Mrs de Winter. He was that sort of person. Even if we had been thrown on a desert island together and lived there in intimacy for the rest of our lives, I should have been Mrs de Winter.

'I've been calling on the bishop,' I said, 'and I found the bishop out, but the bishop's lady was at home. She and the bishop are very fond of walking. Sometimes they do twenty miles a day, in the Pennines.'

'I don't know that part of the world,' said Frank Crawley; 'they say the country round is very fine. An uncle of mine used to live there.'

It was the sort of remark Frank Crawley always made. Safe, conventional, very correct.

'The bishop's wife wants to know when we are going to give a Fancy Dress ball at Manderley,' I said, watching him out of the tail of my eye. 'She came to the last one, she said, and enjoyed it very much. I did not know you have Fancy Dress dances here, Frank.'

He hesitated a moment before replying. He looked a little troubled. 'Oh, yes,' he said after a moment, 'the Manderley ball was generally an annual affair. Everyone in the county came. A lot of people from London too. Quite a big show.'

'It must have taken a lot of organization,' I said.

'Yes,' he said.

'I suppose', I said carelessly, 'Rebecca did most of it?'

I looked straight ahead of me along the drive, but I could see his face was turned towards me, as though he wished to read my expression.

'We all of us worked pretty hard,' he said quietly.

There was a funny reserve in his manner as he said this, a certain shyness that reminded me of my own. I wondered suddenly if he had been in love with Rebecca. His voice was the sort of voice I should have used in his circumstances, had this been so. The idea opened up a new field of possibilities. Frank Crawley being so shy, so dull, he would never have told anyone, least of all Rebecca.

'I'm afraid I should not be much use if we have a dance,' I said, 'I'm no earthly use at organizing anything.'

'There would be no need for you to do anything,' he said, 'you would just be your self and look decorative.'

'That's very polite of you, Frank,' I said, 'but I'm afraid I should not be able to do that very well either.'

'I think you would do it excellently,' he said. Dear Frank Crawley, how tactful he was and considerate. I almost believed him. But he did not deceive me really.

'Will you ask Maxim about the ball?' I said.

'Why don't you ask him?' he answered.

'No,' I said. 'No, I don't like to.'

We were silent then. We went on walking along the drive. Now that I had broken down my reluctance at saying Rebecca's name, first with the bishop's wife and now with Frank Crawley, the urge to continue was strong within me. It gave me a curious satisfaction, it acted upon me like a stimulant. I knew that in a moment or two I should have to say it again. 'I was down on one of the beaches the other day,' I said, 'the one with the breakwater. Jasper was being infuriating,

143

he kept barking at the poor man with the idiot's eyes.'

'You must mean Ben,' said Frank, his voice quite easy now; 'he always potters about on the shore. He's quite a nice fellow, you need never be frightened of him. He would not hurt a fly.'

'Oh, I wasn't frightened,' I said. I waited a moment, humming a tune to give me confidence. 'I'm afraid that cottage place is going to rack and ruin,' I said lightly. 'I had to go in, to find a piece of string or something to tie up Jasper. The china is mouldy and the books are being ruined. Why isn't something done about it? It seems such a pity.'

I knew he would not answer at once. He bent down to tie up his shoe lace.

I pretended to examine a leaf on one of the shrubs. 'I think if Maxim wanted anything done he would tell me,' he said, still fumbling with his shoe.

'Are they all Rebecca's things?' I asked.

'Yes,' he said.

I threw the leaf away and picked another, turning it over in my hands.

'What did she use the cottage for?' I asked; 'it looked quite furnished. I thought from the outside it was just a boat-house.'

'It was a boat-house originally,' he said, his voice constrained again, difficult, the voice of someone who is uncomfortable about his subject. 'Then – then she converted it like that, had furniture put in, and china.'

I thought it funny the way he called her 'she'. He did not say Rebecca or Mrs de Winter, as I expected him to do.

'Did she use it a great deal?' I asked.

'Yes,' he said. 'Yes, she did. Moonlight picnics, and – and one thing and another.'

We were walking again side by side, I still humming my little tune. 'How jolly,' I said brightly. 'Moonlight picnics must be great fun. Did you ever go to them?'

'Once or twice,' he said. I pretended not to notice his manner, how quiet it had become, how reluctant to speak about these things.

'Why is the buoy there in the little harbour place?' I said.

'The boat used to be moored there,' he said.

'What boat?' I asked.

'Her boat,' he said.

A strange sort of excitement was upon me. I had to go on with my questions. He did not want to talk about it. I knew that, but although I was sorry for him and shocked at my own self I had to continue, I could not be silent.

'What happened to it?' I said. 'Was that the boat she was sailing when she was drowned?'

'Yes,' he said quietly, 'it capsized and sank. She was washed overboard.'

'What sort of size boat was it?' I asked.

'About three tons. It had a little cabin.'

'What made it capsize?' I said.

'It can be very squally in the bay,' he said.

I thought of that green sea, foam-flecked, that ran down channel beyond the headland. Did the wind come suddenly, I wondered, in a funnel from the beacon on the hill, and did the little boat heel to it, shivering, the white sail flat against a breaking sea?

'Could not someone have got out to her?' I said.

'Nobody saw the accident, nobody knew she had gone,' he said.

I was very careful not to look at him. He might have seen the surprise in my face. I had always thought it happened in a sailing race, that other boats were there, the boats from Kerrith, and that people were watching from the cliffs. I did not know she had been alone, quite alone, out there in the bay.

'They must have known up at the house!' I said.

'No,' he said. 'She often went out alone like that. She would come back any time of the night, and sleep at the cottage on the beach.'

'Was not she nervous?'

'Nervous?' he said; 'no, she was not nervous of anything.'

'Did – did Maxim mind her going off alone like that?'

He waited a minute, and then 'I don't know,' he said shortly. I had the impression he was being loyal to someone. Either to Maxim or to Rebecca, or perhaps even to himself. He was odd. I did not know what to make of it.

'She must have been drowned, then, trying to swim to shore, after the boat sank?' I said.

'Yes,' he said.

I knew how the little boat would quiver and plunge, the water gushing into the steering well, and how the sails would press her down, suddenly, horribly, in that gust of wind. It must have been very dark out there in the bay. The shore must have seemed very far away to anyone swimming there, in the water.

'How long afterwards was it that they found her?' I said.

'About two months,' he said.

Two months. I thought drowned people were found after two days. I thought they would be washed up close to the shore when the tide came.

'Where did they find her?' I asked.

'Near Edgecoombe, about forty miles up channel,' he said.

I had spent a holiday at Edgecoombe once, when I was seven. It was a big place, with a pier, and donkeys. I remembered riding a donkey along the sands.

'How did they know it was her — after two months, how could they tell?' I said. I wondered why he paused before each sentence, as though he weighed his words. Had he cared for her, then, had he minded so much?

'Maxim went up to Edgecoombe to identify her,' he said.

Suddenly I did not want to ask him any more. I felt sick at myself, sick and disgusted. I was like a curious sightseer standing on the fringe of a crowd after someone had been knocked down. I was like a poor person in a tenement building, when someone had died, asking if I might see the body. I hated myself. My questions had been degrading, shameful. Frank Crawley must despise me.

'It was a terrible time for all of you,' I said rapidly. 'I don't suppose you like being reminded about it. I just wondered if

146

there was anything one could do to the cottage, that's all. It seems such a pity, all the furniture being spoilt by the damp.'

He did not say anything. I felt hot and uncomfortable. He must have sensed that it was not concern for the empty cottage that had prompted me to all these questions, and now he was silent because he was shocked at me. Ours had been a comfortable, steady sort of friendship. I had felt him an ally. Perhaps I had destroyed all this, and he would never feel the same about me again.

'What a long drive this is,' I said; 'it always reminds me of the path in the forest in a Grimm's fairy tale, where the prince gets lost, you know. It's always longer than one expects, and the trees are so dark, and close.'

'Yes, it is rather exceptional,' he said.

I could tell by his manner he was still on his guard, as though waiting for a further question from me. There was an awkwardness between us that could not be ignored. Something had to be done about it, even if it covered me with shame.

'Frank,' I said desperately, 'I know what you are thinking. You can't understand why I asked all those questions just now. You think I'm morbid, and curious, in a rather beastly way. It's not that, I promise you. It's only that – that sometimes I feel myself at such a disadvantage. It's all very strange to me, living here at Manderley. Not the sort of life I've been brought up to. When I go returning these calls, as I did this afternoon, I know people are looking me up and down, wondering what sort of success I'm going to make of it. I can imagine them saying, "What on earth does Maxim see in her?" And then, Frank, I begin to wonder myself, and I begin to doubt, and I have a fearful haunting feeling that I should never have married Maxim, that we are not going to be happy. You see, I know that all the time, whenever I meet anyone new, they are all thinking the same thing – How different she is to Rebecca.'

I stopped breathless, already a little ashamed of my outburst, feeling that now at any rate I had burnt my boats for all time. He turned to me looking very concerned and troubled.

'Mrs de Winter, please don't think that,' he said. 'For my part I can't tell you how delighted I am that you have married Maxim. It will make all the difference to his life. I am positive that you will make a great success of it. From my point of view it's – it's very refreshing and charming to find someone like yourself who is not entirely – er—' he blushed, searching for a word 'not entirely *au fait*, shall we say, with ways at Manderley. And if people around here give you the impression that they are criticizing you, it's – well – it's most damnably offensive of them, that's all. I've never heard a word of criticism, and if I did I should take great care that it was never uttered again.'

'That's very sweet of you, Frank,' I said, 'and what you say helps enormously. I dare say I've been very stupid. I'm not good at meeting people, I've never had to do it, and all the time I keep remembering how – how it must have been at Manderley before, when there was someone there who was born and bred to it, did it all naturally and without effort. And I realize, every day, that things I lack, confidence, grace, beauty, intelligence, wit – Oh, all the qualities that mean most in a woman – she possessed. It doesn't help, Frank, it doesn't help.'

He said nothing. He went on looking anxious, and distressed. He pulled out his handkerchief and blew his nose. 'You must not say that,' he said.

'Why not? It's true,' I said.

'You have qualities that are just as important, far more so, in fact. It's perhaps cheek of me to say so, I don't know you very well. I'm a bachelor, I don't know very much about women, I lead a quiet sort of life down here at Manderley as you know, but I should say that kindness, and sincerity, and – if I may say so – modesty are worth far more to a man, to a husband, than all the wit and beauty in the world.'

He looked very agitated, and blew his nose again. I saw that I had upset him far more than I had upset myself, and the realization of this calmed me and gave me a feeling of superiority. I wondered why he was making such a fuss. After all, I had not said very much. I had only confessed my sense of insecurity, following as I did upon Rebecca. And she must have had these qualities that he presented to me as mine. She must have been kind and sincere, with all her friends, her boundless popularity. I was not sure what he meant by modesty. It was a word I had never understood. I always imagined it had something to do with minding meeting people in a passage on the way to the bathroom. . . Poor Frank. And Beatrice had called him a dull man, with never a word to say for himself.

'Well,' I said, rather embarrassed, 'well, I don't know about all that. I don't think I'm very kind, or particularly sincere, and as for being modest, I don't think I've ever had much of a chance to be anything else. It was not very modest, of course, being married hurriedly like that, down in Monte Carlo, and being alone there in that hotel, beforehand, but perhaps you don't count that?'

'My dear Mrs de Winter, you don't think I imagine for one moment that your meeting down there was not entirely above board?' he said in a low voice.

'No, of course not,' I said gravely. Dear Frank. I think I had shocked him. What a Frank-ish expression, too, 'above board'. It made one think immediately of the sort of things that would happen below board.

'I'm sure,' he began, and hesitated, his expression still troubled, 'I'm sure that Maxim would be very worried, very distressed, if he knew how you felt. I don't think he can have any idea of it.'

'You won't tell him?' I said hastily.

'No, naturally not, what do you take me for? But you see, Mrs de Winter, I know Maxim pretty well, and I've seen him through many . . . moods. If he thought you were worrying about – well – about the past, it would distress him more than anything on earth. I can promise you that. He's looking very well, very fit, but Mrs Lacy was quite right the other day when she said he had been on the verge of a breakdown last year, though it was tactless of her to say so in front of him. That's why you are so good for him. You are fresh and young and – and sensible, you

149

have nothing to do with all that time that has gone. Forget it, Mrs de Winter, forget it, as he has done, thank heaven, and the rest of us. We none of us want to bring back the past. Maxim least of all. And it's up to you, you know, to lead us away from it. Not to take us back there again.'

He was right, of course he was right. Dear good Frank, my friend, my ally. I had been selfish and hypersensitive, a martyr to my own inferiority complex. 'I ought to have told you all this before,' I said.

'I wish you had,' he said. 'I might have spared you some worry.'

'I feel happier,' I said, 'much happier. And I've got you for my friend whatever happens, haven't I, Frank?'

'Yes, indeed,' he said.

We were out of the dark wooded drive and into the light again. The rhododendrons were upon us. Their hour would soon be over. Already they looked a little overblown, a little faded. Next month the petals would fall one by one from the great faces, and the gardeners would come and sweep them away. Theirs was a brief beauty. Not lasting very long.

'Frank,' I said, 'before we put an end to this conversation, for ever let's say, will you promise to answer me one thing, quite truthfully?'

He paused, looking at me a little suspiciously. 'That's not quite fair,' he said, 'you might ask me something that I should not be able to answer, something quite impossible.'

'No,' I said, 'it's not that sort of question. It's not intimate or personal, or anything like that.'

'Very well, I'll do my best,' he said.

We came round the sweep of the drive and Manderley was before us, serene and peaceful in the hollow of the lawns, surprising me as it always did, with its perfect symmetry and grace, its great simplicity.

The sunlight flickered on the mullioned windows, and there was a soft rusted glow about the stone walls where the lichen clung. A thin column of smoke curled from the library chimney. I bit my thumb nail, watching Frank out of the tail of my eye.

'Tell me,' I said, my voice casual, not caring a bit, 'tell me, was Rebecca very beautiful?'

Frank waited a moment. I could not see his face. He was looking away from me towards the house. 'Yes,' he said slowly, 'yes, I suppose she was the most beautiful creature I ever saw in my life.'

We went up the steps then to the hall, and I rang the bell for tea.

I did not see much of Mrs Danvers. She kept very much to herself. She still rang the house telephone to the morning-room every day and submitted the menu to me as a matter of form, but that was the limit of our intercourse. She had engaged a maid for me, Clarice, the daughter of somebody on the estate, a nice quiet well-mannered girl, who, thank heaven, had never been in service before and had no alarming standards. I think she was the only person in the house who stood in awe of me. To her I was the mistress: I was Mrs de Winter. The possible gossip of the others could not affect her. She had been away for some time, brought up by an aunt fifteen miles away, and in a sense she was as new to Manderley as I was. I felt at ease with her. I did not mind saying 'Oh, Clarice, would you mend my stocking?'

The housemaid Alice had been so superior. I used to sneak my chemise and nightgowns out of my drawer and mend them myself rather than ask her to do them. I had seen her once, with one of my chemises over her arm, examining the plain material with its small edging of lace. I shall never forget her expression. She looked almost shocked, as though her own personal pride had received a blow. I had never thought about my underclothes before. As long as they were clean and neat I had not thought the material or the existence of lace mattered. Brides one read about had trousseaux, dozens of sets at a time, and I had never bothered. Alice's face taught me a lesson. I wrote quickly to a shop in London and asked for a catalogue of under-linen. By the time I had made my choice Alice was looking after me no longer and Clarice was installed instead. It seemed such a waste buying new underclothes for Clarice that

I put the catalogue away in a drawer and never wrote to the shop after all.

I often wondered whether Alice told the others, and if my underclothes became a topic of conversation in the servants' hall, something rather dreadful, to be discussed in low tones when the men were nowhere about. She was too superior for it to be made a joking question. Phrases like 'Chemise to you' would never be bandied between her and Frith, for instance.

No, my underclothes were more serious than that. More like a divorce case heard *in camera* . . . At any rate I was glad when Alice surrendered me to Clarice. Clarice would never know real lace from false. It was considerate of Mrs Danvers to have engaged her. She must have thought we would be fit company, one for the other. Now that I knew the reason for Mrs Danvers' dislike and resentment it made things a little easier. I knew it was not just me personally she hated, but what I represented. She would have felt the same towards anyone who had taken Rebecca's place. At least that was what I understood from Beatrice the day she came to lunch.

'Did not you know?' she had said; 'she simply adored Rebecca.'

The words had shocked me at the time. Somehow I had not expected them. But when I thought it over I began to lose my first fear of Mrs Danvers. I began to be sorry for her. I could imagine what she must feel. It must hurt her every time she heard me called 'Mrs de Winter'. Every morning when she took up the house telephone and spoke to me, and I answered 'Yes, Mrs Danvers,' she must be thinking of another voice. When she passed through the rooms and saw traces of me about the place, a beret on a window-seat, a bag of knitting on a chair, she must think of another one, who had done these things before. Even as I did. I, who had never known Rebecca. Mrs Danvers knew how she walked and how she spoke. Mrs Danvers knew the colour of her eyes, her smile, the texture of her hair. I knew none of these things, I had never asked about them, but sometimes I felt Rebecca was as real to me as she was to Mrs Danvers.

Frank had told me to forget the past, and I wanted to forget it. But Frank did not have to sit in the morning-room as I did, every day, and touch the pen she had held between her fingers. He did not have to rest his hands on the blotter, and stare in front of him at her writing on the pigeon-holes. He did not have to look at the candlesticks on the mantelpiece, the clock, the vase in which the flowers stood, the pictures on the walls and remember, every day, that they belonged to her, she had chosen them, they were not mine at all. Frank did not have to sit at her place in the dining-room, hold the knife and fork that she had held, drink from her glass. He did not throw a coat over his shoulders which had been hers, nor find her handkerchief in the pocket. He did not notice, every day, as I did, the blind gaze of the old dog in its basket in the library, who lifted its head when it heard my footstep, the footstep of a woman, and sniffing the air drooped its head again, because I was not the one she sought.

Little things, meaningless and stupid in themselves, but they were there for me to see, for me to hear, for me to feel. Dear God, I did not want to think about Rebecca. I wanted to be happy, to make Maxim happy, and I wanted us to be together. There was no other wish in my heart but that. I could not help it if she came to me in thoughts, in dreams. I could not help it if I felt like a guest in Manderley, my home, walking where she had trodden, resting where she had lain. I was like a guest, biding my time, waiting for the return of the hostess. Little sentences, little reproofs reminding me every hour, every day.

'Frith,' I said, coming into the library on a summer morning, my arms full of lilac, 'Frith, where can I find a tall vase for these? They are all too small in the flower-room.'

'The white alabaster vase in the drawing-room was always used for the lilac, Madam.'

'Oh, wouldn't it be spoilt? It might get broken.'

'Mrs de Winter always used the alabaster vase, Madam.'

'Oh, oh, I see.'

Then the alabaster vase was brought for me, already filled with water, and as I put the sweet lilac in the vase and arranged the

154

sprigs, one by one, the mauve warm scent filling the room, mingling with the smell of the new-mown lawn outside coming from the open window, I thought: 'Rebecca did this. She took the lilac, as I am doing, and put the sprigs one by one in the white vase. I'm not the first to do it. This is Rebecca's vase, this is Rebecca's lilac.' She must have wandered out into the garden as I did, in that floppy garden hat that I had seen once at the back of the cupboard in the flower-room, hidden under some old cushions, and crossed the lawn to the lilac bushes, whistling perhaps, humming a tune, calling to the dogs to follow her, carrying in her hands the scissors that I carried now.

'Frith, could you move that book-stand from the table in the window, and I will put the lilac there?'

'Mrs de Winter always had the alabaster vase on the table behind the sofa, Madam.'

'Oh, well . . .' I hesitated, the vase in my hands, Frith's face impassive. He would obey me of course if I said I preferred to put the vase on the smaller table by the window. He would move the book-stand at once.

'All right,' I said, 'perhaps it would look better on the larger table.' And the alabaster vase stood, as it had always done, on the table behind the sofa . . .

Beatrice remembered her promise of a wedding present. A large parcel arrived one morning, almost too large for Robert to carry. I was sitting in the morning-room, having just read the menu for the day. I have always had a childish love of parcels. I snipped the string excitedly, and tore off the dark brown paper. It looked like books. I was right. It was books. Four big volumes. *A History of Painting.* And a sheet of notepaper in the first volume saying 'I hope this is the sort of thing you like,' and signed 'Love from Beatrice.' I could see her going into the shop in Wigmore Street and buying them. Looking about her in her abrupt, rather masculine way. 'I want a set of books for someone who is keen on Art,' she would say, and the attendant would answer, 'Yes, Madam, will you come this way.' She would finger the volumes a little suspiciously. 'Yes, that's about the price. It's for a wedding

155

present. I want them to look good. Are these all about Art?' 'Yes, this is the standard work on the subject,' the assistant would say. And then Beatrice must have written her note, and paid her cheque, and given the address 'Mrs de Winter, Manderley.'

It was nice of Beatrice. There was something rather sincere and pathetic about her going off to a shop in London and buying me these books because she knew I was fond of painting. She imagined me, I expect, sitting down on a wet day and looking solemnly at the illustrations, and perhaps getting a sheet of drawing-paper and a paint-box and copying one of the pictures. Dear Beatrice. I had a sudden, stupid desire to cry. I gathered up the heavy volumes and looked round the morning-room for somewhere to put them. They were out of place in that fragile delicate room. Never mind, it was my room now, after all. I arranged them in a row on the top of the desk. They swayed dangerously, leaning one against the other. I stood back a bit, to watch the effect. Perhaps I moved too quickly, and it disturbed them. At any rate the foremost one fell, and the others slid after him. They upset a little china cupid who had hitherto stood alone on the desk except for the candle-sticks. He fell to the ground, hitting the waste-paper basket as he did so, and broke into fragments. I glanced hurriedly at the door, like a guilty child. I knelt on the floor and swept up the pieces into my hand. I found an envelope to put them in. I hid the envelope at the back of one of the drawers in the desk. Then I took the books off to the library and found room for them on the shelves.

Maxim laughed when I showed them to him with pride.

'Dear old Bee,' he said, 'you must have had a success with her. She never opens a book if she can help it.'

'Did she say anything about – well – what she thought of me?' I asked.

'The day she came to lunch? No, I don't think so.'

'I thought she might have written or something.'

'Beatrice and I don't correspond unless there's a major event in the family. Writing letters is a waste of time,' said Maxim.

I supposed I was not a major event. Yet if I had been Beatrice, and had a brother, and the brother married, surely one would have said something, expressed an opinion, written two words? Unless of course one had taken a dislike to the wife, or thought her unsuitable. Then of course it would be different. Still, Beatrice had taken the trouble to go up to London and to buy the books for me. She would not have done that if she disliked me.

It was the following day I remember, when Frith, who had brought in the coffee after lunch to the library, waited a moment, hovering behind Maxim, and said,

'Could I speak to you, sir?' Maxim glanced up from his paper.

'Yes, Frith, what is it?' he said, rather surprised. Frith wore a stiff solemn expression, his lips pursed. I thought at once his wife had died.

'It's about Robert, sir. There has been a slight unpleasantness between him and Mrs Danvers. Robert is very upset.'

'Oh, Lord,' said Maxim, making a face at me. I bent down to fondle Jasper, my unfailing habit in moments of embarrassment.

'Yes, sir. It appears Mrs Danvers has accused Robert of secreting a valuable ornament from the morning-room. It is Robert's business to bring in the fresh flowers to the morning-room and place the vases. Mrs Danvers went in this morning after the flowers had been done, and noticed one of the ornaments was missing. It was there yesterday, she said. She accused Robert of either taking the ornament or breaking it and concealing the breakage. Robert denied both accusations most emphatically, and came to me nearly in tears, sir. You may have noticed he was not himself at lunch.'

'I wondered why he handed me the cutlets without giving me a plate,' murmured Maxim. 'I did not know Robert was so sensitive. Well, I suppose someone else did it. One of the maids.'

'No, sir. Mrs Danvers went into the room before the girl had done the room. Nobody had been there since Madam yesterday, and Robert first thing with the flowers. It makes it very unpleasant for Robert and myself, sir.'

'Yes, of course it does. Well you had better ask Mrs Danvers

157

to come here and we'll get to the bottom of it. What ornament was it, anyway?'

'The china cupid, sir, that stands on the writing-table.'

'Oh! Oh, Lord. That's one of our treasures, isn't it? It will have to be found. Get hold of Mrs Danvers at once.'

'Very good, sir.'

Frith left the room and we were alone again. 'What a confounded nuisance,' said Maxim; 'that cupid is worth a hell of a lot. How I loathe servants' rows too. I wonder why they come to me about it. That's your job, sweetheart.'

I looked up from Jasper, my face red as fire. 'Darling,' I said, 'I meant to tell you before, but – but I forgot. The fact is I broke that cupid when I was in the morning-room yesterday.'

'You broke it? Well, why the devil didn't you say so when Frith was here?'

'I don't know. I didn't like to. I was afraid he would think me a fool.'

'He'll think you much more of a fool now. You'll have to explain to him and Mrs Danvers.'

'Oh, no, please, Maxim, you tell them. Let me go upstairs.'

'Don't be a little idiot. Anyone would think you were afraid of them.'

'I am afraid of them. At least, not afraid, but . . .'

The door opened, and Frith ushered Mrs Danvers into the room. I looked nervously at Maxim. He shrugged his shoulders, half amused, half angry.

'It's all a mistake, Mrs Danvers. Apparently Mrs de Winter broke the cupid herself and forgot to say anything,' said Maxim.

They all looked at me. It was like being a child again. I was still aware of my guilty flush. 'I'm so sorry,' I said, watching Mrs Danvers, 'I never thought Robert would get into trouble.'

'Is it possible to repair the ornament, Madam?' said Mrs Danvers. She did not seem to be surprised that I was the culprit. She looked at me with her white skull's face and her dark eyes. I felt she had known it was me all along and had accused Robert to see if I would have the courage to confess.

'I'm afraid not,' I said, 'it's smashed in little pieces.'

'What did you do with the pieces?' said Maxim.

It was like being a prisoner, giving evidence. How paltry and mean my actions sounded, even to myself. 'I put them all into an envelope,' I said.

'Well, what did you do with the envelope?' said Maxim, lighting a cigarette, his tone a mixture of amusement and exasperation.

'I put it at the back of one of the drawers in the writing-desk,' I said.

'It looks as though Mrs de Winter thought you would put her in prison, doesn't it, Mrs Danvers?' said Maxim. 'Perhaps you would find the envelope and send the pieces up to London. If they are too far gone to mend it can't be helped. All right, Frith. Tell Robert to dry his tears.'

Mrs Danvers lingered when Frith had gone. 'I will apologize to Robert of course,' she said, 'but the evidence pointed so strongly to him. It did not occur to me that Mrs de Winter had broken the ornament herself. Perhaps, if such a thing should happen again, Mrs de Winter will tell me personally, and I will have the matter attended to? It would save everybody a lot of unpleasantness.'

'Naturally,' said Maxim impatiently, 'I can't think why she didn't do so yesterday. I was just going to tell her when you came into the room.'

'Perhaps Mrs de Winter was not aware of the value of the ornament?' said Mrs Danvers, turning her eyes upon me.

'Yes,' I said wretchedly. 'Yes, I was afraid it was valuable. That's why I swept the pieces up so carefully.'

'And hid them at the back of a drawer where no one would find them, eh?' said Maxim, with a laugh, and a shrug of the shoulders. 'Is not that the sort of thing the between-maid is supposed to do, Mrs Danvers?'

'The between-maid at Manderley would never be allowed to touch the valuable things in the morning-room, sir,' said Mrs Danvers.

'No, I can't see you letting her,' said Maxim.

'It's very unfortunate,' said Mrs Danvers, 'I don't think we have ever had any breakages in the morning-room before. We were always so particular. I've done the dusting in there myself since — last year. There was no one I could trust. When Mrs de Winter was alive we used to do the valuables together.'

'Yes, well — it can't be helped,' said Maxim. 'All right, Mrs Danvers.'

She went out of the room, and I sat on the window-seat, looking out of the window. Maxim picked up his paper again. Neither of us spoke.

'I'm awfully sorry, darling,' I said, after a moment, 'it was very careless of me. I can't think how it happened. I was just arranging those books on the desk, to see if they would stand, and the cupid slipped.'

'My sweet child, forget it. What does it matter?'

'It does matter. I ought to have been more careful. Mrs Danvers must be furious with me.'

'What the devil has she got to be furious about? It's not her bit of china.'

'No, but she takes such a pride in it all. It's so awful to think nothing in there has ever been broken before. It had to be me.'

'Better you than the luckless Robert.'

'I wish it had been Robert. Mrs Danvers will never forgive me.'

'Damn Mrs Danvers,' said Maxim, 'she's not God Almighty, is she? I can't understand you. What do you mean by saying you are afraid of her?'

'I did not mean afraid exactly. I don't see much of her. It's not that. I can't really explain.'

'You do such extraordinary things,' said Maxim; 'fancy not getting hold of her when you broke the thing and saying, "Here, Mrs Danvers, get this mended." She'd understand that. Instead of which you scrape up the remains in an envelope and hide 'em at the back of a drawer. Just like a between-maid, as I said, and not the mistress of a house.'

'I am like a between-maid,' I said slowly, 'I know I am, in lots of ways. That's why I have so much in common with Clarice. We are on the same sort of footing. And that's why she likes me. I went and saw her mother the other day. And do you know what she said? I asked her if she thought Clarice was happy with us, and she said, "Oh, yes, Mrs de Winter. Clarice seems quite happy. She says, 'It's not like being with a lady, Mum, it's like being with one of ourselves.'" Do you suppose she meant it as a compliment or not?'

'God knows,' said Maxim; 'remembering Clarice's mother, I should take it as a direct insult. Her cottage is generally a shambles and smells of boiled cabbage. At one time she had nine children under eleven, and she herself used to patter about in that patch of garden with no shoes and a stocking round her head. We nearly gave her notice to quit. Why Clarice looks as neat and clean as she does I can't imagine.'

'She's been living with an aunt,' I said, feeling rather subdued. 'I know my flannel skirt has a dirty mark down the front, but I've never walked barefoot with a stocking round my head.' I knew now why Clarice did not disdain my underclothes as Alice had done. 'Perhaps that's why I prefer calling on Clarice's mother to calling on people like the bishop's wife?' I went on. 'The bishop's wife never said I was like one of themselves.'

'If you wear that grubby skirt when you call on her I don't suppose she does,' said Maxim.

'Of course I didn't call on her in my old skirt, I wore a frock,' I said, 'and anyway I don't think much of people who just judge one by one's clothes.'

'I hardly think the bishop's wife cares twopence about clothes,' said Maxim, 'but she may have been rather surprised if you sat on the extreme edge of the chair and answered "Yes" and "No" like someone after a new job, which you did the only time we returned a call together.'

'I can't help being shy.'

'I know you can't, sweetheart. But you don't make an effort to conquer it.'

'I think that's very unfair,' I said. 'I try every day, every time I go out or meet anyone new. I'm always making efforts. You don't understand. It's all very well for you, you're used to that sort of thing. I've not been brought up to it.'

'Rot,' said Maxim; 'it's not a question of bringing up, as you put it. It's a matter of application. You don't think I like calling on people, do you? It bores me stiff. But it has to be done, in this part of the world.'

'We're not talking about boredom,' I said; 'there's nothing to be afraid of in being bored. If I was just bored it would be different. I hate people looking me up and down as though I were a prize cow.'

'Who looks you up and down?'

'All the people down here. Everybody.'

'What does it matter if they do? It gives them some interest in life.'

'Why must I be the one to supply the interest, and have all the criticism?'

'Because life at Manderley is the only thing that ever interests anybody down here.'

'What a slap in the eye I must be to them then.'

Maxim did not answer. He went on looking at his paper.

'What a slap in the eye I must be to them,' I repeated. And then, 'I suppose that's why you married me,' I said; 'you knew I was dull and quiet and inexperienced, so that there would never be any gossip about me.'

Maxim threw his paper on the ground and got up from his chair. 'What do you mean?' he said.

His face was dark and queer, and his voice was rough, not his voice at all.

'I – I don't know,' I said, leaning back against the window, 'I don't mean anything. Why do you look like that?'

'What do you know about any gossip down here?' he said.

'I don't,' I said, scared by the way he looked at me. 'I only said it because – because of something to say. Don't look at me like that. Maxim, what have I said? what's the matter?'

'Who's been talking to you,' he said slowly.

'No one. No one at all.'

'Why did you say what you did?'

'I tell you, I don't know. It just came to my head. I was angry, cross. I do hate calling on these people. I can't help it. And you criticized me for being shy. I didn't mean it. Really, Maxim, I didn't. Please believe me.'

'It was not a particularly attractive thing to say, was it?' he said.

'No,' I said. 'No, it was rude, hateful.'

He stared at me moodily, his hands in his pockets, rocking backwards and forwards on his heels. 'I wonder if I did a very selfish thing in marrying you,' he said. He spoke slowly, thoughtfully.

I felt very cold, rather sick. 'How do you mean?' I said.

'I'm not much of a companion to you, am I?' he said. 'There are too many years between us. You ought to have waited, and then married a boy of your own age. Not someone like myself, with half his life behind him.'

'That's ridiculous,' I said hurriedly, 'you know age doesn't mean anything in marriage. Of course we are companions.'

'Are we? I don't know,' he said.

I knelt up on the window-seat and put my arms round his shoulders. 'Why do you say these things to me?' I said; 'you know I love you more than anything in the world. There has never been anyone but you. You are my father and my brother and my son. All those things.'

'It was my fault,' he said, not listening. 'I rushed you into it. I never gave you a chance to think it over.'

'I did not want to think it over,' I said, 'there was no other choice. You don't understand, Maxim. When one loves a person . . .'

'Are you happy here?' he said, looking away from me, out of the window, 'I wonder sometimes. You've got thinner. Lost your colour.'

'Of course I'm happy,' I said, 'I love Manderley. I love the garden, I love everything. I don't mind calling on people. I just said that to be tiresome. I'll call on people every day, if you want me to. I don't mind what I do. I've never for one moment regretted marrying you, surely you must know that?'

He patted my cheek in his terrible absent way, and bent down, and kissed the top of my head. 'Poor lamb, you don't have much fun, do you? I'm afraid I'm very difficult to live with.'

'You're not difficult,' I said eagerly, 'you are easy, very easy. Much easier than I thought you would be. I used to think it would be dreadful to be married, that one's husband would drink, or use awful language, or grumble if the toast was soft at breakfast, and be rather unattractive altogether, smell possibly. You don't do any of those things.'

'Good God, I hope not,' said Maxim, and he smiled.

I seized advantage of his smile, I smiled too, and took his hands and kissed them. 'How absurd to say we are not companions,' I said; 'why look how we sit here every evening, you with a book or a paper, and me with my knitting. Just like cups of tea. Just like old people, married for years and years. Of course we are companions. Of course we are happy. You talk as though you thought we had made a mistake? You don't mean it like that, do you, Maxim? You know our marriage is a success, a wonderful success?'

'If you say so, then it's all right,' he said.

'No, but you think it too, don't you, darling? It's not just me? We are happy, aren't we? Terribly happy?'

He did not answer. He went on staring out of the window while I held his hands. My throat felt dry and tight, and my eyes were burning. Oh, God, I thought, this is like two people in a play, in a moment the curtain will come down, we shall bow to the audience, and go off to our dressing-rooms. This can't be a real moment in the lives of Maxim and myself. I sat down on the window-seat, and let go of his hands. I heard myself speaking in a hard cool voice. 'If you don't think we are happy it would be much better if you would admit it. I don't want you to pretend anything. I'd much rather go away. Not live with you any more.' It was not really happening of course. It was the girl in the play talking, not me to Maxim. I pictured the type of girl who would play the part. Tall and slim, rather nervy.

'Well, why don't you answer me?' I said.

He took my face in his hands and looked at me, just as he had before, when Frith had come into the room with tea, the day we went to the beach.

'How can I answer you?' he said. 'I don't know the answer myself. If you say we are happy, let's leave it at that. It's something I know nothing about. I take your word for it. We are happy. All right then, that's agreed!' He kissed me again, and then walked away across the room. I went on sitting by the window, stiff and straight, my hands in my lap.

'You say all this because you are disappointed in me,' I said. 'I'm gauche and awkward, I dress badly, I'm shy with people. I warned you in Monte Carlo how it would be. You think I'm not right for Manderley.'

'Don't talk nonsense,' he said. 'I've never said you dressed badly or were gauche. It's your imagination. As for being shy, you'll get over that. I've told you so before.'

'We've argued in a circle,' I said, 'we've come right back to where we started. This all began because I broke the cupid in the morning-room. If I hadn't broken the cupid none of this would have happened. We'd have drunk our coffee, and gone out into the garden.'

'Oh, damn that infernal cupid,' said Maxim wearily. 'Do you really think I care whether it's in ten thousand pieces or not?'

'Was it very valuable?'

'Heaven knows. I suppose so. I've really forgotten.'

'Are all those things in the morning-room valuable?'

'Yes, I believe so.'

'Why were all the most valuable things put in the morning-room?'

'I don't know. I suppose because they looked well there.'

'Were they always there? When your mother was alive?'

'No. No, I don't think they were. They were scattered about the house. The chairs were in a lumber room I believe.'

'When was the morning-room furnished as it is now?'

'When I was married.'

'I suppose the cupid was put there then?'

'I suppose so.'

'Was that found in a lumber room?'

'No. No, I don't think it was. As a matter of fact I believe it was a wedding-present. Rebecca knew a lot about china.'

I did not look at him. I began to polish my nails. He had said the word quite naturally, quite calmly. It had been no effort to him. After a minute I glanced at him swiftly. He was standing by the mantelpiece, his hands in his pockets. He was staring straight in front of him. He is thinking about Rebecca, I said to myself. He is thinking how strange it was that a wedding present to me should have been the cause of destroying a wedding present to Rebecca. He is thinking about the cupid. He is remembering who gave it to Rebecca. He is going over in his mind how the parcel came and how pleased she was. Rebecca knew a lot about china. Perhaps he came into the room, and she was kneeling on the floor, wrenching open the little crate in which the cupid was packed. She must have glanced up at him, and smiled. 'Look, Max,' she would have said, 'look what we've been sent.' And she then would have plunged her hand down into the shavings and brought out the cupid who stood on one foot, his bow in his hand. 'We'll have it in the morning-room,' she must have said, and he must have knelt down beside her, and they must have looked at the cupid together.

I went on polishing my nails. They were scrubby, like a schoolboy's nails. The cuticles grew up over the half moons. The thumb was bitten nearly to the quick. I looked at Maxim again. He was still standing in front of the fireplace.

'What are you thinking about?' I said.

My voice was steady and cool. Not like my heart, thumping inside me. Not like my mind, bitter and resentful. He lit a cigarette, surely the twenty-fifth that day, and we had only just finished lunch; he threw the match into the empty grate, he picked up the paper.

'Nothing very much, why?' he said.

'Oh, I don't know,' I said, 'you looked so serious, so far away.'

He whistled a tune absently, the cigarette twisting in his fingers. 'As a matter of fact I was wondering if they had chosen the Surrey side to play Middlesex at the Oval,' he said.

He sat down in the chair again and folded the paper. I looked out of the window. Presently Jasper came to me and climbed on my lap.

Maxim had to go up to London at the end of June to some public dinner. A man's dinner. Something to do with the county. He was away for two days and I was left alone. I dreaded his going. When I saw the car disappear round the sweep in the drive I felt exactly as though it were to be a final parting and I should never see him again. There would be an accident of course and later on in the afternoon, when I came back from my walk, I should find Frith white and frightened waiting for me with a message. The doctor would have rung up from some cottage hospital. 'You must be very brave,' he would say, 'I'm afraid you must be prepared for a great shock.'

And Frank would come, and we would go to the hospital together. Maxim would not recognize me. I went through the whole thing as I was sitting at lunch, I could see the crowd of local people clustering round the churchyard at the funeral, and myself leaning on Frank's arm. It was so real to me that I could scarcely eat any lunch, and I kept straining my ears to hear the telephone should it ring.

I sat out in the garden under the chestnut tree in the afternoon, with a book on my lap, but I scarcely read at all. When I saw Robert come across the lawn I knew it was the telephone and I felt physically sick. 'A message from the club, Madam, to say Mr de Winter arrived ten minutes ago.'

I shut up my book. 'Thank you, Robert. How quickly he got up.'

'Yes, Madam. A very good run.'

'Did he ask to speak to me, or leave any special message?'

'No, Madam. Just that he had arrived safely. It was the porter speaking.'

'All right, Robert. Thanks very much.'

The relief was tremendous. I did not feel sick any more. The pain had gone. It was like coming ashore after a channel crossing. I began to feel rather hungry, and when Robert had gone back into the house I crept into the dining-room through the long window and stole some biscuits from the sideboard. I had six of them. Bath Olivers. And then an apple as well. I had no idea I was so empty. I went and ate them in the woods, in case one of the servants should see me on the lawn from the windows, and then go and tell the cook that they did not think Mrs de Winter cared for the food prepared in the kitchen, as they had just seen her filling herself with fruit and biscuits. The cook would be offended, and perhaps go to Mrs Danvers.

Now that Maxim was safe in London, and I had eaten my biscuits, I felt very well and curiously happy. I was aware of a sense of freedom, as though I had no responsibilities at all. It was rather like a Saturday when one was a child. No lessons, and no prep. One could do as one liked. One put on an old skirt and a pair of sand-shoes and played Hares and Hounds on the common with the children who lived next door.

I had just the same feeling. I had not felt like this all the time I had been at Manderley. It must be because Maxim had gone to London.

I was rather shocked at myself. I could not understand it at all. I had not wanted him to go. And now this lightness of heart, this spring in my step, this childish feeling that I wanted to run across the lawn, and roll down the bank. I wiped the biscuit crumbs from my mouth and called to Jasper. Perhaps I was just feeling like this because it was a lovely day . . .

We went through the Happy Valley to the little cove. The azaleas were finished now, the petals lay brown and crinkled on the moss. The bluebells had not faded yet, they made a solid carpet in the woods above the valley, and the young bracken was shooting up, curling and green. The moss smelt rich and deep, and the bluebells were earthy, bitter. I lay down in the long grass beside the bluebells with my hands behind my head, and

Jasper at my side. He looked down at me panting, his face foolish, saliva dripping from his tongue and his heavy jowl. There were pigeons somewhere in the trees above. It was very peaceful and quiet. I wondered why it was that places are so much lovelier when one is alone. How commonplace and stupid it would be if I had a friend now, sitting beside me, someone I had known at school, who would say 'By the way, I saw old Hilda the other day. You remember her, the one who was so good at tennis. She's married, with two children.' And the bluebells beside us unnoticed, and the pigeons overhead unheard. I did not want anyone with me. Not even Maxim. If Maxim had been there I should not be lying as I was now, chewing a piece of grass, my eyes shut. I should have been watching him, watching his eyes, his expression. Wondering if he liked it, if he was bored. Wondering what he was thinking. Now I could relax, none of these things mattered. Maxim was in London. How lovely it was to be alone again. No, I did not mean that. It was disloyal, wicked. It was not what I meant. Maxim was my life and my world. I got up from the bluebells and called sharply to Jasper. We set off together down the valley to the beach. The tide was out, the sea very calm and remote. It looked like a great placid lake out there in the bay. I could not imagine it rough now, any more than I could imagine winter in summer. There was no wind, and the sun shone on the lapping water where it ran into the little pools in the rocks. Jasper scrambled up the rocks immediately, glancing back at me, one ear blown back against his head, giving him an odd rakish appearance.

'Not that way, Jasper,' I said.

He cared nothing for me of course. He loped off, deliberately disobedient. 'What a nuisance he is,' I said aloud, and I scrambled up the rocks after him, pretending to myself I did not want to go to the other beach. 'Oh, well,' I thought, 'it can't be helped. After all, Maxim is not with me. It's nothing to do with me.'

I splashed through the pools on the rocks, humming a tune. The cove looked different when the tide was out. Less formidable. There was only about three foot of water in the tiny harbour. A boat would just float there comfortably I supposed, at dead low water. The buoy was still there. It was painted white and green, I had not noticed that before. Perhaps because it had been raining the colouring was indistinct. There was no one on the beach. I walked across the shingle to the other side of the cove, and climbed the low stone wall of the jetty-arm. Jasper ran on ahead as though it was his custom. There was a ring in the wall and an iron ladder descending to the water. That's where the dinghy would be tied, I suppose, and one would climb to it from the ladder. The buoy was just opposite, about thirty feet away. There was something written on it. I craned my neck sideways to read the lettering. 'Je Reviens'. What a funny name. Not like a boat. Perhaps it had been a French boat though, a fishing boat. Fishing boats sometimes had names like that; 'Happy Return', 'I'm Here', those sort of names. 'Je Reviens' – 'I come back.' Yes, I suppose it was quite a good name for a boat. Only it had not been right for that particular boat which would never come back again.

It must be cold sailing out there in the bay, beyond the beacon away on the headland. The sea was calm in the bay, but even today, when it was so still, out there round the headland there was a ripple of white foam on the surface of the water where the tide was racing. A small boat would heel to the wind when she rounded the headland and came out of the landlocked bay. The sea would splash inboard perhaps, run down the deck. The person at the tiller would wipe spray out of her eyes and hair, glance up at the straining mast. I wondered what colour the boat had been. Green and white perhaps, like the buoy. Not very big, Frank had said, with a little cabin.

Jasper was sniffing at the iron ladder. 'Come away,' I said. 'I don't want to go in after you.' I went back along the harbour wall to the beach. The cottage did not seem so remote and sinister at the edge of the wood as it had done before. The sun made such a difference. No rain today, pattering on the roof. I walked slowly up the beach towards it. After all, it was only a cottage, with nobody living in it. There was nothing to be frightened of. Nothing at all. Any place seemed damp and sinister when it had been uninhabited for a certain time. Even new bungalows and places. Besides, they had moonlight picnics and things here. Week-end visitors probably used to come and bathe, and then go for a sail in the boat. I stood looking into the neglected garden choked with nettles. Someone ought to come and tidy it up. One of the gardeners. There was no need to leave it like this. I pushed the little gate and went to the door of the cottage. It was not entirely closed. I was certain I had closed it the last time. Jasper began growling, sniffing under the door.

'Don't, Jasper,' I said. He went on sniffing deeply, his nose thrust to the crack. I pushed the door open and looked inside. It was very dark. Like it had been before. Nothing was changed. The cobwebs still clung to the rigging of the model boats. The door into the boat-store at the end of the room was open though. Jasper growled again, and there was a sound of something falling. Jasper barked furiously, and darting between my legs into the room he tore to the open door of the store. I followed him, heart beating, and then stood uncertainly in the middle of the room. 'Jasper, come back, don't be a fool,' I said. He stood in the doorway, still barking furiously, an hysterical note in his voice. Something was there then, inside the store. Not a rat. He would have gone for a rat. 'Jasper, Jasper. Come here,' I said. He would not come. I went slowly to the door of the store.

'Is there anybody there?' I said.

No one answered. I bent down to Jasper, putting my hand on his collar, and looked round the edge of the door. Someone was sitting in the corner against the wall. Someone who, from his crouching position, was even more frightened than me. It was Ben. He was trying to hide behind one of the sails. 'What is the matter? Do you want something?' I said. He blinked at me stupidly, his mouth slightly open.

'I'm not doing nothing,' he said.

'Quiet, Jasper,' I scolded, putting my hand over his muzzle, and I took my belt off and ran it through his collar as a leash.

'What do you want, Ben?' I said, a little bolder this time.

He did not answer. He watched me with his sly idiot's eyes.

'I think you had better come out,' I said. 'Mr de Winter doesn't like people walking in and out of here.'

He shambled to his feet grinning furtively, wiping his nose with the back of his hand. The other hand he kept behind his back. 'What have you got, Ben?' I said. He obeyed me like a child, showing me the other hand. There was a fishing line in it. 'I'm not doing anything,' he repeated.

'Does that line belong here?' I asked.

'Eh?' he said.

'Listen, Ben,' I said. 'You can take that line if you want to, but you mustn't do it again. It's not honest, taking people's things.'

He said nothing. He blinked at me and wriggled.

'Come along,' I said firmly.

I went into the main room and he followed me. Jasper had stopped barking, and was now sniffing at Ben's heels. I did not want to stop any longer in the cottage. I walked quickly out into the sunshine, Ben shuffling behind me. Then I shut the door.

'You had better go home,' I said to Ben.

He held the fishing line clutched to his heart like a treasure. 'You won't put me to the asylum, will you?' he said.

I saw then that he was trembling with fright. His hands were shaking, and his eyes were fixed on mine in supplication, like a dumb thing.

'Of course not,' I said gently.

'I done nothing,' he repeated, 'I never told no one. I don't want to be put to the asylum.' A tear rolled down his dirty face.

'That's all right, Ben,' I said; 'no one will put you away. But you must not go to the cottage again.'

I turned away, and he came after me, pawing at my hand.

'Here,' he said. 'Here, I got something for you.'

He smiled foolishly, he beckoned with his finger, and turned towards the beach. I went with him, and he bent down and picked up a flat stone by a rock. There was a little heap of shells under the stone. He chose one, and presented it to me. 'That's yourn,' he said.

'Thank you; it's very pretty,' I said.

He grinned again, rubbing his ear, his fright forgotten. 'You've got angel's eyes,' he said.

I glanced down at the shell again, rather taken aback. I did not know what to say.

'You're not like the other one,' he said.

'Who do you mean?' I said. 'What other one?'

He shook his head. His eyes were sly again. He laid his finger against his nose. 'Tall and dark she was,' he said. 'She gave you the feeling of a snake. I seen her here with me own eyes. Be night she'd come. I seen her.' He paused, watching me intently. I did not say anything. 'I looked in on her once,' he said, 'and she turned on me, she did. "You don't know me, do you?" she said. "You've never seen me here, and you won't again. If I catch you looking at me through the windows here I'll have you put to the asylum," she said. "You wouldn't like that would you? They're cruel to people in the asylum," she said. "I won't say nothing, M'am," I said. And I touched me cap, like this here.' He pulled at his sou'wester. 'She's gone now, ain't she?' he said anxiously.

'I don't know who you mean,' I said slowly; 'no one is going to put you in the asylum. Good afternoon, Ben.'

I turned away and walked up the beach to the path dragging Jasper by his belt. Poor wretch, he was potty, of course. He did not know what he was talking about. It was hardly likely that anyone would threaten him with the asylum. Maxim had said he was quite harmless, and so had Frank. Perhaps he had heard himself discussed once, amongst his own people, and the memory of it lingered, like an ugly picture in the mind of a child. He would have a child's mentality too, regarding likes and dislikes. He would take a fancy to a person for no reason, and be friendly one day perhaps and sullen the next. He had been friendly with me because I had said he could keep the fishing line. Tomorrow

174

if I met him he might not know me. It was absurd to notice anything said by an idiot. I glanced back over my shoulder at the cove. The tide had begun to run and was swirling slowly round the arm of the harbour wall. Ben had disappeared over the rocks. The beach was deserted again. I could just see the stone chimney of the cottage through a gap in the dark trees. I had a sudden unaccountable desire to run. I pulled at Jasper's leash and panted up the steep narrow path through the woods, not looking back any more. Had I been offered all the treasures in the world I could not have turned and gone down to the cottage or the beach again. It was as though someone waited down there, in the little garden where the nettles grew. Someone who watched and listened.

Jasper barked as we ran together. He thought it was some new kind of game. He kept trying to bite the belt and worry it. I had not realized how closely the trees grew together here, their roots stretching across the path like tendrils ready to trip one. They ought to clear all this, I thought as I ran, catching my breath, Maxim should get the men on to it. There is no sense or beauty in this undergrowth. That tangle of shrubs there should be cut down to bring light to the path. It was dark, much too dark. That naked eucalyptus tree stifled by brambles looked like the white bleached limb of a skeleton, and there was a black earthy stream running beneath it, choked with the muddied rains of years, trickling silently to the beach below. The birds did not sing here as they did in the valley. It was quiet in a different way. And even as I ran and panted up the path I could hear the wash of the sea as the tide crept into the cove. I understood why Maxim disliked the path and the cove. I disliked it too. I had been a fool to come this way. I should have stayed on the other beach, on the white shingle, and come home by the Happy Valley.

I was glad to come out on to the lawn and see the house there in the hollow, solid and secure. The woods were behind me. I would ask Robert to bring me my tea under the chestnut tree. I glanced at my watch. It was earlier than I thought, not yet four. I would have to wait a bit. It was not the routine at Manderley to have tea before half past. I was glad Frith was out. Robert would not make such a performance of bringing the tea out into the garden. As I wandered across the lawn to the terrace my eye was caught by a gleam of sunshine on something metal showing through the green of the rhododendron leaves at the turn in the drive. I shaded my eyes with my hand to see what it was. It looked like the radiator of a car. I wondered if someone had called. If they had though, they would have driven up to the house, not left their car concealed like that from the house, at the turn of the drive, by the shrubs. I went a little closer. Yes, it was a car all right. I could see the wings now and the hood. What a funny thing. Visitors never did that as a rule. And the tradesmen went round the back way by the old stables and the garage. It was not Frank's Morris. I knew that well. This was a long, low car, a sports car. I wondered what I had better do. If it was a caller Robert would have shown them into the library or the drawing-room. In the drawing-room they would be able to see me as I came across the lawn. I did not want to face a caller dressed like this. I should have to ask them to stay to tea. I hesitated, at the edge of the lawn. For no reason, perhaps because the sunlight flickered a moment on the glass, I looked up at the house, and as I did so I noticed with surprise that the shutters of one of the windows in the west wing had been opened up. Somebody stood by the window. A man. And then he must have caught sight of me because he drew back abruptly, and a figure behind him put up an arm and closed the shutters.

The arm belonged to Mrs Danvers. I recognized the black sleeve. I wondered for a minute if it was a public day and she was showing the rooms. It could not be so though because Frith always did that, and Frith was out. Besides, the rooms in the west wing were not shown to the public. I had not even been into them myself yet. No, I knew it was not a public day. The public never came on a Tuesday. Perhaps it was something to do with a repair in one of the rooms. It was odd though the way the man had been looking out and directly he saw me he whipped back into the room and the shutters were closed. And the car too, drawn up behind the rhododendrons, so that it could not be seen from the house. Still, that was up to Mrs Danvers. It was nothing to do with me. If she had friends she took to the west wing it was not exactly my affair. I had never known it happen before though. Odd that it should occur on the only day Maxim was from home.

I strolled rather self-consciously across the lawn to the house, aware that they might be watching me still from a chink in the shutters.

I went up the steps and through the big front door to the hall. There was no sign of a strange cap or stick, and no card on the salver. Evidently this was not an official visitor. Well, it was not my affair. I went into the flower room and washed my hands in the basin to save going upstairs. It would be awkward if I met them face to face on the stairs or somewhere. I remembered I had left my knitting in the morning-room before lunch, and I went along through the drawing-room to fetch it, the faithful Jasper at my heels. The morning-room door was open. And I noticed that my bag of knitting had been moved. I had left it on the divan, and it had been picked up and pushed behind a cushion. There was the imprint of a person on the fabric of the divan where my knitting had been before. Someone had sat down there recently, and picked up my knitting because it had been in the way. The chair by the desk had also been moved. It looked as though Mrs Danvers entertained her visitors in the morning-room when Maxim and I were out of the way. I felt rather uncomfortable. I would rather not know. Jasper was sniffing under the divan and wagging his tail. He was not suspicious of the visitor anyway. I took my bag of knitting and went out. As I did so the door in the large drawing-room that led to the stone passage and the back premises opened, and I heard voices. I darted back into the morning-room again, just in time. I had not been seen. I waited behind the door frowning at Jasper who stood in the doorway looking at me, his tongue hanging out, wagging his tail. The little wretch would give me away. I stood very still, holding my breath.

Then I heard Mrs Danvers speak. 'I expect she has gone to the library,' she said. 'She's come home early for some reason. If she has gone to the library you will be able to go through the hall without her seeing you. Wait here while I go and see.'

I knew they were talking about me. I began to feel more uncomfortable than ever. It was so furtive, the whole business. And I did not want to catch Mrs Danvers in the wrong. Then Jasper turned his head sharply towards the drawing-room. He trotted out, wagging his tail.

'Hullo, you little tyke,' I heard the man say. Jasper began to bark excitedly. I looked round desperately for somewhere to hide. Hopeless of course. And then I heard a footstep quite close to my ear, and the man came into the room. He did not see me at first because I was behind the door, but Jasper made a dive at me, still barking with delight.

The man wheeled round suddenly and saw me. I have never seen anyone look more astonished. I might have been the burglar and he the master of the house.

'I beg your pardon,' he said, looking me up and down.

He was a big, hefty fellow, good-looking in a rather flashy, sunburnt way. He had the hot, blue eyes usually associated with heavy drinking and loose living. His hair was reddish like his skin. In a few years he would run to fat, his neck bulging over the back of his collar. His mouth gave him away, it was too soft, too pink. I could smell the whisky in his breath from where I stood. He began to smile. The sort of smile he would give to every woman.

'I hope I haven't startled you,' he said.

I came out from behind the door looking no doubt as big a fool as I felt. 'No, of course not,' I said, 'I heard voices, I was not quite sure who it was. I did not expect any callers this afternoon.'

'What a shame,' he said heartily, 'it's too bad of me to butt in on you like this. I hope you'll forgive me. The fact is I just popped in to see old Danny, she's a very old friend of mine.'

'Oh, of course, it's quite all right,' I said.

'Dear old Danny,' he said, 'she's so anxious, bless her, not to disturb anyone. She didn't want to worry you.'

'Oh, it does not matter at all,' I said. I was watching Jasper who was jumping up and pawing at the man in delight.

'This little beggar hasn't forgotten me, has he?' he said. 'Grown into a jolly little beast. He was quite a youngster when I saw him last. He's too fat though. He needs more exercise.'

'I've just taken him for a long walk,' I said.

'Have you really? How sporting of you,' he said. He went on patting Jasper and smiling at me in a familiar way. Then he pulled out his cigarette case. 'Have one?' he said.

'I don't smoke,' I told him.

'Don't you really?' He took one himself and lighted it.

I never minded those things, but it seemed odd to me, in somebody else's room. It was surely rather bad manners? Not polite to me.

'How's old Max?' he said.

I was surprised at his tone. It sounded as though he knew him well. It was queer, to hear Maxim talked of as Max. No one called him that.

'He's very well, thank you,' I said. 'He's gone up to London.'

'And left the bride all alone? Why, that's too bad. Isn't he afraid someone will come and carry you off?'

He laughed, opening his mouth. I did not like his laugh. There was something offensive about it. I did not like him, either. Just then Mrs Danvers came into the room. She turned her eyes upon me and I felt quite cold. Oh, God, I thought, how she must hate me.

'Hullo, Danny, there you are,' said the man; 'all your precautions were in vain. The mistress of the house was hiding behind the door.' And he laughed again. Mrs Danvers did not say anything. She just went on looking at me. 'Well, aren't you going to introduce me?' he said; 'after all it's the usual thing to do, isn't it, to pay one's respect to a bride?'

'This is Mr Favell, Madam,' said Mrs Danvers. She spoke quietly, rather unwillingly. I don't think she wanted to introduce him to me.

'How do you do,' I said, and then, with an effort to be polite, 'Won't you stay to tea?'

He looked very amused. He turned to Mrs Danvers.

'Now isn't that a charming invitation?' he said. 'I've been asked to stay to tea? By heaven, Danny, I've a good mind to.'

I saw her flash a look of warning at him. I felt very uneasy. It was all wrong, this situation. It ought not to be happening at all.

'Well, perhaps you're right,' he said; 'it would have been a lot of fun, all the same. I suppose I had better be going, hadn't I? Come and have a look at my car.' He still spoke in a familiar rather offensive way. I did not want to go and look at his car. I felt very awkward and embarrassed. 'Come on,' he said, 'it's a jolly good little car. Much faster than anything poor old Max ever has.'

I could not think of an excuse. The whole business was so forced and stupid. I did not like it. And why did Mrs Danvers have to stand there looking at me with that smouldering look in her eyes?

'Where is the car?' I said feebly.

'Round the bend in the drive. I didn't drive to the door, I was afraid of disturbing you. I had some idea you probably rested in the afternoon.'

I said nothing. The lie was too obvious. We all walked out through the drawing-room and into the hall. I saw him glance over his shoulder and wink at Mrs Danvers. She did not wink in return. I hardly expected she would. She looked very hard and grim. Jasper frolicked out on to the drive. He seemed delighted with the sudden appearance of this visitor whom he appeared to know so well.

'I left my cap in the car, I believe,' said the man, pretending to glance round the hall. 'As a matter of fact, I didn't come in this way. I slipped round and bearded Danny in her den. Coming out to see the car too?'

He looked inquiringly at Mrs Danvers. She hesitated, watching me out of the tail of her eye.

'No,' she said. 'No, I don't think I'll come out now. Good-bye, Mr Jack.'

He seized her hand and shook it heartily. 'Good-bye, Danny: take care of yourself. You know where to get in touch with me always. It's done me a power of good to see you again.' He walked out on to the drive, Jasper dancing at his heels, and I followed him slowly, feeling very uncomfortable still.

'Dear old Manderley,' he said, looking up at the windows. 'The place hasn't changed much. I suppose Danny sees to that. What a wonderful woman she is, eh?'

'Yes, she's very efficient,' I said.

'And what do you think of it all? Like being buried down here?'

'I'm very fond of Manderley,' I said stiffly.

'Weren't you living somewhere down in the south of France when Max met you? Monte, wasn't it? I used to know Monte well.'

'Yes, I was in Monte Carlo,' I said.

We had come to his car now. A green sports thing, typical of its owner.

'What do you think of it?' he said.

'Very nice,' I said, politely.

'Come for a run to the lodge gates?' he said.

'No, I don't think I will,' I said. 'I'm rather tired.'

'You don't think it would look too good for the mistress of Manderley to be seen driving with someone like me, is that it?' he said, and he laughed, shaking his head at me.

'Oh, no,' I said, turning rather red. 'No, really.'

He went on looking me up and down in his amused way with those familiar, unpleasant blue eyes. I felt like a barmaid.

'Oh, well,' he said, 'we mustn't lead the bride astray, must we, Jasper? It wouldn't do at all.' He reached for his cap, and an enormous pair of motoring gloves. He threw his cigarette away on the drive.

'Good-bye,' he said, holding out his hand; 'it's been a lot of fun meeting you.'

'Good-bye,' I said.

'By the way,' he said carelessly, 'it would be very sporting and grand of you if you did not mention this little visit of mine to Max? He doesn't exactly approve of me, I'm afraid; I don't know why, and it might get poor old Danny into trouble.'

'No,' I said awkwardly. 'No, all right.'

'That's very sporting of you. Sure you won't change your mind and come for a run?'

'No, I don't think I will, if you don't mind.'

'Bye-bye, then. Perhaps I'll come and look you up one day. Get down, Jasper, you devil, you'll scratch my paint. I say, I call it a damn shame Max going up to London and leaving you alone like this!'

'I don't mind. I like being alone,' I said.

'Do you, by Jove? What an extraordinary thing. It's all wrong, you know. Against nature. How long have you been married? Three months, isn't it?'

'About that,' I said.

'I say, I wish I'd got a bride of three months waiting for me at home! I'm a poor lonesome bachelor.' He laughed again, and pulled his cap down over his eyes. 'Fare you well,' he said, starting up the engine, and the car shot down the drive snorting explosive fury from the exhaust, while Jasper stood looking after it, his ears drooping, his tail between his legs.

'Oh, come on, Jasper,' I said, 'don't be so idiotic.' I walked slowly back to the house. Mrs Danvers had disappeared. I stood in the hall and rang the bell. Nothing happened for about five minutes. I rang again. Presently Alice appeared, her face rather aggrieved. 'Yes, Madam?' she said.

'Oh, Alice,' I said, 'isn't Robert there? I rather fancied my tea out under the chestnut tree.'

'Robert went to the post this afternoon, and isn't back yet, Madam,' said Alice. 'Mrs Danvers gave him to understand you would be late for tea. Frith is out too of course. If you want your tea now I can get it for you. I don't think it's quite half past four yet.'

'Oh, it doesn't matter, Alice. I'll wait till Robert comes back,' I said. I supposed when Maxim was away things automatically became slack. I had never known Frith and Robert to be out at the same time. It was Frith's day of course. And Mrs Danvers had sent Robert to the post. And I myself was understood to have gone for a long walk. That man Favell had chosen his time well to pay his call on Mrs Danvers. It was almost too well chosen. There was something not right about it, I was certain of that. And then he had asked me not to say anything to Maxim. It was all very awkward. I did not want to get Mrs Danvers into trouble or make any sort of scene. More important still I did not want to worry Maxim.

I wondered who he was, this man Favell. He had called Maxim 'Max'. No one ever called him Max. I had seen it written once, on the fly-leaf of a book, the letters thin and slanting, curiously pointed, the tail of the M very definite, very long. I thought there was only one person who had ever called him Max . . .

As I stood there in the hall, undecided about my tea, wondering what to do, the thought suddenly came to me that perhaps Mrs Danvers was dishonest, that all this time she was engaged in some business behind Maxim's back, and coming back early as I had today I had discovered her and this man, an accomplice, who had then bluffed his way out by pretending to be familiar with the house and with Maxim. I wondered what they had been doing in the west wing. Why had they closed the shutters when they saw me on the lawn? I was filled with vague disquiet. Frith and Robert had been away. The maids were generally in their bedrooms changing during the afternoon. Mrs Danvers would have the run of the place. Supposing this man was a thief, and Mrs Danvers was in his pay? There were valuable things in the west wing. I had a sudden rather terrifying impulse to creep upstairs now to the west wing and go into those rooms and see for myself.

Robert was not yet back. I would just have time before tea.

I hesitated, glancing at the gallery. The house seemed very still and quiet. The servants were all in their own quarters beyond the kitchen. Jasper lapped noisily at his drinking bowl below the stairs, the sound echoing in the great stone hall. I began to walk upstairs. My heart was beating in a queer excited way.

I found myself in the corridor where I had stood that first morning. I had not been there since, nor had I wished to go. The sun streamed in from the window in the alcove and made gold patterns on the dark panelling.

There was no sound at all. I was aware of the same musty, unused smell that had been before. I was uncertain which way to go. The plan of the rooms was not familiar to me. I remembered then that last time Mrs Danvers had come out of a door here, just behind me, and it seemed to me that the position of the room would make it the one I wanted, whose windows looked out upon the lawns to the sea. I turned the handle of the door and went inside. It was dark of course, because of the shutters. I felt for the electric light switch on the wall and turned it on. I was standing in a little ante-room, a dressing-room I judged, with big wardrobes round the wall, and at the end of this room was another door, open, leading to a larger room. I went through to this room, and turned on the light. My first impression was one of shock because the room was fully furnished, as though in use.

I had expected to see chairs and tables swathed in dust-sheets, and dust-sheets too over the great double bed against the wall. Nothing was covered up. There were brushes and combs on the dressing-table, scent, and powder. The bed was made up, I saw the gleam of white linen on the pillow-case, and the tip of a blanket beneath the quilted coverlet. There were flowers on the dressing-table and on the table beside the bed. Flowers too on the carved mantelpiece. A satin dressing-gown lay on a chair, and a pair of bedroom slippers beneath. For one desperate moment I thought that something had happened to my brain, that I was seeing back into Time, and looking upon the room as it used to be, before she died . . . In a minute Rebecca herself would come back into the room, sit down before the looking-glass at her dressing-table, humming a tune, reach for her comb and run it through her hair. If she sat there I should see her reflection in the glass and she would see me too, standing like this by the door. Nothing happened. I went on standing there, waiting for something to happen. It was the clock ticking on the wall that brought me to reality again. The hands stood at twenty-five past four. My watch said the same. There was something sane and comforting about the ticking of the clock. It reminded me of the present, and that tea would soon be ready for me on the lawn. I walked slowly into the middle of the room. No, it was not used. It was not lived in any more. Even the flowers could not destroy the musty smell. The curtains were drawn and the shutters were closed. Rebecca would never come back to the room again. Even if Mrs Danvers did put the flowers on the mantelpiece and the sheets upon the bed, they would not bring her back. She was dead. She had been dead now for a year. She lay buried in the crypt of the church with all the other dead de Winters.

I could hear the sound of the sea very plainly. I went to the window and swung back the shutter. Yes, I was standing at the same window where Favell and Mrs Danvers had stood, half an hour ago. The long shaft of daylight made the electric light look false and yellow. I opened the shutter a little more. The daylight cast a white beam upon the bed. It shone upon the nighdress-case, lying on the pillow. It shone on the glass top of the dressing-table, on the brushes, and on the scent bottles.

The daylight gave an even greater air of reality to the room. When the shutter was closed and it had been lit by electricity the room had more the appearance of a setting on the stage. The scene set between performances. The curtain having fallen for the night, the evening over, and the first act set for tomorrow's matinée. But the daylight made the room vivid and alive. I forgot the musty smell and the drawn curtains of the other windows.

I was a guest again. An uninvited guest. I had strolled into my hostess's bedroom by mistake. Those were her brushes on the dressing-table, that was her dressing-gown and slippers laid out upon the chair.

I realized for the first time since I had come into the room that my legs were trembling, weak as straw. I sat down on the stool by the dressing-table. My heart no longer beat in a strange excited way. It felt as heavy as lead. I looked about me in the room with a sort of dumb stupidity. Yes, it was a beautiful room. Mrs Danvers had not exaggerated that first evening. It was the most beautiful room in the house. That exquisite mantelpiece, the ceiling, the carved bedstead, and the curtain hangings, even the clock on the wall and the candlesticks up on the dressing-table beside me, all were things I would have loved and almost worshipped had they been mine. They were not mine though. They belonged to somebody else. I put out my hand and touched the brushes. One was more worn than its fellow. I understood it well. There was always one brush that had the greater use. Often you forgot to use the other, and when they were taken to be washed there was one that was still quite clean and untouched. How white and thin my face looked in the glass, my hair hanging lank and straight. Did I always look like this? Surely I had more colour as a rule? The reflection stared back at me, sallow and plain.

I got up from the stool and went and touched the dressing-gown on the chair. I picked up the slippers and held them in my hand. I was aware of a growing sense of horror, of horror turning to despair. I touched the quilt on the bed, traced with my fingers the monogram on the nightdress case, R de W, inter-woven and interlaced. The letters were corded and strong against the golden satin material. The nightdress was inside the case, thin as gossamer, apricot in colour. I touched it, drew it out from the case, put it against my face. It was cold, quite cold. But there was a dim mustiness about it still where the scent had been. The scent of the white azaleas. I folded it, and put it back into the case, and as I did so I noticed with a sick dull aching in my

187

heart that there were creases in the night-dress, the texture was ruffled, it had not been touched or laundered since it was last worn.

On a sudden impulse I moved away from the bed and went back to the little ante-room where I had seen the wardrobes. I opened one of them. It was as I thought. The wardrobe was full of clothes. There were evening dresses here, I caught the shimmer of silver over the top of the white bags that enfolded them. There was a piece of gold brocade. There, next to it, was velvet, wine-coloured and soft. There was a train of white satin, dripping on the floor of the wardrobe. Peeping out from a piece of tissue paper on a shelf above was an ostrich feather fan.

The wardrobe smelt stuffy, queer. The azalea scent, so fragrant and delicate in the air, had turned stale inside the wardrobe, tarnishing the silver dresses and the brocade, and the breath of it wafted towards me now from the open doors, faded and old. I shut the doors. I went back into the bedroom once again. The gleam of light from the shutter still shone white and clear on the golden coverlet of the bed, picking out clearly and distinctly the tall sloping R of the monogram.

Then I heard a step behind me and turning round I saw Mrs Danvers. I shall never forget the expression on her face. Triumphant, gloating, excited in a strange unhealthy way. I felt very frightened.

'Is anything the matter, Madam?' she said.

I tried to smile at her, and could not. I tried to speak.

'Are you feeling unwell?' she said, coming nearer to me, speaking very softly. I backed away from her. I believe if she had come any closer to me I should have fainted. I felt her breath on my face.

'I'm all right, Mrs Danvers,' I said, after a moment, 'I did not expect to see you. The fact is, I was looking up at the windows from the lawn. I noticed one of the shutters was not quite closed. I came up to see if I could fasten it.'

'I will fasten it,' she said, and she went silently across the room and clamped back the shutter. The daylight had gone. The room looked unreal again in the false yellow light. Unreal and ghastly.

Mrs Danvers came back and stood beside me. She smiled, and her manner, instead of being still and unbending as it usually was, became startlingly familiar, fawning even.

'Why did you tell me the shutter was open?' she asked. 'I closed it before I left the room. You opened it yourself, didn't you, now? You wanted to see the room. Why have you never asked me to show it to you before? I was ready to show it to you every day. You had only to ask me.'

I wanted to run away, but I could not move. I went on watching her eyes.

'Now you are here, let me show you everything,' she said, her voice ingratiating and sweet as honey, horrible, false. 'I know you want to see it all, you've wanted to for a long time, and you were too shy to ask. It's a lovely room, isn't it? The loveliest room you have ever seen.'

She took hold of my arm, and walked me towards the bed. I could not resist her, I was like a dumb thing. The touch of her hand made me shudder. And her voice was low and intimate, a voice I hated and feared.

'That was her bed. It's a beautiful bed, isn't it? I keep the golden coverlet on it always, it was her favourite. Here is her nightdress inside the case. You've been touching it, haven't you? This was the nightdress she was wearing for the last time, before she died. Would you like to touch it again?' She took the nightdress from the case and held it before me. 'Feel it, hold it,' she said, 'how soft and light it is, isn't it? I haven't washed it since she wore it for the last time. I put it out like this, and the dressing-gown and slippers, just as I put them out for her the night she never came back, the night she was drowned.' She folded up the nightgown and put it back in the case. 'I did everything for her, you know,' she said, taking my arm again, leading me to the dressing-gown and slippers. 'We tried maid after maid but not one of them suited. "You maid me better than anyone, Danny," she used to say, "I won't have anyone but you." Look, this is her dressing-gown. She was much taller than you, you

189

can see by the length. Put it up against you. It comes down to your ankles. She had a beautiful figure. These are her slippers. "Throw me my slips, Danny," she used to say. She had little feet for her height. Put your hands inside the slippers. They are quite small and narrow, aren't they?'

She forced the slippers over my hands, smiling all the while, watching my eyes. 'You never would have thought she was so tall, would you?' she said, 'these slippers would fit a tiny foot. She was so slim too. You would forget her height, until she stood beside you. She was every bit as tall as me. But lying there in bed she looked quite a slip of a thing, with her mass of dark hair, standing out from her face like a halo.'

She put the slippers back on the floor, and laid the dressing-gown on the chair. 'You've seen her brushes, haven't you?' she said, taking me to the dressing-table; 'there they are, just as she used them, unwashed and untouched. I used to brush her hair for her every evening. "Come on, Danny, hair-drill," she would say, and I'd stand behind her by the stool here, and brush away for twenty minutes at a time. She only wore it short the last few years, you know. It came down below the waist, when she was first married. Mr de Winter used to brush it for her then. I've come into this room time and time again and seen him, in his shirt sleeves, with the two brushes in his hand. "Harder, Max, harder," she would say, laughing up at him, and he would do as she told him. They would be dressing for dinner, you see, and the house filled with guests. "Here, I shall be late," he would say, throwing the brushes to me, and laughing back at her. He was always laughing and gay then.' She paused, her hand still resting on my arm.

'Everyone was angry with her when she cut her hair,' she said, 'but she did not care. "It's nothing to do with anyone but myself," she would say. And of course short hair was much easier for riding and sailing. She was painted on horseback, you know. A famous artist did it. The picture hung in the Academy. Did you ever see it?'

I shook my head. 'No,' I said. 'No.'

'I understood it was the picture of the year,' she went on, 'but Mr de Winter did not care for it, and would not have it at Manderley. I don't think he considered it did her justice. You would like to see her clothes, wouldn't you?' She did not wait for my answer. She led me to the little ante-room and opened the wardrobes, one by one.

'I keep her furs in here,' she said, 'the moths have not got to them yet, and I doubt if they ever will. I'm too careful. Feel that sable wrap. That was a Christmas present from Mr de Winter. She told me the cost once, but I've forgotten it now. This chinchilla she wore in the evenings mostly. Round her shoulders, very often, when the evenings were cold. This wardrobe here is full of her evening clothes. You opened it, didn't you? The latch is not quite closed. I believe Mr de Winter liked her to wear silver mostly. But of course she could wear anything, stand any colour. She looked beautiful in this velvet. Put it against your face. It's soft, isn't it? You can feel it, can't you? The scent is still fresh, isn't it? You could almost imagine she had only just taken it off. I would always know when she had been before me in a room. There would be a little whiff of her scent in the room. These are her underclothes, in this drawer. This pink set here she had never worn. She was wearing slacks of course and a shirt when she died. They were torn from her body in the water though. There was nothing on the body when it was found, all those weeks afterwards.'

Her fingers tightened on my arm. She bent down to me, her skull's face close, her dark eyes searching mine. 'The rocks had battered her to bits, you know,' she whispered, 'her beautiful face unrecognizable, and both arms gone. Mr de Winter identified her. He went up to Edgecoombe to do it. He went quite alone. He was very ill at the time but he would go. No one could stop him. Not even Mr Crawley.'

She paused, her eyes never leaving my face. 'I shall always blame myself for the accident,' she said, 'it was my fault for being out that evening. I had gone into Kerrith for the afternoon and stayed there late, as Mrs de Winter was up in London and not expected back until much later. That's why I did not hurry back. When I came in, about half past nine, I heard she had returned just before seven, had her dinner, and then went out again. Down to the beach of course. I felt worried then. It was blowing from the south-west. She would never have gone if I'd been in. She always listened to me. 'I wouldn't go out this evening, it's not fit,' I should have said, and she would have answered me 'All right, Danny, you old fuss-pot.' And we would have sat up here talking no doubt, she telling me all she had done in London, like she always did.'

My arm was bruised and numb from the pressure of her fingers. I could see how tightly the skin was stretched across her face, showing the cheekbones. There were little patches of yellow beneath her ears.

'Mr de Winter had been dining with Mr Crawley down at his house,' she went on. 'I don't know what time he got back, I dare say it was after eleven. But it began to blow quite hard just before midnight, and she had not come back. I went downstairs, but there were no lights under the library door. I came upstairs again and knocked on the dressing-room door. Mr de Winter answered at once, "Who is it, what do you want?" he said. I told him I was worried about Mrs de Winter not being back. He waited a moment, and then he came and opened the door in his dressing-gown. "She's spending the night down at the cottage I expect," he said. "I should go to bed if I were you. She won't come back here to sleep if it goes on like this." He looked tired, and I did not like to disturb him. After all, she spent many nights at the cottage, and had sailed in every sort of weather. She might not even have gone for a sail, but just wanted the night at the cottage as a change after London. I said good night to Mr de Winter and went back to my room. I did not sleep though. I kept wondering what she was doing.'

She paused again. I did not want to hear any more. I wanted to get away from her, away from the room.

'I sat on my bed until half past five,' she said, 'then I couldn't wait there any longer. I got up and put on my coat and went down through the woods to the beach. It was getting light, but there was still a misty sort of rain falling, although the wind had dropped. When I got to the beach I saw the buoy there in the water and the dinghy, but the boat had gone . . .' It seemed to me that I could see the cove in the grey morning light, feel the thin drizzle on my face, and peering through the mist could make out, shadowy and indistinct, the low dark outline of the buoy.

Mrs Danvers loosened the pressure on my arm. Her hand fell back again to her side. Her voice lost all expression, became the hard mechanical voice of every day.

'One of the life-buoys was washed up at Kerrith in the afternoon,' she said, 'and another was found the next day by some crabbers on the rocks below the headland. Bits and pieces of rigging too would come in with the tide.' She turned away from me, and closed the chest of drawers. She straightened one of the pictures on the wall. She picked up a piece of fluff from the carpet. I stood watching her, not knowing what to do.

'You know now', she said, 'why Mr de Winter does not use these rooms any more. Listen to the sea.'

Even with the windows closed and the shutters fastened I could hear it; a low sullen murmur as the waves broke on the white shingle in the cove. The tide would be coming in fast now and running up the beach nearly to the stone cottage.

'He has not used these rooms since the night she was drowned,' she said. 'He had his things moved out from the dressing-room. We made up one of the rooms at the end of the corridor. I don't think he slept much even there. He used to sit in the arm-chair. There would be cigarette ash all round it in the morning. And in the daytime Frith would hear him in the library pacing up and down. Up and down, up and down.'

I too could see the ash on the floor beside the chair. I too could hear his footsteps; one, two, one, two, backwards and forwards across the library . . . Mrs Danvers closed the door softly between the bedroom and the ante-room where we were standing, and put out the light. I could not see the bed any

193

more, nor the nightdress case upon the pillow, nor the dressing-table, nor the slippers by the chair. She crossed the ante-room and put her hand on the knob of the door and stood waiting for me to follow her.

'I come to the rooms and dust them myself every day,' she said. 'If you want to come again you have only to tell me. Ring me on the house-telephone. I shall understand. I don't allow the maids up here. No one ever comes but me.'

Her manner was fawning again, intimate and unpleasant. The smile on her face was a false, unnatural thing. 'Sometimes when Mr de Winter is away, and you feel lonely, you might like to come up to these rooms and sit here. You have only to tell me. They are such beautiful rooms. You would not think she had gone now for so long, would you, not by the way the rooms are kept? You would think she had just gone out for a little while and would be back in the evening.'

I forced a smile. I could not speak. My throat felt dry and tight.

'It's not only this room,' she said. 'It's in many rooms in the house. In the morning-room, in the hall, even in the little flower-room. I feel her everywhere. You do too, don't you?'

She stared at me curiously. Her voice dropped to a whisper. 'Sometimes, when I walk along the corridor here, I fancy I hear her just behind me. That quick, light footstep. I could not mistake it anywhere. And in the minstrels' gallery above the hall. I've seen her leaning there, in the evenings in the old days, looking down at the hall below and calling to the dogs. I can fancy her there now from time to time. It's almost as though I catch the sound of her dress sweeping the stairs as she comes down to dinner.' She paused. She went on looking at me, watching my eyes. 'Do you think she can see us, talking to one another now?' she said slowly. 'Do you think the dead come back and watch the living?'

I swallowed. I dug my nails into my hands.

'I don't know,' I said. 'I don't know.' My voice sounded high-pitched and unnatural. Not my voice at all.

'Sometimes I wonder,' she whispered. 'Sometimes I wonder if she comes back here to Manderley and watches you and Mr de Winter together.'

We stood there by the door, staring at one another. I could not take my eyes away from hers. How dark and sombre they were in the white skull's face of hers, how malevolent, how full of hatred. Then she opened the door into the corridor. 'Robert is back now,' she said. 'He came back a quarter of an hour ago. He has orders to take your tea out under the chestnut tree.'

She stepped aside for me to pass. I stumbled out on to the corridor, not looking where I was going. I did not speak to her, I went down the stairs blindly, and turned the corner and pushed through the door that led to my own rooms in the east wing. I shut the door of my room and turned the key, and put the key in my pocket.

Then I lay down on my bed and closed my eyes. I felt deadly sick.

Maxim rang up the next morning to say he would be back about seven. Frith took the message. Maxim did not ask to speak to me himself. I heard the telephone ring while I was at breakfast and I thought perhaps Frith would come into the dining-room and say 'Mr de Winter on the telephone, Madam.' I had put down my napkin and had risen to my feet. And then Frith came back into the dining-room and gave me the message.

He saw me push back my chair and go to the door. 'Mr de Winter has rung off, Madam,' he said, 'there was no message. Just that he would be back about seven.'

I sat down in my chair again and picked up my napkin. Frith must have thought me eager and stupid rushing across the dining-room.

'All right, Frith. Thank you,' I said.

I went on eating my eggs and bacon, Jasper at my feet, the old dog in her basket in the corner. I wondered what I should do with my day. I had slept badly; perhaps because I was alone in the room. I had been restless, waking up often, and when I glanced at my clock I saw the hands had scarcely moved. When I did fall asleep I had varied, wandering dreams. We were walking through woods, Maxim and I, and he was always just a little ahead of me. I could not keep up with him. Nor could I see his face. Just his figure, striding away in front of me all the time. I must have cried while I slept, for when I woke in the morning the pillow was damp. My eyes were heavy too, when I looked in the glass. I looked plain, unattractive. I rubbed a little rouge on my cheeks in a wretched attempt to give myself colour. But it made me worse. It gave me a false clown look. Perhaps I did not know the best way to put it on. I noticed Robert staring at me as I crossed the hall and went into breakfast.

About ten o'clock as I was crumbling some pieces for the birds on the terrace the telephone rang again. This time it was for me. Frith came and said Mrs Lacy wanted to speak to me.

'Good morning, Beatrice,' I said.

'Well, my dear, how are you?' she said, her telephone voice typical of herself, brisk, rather masculine, standing no nonsense, and then not waiting for my answer. 'I thought of motoring over this afternoon and looking up Gran. I'm lunching with people about twenty miles from you. Shall I come and pick you up and we'll go together? It's time you met the old lady, you know.'

'I'd like to very much, Beatrice,' I said.

'Splendid. Very well, then. I'll come along for you about half past three. Giles saw Maxim at the dinner. Poor food, he said, but excellent wine. All right, my dear, see you later.'

The click of the receiver, and she was gone. I wandered back into the garden. I was glad she had rung up and suggested the plan of going over to see the grandmother. It made something to look forward to, and broke the monotony of the day. The hours had seemed so long until seven o'clock. I did not feel in my holiday mood today, and I had no wish to go off with Jasper to the Happy Valley and come to the cove and throw stones in the water. The sense of freedom had departed, and the childish desire to run across the lawns in sandshoes. I went and sat down with a book and *The Times* and my knitting in the rose-garden, domestic as a matron, yawning in the warm sun while the bees hummed amongst the flowers.

I tried to concentrate on the bald newspaper columns, and later to lose myself in the racy plot of the novel in my hands. I did not want to think of yesterday afternoon and Mrs Danvers. I tried to forget that she was in the house at this moment, perhaps looking down on me from one of the windows. And now and again, when I looked up from my book or glanced across the garden, I had the feeling I was not alone.

There were so many windows in Manderley, so many rooms

that were never used by Maxim and myself that were empty now; dust-sheeted, silent, rooms that had been occupied in the old days when his father and his grandfather had been alive, when there had been much entertaining, many servants. It would be easy for Mrs Danvers to open those doors softly and close them again, and then steal quietly across the shrouded room and look down upon me from behind the drawn curtains.

I should not know. Even if I turned in my chair and looked up at the windows I would not see her. I remembered a game I had played as a child that my friends next-door had called 'Grandmother's Steps' and myself 'Old Witch'. You had to stand at the end of the garden with your back turned to the rest, and one by one they crept nearer to you, advancing in short furtive fashion. Every few minutes you turned to look at them, and if you saw one of them moving the offender had to retire to the back line and begin again. But there was always one a little bolder than the rest, who came up very close, whose movement was impossible to detect, and as you waited there, your back turned, counting the regulation Ten, you knew, with a fatal terrifying certainty, that before long, before even the Ten was counted, this bold player would pounce upon you from behind, unheralded, unseen, with a scream of triumph. I felt as tense and expectant as I did then. I was playing 'Old Witch' with Mrs Danvers.

Lunch was a welcome break to the long morning. The calm efficiency of Frith, and Robert's rather foolish face, helped me more than my book and my newspaper had done. And at half past three, punctual to the moment, I heard the sound of Beatrice's car round the sweep of the drive and pull up at the steps before the house. I ran out to meet her, ready dressed, my gloves in my hand. 'Well, my dear, here I am, what a splendid day, isn't it?' She slammed the door of the car and came up the steps to meet me. She gave me a hard swift kiss, brushing me somewhere near the ear.

'You don't look well,' she said immediately, looking me up and down, 'much too thin in the face and no colour. What's wrong with you?'

'Nothing,' I said humbly, knowing the fault of my face too well. 'I'm not a person who ever has much colour.'

'Oh, bosh,' she replied, 'you looked quite different when I saw you before.'

'I expect the brown of Italy has worn off,' I said, getting into the car.

'H'mph,' she said shortly, 'you're as bad as Maxim. Can't stand any criticism about your health. Slam the door hard or it doesn't shut.' We started off down the drive, swerving at the corner, going rather too fast. 'You're not by any chance starting an infant, are you?' she said, turning her hawk-brown eyes upon me.

'No,' I said awkwardly. 'No, I don't think so.'

'No morning sickness or anything like that?'

'No.'

'Oh, well – of course it doesn't always follow. I never turned a hair when Roger was born. Felt as fit as a fiddle the whole nine months. I played golf the day before he arrived. There's nothing to be embarrassed about in the facts of nature, you know. If you have any suspicions you had better tell me.'

'No, really, Beatrice,' I said, 'there's nothing to tell.'

'I must say I do hope you will produce a son and heir before long. It would be so terribly good for Maxim. I hope you are doing nothing to prevent it.'

'Of course not,' I said. What an extraordinary conversation.

'Oh, don't be shocked,' she said, 'you must never mind what I say. After all, brides of today are up to everything. It's a damn nuisance if you want to hunt and you land yourself with an infant your first season. Quite enough to break a marriage up if you are both keen. Wouldn't matter in your case. Babies needn't interfere with sketching. How is the sketching, by the way?'

'I'm afraid I don't seem to do much,' I said.

'Oh, really? Nice weather, too, for sitting out of doors. You only need a camp-stool and a box of pencils, don't you? Tell me, were you interested in those books I sent you?'

'Yes, of course,' I said. 'It was a lovely present, Beatrice.'

She looked pleased. 'Glad you liked them,' she said.

The car sped along. She kept her foot permanently on the accelerator, and took every corner at an acute angle. Two motorists we passed looked out of their windows outraged as she swept by, and one pedestrian in a lane waved his stick at her. I felt rather hot for her. She did not seem to notice though. I crouched lower in my seat.

'Roger goes up to Oxford next term,' she said, 'heaven knows what he'll do with himself. Awful waste of time I think, and so does Giles, but we couldn't think what else to do with him. Of course he's just like Giles and myself. Thinks of nothing but horses. What on earth does this car in front think it's doing? Why don't you put out your hand, my good man? Really, some of these people on the road today ought to be shot.'

We swerved into a main road, narrowly avoiding the car ahead of us. 'Had any people down to stay?' she asked.

'No, we've been very quiet,' I said.

'Much better, too,' she said, 'awful bore, I always think, those big parties. You won't find it alarming if you come to stay with us. Very nice lot of people all round, and we all know one another frightfully well. We dine in one another's houses, and have our bridge, and don't bother with outsiders. You do play bridge, don't you?'

'I'm not very good, Beatrice.'

'Oh, we shan't mind that. As long as you can play. I've no patience with people who won't learn. What on earth can one do with them between tea and dinner in the winter, and after dinner? One can't just sit and talk.'

I wondered why. However, it was simpler not to say anything.

'It's quite amusing now Roger is a reasonable age,' she went on, 'because he brings his friends to stay, and we have really good fun. You ought to have been with us last Christmas. We had charades. My dear, it was the greatest fun. Giles was in his element. He adores dressing-up, you know, and after a glass or two of champagne he's the funniest thing you've ever seen. We often say he's missed his vocation and ought to have been on the stage.'

I thought of Giles, and his large moon face, his horn spectacles.

I felt the sight of him being funny after champagne would embarrass me. 'He and another man, a great friend of ours, Dickie Marsh, dressed up as women and sang a duet. What exactly it had to do with the word in the charade nobody knew, but it did not matter. We all roared.'

I smiled politely. 'Fancy, how funny,' I said.

I saw them all rocking from side to side in Beatrice's drawing-room. All these friends who knew one another so well. Roger would look like Giles. Beatrice was laughing again at the memory. 'Poor Giles,' she said. 'I shall never forget his face when Dick squirted the soda syphon down his back. We were all in fits.'

I had an uneasy feeling we might be asked to spend the approaching Christmas with Beatrice. Perhaps I could have influenza.

'Of course our acting was never very ambitious,' she said. 'It was just a lot of fun amongst ourselves. At Manderley now, there is scope for a really fine show. I remember a pageant they had there, some years ago. People from London came down to do it. Of course that type of thing needs terrific organization.'

'Yes,' I said.

She was silent for a while, and drove without speaking.

'How is Maxim?' she said, after a moment.

'Very well, thanks,' I said.

'Quite cheerful and happy?'

'Oh, yes. Yes, rather.'

A narrow village street engaged her attention. I wondered whether I should tell her about Mrs Danvers. About the man Favell. I did not want her to make a blunder though, and perhaps tell Maxim.

'Beatrice,' I said, deciding upon it, 'have you ever heard of someone called Favell? Jack Favell?'

'Jack Favell,' she repeated. 'Yes, I do know the name. Wait a minute. Jack Favell. Of course. An awful bounder. I met him once, ages ago.'

'He came to Manderley yesterday to see Mrs Danvers,' I said.

'Really? Oh, well, perhaps he would . . .'

'Why?' I said.

'I rather think he was Rebecca's cousin,' she said.

I was very surprised. That man her relation? It was not my idea of the sort of cousin Rebecca would have. Jack Favell her cousin. 'Oh,' I said. 'Oh, I hadn't realized that.'

'He probably used to go to Manderley a lot,' said Beatrice. 'I don't know. I couldn't tell you. I was very seldom there.' Her manner was abrupt. It gave me the impression she did not want to pursue the subject.

'I did not take to him much,' I said.

'No,' said Beatrice. 'I don't blame you.'

I waited, but she did not say any more. I thought it wiser not to tell her how Favell had asked me to keep the visit a secret. It might lead to some complication. Besides, we were just coming to our destination. A pair of white gates and a smooth gravel drive.

'Don't forget the old lady is nearly blind,' said Beatrice, 'and she's not very bright these days. I telephoned to the nurse that we were coming, so everything will be all right.'

The house was large, red-bricked, and gabled. Late Victorian I supposed. Not an attractive house. I could tell in a glance it was the sort of house that was aggressively well-kept by a big staff. And all for one old lady who was nearly blind.

A trim parlour-maid opened the door.

'Good afternoon, Norah, how are you?' said Beatrice.

'Very well, thank you, Madam. I hope you are keeping well?'

'Oh, yes, we are all flourishing. How has the old lady been, Norah?'

'Rather mixed, Madam. She has one good day, and then a bad. She's not too bad in herself, you know. She will be pleased to see you I'm sure.' She glanced curiously at me.

'This is Mrs Maxim,' said Beatrice.

'Yes, Madam. How do you do,' said Norah.

We went through a narrow hall and a drawing-room crowded with furniture to a veranda facing a square clipped lawn. There were many bright geraniums in stone vases on the steps of the

202

veranda. In the corner was a bath chair. Beatrice's grandmother was sitting there, propped up with pillows and surrounded by shawls. When we came close to her I saw that she had a strong, rather uncanny, resemblance to Maxim. That was what Maxim would look like, if he was very old, if he was blind. The nurse by her side got up from her chair and put a mark in the book she was reading aloud. She smiled at Beatrice.

'How are you, Mrs Lacy?' she said.

Beatrice shook hands with her and introduced me. 'The old lady looks all right,' she said. 'I don't know how she does it, at eighty-six. Here we are, Gran,' she said, raising her voice, 'arrived safe and sound.'

The grandmother looked in our direction. 'Dear Bee,' she said, 'how sweet of you to come and visit me. We're so dull here, nothing for you to do.'

Beatrice leant over her and kissed her. 'I've brought Maxim's wife over to see you,' she said, 'she wanted to come and see you before, but she and Maxim have been so busy.'

Beatrice prodded me in the back. 'Kiss her,' she murmured. I too bent down and kissed her on the cheek.

The grandmother touched my face with her fingers. 'You nice thing,' she said, 'so good of you to come. I'm very pleased to see you, dear. You ought to have brought Maxim with you.'

'Maxim is in London,' I said, 'he's coming back tonight.'

'You might bring him next time,' she said. 'Sit down, dear, in this chair, where I can see you. And Bee, come the other side. How is dear Roger? He's a naughty boy, he doesn't come and see me.'

'He shall come during August,' shouted Beatrice; 'he's leaving Eton, you know, he's going up to Oxford.'

'Oh, dear, he'll be quite a young man, I shan't know him.'

'He's taller than Giles now,' said Beatrice.

She went on, telling her about Giles, and Roger, and the horses, and the dogs. The nurse brought out some knitting, and clicked her needles sharply. She turned to me, very bright, very cheerful.

'How are you liking Manderley, Mrs de Winter?'

'Very much, thank you,' I said.

'It's a beautiful spot, isn't it?' she said, the needles jabbing one another. 'Of course we don't get over there now, she's not up to it. I am sorry, I used to love our days at Manderley.'

'You must come over yourself some time,' I said.

'Thank you, I should love to. Mr de Winter is well, I suppose?'

'Yes, very well.'

'You spent your honeymoon in Italy, didn't you? We were so pleased with the picture-postcard Mr de Winter sent.'

I wondered whether she used 'we' in the royal sense, or if she meant that Maxim's grandmother and herself were one.

'Did he send one? I can't remember.'

'Oh, yes, it was quite an excitement. We love anything like that. We keep a scrap-book you know, and paste anything to do with the family inside it. Anything pleasant, that is.'

'How nice,' I said.

I caught snatches of Beatrice's conversation on the other side. 'We had to put old Marksman down,' she was saying. 'You remember old Marksman? The best hunter I ever had.'

'Oh, dear, not old Marksman?' said her grandmother.

'Yes, poor old man. Got blind in both eyes, you know.'

'Poor Marksman,' echoed the old lady.

I thought perhaps it was not very tactful to talk about blindness, and I glanced at the nurse. She was still busy clicking her needles.

'Do you hunt, Mrs de Winter?' she said.

'No, I'm afraid I don't,' I said.

'Perhaps you will come to it. We are all very fond of hunting in this part of the world.'

'Yes.'

'Mrs de Winter is very keen on art,' said Beatrice to the nurse. 'I tell her there are heaps of spots in Manderley that would make very jolly pictures.'

'Oh rather,' agreed the nurse, pausing a moment from the fury of knitting. 'What a nice hobby. I had a friend who was a wonder with her pencil. We went to Provence together one Easter and she did such pretty sketches.'

'How nice,' I said.

'We're talking about sketching,' shouted Beatrice to her grandmother, 'you did not know we had an artist in the family, did you?'

'Who's an artist?' said the old lady. 'I don't know any.'

'Your new granddaughter,' said Beatrice: 'you ask her what I gave her for a wedding-present.'

I smiled, waiting to be asked. The old lady turned her head in my direction. 'What's Bee talking about?' she said. 'I did not know you were an artist. We've never had any artists in the family.'

'Beatrice was joking,' I said: 'of course I'm not an artist really. I like drawing as a hobby. I've never had any lessons. Beatrice gave me some lovely books as a present.'

'Oh,' she said, rather bewildered. 'Beatrice gave you some books, did she? Rather like taking coals to Newcastle, wasn't it? There are so many books in the library at Manderley.' She laughed heartily. We all joined in her joke. I hoped the subject would be left at that, but Beatrice had to harp on it. 'You don't understand, Gran,' she said. 'They weren't ordinary books. They were volumes on art. Four of 'em.'

The nurse leant forward to add her tribute. 'Mrs Lacy is trying to explain that Mrs de Winter is very fond of sketching as a hobby. So she gave her four fine volumes all about painting as a wedding-present.'

'What a funny thing to do,' said the grandmother. 'I don't think much of books for a wedding-present. Nobody ever gave me any books when I was married. I should never have read them if they had.'

She laughed again. Beatrice looked rather offended. I smiled at her to show my sympathy. I don't think she saw. The nurse resumed her knitting.

'I want my tea,' said the old lady querulously, 'isn't it half past four yet? Why doesn't Norah bring the tea?'

'What? Hungry again after our big lunch?' said the nurse, rising to her feet and smiling brightly at her charge.

I felt rather exhausted, and wondered, rather shocked at my callous thought, why old people were sometimes such a strain. Worse than young children or puppies because one had to be polite. I sat with my hands in my lap ready to agree with what anybody said. The nurse was thumping the pillows and arranging the shawls.

Maxim's grandmother suffered her in patience. She closed her eyes as though she too were tired. She looked more like Maxim than ever. I knew how she must have looked when she was young, tall, and handsome, going round to the stables at Manderley with sugar in her pockets, holding her trailing skirt out of the mud. I pictured the nipped-in waist, the high collar, I heard her ordering the carriage for two o'clock. That was all finished now for her, all gone. Her husband had been dead for forty years, her son for fifteen. She had to live in this bright, red gabled house with the nurse until it was time for her to die. I thought how little we know about the feelings of old people. Children we understand, their fears and hopes and make-believe. I was a child yesterday. I had not forgotten. But Maxim's grandmother, sitting there in her shawl with her poor blind eyes, what did she feel, what was she thinking? Did she know that Beatrice was yawning and glancing at her watch? Did she guess that we had come to visit her because we felt it right, it was a duty, so that when she got home afterwards Beatrice would be able to say, 'Well, that clears my conscience for three months'?

Did she ever think about Manderley? Did she remember sitting at the dining-room table, where I sat? Did she too have tea under the chestnut-tree? Or was it all forgotten and laid aside, and was there nothing left behind that calm, pale face of hers but little aches and little strange discomforts, a blurred thankfulness when the sun shone, a tremor when the wind blew cold?

I wished that I could lay my hands upon her face and take the years away. I wished I could see her young, as she was once, with colour in her cheeks and chestnut hair, alert and active as

Beatrice by her side, talking as she did about hunting, hounds, and horses. Not sitting there with her eyes closed while the nurse thumped the pillows behind her head.

'We've got a treat today, you know,' said the nurse, 'water-cress sandwiches for tea. We love water-cress, don't we?'

'Is it water-cress day?' said Maxim's grandmother, raising her head from the pillows, and looking towards the door. 'You did not tell me that. Why does not Norah bring in the tea?'

'I wouldn't have your job, Sister, for a thousand a day,' said Beatrice *sotto voce* to the nurse.

'Oh, I'm used to it, Mrs Lacy,' smiled the nurse; 'it's very comfortable here, you know. Of course we have our bad days but they might be a great deal worse. She's very easy, not like some patients. The staff are obliging too, that's really the main thing. Here comes Norah.'

The parlour-maid brought out a little gate-legged table and a snowy cloth.

'What a time you've been, Norah,' grumbled the old lady.

'It's only just turned the half-hour, Madam,' said Norah in a special voice, bright and cheerful like the nurse. I wondered if Maxim's grandmother realized that people spoke to her in this way. I wondered when they had done so for the first time, and if she had noticed then. Perhaps she had said to herself, 'They think I'm getting old, how very ridiculous', and then little by little she had become accustomed to it, and now it was as though they had always done so, it was part of her background. But the young woman with the chestnut hair and the narrow waist who gave sugar to the horses, where was she?

We drew our chairs to the gate-legged table and began to eat the water-cress sandwiches. The nurse prepared special ones for the old lady.

'There, now, isn't that a treat?' she said.

I saw a slow smile pass over the calm, placid face. 'I like water-cress day,' she said.

The tea was scalding, much too hot to drink. The nurse drank hers in tiny sips.

'Boiling water today,' she said, nodding at Beatrice. 'I have such trouble about it. They will let the tea stew. I've told them time and time again about it. They will not listen.'

'Oh, they're all the same,' said Beatrice. 'I've given it up as a bad job.' The old lady stirred hers with a spoon, her eyes very far and distant. I wished I knew what she was thinking about.

'Did you have fine weather in Italy?' said the nurse.

'Yes, it was very warm,' I said.

Beatrice turned to her grandmother. 'They had lovely weather in Italy for their honeymoon, she says. Maxim got quite sunburnt.'

'Why isn't Maxim here today?' said the old lady.

'We told you, darling, Maxim had to go to London,' said Beatrice impatiently. 'Some dinner, you know. Giles went too.'

'Oh, I see. Why did you say Maxim was in Italy?'

'He was in Italy, Gran. In April. They're back at Manderley now.' She glanced at the nurse, shrugging her shoulders.

'Mr and Mrs de Winter are in Manderley now,' repeated the nurse.

'It's been lovely there this month,' I said, drawing nearer to Maxim's grandmother. 'The roses are in bloom now. I wish I had brought you some.'

'Yes, I like roses,' she said vaguely, and then peering closer at me with her dim blue eyes. 'Are you staying at Manderley too?'

I swallowed. There was a slight pause. Then Beatrice broke in with her loud, impatient voice, 'Gran, darling, you know perfectly well she lives there now. She and Maxim are married.'

I noticed the nurse put down her cup of tea and glance swiftly at the old lady. She had relaxed against the pillows, plucking at her shawl, and her mouth began to tremble. 'You talk too much, all of you. I don't understand.' Then she looked across at me, a frown on her face, and began shaking her head. 'Who are you, my dear, I haven't seen you before? I don't know your face. I don't remember you at Manderley. Bee, who is this child? Why did not Maxim bring Rebecca? I'm so fond of Rebecca. Where is dear Rebecca?'

There was a long pause, a moment of agony. I felt my cheeks

grow scarlet. The nurse got to her feet very quickly and went to the bath-chair.

'I want Rebecca,' repeated the old lady, 'what have you done with Rebecca?' Beatrice rose clumsily from the table, shaking the cups and saucers. She too had turned very red, and her mouth twitched.

'I think you'd better go, Mrs Lacy,' said the nurse, rather pink and flustered. 'She's looking a little tired, and when she wanders like this it sometimes lasts a few hours. She does get excited like this from time to time. It's very unfortunate it should happen today. I'm sure you will understand, Mrs de Winter?' She turned apologetically to me.

'Of course,' I said quickly, 'it's much better we should go.'

Beatrice and I groped for our bags and gloves. The nurse had turned to her patient again. 'Now, what's all this about? Do you want your nice water-cress sandwich that I've cut for you?'

'Where is Rebecca? Why did not Maxim come and bring Rebecca?' replied the thin, querulous voice.

We went through the drawing-room to the hall and let ourselves out of the front door. Beatrice started up the car without a word. We drove down the smooth gravel drive and out of the white gates.

I stared straight in front of me down the road. I did not mind for myself. I should not have cared if I had been alone. I minded for Beatrice.

The whole thing had been so wretched and awkward for Beatrice.

She spoke to me when we turned out of the village. 'My dear,' she began, 'I'm so dreadfully sorry. I don't know what to say.'

'Don't be absurd, Beatrice,' I said hurriedly, 'it doesn't matter a bit. It's absolutely all right.'

'I had no idea she would do that,' said Beatrice. 'I would never have dreamt of taking you to see her. I'm so frightfully sorry.'

'There's nothing to be sorry about. Please don't say any more.'

'I can't make it out. She knew all about you. I wrote and told her, and so did Maxim. She was so interested in the wedding abroad.'

'You forget how old she is,' I said. 'Why should she remember that? She doesn't connect me with Maxim. She only connects him with Rebecca.' We went on driving in silence. It was a relief to be in the car again. I did not mind the jerky motion and the swaying corners.

'I'd forgotten she was so fond of Rebecca,' said Beatrice slowly, 'I was a fool not to expect something like this. I don't believe she ever took it in properly about the accident. Oh, Lord, what a ghastly afternoon. What on earth will you think of me?'

'Please, Beatrice, don't. I tell you I don't mind.'

'Rebecca made a great fuss of her always. And she used to have the old lady over to Manderley. Poor darling Gran was much more alert then. She used to rock with laughter at whatever Rebecca said. Of course she was always very amusing, and the old lady loved that. She had an amazing gift, Rebecca I mean, of being attractive to people; men, women, children, dogs. I suppose the old lady has never forgotten her. My dear, you won't thank me for this afternoon.'

'I don't mind, I don't mind,' I repeated mechanically. If only Beatrice could leave the subject alone. It did not interest me. What did it matter after all? What did anything matter?

'Giles will be very upset,' said Beatrice. 'He will blame me for taking you over. "What an idiotic thing to do, Bee." I can hear him saying it. I shall get into a fine row.'

'Don't say anything about it,' I said. 'I would much rather it was forgotten. The story will only get repeated and exaggerated.'

'Giles will know something is wrong from my face. I never have been able to hide anything from him.'

I was silent. I knew how the story would be tossed about in their immediate circle of friends. I could imagine the little crowd at Sunday lunch. The round eyes, the eager ears, and the gasps and exclamations—

'My Lord, how awful, what on earth did you do?' and then, 'How did she take it? How terribly embarrassing for everyone!'

The only thing that mattered to me was that Maxim should never come to hear of it. One day I might tell Frank Crawley, but not yet, not for quite a while.

It was not long before we came to the high road at the top of the hill. In the distance I could see the first grey roofs of Kerrith, while to the right, in a hollow, lay the deep woods of Manderley and the sea beyond.

'Are you in a frightful hurry to get home?' said Beatrice.

'No,' I said. 'I don't think so. Why?'

'Would you think me a perfect pig if I dropped you at the lodge gates? If I drive like hell now I shall just be in time to meet Giles by the London train, and it will save him taking the station taxi.'

'Of course,' I said. 'I can walk down the drive.'

'Thanks awfully,' she said gratefully.

I felt the afternoon had been too much for her. She wanted to be alone again, and did not want to face another belated tea at Manderley.

I got out of the car at the lodge gates and we kissed goodbye.

'Put on some weight next time I see you,' she said; 'it doesn't suit you to be so thin. Give Maxim my love, and forgive me for today.' She vanished in a cloud of dust and I turned in down the drive.

I wondered if it had altered much since Maxim's grandmother had driven down it in her carriage. She had ridden here as a young woman, she had smiled at the woman at the lodge as I did now. And in her day the lodge-keeper's wife had curtseyed, sweeping the path with her full wide skirt. This woman nodded to me briefly, and then called to her little boy, who was grubbing with some kittens at the back. Maxim's grandmother had bowed her head to avoid the sweeping branches of the trees, and the horse had trotted down the twisting drive where I now walked. The drive had been wider then, and smoother too, better kept. The woods did not encroach upon it.

I did not think of her as she was now, lying against those pillows, with that shawl around her. I saw her when she was

211

young, and when Manderley was her home. I saw her wandering in the gardens with a small boy, Maxim's father, clattering behind her on his hobby horse. He would wear a stiff Norfolk jacket and a round white collar. Picnics to the cove would be an expedition, a treat that was not indulged in very often. There would be a photograph somewhere, in an old album – all the family sitting very straight and rigid round a tablecloth set upon the beach, the servants in the background beside a huge lunchbasket. And I saw Maxim's grandmother when she was older too, a few years ago. Walking on the terrace at Manderley, leaning on a stick. And someone walked beside her, laughing, holding her arm. Someone tall and slim and very beautiful, who had a gift, Beatrice said, of being attractive to people. Easy to like, I supposed, easy to love.

When I came to the end of the long drive at last I saw that Maxim's car was standing in front of the house. My heart lifted, I ran quickly into the hall. His hat and gloves were lying on the table. I went towards the library, and as I came near I heard the sound of voices, one raised louder than the other, Maxim's voice. The door was shut. I hesitated a moment before going in.

'You can write and tell him from me to keep away from Manderley in future, do you hear? Never mind who told me, that's of no importance. I happen to know his car was seen here yesterday afternoon. If you want to meet him you can meet him outside Manderley. I won't have him inside the gates, do you understand? Remember, I'm warning you for the last time.'

I slipped away from the door to the stairs. I heard the door of the library open. I ran swiftly up the stairs and hid in the gallery. Mrs Danvers came out of the library, shutting the door behind her. I crouched against the wall of the gallery so that I should not be seen. I had caught one glimpse of her face. It was grey with anger, distorted, horrible.

She passed up the stairs swiftly and silently and disappeared through the door leading to the west wing.

I waited a moment. Then I went slowly downstairs to the library. I opened the door and went in. Maxim was standing by the window, some letters in his hand. His back was turned to me. For a moment I thought of creeping out again, and going upstairs to my room and sitting there. He must have heard me though, for he swung round impatiently.

'Who is it now?' he said.

I smiled, holding out my hands. 'Hullo!' I said.

'Oh, it's you . . .'

I could tell in a glance that something had made him very angry. His mouth was hard, his nostrils white and pinched. 'What have you been doing with yourself?' he said. He kissed the top of my head and put his arm round my shoulder. I felt as if a very long time had passed since he had left me yesterday.

'I've been to see your grandmother,' I said. 'Beatrice drove me over this afternoon.'

'How was the old lady?'

'All right.'

'What's happened to Bee?'

'She had to get back to meet Giles.'

We sat down together on the window-seat. I took his hand in mine. 'I hated you being away, I've missed you terribly,' I said.

'Have you?' he said.

We did not say anything for a bit. I just held his hand.

'Was it hot up in London?' I said.

'Yes, pretty awful. I always hate the place.'

I wondered if he would tell me what had happened just now in the library with Mrs Danvers. I wondered who had told him about Favell.

'Are you worried about something?' I said.

'I've had a long day,' he said, 'that drive twice in twenty-four hours is too much for anyone.'

He got up and wandered away, lighting a cigarette. I knew then that he was not going to tell me about Mrs Danvers.

'I'm tired too,' I said slowly, 'it's been a funny sort of day.'

16

It was one Sunday, I remember, when we had an invasion of visitors during the afternoon, that the subject of the fancy dress ball was first brought up. Frank Crawley had come over to lunch, and we were all three of us looking forward to a peaceful afternoon under the chestnut tree when we heard the fatal sound of a car rounding the sweep in the drive. It was too late to warn Frith, the car itself came upon us standing on the terrace with cushions and papers under our arms.

We had to come forward and welcome the unexpected guests. As often happens in such cases, these were not to be the only visitors. Another car arrived about half an hour afterwards, followed by three local people who had walked from Kerrith, and we found ourselves, with the peace stripped from our day, entertaining group after group of dreary acquaintances, doing the regulation walk in the grounds, the tour of the rose-garden, the stroll across the lawns, and the formal inspection of the Happy Valley.

They stayed for tea of course, and instead of a lazy nibbling of cucumber sandwiches under the chestnut tree, we had the paraphernalia of a stiff tea in the drawing-room, which I always loathed. Frith in his element of course, directing Robert with a lift of his eyebrows, and myself rather hot and flustered with a monstrous silver tea-pot and kettle that I never knew how to manage. I found it very difficult to gauge the exact moment when it became imperative to dilute the tea with the boiling water, and more difficult still to concentrate on the small talk that was going on at my side.

Frank Crawley was invaluable at a moment like this. He took the cups from me and handed them to people, and when my answers seemed more than usually vague owing to my concentration on the silver tea-pot he quietly and unobtrusively put in his small wedge to the conversation, relieving me of responsibility. Maxim was always at the other end of the room, showing a book to a bore, or pointing out a picture, playing the perfect host in his own inimitable way, and the business of tea was a side-issue that did not matter to him. His own cup of tea grew cold, left on a side table behind some flowers, and I, steaming behind my kettle, and Frank gallantly juggling with scones and angel cake, were left to minister to the common wants of the herd. It was Lady Crowan, a tiresome gushing woman who lived in Kerrith, who introduced the matter. There was one of those pauses in conversation that happen in every tea-party, and I saw Frank's lips about to form the inevitable and idiotic remark about an angel passing overhead, when Lady Crowan, balancing a piece of cake on the edge of her saucer, looked up at Maxim who happened to be beside her.

'Oh, Mr de Winter,' she said, 'there is something I've been wanting to ask you for ages. Now tell me, is there any chance of you reviving the Manderley fancy dress ball?' She put her head on one side as she spoke, flashing her too prominent teeth in what she supposed was a smile. I lowered my head instantly, and became very busy with the emptying of my own tea-cup, screening myself behind the cosy.

It was a moment or two before Maxim replied, and when he did his voice was quite calm and matter-of-fact. 'I haven't thought about it,' he said, 'and I don't think anyone else has.'

'Oh, but I assure you we have all thought of it so much,' continued Lady Crowan. 'It used to make the summer for all of us in this part of the world. You have no idea of the pleasure it used to give. Can't I persuade you to think about it again?'

'Well, I don't know,' said Maxim drily. 'It was all rather a business to organize. You had better ask Frank Crawley, he'd have to do it.'

'Oh, Mr Crawley, do be on my side,' she persisted, and one or two of the others joined in. 'It would be a most popular move, you know, we all miss the Manderley gaiety.'

I heard Frank's quiet voice beside me. 'I don't mind organizing the ball if Maxim has no objection to giving it. It's up to him and Mrs de Winter. It's nothing to do with me.'

Of course I was bombarded at once. Lady Crowan moved her chair so that the cosy no longer hid me from view. 'Now, Mrs de Winter, you get round your husband. You are the person he will listen to. He should give the ball in your honour as the bride.'

'Yes, of course,' said somebody else, a man. 'We missed the fun of the wedding, you know; it's a shame to deprive us of all excitement. Hands up for the Manderley fancy-dress ball. There you see, de Winter? Carried unanimously.' There was much laughter and clapping of hands.

Maxim lit a cigarette and his eyes met mine over the tea-pot.

'What do you think about it?' he said.

'I don't know,' I said uncertainly. 'I don't mind.'

'Of course she longs to have a ball in her honour,' gushed Lady Crowan. 'What girl wouldn't? You'd look sweet, Mrs de Winter, dressed as a little Dresden shepherdess, your hair tucked under a big three-cornered hat.'

I thought of my clumsy hands and feet and the slope of my shoulders. A fine Dresden shepherdess I should make! What an idiot the woman was. I was not surprised when nobody agreed with her, and once more I was grateful to Frank for turning the conversation away from me.

'As a matter of fact, Maxim, someone was talking about it the other day. "I suppose we shall be having some sort of celebration for the bride, shan't we, Mr Crawley?" he said. "I wish Mr de Winter would give a ball again. It was rare fun for all of us." It was Tucker at the Home farm,' he added, to Lady Crowan. 'Of course they do adore a show of any kind. I don't know, I told him. Mr de Winter hasn't said anything to me.'

'There you are,' said Lady Crowan triumphantly to the drawing-room in general. 'What did I say? Your own people are asking for a ball. If you don't care for us, surely you care about them.'

Maxim still watched me doubtfully over the tea-pot. It occurred to me that perhaps he thought I could not face it, that being shy, as he knew only too well, I should find myself unable to cope. I did not want him to think that. I did not want him to feel I should let him down.

'I think it would be rather fun,' I said.

Maxim turned away, shrugging his shoulders. 'That settles it of course,' he said. 'All right, Frank, you will have to go ahead with the arrangements. Better get Mrs Danvers to help you. She will remember the form.'

'That amazing Mrs Danvers is still with you then?' said Lady Crowan.

'Yes,' said Maxim shortly, 'have some more cake, will you? Or have you finished? Then let's all go into the garden.'

We wandered out on to the terrace, everyone discussing the prospect of the ball and suitable dates, and then, greatly to my relief, the car parties decided it was time to take their departure, and the walkers went too, on being offered a lift. I went back into the drawing-room and had another cup of tea which I thoroughly enjoyed now that the burden of entertaining had been taken from me, and Frank came too, and we crumbled up the remains of the scones and ate them, feeling like conspirators.

Maxim was throwing sticks for Jasper on the lawn. I wondered if it was the same in every home, this feeling of exuberance when visitors had gone. We did not say anything about the ball for a little while, and then, when I had finished my cup of tea and wiped my sticky fingers on a handkerchief, I said to Frank: 'What do you truthfully think about this fancy dress business?'

Frank hesitated, half glancing out of the window at Maxim on the lawn. 'I don't know,' he said. 'Maxim did not seem to object, did he? I thought he took the suggestion very well.'

'It was difficult for him to do anything else,' I said. 'What a tiresome person Lady Crowan is. Do you really believe all the people round here are talking and dreaming of nothing but a fancy dress ball at Manderley?'

'I think they would all enjoy a show of some sort,' said Frank.

'We're very conventional down here, you know, about these things. I don't honestly think Lady Crowan was exaggerating when she said something should be done in your honour. After all, Mrs de Winter, you are a bride.'

How pompous and stupid it sounded. I wished Frank would not always be so terribly correct.

'I'm not a bride,' I said. 'I did not even have a proper wedding. No white dress or orange blossom or trailing bridesmaids. I don't want any silly dance given in my honour.'

'It's a very fine sight, Manderley *en fête*,' said Frank. 'You'll enjoy it, you see. You won't have to do anything alarming. You just receive the guests and there's nothing in that. Perhaps you'll give me a dance?'

Dear Frank. I loved his little solemn air of gallantry.

'You shall have as many dances as you like,' I said. 'I shan't dance with anyone except you and Maxim.'

'Oh, but that would not look right at all,' said Frank seriously. 'People would be very offended. You must dance with the people who ask you.'

I turned away to hide my smile. It was a joy to me the way he never knew when his leg had been pulled.

'Do you think Lady Crowan's suggestion about the Dresden shepherdess was a good one?' I said slyly.

He considered me solemnly without the trace of a smile. 'Yes, I do,' he said. 'I think you'd look very well indeed.'

I burst into laughter. 'Oh, Frank, dear, I do love you,' I said, and he turned rather pink, a little shocked I think at my impulsive words, and a little hurt too that I was laughing at him.

'I don't see that I've said anything funny,' he said stiffly.

Maxim came in at the window, Jasper dancing at his heels. 'What's all the excitement about?' he said.

'Frank is being so gallant,' I said. 'He thinks Lady Crowan's idea of my dressing up as a Dresden shepherdess is nothing to laugh at.'

'Lady Crowan is a damned nuisance,' said Maxim. 'If she had to write out all the invitations and organize the affair she would not be so enthusiastic. It's always been the same though. The locals look upon Manderley as if it was a pavilion on the end of a pier, and expect us to put up a turn for their benefit. I suppose we shall have to ask the whole county.'

'I've got the records in the office,' said Frank. 'It won't really entail much work. Licking the stamps is the longest job.'

'We'll give that to you to do,' said Maxim, smiling at me.

'Oh, we'll do that in the office,' said Frank. 'Mrs de Winter need not bother her head about anything at all.' I wondered what they would say if I suddenly announced my intention of running the whole affair. Laugh, I supposed, and then begin talking of something else. I was glad, of course, to be relieved of responsibility, but it rather added to my sense of humility to feel that I was not even capable of licking stamps. I thought of the writing-desk in the morning-room, the docketed pigeon-holes all marked in ink by that slanting pointed hand.

'What will you wear?' I said to Maxim.

'I never dress up,' said Maxim. 'It's the one perquisite allowed to the host, isn't it, Frank?'

'I can't really go as a Dresden shepherdess,' I said, 'what on earth shall I do? I'm not much good at dressing-up.'

'Put a ribbon round your hair and be Alice-in-Wonderland,' said Maxim lightly; 'you look like it now, with your finger in your mouth.'

'Don't be so rude,' I said. 'I know my hair is straight, but it isn't as straight as that. I tell you what, I'll give you and Frank the surprise of your lives, and you won't know me.'

'As long as you don't black your face and pretend to be a monkey I don't mind what you do,' said Maxim.

'All right, that's a bargain,' I said. 'I'll keep my costume a secret to the last minute, and you won't know anything about it. Come on, Jasper, we don't care what they say, do we?' I heard Maxim laughing as I went out into the garden, and he said something to Frank which I did not catch.

I wished he would not always treat me as a child, rather spoilt, rather irresponsible, someone to be petted from time to time when the mood came upon him but more often forgotten, more often patted on the shoulder and told to run away and play. I wished something would happen to make me look wiser, more mature. Was it always going to be like this? He away ahead of me, with his own moods that I did not share, his secret troubles that I did not know? Would we never be together, he a man and I a woman, standing shoulder to shoulder, hand in hand, with no gulf between us? I did not want to be a child. I wanted to be his wife, his mother. I wanted to be old.

I stood on the terrace, biting my nails, looking down towards the sea, and as I stood there I wondered for the twentieth time that day whether it was by Maxim's orders that those rooms in the west wing were kept furnished and untouched. I wondered if he went, as Mrs Danvers did, and touched the brushes on the dressing-table, opened the wardrobe doors, and put his hands amongst the clothes.

'Come on, Jasper,' I shouted, 'run, run with me, come on, can't you?' and I tore across the grass, savagely, angrily, the bitter tears behind my eyes, with Jasper leaping at my heels and barking hysterically.

The news soon spread about the fancy dress ball. My little maid Clarice, her eyes shining with excitement, talked of nothing else. I gathered from her that the servants in general were delighted. 'Mr Frith says it will be like old times,' said Clarice eagerly. 'I heard him saying so to Alice in the passage this morning. What will you wear, Madam?'

'I don't know, Clarice, I can't think,' I said.

'Mother said I was to be sure and tell her,' said Clarice. 'She remembers the last ball they gave at Manderley, and she has never forgotten it. Will you be hiring a costume from London, do you think?'

'I haven't made up my mind, Clarice,' I said. 'But I tell you what. When I do decide, I shall tell you and nobody else. It will be a dead secret between us both.'

'Oh, Madam, how exciting,' breathed Clarice. 'I don't know how I am going to wait for the day.'

I was curious to know Mrs Danvers' reaction to the news. Since that afternoon I dreaded even the sound of her voice down the house telephone, and by using Robert as mediator between us I was spared this last ordeal. I could not forget the expression of her face when she left the library after that interview with Maxim. I thanked God she had not seen me crouching in the gallery. And I wondered too, if she thought that it was I who had told Maxim about Favell's visit to the house. If so, she would hate me more than ever. I shuddered now when I remembered the touch of her hand on my arm, and that dreadful soft, intimate pitch of her voice close to my ear. I did not want to remember anything about that afternoon. That was why I did not speak to her, not even on the house telephone.

The preparations went on for the ball. Everything seemed to be done down at the estate office. Maxim and Frank were down there every morning. As Frank had said, I did not have to bother my head about anything. I don't think I licked one stamp. I began to get in a panic about my costume. It seemed so feeble not to be able to think of anything, and I kept remembering all the people who would come, from Kerrith and round about, the bishop's wife who had enjoyed herself so much, the last time, Beatrice and Giles, that tiresome Lady Crowan, and many more people I did not know and who had never seen me, they would every one of them have some criticism to offer, some curiosity to know what sort of effort I should make. At last, in desperation, I remembered the books that Beatrice had given me for a wedding-present, and I sat down in the library one morning turning over the pages as a last hope, passing from illustration to illustration in a sort of frenzy. Nothing seemed suitable, they were all so elaborate and pretentious, those gorgeous costumes of velvet and silk in the reproductions given of Rubens, Rembrandt and others. I got hold of a piece of paper and a pencil and copied one or two of them, but they did not please me, and I threw the sketches into the waste paper basket in disgust, thinking no more about them.

In the evening, when I was changing for dinner, there was a

knock at my bedroom door. I called 'Come in,' thinking it was Clarice. The door opened and it was not Clarice. It was Mrs Danvers. She held a piece of paper in her hand. 'I hope you will forgive me disturbing you,' she said, 'but I was not sure whether you meant to throw these drawings away. All the waste paper baskets are always brought to me to check, at the end of the day, in case of mislaying anything of value. Robert told me this was thrown into the library basket.'

I had turned quite cold all over at the sight of her, and at first I could not find my voice. She held out the paper for me to see. It was the rough drawing I had done during the morning.

'No, Mrs Danvers,' I said, after a moment, 'it doesn't matter throwing that away. It was only a rough sketch. I don't want it.'

'Very good,' she said, 'I thought it better to inquire from you personally to save any misunderstanding.'

'Yes,' I said. 'Yes, of course.' I thought she would turn and go, but she went on standing there by the door.

'So you have not decided yet what you will wear?' she said. There was a hint of derision in her voice, a trace of odd satisfaction. I supposed she had heard of my efforts through Clarice in some way.

'No,' I said. 'No, I haven't decided.'

She continued watching me, her hand on the handle of the door.

'I wonder you don't copy one of the pictures in the gallery,' she said.

I pretended to file my nails. They were too short and too brittle, but the action gave me something to do and I did not have to look at her.

'Yes, I might think about that,' I said. I wondered privately why such an idea had never come to me before. It was an obvious and very good solution to my difficulty. I did not want her to know this though. I went on filing my nails.

'All the pictures in the gallery would make good costumes,' said Mrs Danvers, 'especially that one of the young lady in white, with her hat in her hand. I wonder Mr de Winter does not make it a period ball, everyone dressed more or less the same, to be in keeping. I never think it looks right to see a clown dancing with a lady in powder and patches.'

'Some people enjoy the variety,' I said. 'They think it makes it all the more amusing.'

'I don't like it myself,' said Mrs Danvers. Her voice was surprisingly normal and friendly, and I wondered why it was she had taken the trouble to come up with my discarded sketch herself. Did she want to be friends with me at last? Or did she realize that it had not been me at all who had told Maxim about Favell, and this was her way of thanking me for my silence?

'Has not Mr de Winter suggested a costume for you?' she said.

'No,' I said, after a moment's hesitation. 'No, I want to surprise him and Mr Crawley. I don't want them to know anything about it.'

'It's not for me to make a suggestion, I know,' she said, 'but when you do decide, I should advise you to have your dress made in London. There is no one down here can do that sort of thing well. Voce, in Bond Street, is a good place I know.'

'I must remember that,' I said.

'Yes,' she said, and then, as she opened the door, 'I should study the pictures in the gallery, Madam, if I were you, especially the one I mentioned. And you need not think I will give you away. I won't say a word to anyone.'

'Thank you, Mrs Danvers,' I said. She shut the door very gently behind her. I went on with my dressing, puzzled at her attitude, so different from our last encounter, and wondering whether I had the unpleasant Favell to thank for it.

Rebecca's cousin. Why should Maxim dislike Rebecca's cousin? Why had he forbidden him to come to Manderley? Beatrice had called him a bounder. She had not said much about him. And the more I considered him the more I agreed with her. Those hot blue eyes, that loose mouth, and the careless familiar laugh. Some people would consider him attractive. Girls in sweet shops giggling behind the counter, and girls who gave one programmes in a cinema. I knew how he would look at them, smiling, and half whistling a tune under his breath. The sort of look and the type of whistle that would make one feel uncomfortable. I wondered how well he knew Manderley. He seemed quite at home, and Jasper certainly recognized him, but these two facts did not fit in with Maxim's words to Mrs Danvers. And I could not connect him with my idea of Rebecca. Rebecca, with her beauty, her charm, her breeding, why did she have a cousin like Jack Favell? It was wrong, out of all proportion. I decided he must be the skeleton in the family cupboard, and Rebecca with her generosity had taken pity on him from time to time and invited him to Manderley, perhaps when Maxim was from home, knowing his dislike. There had been some argument about it probably, Rebecca defending him, and ever after this perhaps a slight awkwardness whenever his name was mentioned.

As I sat down to dinner in the dining-room in my accustomed place, with Maxim at the head of the table, I pictured Rebecca sitting in where I sat now, picking up her fork for the fish, and then the telephone ringing and Frith coming into the room and saying 'Mr Favell on the phone, Madam, wishing to speak to you,' and Rebecca would get up from her chair with a quick glance at Maxim, who would not say anything, who would go on eating his fish. And when she came back, having finished her conversation, and sat down in her place again, Rebecca would begin talking about something different, in a gay, careless way, to cover up the little cloud between them. At first Maxim would be glum, answering in monosyllables, but little by little she would win his humour back again, telling him some story of her day, about someone she had seen in Kerrith, and when they had finished the next course he would be laughing again, looking at her and smiling, putting out his hand to her across the table.

'What the devil are you thinking about?' said Maxim.

I started, the colour flooding my face, for in that brief moment, sixty seconds in time perhaps, I had so identified myself with

Rebecca that my own dull self did not exist, had never come to Manderley. I had gone back in thought and in person to the days that were gone.

'Do you know you were going through the most extraordinary antics instead of eating your fish?' said Maxim. 'First you listened, as though you heard the telephone, and then your lips moved, and you threw half a glance at me. And you shook your head, and smiled, and shrugged your shoulders. All in about a second. Are you practising your appearance for the fancy dress ball?' He looked across at me, laughing, and I wondered what he would say if he really knew my thoughts, my heart, and my mind, and that for one second he had been the Maxim of another year, and I had been Rebecca. 'You look like a little criminal,' he said, 'what is it?'

'Nothing,' I said quickly, 'I wasn't doing anything.'

'Tell me what you were thinking?'

'Why should I? You never tell me what you are thinking about.'

'I don't think you've ever asked me, have you?'

'Yes, I did once.'

'I don't remember.'

'We were in the library.'

'Very probably. What did I say?'

'You told me you were wondering who had been chosen to play for Surrey against Middlesex.'

Maxim laughed again. 'What a disappointment to you. What did you hope I was thinking?'

'Something very different.'

'What sort of thing?'

'Oh, I don't know.'

'No, I don't suppose you do. If I told you I was thinking about Surrey and Middlesex I was thinking about Surrey and Middlesex. Men are simpler than you imagine, my sweet child. But what goes on in the twisted tortuous minds of women would baffle anyone. Do you know, you did not look a bit like yourself just now? You had quite a different expression on your face.'

'I did? What sort of expression?'

'I don't know that I can explain. You looked older suddenly, deceitful. It was rather unpleasant.'

'I did not mean to.'

'No, I don't suppose you did.'

I drank some water, watching him over the rim of my glass.

'Don't you want me to look older?' I said.

'No.'

'Why not?'

'Because it would not suit you.'

'One day I shall. It can't be helped. I shall have grey hair, and lines and things.'

'I don't mind that.'

'What do you mind then?'

'I don't want you to look like you did just now. You had a twist to your mouth and a flash of knowledge in your eyes. Not the right sort of knowledge.'

I felt very curious, rather excited. 'What do you mean, Maxim? What isn't the right sort of knowledge?'

He did not answer for a moment. Frith had come back into the room and was changing the plates. Maxim waited until Frith had gone behind the screen and through the service door before speaking again.

'When I met you first you had a certain expression on your face,' he said slowly, 'and you have it still. I'm not going to define it, I don't know how to. But it was one of the reasons why I married you. A moment ago, when you were going through that curious little performance, the expression had gone. Something else had taken its place.'

'What sort of thing? Explain to me, Maxim,' I said eagerly.

He considered me a moment, his eyebrows raised, whistling softly. 'Listen, my sweet. When you were a little girl, were you ever forbidden to read certain books, and did your father put those books under lock and key?'

'Yes,' I said.

'Well, then. A husband is not so very different from a father

226

after all. There is a certain type of knowledge I prefer you not to have. It's better kept under lock and key. So that's that. And now eat up your peaches, and don't ask me any more questions, or I shall put you in the corner.'

'I wish you would not treat me as if I was six,' I said.

'How do you want to be treated?'

'Like other men treat their wives.'

'Knock you about, you mean?'

'Don't be absurd. Why must you make a joke of everything?'

'I'm not joking. I'm very serious.'

'No, you're not. I can tell by your eyes. You're playing with me all the time, just as if I was a silly little girl.'

'Alice-in-Wonderland. That was a good idea of mine. Have you bought your sash and your hair-ribbon yet?'

'I warn you. You'll get the surprise of your life when you do see me in my fancy dress.'

'I'm sure I shall. Get on with your peach and don't talk with your mouth full. I've got a lot of letters to write after dinner.' He did not wait for me to finish. He got up and strolled about the room, and asked Frith to bring the coffee in the library. I sat still, sullenly, being as slow as I could, hoping to keep things back and irritate him, but Frith took no notice of me and my peach, he brought the coffee at once and Maxim went off to the library by himself.

When I had finished I went upstairs to the minstrel's gallery to have a look at the pictures. I knew them well of course by now, but had never studied them with a view to reproducing one of them as a fancy-dress. Mrs Danvers was right of course. What an idiot I had been not to think of it before. I always loved the girl in white, with a hat in her hand. It was a Raeburn, and the portrait was of Caroline de Winter, a sister of Maxim's great-great grandfather. She married a great Whig politician, and was a famous London beauty for many years, but this portrait was painted before that, when she was still unmarried. The white dress should be easy to copy. Those puffed sleeves, the flounce, and the little bodice. The hat might be rather difficult, and I should have to wear a wig. My straight hair would never curl in that way. Perhaps that Voce place in London that Mrs Danvers had told me about would do the whole thing. I would send them a sketch of the portrait and tell them to copy it faithfully, sending my measurements.

What a relief it was to have decided at last! Quite a weight off my mind. I began almost to look forward to the ball. Perhaps I should enjoy it after all, almost as much as little Clarice.

I wrote to the shop in the morning, enclosing a sketch of the portrait, and I had a very favourable reply, full of honour at my esteemed order, and saying the work would be put in hand right away, and they would manage the wig as well.

Clarice could hardly contain herself for excitement, and I, too, began to get party fever as the great day approached. Giles and Beatrice were coming for the night, but nobody else, thank heaven, although a lot of people were expected to dinner first. I had imagined we should have to hold a large house-party for the occasion, but Maxim decided against it. 'Having the dance alone is quite enough effort,' he said; and I wondered whether he did it for my sake alone, or whether a large crowd of people really bored him as he said. I had heard so much of the Manderley parties in the old days, with people sleeping in bathrooms and on sofas because of the squash. And here we were alone in the vast house, with only Beatrice and Giles to count as guests.

The house began to wear a new, expectant air. Men came to lay the floor for dancing in the great hall, and in the drawing-room some of the furniture was moved so that the long buffet tables could be placed against the wall. Lights were put up on the terrace, and in the rose-garden too, wherever one walked there would be some sign of preparation for the ball. Workmen from the estate were everywhere, and Frank came to lunch nearly every day. The servants talked of nothing else, and Frith stalked about as though the whole of the evening would depend on him alone. Robert rather lost his head, and kept forgetting things, napkins at lunch, and handing vegetables. He wore a harassed expression, like someone who has got to catch a train. The dogs were miserable. Jasper trailed about the hall with his tail between his legs, and nipped every workman on sight. He used to stand on the terrace, barking idiotically, and then dash madly to one corner of the lawn and eat grass in a sort of frenzy. Mrs Danvers never obtruded herself, but I was aware of her continually. It was her voice I heard in the drawing-room when they came to put the tables, it was she who gave directions for the laying of the floor in the hall. Whenever I came upon the scene she had always just disappeared; I would catch a glimpse of her skirt brushing the door, or hear the sound of her footsteps on the stairs. I was a lay-figure, no use to man or beast. I used to stand about doing nothing except get in the way. 'Excuse me, Madam,' I would hear a man say, just behind me, and he would pass, with a smile of apology, carrying two chairs on his back, his face dripping with perspiration.

'I'm awfully sorry,' I would say, getting quickly to one side, and then as a cover to my idleness, 'Can I help you? What about putting those chairs in the library?' The man would look bewildered. 'Mrs Danvers' orders, Madam, was that we were to take the chairs round to the back, to be out of the way.'

'Oh,' I said, 'yes, of course. How silly of me. Take them round to the back, as she said.' And I would walk quickly away murmuring something about finding a piece of paper and a pencil, in a vain attempt to delude the man into thinking I was busy, while he went on across the hall, looking rather astonished, and I would feel I had not deceived him for a moment.

The great day dawned misty and overcast, but the glass was high and we, had no fears. The mist was a good sign. It cleared about eleven, as Maxim had foretold, and we had a glorious still summer's day without a cloud in the blue sky. All the morning the gardeners were bringing flowers into the house, the last of the white lilac, and great lupins and delphiniums, five foot high, roses in hundreds, and every sort of lily.

Mrs Danvers showed herself at last; quietly, calmly, she told the gardeners where to put the flowers, and she herself arranged them, stacking the vases with quick, deft fingers. I watched her in fascination, the way she did vase after vase, carrying them herself through the flower-room to the drawing-room and the various corners of the house, massing them in just the right numbers and profusion, putting colour where colour was needed, leaving the walls bare where severity paid.

Maxim and I had lunch with Frank at his bachelor establishment next-door to the office to be out of the way. We were all three in the rather hearty, cheerful humour of people after a funeral. We made pointless jokes about nothing at all, our minds eternally on the thought of the next few hours. I felt very much the same as I did the morning I was married. The same stifled feeling that I had gone too far now to turn back.

The evening had got to be endured. Thank heaven Messrs Voce had sent my dress in time. It looked perfect, in its folds of tissue paper. And the wig was a triumph. I had tried it on after breakfast, and was amazed at the transformation. I looked quite attractive, quite different altogether. Not me at all. Someone much more interesting, more vivid and alive. Maxim and Frank kept asking me about my costume.

'You won't know me,' I told them, 'you will both get the shock of your lives.'

'You are not going to dress up as a clown, are you?' said Maxim gloomily. 'No frightful attempt to be funny?'

'No, nothing like that,' I said, full of importance.

'I wish you had kept to Alice-in-Wonderland,' he said.

'Or Joan of Arc with your hair,' said Frank shyly.

'I never thought of that,' I said blankly, and Frank went rather pink. 'I'm sure we shall like whatever you wear,' he said in his most pompous Frank-ish voice.

'Don't encourage her, Frank,' said Maxim. 'She's so full of her precious disguise already there's no holding her. Bee will put you in your place, that's one comfort. She'll soon tell you if she doesn't like your dress. Dear old Bee always looks just wrong on these occasions, bless her. I remember her once as Madame Pompadour and she tripped up going in to supper and her wig came adrift. "I can't stand this damned thing," she said, in that

230

blunt voice of hers, and chucked it on a chair and went through the rest of the evening with her own cropped hair. You can imagine what it looked like, against a pale blue satin crinoline, or whatever the dress was. Poor Giles did not cope that year. He came as a cook, and sat about in the bar all night looking perfectly miserable. I think he felt Bee had let him down.'

'No, it wasn't that,' said Frank, 'he'd lost his front teeth trying out a new mare, don't you remember, and he was so shy about it he wouldn't open his mouth.'

'Oh, was that it? Poor Giles. He generally enjoys dressing-up.'

'Beatrice says he loves playing charades,' I said. 'She told me they always have charades at Christmas.'

'I know,' said Maxim, 'that's why I've never spent Christmas with her.'

'Have some more asparagus, Mrs de Winter, and another potato?'

'No, really, Frank, I'm not hungry, thank you.'

'Nerves,' said Maxim, shaking his head. 'Never mind, this time tomorrow it will all be over.'

'I sincerely hope so,' said Frank seriously. 'I was going to give orders that all cars should stand by for 5 a.m.'

I began to laugh weakly, the tears coming into my eyes. 'Oh dear,' I said, 'let's send wires to everybody not to come.'

'Come on, be brave and face it,' said Maxim. 'We need not give another one for years. Frank, I have an uneasy feeling we ought to be going up to the house. What do you think?'

Frank agreed, and I followed them unwillingly, reluctant to leave the cramped, rather uncomfortable little dining-room that was so typical of Frank's bachelor establishment, and which seemed to me today the embodiment of peace and quietude. When we came to the house we found that the band had arrived, and were standing about in the hall rather pink in the face and self-conscious, while Frith, more important than ever, offered refreshments. The band were to be our guests for the night, and after we had welcomed them and exchanged a few slightly obvious jokes proper to the occasion, the band were borne off to their quarters to be followed by a tour of the grounds.

The afternoon dragged, like the last hour before a journey when one is packed up and keyed to departure, and I wandered from room to room almost as lost as Jasper, who trailed reproachfully at my heels.

There was nothing I could do to help, and it would have been wiser on my part to have kept clear of the house altogether and taken the dog and myself for a long walk. By the time I decided upon this it was too late, Maxim and Frank were demanding tea, and when tea was over Beatrice and Giles arrived. The evening had come upon us all too soon.

'This is like old times,' said Beatrice, kissing Maxim, and looking about her. 'Congratulations to you for remembering every detail. The flowers are exquisite,' she added, turning to me. 'Did you do them?'

'No,' I said, rather ashamed, 'Mrs Danvers is responsible for everything.'

'Oh. Well, after all . . .' Beatrice did not finish her sentence, she accepted a light for her cigarette from Frank, and once it was lit she appeared to have forgotten what she was going to say.

'Have you got Mitchell's to do the catering as usual?' asked Giles.

'Yes,' said Maxim. 'I don't think anything has been altered, has it, Frank? We had all the records down at the office. Nothing has been forgotten, and I don't think we have left anyone out.'

'What a relief to find only ourselves,' said Beatrice. 'I remember once arriving about this time, and there were about twenty-five people in the place already. All going to stop the night.'

'What's everyone going to wear? I suppose Maxim, as always, refuses to play?'

'As always,' said Maxim.

'Such a mistake I think. The whole thing would go with much more swing if you did.'

'Have you ever known a ball at Manderley not to go with a swing?'

232

'No, my dear boy, the organization is too good. But I do think the host ought to give the lead himself.'

'I think it's quite enough if the hostess makes the effort,' said Maxim. 'Why should I make myself hot and uncomfortable and a damn fool into the bargain?'

'Oh, but that's absurd. There's no need to look a fool. With your appearance, my dear Maxim, you could get away with any costume. You don't have to worry about your figure like poor Giles.'

'What is Giles going to wear tonight?' I asked, 'or is it a dead secret?'

'No, rather not,' beamed Giles; 'as a matter-of-fact it's a pretty good effort. I got our local tailor to rig it up. I'm coming as an Arabian sheik.'

'Good God,' said Maxim.

'It's not at all bad,' said Beatrice warmly. 'He stains his face of course, and leaves off his glasses. The head-dress is authentic. We borrowed it off a friend who used to live in the East, and the rest the tailor copied from some paper. Giles looks very well in it.'

'What are you going to be, Mrs Lacy?' said Frank.

'Oh, I'm afraid I haven't coped much,' said Beatrice, 'I've got some sort of Eastern get-up to go with Giles, but I don't pretend it's genuine. Strings of beads, you know, and a veil over my face.'

'It sounds very nice,' I said politely.

'Oh, it's not bad. Comfortable to wear, that's one blessing. I shall take off the veil if I get too hot. What are you wearing?'

'Don't ask her,' said Maxim. 'She won't tell any of us. There has never been such a secret. I believe she even wrote to London for it.'

'My dear,' said Beatrice, rather impressed, 'don't say you have gone a bust and will put us all to shame? Mine is only home-made, you know.'

'Don't worry,' I said, laughing, 'it's quite simple really. But Maxim would tease me, and I've promised to give him the surprise of his life.'

'Quite right too,' said Giles. 'Maxim is too superior altogether. The fact is he's jealous. Wishes he was dressing up like the rest of us, and doesn't like to say so.'

'Heaven forbid,' said Maxim.

'What are you doing, Crawley?' asked Giles.

Frank looked rather apologetic. 'I've been so busy I'm afraid I've left things to the last moment. I hunted up an old pair of trousers last night, and a striped football jersey, and thought of putting a patch over one eye and coming as a pirate.'

'Why on earth didn't you write to us and borrow a costume?' said Beatrice. 'There's one of a Dutchman that Roger had last winter in Switzerland. It would have suited you excellently.'

'I refuse to allow my agent to walk about as a Dutchman,' said Maxim. 'He'd never get rents out of anybody again. Let him stick to his pirate. It might frighten some of them.'

'Anything less like a pirate,' murmured Beatrice in my ear.

I pretended not to hear. Poor Frank, she was always rather down on him.

'How long will it take me to paint my face?' asked Giles.

'Two hours at least,' said Beatrice. 'I should begin thinking about it if I were you. How many shall we be at dinner?'

'Sixteen,' said Maxim, 'counting ourselves. No strangers. You know them all.'

'I'm beginning to get dress fever already,' said Beatrice. 'What fun it all is. I'm so glad you decided to do this again, Maxim.'

'You've got her to thank for it,' said Maxim, nodding at me.

'Oh, it's not true,' I said. 'It was all the fault of Lady Crowan.'

'Nonsense,' said Maxim, smiling at me, 'you know you're as excited as a child at its first party.'

'I'm not.'

'I'm longing to see your dress,' said Beatrice.

'It's nothing out of the way. Really it's not,' I insisted.

'Mrs de Winter says we shan't know her,' said Frank.

Everybody looked at me and smiled. I felt pleased and flushed and rather happy. People were being nice. They were all so friendly. It was suddenly fun, the thought of the dance, and that I was to be the hostess.

The dance was being given for me, in my honour, because I was the bride. I sat on the table in the library, swinging my legs, while the rest of them stood round, and I had a longing to go upstairs and put on my dress, try the wig in front of the looking-glass, turn this way and that before the long mirror on the wall. It was new this sudden unexpected sensation of being important, of having Giles, and Beatrice, and Frank and Maxim all looking at me and talking about my dress. All wondering what I was going to wear. I thought of the soft white dress in its folds of tissue paper, and how it would hide my flat dull figure, my rather sloping shoulders. I thought of my own lank hair covered by the sleek and gleaming curls.

'What's the time?' I said carelessly, yawning a little, pretending I did not care. 'I wonder if we ought to think about going upstairs . . . ?'

As we crossed the great hall on the way to our rooms I realized for the first time how the house lent itself to the occasion, and how beautiful the rooms were looking. Even the drawing-room, formal and cold to my consideration when we were alone, was a blaze of colour now, flowers in every corner, red roses in silver bowls on the white cloth of the supper table, the long windows open to the terrace, where, as soon as it was dusk, the fairy lights would shine. The band had stacked their instruments ready in the minstrel's gallery above the hall, and the hall itself wore a strange, waiting air; there was a warmth about it I had never known before, due to the night itself, so still and clear, to the flowers beneath the pictures, to our own laughter as we hovered on the wide stone stairs.

The old austerity had gone. Manderley had come alive in a fashion I would not have believed possible. It was not the still quiet Manderley I knew. There was a certain significance about it now that had not been before. A reckless air, rather triumphant, rather pleasing. It was as if the house remembered other days, long, long ago, when the hall was a banqueting hall indeed, with weapons and tapestry hanging upon the walls, and men sat at a long narrow table in the centre laughing louder than we laughed now, calling for wine, for song, throwing great pieces of meat upon the flags to the slumbering dogs. Later, in other years, it would still be gay, but with a certain grace and dignity, and Caroline de Winter, whom I should present tonight, would walk down the wide stone stairs in her white dress to dance the minuet. I wished we could sweep away the years and see her. I wished we did not have to degrade the house with our modern jig-tunes, so out-of-place and unromantic. They would not suit Manderley. I found myself in sudden agreement with Mrs Danvers. We should have made it a period ball, not the hotchpotch of humanity it was bound to be, with Giles, poor fellow, well-meaning and hearty in his guise of Arabian sheik. I found Clarice waiting for me in my bedroom, her round face scarlet with excitement. We giggled at one another like schoolgirls, and I bade her lock my door. There was much sound of tissue paper, rustling and mysterious. We spoke to one another softly like conspirators, we walked on tiptoe. I felt like a child again on the eve of Christmas. This padding to and fro in my room with bare feet, the little furtive bursts of laughter, the stifled exclamations, reminded me of hanging up my stocking long ago. Maxim was safe in his dressing-room, and the way through was barred against him. Clarice alone was my ally and favoured friend. The dress fitted perfectly. I stood still, hardly able to restrain my impatience while Clarice hooked me up with fumbling fingers.

'It's handsome, Madam,' she kept saying, leaning back on her heels to look at me. 'It's a dress fit for the Queen of England.'

'What about under the left shoulder there,' I said, anxiously. 'That strap of mine, is it going to show?'

'No, Madam, nothing shows.'

'How is it? How do I look?' I did not wait for her answer, I twisted and turned in front of the mirror, I frowned, I smiled. I felt different already, no longer hampered by my appearance. My own dull personality was submerged at last. 'Give me the wig,' I said excitedly, 'careful, don't crush it, the curls mustn't be flat. They are supposed to stand out from the face.' Clarice stood behind my shoulder, I saw her round face beyond mine in the reflection of the looking-glass, her eyes shining, her mouth a little open. I brushed my own hair sleek behind my ears. I took hold of the soft gleaming curls with trembling fingers, laughing under my breath, looking up at Clarice.

'Oh, Clarice,' I said, 'what will Mr de Winter say?'

I covered my own mousy hair with the curled wig, trying to hide my triumph, trying to hide my smile. Somebody came and hammered on the door.

'Who's there?' I called in panic. 'You can't come in.'

'It's me, my dear, don't alarm yourself,' said Beatrice, 'how far have you got? I want to look at you.'

'No, no,' I said, 'you can't come in, I'm not ready.'

The flustered Clarice stood beside me, her hand full of hair-pins, while I took them from her one by one, controlling the curls that had become fluffed in the box.

'I'll come down when I am ready,' I called. 'Go on down, all of you. Don't wait for me. Tell Maxim he can't come in.'

'Maxim's down,' she said. 'He came along to us. He said he hammered on your bathroom door and you never answered. Don't be too long, my dear, we are all so intrigued. Are you sure you don't want any help?'

'No,' I shouted impatiently, losing my head, 'go away, go on down.'

Why did she have to come and bother just at this moment? It fussed me, I did not know what I was doing. I jabbed with a hair-pin, flattening it against a curl. I heard no more from Beatrice, she must have gone along the passage. I wondered if she was happy in her Eastern robes and if Giles had succeeded in painting his face. How absurd it was, the whole thing. Why did we do it, I wonder, why were we such children?

I did not recognize the face that stared at me in the glass. The eyes were larger surely, the mouth narrower, the skin white and clear? The curls stood away from the head in a little cloud.

I watched this self that was not me at all and then smiled; a new, slow smile.

'Oh, Clarice!' I said. 'Oh, Clarice!' I took the skirt of my dress in my hands and curtseyed to her, the flounces sweeping the ground. She giggled excitedly, rather embarrassed, flushed though, very pleased. I paraded up and down in front of my glass watching my reflection.

'Unlock the door,' I said. 'I'm going down. Run ahead and see if they are there.' She obeyed me, still giggling, and I lifted my skirts off the ground and followed her along the corridor.

She looked back at me and beckoned. 'They've gone down,' she whispered, 'Mr de Winter, and Major and Mrs Lacy. Mr Crawley has just come. They are all standing in the hall.' I peered through the archway at the head of the big staircase, and looked down on the hall below.

Yes, there they were. Giles, in his white Arab dress, laughing loudly, showing the knife at his side; Beatrice swathed in an extraordinary green garment and hung about the neck with trailing beads; poor Frank self-conscious and slightly foolish in his striped jersey and sea-boots; Maxim, the only normal one of the party, in his evening clothes.

'I don't know what she's doing,' he said, 'she's been up in her bedroom for hours. What's the time, Frank? The dinner crowd will be upon us before we know where we are.'

The band were changed, and in the gallery already. One of the men was tuning his fiddle. He played a scale softly, and then plucked at a string. The light shone on the picture of Caroline de Winter.

Yes, the dress had been copied exactly from my sketch of the portrait. The puffed sleeve, the sash and the ribbon, the wide floppy hat I held in my hand. And my curls were her curls, they stood out from my face as hers did in the picture. I don't think I have ever felt so excited before, so happy and so proud. I waved my hand at the man with the fiddle, and then put my finger to my lips for silence. He smiled and bowed. He came across the gallery to the archway where I stood.

'Make the drummer announce me,' I whispered, 'make him beat the drum, you know how they do, and then call out Miss Caroline de Winter. I want to surprise them below.' He nodded his head, he understood. My heart fluttered absurdly, and my cheeks were burning. What fun it was, what mad ridiculous childish fun! I smiled at Clarice still crouching on the corridor. I picked up my skirt in my hands. Then the sound of the drum echoed in the great hall, startling me for a moment, who had waited for it, who knew that it would come. I saw them look up surprised and bewildered from the hall below.

'Miss Caroline de Winter,' shouted the drummer.

I came forward to the head of the stairs and stood there, smiling, my hat in my hand, like the girl in the picture. I waited for the clapping and laughter that would follow as I walked slowly down the stairs. Nobody clapped, nobody moved.

They all stared at me like dumb things. Beatrice uttered a little cry and put her hand to her mouth. I went on smiling, I put one hand on the banister.

'How do you do, Mr de Winter,' I said.

Maxim had not moved. He stared up at me, his glass in his hand. There was no colour in his face. It was ashen white. I saw Frank go to him as though he would speak, but Maxim shook him off. I hesitated, one foot already on the stairs. Something was wrong, they had not understood. Why was Maxim looking like that? Why did they all stand like dummies, like people in a trance?

Then Maxim moved forward to the stairs, his eyes never leaving my face.

'What the hell do you think you are doing?' he asked. His eyes blazed in anger. His face was still ashen white.

I could not move, I went on standing there, my hand on the banister.

'It's the picture,' I said, terrified at his eyes, at his voice. 'It's the picture, the one in the gallery.'

There was a long silence. We went on staring at each other. Nobody moved in the hall. I swallowed, my hand moved to my throat. 'What is it?' I said. 'What have I done?'

If only they would not stare at me like that with dull blank faces. If only somebody would say something. When Maxim spoke again I did not recognize his voice. It was still and quiet, icy cold, not a voice I knew.

'Go and change,' he said, 'it does not matter what you put on. Find an ordinary evening frock, anything will do. Go now, before anybody comes.'

I could not speak, I went on staring at him. His eyes were the only living things in the white mask of his face.

'What are you standing there for?' he said, his voice harsh and queer. 'Didn't you hear what I said?'

I turned and ran blindly through the archway to the corridors beyond. I caught a glimpse of the astonished face of the drummer who had announced me. I brushed past him, stumbling, not looking where I went. Tears blinded my eyes. I did not know what was happening. Clarice had gone. The corridor was deserted. I looked about me stunned and stupid like a haunted thing. Then I saw that the door leading to the west wing was open wide, and that someone was standing there.

It was Mrs Danvers. I shall never forget the expression on her face, loathsome, triumphant. The face of an exulting devil. She stood there, smiling at me.

And then I ran from her, down the long narrow passage to my own room, tripping, stumbling over the flounces of my dress.

Clarice was waiting for me in my bedroom. She looked pale and scared. As soon as she saw me she burst into tears. I did not say anything. I began tearing at the hooks of my dress, ripping the stuff. I could not manage them properly, and Clarice came to help me, still crying noisily.

'It's all right, Clarice, it's not your fault,' I said, and she shook her head, the tears still running down her cheeks.

'Your lovely dress, Madam,' she said, 'your lovely white dress.'

'It doesn't matter,' I said. 'Can't you find the hook? There it is, at the back. And another one somewhere, just below.'

She fumbled with the hooks, her hands trembling, making worse trouble with it than I did myself, and all the time catching at her breath.

'What will you wear instead, Madam?' she said.

'I don't know,' I said, 'I don't know.' She had managed to unfasten the hooks, and I struggled out of the dress. 'I think I'd rather like to be alone, Clarice,' I said, 'would you be a dear and leave me? Don't worry, I shall manage all right. Forget what's happened. I want you to enjoy the party.'

'Can't I press out a dress for you, Madam?' she said, looking up at me with swollen streaming eyes. 'It won't take me a moment.'

'No,' I said, 'don't bother, I'd rather you went, and Clarice . . .'

'Yes, Madam?'

'Don't — don't say anything about what's just happened.'

'No, Madam.' She burst into another torrent of weeping.

'Don't let the others see you like that,' I said. 'Go to your bedroom and do something to your face. There's nothing to cry about, nothing at all.' Somebody knocked on the door. Clarice threw me a quick frightened glance.

'Who is it?' I said. The door opened and Beatrice came into the room. She came to me at once, a strange, rather ludicrous figure in her Eastern drapery, the bangles jangling on her wrists.

'My dear,' she said, 'my dear,' and held out her hands to me.

Clarice slipped out of the room. I felt tired suddenly, and unable to cope. I went and sat down on the bed. I put my hand up to my head and took off the curled wig. Beatrice stood watching me.

'Are you all right?' she said. 'You look very white.'

'It's the light,' I said. 'It never gives one any colour.'

'Sit down for a few minutes and you'll be all right,' she said; 'wait, I'll get a glass of water.'

She went into the bathroom, her bangles jangling with her every movement, and then she came back, the glass of water in her hands.

I drank some to please her, not wanting it a bit. It tasted warm from the tap; she had not let it run.

'Of course I knew at once it was just a terrible mistake,' she said. 'You could not possibly have known, why should you?'

'Known what?' I said.

'Why, the dress, you poor dear, the picture you copied of the girl in the gallery. It was what Rebecca did at the last fancy dress ball at Manderley. Identical. The same picture, the same dress. You stood there on the stairs, and for one ghastly moment I thought . . .'

She did not go on with her sentence, she patted me on the shoulder.

'You poor child, how wretchedly unfortunate, how were you to know?'

'I ought to have known,' I said stupidly, staring at her, too stunned to understand. 'I ought to have known.'

'Nonsense, how could you know? It was not the sort of thing that could possibly enter any of our heads. Only it was such a shock, you see. We none of us expected it, and Maxim . . .'

'Yes, Maxim?' I said.

'He thinks, you see, it was deliberate on your part. You had some bet that you would startle him, didn't you? Some foolish joke. And of course, he doesn't understand. It was such a frightful shock for him. I told him at once you could not have done such a thing, and that it was sheer appalling luck that you had chosen that particular picture.'

'I ought to have known,' I repeated again. 'It's all my fault, I ought to have seen. I ought to have known.'

'No, no. Don't worry, you'll be able to explain the whole thing to him quietly. Everything will be quite all right. The first lot of people were arriving just as I came upstairs to you. They are having drinks. Everything's all right. I've told Frank and Giles to make up a story about your dress not fitting, and you are very disappointed.'

I did not say anything. I went on sitting on the bed with my hands in my lap.

'What can you wear instead?' said Beatrice, going to my wardrobe and flinging open the doors. 'Here. What's this blue? It looks charming. Put this on. Nobody will mind. Quick. I'll help you.'

'No,' I said. 'No, I'm not coming down.'

Beatrice stared at me in great distress, my blue frock over her arm.

'But, my dear, you must,' she said in dismay. 'You can't possibly not appear.'

'No, Beatrice, I'm not coming down. I can't face them, not after what's happened.'

'But nobody will know about the dress,' she said. 'Frank and Giles will never breathe a word. We've got the story all arranged. The shop sent the wrong dress, and it did not fit, so you are wearing an ordinary evening dress instead. Everyone will think it perfectly natural. It won't make any difference to the evening.'

'You don't understand,' I said. 'I don't care about the dress. It's not that at all. It's what has happened, what I did. I can't come down now, Beatrice, I can't.'

'But, my dear, Giles and Frank understand perfectly. They are full of sympathy. And Maxim too. It was just the first shock . . .

I'll try and get him alone a minute, I'll explain the whole thing.'

'No!' I said. 'No!'

She put my blue frock down beside me on the bed. 'Everyone will be arriving,' she said, very worried, very upset. 'It will look so extraordinary if you don't come down. I can't say you've suddenly got a headache.'

'Why not?' I said wearily. 'What does it matter? Make anything up. Nobody will mind, they don't any of them know me.'

'Come now, my dear,' she said, patting my hand, 'try and make the effort. Put on this charming blue. Think of Maxim. You must come down for his sake.'

'I'm thinking about Maxim all the time,' I said.

'Well, then, surely . . . ?'

'No,' I said, tearing at my nails, rocking backwards and forwards on the bed. 'I can't, I can't.'

Somebody else knocked on the door. 'Oh, dear, who on earth is that?' said Beatrice, walking to the door. 'What is it?'

She opened the door. Giles was standing just outside. 'Everyone has turned up. Maxim sent me up to find out what's happening,' he said.

'She says she won't come down,' said Beatrice. 'What on earth are we going to say?'

I caught sight of Giles peering at me through the open door.

'Oh, Lord, what a frightful mix-up,' he whispered. He turned away embarrassed when he noticed that I had seen him.

'What shall I say to Maxim?' he asked Beatrice. 'It's five past eight now.'

'Say she's feeling rather faint, but will try and come down later. Tell them not to wait dinner. I'll be down directly, I'll make it all right.'

'Yes, right you are.' He half glanced in my direction again, sympathetic but rather curious, wondering why I sat there on the bed, and his voice was low, as it might be after an accident, when people are waiting for the doctor.

'Is there anything else I can do?' he said.

'No,' said Beatrice, 'go down now, I'll follow in a minute.'

He obeyed her, shuffling away in his Arabian robes. This is the sort of moment, I thought, that I shall laugh at years afterwards, that I shall say 'Do you remember how Giles was dressed as an Arab, and Beatrice had a veil over her face, and jangling bangles on her wrist?' And time will mellow it, make it a moment for laughter. But now it was not funny, now I did not laugh. It was not the future, it was the present. It was too vivid and too real. I sat on the bed, plucking at the eiderdown, pulling a little feather out of a slit in one corner.

'Would you like some brandy?' said Beatrice, making a last effort. 'I know it's only Dutch courage, but it sometimes works wonders.'

'No,' I said. 'No, I don't want anything.'

'I shall have to go down. Giles says they are waiting dinner. Are you sure it's all right for me to leave you?'

'Yes. And thank you, Beatrice.'

'Oh, my dear, don't thank me. I wish I could do something.' She stooped swiftly to my looking-glass and dabbed her face with powder. 'God, what a sight I look,' she said, 'this damn veil is crooked I know. However it can't be helped.' She rustled out of the room, closing the door behind her. I felt I had forfeited her sympathy by my refusal to go down. I had shown the white feather. She had not understood. She belonged to another breed of men and women, another race than I. They had guts, the women of her race. They were not like me. If it had been Beatrice who had done this thing instead of me she would have put on her other dress and gone down again to welcome her guests. She would have stood by Giles's side, and shaken hands with people, a smile on her face. I could not do that. I had not the pride, I had not the guts. I was badly bred.

I kept seeing Maxim's eyes blazing in his white face, and behind him Giles, and Beatrice and Frank standing like dummies, staring at me.

I got up from my bed and went and looked out of the window. The gardeners were going round to the lights in the rose garden, testing them to see if they all worked. The sky was pale, with a few salmon clouds of evening streaking to the west. When it was dusk the lamps would all be lit. There were tables and chairs in the rose-garden, for the couples who wanted to sit out. I could smell the roses from my window. The men were talking to one another and laughing. 'There's one here gone,' I heard a voice call out; 'can you get me another small bulb? One of the blue ones, Bill.' He fixed the light into position. He whistled a popular tune of the moment with easy confidence, and I thought how tonight perhaps the band would play the same tune in the minstrel's gallery above the hall. 'That's got it,' said the man, switching the light on and off, 'they're all right here. No others gone. We'd better have a look at those on the terrace.' They went off round the corner of the house, still whistling the song. I wished I could be the man. Later in the evening he would stand with his friend in the drive and watch the cars drive up to the house, his hands in his pockets, his cap on the back of his head. He would stand in a crowd with other people from the estate, and then drink cider at the long table arranged for them in one corner of the terrace. 'Like the old days, isn't it?' he would say. But his friend would shake his head, puffing at his pipe. 'This new one's not like our Mrs de Winter, she's different altogether.' And a woman next them in the crowd would agree, other people too, all saying 'That's right,' and nodding their heads.

'Where is she tonight? She's not been on the terrace once.'

'I can't say, I'm sure. I've not seen her.'

'Mrs de Winter used to be here, there, and everywhere.'

'Aye, that's right.'

And the woman would turn to her neighbours nodding mysteriously.

'They say she's not appearing tonight at all.'

'Go on.'

'That's right. One of the servants from the house told me Mrs de Winter hasn't come down from her room all evening.'

'What's wrong with the maid, is she bad?'

'No, sulky I reckon. They say her dress didn't please her.'

A squeal of laughter and a murmur from the little crowd.

'Did you ever hear of such a thing? It's a shame for Mr de Winter.'

'I wouldn't stand for it, not from a chit like her.'

'Maybe it's not true at all.'

'It's true all right. They're full of it up at the house.' One to the other. This one to the next. A smile, a wink, a shrug of the shoulder. One group, and then another group. And then spreading to the guests who walked on the terrace and strolled across the lawns. The couple who in three hours' time would sit in those chairs beneath me in the rose-garden.

'Do you suppose it's true what I heard?'

'What did you hear?'

'Why, that there's nothing wrong with her at all, they've had a colossal row, and she won't appear!'

'I say!' A lift of the eyebrows, a long whistle.

'I know. Well, it does look rather odd, don't you think? What I mean is, people don't suddenly for no reason have violent headaches. I call the whole thing jolly fishy.'

'I thought he looked a bit grim.'

'So did I.'

'Of course I have heard before the marriage is not a wild success.'

'Oh, really?'

'H'm. Several people have said so. They say he's beginning to realize he's made a big mistake. She's nothing to look at, you know.'

'No, I've heard there's nothing much to her. Who was she?'

'Oh, no one at all. Some pick-up in the south of France, a nursery gov., or something.'

'Good Lord!'

'I know. And when you think of Rebecca . . .'

I went on staring at the empty chairs. The salmon sky had turned to grey. Above my head was the evening star. In the woods beyond the rose-garden the birds were making their last little rustling noises before nightfall. A lone gull flew across the sky.

I went away from the window, back to the bed again. I picked up the white dress I had left on the floor and put it back in the box with the tissue paper. I put the wig back in its box too. Then I looked in one of my cupboards for the little portable iron I used to have in Monte Carlo for Mrs Van Hopper's dresses. It was lying at the back of a shelf with some woollen jumpers I had not worn for a long time. The iron was one of those universal kinds that go on any voltage and I fitted it to the plug in the wall. I began to iron the blue dress that Beatrice had taken from the wardrobe, slowly, methodically, as I used to iron Mrs Van Hopper's dresses in Monte Carlo.

When I had finished I laid the dress ready on the bed. Then I cleaned the make-up off my face that I had put on for the fancy dress. I combed my hair, and washed my hands. I put on the blue dress and the shoes that went with it. I might have been my old self again, going down to the lounge of the hotel with Mrs Van Hopper. I opened the door of my room and went along the corridor. Everything was still and silent. There might not have been a party at all. I tiptoed to the end of the passage and turned the corner. The door to the west wing was closed. There was no sound of anything at all. When I came to the archway by the gallery and the staircase I heard the murmur and hum of conversation coming from the dining-room. They were still having dinner. The great hall was deserted. There was nobody in the gallery either. The band must be having their dinner too. I did not know what arrangements had been made for them. Frank had done it – Frank or Mrs Danvers.

From where I stood I could see the picture of Caroline de Winter facing me in the gallery. I could see the curls framing her face, and I could see the smile on her lips. I remembered the bishop's wife who had said to me that day I called, 'I shall never forget her, dressed all in white, with that cloud of dark hair.' I ought to have remembered that, I ought to have known. How queer the instruments looked in the gallery, the little stands for the music, the big drum. One of the men had left his handkerchief on a chair. I leant over the rail and looked down at the hall below. Soon it would be filled with people, like the bishop's wife had said, and Maxim would stand at the bottom of the stairs shaking hands with them as they came into the hall. The sound of their voices would echo to the ceiling, and then the band would play from the gallery where I was leaning now, the man with the violin smiling, swaying to the music.

It would not be quiet like this any more. A board creaked in the gallery. I swung round, looking at the gallery behind me. There was nobody there. The gallery was empty, just as it had been before. A current of air blew in my face though, some-body must have left a window open in one of the passages. The hum of voices continued in the dining-room. I wondered why the board creaked when I had not moved at all. The warmth of the night perhaps, a swelling somewhere in the old wood. The draught still blew in my face though. A piece of music on one of the stands fluttered to the floor. I looked towards the archway above the stairs. The draught was coming from there. I went beneath the arch again, and when I came out on to the long corridor I saw that the door to the west wing had blown open and swung back against the wall. It was dark in the west passage, none of the lights had been turned on. I could feel the wind blowing on my face from an open window. I fumbled for a switch on the wall and could not find one. I could see the window in an angle of the passage, the curtain blowing softly, backwards and forwards. The grey evening light cast queer shadows on the floor. The sound of the sea came to me through the open window, the soft hissing sound of the ebb-tide leaving the shingle.

I did not go and shut the window. I stood there shivering a moment in my thin dress, listening to the sea as it sighed and left the shore. Then I turned quickly and shut the door of the west wing behind me, and came out again through the archway by the stairs.

The murmur of voices had swollen now and was louder than before. The door of the dining-room was open. They were coming out of dinner. I could see Robert standing by the open

249

door, and there was a scraping of chairs, a babble of conversation, and laughter.

I walked slowly down the stairs to meet them.

When I look back at my first party at Manderley, my first and my last, I can remember little isolated things standing alone out of the vast blank canvas of the evening. The background hazy, a sea of dim faces none of whom I knew, and there was the slow drone of the band harping out a waltz that never finished, that went on and on. The same couples swung by in rotation, with the same fixed smiles, and to me, standing with Maxim at the bottom of the stairs to welcome the late-comers, these dancing couples seemed like marionettes twisting and turning on a piece of string, held by some invisible hand.

There was a woman, I never knew her name, never saw her again, but she wore a salmon-coloured gown hooped in crinoline form, a vague gesture to some past century but whether seventeenth, eighteenth, or nineteenth I could not tell, and every time she passed me it coincided with a sweeping bar of the waltz to which she dipped and swayed, smiling as she did so in my direction. It happened again and again until it became automatic, a matter of routine, like those promenades on board ship when we meet the same people bent on exercise like ourselves, and know with deadly certainty that we will pass them by the bridge.

I can see her now, the prominent teeth, the gay spot of rouge placed high upon her cheek-bones, and her smile, vacant, happy, enjoying her evening. Later I saw her by the supper table, her keen eyes searching the food, and she heaped a plate high with salmon and lobster mayonnaise and went off into a corner. There was Lady Crowan too, monstrous in purple, disguised as I know not what romantic figure of the past, it might have been Marie Antoinette or Nell Gwynne for all I knew, or a strange erotic combination of the two, and she kept exclaiming in excited high-pitch tones, a little higher than usual because of the champagne she had consumed, 'You all have me to thank for this, not the de Winters at all.'

I remember Robert dropping a tray of ices, and the expression of Frith's face when he saw Robert was the culprit and not one of the minions hired for the occasion. I wanted to go to Robert and stand beside him and say 'I know how you feel. I understand. I've done worse than you tonight.' I can feel now the stiff, set smile on my face that did not match the misery in my eyes. I can see Beatrice, dear friendly tactless Beatrice, watching me from her partner's arms, nodding encouragement, the bangles jangling on her wrists, the veil slipping continually from her overheated forehead. I can picture myself once more whirled round the room in a desperate dance with Giles, who with dog-like sympathy and kind heart would take no refusal, but must steer me through the stamping crowd as he would one of his own horses at a meet. 'That's a jolly pretty dress you're wearing,' I can hear him say, 'it makes all these people look damn silly,' and I blessed him for his pathetic simple gesture of understanding and sincerity, thinking, dear Giles, that I was disappointed in my dress, that I was worrying about my appearance, that I cared.

It was Frank who brought me a plate of chicken and ham that I could not eat, and Frank who stood by my elbow with a glass of champagne I would not drink.

'I wish you would,' he said quietly, 'I think you need it,' and I took three sips of it to please him. The black patch over his eye gave him a pale odd appearance, it made him look older, different. There seemed to be lines on his face I had not seen before.

He moved amongst the guests like another host, seeing to their comfort, that they were supplied with drink, and food, and cigarettes, and he danced too in solemn painstaking fashion, walking his partners round the room with a set face. He did not wear his pirate costume with abandon, and there was something rather tragic about the side-whiskers he had fluffed under the scarlet handkerchief on his head. I thought of him standing before the looking-glass in his bare bachelor bedroom curling them

251

round his fingers. Poor Frank. Dear Frank. I never asked, I never knew, how much he hated the last fancy dress ball given at Manderley.

The band played on, and the swaying couples twisted like bobbing marionettes, to and fro, to and fro, across the great hall and back again, and it was not I who watched them at all, not someone with feelings, made of flesh and blood, but a dummy-stick of a person in my stead, a prop who wore a smile screwed to its face. The figure who stood beside it was wooden too. His face was a mask, his smile was not his own. The eyes were not the eyes of the man I loved, the man I knew. They looked through me and beyond me, cold, expressionless, to some place of pain and torture I could not enter, to some private, inward hell I could not share.

He never spoke to me. He never touched me. We stood beside one another, the host and the hostess, and we were not together. I watched his courtesy to his guests. He flung a word to one, a jest to another, a smile to a third, a call over his shoulder to a fourth, and no one but myself could know that every utterance he made, every movement, was automatic and the work of a machine. We were like two performers in a play, but we were divided, we were not acting with one another. We had to endure it alone, we had to put up this show, this miserable, sham perform-ance, for the sake of all these people I did not know and did not want to see again.

'I hear your wife's frock never turned up in time,' said someone with a mottled face and a sailor's pigtail, and he laughed, and dug Maxim in the ribs. 'Damn shame, what? I should sue the shop for fraud. Same thing happened to my wife's cousin once.'

'Yes, it was unfortunate,' said Maxim.

'I tell you what,' said the sailor, turning to me, 'you ought to say you are a forget-me-not. They're blue aren't they? Jolly little flowers, forget-me-nots. That's right, isn't it, de Winter? Tell your wife she must call herself a "forget-me-not".' He swept away, roaring with laughter, his partner in his arms. 'Pretty good idea, what? A forget-me-not.' Then Frank again hovering just behind me, another glass in his hand, lemonade this time. 'No, Frank, I'm not thirsty.'

'Why don't you dance? Or come and sit down a moment; there's a corner in the terrace.'

'No, I'm better standing. I don't want to sit down.'

'Can't I get you something, a sandwich, a peach?'

'No, I don't want anything.'

There was the salmon lady again; she forgot to smile at me this time. She was flushed after her supper. She kept looking up into her partner's face. He was very tall, very thin, he had a chin like a fiddle.

The Destiny waltz, the Blue Danube, the Merry Widow, one-two-three, one-two-three, round-and-round, one-two-three, one-two-three, round-and-round. The salmon lady, a green lady, Beatrice again, her veil pushed back off her forehead; Giles, his face streaming with perspiration, and that sailor once more, with another partner; they stopped beside me, I did not know her; she was dressed as a Tudor woman, any Tudor woman; she wore a ruffle round her throat and a black velvet dress.

'When are you coming to see us?' she said, as though we were old friends, and I answered, 'Soon of course; we were talking about it the other day,' wondering why I found it so easy to lie suddenly, no effort at all. 'Such a delightful party; I do congratulate you,' she said, and 'Thank you very much,' I said. 'It's fun, isn't it?'

'I hear they sent you the wrong dress?'

'Yes; absurd, wasn't it?'

'These shops are all the same. No depending on them. But you look delightfully fresh in that pale blue. Much more comfortable than this hot velvet. Don't forget, you must both come and dine at the Palace soon.'

'We should love to.'

What did she mean, where, what palace? Were we entertaining royalty? She swept on to the Blue Danube in the arms of the sailor, her velvet frock brushing the ground like a carpet-sweeper, and it was not until long afterwards, in the middle of some night,

253

when I could not sleep, that I remembered the Tudor woman was the bishop's wife who liked walking in the Pennines.

What was the time? I did not know. The evening dragged on, hour after hour, the same faces and the same tunes. Now and again the bridge people crept out of the library like hermits to watch the dancers, and then returned again. Beatrice, her draperies trailing behind her, whispered in my ear.

'Why don't you sit down? You look like death.'

'I'm all right.'

Giles, the make-up running on his face, poor fellow, and stifling in his Arab blanket, came up to me and said, 'Come and watch the fireworks on the terrace.'

I remember standing on the terrace and staring up at the sky as the foolish rockets burst and fell. There was little Clarice in a corner with some boy off the estate; she was smiling happily, squealing with delight as a squib spluttered at her feet. She had forgotten her tears.

'Hullo, this will be a big 'un.' Giles, his large face upturned, his mouth open. 'Here she comes. Bravo, jolly fine show.'

The slow hiss of the rocket as it sped into the air, the burst of the explosion, the stream of little emerald stars. A murmur of approval from the crowd, cries of delight, and a clapping of hands.

The salmon lady well to the front, her face eager with expectation, a remark for every star that fell. 'Oh, what a beauty . . . look at that one now; I say, how pretty . . . Oh, that one didn't burst . . . take care, it's coming our way . . . what are those men doing over there?' . . . Even the hermits left their lair and came to join the dancers on the terrace. The lawns were black with people. The bursting stars shone on their upturned faces.

Again and again the rockets sped into the air like arrows, and the sky became crimson and gold. Manderley stood out like an enchanted house, every window aflame, the grey walls coloured by the falling stars. A house bewitched, carved out of the dark woods. And when the last rocket burst and the cheering died away, the night that had been fine before seemed dull and heavy in contrast, the sky became a pall. The little groups on the lawns and in the drive broke up and scattered. The guests crowded the long windows in the terrace back to the drawing-room again. It was anti-climax, the aftermath had come. We stood about with blank faces. Someone gave me a glass of champagne. I heard the sound of cars starting up in the drive.

'They're beginning to go,' I thought. 'Thank God, they're beginning to go.' The salmon lady was having some more supper. It would take time yet to clear the hall. I saw Frank make a signal to the band. I stood in the doorway between the drawing-room and the hall beside a man I did not know.

'What a wonderful party it's been,' he said.

'Yes,' I said.

'I've enjoyed every minute of it,' he said.

'I'm so glad,' I said.

'Molly was wild with fury at missing it,' he said.

'Was she?' I said.

The band began to play Auld Lang Syne. The man seized my hand and started swinging it up and down. 'Here,' he said, 'come on, some of you.' Somebody else swung my other hand, and more people joined us. We stood in a great circle singing at the top of our voices. The man who had enjoyed his evening and said Molly would be wild at missing it was dressed as a Chinese mandarin, and his false nails got caught up in his sleeve as we swung our hands up and down. He roared with laughter. We all laughed. 'Should auld acquaintance be forgot,' we sang.

The hilarious gaiety changed swiftly at the closing bars, and the drummer rattled his sticks in the inevitable prelude to God Save the King. The smiles left our faces as though wiped clean by a sponge. The Mandarin sprang to attention, his hands stiff to his sides. I remember wondering vaguely if he was in the Army. How queer he looked with his long poker face, and his drooping Mandarin moustache. I caught the salmon lady's eye. God Save the King had taken her unawares, she was still holding a plate heaped with chicken in aspic. She held it stiffly out in front of her like a church collection. All animation had gone from her face. As the last note of God Save the King died away she relaxed again, and attacked her chicken in a sort of frenzy, chattering over her shoulder to her partner. Somebody came and wrung me by the hand.

'Don't forget, you're dining with us on the fourteenth of next month.'

'Oh, are we?' I stared at him blankly.

'Yes, we've got your sister-in-law to promise too.'

'Oh. Oh, what fun.'

'Eight-thirty, and black tie. So looking forward to seeing you.'

'Yes. Yes, rather.'

People began to form up in queues to say good-bye. Maxim was at the other side of the room. I put on my smile again, which had worn thin after Auld Lang Syne.

'The best evening I've spent for a long time.'

'I'm so glad.'

'Many thanks for a grand party.'

'I'm so glad.'

'Here we are, you see, staying to the bitter end.'

'Yes, I'm so glad.'

Was there no other sentence in the English language? I bowed and smiled like a dummy, my eyes searching for Maxim above their heads. He was caught up in a knot of people by the library. Beatrice too was surrounded, and Giles had led a team of stragglers to the buffet table in the drawing-room. Frank was out in the drive seeing that people got their cars. I was hemmed in by strangers.

'Good-bye, and thanks tremendously.'

'I'm so glad.'

The great hall began to empty. Already it wore that drab deserted air of a vanished evening and the dawn of a tired day. There was a grey light on the terrace, I could see the shapes of the blown firework stands taking form on the lawns.

'Good-bye; a wonderful party.'

'I'm so glad.'

Maxim had gone out to join Frank in the drive. Beatrice came up to me, pulling off her jangling bracelets. 'I can't stand

256

these things a moment longer. Heavens, I'm dead beat. I don't believe I've missed a dance. Anyway, it was a tremendous success.'

'Was it?' I said.

'My dear, hadn't you better go to bed? You look worn out. You've been standing nearly all the evening. Where are the men?'

'Out on the drive.'

'I shall have some coffee, and eggs and bacon. What about you?'

'No, Beatrice, I don't think I will.'

'You looked very charming in your blue. Everyone said so. And nobody had an inkling about – about the other things, so you mustn't worry.'

'No.'

'If I were you I should have a good long lie tomorrow morning. Don't attempt to get up. Have your breakfast in bed.'

'Yes, perhaps.'

'I'll tell Maxim you've gone up, shall I?'

'Please, Beatrice.'

'All right, my dear. Sleep well.' She kissed me swiftly, patting my shoulder at the same time, and then went off to find Giles in the supper room. I walked slowly up the stairs, one step at a time. The band had turned the lights off in the gallery, and had gone down to have eggs and bacon too. Pieces of music lay about the floor. One chair had been upturned. There was an ashtray full of the stubs of their cigarettes. The aftermath of the party. I went along the corridor to my room. It was getting lighter every moment, and the birds had started singing. I did not have to turn on the light to undress. A little chill wind blew in from the open window. It was rather cold. Many people must have used the rose-garden during the evening, for all the chairs were moved, and dragged from their places. There was a tray of empty glasses on one of the tables. Someone had left a bag behind on a chair. I pulled the curtain to darken the room, but the grey morning light found its way through the gaps at the side.

I got into bed, my legs very weary, a niggling pain in the

small of my back. I lay back and closed my eyes, thankful for the cool white comfort of clean sheets. I wished my mind would rest like my body, relax, and pass to sleep. Not hum round in the way it did, jigging to music, whirling in a sea of faces. I pressed my hands over my eyes but they would not go.

I wondered how long Maxim would be. The bed beside me looked stark and cold. Soon there would be no shadows in the room at all, the walls and the ceiling and the floor would be white with the morning. The birds would sing their songs, louder, gayer, less subdued. The sun would make a yellow pattern on the curtain. My little bed-side clock ticked out the minutes one by one. The hand moved round the dial. I lay on my side watching it. It came to the hour and passed it again. It started afresh on its journey. But Maxim did not come.

18

I think I fell asleep a little after seven. It was broad daylight, I remember, there was no longer any pretence that the drawn curtains hid the sun. The light streamed in at the open window and made patterns on the wall. I heard the men below in the rose-garden clearing away the tables and the chairs, and taking down the chain of fairy lights. Maxim's bed was still bare and empty. I lay across my bed, my arms over my eyes, a strange, mad position and the least likely to bring sleep, but I drifted to the border-line of the unconscious and slipped over it at last. When I awoke it was past eleven, and Clarice must have come in and brought me my tea without my hearing her, for there was a tray by my side, and a stone-cold teapot, and my clothes had been tidied, my blue frock put away in the wardrobe.

I drank my cold tea, still blurred and stupid from my short heavy sleep, and stared at the blank wall in front of me. Maxim's empty bed brought me to realization with a queer shock to my heart, and the full anguish of the night before was upon me once again. He had not come to bed at all. His pyjamas lay folded on the turned-down sheet untouched. I wondered what Clarice had thought when she came into the room with my tea. Had she noticed? Would she have gone out and told the other servants, and would they all discuss it over their breakfast? I wondered why I minded that, and why the thought of the servants talking about it in the kitchen should cause me such distress. It must be that I had a small mean mind, a conventional, petty hatred of gossip.

That was why I had come down last night in my blue dress and had not stayed hidden in my room. There was nothing brave or fine about it, it was a wretched tribute to convention. I had not come down for Maxim's sake, for Beatrice's, for the sake of Manderley. I had come down because I did not want the people at the ball to think I had quarrelled with Maxim. I didn't want them to go home and say, 'Of course you know they don't get on. I hear he's not at all happy.' I had come for my own sake, my own poor personal pride. As I sipped my cold tea I thought with a tired bitter feeling of despair that I would be content to live in one corner of Manderley and Maxim in the other so long as the outside world should never know. If he had no more tenderness for me, never kissed me again, did not speak to me except on matters of necessity, I believed I could bear it if I were certain that nobody knew of this but our two selves. If we could bribe servants not to tell, play our part before relations, before Beatrice, and then when we were alone sit apart in our separate rooms, leading our separate lives.

It seemed to me, as I sat there in bed, staring at the wall, at the sunlight coming in at the window, at Maxim's empty bed, that there was nothing quite so shaming, so degrading as a marriage that had failed. Failed after three months, as mine had done. For I had no illusions left now, I no longer made any effort to pretend. Last night had shown me too well. My marriage was a failure. All the things that people would say about it if they knew, were true. We did not get on. We were not companions. We were not suited to one another. I was too young for Maxim, too inexperienced, and, more important still, I was not of his world. The fact that I loved him in a sick, hurt, desperate way, like a child or a dog, did not matter. It was not the sort of love he needed. He wanted something else that I could not give him, something he had had before. I thought of the youthful almost hysterical excitement and conceit with which I had gone into this marriage, imagining I would bring happiness to Maxim, who had known much greater happiness before. Even Mrs Van Hopper, with her cheap views and common outlook, had known I was making a mistake. 'I'm afraid you will regret it,' she said. 'I believe you are making a big mistake.'

I would not listen to her, I thought her hard and cruel. But she was right. She was right in everything. That last mean thrust thrown at me before she said good-bye, 'You don't flatter yourself he's in love with you, do you? He's lonely, he can't bear that great empty house,' was the sanest, most truthful statement she had ever made in her life. Maxim was not in love with me, he had never loved me. Our honeymoon in Italy had meant nothing at all to him, nor our living here together. What I had thought was love for me, for myself as a person, was not love. It was just that he was a man, and I was his wife and was young, and he was lonely. He did not belong to me at all, he belonged to Rebecca. He still thought about Rebecca. He would never love me because of Rebecca. She was in the house still, as Mrs Danvers had said; she was in that room in the west wing, she was in the library, in the morning-room, in the gallery above the hall. Even in the little flower-room, where her mackintosh still hung. And in the garden, and in the woods, and down in the stone cottage on the beach. Her footsteps sounded in the corridors, her scent lingered on the stairs. The servants obeyed her orders still, the food we ate was the food she liked. Her favourite flowers filled the rooms. Her clothes were in the wardrobes in her room, her brushes were on the table, her shoes beneath the chair, her night-dress on her bed. Rebecca was still mistress of Manderley. Rebecca was still Mrs de Winter. I had no business here at all. I had come blundering like a poor fool on ground that was preserved. 'Where is Rebecca?' Maxim's grandmother had cried. 'I want Rebecca. What have you done with Rebecca?' She did not know me, she did not care about me. Why should she? I was a stranger to her. I did not belong to Maxim or to Manderley. And Beatrice at our first meeting, looking me up and down, frank, direct, 'You're so very different from Rebecca.' Frank, reserved, embarrassed when I spoke of her, hating those questions I had poured upon him, even as I had hated them myself, and then answering that final one as we came towards the house, his voice grave and quiet. 'Yes, she was the most beautiful creature I have ever seen.'

Rebecca, always Rebecca. Wherever I walked in Manderley, wherever I sat, even in my thoughts and in my dreams, I met

Rebecca. I knew her figure now, the long slim legs, the small and narrow feet. Her shoulders, broader than mine, the capable clever hands. Hands that could steer a boat, could hold a horse. Hands that arranged flowers, made the models of ships, and wrote 'Max from Rebecca' on the fly-leaf of a book. I knew her face too, small and oval, the clear white skin, the cloud of dark hair. I knew the scent she wore, I could guess her laughter and her smile. If I heard it, even among a thousand others, I should recognize her voice. Rebecca, always Rebecca. I should never be rid of Rebecca.

Perhaps I haunted her as she haunted me; she looked down on me from the gallery as Mrs Danvers had said, she sat beside me when I wrote my letters at her desk. That mackintosh I wore, that handkerchief I used. They were hers. Perhaps she knew and had seen me take them. Jasper had been her dog, and he ran at my heels now. The roses were hers and I cut them. Did she resent me and fear me as I resented her? Did she want Maxim alone in the house again? I could fight the living but I could not fight the dead. If there was some woman in London that Maxim loved, someone he wrote to, visited, dined with, slept with, I could fight with her. We would stand on common ground. I should not be afraid. Anger and jealousy were things that could be conquered. One day the woman would grow old or tired or different, and Maxim would not love her any more. But Rebecca would never grow old. Rebecca would always be the same. And her I could not fight. She was too strong for me.

I got out of bed and pulled the curtains. The sun streamed into the room. The men had cleared the mess away from the rose-garden. I wondered if people were talking about the ball in the way they do the day after a party.

'Did you think it quite up to their usual standard?'

'Oh, I think so.'

'The band dragged a bit, I thought.'

'The supper was damn good.'

'Fireworks weren't bad.'

'Bee Lacy is beginning to look old.'

'Who wouldn't in that get-up?'

'I thought he looked rather ill.'

'He always does.'

'What did you think of the bride?'

'Not much. Rather dull.'

'I wonder if it's a success.'

'Yes, I wonder . . .'

Then I noticed for the first time there was a note under my door. I went and picked it up. I recognized the square hand of Beatrice. She had scribbled it in pencil after breakfast.

I knocked at your door but had no answer so gather you've taken my advice and are sleeping off last night. Giles is anxious to get back early as they have rung up from home to say he's wanted to take somebody's place in a cricket match, and it starts at two. How he is going to see the ball after all the champagne he put away last night heaven only knows! I'm feeling a bit weak in the legs, but slept like a top. Frith says Maxim was down to an early breakfast, and there's now no sign of him! So please give him our love, and many thanks to you both for our evening, which we thoroughly enjoyed. Don't think any more about the dress. [*This last was heavily underlined*] Yours affection-ately, Bee. [*And a postscript*] You must both come over and see us soon.

She had scribbled nine-thirty a.m. at the top of the paper, and it was now nearly half past eleven. They had been gone about two hours. They would be home by now, Beatrice with her suitcase unpacked, going out into her garden and taking up her ordinary routine, and Giles preparing for his match, renewing the whipping on his bat.

In the afternoon Beatrice would change into a cool frock and a shady hat and watch Giles play cricket. They would have tea afterwards in a tent, Giles very hot and red in the face, Beatrice laughing and talking to her friends. 'Yes, we went over for the dance at Manderley; it was great fun. I wonder Giles was able to run a yard.' Smiling at Giles, patting him on the back. They were both middle-aged and unromantic. They had been married for twenty years and had a grown-up son who was going to Oxford. They were very happy. Their marriage was a success. It had not failed after three months as mine had done.

I could not go on sitting in my bedroom any longer. The maids would want to come and do the room. Perhaps Clarice would not have noticed about Maxim's bed after all. I rumpled it, to make it look as though he had slept there. I did not want the housemaids to know, if Clarice had not told them.

I had a bath and dressed, and went downstairs. The men had taken up the floor already in the hall and the flowers had been carried away. The music stands were gone from the gallery. The band must have caught an early train. The gardeners were sweeping the lawns and the drive clear of the spent fireworks. Soon there would be no trace left of the fancy dress ball at Manderley. How long the preparations had seemed, and how short and swift the clearance now.

I remembered the salmon lady standing by the drawing-room door with her plate of chicken, and it seemed to me a thing I must have fancied, or something that had happened very long ago. Robert was polishing the table in the dining-room. He was normal again, stolid, dull, not the fey excited creature of the past few weeks.

'Good morning, Robert,' I said.

'Good morning, Madam.'

'Have you seen Mr de Winter anywhere?'

'He went out soon after breakfast, Madam, before Major and Mrs Lacy were down. He has not been in since.'

'You don't know where he went?'

'No, Madam, I could not say.'

I wandered back again into the hall. I went through the drawing-room to the morning-room. Jasper rushed at me and licked my hands in a frenzy of delight as if I had been away for a long time. He had spent the evening on Clarice's bed and I had not seen him since tea-time yesterday. Perhaps the hours had been as long for him as they had for me.

I picked up the telephone and asked for the number of the estate office. Perhaps Maxim was with Frank. I felt I must speak to him, even if it was only for two minutes. I must explain to him that I had not meant to do what I had done last night. Even if I never spoke to him again, I must tell him that. The clerk answered the telephone, and told me that Maxim was not there.

'Mr Crawley is here, Mrs de Winter,' said the clerk; 'would you speak to him?' I would have refused, but he gave me no chance, and before I could put down the receiver I heard Frank's voice.

'Is anything the matter?' It was a funny way to begin a conversation. The thought flashed through my mind. He did not say good-morning, or did you sleep well? Why did he ask if something was the matter?

'Frank, it's me,' I said; 'where's Maxim?'

'I don't know, I haven't seen him. He's not been in this morning.'

'Not been to the office?'

'No.'

'Oh! Oh, well, it doesn't matter.'

'Did you see him at breakfast?' Frank said.

'No, I did not get up.'

'How did he sleep?'

I hesitated, Frank was the only person I did not mind knowing. 'He did not come to bed last night.'

There was silence at the other end of the line, as though Frank was thinking hard for an answer.

'Oh,' he said at last, very slowly. 'Oh, I see,' and then, after a minute, 'I was afraid something like that would happen.'

'Frank,' I said desperately, 'what did he say last night when everyone had gone? What did you all do?'

'I had a sandwich with Giles and Mrs Lacy,' said Frank. 'Maxim did not come. He made some excuse and went into the library.

265

I came back home almost at once. Perhaps Mrs Lacy can tell you.'

'She's gone,' I said, 'they went after breakfast. She sent up a note. She had not seen Maxim, she said.'

'Oh,' said Frank. I did not like it. I did not like the way he said it. It was sharp, ominous.

'Where do you think he's gone?' I said.

'I don't know,' said Frank; 'perhaps he's gone for a walk.' It was the sort of voice doctors used to relatives at a nursing-home when they came to inquire.

'Frank, I must see him,' I said. 'I've got to explain about last night.'

Frank did not answer. I could picture his anxious face, the lines on his forehead.

'Maxim thinks I did it on purpose,' I said, my voice breaking in spite of myself, and the tears that had blinded me last night and I had not shed came coursing down my cheeks sixteen hours too late. 'Maxim thinks I did it as a joke, a beastly damnable joke!'

'No,' said Frank. 'No.'

'He does, I tell you. You didn't see his eyes, as I did. You didn't stand beside him all the evening, watching him, as I did. He didn't speak to me, Frank. He never looked at me again. We stood there together the whole evening and we never spoke to one another.'

'There was no chance,' said Frank. 'All those people. Of course I saw, don't you think I know Maxim well enough for that? Look here . . .'

'I don't blame him,' I interrupted. 'If he believes I played that vile hideous joke he has a right to think what he likes of me, and never talk to me again, never see me again.'

'You mustn't talk like that,' said Frank. 'You don't know what you're saying. Let me come up and see you. I think I can explain.'

What was the use of Frank coming to see me, and us sitting in the morning-room together, Frank smoothing me down, Frank being tactful, Frank being kind? I did not want kindness from anybody now. It was too late.

'No,' I said. 'No, I don't want to go over it and over it again. It's happened, it can't be altered now. Perhaps it's a good thing; it's made me realize something I ought to have known before, that I ought to have suspected when I married Maxim.'

'What do you mean?' said Frank.

His voice was sharp, queer. I wondered why it should matter to him about Maxim not loving me. Why did he not want me to know?

'About him and Rebecca,' I said, and as I said her name it sounded strange and sour like a forbidden word, a relief to me no longer, not a pleasure, but hot and shaming as a sin confessed.

Frank did not answer for a moment. I heard him draw in his breath at the other end of the wire.

'What do you mean?' he said again, shorter and sharper than before. 'What do you mean?'

'He doesn't love me, he loves Rebecca,' I said. 'He's never forgotten her, he thinks about her still, night and day. He's never loved me, Frank. It's always Rebecca, Rebecca, Rebecca.'

I heard Frank give a startled cry but I did not care how much I shocked him now. 'Now you know how I feel,' I said, 'now you understand.'

'Look here,' he said; 'I've got to come and see you, I've got to, do you hear? It's vitally important; I can't talk to you down the telephone. Mrs de Winter? Mrs de Winter?'

I slammed down the receiver, and got up from the writing-desk. I did not want to see Frank. He could not help me over this. No one could help me but myself. My face was red and blotchy from crying. I walked about the room biting the corner of my handkerchief, tearing at the edge.

The feeling was strong within me that I should never see Maxim again. It was certainty, born of some strange instinct. He had gone away and would not come back. I knew in my heart that Frank believed this too and would not admit it to me on the telephone. He did not want to frighten me. If I rang him up again at the office now I should find that he had gone. The clerk would say, 'Mr Crawley has just gone out, Mrs de Winter', and I could see Frank, hatless, climbing into his small, shabby Morris, driving off in search of Maxim.

I went and stared out of the window at the little clearing where the satyr played his pipes. The rhododendrons were all over now. They would not bloom again for another year. The tall shrubs looked dark and drab now that the colour had gone. A fog was rolling up from the sea, and I could not see the woods beyond the bank. It was very hot, very oppressive. I could imagine our guests of last night saying to one another, 'What a good thing this fog kept off for yesterday, we should never have seen the fireworks.' I went out of the morning-room and through the drawing-room to the terrace. The sun had gone in now behind a wall of mist. It was as though a blight had fallen upon Manderley taking the sky away and the light of the day. One of the gardeners passed me with a barrow full of bits of paper, and litter, and the skins of fruit left on the lawns by the people last night.

'Good morning,' I said.

'Good morning, Madam.'

'I'm afraid the ball last night has made a lot of work for you,' I said.

'That's all right, Madam,' he said. 'I think everyone enjoyed themselves good and hearty, and that's the main thing, isn't it?'

'Yes, I suppose so,' I said.

He looked across the lawns to the clearing in the woods where the valley sloped to the sea. The dark trees loomed thin and indistinct.

'It's coming up very thick,' he said.

'Yes,' I said.

'A good thing it wasn't like this last night,' he said.

'Yes,' I said.

He waited a moment, and then he touched his cap and went off trundling his barrow. I went across the lawns to the edge of the woods. The mist in the trees had turned to moisture and dripped upon my bare head like a thin rain. Jasper stood by my feet dejected, his tail downcast, his pink tongue hanging from his mouth. The clammy oppression of the day made him listless and heavy. I could hear the sea from where I stood, sullen and slow, as it broke in the coves below the woods. The white fog rolled on past me towards the house smelling of damp salt and seaweed. I put my hand on Jasper's coat. It was wringing wet. When I looked back at the house I could not see the chimneys or the contour of the walls, I could only see the vague substance of the house, the windows in the west wing, and the flower tubs on the terrace. The shutter had been pulled aside from the window of the large bedroom in the west wing, and someone was standing there, looking down upon the lawns. The figure was shadowy and indistinct and for one moment of shock and fear I believed it to be Maxim. Then the figure moved, I saw the arm reach up to fold the shutter, and I knew it was Mrs Danvers. She had been watching me as I stood at the edge of the woods bathed in that white wall of fog. She had seen me walk slowly from the terrace to the lawns. She may have listened to my conversation with Frank on the telephone from the connecting line in her own room. She would know that Maxim had not been with me last night. She would have heard my voice, known about my tears. She knew the part I had played through the long hours, standing by Maxim's side in my blue dress at the bottom of the stairs, and that he had not looked at me nor spoken to me. She knew because she had meant it to happen. This was her triumph, hers and Rebecca's.

I thought of her as I had seen her last night, watching me through the open door to the west wing, and that diabolical smile on her white skull's face, and I remembered that she was a living breathing woman like myself, she was made of flesh and blood. She was not dead, like Rebecca. I could speak to her, but I could not speak to Rebecca.

I walked back across the lawns on sudden impulse to the house. I went through the hall and up the great stairs, I turned in under the archway by the gallery, I passed through the door to the west wing, and so along the dark silent corridor to Rebecca's room. I turned the handle of the door and went inside.

Mrs Danvers was still standing by the window, and the shutter was folded back.

'Mrs Danvers,' I said. 'Mrs Danvers.' She turned to look at me, and I saw her eyes were red and swollen with crying, even as mine were, and there were dark shadows in her white face.

'What is it?' she said, and her voice was thick and muffled from the tears she had shed, even as mine had been.

I had not expected to find her so. I had pictured her smiling as she had smiled last night, cruel and evil. Now she was none of these things, she was an old woman who was ill and tired.

I hesitated, my hand still on the knob of the open door, and I did not know what to say to her now or what to do.

She went on staring at me with those red, swollen eyes and I could not answer her. 'I left the menu on the desk as usual,' she said. 'Do you want something changed?' Her words gave me courage, and I left the door and came to the middle of the room.

'Mrs Danvers,' I said. 'I have not come to talk about the menu. You know that, don't you?'

She did not answer me. Her left hand opened and shut.

'You've done what you wanted, haven't you?' I said, 'you meant this to happen, didn't you? Are you pleased now? Are you happy?'

She turned her head away, and looked out of the window as she had done when I first came into the room. 'Why did you ever come here?' she said. 'Nobody wanted you at Manderley. We were all right until you came. Why did you not stay where you were out in France?'

'You seem to forget I love Mr de Winter,' I said.

'If you loved him you would never have married him,' she said.

I did not know what to say. The situation was mad, unreal. She kept talking in that choked muffled way with her head turned from me.

'I thought I hated you but I don't now,' she said; 'it seems to have spent itself, all the feeling I had.'

'Why should you hate me?' I asked; 'what have I ever done to you that you should hate me?'

'You tried to take Mrs de Winter's place,' she said.

Still she would not look at me. She stood there sullen, her head turned from me. 'I had nothing changed,' I said. 'Manderley went on as it had always been. I gave no orders, I left everything to you. I would have been friends with you, if you had let me, but you set yourself against me from the first. I saw it in your face, the moment I shook hands with you.'

She did not answer, and her hand kept opening and shutting against her dress. 'Many people marry twice, men and women,' I said. 'There are thousands of second marriages taking place every day. You talk as though my marrying Mr de Winter was a crime, a sacrilege against the dead. Haven't we as much right to be happy as anyone else?'

'Mr de Winter is not happy,' she said, turning to look at me at last; 'any fool can see that. You have only to look at his eyes. He's still in hell, and he's looked like that ever since she died.'

'It's not true,' I said. 'It's not true. He was happy when we were in France together; he was younger, much younger, and laughing and gay.'

'Well, he's a man, isn't he?' she said. 'No man denies himself on a honeymoon, does he? Mr de Winter's not forty-six yet.'

She laughed contemptuously, and shrugged her shoulders.

'How dare you speak to me like that? How dare you?' I said.

I was not afraid of her any more. I went up to her, shook her by the arm. 'You made me wear that dress last night,' I said, 'I should never have thought of it but for you. You did it because you wanted to hurt Mr de Winter, you wanted to make him suffer. Hasn't he suffered enough without your playing that vile hideous joke upon him? Do you think his agony and pain will bring Mrs de Winter back again?'

She shook herself clear of me, the angry colour flooded her dead white face. 'What do I care for his suffering?' she said, 'he's never cared about mine. How do you think I've liked it, watching you sit in her place, walk in her footsteps, touch the things that were hers? What do you think it's meant to me all these months knowing that you wrote at her desk in the morning-room, using the very pen that she used, speaking down the house telephone, where she used to speak every morning of her life to me, ever since she first came to Manderley? What do you think it meant to me to hear Frith and Robert and the rest of the servants talking about you as "Mrs de Winter"? "Mrs de Winter has gone out for a walk." "Mrs de Winter wants the car this afternoon at three o'clock." "Mrs de Winter won't be in to tea till five o'clock." And all the while my Mrs de Winter, my lady with her smile and her lovely face and brave ways, the real Mrs de Winter, lying dead and cold and forgotten in the church crypt. If he suffers then he deserves to suffer, marrying a young girl like you not ten months afterwards. Well, he's paying for it now, isn't he? I've seen his face, I've seen his eyes. He's made his own hell and there's no one but himself to thank for it. He knows she sees him, he knows she comes by night and watches him. And she doesn't come kindly, not she, not my lady. She was never one to stand mute and still and be wronged. "I'll see them in hell, Danny," she'd say, "I'll see them in hell first." "That's right, my dear," I'd tell her, "no one will put upon you. You were born into this world to take what you could out of it," and she did, she didn't care, she wasn't afraid. She had all the courage and spirit of a boy, had my Mrs de Winter. She ought to have been a boy, I often told her that. I had the care of her as a child. You knew that, didn't you?'

'No!' I said, 'no. Mrs Danvers, what's the use of all this? I don't want to hear any more, I don't want to know. Haven't I got feelings as well as you? Can't you understand what it means to me, to hear her mentioned, to stand here and listen while you tell me about her?'

She did not hear me, she went on raving like a mad woman, a fanatic, her long fingers twisting and tearing the black stuff of her dress.

'She was lovely then,' she said. 'Lovely as a picture; men turning to stare at her when she passed, and she not twelve years old. She knew then, she used to wink at me like the little devil she was. "I'm going to be a beauty, aren't I, Danny?" she said, and

"We'll see about that, my love, we'll see about that," I told her. She had all the knowledge then of a grown person; she'd enter into conversation with men and women as clever and full of tricks as someone of eighteen. She twisted her father round her little finger, and she'd have done the same with her mother, had she lived. Spirit, you couldn't beat my lady for spirit. She drove a four-in-hand on her fourteenth birthday, and her cousin, Mr Jack, got up on the box beside her and tried to take the reins from her hands. They fought it out there together, for three minutes, like a couple of wild cats, and the horses galloping to glory. She won though, my lady won. She cracked her whip over his head and down he came, head-over-heels, cursing and laughing. They were a pair, I tell you, she and Mr Jack. They sent him in the Navy, but he wouldn't stand the discipline, and I don't blame him. He had too much spirit to obey orders, like my lady.'

I watched her, fascinated, horrified; a queer ecstatic smile was on her lips, making her older than ever, making her skull's face vivid and real. 'No one got the better of her, never, never,' she said. 'She did what she liked, she lived as she liked. She had the strength of a little lion too. I remember her at sixteen getting up on one of her father's horses, a big brute of an animal too, that the groom said was too hot for her to ride. She stuck to him, all right. I can see her now, with her hair flying out behind her, slashing at him, drawing blood, digging the spurs into his side, and when she got off his back he was trembling all over, full of froth and blood. "That will teach him, won't it, Danny?" she said, and walked off to wash her hands as cool as you please. And that's how she went at life, when she grew up. I saw her, I was with her. She cared for nothing and for no one. And then she was beaten in the end. But it wasn't a man, it wasn't a woman. The sea got her. The sea was too strong for her. The sea got her in the end.'

She broke off, her mouth working strangely, and dragging at the corners. She began to cry noisily, harshly, her mouth open and her eyes dry.

273

'Mrs Danvers,' I said. 'Mrs Danvers.' I stood before her help-lessly, not knowing what to do. I mistrusted her no longer, I was afraid of her no more, but the sight of her sobbing there, dry-eyed, made me shudder, made me ill. 'Mrs Danvers,' I said, 'you're not well, you ought to be in bed. Why don't you go to your room and rest? Why don't you go to bed?'

She turned on me fiercely. 'Leave me alone, can't you?' she said. 'What's it to do with you if I show my grief? I'm not ashamed of it, I don't shut myself up in my room to cry. I don't walk up and down, up and down, in my room like Mr de Winter, with the door locked on me.'

'What do you mean?' I said. 'Mr de Winter does not do that.'

'He did,' she said, 'after she died. Up and down, up and down in the library. I heard him. I watched him too, through the key-hole, more than once. Backwards and forwards, like an animal in a cage.'

'I don't want to hear,' I said. 'I don't want to know.'

'And then you say you made him happy on his honeymoon,' she said; 'made him happy – you, a young ignorant girl, young enough to be his daughter. What do you know about life? What do you know about men? You come here and think you can take Mrs de Winter's place. You. You take my lady's place. Why, even the servants laughed at you when you came to Manderley. Even the little scullery-maid you met in the back passage there on your first morning. I wonder what Mr de Winter thought when he got you back here at Manderley, after his precious honeymoon was over. I wonder what he thought when he saw you sitting at the dining-room table for the first time.'

'You'd better stop this, Mrs Danvers,' I said; 'you'd better go to your room.'

'Go to my room,' she mimicked, 'go to my room. The mistress of the house thinks I had better go to my room. And after that, what then? You'll go running to Mr de Winter and saying, "Mrs Danvers has been unkind to me, Mrs Danvers has been rude." You'll go running to him like you did before when Mr Jack came to see me.'

'I never told him,' I said.

'That's a lie,' she said. 'Who else told him, if you didn't? No one else was here. Frith and Robert were out, and none of the other servants knew. I made up my mind then I'd teach you a lesson, and him too. Let him suffer, I say. What do I care? What's his suffering to me? Why shouldn't I see Mr Jack here at Manderley? He's the only link I have left now with Mrs de Winter. "I'll not have him here," he said. "I'm warning you, it's the last time." He's not forgotten to be jealous, has he?'

I remembered crouching in the gallery when the library door was open. I remembered Maxim's voice raised in anger, using the words that Mrs Danvers had just repeated. Jealous, Maxim jealous . . .

'He was jealous while she lived, and now he's jealous when she's dead,' said Mrs Danvers. 'He forbids Mr Jack the house now like he did then. That shows you he's not forgotten her, doesn't it? Of course he was jealous. So was I. So was everyone who knew her. She didn't care. She only laughed. "I shall live as I please, Danny," she told me, "and the whole world won't stop me." A man had only to look at her once and be mad about her. I've seen them here, staying in the house, men she'd meet up in London and bring for week-ends. She would take them bathing from the boat, she would have a picnic supper at her cottage in the cove. They made love to her of course; who would not? She laughed, she would come back and tell me what they had said, and what they'd done. She did not mind, it was like a game to her. Like a game. Who wouldn't be jealous? They were all jealous, all mad for her. Mr de Winter, Mr Jack, Mr Crawley, everyone who knew her, everyone who came to Manderley.'

'I don't want to know,' I said. 'I don't want to know.'

Mrs Danvers came close to me, she put her face near to mine. 'It's no use, is it?' she said. 'You'll never get the better of her. She's still mistress here, even if she is dead. She's the real Mrs de Winter, not you. It's you that's the shadow and the ghost. It's you that's forgotten and not wanted and pushed aside. Well, why don't you leave Manderley to her? Why don't you go?'

I backed away from her towards the window, my old fear and horror rising up in me again. She took my arm and held it like a vice.

'Why don't you go?' she said. 'We none of us want you. He doesn't want you, he never did. He can't forget her. He wants to be alone in the house again, with her. It's you that ought to be lying there in the church crypt, not her. It's you who ought to be dead, not Mrs de Winter.'

She pushed me towards the open window. I could see the terrace below me grey and indistinct in the white wall of fog. 'Look down there,' she said. 'It's easy, isn't it? Why don't you jump? It wouldn't hurt, not to break your neck. It's a quick, kind way. It's not like drowning. Why don't you try it? Why don't you go?'

The fog filled the open window, damp and clammy, it stung my eyes, it clung to my nostrils. I held on to the window-sill with my hands.

'Don't be afraid,' said Mrs Danvers. 'I won't push you. I won't stand by you. You can jump of your own accord. What's the use of your staying here at Manderley? You're not happy. Mr de Winter doesn't love you. There's not much for you to live for, is there? Why don't you jump now and have done with it? Then you won't be unhappy any more.'

I could see the flower tubs on the terrace and the blue of the hydrangeas clumped and solid. The paved stones were smooth and grey. They were not jagged and uneven. It was the fog that made them look so far away. They were not far really, the window was not so very high.

'Why don't you jump?' whispered Mrs Danvers. 'Why don't you try?'

The fog came thicker than before and the terrace was hidden from me. I could not see the flower tubs any more, nor the smooth paved stones. There was nothing but the white mist about me, smelling of sea-weed dank and chill. The only reality was the window-sill beneath my hands and the grip of Mrs Danvers on my left arm. If I jumped I should not see the stones rise up to meet me, the fog would hide them from me. The pain would be sharp and sudden as she said. The fall would break my neck. It would not be slow, like drowning. It would soon be over. And Maxim did not love me. Maxim wanted to be alone again, with Rebecca.

'Go on,' whispered Mrs Danvers. 'Go on, don't be afraid.'

I shut my eyes. I was giddy from staring down at the terrace, and my fingers ached from holding to the ledge. The mist entered my nostrils and lay upon my lips rank and sour. It was stifling, like a blanket, like an anaesthetic. I was beginning to forget about being unhappy, and about loving Maxim. I was beginning to forget Rebecca. Soon I would not have to think about Rebecca any more . . .

As I relaxed my hands and sighed, the white mist and the silence that was part of it was shattered suddenly, was rent in two by an explosion that shook the window where we stood. The glass shivered in its frame. I opened my eyes. I stared at Mrs Danvers. The burst was followed by another, and yet a third and fourth. The sound of the explosions stung the air and the birds rose unseen from the woods around the house and made an echo with their clamour.

'What is it?' I said stupidly. 'What has happened?'

Mrs Danvers relaxed her grip upon my arm. She stared out of the window into the fog. 'It's the rockets,' she said; 'there must be a ship gone ashore there in the bay.'

We listened, staring into the white fog together. And then we heard the sound of footsteps running on the terrace beneath us.

19

It was Maxim. I could not see him but I could hear his voice. He was shouting for Frith as he ran. I heard Frith answer from the hall and come out on the terrace. Their figures loomed out of the mist beneath us.

'She's ashore all right,' said Maxim. 'I was watching her from the headland and I saw her come right into the bay, and head for the reef. They'll never shift her, not with these tides. She must have mistaken the bay for Kerrith harbour. It's like a wall out there, in the bay. Tell them in the house to stand by with food and drink in case these fellows want anything, and ring through to the office to Mr Crawley and tell him what's happened. I'm going back to the cove to see if I can do anything. Get me some cigarettes, will you?'

Mrs Danvers drew back from the window. Her face was expressionless once more, the cold white mask that I knew.

'We had better go down,' she said, 'Frith will be looking for me to make arrangements. Mr de Winter may bring the men back to the house as he said. Be careful of your hands, I'm going to shut the window.' I stepped back into the room still dazed and stupid, not sure of myself or of her. I watched her close the window and fasten the shutters, and draw the curtains in their place.

'It's a good thing there is no sea running,' she said, 'there wouldn't have been much chance for them then. But on a day like this there's no danger. The owners will lose their ship, though, if she's run on the reef as Mr de Winter said.'

She glanced round the room to make certain that nothing was disarranged or out of place. She straightened the cover on the double bed. Then she went to the door and held it open for me. 'I will tell them in the kitchen to serve cold lunch in the dining-room after all,' she said, 'and then it won't matter what time you come for it. Mr de Winter may not want to rush back at one o'clock if he's busy down there in the cove.'

I stared at her blankly and then passed out of the open door, stiff and wooden like a dummy.

'When you see Mr de Winter, Madam, will you tell him it will be quite all right if he wants to bring the men back from the ship? There will be a hot meal ready for them any time.'

'Yes,' I said. 'Yes, Mrs Danvers.'

She turned her back on me and went along the corridor to the service staircase, a weird gaunt figure in her black dress, the skirt just sweeping the ground like the full, wide skirts of thirty years ago. Then she turned the corner of the corridor and disappeared.

I walked slowly along the passage to the door by the archway, my mind still blunt and slow as though I had just woken from a long sleep. I pushed through the door and went down the stairs with no set purpose before me. Frith was crossing the hall towards the dining-room. When he saw me he stopped, and waited until I came down into the hall.

'Mr de Winter was in a few moments ago, Madam,' he said. 'He took some cigarettes, and then went back again to the beach. It appears there is a ship gone ashore.'

'Yes,' I said.

'Did you hear the rockets, Madam?' said Frith.

'Yes, I heard the rockets,' I said.

'I was in the pantry with Robert, and we both thought at first that one of the gardeners had let off a firework left over from last night,' said Frith, 'and I said to Robert, "What do they want to do that for in this weather? Why don't they keep them for the kiddies on Saturday night?" And then the next one came, and then the third. "That's not fireworks," says Robert, "that's a ship in distress." "I believe you're right," I said, and I went out to the hall and there was Mr de Winter calling me from the terrace.'

'Yes,' I said.

'Well, it's hardly to be wondered at in this fog, Madam. That's what I said to Robert just now. It's difficult to find your way on the road, let alone on the water.'

'Yes,' I said.

'If you want to catch Mr de Winter he went straight across the lawn only two minutes ago,' said Frith.

'Thank you, Frith,' I said.

I went out on the terrace. I could see the trees taking shape beyond the lawns. The fog was lifting, it was rising in little clouds to the sky above. It whirled above my head in wreaths of smoke. I looked up at the windows above my head. They were tightly closed, and the shutters were fastened. They looked as though they would never open, never be thrown wide.

It was by the large window in the centre that I had stood five minutes before. How high it seemed above my head, how lofty and remote. The stones were hard and solid under my feet. I looked down at my feet and then up again to the shuttered window, and as I did so I became aware suddenly that my head was swimming and I felt hot. A little trickle of perspiration ran down the back of my neck. Black dots jumped about in the air in front of me. I went into the hall again and sat down on a chair. My hands were quite wet. I sat very still, holding my knees.

'Frith,' I called, 'Frith, are you in the dining-room?'

'Yes, Madam?' He came out at once, and crossed the hall towards me.

'Don't think me very odd, Frith, but I rather think I'd like a small glass of brandy.'

'Certainly, Madam.'

I went on holding my knees and sitting very still. He came back with a liqueur glass on a silver salver.

'Do you feel a trifle unwell, Madam?' said Frith. 'Would you like me to call Clarice?'

'No, I'll be all right, Frith,' I said. 'I felt a bit hot, that's all.'

'It's a very warm morning, Madam. Very warm indeed. Oppressive, one might almost say.'

'Yes, Frith. Very oppressive.'

I drank the brandy and put the glass back on the silver salver.

'Perhaps the sound of those rockets alarmed you,' said Frith; 'they went off so very sudden.'

'Yes, they did,' I said.

'And what with the hot morning and standing about all last night, you are not perhaps feeling quite like yourself, Madam,' said Frith.

'No, perhaps not,' I said.

'Will you lie down for half an hour? It's quite cool in the library.'

'No. No, I think I'll go out in a moment or two. Don't bother, Frith.'

'No. Very good, Madam.'

He went away and left me alone in the hall. It was quiet sitting there, quiet and cool. All trace of the party had been cleared away. It might never have happened. The hall was as it had always been, grey and silent and austere, with the portraits and the weapons on the wall. I could scarcely believe that last night I had stood there in my blue dress at the bottom of the stairs, shaking hands with five hundred people. I could not believe that there had been music-stands in the minstrel's gallery, and a band playing there, a man with a fiddle, a man with a drum. I got up and went out on to the terrace again.

The fog was rising, lifting to the tops of the trees. I could see the woods at the end of the lawns. Above my head a pale sun tried to penetrate the heavy sky. It was hotter than ever. Oppressive, as Frith had said. A bee hummed by me in search of scent, bumbling, noisy, and then creeping inside a flower was suddenly silent. On the grass banks above the lawns the gardener started his mowing machine. A startled linnet fled from the whirring blades towards the rose-garden. The gardener bent to the handles of the machine and walked slowly along the bank scattering the short-tipped grass and the pin-point daisy-heads. The smell of the sweet warm grass came towards me on the air, and the sun shone down upon me full and strong from out of the white mist. I whistled for Jasper but he did not come. Perhaps he had followed Maxim when he went down to the beach. I glanced at my watch. It was after half past twelve, nearly twenty to one. This time yesterday Maxim and I were standing with Frank in the little garden in front of his house, waiting for his house-keeper to serve lunch.

Twenty-four hours ago. They were teasing me, baiting me about my dress. 'You'll both get the surprise of your lives,' I had said.

I felt sick with shame at the memory of my words. And then I realized for the first time that Maxim had not gone away as I had feared. The voice I had heard on the terrace was calm and practical. The voice I knew. Not the voice of last night when I stood at the head of the stairs. Maxim had not gone away. He was down there in the cove somewhere. He was himself, normal and sane. He had just been for a walk, as Frank had said. He had been on the headland, he had seen the ship closing in towards the shore. All my fears were without foundation. Maxim was safe. Maxim was all right. I had just experienced something that was degrading and horrible and mad, something that I did not fully understand even now, that I had no wish to remember, that I wanted to bury for evermore, deep in the shadows of my mind with old forgotten terrors of childhood; but even this did not matter as long as Maxim was all right.

Then I, too, went down the steep twisting path through the dark woods to the beach below.

The fog had almost gone, and when I came to the cove I could see the ship at once, lying about two miles off-shore with her bows pointed towards the cliffs. I went along the breakwater and stood at the end of it, leaning against the rounded wall. There was a crowd of people on the cliffs already who must have walked along the coast-guard path from Kerrith. The cliffs and the headland were part of Manderley, but the public had always used the right-of-way along the cliffs. Some of them were scrambling down the cliff face to get a closer view of the stranded ship. She lay at an awkward angle, her stern tilted, and there were a number of rowing-boats already pulling round her. The life-boat was standing off. I saw someone stand up in her and shout through a megaphone. I could not hear what he was saying. It was still misty out in the bay, and I could not see the horizon. Another motor-boat chugged into the light with some men aboard. The motor-boat was dark grey. I could see someone in uniform. That would be the harbour-master from Kerrith, and the Lloyd's agent with him. Another motor-boat followed, a party of holiday-makers from Kerrith aboard. They circled round and round the stranded steamer chatting excitedly. I could hear their voices echoing across the still water.

I left the breakwater and the cove and climbed up the path over the cliffs towards the rest of the people. I did not see Maxim anywhere. Frank was there, talking to one of the coast-guards. I hung back when I saw him, momentarily embarrassed. Barely an hour ago I had been crying to him, down the telephone. I was not sure what I ought to do. He saw me at once and waved his hand. I went over to him and the coast-guard. The coast-guard knew me.

'Come to see the fun, Mrs de Winter?' he said smiling. 'I'm afraid it will be a hard job. The tugs may shift her, but I doubt it. She's hard and fast where she is on that ledge.'

'What will they do?' I said.

'They'll send a diver down directly to see if she's broken her back,' he replied. 'There's the fellow there in the red stocking cap. Like to see through these glasses?'

I took his glasses and looked at the ship. I could see a group of men staring over her stern. One of them was pointing at something. The man in the life-boat was still shouting through the megaphone.

The harbour-master from Kerrith had joined the group of men in the stern of the stranded ship. The diver in his stocking cap was sitting in the grey motor-boat belonging to the harbour-master.

The pleasure-boat was still circling round the ship. A woman was standing up taking a snapshot. A group of gulls had settled on the water and were crying foolishly, hoping for scraps.

I gave the glasses back to the coast-guard.

'Nothing seems to be happening,' I said.

'They'll send him down directly,' said the coast-guard. 'They'll argue a bit first, like all foreigners. Here come the tugs.'

'They'll never do it,' said Frank. 'Look at the angle she's lying at. It's much shallower there than I thought.'

'That reef runs out quite a way,' said the coast-guard; 'you don't notice it in the ordinary way, going over that piece of water in a small boat. But a ship with her depth would touch all right.'

'I was down in the first cove by the valley when they fired the rockets,' said Frank. 'I could scarcely see three yards in front of me where I was. And then the things went off out of the blue.'

I thought how alike people were in a moment of common interest. Frank was Frith all over again, giving his version of the story, as though it mattered, as though we cared. I knew that he had gone down to the beach to look for Maxim. I knew that he had been frightened, as I had been. And now all this was forgotten and put aside: our conversation down the telephone, our mutual anxiety, his insistence that he must see me. All because a ship had gone ashore in the fog.

A small boy came running up to us. 'Will the sailors be drowned?' he asked.

'Not them. They're all right, sonny,' said the coast-guard. 'The sea's as flat as the back of my hand. No one's going to be hurt this time.'

'If it had happened last night we should never have heard them,' said Frank. 'We must have let off more than fifty rockets at our show, beside all the smaller things.'

'We'd have heard all right,' said the coast-guard. 'We'd have seen the flash and known the direction. There's the diver, Mrs de Winter. See him putting on his helmet?'

'I want to see the diver,' said the small boy.

'There he is,' said Frank, bending and pointing – 'that chap there putting on the helmet. They're going to lower him into the water.'

'Won't he be drowned?' said the child.

'Divers don't drown,' said the coast-guard. 'They have air pumped into them all the time. Watch him disappear. There he goes.'

The surface of the water was disturbed a minute and then was clear again. 'He's gone,' said the small boy.

'Where's Maxim?' I said.

'He's taken one of the crew into Kerrith,' said Frank; 'the fellow lost his head and jumped for it apparently when the ship struck. We found him clinging on to one of the rocks here under the cliff. He was soaked to the skin of course and shaking like a jelly. Couldn't speak a word of English, of course. Maxim went down to him, and found him bleeding like a pig from a scratch on the rocks. He spoke to him in German. Then he hailed one of the motor-boats from Kerrith that was hanging around like a hungry shark, and he's gone off with him to get him bandaged by a doctor. If he's lucky he'll just catch old Phillips sitting down to lunch.'

'When did he go?' I said.

'He went just before you turned up,' said Frank, 'about five minutes ago. I wonder you didn't see the boat. He was sitting in the stern with this German fellow.'

'He must have gone while I was climbing up the cliff,' I said.

'Maxim is splendid at anything like this,' said Frank. 'He always gives a hand if he can. You'll find he will invite the whole crew back to Manderley, and feed them, and give them beds into the bargain.'

'That's right,' said the coast-guard. 'He'd give the coat off his back for any of his own people, I know that. I wish there was more like him in the county.'

'Yes, we could do with them,' said Frank.

We went on staring at the ship. The tugs were standing off still, but the life-boat had turned and gone back towards Kerrith.

'It's not their turn today,' said the coast-guard.

'No,' said Frank, 'and I don't think it's a job for the tugs either. It's the ship-breaker who's going to make money this time.'

The gulls wheeled overhead, mewing like hungry cats; some of them settled on the ledges of the cliff, while others, bolder, rode the surface of the water beside the ship.

The coast-guard took off his cap and mopped his forehead.

'Seems kind of airless, doesn't it?' he said.

'Yes,' I said.

The pleasure-boat with the camera people went chugging off towards Kerrith. 'They've got fed up,' said the coast-guard.

'I don't blame them,' said Frank. 'I don't suppose anything will happen for hours. The diver will have to make his report before they try to shift her.'

'That's right,' said the coast-guard.

'I don't think there's much sense in hanging about here,' said Frank; 'we can't do anything. I want my lunch.'

I did not say anything. He hesitated. I felt his eyes upon me.

'What are you going to do?' he said.

'I think I shall stay here a bit,' I said. 'I can have lunch any time. It's cold. It doesn't matter. I want to see what the diver's going to do.' Somehow I could not face Frank just at the moment. I wanted to be alone, or with someone I did not know, like the coast-guard.

'You won't see anything,' said Frank; 'there won't be anything to see. Why not come back and have some lunch with me?'

'No,' I said. 'No, really . . .'

'Oh, well,' said Frank, 'you know where to find me if you do want me. I shall be at the office all the afternoon.'

'All right,' I said.

He nodded to the coast-guard and went off down the cliff towards the cove. I wondered if I had offended him. I could not help it. All these things would be settled some day, one day. So much seemed to have happened since I spoke to him on the telephone, and I did not want to think about anything any more. I just wanted to sit there on the cliff and stare at the ship.

'He's a good sort, Mr Crawley,' said the coast-guard.

'Yes,' I said.

'He'd give his right hand for Mr de Winter too,' he said.

'Yes, I think he would,' I said.

The small boy was still hopping around on the grass in front of us.

'When's the diver coming up again?' he said.

'Not yet, sonny,' said the coast-guard.

A woman in a pink striped frock and a hair-net came across the grass towards us. 'Charlie? Charlie? Where are you?' she called.

'Here's your mother coming to give you what-for,' said the coast-guard.

'I've seen the diver, Mum,' shouted the boy.

The woman nodded to us and smiled. She did not know me. She was a holiday-maker from Kerrith. 'The excitement all seems to be over doesn't it?' she said; 'they are saying down on the cliff there the ship will be there for days.'

'They're waiting for the diver's report,' said the coast-guard.

'I don't know how they get them to go down under the water like that,' said the woman; 'they ought to pay them well.'

'They do that,' said the coast-guard.

'I want to be a diver, Mum,' said the small boy.

'You must ask your Daddy, dear,' said the woman, laughing at us. 'It's a lovely spot up here, isn't it?' she said to me. 'We brought a picnic lunch, never thinking it would turn foggy and we'd have a wreck into the bargain. We were just thinking of going back to Kerrith when the rockets went off under our noses, it seemed. I nearly jumped out of my skin. "Why, whatever's that?" I said to my husband. "That's a distress signal," he said; "let's stop and see the fun." There's no dragging him away; he's as bad as my little boy. I don't see anything in it myself.'

'No, there's not much to see now,' said the coast-guard.

'Those are nice-looking woods over there; I suppose they're private,' said the woman.

The coast-guard coughed awkwardly, and glanced at me. I began eating a piece of grass and looked away.

'Yes, that's all private in there,' he said.

'My husband says all these big estates will be chopped up in time and bungalows built,' said the woman. 'I wouldn't mind a nice little bungalow up here facing the sea. I don't know that I'd care for this part of the world in the winter though.'

'No, it's very quiet here winter times,' said the coast-guard.

I went on chewing my piece of grass. The little boy kept running round in circles. The coast-guard looked at his watch. 'Well, I must be getting on,' he said; 'good afternoon!' He saluted me, and turned back along the path towards Kerrith. 'Come on, Charlie, come and find Daddy,' said the woman.

She nodded to me in friendly fashion, and sauntered off to the edge of the cliff, the little boy running at her heels. A thin man in khaki shorts and a striped blazer waved to her. They sat down by a clump of gorse bushes and the woman began to undo paper packages.

I wished I could lose my own identity and join them. Eat hard-boiled eggs and potted meat sandwiches, laugh rather loudly, enter their conversation, and then wander back with them during the afternoon to Kerrith and paddle on the beach, run races across the stretch of sand, and so to their lodgings and have shrimps for tea. Instead of which I must go back alone through the woods to Manderley and wait for Maxim. And I did not know what we should say to one another, how he would look at me, what would be his voice. I went on sitting there on the cliff. I was not hungry. I did not think about lunch.

More people came and wandered over the cliffs to look at the ship. It made an excitement for the afternoon. There was nobody I knew. They were all holiday-makers from Kerrith. The sea was glassy calm. The gulls no longer wheeled overhead, they had settled on the water a little distance from the ship. More pleasure boats appeared during the afternoon. It must be a field day for Kerrith boat-men. The diver came up and then went down again. One of the tugs steamed away while the other still stood by. The harbour-master went back in his grey motor-boat, taking some men with him, and the diver who had come to the surface for the second time. The crew of the ship leant against the side throwing scraps to the gulls, while visitors in pleasure-boats rowed slowly round the ship. Nothing happened at all. It was dead low water now, and the ship was heeled at an angle, the propeller showing clean. Little ridges of white cloud formed in the western sky and the sun became pallid. It was still very hot. The woman in the pink striped frock with the little boy got up and wandered off along the path towards Kerrith, the man in the shorts following with the picnic basket.

I glanced at my watch. It was after three o'clock. I got up and went down the hill to the cove. It was quiet and deserted as always. The shingle was dark and grey. The water in the little harbour was glassy like a mirror. My feet made a queer crunching noise as I crossed the shingle. The ridges of white cloud now covered all the sky above my head, and the sun was hidden. When I came to the further side of the cove I saw Ben crouching by a little pool between two rocks scraping winkles into his hand. My shadow fell upon the water as I passed, and he looked up and saw me.

'G' day,' he said, his mouth opening in a grin.

'Good afternoon,' I said.

He scrambled to his feet and opened a dirty handkerchief he had filled with winkles.

'You eat winkles?' he said.

I did not want to hurt his feelings. 'Thank you,' I said.

He emptied about a dozen winkles into my hand, and I put them in the two pockets of my skirt. 'They'm all right with bread-an'-butter,' he said, 'you must boil 'em first.'

'Yes, all right,' I said.

He stood there grinning at me. 'Seen the steamer?' he said.

'Yes,' I said, 'she's gone ashore, hasn't she?'

'Eh?' he said.

'She's run aground,' I repeated. 'I expect she's got a hole in her bottom.'

His face went blank and foolish. 'Aye,' he said, 'she's down there all right. She'll not come back again.'

'Perhaps the tugs will get her off when the tide makes,' I said.

He did not answer. He was staring out towards the stranded ship. I could see her broadside on from here, the red underwater

289

section showing against the black of the top-sides, and the single funnel leaning rakishly towards the cliffs beyond. The crew were still leaning over her side feeding the gulls and staring into the water. The rowing boats were pulling back to Kerrith.

'She's a Dutchman, ain't she?' said Ben.

'I don't know,' I said. 'German or Dutch.'

'She'll break up there where she's to,' he said.

'I'm afraid so,' I said.

He grinned again, and wiped his nose with the back of his hand.

'She'll break up bit by bit,' he said, 'she'll not sink like a stone like the little 'un.' He chuckled to himself, picking his nose. I did not say anything. 'The fishes have eaten her up by now, haven't they?' he said.

'Who?' I said.

He jerked his thumb towards the sea. 'Her,' he said, 'the other one.'

'Fishes don't eat steamers, Ben,' I said.

'Eh?' he said. He stared at me, foolish and blank once more.

'I must go home now,' I said; 'good-afternoon.'

I left him and walked towards the path through the woods. I did not look at the cottage. I was aware of it on my right hand; grey and quiet. I went straight to the path and up through the trees. I paused to rest half-way and looking through the trees I could still see the stranded ship leaning towards the shore. The pleasure boats had all gone. Even the crew had disappeared below. The ridges of cloud covered the whole sky. A little wind sprang from nowhere and blew into my face. A leaf fell onto my hand from the tree above. I shivered for no reason. Then the wind went again, it was hot and sultry as before. The ship looked desolate there upon her side, with no one on her decks, and her thin black funnel pointing to the shore. The sea was so calm that when it broke upon the shingle in the cove it was like a whisper, hushed and still. I turned once more to the steep path through the woods, my legs reluctant, my head heavy, a strange sense of foreboding in my heart.

The house looked very peaceful as I came upon it from the woods and crossed the lawns. It seemed sheltered and protected, more beautiful than I had ever seen it. Standing there, looking down upon it from the banks, I realized, perhaps for the first time, with a funny feeling of bewilderment and pride that it was my home, I belonged there, and Manderley belonged to me. The trees and the grass and the flower tubs on the terrace were reflected in the mullioned windows. A thin column of smoke rose in the air from one of the chimneys. The new-cut grass on the lawn smelt sweet as hay. A blackbird was singing on the chestnut tree. A yellow butterfly winged his foolish way before me to the terrace.

I went into the hall and through to the dining-room. My place was still laid, but Maxim's had been cleared away. The cold meat and salad awaited me on the sideboard. I hesitated, and then rang the dining-room bell. Robert came in from behind the screen.

'Has Mr de Winter been in?' I said.

'Yes, Madam,' said Robert; 'he came in just after two, and had a quick lunch, and then went out again. He asked for you and Frith said he thought you must have gone down to see the ship.'

'Did he say when he would be back again?' I asked.

'No, Madam.'

'Perhaps he went to the beach another way,' I said; 'I may have missed him.'

'Yes, Madam,' said Robert.

I looked at the cold meat and the salad. I felt empty but not hungry. I did not want cold meat now. 'Will you be taking lunch?' said Robert.

'No,' I said, 'No, you might bring me some tea, Robert, in the library. Nothing like cakes or scones. Just tea and bread-and-butter.'

'Yes, Madam.'

I went and sat on the window-seat in the library. It seemed funny without Jasper. He must have gone with Maxim. The old dog lay asleep in her basket. I picked up *The Times* and turned the pages without reading it. It was queer this feeling of marking time, like sitting in a waiting-room at a dentist's. I knew I should never settle to my knitting or to a book. I was waiting for something to happen, something unforeseen. The horror of my morning and the stranded ship and not having any lunch had all combined to give birth to a latent sense of excitement at the back of my mind that I did not understand. It was as though I had entered into a new phase of my life and nothing would be quite the same again. The girl who had dressed for the fancy dress ball the night before had been left behind. It had all happened a very long time ago. This self who sat on the window-seat was new, was different ... Robert brought in my tea, and I ate my bread-and-butter hungrily. He had brought scones as well, and some sandwiches, and an angel cake. He must have thought it derogatory to bring bread-and-butter alone, nor was it Manderley routine. I was glad of the scones and the angel cake. I remembered I had only had cold tea at half past eleven, and no breakfast. Just after I had drunk my third cup Robert came in again.

'Mr de Winter is not back yet is he, Madam?' he said.

'No,' I said. 'Why? Does someone want him?'

'Yes, Madam,' said Robert, 'it's Captain Searle, the harbour-master of Kerrith, on the telephone. He wants to know if he can come up and see Mr de Winter personally.'

'I don't know what to say,' I said. 'He may not be back for ages.'

'No, Madam.'

'You'd better tell him to ring again at five o'clock,' I said. Robert went out of the room and came back again in a few minutes.

'Captain Searle would like to see you, if it would be convenient, Madam,' said Robert. 'He says the matter is rather urgent. He tried to get Mr Crawley, but there was no reply.'

'Yes, of course I must see him if it's urgent,' I said. 'Tell him to come along at once if he likes. Has he got a car?'

'Yes, I believe so, Madam.'

Robert went out of the room. I wondered what I should say to Captain Searle. His business must be something to do with the stranded ship. I could not understand what concern it was of Maxim's. It would have been different if the ship had gone ashore in the cove. That was Manderley property. They might have to ask Maxim's permission to blast away rocks or whatever it was that was done to move a ship. But the open bay and the ledge of rock under the water did not belong to Maxim. Captain Searle would waste his time talking to me about it all.

He must have got into his car right away after talking to Robert because in less than quarter of an hour he was shown into the room.

He was still in his uniform as I had seen him through the glasses in the early afternoon. I got up from the window-seat and shook hands with him. 'I'm sorry my husband isn't back yet, Captain Searle,' I said; 'he must have gone down to the cliffs again, and he went into Kerrith before that. I haven't seen him all day.'

'Yes, I heard he'd been to Kerrith but I missed him there,' said the harbour-master. 'He must have walked back across the cliffs when I was in my boat. And I can't get hold of Mr Crawley either.'

'I'm afraid the ship has disorganized everybody,' I said. 'I was out on the cliffs and went without my lunch, and I know Mr Crawley was there earlier on. What will happen to her? Will tugs get her off, do you think?'

Captain Searle made a great circle with his hands. 'There's a hole that deep in her bottom,' he said, 'she'll not see Hamburg again. Never mind the ship. Her owner and Lloyd's agent will settle that between them. No, Mrs de Winter, it's not the ship that's brought me here. Indirectly of course she's the cause of my coming. The fact is, I've got some news for Mr de Winter, and I hardly know how to break it to him.' He looked at me very straight with his bright blue eyes.

'What sort of news, Captain Searle?'

He brought a large white handkerchief out of his pocket and

293

blew his nose. 'Well, Mrs de Winter, it's not very pleasant for me to tell you either. The last thing I want to do is to cause distress or pain to you and your husband. We're all very fond of Mr de Winter in Kerrith, you know, and the family has always done a lot of good. It's hard on him and hard on you that we can't let the past lie quiet. But I don't see how we can under the circumstances.' He paused, and put his handkerchief back in his pocket. He lowered his voice, although we were alone in the room.

'We sent the diver down to inspect the ship's bottom,' he said, 'and while he was down there he made a discovery. It appears he found the hole in the ship's bottom and was working round to the other side to see what further damage there was when he came across the hull of a little sailing boat, lying on her side, quite intact and not broken up at all. He's a local man, of course, and he recognized the boat at once. It was the little boat belonging to the late Mrs de Winter.'

My first feeling was one of thankfulness that Maxim was not there to hear. This fresh blow coming swiftly upon my masquerade of the night before was ironic, and rather horrible.

'I'm so sorry,' I said slowly, 'it's not the sort of thing one expected would happen. Is it necessary to tell Mr de Winter? Couldn't the boat be left there, as it is? It's not doing any harm, is it?'

'It would be left, Mrs de Winter, in the ordinary way. I'm the last man in the world to want to disturb it. And I'd give anything, as I said before, to spare Mr de Winter's feelings. But that wasn't all, Mrs de Winter. My man poked round the little boat and he made another, more important discovery. The cabin door was tightly closed, it was not stove in, and the portlights were closed too. He broke one of the ports with a stone from the sea bed, and looked into the cabin. It was full of water, the sea must have come through some hole in the bottom, there seemed no damage elsewhere. And then he got the fright of his life, Mrs de Winter.'

Captain Searle paused, he looked over his shoulder as though one of the servants might hear him. 'There was a body in there, lying on the cabin floor,' he said quietly. 'It was dissolved of course, there was no flesh on it. But it was a body all right. He saw the head and the limbs. He came up to the surface then and reported it direct to me. And now you understand, Mrs de Winter, why I've got to see your husband.'

I stared at him, bewildered at first, then shocked, then rather sick.

'She was supposed to be sailing alone?' I whispered, 'there must have been someone with her then, all the time, and no one ever knew?'

'It looks like it,' said the harbour-master.

'Who could it have been?' I said. 'Surely relatives would know if anyone had been missing? There was so much about it at the time, it was all in the papers. Why should one of them be in the cabin and Mrs de Winter herself be picked up many miles away, months afterwards?'

Captain Searle shook his head. 'I can't tell any more than you,' he said. 'All we know is that the body is there, and it has got to be reported. There'll be publicity, I'm afraid, Mrs de Winter. I don't know how we're going to avoid it. It's very hard on you and Mr de Winter. Here you are, settled down quietly, wanting to be happy, and this has to happen.'

I knew now the reason for my sense of foreboding. It was not the stranded ship that was sinister, nor the crying gulls, nor the thin black funnel pointing to the shore. It was the stillness of the black water, and the unknown things that lay beneath. It was the diver going down into those cool quiet depths and stumbling upon Rebecca's boat, and Rebecca's dead companion. He had touched the boat, had looked into the cabin, and all the while I sat on the cliffs and had not known.

'If only we did not have to tell him,' I said. 'If only we could keep the whole thing from him.'

'You know I would if it were possible, Mrs de Winter,' said the harbour-master, 'but my personal feelings have to go, in a matter like this. I've got to do my duty. I've got to report that body.' He broke off short as the door opened, and Maxim came into the room.

'Hullo,' he said, 'what's happening? I didn't know you were here, Captain Searle? Is anything the matter?'

I could not stand it any longer. I went out of the room like the coward I was and shut the door behind me. I had not even glanced at Maxim's face. I had the vague impression that he looked tired, untidy, hatless.

I went and stood in the hall by the front door. Jasper was drinking noisily from his bowl. He wagged his tail when he saw me and went on drinking. Then he loped towards me, and stood up, pawing at my dress. I kissed the top of his head and went and sat on the terrace. The moment of crisis had come, and I must face it. My old fears, my diffidence, my shyness, my hopeless sense of inferiority, must be conquered now and thrust aside. If I failed now I should fail for ever. There would never be another chance. I prayed for courage in a blind despairing way, and dug my nails into my hands. I sat there for five minutes staring at the green lawns and the flower tubs on the terrace. I heard the sound of a car starting up in the drive. It must be Captain Searle. He had broken his news to Maxim and had gone. I got up from the terrace and went slowly through the hall to the library. I kept turning over in my pockets the winkles that Ben had given me. I clutched them tight in my hands.

Maxim was standing by the window. His back was turned to me. I waited by the door. Still he did not turn round. I took my hands out of my pockets and went and stood beside him. I reached out for his hand and laid it against my cheek. He did not say anything. He went on standing there.

'I'm so sorry,' I whispered, 'so terribly, terribly sorry.' He did not answer. His hand was icy cold. I kissed the back of it, and then the fingers, one by one. 'I don't want you to bear this alone,' I said. 'I want to share it with you. I've grown up, Maxim, in twenty-four hours. I'll never be a child again.'

He put his arm round me and pulled me to him very close. My reserve was broken, and my shyness too. I stood there with my face against his shoulder. 'You've forgiven me, haven't you?' I said.

He spoke to me at last. 'Forgiven you?' he said. 'What have I got to forgive you for?'

'Last night,' I said; 'you thought I did it on purpose.'

'Ah, that,' he said. 'I'd forgotten. I was angry with you, wasn't I?'

'Yes,' I said.

He did not say any more. He went on holding me close to his shoulder. 'Maxim,' I said, 'can't we start all over again? Can't we begin from today, and face things together? I don't want you to love me, I won't ask impossible things. I'll be your friend and your companion, a sort of boy. I don't ever want more than that.'

He took my face between his hands and looked at me. For the first time I saw how thin his face was, how lined and drawn. And there were great shadows beneath his eyes.

'How much do you love me?' he said.

I could not answer. I could only stare back at him, at his dark tortured eyes, and his pale drawn face.

'It's too late, my darling, too late,' he said. 'We've lost our little chance of happiness.'

'No, Maxim. No,' I said.

'Yes,' he said. 'It's all over now. The thing has happened.'

'What thing?' I said.

'The thing I've always foreseen. The thing I've dreamt about, day after day, night after night. We're not meant for happiness, you and I.' He sat down on the window-seat, and I knelt in front of him, my hands on his shoulders.

'What are you trying to tell me?' I said.

He put his hands over mine and looked into my face. 'Rebecca has won,' he said.

I stared at him, my heart beating strangely, my hands suddenly cold beneath his hands.

'Her shadow between us all the time,' he said. 'Her damned shadow keeping us from one another. How could I hold you like this, my darling, my little love, with the fear always in my heart that this would happen? I remembered her eyes as she looked at me before she died. I remembered that slow treacherous smile.

297

She knew this would happen even then. She knew she would win in the end.'

'Maxim,' I whispered, 'what are you saying, what are you trying to tell me?'

'Her boat,' he said, 'they've found it. The diver found it this afternoon.'

'Yes,' I said. 'I know. Captain Searle came to tell me. You are thinking about the body, aren't you, the body the diver found in the cabin?'

'Yes,' he said.

'It means she was not alone,' I said. 'It means there was somebody sailing with Rebecca at the time. And you have to find out who it was. That's it, isn't it, Maxim?'

'No,' he said. 'No, you don't understand.'

'I want to share this with you, darling,' I said. 'I want to help you.'

'There was no one with Rebecca, she was alone,' he said.

I knelt there watching his face, watching his eyes.

'It's Rebecca's body lying there on the cabin floor,' he said.

'No,' I said. 'No.'

'The woman buried in the crypt is not Rebecca,' he said. 'It's the body of some unknown woman, unclaimed, belonging nowhere. There never was an accident. Rebecca was not drowned at all. I killed her. I shot Rebecca in the cottage in the cove. I carried her body to the cabin, and took the boat out that night and sunk it there, where they found it today. It's Rebecca who's lying dead there on the cabin floor. Will you look into my eyes and tell me that you love me now?'

20

It was very quiet in the library. The only sound was that of Jasper licking his foot. He must have caught a thorn in his pads, for he kept biting and sucking at the skin. Then I heard the watch on Maxim's wrist ticking close to my ear. The little normal sounds of every day. And for no reason the stupid proverb of my schooldays ran through my mind, 'Time and Tide wait for no man.' The words repeated themselves over and over again. 'Time and Tide wait for no man.' These were the only sounds then, the ticking of Maxim's watch and Jasper licking his foot on the floor beside me.

When people suffer a great shock, like death, or the loss of a limb, I believe they don't feel it just at first. If your hand is taken from you you don't know, for a few minutes, that your hand is gone. You go on feeling the fingers. You stretch and beat them on the air, one by one, and all the time there is nothing there, no hand, no fingers. I knelt there by Maxim's side, my body against his body, my hands upon his shoulders, and I was aware of no feeling at all, no pain and no fear, there was no horror in my heart. I thought how I must take the thorn out of Jasper's foot and I wondered if Robert would come in and clear the tea-things. It seemed strange to me that I should think of these things, Jasper's foot, Maxim's watch, Robert and the tea things. I was shocked at my lack of emotion and this queer cold absence of distress. Little by little the feeling will come back to me, I said to myself, little by little I shall understand. What he has told me and all that has happened will tumble into place like pieces of a jig-saw puzzle. They will fit themselves into a pattern. At the moment I am nothing, I have no heart, and no mind, and no senses, I am just a wooden thing in Maxim's arms.

Then he began to kiss me. He had not kissed me like this before. I put my hands behind his head and shut my eyes.

'I love you so much,' he whispered. 'So much.'

This is what I have wanted him to say every day and every night, I thought, and now he is saying it at last. This is what I imagined in Monte Carlo, in Italy, here in Manderley. He is saying it now. I opened my eyes and looked at a little patch of curtain above his head. He went on kissing me, hungry, desperate, murmuring my name. I kept on looking at the patch of curtain, and saw where the sun had faded it, making it lighter than the piece above. 'How calm I am,' I thought. 'How cool. Here I am looking at the piece of curtain, and Maxim is kissing me. For the first time he is telling me he loves me.'

Then he stopped suddenly, he pushed me away from him, and got up from the window-seat. 'You see, I was right,' he said. 'It's too late. You don't love me now. Why should you?' He went and stood over by the mantelpiece. 'We'll forget that,' he said, 'it won't happen again.'

Realization flooded me at once, and my heart jumped in quick and sudden panic. 'It's not too late,' I said swiftly, getting up from the floor and going to him, putting my arms about him; 'you're not to say that, you don't understand. I love you more than anything in the world. But when you kissed me just now I felt stunned and shaken. I could not feel anything. I could not grasp anything. It was just as though I had no more feeling left in me at all.'

'You don't love me,' he said, 'that's why you did not feel anything. I know. I understand. It's come too late for you, hasn't it?'

'No,' I said.

'This ought to have happened four months ago,' he said. 'I should have known. Women are not like men.'

'I want you to kiss me again,' I said; 'please, Maxim.'

'No,' he said, 'it's no use now.'

'We can't lose each other now,' I said. 'We've got to be together always, with no secrets, no shadows. Please, darling, please.'

'There's no time,' he said. 'We may only have a few hours, a few days. How can we be together now that this has happened? I've told you they've found the boat. They've found Rebecca.'

I stared at him stupidly, not understanding. 'What will they do?' I said.

'They'll identify her body,' he said, 'there's everything to tell them, there in the cabin. The clothes she had, the shoes, the rings on her fingers. They'll identify her body; and then they will remember the other one, the woman buried up there, in the crypt.'

'What are you going to do?' I whispered.

'I don't know,' he said. 'I don't know.'

The feeling was coming back to me, little by little, as I knew it would. My hands were cold no longer. They were clammy, warm. I felt a wave of colour come into my face, my throat. My cheeks were burning hot. I thought of Captain Searle, the diver, the Lloyd's agent, all those men on the stranded ship leaning against the side, staring down into the water. I thought of the shopkeepers in Kerrith, of errand boys whistling in the street, of the vicar walking out of church, of Lady Crowan cutting roses in her garden, of the woman in the pink dress and her little boy on the cliffs. Soon they would know. In a few hours. By breakfast time tomorrow. 'They've found Mrs de Winter's boat, and they say there is a body in the cabin.' A body in the cabin. Rebecca was lying there on the cabin floor. She was not in the crypt at all. Some other woman was lying in the crypt. Maxim had killed Rebecca. Rebecca had not been drowned at all. Maxim had killed her. He had shot her in the cottage in the woods. He had carried her body to the boat, and sunk the boat there in the bay. That grey, silent cottage, with the rain pattering on the roof. The jig-saw pieces came tumbling thick and fast upon me. Disjointed pictures flashed one by one through my bewildered mind. Maxim sitting in the car beside me in the south of France. 'Something happened nearly a year ago that altered my whole life. I had to begin living all over again . . .' Maxim's silence, Maxim's moods. The way he never

301

talked about Rebecca. The way he never mentioned her name. Maxim's dislike of the cove, the stone cottage. 'If you had my memories you would not go there either.' The way he climbed the path through the woods not looking behind him. Maxim pacing up and down the library after Rebecca died. Up and down. Up and down. 'I came away in rather a hurry,' he said to Mrs Van Hopper, a line, thin as gossamer, between his brows. 'They say he can't get over his wife's death.' The fancy dress dance last night, and I coming down to the head of the stairs, in Rebecca's dress. 'I killed Rebecca,' Maxim had said. 'I shot Rebecca in the cottage in the woods.' and the diver had found her lying there, on the cabin floor . . .

'What are we going to do?' I said. 'What are we going to say?'

Maxim did not answer. He stood there by the mantelpiece, his eyes wide and staring, looking in front of him, not seeing anything.

'Does anyone know?' I said, 'anyone at all?'

He shook his head. 'No,' he said.

'No one but you and me?' I asked.

'No one but you and me,' he said.

'Frank,' I said suddenly, 'are you sure Frank does not know?'

'How could he?' said Maxim. 'There was nobody there but myself. It was dark . . .' He stopped. He sat down on a chair, he put his hand up to his forehead. I went and knelt beside him. He sat very still a moment. I took his hands away from his face and looked into his eyes. 'I love you,' I whispered, 'I love you. Will you believe me now?' He kissed my face and my hands. He held my hands very tightly like a child who would gain confidence.

'I thought I should go mad,' he said, 'sitting here, day after day, waiting for something to happen. Sitting down at the desk there, answering those terrible letters of sympathy. The notices in the papers, the interviews, all the little aftermath of death. Eating and drinking, trying to be normal, trying to be sane. Frith, the servants, Mrs Danvers. Mrs Danvers, who I had not the courage to turn away, because with her knowledge of

302

Rebecca she might have suspected, she might have guessed . . . Frank, always by my side, discreet, sympathetic. "Why don't you get away?" he used to say, "I can manage here. You ought to get away." And Giles, and Bee, poor dear tactless Bee. "You're looking frightfully ill, can't you go and see a doctor?" I had to face them all, these people, knowing every word I uttered was a lie.'

I went on holding his hands very tight. I leant close to him, quite close. 'I nearly told you, once,' he said, 'that day Jasper ran to the cove, and you went to the cottage for some string. We were sitting here, like this, and then Frith and Robert came in with the tea.'

'Yes,' I said. 'I remember. Why didn't you tell me? The time we've wasted when we might have been together. All these weeks and days.'

'You were so aloof,' he said, 'always wandering into the garden with Jasper, going off on your own. You never came to me like this.'

'Why didn't you tell me?' I whispered. 'Why didn't you tell me?'

'I thought you were unhappy, bored,' he said. 'I'm so much older than you. You seemed to have more to say to Frank than you ever had to me. You were funny with me, awkward, shy.'

'How could I come to you when I knew you were thinking about Rebecca?' I said. 'How could I ask you to love me when I knew you loved Rebecca still?'

He pulled me close to him and searched my eyes.

'What are you talking about? What do you mean?' he said.

I knelt up straight beside him. 'Whenever you touched me I thought you were comparing me to Rebecca,' I said. 'Whenever you spoke to me or looked at me, walked with me in the garden, sat down to dinner, I felt you were saying to yourself, "This I did with Rebecca, and this, and this."' He stared at me bewildered as though he did not understand.

'It was true, wasn't it?' I said.

'Oh, my God,' he said. He pushed me away, he got up and began walking up and down the room, clasping his hands.

'What is it? What's the matter?' I said.

He whipped round and looked at me as I sat there huddled on the floor. 'You thought I loved Rebecca?' he said. 'You thought I killed her, loving her? I hated her, I tell you. Our marriage was a farce from the very first. She was vicious, damnable, rotten through and through. We never loved each other, never had one moment of happiness together. Rebecca was incapable of love, of tenderness, of decency. She was not even normal.'

I sat on the floor, clasping my knees, staring at him.

'She was clever of course,' he said. 'Damnably clever. No one would guess meeting her that she was not the kindest, most generous, most gifted person in the world. She knew exactly what to say to different people, how to match her mood to theirs. Had she met you, she would have walked off into the garden with you, arm-in-arm, calling to Jasper, chatting about flowers, music, painting, whatever she knew to be your particular hobby; and you would have been taken in, like the rest. You would have sat at her feet and worshipped her.'

Up and down he walked, up and down across the library floor.

'When I married her I was told I was the luckiest man in the world,' he said. 'She was so lovely, so accomplished, so amusing. Even Gran, the most difficult person to please in those days, adored her from the first. "She's got the three things that matter in a wife," she told me: "breeding, brains, and beauty." And I believed her, or forced myself to believe her. But all the time I had a seed of doubt at the back of my mind. There was something about her eyes . . .'

The jig-saw pieces came together piece by piece, the real Rebecca took shape and form before me, stepping from her shadow world like a living figure from a picture frame. Rebecca slashing at her horse; Rebecca seizing life with her two hands; Rebecca, triumphant, leaning down from the minstrel's gallery with a smile on her lips.

Once more I saw myself standing on the beach beside poor startled Ben. 'You're kind,' he said, 'not like the other one. You won't put me to the asylum, will you?' There was someone who walked through the woods by night, someone tall and slim. She gave you the feeling of a snake . . .

Maxim was talking though. Maxim was walking up and down the library floor. 'I found her out at once,' he was saying, 'five days after we were married. You remember that time I drove you in the car, to the hills above Monte Carlo? I wanted to stand there again, to remember. She sat there, laughing, her black hair blowing in the wind; she told me about herself, told me things I shall never repeat to a living soul. I knew then what I had done, what I had married. Beauty, brains, and breeding. Oh, my God!'

He broke off abruptly. He went and stood by the window, looking out upon the lawns. He began to laugh. He stood there laughing. I could not bear it, it made me frightened, ill. I could not stand it.

'Maxim!' I cried. 'Maxim!'

He lit a cigarette, and stood there smoking, not saying anything. Then he turned away again, and paced up and down the room once more. 'I nearly killed her then,' he said. 'It would have been so easy. One false step, one slip. You remember the precipice. I frightened you, didn't I? You thought I was mad. Perhaps I was. Perhaps I am. It doesn't make for sanity, does it, living with the devil.'

I sat there watching him, up and down, up and down.

'She made a bargain with me up there, on the side of the precipice,' he said. '"I'll run your house for you," she told me, "I'll look after your precious Manderley for you, make it the most famous show-place in all the country, if you like. And people will visit us, and envy us, and talk about us; they'll say we are the luckiest, happiest, handsomest couple in all England. What a leg-pull, Max!" she said, "what a God-damn triumph!" She sat there on the hillside, laughing, tearing a flower to bits in her hands.'

Maxim threw his cigarette away, a quarter smoked, into the empty grate.

305

'I did not kill her,' he said. 'I watched her, I said nothing, I let her laugh. We got into the car together and drove away. And she knew I would do as she suggested: come here to Manderley, throw the place open, entertain, have our marriage spoken of as the success of the century. She knew I would sacrifice pride, honour, personal feelings, every damned quality on earth, rather than stand before our little world after a week of marriage and have them know the things about her that she had told me then. She knew I would never stand in a divorce court and give her away, have fingers pointing at us, mud flung at us in the newspapers, all the people who belong down here whispering when my name was mentioned, all the trippers from Kerrith trooping to the lodge gates, peering into the grounds and saying, "That's where he lives, in there. That's Manderley. That's the place that belongs to the chap who had that divorce case we read about. Do you remember what the judge said about his wife . . . ?"'

He came and stood before me. He held out his hands. 'You despise me, don't you?' he said. 'You can't understand my shame, and loathing and disgust?'

I did not say anything. I held his hands against my heart. I did not care about his shame. None of the things that he had told me mattered to me at all. I clung to one thing only, and repeated it to myself, over and over again. Maxim did not love Rebecca. He had never loved her, never, never. They had never known one moment's happiness together. Maxim was talking and I listened to him, but his words meant nothing to me. I did not really care. 'I thought about Manderley too much,' he said. 'I put Manderley first, before anything else. And it does not prosper, that sort of love. They don't preach about it in the churches. Christ said nothing about stones, and bricks, and walls, the love that a man can bear for his plot of earth, his soil, his little kingdom. It does not come into the Christian creed.'

'My darling,' I said, 'my Maxim, my love.' I laid his hands against my face, I put my lips against them.

'Do you understand?' he said, 'do you, do you?'

306

'Yes,' I said, 'my sweet, my love.' But I looked away from him so he should not see my face. What did it matter whether I understood him or not? My heart was light like a feather floating in the air. He had never loved Rebecca.

'I don't want to look back on those years,' he said slowly. 'I don't want even to tell you about them. The shame and the degradation. The lie we lived, she and I. The shabby, sordid farce we played together. Before friends, before relations, even before the servants, before faithful, trusting creatures like old Frith. They all believed in her down here, they all admired her, they never knew how she laughed at them behind their backs, jeered at them, mimicked them. I can remember days when the place was full for some show or other, a garden-party, a pageant, and she walked about with a smile like an angel on her face, her arm through mine, giving prizes afterwards to a little troop of children; and then the day afterwards she would be up at dawn driving to London, streaking to that flat of hers by the river like an animal to its hole in the ditch, coming back here at the end of the week, after five unspeakable days. Oh, I kept to my side of the bargain all right. I never gave her away. Her blasted taste made Manderley the thing it is today. The gardens, the shrubs, even the azaleas in the Happy Valley; do you think they existed when my father was alive? God, the place was a wilderness; lovely, yes, wild and lonely with a beauty of its own, yes, but crying out for skill and care and the money that he would never give to it, that I would not have thought of giving to it – but for Rebecca. Half the stuff you see here in the rooms was never here originally. The drawing room as it is today, the morning-room – that's all Rebecca. Those chairs that Frith points out so proudly to the visitors on the public day, and that panel of tapestry – Rebecca again. Oh, some of the things were here admittedly, stored away in back rooms – my father knew nothing about furniture or pictures – but the majority was bought by Rebecca. The beauty of Manderley that you see today, the Manderley that people talk about and photograph and paint, it's all due to her, to Rebecca.'

I did not say anything. I held him close. I wanted him to go on talking like this, that his bitterness might loosen and come away, carrying with it all the pent-up hatred and disgust and muck of the lost years.

'And so we lived,' he said, 'month after month, year after year. I accepted everything – because of Manderley. What she did in London did not touch me – because it did not hurt Manderley. And she was careful those first years; there was never a murmur about her, never a whisper. Then little by little she began to grow careless. You know how a man starts drinking? He goes easy at first, just a little at a time, a bad bout perhaps every five months or so. And then the period between grows less and less. Soon it's every month, every fortnight, every few days. There's no margin of safety left and all his secret cunning goes. It was like that with Rebecca. She began to ask her friends down here. She would have one or two of them and mix them up at a week-end party so that at first I was not quite sure, not quite certain. She would have picnics down at her cottage in the cove. I came back once, having been away shooting in Scotland, and found her there, with half a dozen of them; people I had never seen before. I warned her, and she shrugged her shoulders. "What the hell's it got to do with you?" she said. I told her she could see her friends in London, but Manderley was mine. She must stick to that part of the bargain. She smiled, she did not say anything. Then she started on Frank, poor shy faithful Frank. He came to me one day and said he wanted to leave Manderley and take another job. We argued for two hours, here in the library, and then I understood. He broke down and told me. She never left him alone, he said, she was always going down to his house, trying to get him to the cottage. Dear, wretched Frank, who had not understood, who had always thought we were the normal happy married couple we pretended to be.

'I accused Rebecca of this, and she flared up at once, cursing me, using every filthy word in her particular vocabulary. We had a sickening, loathsome scene. She went up to London after that and stayed there for a month. When she came back again she was quiet at first; I thought she had learnt her lesson. Bee and Giles came for a week-end, and I realized then what I had some-times suspected before, that Bee did not like Rebecca. I believe, in her funny abrupt, downright way she saw through her, guessed something was wrong. It was a tricky, nervy sort of week-end. Giles went out sailing with Rebecca, Bee and I lazed on the lawn. And when they came back I could tell by Giles's rather hearty jovial manner and by a look in Rebecca's eye that she had started on him, as she had done on Frank. I saw Bee watching Giles at dinner, who laughed louder than usual, talked a little too much. And all the while Rebecca sitting there at the head of the table, looking like an angel.'

They were all fitting into place, the jig-saw pieces. The odd strained shapes that I had tried to piece together with my fumbling fingers and they had never fitted. Frank's odd manner when I spoke about Rebecca. Beatrice, and her rather diffident negative attitude. The silence that I had always taken for sympathy and regret was a silence born of shame and embarrassment. It seemed incredible to me now that I had never understood. I wondered how many people there were in the world who suffered, and continued to suffer, because they could not break out from their own web of shyness and reserve, and in their blindness and folly built up a great distorted wall in front of them that hid the truth. This was what I had done. I had built up false pictures in my mind and sat before them. I had never had the courage to demand the truth. Had I made one step forward out of my own shyness, Maxim would have told me these things four months, five months ago.

'That was the last week-end Bee and Giles ever spent at Manderley,' said Maxim. 'I never asked them alone again. They came officially, to garden-parties, and dances. Bee never said a word to me or I to her. But I think she guessed my life, I think she knew. Even as Frank did. Rebecca grew cunning again. Her behaviour was faultless, outwardly. But if I happened to be away when she was here at Manderley I could never be certain what might happen. There had been Frank, and Giles. She might get hold of one of the workmen on the estate, someone from Kerrith, anyone . . . And then the bomb would have to fall. The gossip, the publicity I dreaded.'

It seemed to me I stood again by the cottage in the woods, and I heard the drip-drip of the rain upon the roof. I saw the dust on the model ships, the rat holes on the divan. I saw Ben with his poor staring idiot's eyes. 'You'll not put me to the asylum, will you?' And I thought of the dark steep path through the woods, and how, if a woman stood there behind the trees, her evening dress would rustle in the thin night breeze.

'She had a cousin,' said Maxim slowly, 'a fellow who had been abroad, and was living in England again. He took to coming here, if ever I was away. Frank used to see him. A fellow called Jack Favell.'

'I know him,' I said; 'he came here the day you went to London.'

'You saw him too?' said Maxim. 'Why didn't you tell me? I heard it from Frank, who saw his car turn in at the lodge gates.'

'I did not like to,' I said, 'I thought it would remind you of Rebecca.'

'Remind me?' whispered Maxim. 'Oh, God, as if I needed reminding.'

He stared in front of him, breaking off from his story, and I wondered if he was thinking, as I was, of that flooded cabin beneath the waters in the bay.

'She used to have this fellow Favell down to the cottage,' said Maxim, 'she would tell the servants she was going to sail, and would not be back before the morning. Then she would spend the night down there with him. Once again I warned her. I said if I found him here, anywhere on the estate, I'd shoot him. He had a black, filthy record . . . The very thought of him walking about the woods in Manderley, in places like the Happy Valley, made me mad. I told her I would not stand for it. She shrugged her shoulders. She forgot to blaspheme. And I noticed she was looking paler than usual, nervy, rather haggard. I wondered then what the hell would happen to her when she began to look old, feel old. Things drifted on. Nothing very much happened. Then one day she went up to London, and came back again the same day, which she did not do as a rule. I did not expect her. I dined that night with Frank at his house, we had a lot of work on at the time.' He was speaking now in short, jerky sentences. I had his hands very tightly between my two hands.

'I came back after dinner, about half past ten, and I saw her scarf and gloves lying on a chair in the hall. I wondered what the devil she had come back for. I went into the morning-room, but she was not there. I guessed she had gone off there then, down to the cove. And I knew then I could not stand this life of lies and filth and deceit any longer. The thing had got to be settled, one way or the other. I thought I'd take a gun and frighten the fellow, frighten them both. I went down right away to the cottage. The servants never knew I had come back to the house at all. I slipped out into the garden and through the woods. I saw the light in the cottage window, and I went straight in. To my surprise Rebecca was alone. She was lying on the divan with an ash-tray full of cigarette stubs beside her. She looked ill, queer.

'I began at once about Favell and she listened to me without a word. "We've lived this life of degradation long enough, you and I," I said. "This is the end, do you understand? What you do in London does not concern me. You can live with Favell there, or with anyone you like. But not here. Not at Manderley."

'She said nothing for a moment. She stared at me, and then she smiled. "Suppose it suits me better to live here, what then?" she said.

'"You know the conditions," I said. "I've kept my part of our dirty, damnable bargain, haven't I? But you've cheated. You think you can treat my house and my home like your own sink in London. I've stood enough, but my God, Rebecca, this is your last chance."

'I remember she squashed out her cigarette in the tub by the divan, and then she got up, and stretched herself, her arms above her head.

311

'"You're right, Max," she said. "It's time I turned over a new leaf."

'She looked very pale, very thin. She began walking up and down the room, her hands in the pockets of her trousers. She looked like a boy in her sailing kit, a boy with a face like a Botticelli angel.

'"Have you ever thought", she said, "how damned hard it would be for you to make a case against me? In a court of law, I mean. If you wanted to divorce me. Do you realize that you've never had one shred of proof against me, from the very first? All your friends, even the servants, believe our marriage to be a success."

'"What about Frank?" I said. "What about Beatrice?"

'She threw back her head and laughed. "What sort of a story could Frank tell against mine?" she said. "Don't you know me well enough for that? As for Beatrice, wouldn't it be the easiest thing in the world for her to stand in a witness-box as the ordinary jealous woman whose husband once lost his head and made a fool of himself? Oh, no, Max, you'd have a hell of a time trying to prove anything against me."

'She stood watching me, rocking on her heels, her hands in her pockets and a smile on her face. "Do you realize that I could get Danny, as my personal maid, to swear anything I asked her to swear, in a court of law? And that the rest of the servants, in blind ignorance, would follow her example and swear too? They think we live together at Manderley as husband and wife, don't they? And so does everyone, your friends, all our little world. Well, how are you going to prove that we don't?"

'She sat down on the edge of the table, swinging her legs, watching me.

'"Haven't we acted the parts of a loving husband and wife rather too well?" she said. I remember watching that foot of hers in its striped sandal swinging backwards and forwards, and my eyes and brain began to burn in a strange quick way.

'"We could make you look very foolish, Danny and I," she said softly. "We could make you look so foolish that no one

312

would believe you, Max, nobody at all." Still that foot of hers, swinging to and fro, that damned foot in its blue and white striped sandal.

'Suddenly she slipped off the table and stood in front of me, smiling still, her hands in her pockets.

'"If I had a child, Max," she said, "neither you, nor anyone in the world, would ever prove that it was not yours. It would grow up here in Manderley, bearing your name. There would be nothing you could do. And when you died Manderley would be his. You could not prevent it. The property's entailed. You would like an heir, wouldn't you, for your beloved Manderley? You would enjoy it, wouldn't you, seeing my son lying in his pram under the chestnut tree, playing leap-frog on the lawn, catching butterflies in the Happy Valley? It would give you the biggest thrill of your life, wouldn't it, Max, to watch my son grow bigger day by day, and to know that when you died, all this would be his?"

'She waited a minute, rocking on her heels, and then she lit a cigarette and went and stood by the window. She began to laugh. She went on laughing. I thought she would never stop. "God, how funny," she said, "how supremely, wonderfully funny! Well, you heard me say I was going to turn over a new leaf, didn't you? Now you know the reason. They'll be happy, won't they, all these smug locals, all your blasted tenants? 'It's what we've always hoped for, Mrs de Winter,' they will say. I'll be the perfect mother, Max, like I've been the perfect wife. And none of them will ever guess, none of them will ever know."

'She turned round and faced me, smiling, one hand in her pocket, the other holding her cigarette. When I killed her she was smiling still. I fired at her heart. The bullet passed right through. She did not fall at once. She stood there, looking at me, that slow smile on her face, her eyes wide open . . .'

Maxim's voice had sunk low, so low that it was like a whisper. The hand that I held between my own was cold. I did not look at him. I watched Jasper's sleeping body on the carpet beside me, the little thump of his tail, now and then, upon the floor.

'I'd forgotten,' said Maxim, and his voice was slow now, tired, without expression, 'that when you shot a person there was so much blood.'

There was a hole there on the carpet beneath Jasper's tail. The burnt hole from a cigarette. I wondered how long it had been there. Some people said ash was good for the carpets.

'I had to get water from the cove,' said Maxim. 'I had to keep going backwards and forwards to the cove for water. Even by the fireplace, where she had not been, there was a stain. It was all round where she lay on the floor. It began to blow too. There was no catch on the window. The window kept banging backwards and forwards, while I knelt there on the floor with that dishcloth, and the bucket beside me.'

And the rain on the roof, I thought, he does not remember the rain on the roof. It pattered thin and light and very fast.

'I carried her out to the boat,' he said; 'it must have been half past eleven by then, nearly twelve. It was quite dark. There was no moon. The wind was squally, from the west. I carried her down to the cabin and left her there. Then I had to get under way, with the dinghy astern, and beat out of the little harbour against the tide. The wind was with me, but it came in puffs, and I was in the lee there, under cover of the headland. I remember I got the mainsail jammed half-way up the mast. I had not done it, you see, for a long time. I never went out with Rebecca.

'And I thought of the tide, how swift it ran and strong into the little cove. The wind blew down from the headland like a funnel. I got the boat out into the bay. I got her out there, beyond the beacon, and I tried to go about, to clear the ridge of rocks. The little jib fluttered. I could not sheet it in. A puff of wind came and the sheet tore out of my hands, went twisting round the mast. The sail thundered and shook. It cracked like a whip above my head. I could not remember what one had to do. I could not remember. I tried to reach that sheet and it blew above me in the air. Another blast of wind came straight ahead. We began to drift sideways, closer to the ridge. It was dark, so damned dark I couldn't see anything on the black, slippery deck.

Somehow I blundered down into the cabin. I had a spike with me. If I didn't do it now it would be too late. We were getting so near to the ridge, and in six or seven minutes, drifting like this, we should be out of deep water. I opened the sea-cocks. The water began to come in. I drove the spike into the bottom boards. One of the planks split right across. I took the spike out and began to drive in another plank. The water came up over my feet. I left Rebecca lying on the floor. I fastened both the scuttles. I bolted the door. When I came up on deck I saw we were within twenty yards of the ridge. I threw some of the loose stuff on the deck into the water. There was a lifebuoy, a pair of sweeps, a coil of rope. I climbed into the dinghy. I pulled away, and lay back on the paddles, and watched. The boat was drifting still. She was sinking too. Sinking by the head. The jib was still shaking and cracking like a whip. I thought someone must hear it, someone walking the cliffs late at night, some fisherman from Kerrith away beyond me in the bay, whose boat I could not see. The boat was smaller, like a black shadow on the water. The mast began to shiver, began to crack. Suddenly she heeled right over and as she went the mast broke in two, split right down the centre. The lifebuoy and the sweeps floated away from me on the water. The boat was not there any more. I remember staring at the place where she had been. Then I pulled back to the cove. It started raining.'

Maxim waited. He stared in front of him still. Then he looked at me, sitting beside him on the floor.

'That's all,' he said, 'there's no more to tell. I left the dinghy on the buoy, as she would have done. I went back and looked at the cottage. The floor was wet with the salt water. She might have done it herself. I walked up the path through the woods. I went into the house. Up the stairs to the dressing-room. I remember undressing. It began to blow and rain very hard. I was sitting there, on the bed, when Mrs Danvers knocked on the door. I went and opened it, in my dressing-gown, and spoke to her. She was worried about Rebecca. I told her to go back to bed. I shut the door again. I went back and sat by the window in my dressing-gown, watching the rain, listening to the sea as it broke there, in the cove.'

We sat there together without saying anything. I went on holding his cold hands. I wondered why Robert did not come to clear the tea.

'She sank too close in,' said Maxim. 'I meant to take her right out in the bay. They would never have found her there. She was too close in.'

'It was the ship,' I said; 'it would not have happened but for the ship. No one would have known.'

'She was too close in,' said Maxim.

We were silent again. I began to feel very tired.

'I knew it would happen one day,' said Maxim, 'even when I went up to Edgecoombe and identified that body as hers. I knew it meant nothing, nothing at all. It was only a question of waiting, of marking time. Rebecca would win in the end. Finding you has not made any difference has it? Loving you does not alter things at all. Rebecca knew she would win in the end. I saw her smile, when she died.'

'Rebecca is dead,' I said. 'That's what we've got to remember. Rebecca is dead. She can't speak, she can't bear witness. She can't harm you any more.'

'There's her body,' he said, 'the diver has seen it. It's lying there, on the cabin floor.'

'We've got to explain it,' I said. 'We've got to think out a way to explain it. It's got to be the body of someone you don't know. Someone you've never seen before.'

'Her things will be there still,' he said. 'The rings on her fingers. Even if her clothes have rotted in the water there will be something there to tell them. It's not like a body lost at sea, battered against rocks. The cabin is untouched. She must be lying there on the floor as I left her. The boat has been there, all these months. No one has moved anything. There is the boat, lying on the sea-bed where she sank.'

'A body rots in water, doesn't it?' I whispered; 'even if it's lying there, undisturbed, the water rots it, doesn't it?'

316

'I don't know,' he said. 'I don't know.'

'How will you find out? how will you know?' I said.

'The diver is going down again at five-thirty tomorrow morning,' said Maxim. 'Searle has made all the arrangements. They are going to try to raise the boat. No one will be about. I'm going with them. He's sending his boat to pick me up in the cove. Five-thirty tomorrow morning.'

'And then?' I said, 'if they get it up, what then?'

'Searle's going to have his big lighter anchored there, just out in the deep water. If the boat's wood has not rotted, if it still holds together, his crane will be able to lift it on to the lighter. They'll go back to Kerrith then. Searle says he will moor the lighter at the head of that disused creek half-way up Kerrith harbour. It drives out very easily. It's mud there at low water and the trippers can't row up there. We shall have the place to ourselves. He says we'll have to let the water drain out of the boat, leaving the cabin bare. He's going to get hold of a doctor.'

'What will he do?' I said. 'What will the doctor do?'

'I don't know,' he said.

'If they find out it's Rebecca you must say the other body was a mistake,' I said. 'You must say that the body in the crypt was a mistake, a ghastly mistake. You must say that when you went to Edgecoombe you were ill, you did not know what you were doing. You were not sure, even then. You could not tell. It was a mistake, just a mistake. You will say that, won't you?'

'Yes,' he said. 'Yes.'

'They can't prove anything against you,' I said. 'Nobody saw you that night. You had gone to bed. They can't prove anything. No one knows but you and I. No one at all. Not even Frank. We are the only two people in the world to know, Maxim. You and I.'

'Yes,' he said. 'Yes.'

'They will think the boat capsized and sank when she was in the cabin,' I said; 'they will think she went below for a rope, for something, and while she was there the wind came from the headland, and the boat heeled over, and Rebecca was trapped. They'll think that, won't they?'

'I don't know,' he said. 'I don't know.'

Suddenly the telephone began ringing in the little room behind the library.

21

Maxim went into the little room and shut the door. Robert came in a few minutes afterwards to clear away the tea. I stood up, my back turned to him so that he should not see my face. I wondered when they would begin to know, on the estate, in the servants' hall, in Kerrith itself. I wondered how long it took for news to trickle through.

I could hear the murmur of Maxim's voice in the little room beyond. I had a sick expectant feeling at the pit of my stomach. The sound of the telephone ringing seemed to have woken every nerve in my body. I had sat there on the floor beside Maxim in a sort of dream, his hand in mine, my face against his shoulder. I had listened to his story, and part of me went with him like a shadow in his tracks. I too had killed Rebecca, I too had sunk the boat there in the bay. I had listened beside him to the wind and water. I had waited for Mrs Danvers' knocking on the door. All this I had suffered with him, all this and more beside. But the rest of me sat there on the carpet, unmoved and detached, thinking and caring for one thing only, repeating a phrase over and over again, 'He did not love Rebecca, he did not love Rebecca.' Now, at the ringing of the telephone, these two selves merged and became one again. I was the self that I had always been, I was not changed. But something new had come upon me that had not been before. My heart, for all its anxiety and doubt, was light and free. I knew then that I was no longer afraid of Rebecca. I did not hate her any more. Now that I knew her to have been evil and vicious and rotten I did not hate her any more. She could not hurt me. I could go to the morning-room and sit down at her desk and touch her pen and look at her writing on the pigeon-holes, and I should not mind. I could go to her room in the west wing, stand by the window even as I had done this morning, and I should not be afraid. Rebecca's power had dissolved into the air, like the mist had done. She would never haunt me again. She would never stand behind me on the stairs, sit beside me in the dining-room, lean down from the gallery and watch me standing in the hall. Maxim had never loved her. I did not hate her any more. Her body had come back, her boat had been found with its queer prophetic name, *Je Reviens*, but I was free of her forever.

I was free now to be with Maxim, to touch him, and hold him, and love him. I would never be a child again. It would not be I, I, I any longer; it would be we, it would be us. We would be together. We would face this trouble together, he and I. Captain Searle, and the diver, and Frank, and Mrs Danvers, and Beatrice, and the men and women of Kerrith reading their newspapers, could not break us now. Our happiness had not come too late. I was not young any more. I was not shy. I was not afraid. I would fight for Maxim. I would lie and perjure and swear, I would blaspheme and pray. Rebecca had not won. Rebecca had lost.

Robert had taken away the tea and Maxim came back into the room.

'It was Colonel Julyan,' he said; 'he's just been talking to Searle. He's coming out with us to the boat tomorrow. Searle has told him.'

'Why Colonel Julyan, why?' I said.

'He's the magistrate for Kerrith. He has to be present.'

'What did he say?'

'He asked me if I had any idea whose body it could be.'

'What did you say?'

'I said I did not know. I said we believed Rebecca to be alone. I said I did not know of any friend.'

'Did he say anything after that?'

'Yes.'

'What did he say?'

'He asked me if I thought it possible that I made a mistake when I went up to Edgecoombe?'

'He said that? He said that already?'

'Yes.'

'And you?'

'I said it might be possible. I did not know.'

'He'll be with you then tomorrow when you look at the boat? He, and Captain Searle, and a doctor.'

'Inspector Welch too.'

'Inspector Welch?'

'Yes.'

'Why? Why Inspector Welch?'

'It's the custom, when a body has been found.'

I did not say anything. We stared at one another. I felt the little pain come again at the pit of my stomach.

'They may not be able to raise the boat,' I said.

'No.' he said.

'They couldn't do anything then about the body, could they?' I said.

'I don't know,' he said.

He glanced out of the window. The sky was white and overcast as it had been when I came away from the cliffs. There was no wind though. It was still and quiet.

'I thought it might blow from the south-west about an hour ago but the wind has died away again,' he said.

'Yes,' I said.

'It will be a flat calm tomorrow for the diver,' he said.

The telephone began ringing again from the little room. There was something sickening about the shrill urgent summons of the bell. Maxim and I looked at one another. Then he went into the room to answer it, shutting the door behind him as he had done before. The queer nagging pain had not left me yet. It returned again in greater force with the ringing of the bell. The feel of it took me back across the years to my childhood. This was the pain I had known when I was very small and the maroons had sounded in the streets of London, and I had sat, shivering, not understanding, under a little cupboard beneath the stairs. It was the same feeling, the same pain.

Maxim came back into the library. 'It's begun,' he said slowly.

'What do you mean? What's happened?' I said, grown suddenly cold.

'It was a reporter,' he said, 'the fellow from the *County Chronicle*. Was it true, he said, that the boat belonging to the late Mrs de Winter had been found.'

'What did you say?'

'I said yes, a boat had been found, but that was all we know. It might not be her boat at all.'

'Was that all he said?'

'No. He asked if I could confirm the rumour that a body had been found in the cabin.'

'No!'

'Yes. Someone must have been talking. Not Searle, I know that. The diver, one of his friends. You can't stop these people. The whole story will be all over Kerrith by breakfast time tomorrow.'

'What did you say, about the body?'

'I said I did not know. I had no statement to make. And I should be obliged if he did not ring me up again.'

'You will irritate them. You will have them against you.'

'I can't help that. I don't make statements to newspapers. I won't have those fellows ringing up and asking questions.'

'We might want them on our side,' I said.

'If it comes to fighting, I'll fight alone,' he said. 'I don't want a newspaper behind me.'

'The reporter will ring up someone else,' I said. 'He will get on to Colonel Julyan or Captain Searle.'

'He won't get much change out of them,' said Maxim.

'If only we could do something,' I said, 'all these hours ahead of us, and we sit here, idle, waiting for tomorrow morning.'

'There's nothing we can do,' said Maxim.

We went on sitting in the library. Maxim picked up a book but I know he did not read. Now and again I saw him lift his head and listen, as though he heard the telephone again. But it did not ring again. No one disturbed us. We dressed for dinner as usual. It seemed incredible to me that this time last night I had been putting on my white dress, sitting before the mirror at my dressing-table, arranging the curled wig. It was like an old forgotten nightmare, something remembered months afterwards with doubt and disbelief. We had dinner. Frith served us, returned from his afternoon. His face was solemn, expressionless. I wondered if he had been in Kerrith, if he had heard anything.

After dinner we went back again to the library. We did not talk much. I sat on the floor at Maxim's feet, my head against his knees. He ran his fingers through my hair. Different from his old abstracted way. It was not like stroking Jasper any more. I felt his finger tips on the scalp of my head. Sometimes he kissed me. Sometimes he said things to me. There were no shadows between us any more, and when we were silent it was because the silence came to us of our own asking. I wondered how it was I could be so happy when our little world about us was so black. It was a strange sort of happiness. Not what I had dreamt about or expected. It was not the sort of happiness I had imagined in the lonely hours. There was nothing feverish or urgent about this. It was a quiet, still happiness. The library windows were open wide, and when we did not talk or touch one another we looked out at the dark dull sky.

It must have rained in the night, for when I woke the next morning, just after seven, and got up, and looked out of the window, I saw the roses in the garden below were folded and drooping, and the grass banks leading to the woods were wet and silver. There was a little smell in the air of mist and damp, the smell that comes with the first fall of the leaf. I wondered if autumn would come upon us two months before her time. Maxim had not woken me when he got up at five. He must have crept from his bed and gone through the bathroom to his dressing-room without a sound. He would be down there now, in the bay, with Colonel Julyan, and Captain Searle, and the men from the lighter. The lighter would be there, the crane and the chain, and Rebecca's boat coming to the surface. I thought about it calmly, coolly, without feeling. I pictured them all down there in the bay, and the little dark hull of the boat rising slowly to the surface, sodden, dripping, the grass-green seaweed and shells clinging to her sides. When they lifted her on to the lighter the water would stream from her sides, back into the sea again. The wood of the little boat would look soft and grey, pulpy in places. She would smell of mud and rust, and that dark weed that grows deep beneath the sea beside rocks that are never uncovered. Perhaps the name-board still hung upon her stern. *Je Reviens*. The lettering green and faded. The nails rusted through. And Rebecca herself was there, lying on the cabin floor.

I got up and had my bath and dressed, and went down to breakfast at nine o'clock as usual. There were a lot of letters on my plate. Letters from people thanking us for the dance. I skimmed through them, I did not read them all. Frith wanted to know whether to keep the breakfast hot for Maxim. I told him I did not know when he would be back. He had to go out very early, I said. Frith did not say anything. He looked very solemn, very grave. I wondered again if he knew.

After breakfast I took my letters along to the morning-room. The room smelt fusty, the windows had not been opened. I flung them wide, letting in the cool fresh air. The flowers on the mantelpiece were drooping, many of them dead. The petals lay on the floor. I rang the bell, and Maud, the under-housemaid, came into the room.

'This room has not been touched this morning,' I said, 'even the windows were shut. And the flowers are dead. Will you please take them away?'

She looked nervous and apologetic. 'I'm very sorry, Madam,' she said. She went to the mantelpiece and took the vases.

'Don't let it happen again,' I said.

'No, Madam,' she said. She went out of the room, taking the flowers with her. I had not thought it would be so easy to be severe. I wondered why it had seemed hard for me before. The menu for the day lay on the writing-desk. Cold salmon and mayonnaise, cutlets in aspic, galantine of chicken, soufflé. I recognized them all from the buffet-supper of the night of the ball. We were evidently still living on the remains. This must be the cold lunch that was put out in the dining-room yesterday and I had not eaten. The staff were taking things easily, it seemed. I put a pencil through the list and rang for Robert. 'Tell Mrs Danvers to order something hot,' I said. 'If there's still a lot of cold stuff to finish we don't want it in the dining-room.'

'Very good, Madam,' he said.

I followed him out of the room and went to the little flower-room for my scissors. Then I went into the rose-garden and cut some young buds. The chill had worn away from the air. It was going to be as hot and airless as yesterday had been. I wondered if they were still down in the bay or whether they had gone back to the creek in Kerrith harbour. Presently I should hear. Presently Maxim would come back and tell me. Whatever happened I must be calm and quiet. Whatever happened I must not be afraid. I cut my roses and took them back into the morning-room. The carpet had been dusted, and the fallen petals removed. I began to arrange the flowers in the vases that Robert had filled with water. When I had nearly finished there was a knock on the door.

'Come in,' I said.

It was Mrs Danvers. She had the menu list in her hand. She looked pale and tired. There were great rings round her eyes.

'Good morning, Mrs Danvers,' I said.

'I don't understand', she began, 'why you sent the menu out and the message by Robert. Why did you do it?'

I looked across at her, a rose in my hand.

'Those cutlets and that salmon were sent in yesterday,' I said. 'I saw them on the side-board. I should prefer something hot today. If they won't eat the cold in the kitchen you had better throw the stuff away. So much waste goes on in this house anyway that a little more won't make any difference.'

She stared at me. She did not say anything. I put the rose in the vase with the others.

'Don't tell me you can't think of anything to give us, Mrs Danvers,' I said. 'You must have menus for all occasions in your room.'

'I'm not used to having messages sent to me by Robert,' she said. 'If Mrs de Winter wanted anything changed she would ring me personally on the house telephone.'

'I'm afraid it does not concern me very much what Mrs de Winter used to do,' I said. 'I am Mrs de Winter now, you know. And if I choose to send a message by Robert I shall do so.'

Just then Robert came into the room. 'The *County Chronicle* on the telephone, Madam,' he said.

'Tell the *County Chronicle* I'm not at home,' I said.

'Yes, Madam,' he said. He went out of the room.

'Well, Mrs Danvers, is there anything else?' I said.

She went on staring at me. Still she did not say anything. 'If you have nothing else to say you had better go and tell the cook about the hot lunch,' I said. 'I'm rather busy.'

'Why did the *County Chronicle* want to speak to you?' she said.

'I haven't the slightest idea, Mrs Danvers,' I said.

'Is it true,' she said slowly, 'the story Frith brought back with him from Kerrith last night, that Mrs de Winter's boat has been found?'

'Is there such a story?' I said. 'I'm afraid I don't know anything about it.'

'Captain Searle, the Kerrith harbour-master, called here yesterday, didn't he?' she said. 'Robert told me, Robert showed him in. Frith says the story in Kerrith is that the diver who went down about the ship there in the bay found Mrs de Winter's boat.'

'Perhaps so,' I said. 'You had better wait until Mr de Winter himself comes in and ask him about it.'

'Why was Mr de Winter up so early?' she asked.

'That was Mr de Winter's business,' I said.

She went on staring at me. 'Frith said the story goes that there was a body in the cabin of the little boat,' she said. 'Why should there be a body there? Mrs de Winter always sailed alone.'

'It's no use asking me, Mrs Danvers,' I said. 'I don't know any more than you do.'

'Don't you?' she said slowly. She kept on looking at me. I turned away, I put the vase back on the table by the window.

'I will give the orders about the lunch,' she said. She waited a moment. I did not say anything. Then she went out of the room. She can't frighten me any more, I thought. She has lost her power with Rebecca. Whatever she said or did now it could not matter to me or hurt me. I knew she was my enemy and I did not mind. But if she should learn the truth about the body in the boat and become Maxim's enemy too – what then? I sat down in the chair. I put the scissors on the table. I did not feel like doing any more roses. I kept wondering what Maxim was doing. I wondered why the reporter from the *County Chronicle* had rung us up again. The old sick feeling came back inside me. I went and leant out of the window. It was very hot. There was thunder in the air. The gardeners began to mow the grass again. I could see one of the men with his machine walk backwards and forwards on the top of the bank. I could not go on sitting in the morning-room. I left my scissors and my roses and went out on to the terrace. I began to walk up and down. Jasper padded after me, wondering why I did not take him for a walk. I went on walking up and down the terrace. About half past eleven Frith came out to me from the hall.

'Mr de Winter on the telephone, Madam,' he said.

I went through the library to the little room beyond. My hands were shaking as I lifted the receiver.

'Is that you?' he said. 'It's Maxim. I'm speaking from the office. I'm with Frank.'

'Yes?' I said.

There was a pause. 'I shall be bringing Frank and Colonel Julyan back to lunch at one o'clock,' he said.

'Yes,' I said.

I waited. I waited for him to go on. 'They were able to raise the boat,' he said. 'I've just got back from the creek.'

'Yes,' I said.

'Searle was there, and Colonel Julyan, and Frank, and the others,' he said. I wondered if Frank was standing beside him at the telephone, and if that was the reason he was so cool, so distant.

'All right then,' he said; 'expect us about one o'clock.'

I put back the receiver. He had not told me anything. I still did not know what had happened. I went back again to the terrace, telling Frith first that we should be four to lunch instead of two.

An hour dragged past, slow, interminable. I went upstairs and changed into a thinner frock. I came down again. I went and sat in the drawing-room and waited. At five minutes to one I heard the sound of a car in the drive, and then voices in the hall. I patted my hair in front of the looking-glass. My face was very white. I pinched some colour into my cheeks and stood up waiting for them to come into the room. Maxim came in, and Frank, and Colonel Julyan. I remembered seeing Colonel Julyan at the ball dressed as Cromwell. He looked shrunken now, different. A smaller man altogether.

'How do you do?' he said. He spoke quietly, gravely, like a doctor.

'Ask Frith to bring the sherry,' said Maxim. 'I'm going to wash.'

'I'll have a wash too,' said Frank. Before I rang the bell Frith appeared with the sherry. Colonel Julyan did not have any. I took some to give me something to hold. Colonel Julyan came and stood beside me by the window.

'This is a most distressing thing, Mrs de Winter,' he said gently. 'I do feel for you and your husband most acutely.'

'Thank you,' I said. I began to sip my sherry. Then I put the glass back again on the table. I was afraid he would notice that my hand was shaking.

328

'What makes it so difficult was the fact of your husband identifying that first body, over a year ago,' he said.

'I don't quite understand,' I said.

'You did not hear, then, what we found this morning?' he said.

'I knew there was a body. The diver found a body,' I said.

'Yes,' he said. And then, half glancing over his shoulder towards the hall, 'I'm afraid it was her, without a doubt,' he said, lowering his voice. 'I can't go into details with you, but the evidence was sufficient for your husband and Doctor Phillips to identify.'

He stopped suddenly, and moved away from me. Maxim and Frank had come back into the room.

'Lunch is ready; shall we go in?' said Maxim.

I led the way into the hall, my heart like a stone, heavy, numb. Colonel Julyan sat on my right, Frank on my left. I did not look at Maxim. Frith and Robert began to hand the first course. We all talked about the weather. 'I see in *The Times* they had it well over eighty in London yesterday,' said Colonel Julyan.

'Really?' I said.

'Yes. Must be frightful for the poor devils who can't get away.'

'Yes, frightful,' I said.

'Paris can be hotter than London,' said Frank. 'I remember staying a week-end in Paris in the middle of August, and it was quite impossible to sleep. There was not a breath of air in the whole city. The temperature was over ninety.'

'Of course the French always sleep with their windows shut, don't they?' said Colonel Julyan.

'I don't know,' said Frank. 'I was staying in a hotel. The people were mostly Americans.'

'You know France of course, Mrs de Winter?' said Colonel Julyan.

'Not so very well,' I said.

'Oh, I had the idea you had lived many years out there.'

'No,' I said.

'She was staying in Monte Carlo when I met her,' said Maxim. 'You don't call that France, do you?'

'No, I suppose not,' said Colonel Julyan; 'it must be very cosmopolitan. The coast is pretty though, isn't it?'

'Very pretty,' I said.

'Not so rugged as this, eh? Still, I know which I'd rather have. Give me England every time, when it comes to settling down. You know where you are over here.'

'I dare say the French feel that about France,' said Maxim.

'Oh, no doubt,' said Colonel Julyan.

We went on eating awhile in silence. Frith stood behind my chair. We were all thinking of one thing, but because of Frith we had to keep up our little performance. I suppose Frith was thinking about it too, and I thought how much easier it would be if we cast aside convention and let him join in with us, if he had anything to say. Robert came with the drinks. Our plates were changed. The second course was handed. Mrs Danvers had not forgotten my wish for hot food. I took something out of a casserole covered in mushroom sauce.

'I think everyone enjoyed your wonderful party the other night,' said Colonel Julyan.

'I'm so glad,' I said.

'Does an immense amount of good locally, that sort of thing,' he said.

'Yes, I suppose it does,' I said.

'It's a universal instinct of the human species, isn't it, that desire to dress up in some sort of disguise?' said Frank.

'I must be very inhuman, then,' said Maxim.

'It's natural, I suppose,' said Colonel Julyan, 'for all of us to wish to look different. We are all children in some ways.'

I wondered how much pleasure it had given him to disguise himself as Cromwell. I had not seen much of him at the ball. He had spent most of the evening in the morning-room, playing bridge.

'You don't play golf, do you, Mrs de Winter?' said Colonel Julyan.

'No, I'm afraid I don't,' I said.

'You ought to take it up,' he said. 'My eldest girl is very keen, and she can't find young people to play with her. I gave her a small car for her birthday, and she drives herself over to the north coast nearly every day. It gives her something to do.'

'How nice,' I said.

'She ought to have been the boy,' he said. 'My lad is different altogether. No earthly use at games. Always writing poetry. I suppose he'll grow out of it.'

'Oh, rather,' said Frank. 'I used to write poetry myself when I was his age. Awful nonsense too. I never write any now.'

'Good heavens, I should hope not,' said Maxim.

'I don't know where my boy gets it from,' said Colonel Julyan; 'certainly not from his mother or from me.'

There was another long silence. Colonel Julyan had a second dip into the casserole. 'Mrs Lacy looked very well the other night,' he said.

'Yes,' I said.

'Her dress came adrift as usual,' said Maxim.

'Those Eastern garments must be the devil to manage,' said Colonel Julyan, 'and yet they say, you know, they are far more comfortable and far cooler than anything you ladies wear in England.'

'Really?' I said.

'Yes, so they say. It seems all that loose drapery throws off the hot rays of the sun.'

'How curious,' said Frank; 'you'd think it would have just the opposite effect.'

'No, apparently not,' said Colonel Julyan.

'Do you know the East, sir?' said Frank.

'I know the Far East,' said Colonel Julyan. 'I was in China for five years. Then Singapore.'

'Isn't that where they make the curry?' I said.

'Yes, they gave us very good curry in Singapore,' he said.

'I'm fond of curry,' said Frank.

'Ah, it's not curry at all in England, it's hash,' said Colonel Julyan.

The plates were cleared away. A soufflé was handed, and a

bowl of fruit salad. 'I suppose you are coming to the end of your raspberries,' said Colonel Julyan. 'It's been a wonderful summer for them, hasn't it? We've put down pots and pots of jam.'

'I never think raspberry jam is a great success,' said Frank; 'there are always so many pips.'

'You must come and try some of ours,' said Colonel Julyan. 'I don't think we have a great lot of pips.'

'We're going to have a mass of apples this year at Manderley,' said Frank. 'I was saying to Maxim a few days ago we ought to have a record season. We shall be able to send a lot up to London.'

'Do you really find it pays?' said Colonel Julyan; 'by the time you've paid your men for the extra labour, and then the packing, and carting, do you make any sort of profit worth while?'

'Oh, Lord, yes,' said Frank.

'How interesting. I must tell my wife,' said Colonel Julyan.

The soufflé and the fruit salad did not take long to finish. Robert appeared with cheese and biscuits, and a few minutes later Frith came with the coffee and cigarettes. Then they both went out of the room and shut the door. We drank our coffee in silence. I gazed steadily at my plate.

'I was saying to your wife before luncheon, de Winter,' began Colonel Julyan, resuming his first quiet confidential tone, 'that the awkward part of this whole distressing business is the fact that you identified that original body.'

'Yes, quite,' said Maxim.

'I think the mistake was very natural under the circumstances,' said Frank quickly. 'The authorities wrote to Maxim, asking him to go up to Edgecoombe, presupposing before he arrived there that the body was hers. And Maxim was not well at the time. I wanted to go with him, but he insisted on going alone. He was not in a fit state to undertake anything of the sort.'

'That's nonsense,' said Maxim. 'I was perfectly well.'

'Well, it's no use going into all that now,' said Colonel Julyan. 'You made that first identification, and now the only thing to do is to admit the error. There seems to be no doubt about it this time.'

'No,' said Maxim.

'I wish you could be spared the formality and the publicity of an inquest,' said Colonel Julyan, 'but I'm afraid that's quite impossible.'

'Naturally,' said Maxim.

'I don't think it need take very long,' said Colonel Julyan. 'It's just a case of you re-affirming identification, and then getting Tabb, who you say converted the boat when your wife brought her from France, just to give his piece of evidence that the boat was seaworthy and in good order when he last had her in his yard. It's just red-tape, you know. But it has to be done. No, what bothers me is the wretched publicity of the affair. So sad and unpleasant for you and your wife.'

'That's quite all right,' said Maxim. 'We understand.'

'So unfortunate that wretched ship going ashore there,' said Colonel Julyan, 'but for that the whole matter would have rested in peace.'

'Yes,' said Maxim.

'The only consolation is that now we know poor Mrs de Winter's death must have been swift and sudden, not the dreadful slow lingering affair we all believed it to be. There can have been no question of trying to swim.'

'None,' said Maxim.

'She must have gone down for something, and then the door jammed, and a squall caught the boat without anyone at the helm,' said Colonel Julyan. 'A dreadful thing.'

'Yes,' said Maxim.

'That seems to be the solution, don't you think, Crawley?' said Colonel Julyan, turning to Frank.

'Oh, yes, undoubtedly,' said Frank.

I glanced up, and I saw Frank looking at Maxim. He looked away again immediately but not before I had seen and understood the expression in his eyes. Frank knew. And Maxim did not know that he knew. I went on stirring my coffee. My hand was hot, damp.

'I suppose sooner or later we all make a mistake in judgement,' said Colonel Julyan, 'and then we are for it. Mrs de Winter must have known how the wind comes down like a funnel in that bay, and that it was not safe to leave the helm of a small boat like that. She must have sailed alone over that spot scores of times. And then the moment came, she took a chance – and the chance killed her. It's a lesson to all of us.'

'Accidents happen so easily,' said Frank, 'even to the most experienced people. Think of the number killed out hunting every season.'

'Oh, I know. But then it's the horse falling generally that lets you down. If Mrs de Winter had not left the helm of her boat the accident would never have happened. An extraordinary thing to do. I must have watched her many times in the handicap race on Saturdays from Kerrith, and I never saw her make an elementary mistake. It's the sort of thing a novice would do. In that particular place too, just by the ridge.'

'It was very squally that night,' said Frank; 'something may have happened to the gear. Something may have jammed. And then she slipped down for a knife.'

'Of course. Of course. Well, we shall never know. And I don't suppose we should be any the better for it if we did. As I said before, I wish I could stop this inquest but I can't. I'm trying to arrange it for Tuesday morning, and it will be as short as possible. Just a formal matter. But I'm afraid we shan't be able to keep the reporters out of it.'

There was another silence. I judged the time had come to push back my chair.

'Shall we go into the garden?' I said.

We all stood up, and then I led the way to the terrace. Colonel Julyan patted Jasper.

'He's grown into a nice-looking dog,' he said.

'Yes,' I said.

'They make nice pets,' he said.

'Yes,' I said.

We stood about for a minute. Then he glanced at his watch. 'Thank you for your most excellent lunch,' he said. 'I have rather a busy afternoon in front of me, and I hope you will excuse me dashing away.'

'Of course,' I said.

'I'm so very sorry this should have happened. You have all my sympathy. I consider it's almost harder for you than for your husband. However, once the inquest is over you must both forget all about it.'

'Yes,' I said, 'yes, we must try to.'

'My car is here in the drive. I wonder whether Crawley would like a lift. Crawley? I can drop you at your office if it's any use.'

'Thank you, sir,' said Frank.

He came and took my hand. 'I shall be seeing you again,' he said.

'Yes,' I said.

I did not look at him. I was afraid he would understand my eyes. I did not want him to know that I knew. Maxim walked with them to the car. When they had gone he came back to me on the terrace. He took my arm. We stood looking down at the green lawns towards the sea and the beacon on the headland.

'It's going to be all right,' he said. 'I'm quite calm, quite confident. You saw how Julyan was at lunch, and Frank. There won't be any difficulty at the inquest. It's going to be all right.'

I did not say anything. I held his arm tightly.

'There was never any question of the body being someone unknown,' he said. 'What we saw was enough for Doctor Phillips even to make the identification alone without me. It was straightforward, simple. There was no trace of what I'd done. The bullet had not touched the bone.'

A butterfly sped past us on the terrace, silly and inconsequent.

'You heard what they said,' he went on; 'they think she was trapped there, in the cabin. The jury will believe that at the inquest too. Phillips will tell them so.' He paused. Still I did not speak.

'I only mind for you,' he said. 'I don't regret anything else. If it had to come all over again I should not do anything different. I'm glad I killed Rebecca. I shall never have any remorse for

335

that, never, never. But you. I can't forget what it has done to you. I was looking at you, thinking of nothing else all through lunch. It's gone forever, that funny, young, lost look that I loved. It won't come back again. I killed that too, when I told you about Rebecca . . . It's gone, in twenty-four hours. You are so much older . . .'

22

That evening, when Frith brought in the local paper, there were great headlines right across the top of the page. He brought the paper and laid it down on the table. Maxim was not there; he had gone up early to change for dinner. Frith stood a moment, waiting for me to say something, and it seemed to me stupid and insulting to ignore a matter that must mean so much to everyone in the house.

'This is a very dreadful thing, Frith,' I said.

'Yes, Madam; we are all most distressed outside,' he said.

'It's so sad for Mr de Winter,' I said, 'having to go through it all again.'

'Yes, Madam. Very sad. Such a shocking experience, Madam, having to identify the second body having seen the first. I suppose there is no doubt then, that the remains in the boat are genuinely those of the late Mrs de Winter?'

'I'm afraid not, Frith. No doubt at all.'

'It seems so odd to us, Madam, that she should have let herself be trapped like that in the cabin. She was so experienced in a boat.'

'Yes, Frith. That's what we all feel. But accidents will happen. And how it happened I don't suppose any of us will ever know.'

'I suppose not, Madam. But it's a great shock, all the same. We are most distressed about it outside. And coming suddenly just after the party. It doesn't seem right somehow, does it?'

'No, Frith.'

'It seems there is to be an inquest, Madam?'

'Yes. A formality, you know.'

'Of course, Madam. I wonder if any of us will be required to give evidence?'

'I don't think so.'

'I shall be only too pleased to do anything that might help the family; Mr de Winter knows that.'

'Yes, Frith. I'm sure he does.'

'I've told them outside not to discuss the matter, but it's very difficult to keep an eye on them, especially the girls. I can deal with Robert, of course. I'm afraid the news has been a great shock to Mrs Danvers.'

'Yes, Frith. I rather expected it would.'

'She went up to her room straight after lunch, and has not come down again. Alice took her a cup of tea and the paper a few minutes ago. She said Mrs Danvers looked very ill indeed.'

'It would be better really if she stayed where she is,' I said. 'It's no use her getting up and seeing to things if she is ill. Perhaps Alice would tell her that. I can very well manage the ordering. The cook and I between us.'

'Yes, Madam. I don't think she is physically ill, Madam; it's just the shock of Mrs de Winter being found. She was very devoted to Mrs de Winter.'

'Yes,' I said. 'Yes, I know.'

Frith went out of the room after that, and I glanced quickly at the paper before Maxim came down. There was a great column, all down the front page, and an awful blurred photograph of Maxim that must have been taken at least fifteen years ago. It was dreadful, seeing it there on the front page staring at me. And the little line about myself at the bottom, saying whom Maxim had married as his second wife, and how we had just given the fancy dress ball at Manderley. It sounded so crude and callous, in the dark print of the newspaper. Rebecca, whom they described as beautiful, talented, and loved by all who knew her, having been drowned a year ago, and then Maxim marrying again the following spring, bringing his bride straight to Manderley (so it said) and giving the big fancy dress ball in her honour. And then the following morning the body of his first wife being found, trapped in the cabin of her sailing boat, at the bottom of the bay.

It was true of course, though sprinkled with the little inaccuracies that added to the story, making it strong meat for the hundreds of readers who wanted value for their pennies. Maxim sounded vile in it, a sort of satyr. Bringing back his 'young bride', as it described me, to Manderley, and giving the dance, as though we wanted to display ourselves before the world.

I hid the paper under the cushion of the chair so that Maxim should not see it. But I could not keep the morning editions from him. The story was in our London papers too. There was a picture of Manderley, and the story underneath. Manderley was news, and so was Maxim. They talked about him as Max de Winter. It sounded racy, horrible. Each paper made great play of the fact that Rebecca's body had been found the day after the fancy dress ball, as though there was something deliberate about it. Both papers used the same word, 'ironic'. Yes, I suppose it was ironic. It made a good story. I watched Maxim at the breakfast table getting whiter and whiter as he read the papers, one after the other, and then the local one as well. He did not say anything. He just looked across at me, and I stretched out my hand to him. 'Damn them,' he whispered, 'damn them, damn them.'

I thought of all the things they could say, if they knew the truth. Not one column, but five or six. Placards in London. Newsboys shouting in the streets, outside the underground stations. That frightful word of six letters, in the middle of the placard, large and black.

Frank came up after breakfast. He looked pale and tired, as though he had not slept. 'I've told the exchange to put all calls for Manderley through to the office,' he said to Maxim. 'It doesn't matter who it is. If reporters ring up I can deal with them. And anyone else too. I don't want either of you to be worried at all. We've had several calls already from locals. I gave the same answer to each. Mr and Mrs de Winter were grateful for all sympathetic inquiries, and they hoped their friends would understand that they were not receiving calls during the next few days. Mrs Lacy rang up about eight-thirty. Wanted to come over at once.'

'Oh, my God . . .' began Maxim.

'It's all right, I prevented her. I told her quite truthfully that I did not think she would do any good coming over. That you did not want to see anyone but Mrs de Winter. She wanted to know when they were holding the inquest, but I told her it had not been settled. I don't know that we can stop her from coming to that, if she finds it in the papers.'

'Those blasted reporters,' said Maxim.

'I know,' said Frank; 'we all want to wring their necks, but you've got to see their point of view. It's their bread-and-butter; they've got to do the job for their paper. If they don't get a story the editor probably sacks them. If the editor does not produce a saleable edition the proprietor sacks him. And if the paper doesn't sell, the proprietor loses all his money. You won't have to see them or speak to them, Maxim. I'm going to do all that for you. All you have to concentrate on is your statement at the inquest.'

'I know what to say,' said Maxim.

'Of course you do, but don't forget old Horridge is the Coroner. He's a sticky sort of chap, goes into details that are quite irrelevant, just to show the jury how thorough he is at his job. You must not let him rattle you.'

'Why the devil should I be rattled? I have nothing to be rattled about.'

'Of course not. But I've attended these coroner's inquests before, and it's so easy to get nervy and irritable. You don't want to put the fellow's back up.'

'Frank's right,' I said. 'I know just what he means. The swifter and smoother the whole thing goes the easier it will be for everyone. Then once the wretched thing is over we shall forget all about it, and so will everyone else, won't they, Frank?'

'Yes, of course,' said Frank.

I still avoided his eye, but I was more convinced than ever that he knew the truth. He had always known it. From the very first. I remembered the first time I met him, that first day of mine at Manderley, when he, and Beatrice, and Giles had all been at lunch, and Beatrice had been tactless about Maxim's health. I remembered Frank, his quiet turning of the subject, the way he had come to Maxim's aid in his quiet unobtrusive manner if there was ever any question of difficulty. That strange reluctance of his to talk about Rebecca, his stiff, funny, pompous way of making conversation whenever we had approached anything like intimacy. I understood it all. Frank knew, but Maxim did not know that he knew. And Frank did not want Maxim to know that he knew. And we all stood there, looking at one another, keeping up these little barriers between us.

We were not bothered with the telephone again. All the calls were put through to the office. It was just a question of waiting now. Waiting until the Tuesday.

I saw nothing of Mrs Danvers. The menu was sent through as usual, and I did not change it. I asked little Clarice about her. She said she was going about her work as usual but she was not speaking to anybody. She had all her meals alone in her sitting-room.

Clarice was wide-eyed, evidently curious, but she did not ask me any questions, and I was not going to discuss it with her. No doubt they talked of nothing else, out in the kitchen, and on the estate too, in the lodge, on the farms. I supposed all Kerrith was full of it. We stayed in Manderley, in the gardens close to the house. We did not even walk in the woods. The weather had not broken yet. It was still hot, oppressive. The air was full of thunder, and there was rain behind the white dull sky, but it did not fall. I could feel it, and smell it, pent up there, behind the clouds. The inquest was to be on the Tuesday afternoon at two o'clock.

We had lunch at a quarter to one. Frank came. Thank heaven Beatrice had telephoned that she could not get over. The boy Roger had arrived home with measles; they were all in quarantine. I could not help blessing the measles. I don't think Maxim could have borne it, with Beatrice sitting here, staying in the house, sincere, anxious, and affectionate, but asking questions all the time. Forever asking questions.

Lunch was a hurried, nervous meal. We none of us talked very much. I had that nagging pain again. I did not want anything to eat. I could not swallow. It was a relief when the farce of the meal was over, and I heard Maxim go out on to the drive and start up the car. The sound of the engine steadied me. It meant we had to go, we had to be doing something. Not just sitting at Manderley. Frank followed us in his own car. I had my hand on Maxim's knee all the way as he drove. He seemed quite calm. Not nervous in any way. It was like going with someone to a nursing-home, someone who was to have an operation. And not knowing what would happen. Whether the operation would be successful. My hands were very cold. My heart was beating in a funny, jerky way. And all the time that little nagging pain beneath my heart. The inquest was to be held at Lanyon, the market town six miles the other side of Kerrith. We had to park the cars in the big cobbled square by the market-place. Doctor Phillips' car was there already, and also Colonel Julyan's. Other cars too. I saw a passer-by stare curiously at Maxim, and then nudge her companion's arm.

'I think I shall stay here,' I said. 'I don't think I'll come in with you after all.'

'I did not want you to come,' said Maxim. 'I was against it from the first. You'd much better have stayed at Manderley.'

'No,' I said. 'No, I'll be all right here, sitting in the car.'

Frank came and looked in at the window. 'Isn't Mrs de Winter coming?' he said.

'No,' said Maxim. 'She wants to stay in the car.'

'I think she's right,' said Frank; 'there's no earthly reason why she should be present at all. We shan't be long.'

'It's all right,' I said.

'I'll keep a seat for you,' said Frank, 'in case you should change your mind.'

They went off together and left me sitting there. It was early-closing day. The shops looked drab and dull. There were not many people about. Lanyon was not much of a holiday centre anyway; it was too far inland. I sat looking at the silent shops.

The minutes went by. I wondered what they were doing, the Coroner, Frank, Maxim, Colonel Julyan. I got out of the car and began walking up and down the market square. I went and looked in a shop window. Then I walked up and down again. I saw a policeman watching me curiously. I turned up a side-street to avoid him.

Somehow, in spite of myself, I found I was coming to the building where the inquest was being held. There had been little publicity about the actual time, and because of this there was no crowd waiting, as I had feared and expected. The place seemed deserted. I went up the steps and stood just inside the door.

A policeman appeared from nowhere. 'Do you want anything?' he said.

'No,' I said. 'No.'

'You can't wait here,' he said.

'I'm sorry,' I said. I went back towards the steps into the street.

'Excuse me, Madam,' he said, 'aren't you Mrs de Winter?'

'Yes,' I said.

'Of course that's different,' he said; 'you can wait here if you like. Would you like to take a seat just inside this room?'

'Thank you,' I said.

He showed me into a little bare room with a desk in it. It was like a waiting-room at a station. I sat there, with my hands on my lap. Five minutes passed. Nothing happened. It was worse than being outside, than sitting in the car. I got up and went into the passage. The policeman was still standing there.

'How long will they be?' I said.

'I'll go and inquire if you like,' he said.

He disappeared along the passage. In a moment he came back again. 'I don't think they will be very much longer,' he said. 'Mr de Winter has just given his evidence. Captain Searle, and the diver, and Doctor Phillips have already given theirs. There's only one more to speak. Mr Tabb, the boat-builder from Kerrith.'

'Then it's nearly over,' I said.

'I expect so, Madam,' he said. Then he said, on a sudden thought, 'Would you like to hear the remaining evidence? There is a seat there, just inside the door. If you slip in now nobody will notice you.'

'Yes,' I said. 'Yes, I think I will.'

It was nearly over. Maxim had finished giving his evidence. I did not mind hearing the rest. It was Maxim I had not wanted to hear. I had been nervous of listening to his evidence. That was why I had not gone with him and Frank in the first place. Now it did not matter. His part of it was over.

I followed the policeman, and he opened a door at the end of the passage. I slipped in, I sat down just by the door. I kept my head low so that I did not have to look at anybody. The room was smaller than I had imagined. Rather hot and stuffy. I had pictured a great bare room with benches, like a church. Maxim and Frank were sitting down at the other end. The Coroner was a thin, elderly man in pince-nez. There were people there I did not know. I glanced at them out of the tail of my eye. My heart gave a jump suddenly as I recognized Mrs Danvers. She was sitting right at the back. And Favell was beside her. Jack Favell, Rebecca's cousin. He was leaning forward, his chin in his hands, his eyes fixed on the Coroner, Mr Horridge. I had not expected him to be there. I wondered if Maxim had seen him. James Tabb, the boat-builder, was standing up now and the Coroner was asking him a question.

'Yes, sir,' answered Tabb, 'I converted Mrs de Winter's little boat. She was a French fishing boat originally, and Mrs de Winter bought her for next to nothing over in Brittany, and had her shipped over. She gave me the job of converting her and doing her up like a little yacht.'

'Was the boat in a fit state to put to sea?' said the Coroner.

'She was when I fitted her out in April of last year,' said Tabb. 'Mrs de Winter laid her up as usual at my yard in the October, and then in March I had word from her to fit her up as usual, which I did. That would be Mrs de Winter's fourth season with the boat since I did the conversion job for her.'

'Had the boat ever been known to capsize before?' asked the Coroner.

'No, sir. I should soon have heard of it from Mrs de Winter had there been any question of it. She was delighted with the boat in every way, according to what she said to me.'

'I suppose great care was needed to handle the boat?' said the Coroner.

'Well, sir, everyone has to have their wits about them, when they go sailing boats, I won't deny it. But Mrs de Winter's boat wasn't one of those cranky little craft that you can't leave for a moment, like some of the boats you see in Kerrith. She was a stout seaworthy boat, and could stand a lot of wind. Mrs de Winter had sailed her in worse weather than she ever found that night. Why, it was only blowing in fits and starts at the time. That's what I've said all along. I couldn't understand Mrs de Winter's boat being lost on a night like that.'

'But surely, if Mrs de Winter went below for a coat, as is supposed, and a sudden puff of wind was to come down from that headland, it would be enough to capsize the boat?' asked the Coroner.

James Tabb shook his head. 'No,' he said stubbornly, 'I don't see that it would.'

'Well, I'm afraid that is what must have happened,' said the Coroner. 'I don't think Mr de Winter or any of us suggest that your workmanship was to blame for the accident at all. You fitted the boat out at the beginning of the season, you reported her sound and seaworthy, and that's all I want to know. Unfortunately the late Mrs de Winter relaxed her watchfulness for a moment and she lost her life, the boat sinking with her aboard. Such accidents have happened before. I repeat again we are not blaming you.'

'Excuse me, sir,' said the boat-builder, 'but there is a little bit more to it than that. And if you would allow me I should like to make a further statement.'

'Very well, go on,' said the Coroner.

'It's like this, sir. After the accident last year a lot of people in Kerrith made unpleasantness about my work. Some said I had let Mrs de Winter start the season in a leaky, rotten boat. I lost two or three orders because of it. It was very unfair, but the boat had sunk, and there was nothing I could say to clear myself. Then that steamer went ashore, as we all know, and Mrs de Winter's little boat was found, and brought to the surface. Captain Searle himself gave me permission yesterday to go and look at her, and I did. I wanted to satisfy myself that the work I had put in to her was sound, in spite of the fact that she had been waterlogged for twelve months or more.'

'Well, that was very natural,' said the Coroner, 'and I hope you were satisfied.'

'Yes, sir, I was. There was nothing wrong with that boat as regards the work I did to her. I examined every corner of her there on the lighter up the pill where Captain Searle had put her. She had sunk on sandy bottom. I asked the diver about that, and he told me so. She had not touched the ridge at all. The ridge was a clear five feet away. She was lying on sand, and there wasn't the mark of a rock on her.'

He paused. The Coroner looked at him expectantly.

'Well?' he said, 'is that all you want to say?'

'No, sir,' said Tabb emphatically, 'it's not. What I want to know is this. Who drove the holes in her planking? Rocks didn't do it. The nearest rock was five feet away. Besides, they weren't the sort of marks made by a rock. They were holes. Done with a spike.'

I did not look at him. I was looking at the floor. There was oil-cloth laid on the boards. Green oil-cloth. I looked at it.

I wondered why the Coroner did not say something. Why did the pause last so long? When he spoke at last his voice sounded rather far away.

'What do you mean?' he said, 'what sort of holes?'

'There were three of them altogether,' said the boat-builder, 'one right for'ard, by her chain locker, on her starboard planking, below the water-line. The other two close together amidships, underneath her floor boards in the bottom. The ballast had been shifted too. It was lying loose. And that's not all. The sea-cocks had been turned on.'

'The sea-cocks? What are they?' asked the Coroner.

'The fitting that plugs the pipes leading from a washbasin or lavatory, sir. Mrs de Winter had a little place fitted up right aft. And there was a sink for'ard, where the washing-up was done. There was a sea-cock there, and another in the lavatory. These are always kept tight closed when you're under way, otherwise the water would flow in. When I examined the boat yesterday both sea-cocks were turned full on.'

It was hot, much too hot. Why didn't they open a window? We should be suffocated if we sat here with the air like this, and there were so many people, all breathing the same air, so many people.

'With those holes in her planking, sir, and the sea-cocks not closed, it wouldn't take long for a small boat like her to sink. Not much more than ten minutes, I should say. Those holes weren't there when the boat left my yard. I was proud of my work and so was Mrs de Winter. It's my opinion, sir, that the boat never capsized at all. She was deliberately scuttled.'

I must try and get out of the door. I must try and go back to the waiting-room again. There was no air left in this place, and the person next to me was pressing close, close ... Someone in front of me was standing up, and they were talking, too, they were all talking. I did not know what was happening. I could not see anything. It was hot, so very hot. The Coroner was asking everybody to be silent. And he said something about 'Mr de Winter'. I could not see. That woman's hat was in front of me. Maxim was standing up now. I could not look at him. I must not look at him. I felt like this once before. When was it? I don't know. I don't remember. Oh, yes, with Mrs Danvers. The time Mrs Danvers stood with me by the window. Mrs Danvers was in this place now, listening to the Coroner. Maxim was standing up over there. The heat was coming up at me from the floor, rising in slow waves. It reached my hands, wet and slippery, it touched my neck, my chin, my face.

'Mr de Winter, you heard the statement from James Tabb, who

had the care of Mrs de Winter's boat? Do you know anything of these holes driven in the planking?'

'Nothing whatever.'

'Can you think of any reason why they should be there?'

'No, of course not.'

'It's the first time you have heard them mentioned?'

'Yes.'

'It's a shock to you, of course?'

'It was shock enough to learn that I made a mistake in identification over twelve months ago, and now I learn that my late wife was not only drowned in the cabin of her boat, but that holes were bored in the boat with the deliberate intent of letting in the water so that the boat should sink. Does it surprise you that I should be shocked?'

No, Maxim. No. You will put his back up. You heard what Frank said. You must not put his back up. Not that voice. Not that angry voice, Maxim. He won't understand. Please, darling, please. Oh, God, don't let Maxim lose his temper. Don't let him lose his temper.

'Mr de Winter, I want you to believe that we all feel very deeply for you in this matter. No doubt you have suffered a shock, a very severe shock, in learning that your late wife was drowned in her own cabin, and not at sea as you supposed. And I am inquiring into the matter for you. I want, for your sake, to find out exactly how and why she died. I don't conduct this inquiry for my own amusement.'

'That's rather obvious, isn't it?'

'I hope that it is. James Tabb has just told us that the boat which contained the remains of the late Mrs de Winter had three holes hammered through her bottom. And that the sea-cocks were open. Do you doubt his statement?'

'Of course not. He's a boat-builder, he knows what he is talking about.'

'Who looked after Mrs de Winter's boat?'

'She looked after it herself.'

'She employed no hand?'

'No, nobody at all.'

'The boat was moored in the private harbour belonging to Manderley?'

'Yes.'

'Any stranger who tried to tamper with the boat would be seen? There is no access to the harbour by public footpath?'

'No, none at all.'

'The harbour is quiet, is it not, and surrounded by trees?'

'Yes.'

'A trespasser might not be noticed?'

'Possibly not.'

'Yet James Tabb has told us, and we have no reason to disbelieve him, that a boat with those holes drilled in her bottom and the sea-cocks open could not float for more than ten or fifteen minutes.'

'Quite.'

'Therefore we can put aside the idea that the boat was tampered with maliciously before Mrs de Winter went for her evening sail. Had that been the case the boat would have sunk at her moorings.'

'No doubt.'

'Therefore we must assume that whoever took the boat out that night drove in the planking and opened the sea-cocks.'

'I suppose so.'

'You have told us already that the door of the cabin was shut, the port-holes closed, and your wife's remains were on the floor. This was in your statement, and in Doctor Phillips', and in Captain Searle's?'

'Yes.'

'And now added to this is the information that a spike was driven through the bottom, and the sea-cocks were open. Does not this strike you, Mr de Winter, as being very strange?'

'Certainly.'

'You have no suggestion to make?'

'No, none at all.'

'Mr de Winter, painful as it may be, it is my duty to ask you a very personal question.'

'Yes.'

'Were relations between you and the late Mrs de Winter perfectly happy?'

They had to come of course, those black spots in front of my eyes, dancing, flickering, stabbing the hazy air, and it was hot, so hot, with all these people, all these faces, and no open window; the door, from being near to me, was farther away than I had thought, and all the time the ground coming up to meet me.

And then, out of the queer mist around me, Maxim's voice, clear and strong. 'Will someone take my wife outside? She is going to faint.'

23

I was sitting in the little room again. The room like a waiting-room at the station. The policeman was there, bending over me, giving me a glass of water, and someone's hand was on my arm, Frank's hand. I sat quite still, the floor, the walls, the figures of Frank and the policeman taking solid shape before me.

'I'm so sorry,' I said, 'such a stupid thing to do. It was so hot in that room, so very hot.'

'It gets very airless in there,' said the policeman, 'there's been complaints about it often, but nothing's ever done. We've had ladies fainting in there before.'

'Are you feeling better, Mrs de Winter?' said Frank.

'Yes. Yes, much better. I shall be all right again. Don't wait with me.'

'I'm going to take you back to Manderley.'

'No.'

'Yes. Maxim has asked me to.'

'No. You ought to stay with him.'

'Maxim told me to take you back to Manderley.'

He put his arm through mine and helped me to get up. 'Can you walk as far as the car or shall I bring it round?'

'I can walk. But I'd much rather stay. I want to wait for Maxim.'

'Maxim may be a long time.'

Why did he say that? What did he mean? Why didn't he look at me? He took my arm and walked with me along the passage to the door, and so down the steps into the street. Maxim may be a long time . . .

We did not speak. We came to the little Morris car belonging to Frank. He opened the door, and helped me in. Then he got in himself and started up the engine. We drove away from the cobbled market-place, through the empty town, and out on to the road to Kerrith.

'Why will they be a long time? What are they going to do?'

'They may have to go over the evidence again.' Frank looked straight in front of him along the hard white road.

'They've had all the evidence,' I said. 'There's nothing more anyone can say.'

'You never know,' said Frank, 'the Coroner may put his questions in a different way. Tabb has altered the whole business. The Coroner will have to approach it now from another angle.'

'What angle? How do you mean?'

'You heard the evidence? You heard what Tabb said about the boat? They won't believe in an accident any more.'

'It's absurd, Frank, it's ridiculous. They should not listen to Tabb. How can he tell, after all these months, how holes came to be in a boat? What are they trying to prove?'

'I don't know.'

'That Coroner will go on and on harping at Maxim, making him lose his temper, making him say things he doesn't mean. He will ask question after question, Frank, and Maxim won't stand it, I know he won't stand it.'

Frank did not answer. He was driving very fast. For the first time since I had known him he was at a loss for the usual conventional phrase. That meant he was worried, very worried. And usually he was such a slow careful driver, stopping dead at every cross-roads, peering to right and left, blowing his horn at every bend in the road.

'That man was there,' I said, 'that man who came once to Manderley to see Mrs Danvers.'

'You mean Favell?' asked Frank. 'Yes, I saw him.'

'He was sitting there, with Mrs Danvers.'

'Yes, I know.'

'Why was he there? What right had he to go to the inquest?'

'He was her cousin.'

'It's not right that he and Mrs Danvers should sit there, listening to that evidence. I don't trust them, Frank.'

'No.'

'They might do something; they might make mischief.'

Again Frank did not answer. I realized that his loyalty to Maxim was such that he would not let himself be drawn into a discussion, even with me. He did not know how much I knew. Nor could I tell for certainty how much he knew. We were allies, we travelled the same road, but we could not look at one another. We neither of us dared risk a confession. We were turning in now at the lodge gates, and down the long twisting narrow drive to the house. I noticed for the first time how the hydrangeas were coming into bloom, their blue heads thrusting themselves from the green foliage behind. For all their beauty there was something sombre about them, funereal; they were like the wreaths, stiff and artificial, that you see beneath glass cases in a foreign churchyard. There they were, all the way along the drive, on either side of us, blue, monotonous, like spectators lined up in a street to watch us pass.

We came to the house at last and rounded the great sweep before the steps. 'Will you be all right now?' said Frank. 'You can lie down, can't you?'

'Yes,' I said, 'yes, perhaps.'

'I shall go back to Lanyon,' he said, 'Maxim may want me.'

He did not say anything more. He got quickly back into the car again and drove away. Maxim might want him. Why did he say Maxim might want him? Perhaps the Coroner was going to question Frank as well. Ask him about that evening, over twelve months ago, when Maxim had dined with Frank. He would want to know the exact time that Maxim left his house. He would want to know if anybody saw Maxim when he returned to the house. Whether the servants knew that he was there. Whether anybody could prove that Maxim went straight up to bed and undressed. Mrs Danvers might be questioned. They might ask Mrs Danvers to give evidence. And Maxim beginning to lose his temper, beginning to go white . . .

I went into the hall. I went upstairs to my room, and lay down upon my bed, even as Frank had suggested. I put my hands over my eyes. I kept seeing that room and all the faces. The lined, painstaking, aggravating face of the Coroner, the gold pince-nez on his nose.

'I don't conduct this inquiry for my own amusement.' His slow, careful mind, easily offended. What were they all saying now? What was happening? Suppose in a little while Frank came back to Manderley alone?

I did not know what happened. I did not know what people did. I remembered pictures of men in the papers, leaving places like that, and being taken away. Suppose Maxim was taken away? They would not let me go to him. They would not let me see him. I should have to stay here at Manderley day after day, night after night, waiting, as I was waiting now. People like Colonel Julyan being kind. People saying 'You must not be alone. You must come to us.' The telephone, the newspapers, the telephone again. 'No, Mrs de Winter can't see anyone. Mrs de Winter has no story to give the *County Chronicle*.' And another day. And another day. Weeks that would be blurred and non-existent. Frank at last taking me to see Maxim. He would look thin, queer, like people in hospital . . .

Other women had been through this. Women I had read about in papers. They sent letters to the Home Secretary and it was not any good. The Home Secretary always said that justice must take its course. Friends sent petitions too, everybody signed them, but the Home Secretary could never do anything. And the ordinary people who read about it in the papers said why should the fellow get off, he murdered his wife, didn't he? What about the poor, murdered wife? This sentimental business about abolishing the death penalty simply encourages crime. This fellow ought to have thought about that before he killed his wife. It's too late now. He will have to hang for it, like any other murderer. And serve him right too. Let it be a warning to others.

I remember seeing a picture on the back of a paper once, of a little crowd collected outside a prison gate, and just after nine o'clock a policeman came and pinned a notice on the gate for the people to read. The notice said something about the sentence being carried out. 'Sentence of death was carried out this morning at nine o'clock. The Governor, the Prison Doctor, and the Sheriff of the County were present.' Hanging was quick. Hanging did not hurt. It broke your neck at once. No, it did not. Someone said once it did not always work. Someone who had known the Governor of a prison. They put that bag over your head, and you stand on the little platform, and then the floor gives way beneath you. It takes exactly three minutes to go from the cell to the moment you are hanged. No, fifty seconds, someone said. No, that's absurd. It could not be fifty seconds. There's a little flight of steps down the side of the shed, down to the pit. The doctor goes down there to look. They die instantly. No, they don't. The body moves for some time, the neck is not always broken. Yes, but even so they don't feel anything. Someone said they did. Someone who had a brother who was a prison doctor said it was not generally known, because it would be such a scandal, but they did not always die at once. Their eyes were open, they stay open for quite a long time.

God, don't let me go on thinking about this. Let me think about something else. About other things. About Mrs Van Hopper in America. She must be staying with her daughter now. They had that house on Long Island in the summer. I expect they played a lot of bridge. They went to the races. Mrs Van Hopper was fond of the races. I wonder if she still wears that little yellow hat. It was too small for her. Much too small on that big face. Mrs Van Hopper sitting about in the garden of that house on Long Island, with novels, and magazines, and papers on her lap. Mrs Van Hopper putting up her lorgnette and calling to her daughter. 'Look at this, Helen. They say Max de Winter murdered his first wife. I always did think there was something peculiar about him. I warned that fool of a girl she was making a mistake, but she wouldn't listen to me. Well, she's cooked her goose now all right. I suppose they'll make her a big offer to go on the pictures.'

Something was touching my hand. It was Jasper. It was Jasper, thrusting his cold damp nose in my hands. He had followed me up from the hall. Why did dogs make one want to cry? There was something so quiet and hopeless about their sympathy. Jasper, knowing something was wrong, as dogs always do. Trunks being packed. Cars being brought to the door. Dogs standing with drooping tails, dejected eyes. Wandering back to their baskets in the hall when the sound of the car dies away . . .

I must have fallen asleep because I woke suddenly with a start, and heard that first crack of thunder in the air. I sat up. The clock said five. I got up and went to the window. There was not a breath of wind. The leaves hung listless on the trees, waiting. The sky was slatey grey. The jagged lightning split the sky. Another rumble in the distance. No rain fell. I went out into the corridor and listened. I could not hear anything. I went to the head of the stairs. There was no sign of anybody. The hall was dark because of the menace of thunder overhead. I went down and stood on the terrace. There was another burst of thunder. One spot of rain fell on my hand. One spot. No more. It was very dark. I could see the sea beyond the dip in the valley like a black lake. Another spot fell on my hands, and another crack of thunder came. One of the housemaids began shutting the windows in the rooms upstairs. Robert appeared and shut the windows of the drawing-room behind me.

'The gentlemen are not back yet, are they, Robert?' I asked.

'No, Madam, not yet. I thought you were with them, Madam.'

'No. No, I've been back some time.'

'Will you have tea, Madam?'

'No, no, I'll wait.'

'It looks as though the weather was going to break at last, Madam.'

'Yes.'

No rain fell. Nothing since those two drops on my hand. I went back and sat in the library. At half past five Robert came into the room.

'The car has just driven up to the door now, Madam,' he said.

'Which car?' I said.

'Mr de Winter's car, Madam,' he said.

'Is Mr de Winter driving it himself?'

'Yes, Madam.'

I tried to get up but my legs were things of straw, they would not bear me. I stood leaning against the sofa. My throat was very dry. After a minute Maxim came into the room. He stood just inside the door.

He looked very tired, old. There were lines at the corner of his mouth I had never noticed before.

'It's all over,' he said.

I waited. Still I could not speak or move towards him.

'Suicide,' he said, 'without sufficient evidence to show the state of mind of the deceased. They were all at sea of course, they did not know what they were doing.'

I sat down on the sofa. 'Suicide,' I said, 'but the motive? Where was the motive?'

'God knows,' he said. 'They did not seem to think a motive was necessary. Old Horridge, peering at me, wanting to know if Rebecca had any money troubles. Money troubles. God in heaven.'

He went and stood by the window, looking out at the green lawns. 'It's going to rain,' he said. 'Thank God it's going to rain at last.'

'What happened?' I said, 'what did the Coroner say? Why have you been there all this time?'

'He went over and over the same ground again,' said Maxim. 'Little details about the boat that no one cared about a damn. Were the sea-cocks hard to turn on? Where exactly was the first hole in relation to the second? What was ballast? What effect upon the stability of the boat would the shifting of the ballast have? Could a woman do this unaided? Did the cabin door shut firmly? What pressure of water was necessary to burst open the door? I thought I should go mad. I kept my temper though. Seeing you there, by the door, made me remember what I had to do. If you had not fainted like that, I should never have done

357

it. It brought me up with a jerk. I knew exactly what I was going to say. I faced Horridge all the time. I never took my eyes off his thin, pernickety, little face and those gold-rimmed pince-nez. I shall remember that face of his to my dying day. I'm tired, darling; so tired I can't see, or hear or feel anything.'

He sat down on the window-seat. He leant forward, his head in his hands. I went and sat beside him. In a few minutes Frith came in, followed by Robert carrying the table for tea. The solemn ritual went forward as it always did, day after day, the leaves of the table pulled out, the legs adjusted, the laying of the snowy cloth, the putting down of the silver tea-pot and the kettle with the little flame beneath. Scones, sandwiches, three different sorts of cake. Jasper sat close to the table, his tail thumping now and again upon the floor, his eyes fixed expectantly on me. It's funny, I thought, how the routine of life goes on, whatever happens, we do the same things, go through the little performance of eating, sleeping, washing. No crisis can break through the crust of habit. I poured out Maxim's tea, I took it to him on the window-seat, gave him his scone, and buttered one for myself.

'Where's Frank?' I asked.

'He had to go and see the vicar. I would have gone too but I wanted to come straight back to you. I kept thinking of you, waiting here, all by yourself, not knowing what was going to happen.'

'Why the vicar?' I said.

'Something has to happen this evening,' he said. 'Something at the church.'

I stared at him blankly. Then I understood. They were going to bury Rebecca. They were going to bring Rebecca back from the mortuary.

'It's fixed for six-thirty,' he said. 'No one knows but Frank, and Colonel Julyan, and the vicar, and myself. There won't be anyone hanging about. This was arranged yesterday. The verdict doesn't make any difference.'

'What time must you go?'

'I'm meeting them there at the church at twenty-five past six.'

I did not say anything. I went on drinking my tea. Maxim put his sandwich down untasted. 'It's still very hot, isn't it,' he said.

'It's the storm,' I said. 'It won't break. Only little spots at a time. It's there in the air. It won't break.'

'It was thundering when I left Lanyon,' he said, 'the sky was like ink over my head. Why in the name of God doesn't it rain?'

The birds were hushed in the trees. It was still very dark.

'I wish you did not have to go out again,' I said.

He did not answer. He looked tired, so deathly tired.

'We'll talk over things this evening when I get back,' he said presently. 'We've got so much to do together, haven't we? We've got to begin all over again. I've been the worst sort of husband for you.'

'No!' I said. 'No!'

'We'll start again, once this thing is behind us. We can do it, you and I. It's not like being alone. The past can't hurt us if we are together. You'll have children too.' After a while he glanced at his watch. 'It's ten past six,' he said, 'I shall have to be going. It won't take long, not more than half an hour. We've got to go down to the crypt.'

I held his hand. 'I'll come with you. I shan't mind. Let me come with you.'

'No,' he said. 'No, I don't want you to come.'

Then he went out of the room. I heard the sound of the car starting up in the drive. Presently the sound died away, and I knew he had gone.

Robert came to clear away the tea. It was like any other day. The routine was unchanged. I wondered if it would have been so had Maxim not come back from Lanyon. I wondered if Robert would have stood there, that wooden expression on his young sheep's face, brushing the crumbs from the snow-white cloth, picking up the table, carrying it from the room.

It seemed very quiet in the library when he had gone. I began to think of them down at the church, going through that door and down the flight of stairs to the crypt. I had never been there. I had only seen the door. I wondered what a crypt was like, if there were coffins standing there. Maxim's father and mother. I wondered what would happen to the coffin of that other woman who had been put there by mistake. I wondered who she was, poor unclaimed soul, washed up by the wind and tide. Now another coffin would stand there. Rebecca would lie there in the crypt as well. Was the vicar reading the burial service there, with Maxim, and Frank, and Colonel Julyan standing by his side? Ashes to ashes. Dust to dust. It seemed to me that Rebecca had no reality any more. She had crumbled away when they had found her on the cabin floor. It was not Rebecca who was lying in the crypt, it was dust. Only dust.

Just after seven the rain began to fall. Gently at first, a light pattering in the trees, and so thin I could not see it. Then louder and faster, a driving torrent falling slantways from the slate sky, like water from a sluice. I left the windows open wide. I stood in front of them and breathed the cold clean air. The rain splashed into my face and on my hands. I could not see beyond the lawns, the falling rain came thick and fast. I heard it sputtering in the gutter-pipes above the window, and splashing on the stones of the terrace. There was no more thunder. The rain smelt of moss and earth and of the black bark of trees.

I did not hear Frith come in at the door. I was standing by the window, watching the rain. I did not see him until he was beside me.

'Excuse me, Madam,' he said, 'do you know if Mr de Winter will be long?'

'No,' I said, 'not very long.'

'There's a gentleman to see him, Madam,' said Frith after a moment's hesitation. 'I'm not quite sure what I ought to say. He's very insistent about seeing Mr de Winter.'

'Who is it?' I said. 'Is it anyone you know?'

Frith looked uncomfortable. 'Yes, Madam,' he said, 'it's a gentleman who used to come here frequently at one time, when Mrs de Winter was alive. A gentleman called Mr Favell.'

I knelt on the window-seat and shut the window. The rain was coming in on the cushions. Then I turned round and looked at Frith.

'I think perhaps I had better see Mr Favell,' I said.

'Very good, Madam.'

I went and stood over on the rug beside the empty fireplace. It was just possible that I should be able to get rid of Favell before Maxim came back. I did not know what I was going to say to him, but I was not frightened.

In a few moments Frith returned and showed Favell into the library. He looked much the same as before but a little rougher if possible, a little more untidy. He was the sort of man who invariably went hatless, his hair was bleached from the sun of the last days and his skin was deeply tanned. His eyes were rather bloodshot. I wondered if he had been drinking.

'I'm afraid Maxim is not here,' I said. 'I don't know when he will be back. Wouldn't it be better if you made an appointment to see him at the office in the morning?'

'Waiting doesn't worry me,' said Favell, 'and I don't think I shall have to wait very long, you know. I had a look in the dining-room as I came along, and I see Max's place is laid for dinner all right.'

'Our plans have been changed,' I said. 'It's quite possible Maxim won't be home at all this evening.'

'He's run off, has he?' said Favell, with a half smile I did not like. 'I wonder if you really mean it. Of course under the circumstances it's the wisest thing he can do. Gossip is an unpleasant thing to some people. It's more pleasant to avoid it, isn't it?'

'I don't know what you mean,' I said.

'Don't you?' he said. 'Oh, come, you don't expect me to believe that, do you? Tell me, are you feeling better? Too bad fainting like that at the inquest this afternoon. I would have come and helped you out but I saw you had one knight-errant already. I bet Frank Crawley enjoyed himself. Did you let him drive you home? You wouldn't let me drive you five yards when I offered to.'

361

'What do you want to see Maxim about?' I asked.

Favell leant forward to the table and helped himself to a ciga-rette. 'You don't mind my smoking, I suppose?' he said, 'it won't make you sick, will it? One never knows with brides.'

He watched me over his lighter. 'You've grown up a bit since I saw you last, haven't you?' he said. 'I wonder what you have been doing. Leading Frank Crawley up the garden-path?' He blew a cloud of smoke in the air. 'I say, do you mind asking old Frith to get me a whisky-and-soda?'

I did not say anything. I went and rang the bell. He sat down on the edge of the sofa, swinging his legs, that half-smile on his lips. Robert answered the bell. 'A whisky-and-soda for Mr Favell,' I said.

'Well, Robert?' said Favell, 'I haven't seen you for a very long time. Still breaking the hearts of the girls in Kerrith?'

Robert flushed. He glanced at me, horribly embarrassed.

'All right, old chap, I won't give you away. Run along and get me a double whisky, and jump on it.'

Robert disappeared. Favell laughed, dropping ash all over the floor.

'I took Robert out once on his half-day,' he said. 'Rebecca bet me a fiver I wouldn't ask him. I won my fiver all right. Spent one of the funniest evenings of my life. Did I laugh? Oh, boy! Robert on the razzle takes a lot of beating, I tell you. I must say he's got a good eye for a girl. He picked the prettiest of the bunch we saw that night.'

Robert came back again with the whisky-and-soda on a tray. He still looked very red, very uncomfortable. Favell watched him with a smile as he poured out his drink, and then he began to laugh, leaning back on the arm of the sofa. He whistled the bar of a song, watching Robert all the while.

'That was the one, wasn't it?' he said, 'that was the tune? Do you still like ginger hair, Robert?'

Robert gave him a flat weak smile. He looked miserable. Favell laughed louder still. Robert turned and went out of the room.

'Poor kid,' said Favell. 'I don't suppose he's been on the loose since. That old ass Frith keeps him on a leading string.'

He began drinking his whisky-and-soda, glancing round the room, looking at me every now and again, and smiling.

'I don't think I shall mind very much if Max doesn't get back to dinner,' he said. 'What say you?'

I did not answer. I stood by the fireplace my hands behind my back. 'You wouldn't waste that place at the dining-room table, would you?' he said. He looked at me, smiling still, his head on one side.

'Mr Favell,' I said, 'I don't want to be rude, but as a matter of fact I'm very tired. I've had a long and fairly exhausting day. If you can't tell me what you want to see Maxim about it's not much good your sitting here. You had far better do as I suggest, and go round to the estate office in the morning.'

He slid off the arm of the sofa and came towards me, his glass in his hand. 'No, no,' he said. 'No, no, don't be a brute. I've had an exhausting day too. Don't run away and leave me, I'm quite harmless, really I am. I suppose Max has been telling tales about me to you?'

I did not answer. 'You think I'm the big, bad wolf, don't you?' he said, 'but I'm not, you know. I'm a perfectly ordinary, harmless bloke. And I think you are behaving splendidly over all this, perfectly splendidly. I take off my hat to you, I really do.' This last speech of his was very slurred and thick. I wished I had never told Frith I would see him.

'You come down here to Manderley,' he said, waving his arm vaguely, 'you take on all this place, meet hundreds of people you've never seen before, you put up with old Max and his moods, you don't give a fig for anyone, you just go your own way. I call it a damn good effort, and I don't care who hears me say so. A damn good effort.' He swayed a little as he stood. He steadied himself, and put the empty glass down on the table. 'This business has been a shock to me, you know,' he said. 'A bloody awful shock. Rebecca was my cousin. I was damn fond of her.'

'Yes,' I said. 'I'm very sorry for you.'

'We were brought up together,' he went on. 'Always tremendous pals. Liked the same things, the same people. Laughed at the same jokes. I suppose I was fonder of Rebecca than anyone else in the world. And she was fond of me. All this has been a bloody shock.'

'Yes,' I said. 'Yes, of course.'

'And what is Max going to do about it, that's what I want to know? Does he think he can sit back quietly now that sham inquest is over? Tell me that?' He was not smiling any more. He bent towards me.

'I'm going to see justice is done to Rebecca,' he said, his voice growing louder. 'Suicide . . . God Almighty, that doddering old fool of a Coroner got the jury to say suicide. You and I know it wasn't suicide, don't we?' He leant closer to me still. 'Don't we?' he said slowly.

The door opened and Maxim came into the room, with Frank just behind him. Maxim stood quite still, with the door open, staring at Favell. 'What the hell are you doing here?' he said.

Favell turned round, his hands in his pockets. He waited a moment, and then he began to smile. 'As a matter of fact, Max, old chap, I came to congratulate you on the inquest this afternoon.'

'Do you mind leaving the house?' said Max, 'or do you want Crawley and me to chuck you out?'

'Steady a moment, steady a moment,' said Favell. He lit another cigarette, and sat down once more on the arm of the sofa.

'You don't want Frith to hear what I'm going to say, do you?' he said. 'Well, he will, if you don't shut that door.'

Maxim did not move. I saw Frank close the door very quietly.

'Now, listen here, Max,' said Favell, 'you've come very well out of this affair, haven't you? Better than you ever expected. Oh, yes, I was in the court this afternoon, and I dare say you saw me. I was there from start to finish. I saw your wife faint, at a rather critical moment, and I don't blame her. It was touch and go, then, wasn't it, Max, what way the inquiry would go?

364

And luckily for you it went the way it did. You hadn't squared those thick-headed fellows who were acting jury, had you? It looked damn like it to me.'

Maxim made a move towards Favell, but Favell held up his hand.

'Wait a bit, can't you?' he said. 'I haven't finished yet. You realize, don't you, Max, old man, that I can make things damned unpleasant for you if I choose. Not only unpleasant, but shall I say dangerous?'

I sat down on the chair beside the fireplace. I held the arms of the chair very tight. Frank came over and stood behind the chair. Still Maxim did not move. He never took his eyes off Favell.

'Oh, yes?' he said, 'in what way can you make things dangerous?'

'Look here, Max,' said Favell, 'I suppose there are no secrets between you and your wife and from the look of things Crawley there just makes the happy trio. I can speak plainly then, and I will. You all know about Rebecca and me. We were lovers, weren't we? I've never denied it, and I never will. Very well then. Up to the present I believed, like every other fool, that Rebecca was drowned sailing in the bay, and that her body was picked up at Edgecoombe weeks afterwards. It was a shock to me then, a bloody shock. But I said to myself, That's the sort of death Rebecca would choose, she'd go out like she lived, fighting.' He paused, he sat there on the edge of the sofa, looking at all of us in turn. 'Then I pick up the evening paper a few days ago and I read that Rebecca's boat had been stumbled on by the local diver and that there was a body in the cabin. I couldn't understand it. Who the hell would Rebecca have as a sailing companion? It didn't make sense. I came down here, and put up at a pub just outside Kerrith. I got in touch with Mrs Danvers. She told me then that the body in the cabin was Rebecca's. Even so I thought like everyone else that the first body was a mistake and Rebecca had somehow got shut in the cabin when she went to fetch a coat. Well, I attended that inquest today, as

365

you know. And everything went smoothly, didn't it, until Tabb gave his evidence? But after that? Well, Max, old man, what have you got to say about those holes in the floor-boards, and those sea-cocks turned full on?'

'Do you think,' said Maxim slowly, 'that after those hours of talk this afternoon I am going into it again – with you? You heard the evidence, and you heard the verdict. It satisfied the Coroner, and it must satisfy you.'

'Suicide, eh?' said Favell. 'Rebecca committing suicide. The sort of thing she would do, wasn't it? Listen; you never knew I had this note, did you? I kept it, because it was the last thing she ever wrote to me. I'll read it to you. I think it will interest you.'

He took a piece of paper out of his pocket. I recognized that thin, pointed, slanting hand.

I tried to ring you from the flat, but could get no answer [*he read*]. I'm going down to Manders right away. I shall be at the cottage this evening, and if you get this in time will you get the car and follow me. I'll spend the night at the cottage, and leave the door open for you. I've got something to tell you and I want to see you as soon as possible. Rebecca.

He put the note back in his pocket. 'That's not the sort of note you write when you're going to commit suicide, is it?' he said. 'It was waiting for me at my flat when I got back about four in the morning. I had no idea Rebecca was to be in London that day or I should have got in touch with her. It happened, by a vile stroke of fortune, I was on a party that night. When I read the note at four in the morning I decided it was too late to go crashing down on a six-hour run to Manderley. I went to bed, determined to put a call through later in the day. I did. About twelve o'clock. And I heard Rebecca had been drowned!'

He sat there, staring at Maxim. None of us spoke.

'Supposing the Coroner this afternoon had read that note, it would have made it a little bit more tricky for you, wouldn't it, Max, old man?' said Favell.

'Well,' said Maxim, 'why didn't you get up and give it to him?'

'Steady, old boy, steady. No need to get rattled. I don't want to smash you, Max. God knows you've never been a friend to me, but I don't bear malice about it. All married men with lovely wives are jealous, aren't they? And some of 'em just can't help playing Othello. They're made that way. I don't blame them. I'm sorry for them. I'm a bit of a Socialist in my way, you know, and I can't think why fellows can't share their women instead of killing them. What difference does it make? You can get your fun just the same. A lovely woman isn't like a motor tyre, she doesn't wear out. The more you use her the better she goes. Now, Max, I've laid all my cards on the table. Why can't we come to some agreement? I'm not a rich man. I'm too fond of gambling for that. But what gets me down is never having any capital to fall back upon. Now if I had a settlement of two or three thousand a year for life I could jog along comfortably. And I'd never trouble you again. I swear before God I would not.'

'I've asked you before to leave the house,' said Maxim. 'I'm not going to ask you again. There's the door behind me. You can open it yourself.'

'Half a minute, Maxim,' said Frank; 'it's not quite so easy as all that.' He turned to Favell. 'I see what you're driving at. It happens, very unfortunately, that you could, as you say, twist things round and make it difficult for Maxim. I don't think he sees it as clearly as I do. What is the exact amount you propose Maxim should settle on you?'

I saw Maxim go very white, and a little pulse began to show on his forehead. 'Don't interfere with this, Frank,' he said, 'this is my affair entirely. I'm not going to give way to blackmail.'

'I don't suppose your wife wants to be pointed out as Mrs de Winter, the widow of a murderer, of a fellow who was hanged,' said Favell. He laughed, and glanced towards me.

'You think you can frighten me, don't you, Favell?' said Maxim. 'Well, you are wrong. I'm not afraid of anything you can do.

There is the telephone, in the next room. Shall I ring up Colonel Julyan and ask him to come over? He's the magistrate. He'll be interested in your story.'

Favell stared at him, and laughed.

'Good bluff,' he said, 'but it won't work. You wouldn't dare ring up old Julyan. I've got enough evidence to hang you, Max, old man.'

Maxim walked slowly across the room and passed through to the little room beyond. I heard the click of the telephone.

'Stop him!' I said to Frank. 'Stop him, for God's sake.'

Frank glanced at my face, he went swiftly towards the door.

I heard Maxim's voice, very cool, very calm. 'I want Kerrith 17,' he said.

Favell was watching the door, his face curiously intense.

'Leave me alone,' I heard Maxim say to Frank. And then, two minutes afterwards. 'Is that Colonel Julyan speaking? It's de Winter here. Yes. Yes, I know. I wonder if you could possibly come over here at once. Yes, to Manderley. It's rather urgent. I can't explain why on the telephone, but you shall hear everything directly you come. I'm very sorry to have to drag you out. Yes. Thank you very much. Good-bye.'

He came back again into the room. 'Julyan is coming right away,' he said. He crossed over and threw open the windows. It was still raining very hard. He stood there, with his back to us, breathing the cold air.

'Maxim,' said Frank quietly. 'Maxim.'

He did not answer. Favell laughed, and helped himself to another cigarette. 'If you want to hang yourself, old fellow, it's all the same to me,' he said. He picked up a paper from the table and flung himself down on the sofa, crossed his legs, and began to turn over the pages. Frank hesitated, glancing from me to Maxim. Then he came beside me.

'Can't you do something?' I whispered. 'Go out and meet Colonel Julyan, prevent him from coming, say it was all a mistake?'

Maxim spoke from the window without turning round.

'Frank is not to leave this room,' he said. 'I'm going to manage this thing alone. Colonel Julyan will be here in exactly ten minutes.'

We none of us said anything. Favell went on reading his paper. There was no sound but the steady falling rain. It fell without a break, steady, straight, and monotonous. I felt helpless, without strength. There was nothing I could do. Nothing that Frank could do. In a book or in a play I would have found a revolver, and we should have shot Favell, hidden his body in a cupboard. There was no revolver. There was no cupboard. We were ordinary people. These things did not happen. I could not go to Maxim now and beg him on my knees to give Favell the money. I had to sit there, with my hands in my lap, watching the rain, watching Maxim with his back turned to me, standing by the window.

It was raining too hard to hear the car. The sound of the rain covered all other sounds. We did not know Colonel Julyan had arrived until the door opened, and Frith showed him into the room.

Maxim swung round from the window. 'Good evening,' he said. 'We meet again. You've made very good time.'

'Yes,' said Colonel Julyan, 'you said it was urgent, so I came at once. Luckily, my man had left the car handy. What an evening.'

He glanced at Favell uncertainly, and then came over and shook hands with me, nodding to Maxim. 'A good thing the rain has come,' he said. 'It's been hanging about too long. I hope you're feeling better.'

I murmured something, I don't know what, and he stood there looking from one to the other of us, rubbing his hands.

'I think you realize,' Maxim said, 'that I haven't brought you out on an evening like this for a social half-hour before dinner. This is Jack Favell, my late wife's first cousin. I don't know if you have ever met.'

Colonel Julyan nodded. 'Your face seems familiar. I've probably met you here in the old days.'

'Quite,' said Maxim. 'Go ahead, Favell.'

Favell got up from the sofa and chucked the paper back on the table. The ten minutes seemed to have sobered him. He walked quite steadily. He was not smiling any longer. I had the impression that he was not entirely pleased with the turn in the events, and he was ill-prepared for the encounter with Colonel Julyan. He began speaking in a loud, rather domineering voice. 'Look here, Colonel Julyan,' he said, 'there's no sense in beating about the bush. The reason why I'm here is that I'm not satisfied with the verdict given at the inquest this afternoon.'

'Oh?' said Colonel Julyan, 'isn't that for de Winter to say, not you?'

'No, I don't think it is,' said Favell. 'I have a right to speak, not only as Rebecca's cousin, but as her prospective husband, had she lived.'

Colonel Julyan looked rather taken aback. 'Oh,' he said. 'Oh, I see. That's rather different. Is this true, de Winter?'

Maxim shrugged his shoulders. 'It's the first I've heard of it,' he said.

Colonel Julyan looked from one to the other doubtfully. 'Look here, Favell,' he said, 'what exactly is your trouble?'

Favell stared at him a moment. I could see he was planning something in his mind, and he was still not sober enough to carry it through. He put his hand slowly in his waistcoat pocket and brought out Rebecca's note. 'This note was written a few hours before Rebecca was supposed to have set out on that suicidal sail. Here it is. I want you to read it, and say whether you think a woman who wrote that note had made up her mind to kill herself.'

Colonel Julyan took a pair of spectacles from a case in his pocket and read the note. Then he handed it back to Favell. 'No,' he said, 'on the face of it, no. But I don't know what the note refers to. Perhaps you do. Or perhaps de Winter does?'

Maxim did not say anything. Favell twisted the piece of paper in his fingers, considering Colonel Julyan all the while. 'My cousin made a definite appointment in that note, didn't she?' he said. 'She deliberately asked me to drive down to Manderley that night because she had something to tell me. What it actually was I don't suppose we shall ever know, but that's beside the point.

She made the appointment, and she was to spend the night in the cottage on purpose to see me alone. The mere fact of her going for a sail never surprised me. It was the sort of thing she did, for an hour or so, after a long day in London. But to plug holes in the cabin and deliberately drown herself, the hysterical impulsive freak of a neurotic girl – oh, no, Colonel Julyan, by Christ no!' The colour had flooded into his face, and the last words were shouted. His manner was not helpful to him, and I could see by the thin line of Colonel Julyan's mouth that he had not taken to Favell.

'My dear fellow,' he said, 'it's not the slightest use your losing your temper with me. I'm not the Coroner who conducted the inquiry this afternoon, nor am I a member of the jury who gave the verdict. I'm merely the magistrate of the district. Naturally I want to help you all I can, and de Winter, too. You say you refuse to believe your cousin committed suicide. On the other hand you heard, as we all did, the evidence of the boat-builder. The sea-cocks were open, the holes were there. Very well. Suppose we get to the point. What do you suggest really happened?'

Favell turned his head and looked slowly towards Maxim. He was still twisting the note between his fingers. 'Rebecca never opened those sea-cocks, nor split the holes in the planking. Rebecca never committed suicide. You've asked for my opinion, and by God you shall have it. Rebecca was murdered. And if you want to know who the murderer is, why there he stands, by the window there, with that God-damned superior smile on his face. He couldn't even wait could he, until the year was out, before marrying the first girl he set eyes on? There he is, there's your murderer for you, Mr Maximilian de Winter. Take a good long look at him. He'd look well hanging, wouldn't he?'

And Favell began to laugh, the laugh of a drunkard, high-pitched, forced, and foolish, and all the while twisting Rebecca's note between his fingers.

Thank God for Favell's laugh. Thank God for his pointing finger, his flushed face, his staring bloodshot eyes. Thank God for the way he stood there swaying on his two feet. Because it made Colonel Julyan antagonistic, it put him on our side. I saw the disgust on his face, the quick movement of his lips. Colonel Julyan did not believe him. Colonel Julyan was on our side.

'The man's drunk,' he said quickly. 'He doesn't know what he's saying.'

'Drunk, am I?' shouted Favell. 'Oh, no, my fine friend. You may be a magistrate and a colonel into the bargain, but it won't cut any ice with me. I've got the law on my side for a change, and I'm going to use it. There are other magistrates in this bloody county besides you. Fellows with brains in their heads, who understand the meaning of justice. Not soldiers who got the sack years ago for incompetence and walk about with a string of putty medals on their chest. Max de Winter murdered Rebecca and I'm going to prove it.'

'Wait a minute, Mr Favell,' said Colonel Julyan quietly, 'you were present at the inquiry this afternoon, weren't you? I remember you now. I saw you sitting there. If you felt so deeply about the injustice of the verdict why didn't you say so then, to the jury, to the Coroner himself? Why didn't you produce that letter in court?'

Favell stared at him, and laughed. 'Why?' he said, 'because I did not choose to, that's why. I preferred to come and tackle de Winter personally.'

'That's why I rang you up,' said Maxim, coming forward from the window; 'we've already heard Favell's accusations. I asked him the same question. Why didn't he tell his suspicions to the Coroner? He said he was not a rich man, and that if I cared to settle two or three thousand on him for life he would never worry me again. Frank was here, and my wife. They both heard him. Ask them.'

'It's perfectly true, sir,' said Frank. 'It's blackmail, pure and simple.'

'Yes, of course,' said Colonel Julyan, 'the trouble is that blackmail is not very pure, nor is it particularly simple. It can make a lot of unpleasantness for a great many people, even if the blackmailer finds himself in jail at the end of it. Sometimes innocent people find themselves in jail as well. We want to avoid that, in this case. I don't know whether you are sufficiently sober, Favell, to answer my questions, and if you keep off irrelevant personalities we may get through with the business quicker. You have just made a serious accusation against de Winter. Have you any proof to back that accusation?'

'Proof?' said Favell. 'What the hell do you want with proof? Aren't those holes in the boat proof enough?'

'Certainly not,' said Colonel Julyan, 'unless you can bring a witness who saw him do it. Where's your witness?'

'Witness be damned,' said Favell. 'Of course de Winter did it. Who else would kill Rebecca?'

'Kerrith has a large population,' said Colonel Julyan. 'Why not go from door to door making inquiries? I might have done it myself. You appear to have no more proof against de Winter there than you would have against me.'

'Oh, I see,' said Favell, 'you're going to hold his hand through this. You're going to back de Winter. You won't let him down because you've dined with him, and he's dined with you. He's a big name down here. He's the owner of Manderley. You poor bloody little snob.'

'Take care, Favell, take care.'

'You think you can get the better of me, don't you? You think I've got no case to bring to a court of law. I'll get my proof for you all right. I tell you de Winter killed Rebecca because of me.

He knew I was her lover; he was jealous, madly jealous. He knew she was waiting for me at the cottage on the beach, and he went down that night and killed her. Then he put her body in the boat and sank her.'

'Quite a clever story, Favell, in its way, but I repeat again you have no proof. Produce your witness who saw it happen and I might begin to take you seriously. I know that cottage on the beach. A sort of picnic place, isn't it? Mrs de Winter used to keep the gear there for the boat. It would help your story if you could turn it into a bungalow with fifty replicas alongside of it. There would be a chance then that one of the inhabitants might have seen the whole affair.'

'Hold on,' said Favell slowly, 'hold on . . . There is a chance de Winter might have been seen that night. Quite a good chance too. It's worth finding out. What would you say if I did produce a witness?'

Colonel Julyan shrugged his shoulders. I saw Frank glance inquiringly at Maxim. Maxim did not say anything. He was watching Favell. I suddenly knew what Favell meant. I knew who he was talking about. And in a flash of fear and horror I knew that he was right. There had been a witness that night. Little sentences came back to me. Words I had not understood, phrases I believed to be the fragments of a poor idiot's mind. 'She's down there isn't she? She won't come back again.' 'I didn't tell no one.' 'They'll find her there, won't they? The fishes have eaten her, haven't they?' 'She'll not come back no more.' Ben knew. Ben had seen. Ben, with his queer crazed brain, had been a witness all the time. He had been hiding in the woods that night. He had seen Maxim take the boat from the moorings, and pull back in the dinghy, alone. I knew all the colour was draining away from my face. I leant back against the cushion of the chair.

'There's a local half-wit who spends his time on the beach,' said Favell. 'He was always hanging about, when I used to come down and meet Rebecca. I've often seen him. He used to sleep in the woods, or on the beach when the nights were hot. The fellow's cracked, he would never have come forward on his own. But I could make him talk if he did see anything that night. And there's a bloody big chance he did.'

'Who is this? What's he talking about?' said Colonel Julyan.

'He must mean Ben,' said Frank, with another glance at Maxim. 'He's the son of one of our tenants. But the man's not responsible for what he says or does. He's been an idiot since birth.'

'What the hell does that matter?' said Favell. 'He's got eyes, hasn't he? He knows what he sees. He's only got to answer yes or no. You're getting windy now, aren't you? Not so mighty confident?'

'Can we get hold of this fellow and question him?' asked Colonel Julyan.

'Of course,' said Maxim. 'Tell Robert to cut down to his mother's cottage, Frank, and bring him back.'

Frank hesitated, I saw him glance at me out of the tail of his eye.

'Go on, for God's sake,' said Maxim. 'We want to end this thing, don't we?' Frank went out of the room. I began to feel the old nagging pain beneath my heart.

In a few minutes Frank came back again into the room.

'Robert's taken my car,' he said. 'If Ben is at home he won't be more than ten minutes.'

'The rain will keep him at home all right,' said Favell; 'he'll be there. And I think you will find I shall be able to make him talk.' He laughed, and looked at Maxim. His face was still very flushed. Excitement had made him sweat; there were beads of perspiration on his forehead. I noticed how his neck bulged over the back of his collar, and how low his ears were set on his head. Those florid good looks would not last him very long. Already he was out of condition, puffy. He helped himself to another cigarette. 'You're like a little trade union here at Manderley, aren't you?' he said; 'no one going to give anyone else away. Even the local magistrate is on the same racket. We must exempt the bride of course. A wife doesn't give evidence against her husband. Crawley of course has been squared. He knows he would lose his job if he told the truth. And if I guess rightly there's a spice of malice in his soul towards me too. You didn't have much success with Rebecca, did you, Crawley? That garden path wasn't quite long enough, eh? It's a bit easier this time, isn't it. The bride will be grateful for your fraternal arm every time she faints. When she hears the judge sentence her husband to death that arm of yours will come in very handy.'

It happened very quickly. Too quick for me to see how Maxim did it. But I saw Favell stagger and fall against the arm of the sofa, and down on to the floor. And Maxim was standing just beside him. I felt rather sick. There was something degrading in the fact that Maxim had hit Favell. I wished I had not known. I wished I had not been there to see. Colonel Julyan did not say anything. He looked very grim. He turned his back on them and came and stood beside me.

'I think you had better go upstairs,' he said quietly.

I shook my head. 'No,' I whispered. 'No.'

'That fellow is in a state capable of saying anything,' he said. 'What you have just seen was not very attractive, was it? Your husband was right of course, but it's a pity you saw it.'

I did not answer. I was watching Favell who was getting slowly to his feet. He sat down heavily on the sofa and put his hand-kerchief to his face.

'Get me a drink,' he said, 'get me a drink.'

Maxim looked at Frank. Frank went out of the room. None of us spoke. In a moment Frank came back with the whisky and soda on a tray. He mixed some in a glass and gave it to Favell. Favell drank it greedily, like an animal. There was something sensual and horrible the way he put his mouth to the glass. His lips folded upon the glass in a peculiar way. There was a dark red patch on his jaw where Maxim had hit him. Maxim had turned his back on him again and had returned to the window. I glanced at Colonel Julyan and saw that he was looking at Maxim. His gaze was curious, intent. My heart began beating very quickly. Why did Colonel Julyan look at Maxim in that way?

Did it mean that he was beginning to wonder, to suspect?

Maxim did not see. He was watching the rain. It fell straight and steady as before. The sound filled the room. Favell finished his whisky and soda and put the glass back on the table beside the sofa. He was breathing heavily. He did not look at any of us. He was staring straight in front of him at the floor.

The telephone began ringing in the little room. It struck a shrill, discordant note. Frank went to answer it.

He came back at once and looked at Colonel Julyan. 'It's your daughter,' he said; 'they want to know if they are to keep dinner back.'

Colonel Julyan waved his hand impatiently. 'Tell them to start,' he said, 'tell them I don't know when I shall be back.' He glanced at his watch. 'Fancy ringing up,' he muttered; 'what a moment to choose.'

Frank went back into the little room to give the message. I thought of the daughter at the other end of the telephone. It would be the one who played golf. I could imagine her calling to her sister, 'Dad says we're to start. What on earth can he be doing? The steak will be like leather.' Their little household disorganized because of us. Their evening routine upset. All these foolish inconsequent threads hanging upon one another, because Maxim had killed Rebecca. I looked at Frank. His face was pale and set.

'I heard Robert coming back with the car,' he said to Colonel Julyan. 'The window in there looks on to the drive.'

He went out of the library to the hall. Favell had lifted his head when he spoke. Then he got to his feet once more and stood looking towards the door. There was a queer ugly smile on his face.

The door opened, and Frank came in. He turned and spoke to someone in the hall outside.

'All right, Ben,' he said quietly, 'Mr de Winter wants to give you some cigarettes. There's nothing to be frightened of.'

Ben stepped awkwardly into the room. He had his sou'wester in his hands. He looked odd and naked without his hat. I realized for the first time that his head was shaved all over, and he had no hair. He looked different, dreadful.

The light seemed to daze him. He glanced foolishly round the room, blinking his small eyes. He caught sight of me, and I gave him a weak, rather tremulous smile. I don't know if he recognized me or not. He just blinked his eyes. Then Favell walked slowly towards him and stood in front of him.

'Hullo,' he said; 'how's life treated you since we last met?'

Ben stared at him. There was no recognition on his face. He did not answer.

'Well?' said Favell, 'you know who I am, don't you?'

Ben went on twisting his sou'wester. 'Eh?' he said.

'Have a cigarette,' said Favell, handing him the box. Ben glanced at Maxim and Frank.

'All right,' said Maxim, 'take as many as you like.'

Ben took four and stuck two behind each ear. Then he stood twisting his cap again.

'You know who I am don't you?' repeated Favell.

Still Ben did not answer. Colonel Julyan walked across to him. 'You shall go home in a few moments, Ben,' he said. 'No one is going to hurt you. We just want you to answer one or two questions. You know Mr Favell, don't you?'

This time Ben shook his head. 'I never seen 'un,' he said.

'Don't be a bloody fool,' said Favell roughly; 'you know you've seen me. You've seen me go to the cottage on the beach, Mrs de Winter's cottage. You've seen me there, haven't you?'

'No,' said Ben. 'I never seen no one.'

'You damned half-witted liar,' said Favell, 'are you going to stand there and say you never saw me, last year, walk through those woods with Mrs de Winter, and go into the cottage? Didn't we catch you once, peering at us from the window?'

'Eh?' said Ben.

'A convincing witness,' said Colonel Julyan sarcastically.

Favell swung round on him. 'It's a put-up job,' he said. 'Someone has got at this idiot and bribed him too. I tell you he's seen me scores of times. Here. Will this make you remember?' He fumbled in his hip-pocket and brought out a note-case. He flourished a pound note in front of Ben. 'Now do you remember me?' he said.

Ben shook his head. 'I never seen 'un,' he said, and then he took hold of Frank's arm. 'Has he come here to take me to the asylum?' he said.

'No,' said Frank. 'No, of course not, Ben.'

'I don't want to go to the asylum,' said Ben. 'They'm cruel to folk in there. I want to stay home. I done nothing.'

'That's all right, Ben,' said Colonel Julyan. 'No one's going to put you in the asylum. Are you quite sure you've never seen this man before?'

'No,' said Ben. 'I've never seen 'un.'

'You remember Mrs de Winter, don't you?' said Colonel Julyan.

Ben glanced doubtfully towards me.

'No,' said Colonel Julyan gently, 'not this lady. The other lady, who used to go to the cottage.'

'Eh?' said Ben.

'You remember the lady who had the boat?'

Ben blinked his eyes. 'She's gone,' he said.

'Yes, we know that,' said Colonel Julyan. 'She used to sail the boat, didn't she? Were you on the beach when she sailed the boat the last time? One evening, over twelve months ago. When she didn't come back again?'

Ben twisted his sou'wester. He glanced at Frank, and then at Maxim.

'Eh?' he said.

'You were there, weren't you?' said Favell, leaning forward. 'You saw Mrs de Winter come down to the cottage, and presently you saw Mr de Winter too. He went into the cottage after her. What happened then? Go on. What happened?'

Ben shrank back against the wall. 'I seen nothing,' he said. 'I want to stay home. I'm not going to the asylum. I never seen you. Never before. I never seen you and she in the woods.' He began to blubber like a child.

'You crazy little rat,' said Favell slowly, 'you bloody crazy little rat.'

Ben was wiping his eyes with the sleeve of his coat.

'Your witness does not seem to have helped you,' said Colonel Julyan. 'The performance has been rather a waste of time, hasn't it? Do you want to ask him anything else?'

'It's a plot,' shouted Favell. 'A plot against me. You're all in it, every one of you. Someone's paid this half-wit, I tell you. Paid him to tell his string of dirty lies.'

'I think Ben might be allowed to go home,' said Colonel Julyan.

'All right, Ben,' said Maxim. 'Robert shall take you back. And no one will put you in the asylum, don't be afraid. Tell Robert to find him something in the kitchen,' he added to Frank. 'Some cold meat, whatever he fancies.'

'Payment for services rendered, eh?' said Favell. 'He's done a good day's work for you, Max, hasn't he?'

Frank took Ben out of the room. Colonel Julyan glanced at Maxim. 'The fellow appeared to be scared stiff,' he said; 'he was shaking like a leaf. I was watching him. He's never been ill-treated, has he?'

'No,' said Maxim, 'he's perfectly harmless, and I've always let him have the run of the place.'

'He's been frightened at some time,' said Colonel Julyan. 'He was showing the whites of his eyes, just like a dog does when you're going to whip him.'

'Well, why didn't you?' said Favell. 'He'd have remembered me all right if you'd whipped him. Oh, no, he's going to be given a good supper for his work tonight. Ben's not going to be whipped.'

'He has not helped your case, has he?' said Colonel Julyan quietly; 'we're still where we were. You can't produce one shred of evidence against de Winter and you know it. The very motive you gave won't stand the test. In a court of law, Favell, you wouldn't have a leg to stand on. You say you were Mrs de Winter's prospective husband, and that you held clandestine meetings with her in that cottage on the beach. Even the poor idiot we have just had in this room swears he never saw you. You can't even prove your own story, can you?'

'Can't I?' said Favell. I saw him smile. He came across to the fireplace and rang the bell.

'What are you doing?' said Colonel Julyan.

'Wait a moment and you'll see,' said Favell.

I guessed already what was going to happen. Frith answered the bell.

'Ask Mrs Danvers to come here,' said Favell.

Frith glanced at Maxim. Maxim nodded shortly.

Frith went out of the room. 'Isn't Mrs Danvers the house-keeper?' said Colonel Julyan.

'She was also Rebecca's personal friend,' said Favell. 'She was with her for years before she married and practically brought her up. You are going to find Danny a very different sort of witness to Ben.'

Frank came back into the room. 'Packed Ben off to bed?' said Favell. 'Given him his supper and told him he was a good boy? This time it won't be quite so easy for the trade union.'

'Mrs Danvers is coming down,' said Colonel Julyan. 'Favell seems to think he will get something out of her.'

Frank glanced quickly at Maxim. Colonel Julyan saw the glance. I saw his lips tighten. I did not like it. No, I did not like it. I began biting my nails.

We all waited, watching the door. And Mrs Danvers came into the room. Perhaps it was because I had generally seen her alone, and beside me she had seemed tall and gaunt, but she looked shrunken now in size, more wizened, and I noticed she had to look up to Favell and to Frank and Maxim. She stood by the door, her hands folded in front of her, looking from one to the other of us.

'Good evening, Mrs Danvers,' said Colonel Julyan.

'Good evening, sir,' she said.

Her voice was that old, dead, mechanical one I had heard so often.

'First of all, Mrs Danvers, I want to ask you a question,' said Colonel Julyan, 'and the question is this. Were you aware of the relationship between the late Mrs de Winter and Mr Favell here?'

'They were first cousins,' said Mrs Danvers.

'I was not referring to blood-relationship, Mrs Danvers,' said Colonel Julyan. 'I mean something closer than that.'

'I'm afraid I don't understand, sir,' said Mrs Danvers.

'Oh, come off it, Danny,' said Favell; 'you know damn well what he's driving at. I've told Colonel Julyan already, but he doesn't seem to believe me. Rebecca and I had lived together off and on for years, hadn't we? She was in love with me, wasn't she?'

To my surprise Mrs Danvers considered him a moment without speaking, and there was something of scorn in the glance she gave him.

'She was not,' she said.

'Listen here, you old fool . . .' began Favell, but Mrs Danvers cut him short.

'She was not in love with you, or with Mr de Winter. She was not in love with anyone. She despised all men. She was above all that.'

Favell flushed angrily. 'Listen here. Didn't she come down the path through the woods to meet me, night after night? Didn't you wait up for her? Didn't she spend the week-ends with me in London?'

'Well?' said Mrs Danvers, with sudden passion, 'and what if she did? She had a right to amuse herself, hadn't she. Love-making was a game with her, only a game. She told me so. She did it because it made her laugh. It made her laugh, I tell you. She laughed at you like she did at the rest. I've known her come back and sit upstairs in her bed and rock with laughter at the lot of you.'

There was something horrible in the sudden torrent of words, something horrible and unexpected. It revolted me, even though I knew. Maxim had gone very white. Favell stared at her blankly, as though he had not understood. Colonel Julyan tugged at his small moustache. No one said anything for a few minutes. And there was no sound but that inevitable falling rain. Then Mrs Danvers began to cry. She cried like she had done that morning

382

in the bedroom. I could not look at her. I had to turn away. No one said anything. There were just the two sounds in the room, the falling rain and Mrs Danvers crying. It made me want to scream. I wanted to run out of the room and scream and scream.

No one moved towards her, to say anything, or to help her. She went on crying. Then at last, it seemed eternity, she began to control herself. Little by little the crying ceased. She stood quite still, her face working, her hands clutching the black stuff of her frock. At last she was silent again. Then Colonel Julyan spoke, quietly, slowly.

'Mrs Danvers,' he said, 'can you think of any reason, however remote, why Mrs de Winter should have taken her own life?'

Mrs Danvers swallowed. She went on clutching at her frock. She shook her head. 'No,' she said. 'No.'

'There, you see?' Favell said swiftly. 'It's impossible. She knows that as well as I do. I've told you already.'

'Be quiet, will you?' said Colonel Julyan. 'Give Mrs Danvers time to think. We all of us agree that on the face of it the thing's absurd, out of the question. I'm not disputing the truth or veracity of that note of yours. It's plain for us to see. She wrote you that note some time during those hours she spent in London. There was something she wanted to tell you. It's just possible that if we knew what that something was we might have the answer to the whole appalling problem. Let Mrs Danvers read the note. She may be able to throw light on it.' Favell shrugged his shoulders. He felt in his pocket for the note and threw it on the floor at Mrs Danvers' feet. She stooped and picked it up. We watched her lips move as she read the words. She read it twice. Then she shook her head. 'It's no use,' she said. 'I don't know what she meant. If there was something important she had to tell Mr Jack she would have told me first.'

'You never saw her that night?'

'No, I was out. I was spending the afternoon and evening in Kerrith. I shall never forgive myself for that. Never till my dying day.'

'Then you know of nothing on her mind, you can't suggest a solution, Mrs Danvers? Those words "*I have something to tell you*" do not convey anything to you at all?'

'No,' she answered. 'No, sir, nothing at all.'

'Does anybody know how she spent that day in London?'

Nobody answered. Maxim shook his head. Favell swore under his breath. 'Look here, she left that note at my flat at three in the afternoon,' he said. 'The porter saw her. She must have driven down here straight after that, and gone like the wind too.'

'Mrs de Winter had a hair appointment from twelve until one thirty,' said Mrs Danvers. 'I remember that, because I had to telephone through to London from here earlier in the week and book it for her. I remember doing it. Twelve to one thirty. She always lunched at her club after a hair appointment so that she could leave the pins in her hair. It's almost certain she lunched there that day.'

'Say it took her half-an-hour to have lunch; what was she doing from two until three? We ought to verify that,' said Colonel Julyan.

'Oh, Christ Jesus, who the hell cares what she was doing?' shouted Favell. 'She didn't kill herself, that's the only thing that matters, isn't it?'

'I've got her engagement diary locked in my room,' said Mrs Danvers slowly. 'I kept all those things. Mr de Winter never asked me for them. It's just possible she may have noted down her appointments for that day. She was methodical in that way. She used to put everything down and then tick the items off with a cross. If you think it would be helpful I'll go and fetch the diary.'

'Well, de Winter?' said Colonel Julyan, 'what do you say? Do you mind us seeing this diary?'

'Of course not,' said Maxim. 'Why on earth should I?'

Once again I saw Colonel Julyan give him that swift, curious glance. And this time Frank noticed it. I saw Frank look at Maxim too. And then back again to me. This time it was I who got up and went towards the window. It seemed to me that it was no longer raining quite so hard. The fury was spent. The rain that was falling now had a quieter, softer note. The grey light of evening had come into the sky. The lawns were dark and drenched with the heavy rain, and the trees had a shrouded humped appearance. I could hear the housemaid overhead drawing the curtains for the night, shutting down the windows that had not been closed already. The little routine of the day going on inevitably as it had always done. The curtains drawn, shoes taken down to be cleaned, the towel laid out on the chair in the bathroom, and the water run for my bath. Beds turned down, slippers put beneath a chair. And here were we in the library, none of us speaking, knowing in our hearts that Maxim was standing trial here for his life.

I turned round when I heard the soft closing of the door. It was Mrs Danvers. She had come back again with the diary in her hand.

'I was right,' she said quietly. 'She had marked down the engagements as I said she would. Here they are on the date she died.'

She opened the diary, a small, red leather book. She gave it to Colonel Julyan. Once more he brought his spectacles from his case. There was a long pause while he glanced down the page. It seemed to me then that there was something about that particular moment, while he looked at the page of the diary, and we stood waiting, that frightened me more than anything that had happened that evening.

I dug my nails in my hands. I could not look at Maxim. Surely Colonel Julyan must hear my heart beating and thumping in my breast?

'Ah!' he said. His finger was in the middle of the page. Something is going to happen, I thought, something terrible is going to happen. 'Yes,' he said, 'yes, here it is. Hair at twelve, as Mrs Danvers said. And a cross beside it. She kept her appointment, then. Lunch at the club, and a cross beside that. What have we here, though? Baker, two o'clock. Who was Baker?' He looked at Maxim. Maxim shook his head. Then at Mrs Danvers.

'Baker?' repeated Mrs Danvers. 'She knew no one called Baker. I've never heard the name before.'

'Well, here it is,' said Colonel Julyan, handing her the diary. 'You can see for yourself, Baker. And she's put a great cross beside it as though she wanted to break the pencil. She evidently saw this Baker, whoever he may have been.'

Mrs Danvers was staring at the name written in the diary, and the black cross beside it. 'Baker,' she said. 'Baker.'

'I believe if we knew who Baker was we'd be getting to the bottom of the whole business,' said Colonel Julyan. 'She wasn't in the hands of money-lenders, was she?'

Mrs Danvers looked at him with scorn. 'Mrs de Winter?' she said.

'Well, blackmailers perhaps?' said Colonel Julyan, with a glance at Favell.

Mrs Danvers shook her head. 'Baker,' she repeated. 'Baker.'

'She had no enemy, no one who had ever threatened her, no one she was afraid of?'

'Mrs de Winter afraid?' said Mrs Danvers. 'She was afraid of nothing and no one. There was only one thing ever worried her, and that was the idea of getting old, of illness, of dying in her bed. She has said to me a score of times, "When I go, Danny, I want to go quickly, like the snuffing out of a candle." That used to be the only thing that consoled me, after she died. They say drowning is painless, don't they?'

She looked searchingly at Colonel Julyan. He did not answer. He hesitated, tugging at his moustache. I saw him throw another glance at Maxim.

'What the hell's the use of all this?' said Favell, coming forward. 'We're streaking away from the point the whole bloody time. Who cares about this Baker fellow? What's he got to do with it? It was probably some damn merchant who sold stockings, or face-cream. If he had been anyone important Danny here would know him. Rebecca had no secrets from Danny.'

But I was watching Mrs Danvers. She had the book in her

hands and was turning the leaves. Suddenly she gave an exclamation.

'There's something here,' she said, 'right at the back among the telephone numbers. Baker. And there's a number beside it: 0488. But there is no exchange.'

'Brilliant Danny,' said Favell: 'becoming quite a sleuth in your old age, aren't you? But you're just twelve months too late. If you'd done this a year ago there might have been some use in it.'

'That's his number all right,' said Colonel Julyan, '0488, and the name Baker beside it. Why didn't she put the exchange?'

'Try every exchange in London,' jeered Favell. 'It will take you through the night but we don't mind. Max doesn't care if his telephone bill is a hundred pounds, do you, Max? You want to play for time, and so should I, if I were in your shoes.'

'There is a mark beside the number but it might mean anything,' said Colonel Julyan; 'take a look at it, Mrs Danvers. Could it possibly be an M?'

Mrs Danvers took the diary in her hands again. 'It might be,' she said doubtfully. 'It's not like her usual M but she may have scribbled it in a hurry. Yes, it might be M.'

'Mayfair 0488,' said Favell; 'what a genius, what a brain!'

'Well?' said Maxim, lighting his first cigarette, 'something had better be done about it. Frank? Go through and ask the exchange for Mayfair 0488.'

The nagging pain was strong beneath my heart. I stood quite still, my hands by my side. Maxim did not look at me.

'Go on, Frank,' he said. 'What are you waiting for?'

Frank went through to the little room beyond. We waited while he called the exchange. In a moment he was back again. 'They're going to ring me,' he said quietly. Colonel Julyan clasped his hands behind his back and began walking up and down the room. No one said anything. After about four minutes the telephone rang shrill and insistent, that irritating, monotonous note of a long-distance call. Frank went through to answer it. 'Is that Mayfair 0488?' he said. 'Can you tell me if anyone of the name

387

of Baker lives there? Oh, I see. I'm so sorry. Yes, I must have got the wrong number. Thank you very much.'

The little click as he replaced the receiver. Then he came back into the room. 'Someone called Lady Eastleigh lives at Mayfair 0488. It's an address in Grosvenor Street. They've never heard of Baker.'

Favell gave a great cackle of laughter. 'The butcher, the baker, the candlestick-maker, they all jumped out of a rotten potato,' he said. 'Carry on, detective Number One, what's the next exchange on the list?'

'Try Museum,' said Mrs Danvers.

Frank glanced at Maxim. 'Go ahead,' said Maxim.

The farce was repeated all over again. Colonel Julyan repeated his walk up and down the room. Another five minutes went by, and the telephone rang again. Frank went to answer it. He left the door wide open, I could see him lean down to the table where the telephone stood, and bend to the mouth-piece.

'Hullo? Is that Museum 0488? Can you tell me if anyone of the name of Baker lives there? Oh; who is that speaking? A night porter. Yes. Yes, I understand. Not offices. No, no of course. Can you give me the address? Yes, it's rather important.' He paused. He called to us over his shoulder. 'I think we've got him,' he said.

Oh, God, don't let it be true. Don't let Baker be found. Please God make Baker be dead. I knew who Baker was. I had known all along. I watched Frank through the door, I watched him lean forward suddenly, reach for a pencil and a piece of paper. 'Hullo? Yes, I'm still here. Could you spell it? Thank you. Thank you very much. Good night.' He came back into the room, the piece of paper in his hands. Frank who loved Maxim, who did not know that the piece of paper he held was the one shred of evidence that was worth a damn in the whole nightmare of our evening, and that by producing it he could destroy Maxim as well and truly as though he had a dagger in his hand and stabbed him in the back.

'It was the night porter from an address in Bloomsbury,' he

said. 'There are no residents there at all. The place is used during the day as a doctor's consulting rooms. Apparently Baker's given up practice, and left six months ago. But we can get hold of him all right. The night porter gave me his address. I wrote it down on this piece of paper.'

It was then that Maxim looked at me. He looked at me for the first time that evening. And in his eyes I read a message of farewell. It was as though he leant against the side of a ship, and I stood below him on the quay. There would be other people touching his shoulder, and touching mine, but we would not see them. Nor would we speak or call to one another, for the wind and the distance would carry away the sound of our voices. But I should see his eyes and he would see mine before the ship drew away from the side of the quay. Favell, Mrs Danvers, Colonel Julyan, Frank with the slip of paper in his hands, they were all forgotten at this moment. It was ours, inviolate, a fraction of time suspended between two seconds. And then he turned away and held out his hand to Frank.

'Well done,' he said. 'What's the address?'

'Somewhere near Barnet, north of London,' said Frank, giving him the paper. 'But it's not on the telephone. We can't ring him up.'

'Satisfactory work, Crawley,' said Colonel Julyan, 'and from you too, Mrs Danvers. Can you throw any light on the matter now?'

Mrs Danvers shook her head. 'Mrs de Winter never needed a doctor. Like all strong people she despised them. We only had Doctor Phillips from Kerrith here once, that time she sprained her wrist. I've never heard her speak of this Doctor Baker, she never mentioned his name to me.'

'I tell you the fellow was a face-cream mixer,' said Favell. 'What the hell does it matter who he was? If there was anything to it Danny would know. I tell you it's some fool fellow who had discovered a new way of bleaching the hair or whitening the skin, and Rebecca had probably got the address from her hairdresser that morning and went along after lunch out of curiosity.'

'No,' said Frank. 'I think you're wrong there. Baker wasn't a quack. The night porter at Museum 0488 told me he was a very well-known woman's specialist.'

'H'm,' said Colonel Julyan, pulling at his moustache, 'there must have been something wrong with her after all. It seems very curious that she did not say a word to anybody, not even to you, Mrs Danvers.'

'She was too thin,' said Favell. 'I told her about it, but she only laughed. Said it suited her. Banting I suppose, like all these women. Perhaps she went to this chap Baker for a diet sheet.'

'Do you think that's possible, Mrs Danvers?' asked Colonel Julyan.

Mrs Danvers shook her head slowly. She seemed dazed, bewildered by this sudden news about Baker. 'I can't understand it,' she said. 'I don't know what it means. Baker. A Doctor Baker. Why didn't she tell me? Why did she keep it from me? She told me everything.'

'Perhaps she didn't want to worry you,' said Colonel Julyan. 'No doubt she made an appointment with him, and saw him, and then when she came down that night she was going to have told you all about it.'

'And the note to Mr Jack,' said Mrs Danvers suddenly. 'That note to Mr Jack, "*I have something to tell you. I must see you*"; she was going to tell him too?'

'That's true,' said Favell slowly. 'We were forgetting the note.' Once more he pulled it out of his pocket and read it to us aloud. '"*I've got something to tell you, and I want to see you as soon as possible. Rebecca.*"'

'Of course, there's no doubt about it,' said Colonel Julyan, turning to Maxim. 'I wouldn't mind betting a thousand pounds on it. She was going to tell Favell the result of that interview with this Doctor Baker.'

'I believe you're right after all,' said Favell. 'The note and that appointment seem to hang together. But what the hell was it all about, that's what I want to know? What was the matter with her?'

The truth screamed in their faces and they did not see. They all stood there, staring at one another, and they did not understand. I dared not look at them. I dared not move lest I betray my knowledge. Maxim said nothing. He had gone back to the window and was looking out into the garden that was hushed and dark and still. The rain had ceased at last, but the spots fell from the dripping leaves and from the gutter above the window.

'It ought to be quite easy to verify,' said Frank. 'Here is the doctor's present address. I can write him a letter and ask him if he remembers an appointment last year with Mrs de Winter.'

'I don't know if he would take any notice of it,' said Colonel Julyan, 'there is so much of this etiquette in the medical profession. Every case is confidential, you know. The only way to get anything out of him would be to get de Winter to see him privately and explain the circumstances. What do you say, de Winter?'

Maxim turned round from the window. 'I'm ready to do whatever you care to suggest,' he said quietly.

'Anything for time, eh?' said Favell; 'a lot can be done in twenty-four hours, can't it? Trains can be caught, ships can sail, aeroplanes can fly.'

I saw Mrs Danvers look sharply from Favell to Maxim, and I realized then, for the first time, that Mrs Danvers had not known about Favell's accusation. At last she was beginning to understand. I could tell from the expression on her face. There was doubt written on it, then wonder and hatred mixed, and then conviction. Once again those lean long hands of hers clutched convulsively at her dress, and she passed her tongue over her lips. She went on staring at Maxim. She never took her eyes away from Maxim. It's too late, I thought, she can't do anything to us now, the harm is done. It does not matter what she says to us now, or what she does. The harm is done. She can't hurt us any more. Maxim did not notice her, or if he did he gave no sign. He was talking to Colonel Julyan.

'What do you suggest?' he said. 'Shall I go up in the morning, drive to this address at Barnet? I can wire Baker to expect me.'

'He's not going alone,' said Favell, with a short laugh. 'I have a right to insist on that, haven't I? Send him up with Inspector Welch and I won't object.'

If only Mrs Danvers would take her eyes away from Maxim. Frank had seen her now. He was watching her, puzzled, anxious. I saw him glance once more at the slip of paper in his hands, on which he had written Doctor Baker's address. Then he too glanced at Maxim. I believe then that some faint idea of the truth began to force itself to his conscience, for he went very white and put the paper down on the table.

'I don't think there is any necessity to bring Inspector Welch into the affair – yet,' said Colonel Julyan. His voice was different, harder. I did not like the way he used the word 'yet'. Why must he use it at all? I did not like it. 'If I go with de Winter, and stay with him the whole time, and bring him back, will that satisfy you?' he said.

Favell looked at Maxim, and then at Colonel Julyan. The expression on his face was ugly, calculating, and there was something of triumph too in his light blue eyes. 'Yes,' he said slowly, 'yes, I suppose so. But for safety's sake do you mind if I come with you too?'

'No,' said Colonel Julyan, 'unfortunately I think you have the right to ask that. But if you do come, I have the right to insist on your being sober.'

'You needn't worry about that,' said Favell, beginning to smile; 'I'll be sober all right. Sober as the judge will be when he sentences Max in three months' time. I rather think this Doctor Baker is going to prove my case, after all.'

He looked around at each one of us and began to laugh. I think he too had understood at last the significance of that visit to the doctor.

'Well,' he said, 'what time are we going to start in the morning?'

Colonel Julyan looked at Maxim. 'How early can you be ready?'

'Any time you say,' said Maxim.

'Nine o'clock?'

'Nine o'clock,' said Maxim.

'How do we know he won't do a bolt in the night?' said Favell. 'He's only to cut round to the garage and get his car.'

'Is my word enough for you?' said Maxim, turning to Colonel Julyan. And for the first time Colonel Julyan hesitated. I saw him glance at Frank. And a flush came over Maxim's face. I saw the little pulse beating on his forehead. 'Mrs Danvers,' he said slowly, 'when Mrs de Winter and I go to bed tonight will you come up yourself and lock the door on the outside? And call us yourself, at seven in the morning?'

'Yes, sir,' said Mrs Danvers. Still she kept her eyes on him, still her hands clutched at her dress.

'Very well, then,' said Colonel Julyan brusquely. 'I don't think there is anything else we need discuss, tonight. I shall be here sharp at nine in the morning. You will have room for me in your car, de Winter?'

'Yes,' said Maxim.

'And Favell will follow us in his?'

'Right on your tail, my dear fellow, right on your tail,' said Favell.

Colonel Julyan came up to me and took my hand. 'Good night,' he said. 'You know how I feel for you in all this, there's no need for me to tell you. Get your husband to bed early, if you can. It's going to be a long day.' He held my hand a minute and then he turned away. It was curious how he avoided my eye. He looked at my chin. Frank held the door for him as he went out. Favell leant forward and filled his case with cigarettes from the box on the table.

'I suppose I'm not going to be asked to stop to dinner?' he said.

Nobody answered. He lit one of the cigarettes, and blew a cloud of smoke into the air. 'It means a quiet evening at the pub on the highroad then,' he said, 'and the barmaid has a squint. What a hell of a night I'm going to spend! Never mind, I'm looking forward to tomorrow. Good night, Danny old lady, don't forget to turn the key on Mr de Winter, will you?'

He came over to me and held out his hand.

Like a foolish child I put my hands behind my back. He laughed, and bowed.

'It's just too bad, isn't it?' he said. 'A nasty man like me coming and spoiling all your fun. Don't worry, it will be a great thrill for you when the yellow Press gets going with your life story, and you see the headlines "From Monte Carlo to Manderley. Experiences of murderer's girl-bride," written across the top. Better luck next time.'

He strolled across the room to the door, waving his hand to Maxim by the window. 'So long, old man,' he said, 'pleasant dreams. Make the most of your night behind that locked door.' He turned and laughed at me, and then he went out of the room. Mrs Danvers followed him. Maxim and I were alone. He went on standing by the window. He did not come to me. Jasper came trotting in from the hall. He had been shut outside all the evening. He came fussing up to me, biting the edge of my skirt.

'I'm coming with you in the morning,' I said to Maxim. 'I'm coming up to London with you in the car.'

He did not answer for a moment. He went on looking out of the window. Then 'Yes,' he said, his voice without expression. 'Yes, we must go on being together.'

Frank came back into the room. He stood in the entrance, his hand on the door. 'They've gone,' he said, 'Favell and Colonel Julyan, I watched them go.'

'All right, Frank,' said Maxim.

'Is there anything I can do?' said Frank, 'anything at all? Wire to anyone, arrange anything? I'll stay up all night if only there's anything I can do. I'll get that wire off to Baker of course.'

'Don't worry,' said Maxim, 'there's nothing for you to do – yet. There may be plenty – after tomorrow. We can go into all

395

that when the time comes. Tonight we want to be together. You understand, don't you?'

'Yes,' said Frank. 'Yes, of course.'

He waited a moment, his hand on the door. 'Good night,' he said.

'Good night,' said Maxim.

When he had gone, and shut the door behind him, Maxim came over to me where I was standing by the fireplace. I held out my arms to him and he came to me like a child. I put my arms round him and held him. We did not say anything for a long time. I held him and comforted him as though he were Jasper. As though Jasper had hurt himself in some way and he had come to me to take his pain away.

'We can sit together,' he said, 'driving up in the car.'

'Yes,' I said.

'Julyan won't mind,' he said.

'No,' I said.

'We shall have tomorrow night too,' he said. 'They won't do anything at once, not for twenty-four hours perhaps.'

'No,' I said.

'They aren't so strict now,' he said. 'They let one see people. And it all takes such a long time. If I can I shall try and get hold of Hastings. He's the best. Hastings or Birkett. Hastings used to know my father.'

'Yes,' I said.

'I shall have to tell him the truth,' he said. 'It makes it easier for them. They know where they are.'

'Yes,' I said.

The door opened and Frith came into the room. I pushed Maxim away, I stood up straight and conventional, patting my hair into place.

'Will you be changing, Madam, or shall I serve dinner at once?'

'No, Frith, we won't be changing, not tonight,' I said.

'Very good, Madam,' he said.

He left the door open. Robert came in and began drawing

the curtains. He arranged the cushions, straightened the sofa, tidied the books and papers on the table. He took away the whisky and soda and the dirty ash-trays. I had seen him do these things as a ritual every evening I had spent at Manderley, but tonight they seemed to take on a special significance, as though the memory of them would last for ever and I would say, long after, in some other time, 'I remember this moment.'

Then Frith came in and told us that dinner was served.

I remember every detail of that evening. I remember the ice-cold consommé in the cups, and the fillets of sole, and the hot shoulder of lamb.

I remember the burnt sugar sweet, the sharp savoury that followed.

We had new candles in the silver candlesticks, they looked white and slim and very tall. The curtains had been drawn here too against the dull grey evening. It seemed strange to be sitting in the dining-room and not look out on to the lawns. It was like the beginning of autumn.

It was while we were drinking our coffee in the library that the telephone rang. This time it was I who answered it. I heard Beatrice speaking at the other end. 'Is that you?' she said, 'I've been trying to get through all the evening. Twice it was engaged.'

'I'm so sorry,' I said, 'so very sorry.'

'We had the evening papers about two hours ago,' she said, 'and the verdict was a frightful shock to both Giles and myself. What does Maxim say about it?'

'I think it was a shock to everybody,' I said.

'But, my dear, the thing is preposterous. Why on earth should Rebecca have committed suicide? The most unlikely person in the world. There must have been a blunder somewhere.'

'I don't know,' I said.

'What does Maxim say? Where is he?' she said.

'People have been here,' I said – 'Colonel Julyan, and others. Maxim is very tired. We're going up to London tomorrow.'

'What on earth for?'

'Something to do with the verdict. I can't very well explain.'

'You ought to get it quashed,' she said. 'It's ridiculous, quite ridiculous. And so bad for Maxim, all this frightful publicity. It's going to reflect on him.'

'Yes,' I said.

'Surely Colonel Julyan can do something?' she said. 'He's a magistrate. What are magistrates for? Old Horridge from Lanyon must have been off his head. What was her motive supposed to be? It's the most idiotic thing I've ever heard in my life. Someone ought to get hold of Tabb. How can he tell whether those holes in the boat were made deliberately or not? Giles said of course it must have been the rocks.'

'They seemed to think not,' I said.

'If only I could have been there,' she said. 'I should have insisted on speaking. No one seems to have made any effort. Is Maxim very upset?'

'He's tired,' I said, 'more tired than anything else.'

'I wish I could come up to London and join you,' she said, 'but I don't see how I can. Roger has a temperature of 103, poor old boy, and the nurse we've got in is a perfect idiot, he loathes her. I can't possibly leave him.'

'Of course not,' I said. 'You mustn't attempt it.'

'Whereabouts in London will you be?'

'I don't know,' I said. 'It's all rather vague.'

'Tell Maxim he must try and do something to get that verdict altered. It's so bad for the family. I'm telling everybody here it's absolutely wicked. Rebecca would never have killed herself, she wasn't the type. I've got a good mind to write to the Coroner myself.'

'It's too late,' I said. 'Much better leave it. It won't do any good.'

'The stupidity of it gets my goat,' she said. 'Giles and I think it much more likely that if those holes weren't done by the rocks they were done deliberately, by some tramp or other. A Communist perhaps. There are heaps of them about. Just the sort of thing a Communist would do.'

Maxim called to me from the library. 'Can't you get rid of her? What on earth is she talking about?'

'Beatrice,' I said desperately, 'I'll try and ring you up from London.'

'Is it any good my tackling Dick Godolphin?' she said. 'He's your M.P. I know him very well, much better than Maxim does. He was at Oxford with Giles. Ask Maxim whether he would like me to telephone Dick and see if he can do anything to quash the verdict? Ask Maxim what he thinks of this Communist idea.'

'It's no use,' I said. 'It can't do any good. Please, Beatrice, don't try and do anything. It will make it worse, much worse. Rebecca may have had some motive we don't know anything about. And I don't think Communists go ramming holes in boats, what would be the use? Please, Beatrice, leave it alone.'

Oh, thank God she had not been with us today. Thank God for that at least. Something was buzzing in the telephone. I heard Beatrice shouting, 'Hullo, hullo, don't cut us off, exchange,' and then there was a click, and silence.

I went back into the library, limp and exhausted. In a few minutes the telephone began ringing again. I did not do anything. I let it ring. I went and sat down at Maxim's feet. It went on ringing. I did not move. Presently it stopped, as though cut suddenly in exasperation. The clock on the mantelpiece struck ten o'clock. Maxim put his arms round me and lifted me against him. We began to kiss one another, feverishly, desperately, like guilty lovers who have not kissed before.

Whn I awoke the next morning, just after six o'clock, and got up and went to the window there was a foggy dew upon the grass like frost, and the trees were shrouded in a white mist. There was a chill in the air and a little, fresh wind, and the cold, quiet smell of autumn.

As I knelt by the window looking down on to the rose-garden where the flowers themselves drooped upon their stalks, the petals brown and dragging after last night's rain, the happenings of the day before seemed remote and unreal. Here at Manderley a new day was starting, the things of the garden were not concerned with our troubles. A blackbird ran across the rose-garden to the lawns in swift, short rushes, stopping now and again to stab at the earth with his yellow beak. A thrush, too, went about his business, and two stout little wagtails, following one another, and a little cluster of twittering sparrows. A gull poised himself high in the air, silent and alone, and then spread his wings wide and swooped beyond the lawns to the woods and the Happy Valley. These things continued, our worries and anxieties had no power to alter them. Soon the gardeners would be astir, brushing the first leaves from the lawns and the paths, raking the gravel in the drive. Pails would clank in the courtyard behind the house, the hose would be turned on the car, the little scullery maid would begin to chatter through the open door to the men in the yard. There would be the crisp, hot smell of bacon. The housemaids would open up the house, throw wide the windows, draw back the curtains.

The dogs would crawl from their baskets, yawn and stretch themselves, wander out on to the terrace and blink at the first struggles of the pale sun coming through the mist. Robert would lay the table for breakfast, bring in those piping scones, the clutch of eggs, the glass dishes of honey, jam, and marmalade, the bowl of peaches, the cluster of purple grapes with the bloom upon them still, hot from the greenhouses.

Maids sweeping in the morning-room, the drawing-room, the fresh clean air pouring into the long open windows. Smoke curling from the chimneys, and little by little the autumn mist fading away and the trees and the banks and the woods taking shape, the glimmer of the sea showing with the sun upon it below the valley, the beacon standing tall and straight upon the headland.

The peace of Manderley. The quietude and the grace. Whoever lived within its walls, whatever trouble there was and strife, however much uneasiness and pain, no matter what tears were shed, what sorrows borne, the peace of Manderley could not be broken or the loveliness destroyed. The flowers that died would bloom again another year, the same birds build their nests, the same trees blossom. The old quiet moss smell would linger in the air, and bees would come, and crickets, and herons build their nests in the deep dark woods. The butterflies would dance their merry jig across the lawns, and spiders spin foggy webs, and small startled rabbits who had no business to come trespassing poke their faces through the crowded shrubs. There would be lilac and honeysuckle still, and the white magnolia buds unfolding slow and tight beneath the dining-room window. No one would ever hurt Manderley. It would lie always in a hollow like an enchanted thing, guarded by the woods, safe, secure, while the sea broke and ran and came again in the little shingle bays below.

Maxim slept on and I did not wake him. The day ahead of us would be a weary thing and long. Highroads, and telegraph poles, and the monotony of passing traffic, the slow crawl into London. We did not know what we should find at the end of our journey. The future was unknown. Somewhere to the north of London lived a man called Baker who had never heard of us, but he held our future in the hollow of his hand. Soon he too would be waking, stretching, yawning, going about the business of his day. I got up, and went into the bathroom, and began to run my bath. These actions held for me the same significance as Robert and his clearing of the library had the night before. I had done these things before mechanically, but now I was aware as I dropped my sponge into the water, as I spread my towel on the chair from the hot rail, as I lay back and let the water run over my body. Every moment was a precious thing, having in it the essence of finality. When I went back to the bedroom and began to dress I heard a soft footstep come and pause outside the door, and the key turn quietly in the lock. There was silence a moment, and then the footsteps went away. It was Mrs Danvers.

She had not forgotten. I had heard the same sound the night before after we had come up from the library. She had not knocked upon the door, she had not made herself known; there was just the sound of footsteps and the turning of the key in the lock. It brought me to reality and the facing of the immediate future.

I finished dressing, and went and turned on Maxim's bath. Presently Clarice came with our tea. I woke Maxim. He stared at me at first like a puzzled child, and then he held out his arms. We drank our tea. He got up and went to his bath and I began putting things methodically in my suit-case. It might be that we should have to stay in London.

I packed the brushes Maxim had given me, a nightdress, my dressing-gown and slippers, and another dress too and a pair of shoes. My dressing-case looked unfamiliar as I dragged it from the back of a wardrobe. It seemed so long since I had used it, and yet it was only four months ago. It still had the Customs mark upon it they had chalked at Calais. In one of the pockets was a concert ticket from the casino in Monte Carlo. I crumpled it and threw it into the waste-paper basket. It might have belonged to another age, another world. My bedroom began to take on the appearance of all rooms when the owner goes away. The dressing-table was bare without my brushes. There was tissue-paper lying on the floor, and an old label. The beds where

402

we had slept had a terrible emptiness about them. The towels lay crumpled on the bathroom floor. The wardrobe doors gaped open. I put on my hat so that I should not have to come up again, and I took my bag and my gloves and my suit-case. I glanced round the room to see if there was anything I had forgotten. The mist was breaking, the sun was forcing its way through and throwing patterns on the carpet. When I was half-way down the passage I had a curious, inexplicable feeling that I must go back and look in my room again. I went without reason, and stood a moment looking at the gaping wardrobe and the empty bed, and the tray of tea upon the table. I stared at them, impressing them for ever on my mind, wondering why they had the power to touch me, to sadden me, as though they were children that did not want me to go away.

Then I turned and went downstairs to breakfast. It was cold in the dining-room, the sun not yet on the windows, and I was grateful for the scalding bitter coffee and heartening bacon. Maxim and I ate in silence. Now and again he glanced at the clock. I heard Robert put the suit-cases in the hall with the rug, and presently there was the sound of the car being brought to the door.

I went out and stood on the terrace. The rain had cleared the air, and the grass smelt fresh and sweet. When the sun was higher it would be a lovely day. I thought how we might have wandered in the valley before lunch, and then sat out afterwards under the chestnut tree with books and papers. I closed my eyes a minute and felt the warmth of the sun on my face and on my hands.

I heard Maxim calling to me from the house. I went back, and Frith helped me into my coat. I heard the sound of another car. It was Frank.

'Colonel Julyan is waiting at the lodge gates,' he said. 'He did not think it worth while to drive up to the house.'

'No,' said Maxim.

'I'll stand by in the office all day and wait for you to tele-phone,' said Frank. 'After you've seen Baker you may find you want me, up in London.'

'Yes,' said Maxim. 'Yes, perhaps.'

'It's just nine now,' said Frank. 'You're up to time. It's going to be fine too. You should have a good run.'

'Yes.'

'I hope you won't get over-tired, Mrs de Winter,' he said to me. 'It's going to be a long day for you.'

'I shall be all right,' I said. I looked at Jasper who was standing by my feet with ears drooping and sad reproachful eyes.

'Take Jasper back with you to the office,' I said. 'He looks so miserable.'

'Yes,' he said. 'Yes, I will.'

'We'd better be off,' said Maxim. 'Old Julyan will be getting impatient. All right, Frank.'

I climbed in the car beside Maxim. Frank slammed the door.

'You will telephone, won't you?' he said.

'Yes, of course,' said Maxim.

I looked back at the house. Frith was standing at the top of the steps, and Robert just behind. My eyes filled with tears for no reason. I turned away and groped with my bag on the floor of the car so that nobody should see. Then Maxim started up the car and we swept round and into the drive and the house was hidden.

We stopped at the lodge-gates and picked up Colonel Julyan. He got in at the back. He looked doubtful when he saw me.

'It's going to be a long day,' he said. 'I don't think you should have attempted it. I would have taken care of your husband you know.'

'I wanted to come,' I said.

He did not say any more about it. He settled himself in the corner. 'It's fine, that's one thing,' he said.

'Yes,' said Maxim.

'That fellow Favell said he would pick us up at the cross-roads. If he's not there don't attempt to wait, we'd do much better without him. I hope the damned fellow has overslept himself.'

When we came to the cross-roads though I saw the long

green body of his car, and my heart sank. I had thought he might not be on time. Favell was sitting at the wheel, hatless, a cigarette in his mouth. He grinned when he saw us, and waved us on. I settled down in my seat for the journey ahead, one hand on Maxim's knee. The hours passed, and the miles were covered. I watched the road ahead in a kind of stupor. Colonel Julyan slept at the back from time to time. I turned occasionally and saw his head loll against the cushions, and his mouth open. The green car kept close beside us. Sometimes it shot ahead, sometimes it dropped behind. But we never lost it. At one we stopped for lunch at one of those inevitable old-fashioned hotels in the main street of a county town. Colonel Julyan waded through the whole set lunch, starting with soup and fish, and going on to roast beef and Yorkshire pudding. Maxim and I had cold ham and coffee.

I half expected Favell to wander into the dining-room and join us, but when we came out to the car again I saw his car had been drawn up outside a café on the opposite side of the road. He must have seen us from the window, for three minutes after we had started he was on our tail again.

We came to the suburbs of London about three o'clock. It was then that I began to feel tired, the noise and the traffic blocks started a humming in my head. It was warm in London too. The streets had that worn dusty look of August, and the leaves hung listless on dull trees. Our storm must have been local, there had been no rain here.

People were walking about in cotton frocks and the men were hatless. There was a smell of waste-paper, and orange-peel, and feet, and burnt dried grass. Buses lumbered slowly, and taxis crawled. I felt as though my coat and skirt were sticking to me, and my stockings pricked my skin.

Colonel Julyan sat up and looked out through his window. 'They've had no rain here,' he said.

'No,' said Maxim.

'Looks as though the place needed it, too.'

'Yes.'

'We haven't succeeded in shaking Favell off. He's still on our tail.'

'Yes.'

Shopping centres on the outskirts seemed congested. Tired women with crying babies in prams stared into windows, hawkers shouted, small boys hung on to the backs of lorries. There were too many people, too much noise. The very air was irritable and exhausted and spent.

The drive through London seemed endless, and by the time we had drawn clear again and were out beyond Hampstead there was a sound in my head like the beating of a drum, and my eyes were burning.

I wondered how tired Maxim was. He was pale, and there were shadows under his eyes, but he did not say anything. Colonel Julyan kept yawning at the back. He opened his mouth very wide and yawned aloud, sighing heavily afterwards. He would do this every few minutes. I felt a senseless stupid irritation come over me, and I did not know how to prevent myself from turning round and screaming to him to stop.

Once we had passed Hampstead he drew out a large-scale map from his coat-pocket and began directing Maxim to Barnet. The way was clear and there were sign-posts to tell us, but he kept pointing out every turn and twist in the road, and if there was any hesitation on Maxim's part Colonel Julyan would turn down the window and call for information from a passer-by.

When we came to Barnet itself he made Maxim stop every few minutes. 'Can you tell us where a house called Roselands is? It belongs to a Doctor Baker, who's retired, and come to live there lately,' and the passer-by would stand frowning a moment, obviously at sea, ignorance written plain upon his face.

'Doctor Baker? I don't know a Doctor Baker. There used to be a house called Rose Cottage near the church, but a Mrs Wilson lives there.'

'No, it's Roselands we want, Doctor Baker's house,' said Colonel Julyan, and then we would go on and stop again in front of a nurse and a pram. 'Can you tell us where Roselands is?'

'I'm sorry. I'm afraid I've only just come to live here.'

'You don't know a Doctor Baker?'

'Doctor Davidson. I know Doctor Davidson.'

'No, it's Doctor Baker we want.'

I glanced up at Maxim. He was looking very tired. His mouth was set hard. Behind us crawled Favell, his green car covered in dust.

It was a postman who pointed out the house in the end. A square house, ivy covered, with no name on the gate, which we had already passed twice. Mechanically I reached for my bag and dabbed my face with the end of the powder puff. Maxim drew up outside at the side of the road. He did not take the car into the short drive. We sat silently for a few minutes.

'Well, here we are,' said Colonel Julyan, 'and it's exactly twelve minutes past five. We shall catch them in the middle of their tea. Better wait for a bit.'

Maxim lit a cigarette, and then stretched out his hand to me. He did not speak. I heard Colonel Julyan crinkling his map.

'We could have come right across without touching London,' he said, 'saved us forty minutes I dare say. We made good time the first two hundred miles. It was from Chiswick on we took the time.'

An errand-boy passed us whistling on his bicycle. A motor-coach stopped at the corner and two women got out. Somewhere a church clock chimed the quarter. I could see Favell leaning back in his car behind us and smoking a cigarette. I seemed to have no feeling in me at all. I just sat and watched the little things that did not matter. The two women from the bus walk along the road. The errand-boy disappears round the corner. A sparrow hops about in the middle of the road pecking at dirt.

'This fellow Baker can't be much of a gardener,' said Colonel Julyan. 'Look at those shrubs tumbling over his wall. They ought to have been pruned right back.' He folded up the map and put it back in his pocket. 'Funny sort of place to choose to retire in,' he said. 'Close to the main road and overlooked by other houses. Shouldn't care about it myself. I dare say it was quite pretty once before they started building. No doubt there's a good golf-course somewhere handy.'

He was silent for a while, then he opened the door and stood out in the road. 'Well, de Winter,' he said, 'what do you think about it?'

'I'm ready,' said Maxim.

We got out of the car. Favell strolled up to meet us.

'What were you all waiting for, cold feet?' he said.

Nobody answered him. We walked up the drive to the front door, a strange incongruous little party. I caught sight of a tennis lawn beyond the house, and I heard the thud of balls. A boy's voice shouted 'Forty-fifteen, not thirty all. Don't you remember hitting it out, you silly ass?'

'They must have finished tea,' said Colonel Julyan.

He hesitated a moment, glancing at Maxim. Then he rang the bell.

It tinkled somewhere in the back premises. There was a long pause. A very young maid opened the door to us. She looked startled at the sight of so many of us.

'Doctor Baker?' said Colonel Julyan.

'Yes, sir, will you come in?'

She opened the door on the left of the hall as we went in. It would be the drawing-room, not used much in the summer. There was a portrait of a very plain dark woman on the wall. I wondered if it was Mrs Baker. The chintz covers on the chairs and on the sofa were new and shiny. On the mantelpiece were photographs of two schoolboys with round, smiling faces. There was a very large wireless in the corner of the room by the window. Cords trailed from it, and bits of aerial. Favell examined the portrait on the wall. Colonel Julyan went and stood by the empty fireplace. Maxim and I looked out of the window. I could see a deck-chair under a tree, and the back of a woman's head. The tennis court must be round the corner. I could hear

408

the boys shouting to each other. A very old Scotch terrier was scratching himself in the middle of the path. We waited there for about five minutes. It was as though I was living the life of some other person and had come to this house to call for a subscription to a charity. It was unlike anything I had ever known. I had no feeling, no pain.

Then the door opened and a man came into the room. He was medium height, rather long in the face, with a keen chin. His hair was sandy, turning grey. He wore flannels, and a dark blue blazer.

'Forgive me for keeping you waiting,' he said, looking a little surprised, as the maid had done, to see so many of us. 'I had to run up and wash. I was playing tennis when the bell rang. Won't you sit down?' He turned to me. I sat down in the nearest chair and waited.

'You must think this a very unorthodox invasion, Doctor Baker,' said Colonel Julyan, 'and I apologize very humbly for disturbing you like this. My name is Julyan. This is Mr de Winter, Mrs de Winter, and Mr Favell. You may have seen Mr de Winter's name in the papers recently.'

'Oh,' said Doctor Baker, 'yes, yes, I suppose I have. Some inquest or other, wasn't it? My wife was reading all about it.'

'The jury brought in a verdict of suicide,' said Favell coming forward, 'which I say is absolutely out of the question. Mrs de Winter was my cousin, I knew her intimately. She would never have done such a thing, and what's more she had no motive. What we want to know is what the devil she came to see you about the very day she died?'

'You had better leave this to Julyan and myself,' said Maxim quietly. 'Doctor Baker has not the faintest idea what you are driving at.'

He turned to the doctor who was standing between them with a line between his brows, and his first polite smile frozen on his lips. 'My late wife's cousin is not satisfied with the verdict,' said Maxim, 'and we've driven up to see you today because we found your name, and the telephone number of your old consulting-rooms, in my wife's engagement diary. She seems to have made an appointment with you, and kept it, at two o'clock on the last day she ever spent in London. Could you possibly verify this for us?'

Doctor Baker was listening with great interest, but when Maxim had finished he shook his head. 'I'm most awfully sorry,' he said, 'but I think you've made a mistake. I should have remembered the name de Winter. I've never attended a Mrs de Winter in my life.'

Colonel Julyan brought out his note case and gave him the page he had torn from the engagement diary. 'Here it is, written down,' he said, 'Baker, two o'clock. And a big cross beside it, to show that the appointment was kept. And here is the telephone address. Museum 0488.'

Doctor Baker stared at the piece of paper. 'That's very odd, very odd indeed. Yes, the number is quite correct as you say.'

'Could she have come to see you and given a false name?' said Colonel Julyan.

'Why, yes, that's possible. She may have done that. It's rather unusual of course. I've never encouraged that sort of thing. It doesn't do us any good in the profession if people think they can treat us like that.'

'Would you have any record of the visit in your files?' said Colonel Julyan. 'I know it's not etiquette to ask, but the circumstances are very unusual. We do feel her appointment with you must have some bearing on the case and her subsequent – suicide.'

'Murder,' said Favell.

Doctor Baker raised his eyebrows, and looked inquiringly at Maxim. 'I'd no idea there was any question of that,' he said quietly. 'Of course I understand, and I'll do anything in my power to help you. If you will excuse me a few minutes I will go and look up my files. There should be a record of every appointment booked throughout the year, and a description of the case. Please help yourself to cigarettes. It's too early to offer you sherry, I suppose?'

Colonel Julyan and Maxim shook their heads. I thought Favell was going to say something but Doctor Baker had left the room before he had a chance.

'Seems a decent sort of fellow,' said Colonel Julyan.

'Why didn't he offer us whisky and soda?' said Favell. 'Keeps it locked up, I suppose. I didn't think much of him. I don't believe he's going to help us now.'

Maxim did not say anything. I could hear the sound of the tennis balls from the court. The Scotch terrier was barking. A woman's voice shouted to him to be quiet. The summer holidays. Baker playing with his boys. We had interrupted their routine. A high-pitched, gold clock in a glass case ticked very fast on the mantelpiece. There was a postcard of the Lake of Geneva leaning against it. The Bakers had friends in Switzerland.

Doctor Baker came back into the room with a large book and a file-case in his hands. He carried them over to the table. 'I've brought the collection for last year,' he said. 'I haven't been through them yet since we moved. I only gave up practice six months ago you know.' He opened the book and began turning the pages. I watched him fascinated. He would find it of course. It was only a question of moments now, of seconds. 'The seventh, eighth, tenth,' he murmured, 'nothing here. The twelfth did you say? At two o'clock? Ah!'

We none of us moved. We all watched his face.

'I saw a Mrs Danvers on the twelfth at two o'clock,' he said.

'Danny? What on earth ...' began Favell, but Maxim cut him short.

'She gave a wrong name, of course,' he said. 'That was obvious from the first. Do you remember the visit now, Doctor Baker?'

But Doctor Baker was already searching his files. I saw his fingers delve into the pocket marked with D. He found it almost at once. He glanced down rapidly at his handwriting. 'Yes,' he said slowly. 'Yes, Mrs Danvers. I remember now.'

'Tall, slim, dark, very handsome?' said Colonel Julyan quietly.

'Yes,' said Doctor Baker. 'Yes.'

He read through the files, and then replaced them in the case. 'Of course,' he said, glancing at Maxim, 'this is unprofessional you

411

know? We treat patients as though they were in the confessional. But your wife is dead, and I quite understand the circumstances are exceptional. You want to know if I can suggest any motive why your wife should have taken her life? I think I can. The woman who called herself Mrs Danvers was very seriously ill.'

He paused. He looked at every one of us in turn.

'I remember her perfectly well,' he said, and he turned back to the files again. 'She came to me for the first time a week previously to the date you mentioned. She complained of certain symptoms, and I took some X-rays of her. The second visit was to find out the result of those X-rays. The photographs are not here, but I have the details written down. I remember her standing in my consulting-room and holding out her hand for the photographs. "I want to know the truth," she said; "I don't want soft words and a bedside manner. If I'm for it, you can tell me right away."' He paused, he glanced down at the files once again.

I waited, waited. Why couldn't he get done with it and finish and let us go? Why must we sit there, waiting, our eyes upon his face.

'Well,' he said, 'she asked for the truth, and I let her have it. Some patients are better for it. Shirking the point does them no good. This Mrs Danvers, or Mrs de Winter rather, was not the type to accept a lie. You must have known that. She stood it very well. She did not flinch. She said she had suspected it for some time. Then she paid my fee and went out. I never saw her again.'

He shut up the box with a snap, and closed the book. 'The pain was slight as yet, but the growth was deep-rooted,' he said, 'and in three or four months' time she would have been under morphia. An operation would have been no earthly use at all. I told her that. The thing had got too firm a hold. There is nothing anyone can do in a case like that, except give morphia, and wait.'

No one said a word. The little clock ticked on the mantelpiece, and the boys played tennis in the garden. An aeroplane hummed overhead.

'Outwardly of course she was a perfectly healthy woman,' he said – 'rather too thin, I remember, rather pale; but then that's the fashion nowadays, pity though it is. It's nothing to go upon with a patient. No, the pain would increase week by week, and as I told you, in four or five months' time she would have had to be kept under morphia. The X-rays showed a certain malformation of the uterus, I remember, which meant she could never have had a child; but that was quite apart, it had nothing to do with the disease.'

I remember hearing Colonel Julyan speak, saying something about Doctor Baker being very kind to have taken so much trouble. 'You have told us all we want to know,' he said, 'and if we could possibly have a copy of the memoranda in your file it might be very useful.'

'Of course,' said Doctor Baker. 'Of course.'

Everyone was standing up. I got up from my chair too, I shook hands with Doctor Baker. We all shook hands with him. We followed him out into the hall. A woman looked out of the room on the other side of the hall and darted back when she saw us. Someone was running a bath upstairs, the water ran loudly. The Scotch terrier came in from the garden and began sniffing at my heels.

'Shall I send the report to you or to Mr de Winter?' said Doctor Baker.

'We may not need it at all,' said Colonel Julyan. 'I rather think it won't be necessary. Either de Winter or I will write. Here is my card.'

'I'm so glad to have been of use,' said Doctor Baker; 'it never entered my head for a moment that Mrs de Winter and Mrs Danvers could be the same person.'

'No, naturally,' said Colonel Julyan.

'You'll be returning to London, I suppose?'

'Yes. Yes, I imagine so.'

'Your best way then is to turn sharp left by that pillar-box, and then right by the church. After that it's a straight road.'

'Thank you. Thank you very much.'

413

We came out on to the drive and went towards the cars. Doctor Baker pulled the Scotch terrier inside the house. I heard the door shut. A man with one leg and a barrel-organ began playing 'Roses in Picardy', at the end of the road.

We went and stood by the car. No one said anything for a few minutes. Colonel Julyan handed round his cigarette case. Favell looked grey, rather shaken. I noticed his hands were trembling as he held the match. The man with the barrel organ ceased playing for a moment and hobbled towards us, his cap in his hand. Maxim gave him two shillings. Then he went back to the barrel-organ and started another tune. The church clock struck six o'clock. Favell began to speak. His voice was diffident, careless, but his face was still grey. He did not look at any of us, he kept glancing down at his cigarette and turning it over in his fingers. 'This cancer business,' he said; 'does anybody know if it's contagious?'

No one answered him. Colonel Julyan shrugged his shoulders.

'I never had the remotest idea,' said Favell jerkily. 'She kept it a secret from everyone, even Danny. What a God-damned appalling thing, eh? Not the sort of thing one would ever connect with Rebecca. Do you fellows feel like a drink? I'm all out over this, and I don't mind admitting it. Cancer! Oh, my God!'

He leant up against the side of the car and shaded his eyes with his hands. 'Tell that bloody fellow with the barrel organ to clear out,' he said. 'I can't stand that God-damned row.'

'Wouldn't it be simpler if we went ourselves?' said Maxim. 'Can you manage your own car, or do you want Julyan to drive it for you?'

'Give me a minute,' muttered Favell. 'I'll be all right. You don't understand. This thing has been a damned unholy shock to me.'

'Pull yourself together, man, for heaven's sake,' said Colonel Julyan. 'If you want a drink go back to the house and ask Baker.

He knows how to treat for shock, I dare say. Don't make an exhibition of yourself in the street.'

'Oh, you're all right, you're fine,' said Favell, standing straight and looking at Colonel Julyan and Maxim. 'You've got nothing to worry about any more. Max is on a good wicket now, isn't he? You've got your motive, and Baker will supply it in black and white free of cost, whenever you send the word. You can dine at Manderley once a week on the strength of it and feel proud of yourself. No doubt Max will ask you to be godfather to his first child.'

'Shall we get into the car and go?' said Colonel Julyan to Maxim. 'We can make our plans going along.'

Maxim held open the door of the car, and Colonel Julyan climbed in. I sat down in my seat in the front. Favell still leant against the car and did not move. 'I should advise you to get straight back to your flat and go to bed,' said Colonel Julyan shortly, 'and drive slowly, or you will find yourself in jail for manslaughter. I may as well warn you now, as I shall not be seeing you again, that as a magistrate I have certain powers that will prove effective if you ever turn up in Kerrith or the district. Blackmail is not much of a profession, Mr Favell. And we know how to deal with it in our part of the world, strange though it may seem to you.'

Favell was watching Maxim. He had lost the grey colour now, and the old unpleasant smile was forming on his lips. 'Yes, it's been a stroke of luck for you, Max, hasn't it?' he said slowly; 'you think you've won, don't you? The law can get you yet, and so can I, in a different way . . .'

Maxim switched on the engine. 'Have you anything else you want to say?' he said; 'because if you have you had better say it now.'

'No,' said Favell. 'No, I won't keep you. You can go.' He stepped back on to the pavement, the smile still on his lips. The car slid forward. As we turned the corner I looked back and saw him standing there, watching us, and he waved his hand and he was laughing.

416

We drove on for a while in silence. Then Colonel Julyan spoke. 'He can't do anything,' he said. 'That smile and that wave were part of his bluff. They're all alike, those fellows. He hasn't a thread of a case to bring now. Baker's evidence would squash it.'

Maxim did not answer. I glanced sideways at his face but it told me nothing. 'I always felt the solution would lie in Baker,' said Colonel Julyan; 'the furtive business of that appointment, and the way she never even told Mrs Danvers. She had her suspicions, you see. She knew something was wrong. A dreadful thing, of course. Very dreadful. Enough to send a young and lovely woman right off her head.'

We drove on along the straight main road. Telegraph poles, motor coaches, open sports cars, little semi-detached villas with new gardens, they flashed past making patterns in my mind I should always remember.

'I suppose you never had any idea of this, de Winter?' said Colonel Julyan.

'No,' said Maxim. 'No.'

'Of course some people have a morbid dread of it,' said Colonel Julyan. 'Women especially. That must have been the case with your wife. She had courage for every other thing but that. She could not face pain. Well, she was spared that at any rate.'

'Yes,' said Maxim.

'I don't think it would do any harm if I quietly let it be known down in Kerrith and in the county that a London doctor has supplied us with a motive,' said Colonel Julyan. 'Just in case there should be any gossip. You never can tell, you know. People are odd, sometimes. If they knew about Mrs de Winter it might make it a lot easier for you.'

'Yes,' said Maxim, 'yes, I understand.'

'It's curious and very irritating,' said Colonel Julyan slowly, 'how long stories spread in country districts. I never know why they should, but unfortunately they do. Not that I anticipate any trouble over this, but it's as well to be prepared. People are inclined to say the wildest things if they are given half a chance.'

417

'Yes,' said Maxim.

'You and Crawley of course can squash any nonsense in Manderley or the estate, and I can deal with it effectively in Kerrith. I shall say a word to my girl too. She sees a lot of the younger people, who very often are the worst offenders in story-telling. I don't suppose the newspapers will worry you any more, that's one good thing. You'll find they will drop the whole affair in a day or two.'

'Yes,' said Maxim.

We drove on through the northern suburbs and came once more to Finchley and Hampstead.

'Half past six,' said Colonel Julyan; 'what do you propose doing? I've got a sister living in St John's Wood, and feel inclined to take her unawares and ask for dinner, and then catch the last train from Paddington. I know she doesn't go away for another week. I'm sure she would be delighted to see you both as well.'

Maxim hesitated, and glanced at me. 'It's very kind of you,' he said, 'but I think we had better be independent. I must ring up Frank, and one thing and another. I dare say we shall have a quiet meal somewhere and start off again afterwards, spending the night at a pub on the way, I rather think that's what we shall do.'

'Of course,' said Colonel Julyan, 'I quite understand. Could you throw me out at my sister's? It's one of those turnings off the Avenue Road.'

When we came to the house Maxim drew up a little way ahead of the gate. 'It's impossible to thank you,' he said, 'for all you've done today. You know what I feel about it without my telling you.'

'My dear fellow,' said Colonel Julyan, 'I've been only too glad. If only we'd known what Baker knew of course there would have been none of this at all. However, never mind about that now. You must put the whole thing behind you as a very unpleasant and unfortunate episode. I'm pretty sure you won't have any more trouble from Favell. If you do, I count on you

418

to tell me at once. I shall know how to deal with him.' He climbed out of the car, collecting his coat and his map. 'I should feel inclined,' he said, not looking directly at us, 'to get away for a bit. Take a short holiday. Go abroad, perhaps.'

We did not say anything. Colonel Julyan was fumbling with his map. 'Switzerland is very nice this time of year,' he said. 'I remember we went once for the girl's holidays, and thoroughly enjoyed ourselves. The walks are delightful.' He hesitated, cleared his throat. 'It is just faintly possible certain little difficulties might arise,' he said, 'not from Favell, but from one or two people in the district. One never knows quite what Tabb has been saying, and repeating, and so on. Absurd of course. But you know the old saying? Out of sight, out of mind. If people aren't there to be talked about the talk dies. It's the way of the world.'

He stood for a moment, counting his belongings. 'I've got everything, I think. Map, glasses, stick, coat. Everything complete. Well, good-bye, both of you. Don't get over-tired. It's been a long day.'

He turned in at the gate and went up the steps. I saw a woman come to the window and smile and wave her hand. We drove away down the road and turned the corner. I leant back in my seat and closed my eyes. Now that we were alone again and the strain was over, the sensation was one of almost unbearable relief. It was like the bursting of an abscess. Maxim did not speak. I felt his hand cover mine. We drove on through the traffic and I saw none of it. I heard the rumble of the buses, the hooting of taxis, that inevitable, tireless London roar, but I was not part of it. I rested in some other place that was cool and quiet and still. Nothing could touch us any more. We had come through our crisis.

When Maxim stopped the car I opened my eyes and sat up. We were opposite one of those numerous little restaurants in a narrow street in Soho. I looked about me, dazed and stupid.

'You're tired,' said Maxim briefly. 'Empty and tired and fit for nothing. You'll be better when you've had something to eat. So shall I. We'll go in here and order dinner right away. I can telephone to Frank too.'

We got out of the car. There was no one in the restaurant but the *maître d'hôtel* and a waiter and a girl behind a desk. It was dark and cool. We went to a table right in the corner. Maxim began ordering the food. 'Favell was right about wanting a drink,' he said. 'I want one too and so do you. You're going to have some brandy.'

The *maître d'hotel* was fat and smiling. He produced long thin rolls in paper envelopes. They were very hard, very crisp. I began to eat one ravenously. My brandy and soda was soft, warming, curiously comforting.

'When we've had dinner we'll drive slowly, very quietly,' said Maxim. 'It will be cool, too, in the evening. We'll find somewhere on the road we can put up for the night. Then we can get along to Manderley in the morning.'

'Yes,' I said.

'You didn't want to dine with Julyan's sister and go down by the late train?'

'No.'

Maxim finished his drink. His eyes looked large and they were ringed with the shadows. They seemed very dark against the pallor of his face.

'How much of the truth', he said, 'do you think Julyan guessed?'

I watched him over the rim of my glass. I did not say anything.

'He knew,' said Maxim slowly, 'of course he knew.'

'If he did,' I said, 'he will never say anything. Never, never.'

'No,' said Maxim. 'No.'

He ordered another drink from the *maître d'hôtel*. We sat silent and peaceful in our dark corner.

'I believe', said Maxim, 'that Rebecca lied to me on purpose. The last supreme bluff. She wanted me to kill her. She foresaw the whole thing. That's why she laughed. That's why she stood there laughing when she died.'

I did not say anything. I went on drinking my brandy and

soda. It was all over. It was all settled. It did not matter any more. There was no need for Maxim to look white and troubled.

'It was her last practical joke,' said Maxim, 'the best of them all. And I'm not sure if she hasn't won, even now.'

'What do you mean? How can she have won?' I said.

'I don't know,' he said. 'I don't know.' He swallowed his second drink. Then he got up from the table. 'I'm going to ring up Frank,' he said.

I sat there in my corner, and presently the waiter brought me my fish. It was lobster. Very hot and good. I had another brandy and soda, too. It was pleasant and comfortable sitting there and nothing mattered very much. I smiled at the waiter. I asked for some more bread in French for no reason. It was quiet and happy and friendly in the restaurant. Maxim and I were together. Everything was over. Everything was settled. Rebecca was dead. Rebecca could not hurt us. She had played her last joke as Maxim had said. She could do no more to us now. In ten minutes Maxim came back again.

'Well,' I said, my own voice sounding far away, 'how was Frank?'

'Frank was all right,' said Maxim. 'He was at the office, been waiting there for me to telephone him ever since four o'clock. I told him what had happened. He sounded glad, relieved.'

'Yes,' I said.

'Something rather odd though,' said Maxim slowly, a line between his brows. 'He thinks Mrs Danvers has cleared out. She's gone, disappeared. She said nothing to anyone, but apparently she'd been packing up all day, stripping her room of things, and the fellow from the station came for her boxes at about four o'clock. Frith telephoned down to Frank about it, and Frank told Frith to ask Mrs Danvers to come down to him at the office. He waited, and she never came. About ten minutes before I rang up, Frith telephoned to Frank again and said there had been a long-distance call for Mrs Danvers which he had switched through to her room, and she had answered. This must have been about ten past six. At a quarter to seven he knocked on the door

421

and found her room empty. Her bedroom too. They looked for her and could not find her. They think she's gone. She must have gone straight out of the house and through the woods. She never passed the lodge-gates.'

'Isn't it a good thing?' I said. 'It saves us a lot of trouble. We should have had to send her away, anyway. I believe she guessed, too. There was an expression on her face last night. I kept thinking of it, coming up in the car.'

'I don't like it,' said Maxim. 'I don't like it.'

'She can't do anything,' I argued. 'If she's gone, so much the better. It was Favell who telephoned of course. He must have told her about Baker. He would tell her what Colonel Julyan said. Colonel Julyan said if there was any attempt at blackmail we were to tell him. They won't dare do it. They can't. It's too dangerous.'

'I'm not thinking of blackmail,' said Maxim.

'What else can they do?' I said. 'We've got to do what Colonel Julyan said. We've got to forget it. We must not think about it any more. It's all over, darling, it's finished. We ought to go down on our knees and thank God that it's finished.'

Maxim did not answer. He was staring in front of him at nothing.

'Your lobster will be cold,' I said; 'eat it, darling. It will do you good, you want something inside you. You're tired.' I was using the words he had used to me. I felt better and stronger. It was I now who was taking care of him. He was tired, pale. I had got over my weakness and fatigue and now he was the one to suffer from reaction. It was just because he was empty, because he was tired. There was nothing to worry about at all. Mrs Danvers had gone. We should praise God for that, too. Everything had been made so easy for us, so very easy. 'Eat up your fish,' I said.

It was going to be very different in the future. I was not going to be nervous and shy with the servants any more. With Mrs Danvers gone I should learn bit by bit to control the house. I would go and interview the cook in the kitchen. They would like me, respect me. Soon it would be as though Mrs Danvers had never had command. I would learn more about the estate, too. I should ask Frank to explain things to me. I was sure Frank liked me. I liked him, too. I would go into things, and learn how they were managed. What they did at the farm. How the work in the grounds was planned. I might take to gardening myself, and in time have one or two things altered. That little square lawn outside the morning-room with the statue of the satyr. I did not like it. We would give the satyr away. There were heaps of things that I could do, little by little. People would come and stay and I should not mind. There would be the interest of seeing to their rooms, having flowers and books put, arranging the food. We would have children. Surely we would have children.

'Have you finished?' said Maxim suddenly. 'I don't think I want any more. Only coffee. Black, very strong, please, and the bill,' he added to the *maître d'hôtel.*

I wondered why we must go so soon. It was comfortable in the restaurant, and there was nothing to take us away. I liked sitting there, with my head against the sofa back, planning the future idly in a hazy pleasant way. I could have gone on sitting there for a long while.

I followed Maxim out of the restaurant, stumbling a little, and yawning. 'Listen,' he said, when we were on the pavement, 'do you think you could sleep in the car if I wrapped you up with the rug, and tucked you down in the back. There's the cushion there, and my coat as well.'

'I thought we were going to put up somewhere for the night?' I said blankly. 'One of those hotels one passes on the road.'

'I know,' he said, 'but I have this feeling I must get down tonight. Can't you possibly sleep in the back of the car?'

'Yes,' I said doubtfully. 'Yes, I suppose so.'

'If we start now, it's a quarter to eight, we ought to be there by half past two,' he said. 'There won't be much traffic on the road.'

'You'll be so tired,' I said. 'So terribly tired.'

'No,' he shook his head. 'I shall be all right. I want to get home. Something's wrong. I know it is. I want to get home.'

His face was anxious, strange. He pulled open the door and began arranging the rugs and the cushion at the back of the car.

'What can be wrong?' I said. 'It seems so odd to worry now, when everything's over. I can't understand you.'

He did not answer. I climbed into the back of the car and lay down with my legs tucked under me. He covered me with the rug. It was very comfortable. Much better than I imagined. I settled the pillow under my head.

'Are you all right?' he said; 'are you sure you don't mind?'

'No,' I said, smiling. 'I'm all right. I shall sleep. I don't want to stay anywhere on the road. It's much better to do this and get home. We'll be at Manderley long before sunrise.'

He got in in front and switched on the engine. I shut my eyes. The car drew away and I felt the slight jolting of the springs under my body. I pressed my face against the cushion. The motion of the car was rhythmic, steady, and the pulse of my mind beat with it. A hundred images came to me when I closed my eyes, things seen, things known, and things forgotten. They were jumbled together in a senseless pattern. The quill of Mrs Van Hopper's hat, the hard straight-backed chairs in Frank's dining-room, the wide window in the west wing at Manderley, the salmon-coloured frock of the smiling lady at the fancy-dress ball, a peasant-girl in a road near Monte Carlo.

Sometimes I saw Jasper chasing butterflies across the lawns; sometimes I saw Doctor Baker's Scotch terrier scratching his ear beside a deck-chair. There was the postman who had pointed out the house to us today, and there was Clarice's mother wiping a chair for me in the back parlour. Ben smiled at me, holding winkles in his hands, and the bishop's wife asked me if I would stay to tea. I could feel the cold comfort of my sheets in my own bed, and the gritty shingle in the cove. I could smell the bracken in the woods, the wet moss, and the dead azalea petals. I fell into a strange broken sleep, waking now and again to the reality of my narrow cramped position and the sight of Maxim's

424

back in front of me. The dusk had turned to darkness. There were the lights of passing cars upon the road. There were villages with drawn curtains and little lights behind them. And I would move, and turn upon my back, and sleep again.

I saw the staircase at Manderley, and Mrs Danvers standing at the top in her black dress, waiting for me to go to her. As I climbed the stairs she backed under the archway and disappeared. I looked for her and I could not find her. Then her face looked at me through a hollow door and I cried out and she had gone again.

'What's the time?' I called. 'What's the time?'

Maxim turned round to me, his face pale and ghostly in the darkness of the car. 'It's half past eleven,' he said. 'We're over half-way already. Try and sleep again.'

'I'm thirsty,' I said.

He stopped at the next town. The man at the garage said his wife had not gone to bed and she would make us some tea. We got out of the car and stood inside the garage. I stamped up and down to bring the blood back to my hands and feet. Maxim smoked a cigarette. It was cold. A bitter wind blew in through the open garage door, and rattled the corrugated roof. I shivered, and buttoned up my coat.

'Yes, it's nippy tonight,' said the garage man, as he wound the petrol pump. 'The weather seemed to break this afternoon. It's the last of the heat waves for this summer. We shall be thinking of fires soon.'

'It was hot in London,' I said.

'Was it?' he said. 'Well, they always have the extremes up there, don't they? We get the first of the bad weather down here. It will blow hard on the coast before morning.'

His wife brought us the tea. It tasted of bitter wood, but it was hot. I drank it greedily, thankfully. Already Maxim was glancing at his watch.

'We ought to be going,' he said. 'It's ten minutes to twelve.' I left the shelter of the garage reluctantly. The cold wind blew in my face. The stars raced across the sky. There were threads of cloud too. 'Yes,' said the garage man, 'summer's over for this year.'

We climbed back into the car. I settled myself once more under the rug. The car went on. I shut my eyes. There was the man with the wooden leg winding his barrel organ, and the tune of 'Roses in Picardy' hummed in my head against the jolting of the car. Frith and Robert carried the tea into the library. The woman at the lodge nodded to me abruptly, and called her child into the house. I saw the model boats in the cottage in the cove, and the feathery dust. I saw the cobwebs stretching from the little masts. I heard the rain upon the roof and the sound of the sea. I wanted to get to the Happy Valley and it was not there. There were woods about me, there was no Happy Valley. Only the dark trees and the young bracken. The owls hooted. The moon was shining in the windows of Manderley. There were nettles in the garden, ten foot, twenty foot high.

'Maxim!' I cried. 'Maxim!'

'Yes,' he said. 'It's all right, I'm here.'

'I had a dream,' I said. 'A dream.'

'What was it?' he said.

'I don't know. I don't know.'

Back again into the moving unquiet depths. I was writing letters in the morning-room. I was sending out invitations. I wrote them all myself with a thick black pen. But when I looked down to see what I had written it was not my small square handwriting at all, it was long, and slanting, with curious pointed strokes. I pushed the cards away from the blotter and hid them. I got up and went to the looking-glass. A face stared back at me that was not my own. It was very pale, very lovely, framed in a cloud of dark hair. The eyes narrowed and smiled. The lips parted. The face in the glass stared back at me and laughed. And I saw then that she was sitting on a chair before the dressing-table in her bedroom, and Maxim was brushing her hair. He held her hair in his hands, and as he brushed it he wound it slowly into a thick rope. It twisted like a snake, and he took hold of it with both hands and smiled at Rebecca and put it round his neck.

'No,' I screamed. 'No, no. We must go to Switzerland. Colonel Julyan said we must go to Switzerland.'

I felt Maxim's hand upon my face. 'What is it?' he said. 'What's the matter?'

I sat up and pushed my hair away from my face.

'I can't sleep,' I said. 'It's no use.'

'You've been sleeping,' he said. 'You've slept for two hours. It's quarter past two. We're four miles the other side of Lanyon.'

It was even colder than before. I shuddered in the darkness of the car.

'I'll come beside you,' I said. 'We shall be back by three.'

I climbed over and sat beside him, staring in front of me through the wind-screen. I put my hand on his knee. My teeth were chattering.

'You're cold,' he said.

'Yes,' I said.

The hills rose in front of us, and dipped, and rose again. It was quite dark. The stars had gone.

'What time did you say it was?' I asked.

'Twenty past two,' he said.

'It's funny,' I said. 'It looks almost as though the dawn was breaking over there, beyond those hills. It can't be though, it's too early.'

'It's the wrong direction,' he said, 'you're looking west.'

'I know,' I said. 'It's funny, isn't it?'

He did not answer and I went on watching the sky. It seemed to get lighter even as I stared. Like the first red streak of sunrise. Little by little it spread across the sky.

'It's in winter you see the northern lights, isn't it?' I said. 'Not in summer?'

'That's not the northern lights,' he said. 'That's Manderley.'

I glanced at him and saw his face. I saw his eyes.

'Maxim,' I said. 'Maxim, what is it?'

He drove faster, much faster. We topped the hill before us and saw Lanyon lying in a hollow at our feet. There to the left of us was the silver streak of the river, widening to the estuary at

Kerrith six miles away. The road to Manderley lay ahead. There was no moon. The sky above our heads was inky black. But the sky on the horizon was not dark at all. It was shot with crimson, like a splash of blood. And the ashes blew towards us with the salt wind from the sea.

Afterword

Rebecca, first published in 1938, was Daphne du Maurier's fifth novel. It was to become the most famous of her many books; over sixty years later, it continues to haunt, fascinate and perplex a new generation of readers. Yet its enduring popularity has not been matched by critical acclaim: *Rebecca*, from the time of first publication, has been woefully and wilfully underestimated. It has been dismissed as a gothic romance, as 'women's fiction' – with such prejudicial terms, of course, giving clues as to why the novel has been so unthinkingly misinterpreted. Re-examination of this strange, angry and prescient novel is long overdue. A re-appraisal of it should begin, perhaps, with the circumstances under which it was written.

Du Maurier began planning it at a difficult point in her life: only a few years had passed since the death of her adored but dominating father, the actor-manager Gerald du Maurier. She was pregnant with her second child when at the planning stage of the book, and, by the time she actually began writing, at the age of thirty, she was in Egypt, where her husband, Frederick Browning, an officer in the Grenadier Guards, had been posted with his battalion. What many would regard as the quintessential Cornish novel was therefore begun, and much of it written, not in Cornwall, not even in England, but in the fierce heat of an Egyptian summer, in a city du Maurier came to loathe: Alexandria.

Du Maurier was desperately homesick; her longing for her home by the sea in Cornwall was, she wrote, 'like a pain under the heart continually'. She was also unhappy: this was the first time she had ever accompanied her husband on a posting, and she hated the role forced upon her in Egypt by her marriage.

Shy, and socially reclusive, she detested the small talk and the endless receptions she was expected to attend and give, in her capacity of commanding officer's wife. This homesickness and her resentment of wifely duties, together with a guilty sense of her own ineptitude when performing them, were to surface in *Rebecca*: they cluster around the two female antagonists of the novel, the living and obedient second wife, Mrs de Winter, and the dead, rebellious and indestructible first wife, Rebecca. Both women reflect aspects of du Maurier's own complex personality: she divided herself between them, and the splitting, doubling and mirroring devices she uses throughout the text destabilise it but give it resonance. With *Rebecca* we enter a world of dreams and daydreams, but they always threaten to tip over into nightmare.

At first, du Maurier struggled with her material. The novel had a false start, which she described as a 'literary miscarriage' – a revealing metaphor, given the centrality of pregnancy and childbirth to the plot and themes of *Rebecca*, and given the fact that du Maurier's second child, another daughter – she had hoped for a son – was born during the time she worked on it. She tore up the initial (fifteen-thousand-word-long) attempt at the book, the first time she had ever done this, and an indication, perhaps, of the difficulties she sensed in this material. She began again while still in Egypt, and finally completed it on her return to England.

She sent it off to her publisher, Victor Gollancz, in April 1938. He knew little about the novel at that stage: du Maurier had briefly described it to him as 'a sinister tale about a woman who marries a widower . . . Psychological and rather macabre'. Gollancz must have been somewhat nervous as he awaited that manuscript. Du Maurier's previous novel, *Jamaica Inn*, had sold more copies than any of her previous books, bringing her to the brink of bestsellerdom; but she was an unpredictable author, and difficult to categorise. Two of her earlier novels, *I'll Never Be Young Again* and *The Progress of Julius*, had sold much less well, and the sexual frankness of both books – especially the latter,

430

which dealt with father-daughter incest – had been met with distaste from critics.

Gollancz's reaction to *Rebecca* was relief, and jubilation. A 'rollicking success' was forecast by him, by his senior editor, and by everyone to whom advance copies were sent. Prior to publication, du Maurier's was the lone dissenting voice in this chorus of approbation. She feared her novel was 'too gloomy' to be popular, and she believed the ending was 'too grim' to appeal to readers. Gollancz ignored such pessimism: *Rebecca* was touted to booksellers as an 'exquisite love story' with a 'brilliantly created atmosphere of suspense'. It was promoted and sold, in short, as a gothic romance.

On publication, some critics acknowledged the book's haunting power and its vice-like narrative grip, but – perhaps misled by the book's presentation, or prejudiced by the gender of the author – they delved no deeper. Most reviews dismissed the novel with that belittling diminutive only ever used for novels by women: it was just a 'novelette'. Readers ignored them: *Rebecca* became an immediate and overwhelming commercial success.

The novel went through twenty-eight printings in four years in Britain alone. It became a bestseller in America, and it sold in vast numbers throughout Europe. It continues to sell well to this day: in the sixty-four years since first publication, it has never been out of print. Its readership was swelled by the Oscar-winning success of Hitchcock's memorable expressionistic film version, and has been increased since by countless theatre, radio and television dramatisations. Like Margaret Mitchell's *Gone With the Wind* (1936, and another novel that concerns women and property), *Rebecca* has made a transition rare in popular fiction: it has passed from bestseller, to cult novel, to cultural classic status. Why is that? What is it about this novel that has *always* spoken to readers, if not to critics?

Rebecca is the story of two women, one man, and a house. Of the four, as Hitchcock once observed, the house, Manderley, is the dominant presence. Although never precisely located (the word 'Cornwall' is never actually used in the novel), its minutely detailed setting is clearly that of an actual house, Menabilly. Du Maurier discovered Menabilly, on its isolated headland near Fowey, as a young woman, when she first went to live in Cornwall; she wrote a magical account of the first time she saw it. Eventually, after the war, and after *Rebecca*, she was able to lease the house. She lived there for over twenty years, using it as the location for several other novels; it lit her imagination, and obsessed her, for much of her life. Du Maurier's own term for Menabilly was the 'House of Secrets', and when she placed it at the heart of *Rebecca*, she created an elliptical, shifting, and deeply secretive book. The plot hinges upon secrets; the novel's milieu is that of an era and social class that, in the name of good manners, rarely allowed the truth to be expressed; and suppression coupled with a fearful secretiveness are its female narrator's most marked characteristics.

By the time du Maurier wrote *Rebecca*, she had mastered the techniques of popular fiction. Her novel came well disguised as bestseller material: an intriguing story of love and murder – a 'page-turner' in modern parlance. But examine the subtext of *Rebecca* and you find a perturbing, darker construct, part Grimm's fairytale, part Freudian family romance. You also find a very interesting literary mirroring, of course, an early example of intertextuality – and that is rare in a 'popular' novel, certainly one this early. *Rebecca* reflects *Jane Eyre*, but the reflection is imperfect, and deliberately so, forcing us to re-examine our assumptions about both novels, and in particular, their treatment of insanity and women.

None of these aspects of *Rebecca* was noticed by critics at the time of publication – and few have paused to examine them since. Instead, Charlotte Brontë's gifts were used as a stick with which to beat an impious, hubristic du Maurier over the head: she was Brontë's inferior, how could she dare to annex a classic novel? The critics moved swiftly on, not pausing for thought, and shunted du Maurier into the category of 'romance' writer – a category she detested and resented, but from which she was never able to escape. Thus was du Maurier 'named' as a writer. The question of how we name and identify – and the ironies and inexactitudes inherent in that process – is, of course, of central importance in *Rebecca*. Both female characters – one dead, one alive – derive their surname, as they do their status, from their husband. The first wife, Rebecca, is vivid and vengeful and, though dead, indestructible: her name lives on in the book's title. The second wife, the drab shadowy creature who narrates this story, remains nameless. We learn that she has a 'lovely and unusual' name, and that it was her father who gave it her. The only other identity she has, was also bestowed by a man – she is a *wife*, she is Mrs de Winter.

That a narrator perceived as a heroine should be *nameless* was a source of continuing fascination to du Maurier's readers. It also fascinated other writers – Agatha Christie corresponded with du Maurier on the subject – and throughout her life, du Maurier was plagued with letters seeking an explanation. Her stock reply was that she found the device technically interesting. The question is not a trivial one, for it takes us straight to the core of *Rebecca* – and that may well be the reason why du Maurier, a secretive woman and a secretive artist, avoided answering it.

The unnamed narrator of *Rebecca* begins her story with a dream, with a first sentence that has become famous: *Last night I dreamt I went to Manderley again.* Almost all the brief first chapter is devoted to that dream, describing her progress up the long winding drive, by moonlight, to Manderley itself. The imagery, of entwined trees and encroaching undergrowth that have 'mated', is sexual; the style is slightly scented and overwritten, that of a schoolgirl, trying to speak poetically, and struggling to impress. Moving forward, with a sense of anticipation and revulsion, the dream narrator first sees Manderley as intact; then, coming closer, she realises her mistake: she is looking at a ruin, at the shell of a once-great house. With this realisation – one of key importance to the novel – the dreamer wakes. She confirms that Manderley has indeed been destroyed, and that the dream was a true one. ('Dreaming true' was a term invented by du Maurier's grandfather, George du Maurier, author of *Trilby*; it was a concept that fascinated her all her life. Daphne was aware of Freud and Jung: George was not.)

Du Maurier's narrator can now begin to tell her story – and she does so in cyclic way; she begins at the end, with herself and her husband Maxim de Winter living in exile in Europe, for reasons that as yet are unclear. Their activities, as they move from hotel to hotel, sound like those of two elderly ex-pats. They follow the cricket, take afternoon tea; the wife selects dull newspaper articles to read to her husband, since – again for reasons unexplained – both find dullness reassuring and safe. The narrator describes a routine of stifling monotony, but does so in terms that are relentlessly optimistic and trite. This may be a marriage but it is one carefully devoid of passion, and apparently without sex.

It therefore comes as a considerable shock to the reader to discover, as the story loops back to this couple's first meeting, that this narrator is *young*. The lapse of time between this present and the past she will now describe is unspecified, but it is clearly only a few years. This makes de Winter a man of about fifty, and his childless friendless wife around twenty-five. Their life in Europe is never mentioned again, but *this* is the 'grim ending' to which du Maurier referred. It is easy to forget, as the drama unfolds, that the aftermath for the de Winters will be exile, ennui, and putting a brave face on a living death.

The plot of *Rebecca* thereafter will be familiar: it has echoes of *Cinderella* and *Bluebeard* as well as *Jane Eyre*. The narrator, working as a paid companion to a monstrous and tyrannical American, and staying with her in a palatial hotel in Monte Carlo, meets Maxim de Winter, a widower twice her age, who is the owner of a legendary house, Manderley. She marries him after a few weeks' acquaintanceship, returns with him to Manderley, and there becomes obsessed with Rebecca, his first wife. Patching together a portrait of Rebecca in her mind, she creates a chimera – and an icon of womanhood. Rebecca, she comes to believe, was everything she herself is not: she was a perfect hostess, a perfect sexual partner, a perfect chatelaine and a perfect wife. This image she later understands is false, but before she can grasp the truth about Rebecca's life, she has first to be told the truth about her death. Rebecca did not drown in a yachting accident, as everyone believes: she was killed by de Winter, who from the days of his honeymoon (also in Monte Carlo) loathed his wife.

Mrs de Winter, once enlightened, accepts without question her husband's version of her predecessor as a promiscuous (possibly bisexual) woman, who was pregnant with another man's child when he killed her, and who taunted him that she would pass off this child as his. De Winter's confession – and a very hollow melodramatic confession it is – is accompanied by a declaration of love – the first he has made, despite months of marriage. There is also the suggestion – very subtle but it is there – that their marriage is consummated, and for the first time, after this confession (note the references to single beds in the novel, and the heroine's embarrassment when there is speculation as to whether she is yet pregnant – something that recurs frequently. Modesty may explain that embarrassment, but in a du Maurier novel, it may well not).

Without hesitation, Mrs de Winter then gives her husband her full support – her one concern from then onwards is to conceal the truth and protect her husband. Thus, she becomes, in legal terms, an accessory after the fact: more importantly, she makes a moral choice. This is the crux of du Maurier's novel: de Winter has confessed, after all, to a *double* murder. He believes he has killed not only Rebecca, but also the child she was carrying – a heinous crime, by any standards. Here, du Maurier was taking a huge risk, particularly in a novel aimed at a popular market. To have an apparent 'hero' revealed as a double murderer, one prepared to perjure himself, moreover, to save his neck, could have shocked and alienated readers in their thousands. Hitchcock, when he came to film the novel two years later, ran a mile from this scenario, which he knew would be unacceptable. In his version, there *is* no murder, and Maxim's crime is at worst manslaughter since, during a quarrel, Rebecca falls, and (conveniently and mortally) injures herself.

How does du Maurier occlude this issue? She does it with immense cleverness: so involved have we, the readers, become in Mrs de Winter's predicament, and so sympathetic to her, that we conjoin with her. Because she loves her guilty husband, and he appears to love her, we too begin to hope that he will escape justice. If Mrs de Winter is culpable, therefore, so is the reader who endorses her actions – and that issue ticks away like a time bomb under the remaining chapters of the book.

This final section of the novel, which is brilliantly plotted, concerns de Winter's attempts to suppress the truth, and – with his loyal wife's assistance – escape the hangman. And so he does, but not without cost. Returning to Manderley from London, with information that gives Rebecca a motive for suicide and thus saves him, both partners are uneasy. De Winter senses impending disaster; in the back of the car, his wife is asleep, dreaming that she and Rebecca have become one, and that their hair, long and black, as Rebecca's was, is winding about de Winter's neck, like a noose.

Mrs de Winter dreams vividly twice in the novel, once at the beginning and once at the end: each time, the dream conveys a truth to her that her conscious mind cannot, or will not, accept. She prefers the sketchy and cliché-ridden visions she summons up when she daydreams – and she daydreams incessantly. The vision she has just had, of Rebecca and herself united, of first and second wives merged into one dangerous female avatar, she instantly rejects. Her husband halts the car on a crest near their home; the night sky beyond is lit with a red glow. (The colour red is linked with Rebecca throughout the novel.) His wife assumes it is the dawn, but de Winter understands at once: Manderley, his ancestral home, is burning. This destruction was prefigured in the dream with which the novel opened, and the literal agent of the destruction (possibly Mrs Danvers) is far less important than the poetic agent, which is Rebecca. Like some avenging angel, Rebecca has marshalled the elements: she has risen from the sea to wreak revenge by fire – thus echoing, and not for the first time, her literary ancestress, that madwoman in the attic, the first Mrs Rochester.

In this way, and very abruptly, the novel ends; it has come full circle. It is melodramatic in places, of course (even *Jane Eyre* cannot entirely escape that criticism). But it is remarkable, given the plot, how consistently and skilfully du Maurier skirts melodrama. What interested her as a novelist can be summarised by the distinction that Charlotte Brontë drew between writing that was 'real' and writing that was 'true'. There *is* realism in *Rebecca*; the mores, snobberies and speech patterns of the class and era du Maurier is describing are, for instance, sharply observed. The elements that give *Rebecca* its force, however, owe nothing to realism: its power lies in its imagery, its symmetry, its poetry – and that poetry is intensely female. The plot of *Rebecca* may be as unlikely as the plot of a fairytale, but that does not alter the novel's mythic resonance and psychological truth.

One way of reading *Rebecca* is as a convention-ridden love story, in which the good woman triumphs over the bad by winning a man's love: this version is the one our nameless narrator would have us accept, and it is undoubtedly the reading that made *Rebecca* a bestseller. Another approach is to see the novel's imaginative links, not just with the work of earlier female novelists, such as Charlotte Brontë, but also with later work, in particular Sylvia Plath's late poems. *Rebecca* is narrated by a masochistic woman, who is desperate for the validation provided by a man's love – a woman seeking an authoritarian father surrogate, or, as Plath expressed it, a 'man in black with a Meinkampf look'. Her search for this man involves both self-effacement and abnegation, as it does for any woman who 'adores a Fascist'. She duly finds her ideal in de Winter, whose last name indicates sterility, coldness, an unfruitful season, and whose Christian name – Maxim, as she always abbreviates it – is a synonym for a rule of conduct. It is also the name of a weapon – a machine gun.

This woman, not surprisingly, views Rebecca as a rival; what she refuses to perceive is that Rebecca is also her twin, and ultimately her alter ego. The two wives have actually suffered very similar fates. Both were taken as brides to Manderley – a male preserve, as the first syllable of its name (like Menabilly's) suggests. Both were marginalised within the confines of the house – Rebecca in the west wing with its view of her symbol, the sea, and the second wife in the east wing, overlooking the confines of a rose garden. The difference between them lies in their reactions: the second wife gladly submits, allowing her identity to be determined by her husband, and by the class attitudes and value systems he embraces. Rebecca has dared to be an unchaste wife; she has broken the 'rules of conduct' Maxim lives by. Her ultimate sin is to threaten the system of primogeniture. That sin, undermining the entire patriarchal edifice that is Manderley, cannot be forgiven – and Rebecca dies for it.

The response of Mrs de Winter to Rebecca's rebellion is deeply ambivalent, and it is this ambivalence that fuels the novel. Her apparent reaction is that of a conventional woman of her time: abhorrence. Yet there are indications throughout the text that the second Mrs de Winter would like to emulate Rebecca, even to be her – and these continue, even when she knows Rebecca has broken every male-determined rule as to a woman's behaviour. Although Rebecca is dead, is never seen, and has in theory been forever silenced, Mrs de Winter's obsession with her insures that Rebecca will triumph over anonymity and effacement. Even a bullet through the heart, and burial at sea cannot quench her vampiric power. Again, one is reminded of Plath's embodiment of amoral, anarchic female force – *I rise with my red hair/And I eat men like air.* Within the conventions of a story, Rebecca's pallid successor is able to do what she dare not do in life: celebrate her predecessor.

She does so with cunning and with power (du Maurier, of course, is pulling the strings here). Long after the book has been closed, which character reverberates in the memory? Rebecca. And which of the two women are readers drawn to, which of these polar opposites fascinates and attracts? Rebecca, again, I would say – certainly for modern readers. But I think that was probably true for readers in 1938 too: thanks to the cunning of du Maurier's narrative structure, they were able to condemn Rebecca (a promiscuous woman – what other option did they have?); but secretly respond to the anger, rebellion and vengefulness she embodies.

There is a final twist to *Rebecca* and it is a covert one. Maxim de Winter kills not one wife, but *two*. He murders the first with a gun, and the second by slower, more insidious methods. The second Mrs de Winter's fate, for which she prepares herself throughout the novel, is to be subsumed by her husband. Following him into that hellish exile glimpsed in the opening chapters, she becomes again what she was when she first met him – the paid companion to a petty tyrant. For humouring his whims, and obeying his every behest, her recompense is not money, but 'love' – and the cost is her identity. This is the final bitter irony of this novel, and the last of its many reversals. A story that ostensibly attempts to bury Rebecca, in fact resurrects her, and renders her unforgettable, whereas Mrs de Winter, our pale, ghostly and timid narrator, fades from our view; it is *she* who is the dying woman in this novel. By extension – and this is daring on du Maurier's part – her obedient beliefs, her unquestioning subservience to the male, are dying with her.

The themes of *Rebecca* – identity, doubling, the intimate linkage between love and murder – recur again and again in du Maurier's work. That the circumstances of her own life were the source of many of those themes is, I think, unquestionable. That she often chose to explore those themes within the confines of a story about love and marriage is perhaps not accidental either; there had always been duality in her life – her bisexuality ensured that; after her marriage, that sense of a dual identity deepened, and was to feed all her fiction.

Du Maurier had been born into a rich, privileged but unconventional and bohemian family. Her father, Gerald, was notorious for his affairs – and for running back to his wife after them. She and her sisters grew up surrounded by the writers, actors and artists who were their parents' close friends. Before du Maurier was twenty-one, she had had several affairs with men and at least one with a woman. Yet she chose to marry a career soldier in one of England's most elite regiments, a man who was a traditionalist to his fingertips, a stickler for correct dress and behaviour, a man who was deeply shocked when – prior to their marriage – she suggested they should sleep together. After a long and distinguished military career, 'Boy' Browning, as he was nicknamed, was to go on to become a courtier, spending much of his time in London, while his wife remained at Menabilly. There can be no question of their love and loyalty for each other: long after he died, du Maurier remained fiercely defensive of her husband. But the differences between them were marked, and their expectations of marriage perhaps very different. Eventually that caused problems: there were infidelities on both sides, and later in life, Browning began to drink heavily. Meanwhile, du Maurier had two identities: she was a Lieutenant General's wife, and later, Lady Browning: she was also an internationally celebrated writer, and finally a Dame of the British Empire. That she found it difficult to reconcile the demands of two *personae* is apparent in her fiction, above all in *Rebecca*, but also in her often bitter, and shocking, short stories.

Throughout her life, she was torn between the need to be a wife and the necessity of being a writer – and she seems to have regarded those roles as irreconcilable. Half accepting society's (and her husband's) interpretation of ideal womanhood, yet rebelling against it and rejecting it, she came to regard herself as a 'half-breed' who was 'unnatural'. To her, both her lesbianism and her art were a form of aberrance: they both sprang, she believed, from a force inside her that she referred to as the 'boy in the box'. Sometimes she fought against this incubus – and sometimes she gloried in him.

Given those beliefs, the dualism, the gender-blurring and the *splitting* that are so apparent in *Rebecca* become more understandable. Du Maurier was wrestling with her own demons here, and when she gave aspects of herself to the two women who are the pillars of her narrative she was entering into an area of deeply personal psychological struggle. She gave her own shyness and social awkwardness to Mrs de Winter. She gave her independence, her love of the sea, her expertise as a sailor, her sexual fearlessness, and even her bisexuality (strongly hinted at in the novel, if not spelled out) to Rebecca. It is for readers to decide where their own sympathies lie – and du Maurier's.

I would say that ultimately it is with Rebecca, with the angry voice of female dissent, that du Maurier's instinctive sympathy lies. But it is possible to argue the opposite view – one of the factors that makes *Rebecca* such a rewarding novel to reread and re-examine. One thing is certain: *Rebecca* is a deeply subversive work, one that undermines the very genre to which critics consigned it. Far from being an 'exquisite' love story, *Rebecca* raises questions about women's acquiescence to male values that are as pertinent today as they were sixty-four years ago. We may have moved on from the subservience of Mrs de Winter, but our enfranchisement is scarcely complete. A glance at the current bestseller lists will only confirm that the sly suggestion underlying *Rebecca* remains valid after sixty-four years: both in life and in bookstores, women continue to buy romance.

Sally Beauman
London 2002

441

VIRAGO MODERN CLASSICS

The first Virago Modern Classic, *Frost in May* by Antonia White, was published in 1978. It launched a list dedicated to the celebration of women writers and to the rediscovery and reprinting of their works. Its aim was, and is, to demonstrate the existence of a female tradition in literature, and to broaden the sometimes narrow definition of a 'classic'. Published with new introductions by some of today's best writers, the books are chosen for many reasons: they may be great works of literature; they may be wonderful period pieces; they may reveal particular aspects of women's lives; they may be classics of comedy, storytelling, letter-writing or autobiography.

'The Virago Modern Classics list contains some of the greatest fiction and non-fiction of the modern age, by authors whose lives were frequently as significant as their writing. Still captivating, still memorable, still utterly essential reading' SARAH WATERS

'The Virago Modern Classics list is wonderful. It's quite simply one of the best and most essential things that has happened in publishing in our time. I hate to think where we'd be without it' ALI SMITH

'The Virago Modern Classics have reshaped literary history and enriched the reading of us all. No library is complete without them' MARGARET DRABBLE

'The writers are formidable, the production handsome. The whole enterprise is thoroughly grand' LOUISE ERDRICH

'Good news for everyone writing and reading today'
HILARY MANTEL

VIRAGO MODERN CLASSICS

AUTHORS INCLUDE:

Elizabeth von Arnim, Beryl Bainbridge,
Pat Barker, Nina Bawden, Vera Brittain, Angela Carter,
Willa Cather, Barbara Comyns, E. M. Delafield, Polly Devlin,
Monica Dickens, Elaine Dundy, Nell Dunn, Nora Ephron,
Janet Flanner, Janet Frame, Miles Franklin, Marilyn French,
Stella Gibbons, Charlotte Perkins Gilman, Rumer Godden,
Radclyffe Hall, Helene Hanff, Josephine Hart, Shirley Hazzard,
Bessie Head, Patricia Highsmith, Winifred Holtby, Zora Neale
Hurston, Elizabeth Jenkins, Molly Keane, Rosamond Lehmann,
Anne Lister, Rose Macaulay, Shena Mackay, Beryl Markham,
Daphne du Maurier, Mary McCarthy, Kate O'Brien, Grace
Paley, Barbara Pym, Mary Renault, Stevie Smith, Muriel Spark,
Elizabeth Taylor, Angela Thirkell, Sylvia Townsend Warner,
Mary Webb, Eudora Welty, Rebecca West,
Edith Wharton, Antonia White

CHILDREN'S CLASSICS INCLUDE:

Joan Aiken, Nina Bawden, Frances Hodgson Burnett,
Susan Coolidge, Rumer Godden, L. M. Montgomery,
Edith Nesbit, Noel Streatfeild, P. L. Travers

To buy any of our books and to find out more
about Virago Press and Virago Modern Classics,
our authors and titles, visit our websites

www.virago.co.uk
www.littlebrown.co.uk

and follow us on Twitter

@ViragoBooks